BERNARD MALAMUD

BERNARD MALAMUD

NOVELS AND STORIES OF
THE 1940S & 50S

The Natural
The Assistant
Twenty Stories
Posthumously Published Stories

Philip Davis, *editor*

THE LIBRARY OF AMERICA

The paper used in this publication meets the
minimum requirements of the American National Standard for
Information Sciences—Permanence of Paper for Printed
Library Materials, ANSI Z39.48—1984.

Distributed to the trade in the United States
by Penguin Group (USA) Inc.
and in Canada by Penguin Books Canada Ltd.

Library of Congress Control Number: 2013941528
ISBN 978-1-59853-292-0

First Printing
The Library of America—248

Manufactured in the United States of America

Contents

THE NATURAL

For My Father

PRE-GAME

Roy Hobbs pawed at the glass before thinking to prick a match with his thumbnail and hold the spurting flame in his cupped palm close to the lower berth window, but by then he had figured it was a tunnel they were passing through and was no longer surprised at the bright sight of himself holding a yellow light over his head, peering back in. As the train yanked its long tail out of the thundering tunnel, the kneeling reflection dissolved and he felt a splurge of freedom at the view of the moon-hazed Western hills bulked against night broken by sprays of summer lightning, although the season was early spring. Lying back, elbowed up on his long side, sleepless still despite the lulling train, he watched the land flowing and waited with suppressed expectancy for a sight of the Mississippi, a thousand miles away.

Having no timepiece he appraised the night and decided it was moving toward dawn. As he was looking, there flowed along this bone-white farmhouse with sagging skeletal porch, alone in untold miles of moonlight, and before it this white-faced, long-boned boy whipped with train-whistle yowl a glowing ball to someone hidden under a dark oak, who shot it back without thought, and the kid once more wound and returned. Roy shut his eyes to the sight because if it wasn't real it was a way he sometimes had of observing himself, just as in this dream he could never shake off—that had hours ago waked him out of sound sleep—of him standing at night in a strange field with a golden baseball in his palm that all the time grew heavier as he sweated to settle whether to hold on or fling it away. But when he had made his decision it was too heavy to lift or let fall (who wanted a hole that deep?) so he changed his mind to keep it and the thing grew fluffy light, a white rose breaking out of its hide, and all but soared off by itself, but he had already sworn to hang on forever.

As dawn tilted the night, a gust of windblown rain blinded him—no, there was a window—but the sliding drops made him thirsty and from thirst sprang hunger. He reached into the hammock for his underwear to be first at breakfast in the dining car and make his blunders of ordering and eating more or less in private, since it was doubtful Sam would be up to tell him what to do. Roy peeled his gray sweatshirt and bunched down the white ducks he was wearing for pajamas in case there was a wreck and he didn't have time to dress. He acrobated into a shirt, pulled up the pants of his good suit, arching to draw them high, but he had crammed both feet into one leg and was trapped so tight wriggling got him nowhere. He worried because here he was straitjacketed in the berth without much room to twist around in and might bust his pants or have to buzz the porter, which he dreaded. Grunting, he contorted himself this way and that till he was at last able to grab and pull down the cuff and with a gasp loosened his feet and got the caught one where it belonged. Sitting up, he gartered his socks, tied laces, got on a necktie and even squirmed into a suit coat so that when he parted the curtains to step out he was fully dressed.

Dropping to all fours, he peered under the berth for his bassoon case. Though it was there he thought he had better open it and did but quickly snapped it shut as Eddie, the porter, came walking by.

"Morning, maestro, what's the tune today?"

"It ain't a musical instrument." Roy explained it was something he had made himself.

"Animal, vegetable, or mineral?"

"Just a practical thing."

"A pogo stick?"

"No."

"Foolproof lance?"

"No."

"Lemme guess," Eddie said, covering his eyes with his long-fingered hand and pawing the air with the other. "I have it—combination fishing rod, gun, and shovel."

Roy laughed. "How far to Chicago, Eddie?"

"Chi? Oh, a long, long ways. I wouldn't walk."

"I don't intend to."

"Why Chi?" Eddie asked. "Why not New Orleans? That's a lush and Frenchy city."

"Never been there."

"Or that hot and hilly town, San Francisco?"

Roy shook his head.

"Why not New York, colossus of colossuses?"

"Some day I'll visit there."

"Where have you visited?"

Roy was embarrassed. "Boise."

"That dusty sandstone quarry."

"Portland too when I was small."

"In Maine?"

"No, Oregon—where they hold the Festival of Roses."

"Oregon—where the refugees from Minnesota and the Dakotas go?"

"I wouldn't know," Roy said. "I'm going to Chicago, where the Cubs are."

"Lions and tigers in the zoo?"

"No, the ballplayers."

"Oh, the ball—" Eddie clapped a hand to his mouth. "Are you one of them?"

"I hope to be."

The porter bowed low. "My hero. Let me kiss your hand."

Roy couldn't help but smile yet the porter annoyed and worried him a little. He had forgotten to ask Sam when to tip him, morning or night, and how much? Roy had made it a point, since their funds were so low, not to ask for anything at all but last night Eddie had insisted on fixing a pillow behind his back, and once when he was trying to locate the men's room Eddie practically took him by the hand and led him to it. Did you hand him a dime after that or grunt a foolish thanks as he had done? He'd personally be glad when the trip was over, though he certainly hated to be left alone in a place like Chicago. Without Sam he'd feel shaky-kneed and unable to say or do simple things like ask for directions or know where to go once you had dropped a nickel into the subway.

After a troublesome shave in which he twice drew blood he used one thin towel to dry his hands, face, and neck, clean his razor and wipe up the wet of his toothbrush so as not to have to ask for another and this way keep the bill down. From the flaring sky out the window it looked around half-past five, but he couldn't be sure because somewhere near they left Mountain Time and lost—no, picked up—yes, it was lost an hour, what Sam called the twenty-three hour day. He packed his razor, toothbrush, and pocket comb into a chamois drawstring bag, rolled it up small and kept it handy in his coat pocket. Passing through the long sleeper, he entered the diner and would gladly have sat down to breakfast, for his stomach had contracted into a bean at the smell of food, but the shirt-sleeved waiters in stocking caps were joshing around as they gobbled fried kippers and potatoes. Roy hurried through the large-windowed club car, empty for once, through several sleepers, coaches, a lounge and another long line of coaches, till he came to the last one, where amid the gloom of drawn shades and sleeping people tossed every which way, Sam Simpson also slept although Roy had last night begged him to take the berth but the soft-voiced Sam had insisted, "You take the bed, kiddo, you're the one that has to show what you have got on the ball when we pull into the city. It don't matter where I sleep."

Sam lay very still on his back, looking as if the breath of life had departed from him except that it was audible in the ripe snore that could be chased without waking him, Roy had discovered, if you hissed scat. His lean head was held up by a folded pillow and his scrawny legs, shoeless, hung limp over the arm of the double seat he had managed to acquire, for he had started out with a seat partner. He was an expert conniver where his comfort was concerned, and since that revolved mostly around the filled flat bottle his ability to raise them up was this side of amazing. He often said he would not die of thirst though he never failed to add, in Roy's presence, that he wished for nobody the drunkard's death. He seemed now to be dreaming, and his sharp nose was pointed in the direction of a scent that led perhaps to the perfumed presence of Dame Fortune, long past due in his bed. With dry lips puckered, he smiled in expectation of a spectacular kiss though he looked less like a lover than an old scarecrow with his comical, seamed face sprouting prickly stubble in the dark glow of the expiring bulb overhead. A trainman passed who, seeing Sam sniff in his sleep, pretended it was at his own reek and humorously held his nose. Roy frowned, but Sam, who had a moment before been getting in good licks against fate, saw in his sleep, and his expression changed. A tear broke from his eye and slowly slid down his cheek. Roy concluded not to wake Sam and left.

He returned to the vacant club car and sat there with a magazine on his knee, worrying whether the trip wasn't a mistake, when a puzzled Eddie came into the car and handed him a pair of red dice.

"Mate them," he said. "I can't believe my eyes."

Roy paired the dice. "They mate."

"Now roll them."

He rolled past his shoe. "Snake eyes."

"Try again," said Eddie, interested.

Roy rattled the red cubes. "Snake eyes once more."

"Amazing. Again, please."

Again he rolled on the rug. Roy whistled. "Holy cow, three in a row."

"Fantastic."

"Did they do the same for you?"

"No, for me they did sevens."

"Are they loaded?"

"Bewitched," Eddie muttered. "I found them in the wash room and I'm gonna get rid of them pronto."

"Why?—if you could win all the time?"

"I don't crave any outside assistance in games of chance."

The train had begun to slow down.

"Oh oh, duty." Eddie hurried out.

Watching through the double-paned glass, Roy saw the porter swing himself off the train and jog along with it a few paces as it pulled to a stop. The morning was high and bright but the desolate station—wherever they were—gave up a single passenger, a girl in a dressy black dress, who despite the morning chill waited with a coat over her arm, and two suitcases and a zippered golf bag at her feet. Hatless, too, her hair a froth of dark curls, she held by a loose cord a shiny black hat box, which she wouldn't let Eddie touch when he gathered up her things. Her face was striking, a little drawn and pale, and when she stepped up into the train her nyloned legs made Roy's pulses dance. When he could no longer see her, he watched Eddie set down her bags, take the red dice out of his pocket, spit on them and fling them over the depot roof. He hurriedly grabbed the bags and hopped on the moving train.

The girl entered the club car and directed Eddie to carry her suitcases to her compartment and she would stay and have a cigarette. He mentioned the hat box again but she giggled nervously and said no.

"Never lost a female hat yet," Eddie muttered.

"Thank you but I'll carry it myself."

He shrugged and left.

She had dropped a flower. Roy thought it was a gardenia but it turned out to be a white rose she had worn pinned to her dress.

When he handed it to her, her eyes widened with fascination, as if she had recognized him from somewhere, but when she found she hadn't, to his horror her expression changed instantly to one of boredom. Sitting across the aisle from him she fished out of her purse a pack of cigarettes and a lighter. She lit up, and crossing her heartbreaking legs, began to flip through a copy of *Life*.

He figured she was his own age, maybe a year or so older. She looked to him like one of those high-class college girls, only with more zip than most of them, and dressed for 6 A.M. as the girls back home never would. He was marvelously interested in her, so much had her first glance into his eyes meant to him, and already felt a great longing in his life. Anxious to get acquainted, he was flabbergasted how to begin. If she hadn't yet eaten breakfast and he could work up the nerve, he could talk to her in the diner—only he didn't dare.

People were sitting around now and the steward came out and said first call for breakfast.

She snubbed out her cigarette with a wriggling motion of the wrist—her bracelets tinkled—picked up the hat box and went into the diner. Her crumpled white rose lay in the ashtray. He took it out and quickly stuck it in his pants pocket. Though his hunger bit sharp he waited till everyone was maybe served, and then he entered.

Although he had tried to avoid it, for fear she would see how unsure he was of these things, he was put at the same table with her and her black hat box, which now occupied a seat of its own. She glanced up furtively when he sat down but went wordlessly back to her coffee. When the waiter handed Roy the pad, he absently printed his name and date of birth but the waiter imperceptibly nudged him (hey, hayseed) and indicated it was for ordering. He pointed on the menu with his yellow pencil (this is the buck breakfast) but the blushing ballplayer, squinting through the blur, could only think he was sitting on the lone four-bit piece he had in his back pocket. He tried to squelch the impulse but something forced him to look up at her as he attempted to pour water into his ice-filled (this'll kill the fever) glass, spilling some on the tablecloth (whose diapers you wetting, boy?), then all thumbs and butter fingers, the pitcher thumped the pitcher down, fished the fifty cents out of his pants, and after scratching out the vital statistics on the pad, plunked the coin down on the table.

"That's for you," he told the (what did I do to deserve this?) waiter, and though the silver-eyed mermaid was about to speak, he did not stay to listen but beat it fast out of the accursed car.

Tramping highways and byways, wandering everywhere bird dogging the sandlots for months without spotting so much as a fifth-rater he could telegraph about to the head scout of the Cubs, and maybe pick up a hundred bucks in the mail as a token of their appreciation, with also a word of thanks for his good bird dogging and maybe they would sometime again employ him as a scout on the regular payroll—well, after a disheartening long time in which he was not able to roust up a single specimen worthy to be called by the name of ballplayer, Sam had one day lost his way along a dusty country road and when he finally found out where he was, too weary to turn back, he crossed over to an old, dry barn and sat against the haypile in front, to drown his sorrows with a swig. On the verge of dozing he heard these shouts and opened his eyes, shielding them from the hot sun, and as he lived, a game of ball was being played in a pasture by twelve blond-bearded players, six on each side, and even from where Sam sat he could tell they were terrific the way they smacked the pill—one blow banging it so far out the fielder had to run a mile before he could jump high and snag it smack in his bare hand. Sam's mouth popped open, he got up whoozy and watched, finding it hard to believe his eyes, as the teams changed sides and the first hitter that batted the ball did so for a far-reaching distance before it was caught, and the same with the second, a wicked clout, but then the third came up, the one who had made the bare-handed catch, and he really laid on and powdered the pellet a thundering crack so that even the one who ran for it, his beard parted in the wind, before long looked like a pygmy chasing it and quit running, seeing the thing was a speck on the horizon.

Sweating and shivering by turns, Sam muttered if I could ketch the whole twelve of them—and staggered out on the field to cry out the good news but when they saw him they gathered bats and balls and ran in a dozen directions, and though Sam was smart enough to hang on to the fellow who had banged the sphere out to the horizon, frantically shouting to him, "Whoa—whoa," his lungs bursting with the effort to call a giant—he wouldn't stop so Sam never caught him.

He woke with a sob in his throat but swallowed before he could sound it, for by then Roy had come to mind and he mumbled, "Got someone just as good," so that for once waking was better than dreaming.

He yawned. His mouth felt unholy dry and his underclothes were crawling. Reaching down his battered valise from the rack, he pulled out a used bath towel and cake of white soap, and to the surprise of those who saw him go out that way, went through the baggage cars to the car between them and the tender. Once inside there, he peeled to the skin and stepped into the shower stall, where he enjoyed himself for ten minutes, soaping and resoaping his bony body under warm water. But then a trainman happened to come through and after sniffing around Sam's clothes yelled in to him, "Hey, bud, come outa there."

Sam stopped off the shower and poked out his head.

"What's that?"

"I said come outa there, that's only for the train crew."

"Excuse me," Sam said, and he began quickly to rub himself dry.

"You don't have to hurry. Just wanted you to know you made a mistake."

"Thought it went with the ticket."

"Not in the coaches it don't."

Sam sat on a metal stool and laced up his high brown shoes. Pointing to the cracked mirror on the wall, he said, "Mind if I use your glass?"

"Go ahead."

He parted his sandy hair, combed behind the ears, and managed to work in a shave and brushing of his yellow teeth before he apologized again to the trainman and left.

Going up a few cars to the lounge, he ordered a cup of hot coffee and a sandwich, ate quickly, and made for the club car. It was semi-officially out of bounds for coach travelers but Sam had told the passenger agent last night that he had a nephew riding on a sleeper, and the passenger agent had mentioned to the conductor not to bother him.

When he entered the club car, after making sure Roy was elsewhere Sam headed for the bar, already in a fluid state for the train was moving through wet territory, but then he changed his mind and sat down to size up the congregation over a newspaper and spot who looked particularly amiable. The headlines caught his eye at the same time as they did this short, somewhat popeyed gent's sitting next to him, who had just been greedily questioning the husky, massive-shouldered man on his right, who was wearing sun glasses. Popeyes nudged the big one and they all three stared at Sam's paper.

WEST COAST OLYMPIC ATHLETE SHOT
FOLLOWS 24 HOURS AFTER SLAYING OF
ALL-AMERICAN FOOTBALL ACE

The article went on to relate that both of these men had been shot under mysterious circumstances with silver bullets from a .22 caliber pistol by an unknown woman that police were on the hunt for.

"That makes the second sucker," the short man said.

"But why with silver bullets, Max?"

"Beats me. Maybe she set out after a ghost but couldn't find him."

The other fingered his tie knot. "Why do you suppose she goes around pickin' on atheletes for?"

"Not only athletes but also the cream of the crop. She's knocked off a crack football boy, and now an Olympic runner. Better watch out, Whammer, she may be heading for a baseball player for the third victim." Max chuckled.

Sam looked up and almost hopped out of his seat as he recognized them both.

Hiding his hesitation, he touched the short one on the arm. "Excuse me, mister, but ain't you Max Mercy, the sportswriter? I know your face from your photo in the articles you write."

But the sportswriter, who wore a comical mustache and dressed in stripes that crisscrossed three ways—suit, shirt, and tie—a nervous man with voracious eyes, also had a sharp sense of smell and despite Sam's shower and toothbrushing nosed out an alcoholic fragrance that slowed his usual speedy response in acknowledging the spread of his fame.

"That's right," he finally said.

"Well, I'm happy to have the chance to say a few words to you. You're maybe a little after my time, but I am Sam Simpson —Bub Simpson, that is—who played for the St. Louis Browns in the seasons of 1919 to 1921."

Sam spoke with a grin though his insides were afry at the mention of his professional baseball career.

"Believe I've heard the name," Mercy said nervously. After a minute he nodded toward the man Sam knew all along as the leading hitter of the American League, three times winner of the Most Valuable Player award, and announced, "This is Walter (the Whammer) Wambold." It had been in the papers that he was a holdout for $75,000 and was coming East to squeeze it out of his boss.

"Howdy," Sam said. "You sure look different in street clothes."

The Whammer, whose yellow hair was slicked flat, with tie and socks to match, grunted.

Sam's ears reddened. He laughed embarrassedly and then remarked sideways to Mercy that he was traveling with a slam-bang young pitcher who'd soon be laying them low in the big leagues. "Spoke to you because I thought you might want to know about him."

"What's his name?"

"Roy Hobbs."

"Where'd he play?"

"Well, he's not exactly been in organized baseball."

"Where'd he learn to pitch?"

"His daddy taught him years ago—he was once a semipro— and I have been polishin' him up."

"Where's he been pitching?"

"Well, like I said, he's young, but he certainly mowed them down in the Northwest High School League last year. Thought you might of heard of his eight no-hitters."

"Class D is as far down as I go," Mercy laughed. He lit one of the cigars Sam had been looking at in his breast pocket.

"I'm personally taking him to Clarence Mulligan of the Cubs for a tryout. They will probably pay me a few grand for uncovering the coming pitcher of the century but the condition is—and Roy is backing me on this because he is more devoted to me than a son—that I am to go back as a regular scout, like I was in 1925."

Roy popped his head into the car and searched around for the girl with the black hat box (Miss Harriet Bird, Eddie had gratuitously told him, making a black fluttering of wings), and seeing her seated near the card tables restlessly thumbing through a magazine, popped out.

"That's him," said Sam. "Wait'll I bring him back." He got up and chased after Roy.

"Who's the gabber?" said the Whammer.

"Guy named Simpson who once caught for the Brownies. Funny thing, last night I was doing a Sunday piece on drunks in baseball and I had occasion to look up his record. He was in the game three years, batted .340, .260, and .198, but his catching was terrific—not one error listed."

"Get rid of him, he jaws too much."

"Sh, here he comes."

Sam returned with Roy in tow, gazing uncomfortably ahead.

"Max," said Sam, "this is Roy Hobbs that I mentioned to you. Say hello to Max Mercy, the syndicated sportswriter, kiddo."

"Hello," Roy nodded.

"This is the Whammer," Max said.

Roy extended his hand but the Whammer looked through him with no expression whatsoever. Seeing he had his eye hooked on Harriet, Roy conceived a strong dislike for the guy.

The Whammer got up. "Come on, Max, I wanna play cards."

Max rose. "Well, hang onto the water wagon, Bub," he said to Sam.

Sam turned red.

Roy shot the sportswriter a dirty look.

"Keep up with the no-hitters, kid," Max laughed.

Roy didn't answer. He took the Whammer's chair and Sam sat where he was, brooding.

"What'll it be?" they heard Mercy ask as he shuffled the cards. They had joined two men at one of the card tables.

The Whammer, who looked to Sam like an overgrown side of beef wrapped in gabardine, said, "Hearts." He stared at Harriet until she looked up from her magazine, and after a moment of doubt, smiled.

The Whammer fingered his necktie knot. As he scooped up the cards his diamond ring glinted in the sunlight.

"Goddamned millionaire," Sam thought.

"The hell with her," thought Roy.

"I dealt rummy," Max said, and though no one had called him, Sam promptly looked around.

Toward late afternoon the Whammer, droning on about his deeds on the playing field, got very chummy with Harriet Bird and before long had slipped his fat fingers around the back of her chair so Roy left the club car and sat in the sleeper, looking out of the window, across the aisle from where Eddie slept sitting up. Gosh, the size of the forest. He thought they had left it for good yesterday and here it still was. As he watched, the trees flowed together and so did the hills and clouds. He felt a kind of sadness, because he had lost the feeling of a particular place. Yesterday he had come from somewhere, a place he knew was there, but today it had thinned away in space— how vast he could not have guessed—and he felt like he would never see it again.

The forest stayed with them, climbing hills like an army, shooting down like waterfalls. As the train skirted close in, the trees leveled out and he could see within the woodland the only place he had been truly intimate with in his wanderings, a green world shot through with weird light and strange bird cries, muffled in silence that made the privacy so complete his inmost self had no shame of anything he thought there, and it eased the body-shaking beat of his ambitions. Then he thought of here and now and for the thousandth time wondered why they had come so far and for what. Did Sam really know what he was doing? Sometimes Roy had his doubts. Sometimes he wanted to turn around and go back home, where he could at least predict what tomorrow would be like. Remembering the white rose in his pants pocket, he decided to get rid of it. But then the pine trees flowed away from the train and slowly swerved behind blue hills; all at once there was this beaten gold, snow-capped mountain in the distance, and on the plain several miles from its base lay a small city gleaming in the rays of the declining sun. Approaching it, the long train slowly pulled to a stop.

Eddie woke with a jump and stared out the window.

"Oh oh, trouble, we never stop here."

He looked again and called Roy.

"What do you make out of that?"

About a hundred yards ahead, where two dirt roads crossed, a moth-eaten model-T Ford was parked on the farther side of the road from town, and a fat old man wearing a broad-brimmed black hat and cowboy boots, who they could see was carrying a squat doctor's satchel, climbed down from it. To the conductor, who had impatiently swung off the train with a lit red lamp, he flourished a yellow telegram. They argued a minute, then the conductor, snapping open his watch, beckoned him along and they boarded the train. When they passed through Eddie's car the conductor's face was sizzling with irritation but the doctor was unruffled. Before disappearing through the door, the conductor called to Eddie, "Half hour."

"Half hour," Eddie yodeled and he got out the stool and set it outside the car so that anyone who wanted to stretch, could.

Only about a dozen passengers got off the train, including Harriet Bird, still hanging on to her precious hat box, the Whammer, and Max Mercy, all as thick as thieves. Roy hunted up the bassoon case just if the train should decide to take off without him, and when he had located Sam they both got off.

"Well, I'll be jiggered." Sam pointed down about a block beyond where the locomotive had halted. There, sprawled out at the outskirts of the city, a carnival was on. It was made up of try-your-skill booths, kiddie rides, a freak show and a gigantic Ferris wheel that looked like a stopped clock. Though there was still plenty of daylight, the carnival was lit up by twisted ropes of blinking bulbs, and many banners streamed in the breeze as the calliope played.

"Come on," said Roy, and they went along with the people from the train who were going toward the tents.

Once they had got there and fooled around a while, Sam stopped to have a crushed cocoanut drink which he privately spiked with a shot from a new bottle, while Roy wandered over to a place where you could throw three baseballs for a dime at three wooden pins, shaped like pint-size milk bottles and set in pyramids of one on top of two, on small raised platforms about twenty feet back from the counter. He changed the fifty-cent piece Sam had slipped him on leaving the train, and this pretty girl in yellow, a little hefty but with a sweet face and nice ways, who with her peanut of a father was waiting on trade, handed him three balls. Lobbing one of them, Roy easily knocked off the pyramid and won himself a naked kewpie doll. Enjoying the game, he laid down another dime, again clattering the pins to the floor in a single shot and now collecting an alarm clock. With the other three dimes he won a brand-new boxed baseball, a washboard, and a baby potty, which he traded in for a six-inch harmonica. A few kids came over to watch and Sam, wandering by, indulgently changed another half into dimes for Roy. And Roy won a fine leather cigar case for Sam, a "God Bless America" banner, a flashlight, can of coffee, and a two-pound box of sweets. To the kids' delight, Sam, after a slight hesitation, flipped Roy another half dollar, but this time the little man behind the counter nudged his daughter and she asked Roy if he would now take a kiss for every three pins he tumbled.

Roy glanced at her breasts and she blushed. He got embarrassed too. "What do you say, Sam, it's your four bits?"

Sam bowed low to the girl. "Ma'am," he said, "now you see how dang foolish it is to be a young feller."

The girl laughed and Roy began to throw for kisses, flushing each pyramid in a shot or two while the girl counted aloud the kisses she owed him.

Some of the people from the train passed by and stayed to watch when they learned from the mocking kids what Roy was throwing for.

The girl, pretending to be unconcerned, tolled off the third and fourth kisses.

As Roy fingered the ball for the last throw the Whammer

came by holding over his shoulder a Louisville Slugger that he had won for himself in the batting cage down a way. Harriet, her pretty face flushed, had a kewpie doll, and Max Mercy carried a box of cigars. The Whammer had discarded his sun glasses and all but strutted over his performance and the prizes he had won.

Roy raised his arm to throw for the fifth kiss and a clean sweep when the Whammer called out to him in a loud voice, "Pitch it here, busher, and I will knock it into the moon."

Roy shot for the last kiss and missed. He missed with the second and third balls. The crowd oohed its disappointment.

"Only four," said the girl in yellow as if she mourned the fifth.

Angered at what had happened, Sam hoarsely piped, "I got ten dollars that says he can strike you out with three pitched balls, Wambold."

The Whammer looked at Sam with contempt.

"What d'ye say, Max?" he said.

Mercy shrugged.

"Oh, I love contests of skill," Harriet said excitedly. Roy's face went pale.

"What's the matter, hayfoot, you scared?" the Whammer taunted.

"Not of you," Roy said.

"Let's go across the tracks where nobody'll get hurt," Mercy suggested.

"Nobody but the busher and his bazooka. What's in it, busher?"

"None of your business." Roy picked up the bassoon case.

The crowd moved in a body across the tracks, the kids circling around to get a good view, and the engineer and fireman watching from their cab window.

Sam cornered one of the kids who lived nearby and sent him home for a fielder's glove and his friend's catcher's mitt. While they were waiting, for protection he buttoned underneath his coat the washboard Roy had won. Max drew a batter's box alongside a piece of slate. He said he would call the throws and they would count as one of the three pitches only if they were over or if the Whammer swung and missed.

When the boy returned with the gloves, the sun was going

down, and though the sky was aflame with light all the way to the snowy mountain peak, it was chilly on the ground.

Breaking the seal, Sam squeezed the baseball box and the pill shot up like a greased egg. He tossed it to Mercy, who inspected the hide and stitches, then rubbed the shine off and flipped it to Roy.

"Better throw a couple of warm-ups."

"My arm is loose," said Roy.

"It's your funeral."

Placing his bassoon case out of the way in the grass, Roy shed his coat. One of the boys came forth to hold it.

"Be careful you don't spill the pockets," Roy told him.

Sam came forward with the catcher's glove on. It was too small for his big hand but he said it would do all right.

"Sam, I wish you hadn't bet that money on me," Roy said.

"I won't take it if we win, kiddo, but just let it stand if we lose," Sam said, embarrassed.

"We came by it too hard."

"Just let it stand so."

He cautioned Roy to keep his pitches inside, for the Whammer was known to gobble them on the outside corner.

Sam returned to the plate and crouched behind the batter, his knees spread wide because of the washboard. Roy drew on his glove and palmed the ball behind it. Mercy, rubbing his hands to warm them, edged back about six feet behind Sam.

The onlookers retreated to the other side of the tracks, except Harriet, who stood without fear of fouls up close. Her eyes shone at the sight of the two men facing one another.

Mercy called, "Batter up."

The Whammer crowded the left side of the plate, gripping the heavy bat low on the neck, his hands jammed together and legs plunked evenly apart. He hadn't bothered to take off his coat. His eye on Roy said it spied a left-handed monkey.

"Throw it, Rube, it won't get no lighter."

Though he stood about sixty feet away, he loomed up gigantic to Roy, with the wood held like a caveman's ax on his shoulder. His rocklike frame was motionless, his face impassive, unsmiling, dark.

Roy's heart skipped a beat. He turned to gaze at the mountain.

Sam whacked the leather with his fist. "Come on, kiddo, wham it down his whammy."

The Whammer out of the corner of his mouth told the drunk to keep his mouth shut.

"Burn it across his button."

"Close your trap," Mercy said.

"Cut his throat with it."

"If he tries to dust me, so help me I will smash his skull," the Whammer threatened.

Roy stretched loosely, rocked back on his left leg, twirling the right a little like a dancer, then strode forward and threw with such force his knuckles all but scraped the ground on the follow-through.

At thirty-three the Whammer still enjoyed exceptional eyesight. He saw the ball spin off Roy's fingertips and it reminded him of a white pigeon he had kept as a boy, that he would send into flight by flipping it into the air. The ball flew at him and he was conscious of its bird-form and white flapping wings, until it suddenly disappeared from view. He heard a noise like the bang of a firecracker at his feet and Sam had the ball in his mitt. Unable to believe his ears he heard Mercy intone a reluctant strike.

Sam flung off the glove and was wringing his hand.

"Hurt you, Sam?" Roy called.

"No, it's this dang glove."

Though he did not show it, the pitch had bothered the Whammer no end. Not just the speed of it but the sensation of surprise and strangeness that went with it—him batting here on the railroad tracks, the crazy carnival, the drunk catching and a clown pitching, and that queer dame Harriet, who had five minutes ago been patting him on the back for his skill in the batting cage, now eyeing him coldly for letting one pitch go by.

He noticed Max had moved farther back.

"How the hell you expect to call them out there?"

"He looks wild to me." Max moved in.

"Your knees are knockin'," Sam tittered.

"Mind your business, rednose," Max said.

"You better watch your talk, mister," Roy called to Mercy.

"Pitch it, greenhorn," warned the Whammer.

Sam crouched with his glove on. "Do it again, Roy. Give him something simular."

"Do it again," mimicked the Whammer. To the crowd, maybe to Harriet, he held up a vaunting finger showing there were other pitches to come.

Roy pumped, reared and flung.

The ball appeared to the batter to be a slow spinning planet looming toward the earth. For a long light-year he waited for this globe to whirl into the orbit of his swing so he could bust it to smithereens that would settle with dust and dead leaves into some distant cosmos. At last the unseeing eye, maybe a fortuneteller's lit crystal ball—anyway, a curious combination of circles—drifted within range of his weapon, or so he thought, because he lunged at it ferociously, twisting round like a top. He landed on both knees as the world floated by over his head and hit with a *whup* into the cave of Sam's glove.

"Hey, Max," Sam said, as he chased the ball after it had bounced out of the glove, "how do they pernounce Whammer if you leave out the W?"

"Strike," Mercy called long after a cheer (was it a jeer?) had burst from the crowd.

"What's he throwing," the Whammer howled, "spitters?"

"In the pig's poop." Sam thrust the ball at him. "It's drier than your granddaddy's scalp."

"I'm warning him not to try any dirty business."

Yet the Whammer felt oddly relieved. He liked to have his back crowding the wall, when there was a single pitch to worry about and a single pitch to hit. Then the sweat began to leak out of his pores as he stared at the hard, lanky figure of the pitiless pitcher, moving, despite his years and a few waste motions, like a veteran undertaker of the diamond, and he experienced a moment of depression.

Sam must have sensed it, because he discovered an unexpected pity in his heart and even for a split second hoped the idol would not be tumbled. But only for a second, for the Whammer had regained confidence in his known talent and experience and was taunting the greenhorn to throw.

Someone in the crowd hooted and the Whammer raised aloft two fat fingers and pointed where he would murder the ball, where the gleaming rails converged on the horizon and beyond was invisible.

Roy raised his leg. He smelled the Whammer's blood and wanted it, and through him the worms he had with him, for the way he had insulted Sam.

The third ball slithered at the batter like a meteor, the flame swallowing itself. He lifted his club to crush it into a universe of sparks but the heavy wood dragged, and though he willed to destroy the sound he heard a gong bong and realized with sadness that the ball he had expected to hit had long since been part of the past; and though Max could not cough the fatal word out of his throat, the Whammer understood he was, in the truest sense of it, out.

The crowd was silent as the violet evening fell on their shoulders.

For a night game, the Whammer harshly shouted, it was customary to turn on lights. Dropping the bat, he trotted off to the train, an old man.

The ball had caught Sam smack in the washboard and lifted him off his feet. He lay on the ground, extended on his back. Roy pushed everybody aside to get him air. Unbuttoning Sam's coat, he removed the dented washboard.

"Never meant to hurt you, Sam."

"Just knocked the wind outa me," Sam gasped. "Feel better now." He was pulled to his feet and stood steady.

The train whistle wailed, the echo banging far out against the black mountain.

Then the doctor in the broadbrimmed black hat appeared, flustered and morose, the conductor trying to pacify him, and Eddie hopping along behind.

The doctor waved the crumpled yellow paper around. "Got a telegram says somebody on this train took sick. Anybody out here?"

Roy tugged at Sam's sleeve.

"Ixnay."

"What's that?"

"Not me," said Roy.

The doctor stomped off. He climbed into his Ford, whipped it up and drove away.

The conductor popped open his watch. "Be a good hour late into the city."

"All aboard," he called.

"Aboard," Eddie echoed, carrying the bassoon case.

The buxom girl in yellow broke through the crowd and threw her arms around Roy's neck. He ducked but she hit him quick with her pucker four times upon the right eye, yet he could see with the other that Harriet Bird (certainly a snappy goddess) had her gaze fastened on him.

They sat, after dinner, in Eddie's dimmed and empty Pullman, Roy floating through drifts of clouds on his triumph as Harriet went on about the recent tourney, she put it, and the unreal forest outside swung forward like a gate shutting. The odd way she saw things interested him, yet he was aware of the tormented trees fronting the snaky lake they were passing, trees bent and clawing, plucked white by icy blasts from the black water, their bony branches twisting in many a broken direction.

Harriet's face was flushed, her eyes gleaming with new insights. Occasionally she stopped and giggled at herself for the breathless volume of words that flowed forth, to his growing astonishment, but after a pause was on her galloping way again—a girl on horseback—reviewing the inspiring sight (she said it was) of David jawboning the Goliath-Whammer, or was it Sir Percy lancing Sir Maldemer, or the first son (with a rock in his paw) ranged against the primitive papa?

Roy gulped. "My father? Well, maybe I did want to skull him sometimes. After my grandma died, the old man dumped me in one orphan home after the other, wherever he happened to be working—when he did—though he did used to take me out of there summers and teach me how to toss a ball."

No, that wasn't what she meant, Harriet said. Had he ever read Homer?

Try as he would he could only think of four bases and not a book. His head spun at her allusions. He found her lingo strange with all the college stuff and hoped she would stop it because he wanted to talk about baseball.

Then she took a breather. "My friends say I have a fantastic imagination."

He quickly remarked he wouldn't say that. "But the only thing I had on my mind when I was throwing out there was that Sam had bet this ten spot we couldn't afford to lose out on, so I had to make him whiff."

"To whiff—oh, Roy, how droll," and she laughed again.

He grinned, carried away by the memory of how he had done it, the hero, who with three pitched balls had nailed the best the American League had to offer. What didn't that say about the future? He felt himself falling into sentiment in his thoughts and tried to steady himself but couldn't before he had come forth with a pronouncement: "You have to have the right stuff to play good ball and I have it. I bet some day I'll break every record in the book for throwing and hitting."

Harriet appeared startled then gasped, hiding it like a cough behind her tense fist, and vigorously applauded, her bracelets bouncing on her wrists. "Bravo, Roy, how wonderful."

"What I mean," he insisted, "is I feel that I have got it in me— that I am due for something very big. I have to do it. I mean," he said modestly, "that's of course when I get in the game."

Her mouth opened. "You mean you're not—" She seemed, to his surprise, disappointed, almost on the verge of crying.

"No," he said, ashamed. "Sam's taking me for a tryout."

Her eyes grew vacant as she stared out the window. Then she asked, "But Walter—*he* is a successful professional player, isn't he?

"The Whammer?" Roy nodded.

"And he has won that award three times—what was it?"

"The Most Valuable Player." He had a panicky feeling he was losing her to the Whammer.

She bit her lip. "Yet you defeated him," she murmured.

He admitted it. "He won't last much longer I don't think— the most a year or two. By then he'll be too old for the game. Myself, I've got my whole life ahead of me."

Harriet brightened, saying sympathetically, "What will you hope to accomplish, Roy?"

He had already told her but after a minute remarked, "Sometimes when I walk down the street I bet people will say there goes Roy Hobbs, the best there ever was in the game."

She gazed at him with touched and troubled eyes. "Is that all?"

He tried to penetrate her question. Twice he had answered it and still she was unsatisfied. He couldn't be sure what she expected him to say. "Is that all?" he repeated. "What more is there?"

"Don't you know?" she said kindly.

Then he had an idea. "You mean the bucks? I'll get them too."

She slowly shook her head. "Isn't there something over and above earthly things—some more glorious meaning to one's life and activities?"

"In baseball?"

"Yes."

He racked his brain—

"Maybe I've not made myself clear, but surely you can see (I was saying this to Walter just before the train stopped) that yourself alone—alone in the sense that we are all terribly alone no matter what people say—I mean by that perhaps if you understood that our values must derive from—oh, I really suppose—" She dropped her hand futilely. "Please forgive me. I sometimes confuse myself with the little I know."

Her eyes were sad. He felt a curious tenderness for her, a little as if she might be his mother (That bird.) and tried very hard to come up with the answer she wanted—something you said about LIFE.

"I think I know what you mean," he said. "You mean the fun and satisfaction you get out of playing the best way that you know how?"

She did not respond to that.

Roy worried out some other things he might have said but had no confidence to put them into words. He felt curiously deflated and a little lost, as if he had just flunked a test. The worst of it was he still didn't know what she'd been driving at.

Harriet yawned. Never before had he felt so tongue-tied in front of a girl, a looker too. Now if he had her in bed—

Almost as if she had guessed what he was thinking and her mood had changed to something more practical than asking nutty questions that didn't count, she sighed and edged closer to him, concealing the move behind a query about his bassoon case. "Do you play?"

"Not any music," he answered, glad they were talking about

something different. "There's a thing in it that I made for myself."

"What, for instance?"

He hesitated. "A baseball bat."

She was herself again, laughed merrily. "Roy, you are priceless."

"I got the case because I don't want to get the stick all banged up before I got the chance to use it."

"Oh, Roy." Her laughter grew. He smiled broadly.

She was now so close he felt bold. Reaching down he lifted the hat box by the string and lightly hefted it.

"What's in it?"

She seemed breathless. "In it?" Then she mimicked, "—Something I made for myself."

"Feels like a hat."

"Maybe a head?" Harriet shook a finger at him.

"Feels more like a hat." A little embarrassed, he set the box down. "Will you come and see me play sometime?" he asked.

She nodded and then he was aware of her leg against his and that she was all but on his lap. His heart slapped against his ribs and he took it all to mean that she had dropped the last of her interest in the Whammer and was putting it on the guy who had buried him.

As they went through a tunnel, Roy placed his arm around her shoulders, and when the train lurched on a curve, casually let his hand fall upon her full breast. The nipple rose between his fingers and before he could resist the impulse he had tweaked it.

Her high-pitched scream lifted her up and twirling like a dancer down the aisle.

Stricken, he rose—had gone too far.

Crooking her arms like broken branches she whirled back to him, her head turned so far around her face hung between her shoulders.

"Look, I'm a twisted tree."

Sam had sneaked out on the squirming, apologetic Mercy, who, with his back to the Whammer—he with a newspaper raised in front of his sullen eyes—had kept up a leechlike prodding about Roy, asking where he had come from (oh, he's just a home town boy), how it was no major league scout had got at him (they did but he turned them down for me) even with the bonus cash that they are tossing around these days (yep), who's his father (like I said, just an old semipro who wanted awful bad to be in the big leagues) and what, for God's sake, does he carry around in that case (that's his bat, Wonderboy). The sportswriter was greedy to know more, hinting he could do great things for the kid, but Sam, rubbing his side where it pained, at last put him off and escaped into the coach to get some shuteye before they hit Chicago, sometime past 1 A.M.

After a long time trying to settle himself comfortably, he fell snoring asleep flat on his back and was at once sucked into a long dream that he had gone thirsty mad for a drink and was threatening the slickers in the car get him a bottle or else. Then this weasel of a Mercy, pretending he was writing on a pad, pointed him out with his pencil and the conductor snapped him up by the seat of his pants and ran his freewheeling feet lickity-split through the sawdust, giving him the merry heave-ho off the train through the air on a floating trapeze, ploop into a bog where it rained buckets. He thought he better get across the foaming river before it flooded the bridge away so he set out, all bespattered, to cross it, only this queer duck of a doctor in oilskins, an old man with a washable white mustache and a yellow lamp he thrust straight into your eyeballs, swore to him the bridge was gone. You're plumb tootin' crazy, Sam shouted in the storm, I saw it standin' with me own eyes, and he scuffled to get past the geezer, who dropped the light setting the rails afire. They wrestled in the rain until Sam slyly tripped and threw him, and helter-skeltered for the bridge, to find to his crawling horror it was truly down and here he was scratching space till he landed with a splishity-splash in the whirling waters, sobbing (whoa whoa) and the white watchman on the embankment flung him a flare but it was all too late because he heard the roar of the falls below (and restless shifting of the sea) and felt with his red hand where the knife had stabbed him . . .

Roy was dreaming of an enormous mountain—Christ, the size of it—when he felt himself roughly shaken—Sam, he thought, because they were there—only it was Eddie holding a lit candle.

"The fuse blew and I've had no chance to fix it."

"What's the matter?"

"Trou-ble. Your friend has collapsed."

Roy hopped out of the berth, stepped into moccasins and ran, with Eddie flying after him with the snuffed wax, into a darkened car where a pool of people under a blue light hovered over Sam, unconscious.

"What happened?" Roy cried.

"Sh," said the conductor, "he's got a raging fever."

"What from?"

"Can't say. We're picking up a doctor."

Sam was lying on a bench, wrapped in blankets with a pillow tucked under his head, his gaunt face broken out in sweat. When Roy bent over him, his eyes opened.

"Hello, kiddo," he said in a cracked voice.

"What hurts you, Sam?"

"Where the washboard banged me—but it don't hurt so much now."

"Oh, Jesus."

"Don't take it so, Roy. I'll be better."

"Save his strength, son," the conductor said. "Don't talk now."

Roy got up. Sam shut his eyes.

The train whistled and ran slow at the next town then came to a draggy halt. The trainman brought a half-dressed doctor in. He examined Sam and straightened up. "We got to get him off and to the hospital."

Roy was wild with anxiety but Sam opened his eyes and told him to bend down.

Everyone moved away and Roy bent low.

"Take my wallet outa my rear pocket."

Roy pulled out the stuffed cowhide wallet.

"Now you go to the Stevens Hotel—"

"No, oh no, Sam, not without you."

"Go on, kiddo, you got to. See Clarence Mulligan tomorrow and say I sent you—they are expecting you. Give them everything you have got on the ball—that'll make me happy."

"But, Sam—"

"You got to. Bend lower."

Roy bent lower and Sam stretched his withered neck and kissed him on the chin.

"Do like I say."

"Yes, Sam."

A tear splashed on Sam's nose.

Sam had something more in his eyes to say but though he tried, agitated, couldn't say it. Then the trainmen came in with a stretcher and they lifted the catcher and handed him down the steps, and overhead the stars were bright but he knew he was dead.

Roy trailed the anonymous crowd out of Northwest Station and clung to the shadowy part of the wall till he had the courage to call a cab.

"Do you go to the Stevens Hotel?" he asked, and the driver without a word shot off before he could rightly be seated, passed a red light and scuttled a cripple across the deserted street. They drove for miles in a shadow-infested, street-lamped jungle.

He had once seen some stereopticon pictures of Chicago and it was a boxed-up ant heap of stone and crumbling wood buildings in a many-miled spreading checkerboard of streets without much open space to speak of except the railroads, stockyards, and the shore of a windy lake. In the Loop, the offices went up high and the streets were jampacked with people, and he wondered how so many of them could live together in any one place. Suppose there was a fire or something and they all ran out of their houses to see—how could they help but trample all over themselves? And Sam had warned him against strangers, because there were so many bums, sharpers, and gangsters around, people you were dirt to, who didn't know you and didn't want to, and for a dime they would slit your throat and leave you dying in the streets.

"Why did I come here?" he muttered and felt sick for home.

The cab swung into Michigan Avenue, which gave a view of the lake and a white-lit building spiring into the sky, then before he knew it he was standing flatfooted (Christ, the size of it) in front of the hotel, an enormous four-sectioned fortress. He hadn't the nerve to go through the whirling doors but had to because this bellhop grabbed his things—he wrested the bassoon case loose—and led him across the thick-carpeted lobby to a desk where he signed a card and had to count out five of the wallet's pulpy dollars for a room he would give up as soon as he found a house to board in.

But his cubbyhole on the seventeenth floor was neat and private, so after he had stored everything in the closet he lost his nervousness. Unlatching the window brought in the lake breeze. He stared down at the lit sprawl of Chicago, standing higher than he ever had in his life except for a night or two on a mountain. Gazing down upon the city, he felt as if bolts in his knees, wrists, and neck had loosened and he had spread up in height. Here, so high in the world, with the earth laid out in small squares so far below, he knew he would go in tomorrow and wow them with his fast one, and they would know him for the splendid pitcher he was.

The telephone rang. He was at first scared to answer it. In a strange place, so far from everybody he knew, it couldn't possibly be for him.

It rang again. He picked up the phone and listened.

"Hello, Roy? This is Harriet."

He wasn't sure he had got it right. "Excuse me?"

"Harriet Bird, silly."

"Oh, Harriet." He had completely forgotten her.

"Come down to my room," she giggled, "and let me say welcome to the city."

"You mean now?"

"Right away." She gave him the room number.

"Sure." He meant to ask her how she knew he was here but she had hung up.

Then he was elated. So that's how they did it in the city. He combed his hair and got out his bassoon case. In the elevator a drunk tried to take it away from him but Roy was too strong for him.

He walked—it seemed ages because he was impatient— through a long corridor till he found her number and knocked.

"Come on in."

Opening the door, he was astonished at the enormous room. Through the white-curtained window the sight of the endless dark lake sent a shiver down his spine.

Then he saw her standing shyly in the far corner of the room, naked under the gossamer thing she wore, held up on her risen nipples and the puffed wedge of hair beneath her white belly. A great weight went off his mind.

As he shut the door she reached into the hat box which lay open next to a vase of white roses on the table and fitted the black feathered hat on her head. A thick veil fell to her breasts. In her hand she held a squat, shining pistol.

He was greatly confused and thought she was kidding but a grating lump formed in his throat and his blood shed ice. He cried out in a gruff voice, "What's wrong here?"

She said sweetly, "Roy, will you be the best there ever was in the game?"

"That's right."

She pulled the trigger (thrum of bull fiddle). The bullet cut a silver line across the water. He sought with his bare hands to catch it, but it eluded him and, to his horror, bounced into his gut. A twisted dagger of smoke drifted up from the gun barrel. Fallen on one knee he groped for the bullet, sickened as it moved, and fell over as the forest flew upward, and she, making muted noises of triumph and despair, danced on her toes around the stricken hero.

BATTER UP!

"I SHOULDA been a farmer," Pop Fisher said bitterly. "I shoulda farmed since the day I was born. I like cows, sheep, and those hornless goats—I am partial to nanny goats, my daddy wore a beard—I like to feed animals and milk 'em. I like fixing things, weeding poison oak out of the pasture, and seeing to the watering of the crops. I like to be by myself on a farm. I like to stand out in the fields, tending the vegetables, the corn, the winter wheat—greenest looking stuff you ever saw. When Ma was alive she kept urging me to leave baseball and take up farming, and I always meant to but after she died I had no heart for it." Pop's voice all but broke and Red Blow shifted nervously on the bench but Pop didn't cry. He took out his handkerchief, flipped it, and blew his nose. "I have that green thumb," he said huskily, "and I shoulda farmed instead of playing wet nurse to a last place, dead-to-the-neck ball team."

They were sitting in the New York Knights' dugout, scanning the dusty field, the listless game and half-empty stands.

"Tough," said Red. He kept his eye on the pitcher.

Removing his cap, Pop rubbed his bald head with his bandaged fingers. "It's been a blasted dry season. No rains at all. The grass is worn scabby in the outfield and the infield is cracking. My heart feels as dry as dirt for the little I have to show for all my years in the game."

He got up, stooped at the fountain and spat the warm, rusty water into the dust. "When the hell they going to fix this thing so we can have a decent drink of water? Did you speak to that bastard partner I have, like I said to?"

"Says he's working on it."

"Working on it," Pop grunted. "He's so tight that if he was any tighter he'd be too stiff to move. It was one of the darkest days of my life when that snake crawled into this club. He's done me out of more dough than I can count."

"Kid's weakening again," Red said. "He passed two."

Pop watched Fowler for a minute but let him stay. "If those boy scouts could bring in a coupla runs once in a while I'd change pitchers, but they couldn't bring their own grandmother in from across the street. What a butchering we took from the Pirates in the first game and here we are six runs behind in this. It's Memorial Day, all right, but not for the soldiers."

"Should've had some runs. Bump had four for four in the first, and two hits before he got himself chucked out of this."

Pop's face burned. "Don't mention that ape man to me—getting hisself bounced out of the game the only time we had runners on the bases when he come up."

"I'd've thrown him out too if I was the ump and he slid dry ice down my pants."

"I'd like to stuff him with ice. I never saw such a disgusting screwball for practical jokes."

Pop scratched violently under his loosely bandaged fingers. "And to top it off I have to go catch athlete's foot on my hands. Now ain't that one for the books? Everybody I have ever heard of have got it on their feet but I have to go and get it on both of my hands and be itchy and bandaged in this goshdarn hot weather. No wonder I am always asking myself is life worth the living of it."

"Tough," Red said. "He's passed Feeber, bases loaded."

Pop fumed. "My best pitcher and he blows up every time I put him against a first-place team. Yank him."

The coach, a lean and freckled man, got nimbly up on the dugout steps and signaled to the bullpen in right field. He sauntered out to the mound just as somebody in street clothes came up the stairs of the tunnel leading from the clubhouse and asked the player at the end of the bench, "Who's Fisher?" The player jerked his thumb toward the opposite side of the dugout, and the man, dragging a large, beat-up valise and a bassoon case, treaded his way to Pop.

When Pop saw him coming he exclaimed, "Oh, my eight-foot uncle, what have we got here, the Salvation Army band?"

The man set his things on the floor and sat down on a concrete step, facing Pop. He beheld an old geezer of sixty-five with watery blue eyes, a thin red neck and a bitter mouth, who looked like a lost banana in the overgrown baseball suit he wore, especially his skinny legs in loose blue-and-white stockings.

And Pop saw a tall, husky, dark-bearded fellow with old eyes but not bad features. His face was strong-boned, if a trifle meaty, and his mouth seemed pleasant though its expression was grim. For his bulk he looked lithe, and he appeared calmer than he felt, for although he was sitting here on this step he was still in motion. He was traveling (on the train that never stopped). His self, his mind, raced on and he felt he hadn't stopped going wherever he was going because he hadn't yet arrived. Where hadn't he arrived? Here. But now it was time to calm down, ease up on the old scooter, sit still and be quiet, though the inside of him was still streaming through towns and cities, across forests and fields, over long years.

"The only music I make," he answered Pop, patting the bassoon case, "is with my bat." Searching through the pockets of his frayed and baggy suit, worn to threads at the knees and elbows, he located a folded letter that he reached over to the manager. "I'm your new left fielder, Roy Hobbs."

"My what!" Pop exploded.

"It says in the letter."

Red, who had returned from the mound, took the letter, unfolded it, and handed it to Pop. He read it in a single swoop then shook his head in disbelief.

"Scotty Carson sent you?"

"That's right."

"He must be daffy."

Roy wet his dry lips.

Pop shot him a shrewd look. "You're thirty-five if you're a day."

"Thirty-four, but I'm good for ten years."

"Thirty-four—Holy Jupiter, mister, you belong in an old man's home, not baseball."

The players along the bench were looking at him. Roy licked his lips.

"Where'd he pick you up?" Pop asked.

"I was with the Oomoo Oilers."

"In what league?"

"They're semipros."

"Ever been in organized baseball?"

"I only recently got back in the game."

"What do you mean got back?"

"Used to play in high school."

Pop snorted. "Well, it's a helluva mess." He slapped the letter with the back of his fingers. "Scotty signed him and the Judge okayed it. Neither of them consulted me. They can't do that," he said to Red. "That thief in the tower might have sixty per cent of the stock but I have it in writing that I am to manage this team and approve all player deals *as long as I live*."

"I got a contract," said Roy.

"Lemme see it."

Roy pulled a blue-backed paper out of his inside coat pocket.

Pop scanned it. "Where in blazes did he get the figure of three thousand dollars?"

"It was for a five thousand minimum but the Judge said I already missed one-third of the season."

Pop burst into scornful laughter. "Sure, but that entitles you to about thirty-three hundred. Just like that godawful deadbeat. He'd skin his dead father if he could get into the grave."

He returned the contract to Roy. "It's illegal."

"Scotty's your chief scout?" Roy asked.

"That's right."

"He signed me to a contract with an open figure and the Judge filled it in. I asked about that and Scotty said he had the authority to sign me."

"He has," Red said to Pop. "You said so yourself if he found anybody decent."

"That's right, that's what I said, but who needs a fielder old enough to be my son? I got a left fielder," he said to Roy, "a darn good one when he feels like it and ain't playing practical jokes on everybody."

Roy stood up. "If you don't want me, Merry Christmas."

"Wait a second," said Red. He fingered Pop up close to the fountain and spoke to him privately.

Pop calmed down. "I'm sorry, son," he apologized to Roy when he returned to the bench, "but you came across me at a bad time. Also thirty-four years for a rookie is starting with one foot in the grave. But like Red says, if our best scout sent you, you musta showed him something. Go on in the clubhouse and have Dizzy fit you up with a monkey suit. Then report back here and I will locate you a place on this bench with the rest of my All-Stars." He threw the players a withering look and they quickly turned away.

"Listen, mister," Roy said, "I know my way out of this jungle if you can't use me. I don't want any second pickings."

"Do as he told you," Red said.

Roy rose, got his valise and bassoon case together, and headed into the tunnel. His heart was thumping like a noisy barrel.

"I shoulda bought a farm," Pop muttered.

The pitcher in the shower had left the door wide open so the locker room was clouded with steam when Roy came in. Unable to find anybody he yelled into the shower room where was the prop man, and the one in the shower yelled back in the equipment room and close the door it was drafty. When the steam had thinned out and Roy could see his way around he located the manager's office, so labeled in black letters on the door, but not the equipment room. In the diagonally opposite corner were the trainer's quarters, and here the door was ajar and gave forth an oil of wintergreen smell that crawled up his nose. He could see the trainer, in a gray sweat shirt with KNIGHTS stenciled across his chest, working on a man mountain on the rubbing table. Catching sight of Roy, the trainer called out in an Irish brogue who was he looking for?

"Prop man," Roy said.

"That's Dizzy—down the hall." The trainer made with his eyes to the left so Roy opened the door there and went down the hall. He located a sign, "Equipment," and through the window under it saw the prop man in a baseball jersey sitting on a uniform trunk with his back to the wall. He was reading the sports page of the *Mirror*.

Roy rapped on the ledge and Dizzy, a former utility pitcher, hastily put the paper down. "Caught me at an interesting moment," he grinned. "I was reading about this catcher that got beaned in Boston yesterday. Broke the side of his skull."

"The name's Roy Hobbs, new hand here. Fisher told me to get outfitted."

"New man—fielder, eh?"

Roy nodded.

"Yeah, we been one man short on the roster for two weeks. One of our guys went and got himself hit on the head with a fly ball and both of his legs are now paralyzed."

Roy winked.

"Honest to God. And just before that our regular third baseman stepped on a bat and rolled down the dugout steps. Snapped his spine in two places." Dizzy grimaced. "We sure been enjoying an unlucky season."

He came forth with a tape measure and took Roy's measurements, then he went back and collected a pile of stuff from the shelves.

"Try this for size." He handed him a blue cap with a white K stitched on the front of it.

Roy tried it. "Too small."

"You sure got some size noggin there."

"Seven and a half." Roy looked at him.

"Just a social remark. No offense meant or intended." He gave Roy a size that fitted.

"How's it look?" Roy asked.

"A dream but why the tears?"

"I have a cold." He turned away.

Dizzy asked him to sign for the stuff—Judge Banner insisted. He helped Roy carry it to his locker.

"Keep anything you like inside of here but for goodness' sakes no booze. Pop throws fits if any of the players drink."

Roy stood the bassoon case in upright. "Got a lock for the door?"

"Nobody locks their doors here. Before the game you deposit your valuables in that trunk there and I will lock them up."

"Okay, skip it."

Dizzy excused himself to get back to his paper and Roy began to undress.

The locker room was tomblike quiet. The pitcher who had been in the showers—his footsteps were still wet on the floor—had dressed rapidly and vanished. As he put his things away, Roy found himself looking around every so often to make sure he was here. He was, all right, yet in all his imagining of how it would be when he finally hit the majors, he had not expected to feel so down in the dumps. It was different than he had thought it would be. So different he almost felt like walking out, jumping back on a train, and going wherever people went when they were running out on something.

Maybe for a long rest in one of those towns he had lived in as a kid. Like the place where he had that shaggy mutt that used to scamper through the woods, drawing him after it to the deepest, stillest part, till the silence was so pure you could crack it if you threw a rock. Roy remained lost in the silence till the dog's yapping woke him, though as he came out of it, it was not barking he heard but the sound of voices through the trainer's half-open door.

He listened closely because he had the weird impression that he knew all the voices in there, and as he sorted them he recognized first the trainer's brogue and then a big voice that he did not so much recall, as remember having heard throughout his life—a strong, rawboned voice, familiar from his boyhood and some of the jobs he had worked at later, and the different places he had bummed around in, slop joints, third-rate hotels, prize fight gyms and such; the big voice of a heavy, bull-necked, strong-muscled guy, the kind of gorilla he had more than once fought half to death for no reason he could think of. Oh, the Whammer, he thought, and quickly ducked but straightened up when he remembered the Whammer was almost fifty and long since retired out of the game. But what made him most uneasy was a third voice, higher than the other two, a greedy, penetrating, ass-kissing voice he had definitely heard before. He strained his ears to hear it again but the big voice was talking about this gag he had pulled on Pop Fisher, in particular, spraying white pepper in Pop's handkerchief, which made him sneeze and constantly blow his beak. That commenced an epidemic of base stealing, to Pop's fury, because the signal to steal that day was for him to raise his handkerchief to his schnozzle.

At the end of the story there was a guffaw and a yelp of laughter, then the trainer remarked something and this other voice, one that stood on stilts, commented that Bump certainly got a kick out of his jokes, and Bump, he must have been, said Pop wouldn't agree to his release, so if he was going to be stuck in this swamp he would at least have a little fun.

He laughed loudly and said, "Here's one for your colyum, kid. We were in Cincy in April and had a free day on our hands because this exhibition game was called off, so in the Plaza lobby that morning we get to bulling about players and records, and you know Pop and this line of his about how lousy the modern player is compared to those mustached freaks he played with in the time of King Tut. He was saying that the average fielder nowadays could maybe hit the kangaroo ball we got—he was looking at me—but you couldn't count on him to catch a high fly. 'How high?' I ask him, innocent, and he points up and says, 'Any decent height. They either lose them in the sun or misjudge them in the wind.' So I say, 'Could you catch the real high ones, Pop?' And he pipes up, 'As high as they went up I could catch them.' He thinks a minute and says, 'I bet I could catch a ball that is dropped from the top of the Empire State Building.' 'No,' I says, like I was surprised, and 'Yes,' he says. So I say, 'We have nothing on for today, and although there isn't any Empire State Building in Cincinnati, yet I do have this friend of mine at the airport who owns a Piper Cub. I will give him a National League baseball and he will drop it at the height of the building if you will catch it.' 'Done,' he says, as perky as a turkey, so I call up this guy I know and arrange it and off we go across the bridge to the Kentucky side of the river, where there is plenty of room to move around in. Well, sir, soon this yellow plane comes over and circles a couple of times till he has the right height, and then he lets go with something that I didn't tell Pop, but which the boys are onto, is a grapefruit so that if it hits him it will not crack his skull open and kill him. Down the thing comes like a cannonball and Pop, in his black two-piece bathing suit, in case he has to go a little in the water, and wearing a mitt the size of a basket, circles under it like a dizzy duck, holding the sun out of his eyes as he gets a line on where it is coming down. Faster it falls, getting bigger by the second, then Pop, who is now set for the catch, suddenly lets out a howl, 'My Christ, the moon is falling on me,' and the next second, bong—the grapefruit busts him on the conk and we have all we can do to keep him from drowning in the juice."

Now there was a loud cackle of laughter in the trainer's room. The voice Roy didn't like—the frightening thought dawned on him that the voice *knew* what he was hiding—it changed the subject and wanted to know from Bump if there was any truth to the rumor about him and Pop's niece.

"Naw," Bump said, and cagily asked, "What rumor?"

"That you and Memo are getting hitched."

Bump laughed. "She must've started that one herself."

"Then you deny it?"

The door was shoved open and Bump waltzed out in his shorts, as husky, broadbacked, and big-shouldered as Roy had thought, followed by the trainer and a slightly popeyed gent dressed in an expensive striped suit, whose appearance gave Roy a shooting pain in the pit of the stomach—Max Mercy.

Ashamed to be recognized, to have his past revealed like an egg spattered on the floor, Roy turned away, tucking his jersey into his pants.

But Bump paraded over with his hairy arm outstretched. "Hiya, Buster, you the latest victim they have trapped?"

Roy felt an irritable urge to pitch his fist at the loudmouth, but he nodded and shook hands.

"Welcome to the lousiest team in the world, barring none," Bump said. "And this is ol' Doc Casey, the trainer, who has got nobody but cripples on his hands except me. And the hawk-shaw with the eyes is Max Mercy, the famous sports colyumist. Most newspaper guys are your pals and know when to keep their traps shut, but to Max a private life is a personal insult. Before you are here a week he will tell the public how much of your salary you send to your grandma and how good is your sex life."

Max, whose mustache and sideboards were graying, laughed hollowly. He said to Roy, "Didn't catch the name."

"Roy Hobbs," he said stiffly, but no one seemed to think it mattered very much.

The game was over and the players hoofed through the tunnel into the locker room. They tore out of their uniforms and piled into the showers. Some stayed in only long enough to wet their skins. Wiping themselves dry, they tumbled into street clothes. Their speed, however, did them no good, for Red, after courteously asking Mercy to leave, posted himself and Earl Wilson, the third base coach, at the door and they let nobody else out. The players waited nervously, except Bump, who slapped backs and advised everybody to cheer up. A few of the boys were working the strategy of staying in the showers so long they hoped Pop would grow sick and tired and leave.

But Pop, a self-sustaining torch in the shut managerial office, outwaited them, and when he got the quiet knock from Red that the lobsters were in the pot, yanked open the door and strode sulphurously forth. The team shriveled.

Pop stepped up on a chair where for once, a bald, bristling figure, he towered over them. Waving his bandaged hands he began to berate them but immediately stopped, choked by his rage into silence.

"If he coughs now," Bump boomed, "he will bust into dust."

Pop glared at him, his head glowing like a red sun. He savagely burst out that not a single blasted one of them here was a true ballplayer. They were sick monkeys, broken-down mules, pigeon-chested toads, slimy horned worms, but not real, honest-to-god baseball players.

"How's about flatfooted fish?" Bump wisecracked. "Get it, boys, fish—Fisher," and he fell into a deep gargle of laughter at his wit, but the semi-frozen players in the room did not react.

"How's he get away with it?" Roy asked the ghost standing next to him. The pale player whispered out of the corner of his mouth that Bump was presently the leading hitter in the league.

Pop ignored Bump and continued to give the team the rough side of his tongue. "What beats me is that I have spent thousands of dollars for the best players I could lay my hands on. I hired two of the finest coaches in the game. I sweat myself sick trying to direct you, and all you can deliver is those goddamn goose eggs." His voice rose. "Do you dimwits realize that we have been skunked for the last forty-five innings in a row?"

"Not Bumpsy," the big voice said, "I am terrific."

"You now hold the record of the most consecutive games lost in the whole league history, the most strikeouts, the most errors—"

"Not Bumpsy—"

"—the most foolishness and colossal stupidities. In plain words, you all stink. I am tempted to take pity on those poor dopes who spend a buck and a half to watch you play and trade the whole lousy lot of you away."

Bump dropped down on his knees and raised his clasped hands. "Me first, Lawdy, me first."

"—and start from scratch to build up a team that will know how to play together and has guts and will fight the other guy to death before they drop seventeen games in the cellar."

The players in the locker room were worn out but Bump was singing, "Many brave hearts are asleep in the deep."

"Beware," he croaked low in his throat, "bewaaare—"

Pop shook a furious finger at him that looked as if it would fly off and strike him in the face. "As for you, Bump Baily, high and mighty though you are, some day you'll pay for your sassifras. Remember that lightning cuts down the tallest trees too."

Bump didn't like warnings of retribution. His face turned surly.

"Lightning, maybe, but no burnt out old fuse."

Pop tottered. "Practice at eight in the morning," he said brokenly. But for Red he would have tumbled off the chair. In his office behind the slammed and smoking door they could hear him sobbing, "Sometimes I could cut my own throat."

It took the Knights a while to grow bones and crawl out after Bump. But when everybody had gone, including the coaches and Dizzy, Roy remained behind. His face was flaming hot, his clothes soaked in sweat and shame, as if the old man's accusations had been leveled at his head.

When Pop came out in his street clothes, a yellowed Panama and a loud sport jacket, he was startled to see Roy sitting there in the gloom and asked what he was waiting for.

"No place to go," Roy said.

"Whyn't you get a room?"

"Ain't got what it takes."

Pop looked at him. "Scotty paid you your bonus cash, didn't he?"

"Two hundred, but I had debts."

"You shoulda drawn an advance on your first two weeks' pay from the office when you came in today. It's too late now, they quit at five, so I will write you out my personal check for twenty-five dollars and you can pay me back when you get the money."

Pop balanced his checkbook on his knee. "You married?"

"No."

"Why'n't you ask around among the married players to see who has got a spare room? That way you'd have a more regular life. Either that, or in a respectable boarding house. Some of the boys who have their homes out of town prefer to stay at a moderate-priced hotel, which I myself have done since my wife passed away, but a boarding house is more homelike and cheaper. Anyway," Pop advised, "tonight you better come along with me to the hotel and tomorrow you can find a place to suit your needs."

Roy remarked he wasn't particularly crazy about hotels.

They left the ball park, got into a cab and drove downtown. The sky over the Hudson was orange. Once Pop broke out of his reverie to point out Grant's Tomb.

At the Midtown Hotel, Pop spoke to the desk clerk and he assigned Roy a room on the ninth floor, facing toward the Empire State Building. Pop went up with him and pumped the mattress.

"Not bad," he said.

After the bellhop had left he said he hoped Roy wasn't the shenanigan type.

"What kind?" Roy asked.

"There are all sorts of nuts in this game and I remember one of my players—seems to me it was close to twenty years ago—who used to walk out on the fifteenth floor ledge and scare fits out of people in the other rooms. One day when he was walking out there he fell and broke his leg and only the darndest luck kept him from rolling right overboard. It was beginning to rain and he pulled himself around from window to window, begging for help, and everybody went into stitches at his acting but kept their windows closed. He finally rolled off and hit bottom."

Roy had unpacked his valise and was washing up.

"Lemme tell you one practical piece of advice, son," Pop went on. "You're starting way late—I was finished after fifteen years as an active player one year after the age you're coming in, but if you want to get along the best way, behave and give the game all you have got, and when you can't do that, quit. We don't need any more goldbrickers or fourflushers or practical jokers around. One Bump Baily is too much for any team."

He left the room, looking wretched.

The phone jangled and after a minute Roy got around to lifting it.

"What's the matter?" Red Blow barked. "Don't you answer your telephone?"

"I like it to ring a little, gives 'em a chance to change their mind."

"Who?"

"Anybody."

Red paused. "Pop asked me to show you around. When are you eating?"

"I am hungry now."

"Meet me in the lobby, half past six."

As Roy hung up there was a loud dum-diddy-um-dum on the door and Bump Baily in a red-flowered Hollywood shirt breezed in.

"Hiya, buster. Saw you pull in with the old geezer and tracked you down. I would like for you to do me a favor."

"Roy is the name."

"Roy is fine. Listen, I got my room on the fourth floor, which is a damn sight classier than this mouse trap. I would like you to borrow it and I will borrow this for tonight."

"What's the pitch?"

"I am having a lady friend visit me and there are too many nosy people on my floor."

Roy considered and said okay. He unconsciously wet his lips.

Bump slapped him between the shoulders. "Stick around, buster, you will get yours."

Roy knew he would never like the guy.

Bump told him his room number and they exchanged keys, then Roy put a few things into his valise and went downstairs.

Coming along the fourth floor hall he saw a door half open and figured this was it. As he pulled the knob he froze, for there with her back to him stood a slim, redheaded girl in black panties and brassiere. She was combing her hair before a mirror on the wall as the light streamed in around her through the billowy curtains. When she saw him in the mirror she let out a scream. He stepped back as if he had been kicked in the face. Then the door slammed and he had a splitting headache.

Bump's room was next door so Roy went in and lay down

on the bed, amid four purple walls traced through with leaves flying among white baskets of fruit, some loaded high and some spilled over. He lay there till the pain in his brain eased.

At 6:30 he went down and met Red, in a droopy linen suit, and they had steaks in a nearby chophouse. Roy had two and plenty of mashed potatoes. Afterwards they walked up Fifth Avenue. He felt better after the meal.

"Want to see the Village?" Red said.

"What's in it?"

Red picked his teeth. "Beats me. Whatever they got I can't find it. How about a picture?"

Roy was agreeable so they dropped into a movie. It was a picture about a city guy who came to the country, where he had a satisfying love affair with a girl he met. Roy enjoyed it. As they walked back to the hotel the night was soft and summery. He thought about the black-brassiered girl in the next room.

Red talked about the Knights. "They are not a bad bunch of players, but they aren't playing together and it's mostly Bump's fault. He is for Bump and not for the team. Fowler, Schultz, Hinkle, and Hill are all good pitchers and could maybe be fifteen or twenty game winners if they got some support in the clutches, which they don't, and whatever Bump gives them in hitting he takes away with his lousy fielding."

"How's that?"

"He's just so damn lazy. Pop has thrown many a fine and suspension at him, but after that he will go into a slump on purpose and we don't win a one. If I was Pop I'da had his ass long ago, but Pop thinks a hitter like him could be a bell cow and lead the rest ahead, so he keeps hoping he will reform. If we could get the team rolling we'd be out of the cellar in no time."

They were approaching the hotel and Roy counted with his eyes up to the fourth floor and watched the curtains in the windows.

"I read Scotty's report on you," Red said. "He says you are a terrific hitter. How come you didn't start playing when you were younger?"

"I did but I flopped." Roy was evasive.

Red cringed. "Don't say that word around here."

"What word?"

"Flopped—at least not anywhere near Pop. He starts to cry when he hears it."

"What for?"

"Didn't you ever hear about Fisher's Flop?"

"Seems to me I did but I am not sure."

Red told him the story. "About forty years ago Pop was the third sacker for the old Sox when they got into their first World Series after twenty years. They sure wanted to take the flag that year but so did the Athletics, who they were playing, and it was a rough contest all the way into the seventh game. That one was played at Philly and from the first inning the score stood at 3–3, until the Athletics drove the tie-breaker across in the last of the eighth. In the ninth the Sox's power was due up but they started out bad. The leadoffer hit a blooper to short, the second struck out, and the third was Pop. It was up to him. He let one go for a strike, then he slammed a low, inside pitch for a tremendous knock.

"The ball sailed out to deep center," Red said, "where the center fielder came in too fast and it rolled through him to the fence and looked good for an inside-the-park homer, or at least a triple. Meanwhile, Pop, who is of course a young guy at this time, was ripping around the bags, and the crowd was howling for him to score and tie up the game, when in some crazy way as he was heading for home, his legs got tangled under him and he fell flat on his stomach, the living bejesus knocked out of him. By the time he was up again the ball was in the catcher's glove and he ran up the baseline after Pop. In the rundown that followed, the third baseman tagged him on the behind and the game was over."

Red spat into the street. Roy tried to say something but couldn't.

"That night Fisher's Flop, or as they mostly call it, 'Fisher's Famous Flop,' was in every newspaper in the country and was talked about by everybody. Naturally Pop felt like hell. I understand that Ma Fisher had the phone out and hid him up in the attic. He stayed there two weeks, till the roof caught fire and he had to come out or burn. After that they went to Florida for a vacation but it didn't help much. His picture was known to all and wherever he went they yelled after him,

'Flippity-flop, flippity-flop.' It was at this time that Pop lost his hair. After a while people no longer recognized him, except on the ball field, yet though the kidding died down, Pop was a marked man."

Roy mopped his face. "Hot," he said.

"But he had his guts in him," Red said, "and stayed in the game for ten years more and made a fine record. Then he retired from baseball for a couple of years, which was a good thing but he didn't know it. Soon one of Ma's rich relatives died and left them a pile of dough that Pop used to buy himself a half share of the Knights. He was made field manager and the flop was forgotten by now except for a few wise-egg sportswriters that, when they are too drunk to do an honest day's work, would raise up the old story and call it Fisher's Fizzle, or Farce, or Fandango—you wouldn't guess there are so many funny words beginning with an f—which some of them do to this day when the Knights look foolish. The result is that Pop has the feeling he has been jinxed since the time of his flop, and he has spent twenty-five years and practically all of his pile trying to break the jinx, which he thinks he can do by making the Knights into the world champs that the old Sox never did become. Eight times he has finished in second place, five in third, and the rest in fourth or fifth, but last season when the Judge bought into the club and then took advantage of Pop's financial necessity to get hold of ten per cent of his shares and make himself the majority stockholder, was our worst season. We ended up in the sewer and this year it looks like a repeat."

"How come?"

"The Judge is trying to push Pop out of his job although he has a contract to manage for life—that's what the Judge had to promise to get that ten per cent of stock. Anyway, he's been trying everything he can think of to make things tough for Pop. He has by his sly ways forced all sorts of trades on us which make money all right but hurt the team. It burns me up," Red said, "because I would give my right arm if I could get Pop the pennant. I am sure that if he took one and the Series after that, he would feel satisfied, quit baseball, and live in peace. He is one helluva white guy and deserves better than he got. That's why I am asking you to give him the best you have in you."

"Let him play me," Roy said, "and he will get the best."

In the lobby Red said he had enjoyed Roy's company and they should eat together more. Before he left he warned Roy to be careful with his earnings. They weren't much, he knew, but if in the future Roy had a chance to invest in something good, he advised him to do so. "There is a short life in baseball and we have to think of the future. Anything can happen to you in this game. Today you are on top and tomorrow you will be on your way out to Dubuque. Try to protect your old age. It don't pay to waste what you earn."

To his surprise, Roy answered, "To hell with my old age. I will be in this game a long time."

Red rubbed his chin. "How are you so sure?"

"It wasn't for nothing it took me fifteen years to get here. I came for more than the ride and I will leave my mark around here."

Red waited to hear more but Roy shut up.

Red shrugged, "Well, each to their choice."

Roy said good night and went upstairs. Entering Bump's room, he picked up a gilt hairpin from the carpet and put it into his wallet because some claimed it brought luck. For a while he stood at the window and watched the lit Empire State Building. It was a great big city, all right. He undressed, thinking of Pop's flop that changed his whole life, and got into bed.

In the dark the bed was in motion, going round in wide, sweeping circles. He didn't like the feeling so he lay deathly still and let everything go by—the trees, mountains, states. Then he felt he was headed into a place where he did not want to go and tried urgently to think of ways to stop the bed. But he couldn't and it went on, a roaring locomotive now, screaming into the night, so that he was tensed and sweating and groaned aloud why did it have to be me? what did I do to deserve it? seeing himself again walking down the long, lonely corridor, carrying the bassoon case, the knock, the crazy Harriet (less and more than human) with the shiny pistol, and him, cut down in the very flower of his youth, lying in a red pool of his own blood.

No, he cried, oh no, and lashed at his pillow, as he had a thousand times before.

Finally, as the sight of him through the long long years of

suffering faded away, he quieted down. The noise of the train eased off as it came to a stop, and Roy found himself set down in a field somewhere in the country, where he had a long and satisfying love affair with this girl he had seen in the picture tonight.

He thought of her till he had fallen all but deep asleep, when a door seemed to open in the mind and this naked redheaded lovely slid out of a momentary flash of light, and the room was dark again. He thought he was still dreaming of the picture but the funny part of it was when she got into bed with him he almost cried out in pain as her icy hands and feet, in immediate embrace, slashed his hot body, but there among the apples, grapes, and melons, he found what he wanted and had it.

AT THE clubhouse the next morning the unshaven Knights were glum and redeyed. They moved around listlessly and cursed each step. Angry fist fights broke out among them. They were sore at themselves and the world, yet when Roy came in and headed for his locker they looked up and watched with interest. He opened the door and found his new uniform knotted up dripping wet on a hook. His sanitary socks and woolen stockings were slashed to shreds and all the other things were smeared black with shoe polish. He located his jock, with two red apples in it, swinging from a cord attached to the light globe, and both his shoes were nailed to the ceiling. The boys let out a bellow of laughter. Bump just about doubled up howling, but Roy yanked the wet pants off the hook and caught him with it smack in the face. The players let out another yowl.

Bump comically dried himself with a bath towel, digging deep into his ears, wiping under the arms, and shimmying as he rubbed it across his fat behind.

"Fast guesswork, buster, and to show you there's no hard feelings, how's about a Camel?"

Roy wanted nothing from the bastard but took the cigarette because everyone was looking on. When he lit it, someone in the rear yelled, "Fire!" and ducked as it burst in Roy's face. Bump had disappeared. The players fell into each other's arms. Tears streamed down their cheeks. Some of them could not unbend and limped around from laughing so.

Roy flipped the ragged butt away and began to mop up his wet locker.

Allie Stubbs, the second baseman, danced around the room in imitation of a naked nature dancer. He pretended to discover a trombone at the foot of a tree and marched around blowing oompah, oompah, oompah.

Roy then realized the bassoon case was missing. It startled him that he hadn't thought of it before.

"Who's got it, boys?"—but no one answered. Allie now made out like he was flinging handfuls of rose petals into the trainer's office.

Going in there, Roy saw that Bump had broken open the bassoon case and was about to attack Wonderboy with a hacksaw.

"Lay off of that, you goon."

Bump turned and stepped back with the bat raised. Roy grabbed it and with a quick twist tore it out of his sweaty hands, turning him around as he did and booting him hard with his knee. Bump grunted and swung but Roy ducked. The team crowded into the trainer's office, roaring with delight.

But Doc Casey pushed his way through them and stepped between Roy and Bump. "That'll do, boys. We want no trouble here. Go on outside or Pop will have your hides."

Bump was sweaty and sore. "You're a lousy sport, alfalfa."

"I don't like the scummy tricks you play on people you have asked for a favor," Roy said.

"I hear you had a swell time, wonderboy."

Again they grappled for each other, but Doc, shouting for help, kept them apart until the players pinned Roy's arms and held on to Bump.

"Lemme at him," Bump roared, "and I will skin the skunk."

Held back by the team, they glared at one another over the trainer's head.

"What's going on in there?" Pop's shrill blast came from inside the locker room. Earl Wilson poked his grayhaired, sunburned head in and quickly called, "All out, men, on the double." The players scurried past Pop and through the tunnel. They felt better.

Dizzy hustled up a makeshift rig for Roy. He dressed and polished his bat, a little sorry he had lost his temper, because he had wanted to speak quietly to the guy and find out whether he was expecting the redhead in his room last night.

Thinking about her made him uneasy. He reported to Pop in the dugout.

"What was that trouble in there between Bump and you?" Pop asked.

Roy didn't say and Pop got annoyed. "I won't stand for any ructions between players so cut it out or you will find yourself chopping wood back in the sticks. Now report to Red."

Roy went over to where Red was catching Chet Schultz,

today's pitcher, and Red said to wait his turn at the batting cage.

The field was overrun with droopy players. Half a dozen were bunched near the gate of the cage, waiting to be pitched to by Al Fowler, whom Pop had ordered to throw batting practice for not bearing down in the clutches yesterday. Some of the men were at the sidelines, throwing catch. A few were shagging flies in the field, a group was playing pepper. On the line between home and first Earl Wilson was hacking out grounders to Allie Stubbs, Cal Baker at short, Hank Benz, the third baseman, and Emil Lajong, who played first. At the edge of the outfield, Hinkle and Hill, two of the regular starters, and McGee, the reliefer, were doing a weak walk-run-walk routine. No one seemed to be thoroughly awake, but when Roy went into the batting cage they came to life and observed him.

Fowler, a southpaw, was in a nasty mood. He didn't like having his ears burned by Pop, called a showboat in front of the other men, and then shoved into batting practice the day after he had pitched. Fowler was twenty-three but looked thirty. He was built rangy, with very light hair and eyelashes, and small blue eyes. As a pitcher he had the stuff and knew it, but all season long he had been erratic and did a great amount of griping. He was palsy with Bump, who as a rule had no friends.

When Roy came up with Wonderboy, he hugged the plate too close to suit Fowler, who was in there anyway only to help the batters find their timing. In annoyance Fowler pitched the ball at Roy's head. Roy hit the dirt.

Pop shrieked, "Cut that out, you blasted fool." Fowler mumbled something about the ball slipping. Yet he wanted to make Roy look silly and burned the next one in. Roy swung and the ball sailed over the right field fence. Red-faced, Fowler tried a hard, sharp-breaking curve. Roy caught it at the end of his bat and pulled it into the left field stands.

"Try this one, grandpa." Fowler flung a stiff-wrist knuckler that hung in the air without spin before it took a sudden dip, but Roy scooped it up with the stick and lifted it twenty rows up into the center field stands. Then he quit. Fowler was scowling at his feet. Everybody else stared at Roy.

Pop called out, "Lemme see that bat, son."

Both he and Red examined it, hefting it and rubbing along the grain with their fingers.

"Where'd you get it?" Pop asked.

Roy cleared his throat. He said he had made it himself.

"Did you brand this name Wonderboy on it?"

"That's right."

"What's it mean?"

"I made it long ago," Roy said, "when I was a kid. I wanted it to be a very good bat and that's why I gave it that name."

"A bat's cheap to buy," Red said.

"I know it but this tree near the river where I lived was split by lightning. I liked the wood inside of it so I cut me out a bat. Hadn't used it much until I played semipro ball, but I always kept it oiled with sweet oil and boned it so it wouldn't chip."

"Sure is white. Did you bleach the wood?"

"No, that's the true color."

"How long ago d'you make it?" Pop asked.

"A long time—I don't remember."

"Whyn't you get into the game then?"

Roy couldn't answer for a minute. "I sorta got sidetracked."

But Pop was all smiles. "Red'll measure and weigh it. If there's no filler and it meets specifications you'll be allowed to use it."

"There's nothing in it but wood."

Red clapped him on the back. "I feel it in my bones that you will have luck with it." He said to Pop, "Maybe we can start Roy in the line-up soon?"

Pop said they would see how it worked out.

But he sent Roy out to left field and Earl hit fungos to him all over the lot. Roy ran them down well. He took one shot over his shoulder and two caroming off the wall below the stands. His throwing was quick, strong, and bull's eye.

When Bump got around to his turn in the cage, though he did not as a rule exert himself in practice, he now whammed five of Fowler's fast pitches into the stands. Then he trotted out to his regular spot in the sun field and Earl hit him some long flies, all of which he ran for and caught with gusto, even those that went close to the wall, which was unusual for him because he didn't like to go too near it.

Practice picked up. The men worked faster and harder than they had in a long time. Pop suddenly felt so good, tears came to his eyes and he had to blow his nose.

In the clubhouse about an hour and a half before game time, the boys were sitting around in their underwear after showers. They were bulling, working crossword puzzles, shaving and writing letters. Two were playing checkers, surrounded by a circle of others, and the rest were drinking soda, looking at the *Sporting News*, or just resting their eyes. Though they tried to hide it they were all nervous, always glancing up whenever someone came into the room. Roy couldn't make sense of it.

Red took him around to meet some of the boys and Roy spoke a few words to Dave Olson, the squat catcher, also to the shy Mexican center fielder, Juan Flores, and to Gabby Laslow, who patrolled right field. They sidestepped Bump, sitting in front of his locker with a bath towel around his rump, as he worked a red thread across the yellowed foot of a sanitary sock.

"Changes that thread from sock to sock every day," Red said in a low voice. "Claims it keeps him hitting."

As the players began to get into clean uniforms, Pop, wearing half-moon specs, stepped out of his office. He read aloud the batting order, then flipping through his dog-eared, yellow-paged notebook he read the names of the players opposing them and reminded them how the pitchers were to pitch and the fielders field them. This information was scribbled all over the book and Pop had to thumb around a lot before he had covered everybody. Roy then expected him to lay on with a blistering mustard plaster for all, but he only glanced anxiously at the door and urged them all to be on their toes and for gosh sakes get some runs.

Just as Pop finished his pep talk the door squeaked open and a short and tubby man in a green suit peeked in. Seeing they were ready, he straightened up and entered briskly, carrying a briefcase in his hand. He beamed at the players and without a word from anybody they moved chairs and benches and arranged themselves in rows before him. Roy joined the rest, expecting to hear some kind of talk. Only Pop and the coaches sat behind the man, and Dizzy lounged, half open-mouthed, at the door leading to the hall.

"What's the act?" Roy asked Olson.

"It's Doc Knobb." The catcher looked sleepy.

"What's he do?"

"Pacifies us."

The players were attentive, sitting as if they were going to have their pictures snapped. The nervousness Roy had sensed among them was all but gone. They looked like men whose worries had been lifted, and even Bump gave forth a soft grunt of contentment.

The doctor removed his coat and rolled up his shirtsleeves. "Got to hurry today," he told Pop, "got a polo team to cheer up in Brooklyn."

He smiled at the men and then spoke so softly, at first they couldn't hear him. When he raised his voice it exuded calm.

"Now, men," he purred, "all of you relax and let me have your complete attention. Don't think of a thing but me." He laughed, brushed a spot off his pants, and continued. "You know what my purpose is. You're familiar with that. It's to help you get rid of the fears and the personal inferiorities that tie you into knots and keep you from being aces in this game. Who are the Pirates? Not supermen, only mortals. What have they got that you haven't got? I can't think of a thing, absolutely not one. It's the attitude that's licking you—your own, not the Pirates'. What do you mean to yourselves? Are you a flock of bats flying around in a coffin, or the sun shining calmly on a blue lake? Are you sardines being swallowed up in the sea, or the whale that does the swallowing? That's why I'm here, to help you answer that question in the affirmative, to help you by mesmerism and autosuggestion, meaning you do the suggesting, not I. I only assist by making you receptive to your own basic thoughts. If you think you are winners, you will be. If you don't, you won't. That's psychology. That's the way the world works. Give me your whole attention and look straight into my eyes. What do you see there? You see sleep. That's right, sleep. So relax, sleep, relax . . ."

His voice was soft, lulling, peaceful. He had raised his pudgy arms and with stubby fingers was making ripples on a vast calm sea. Already Olson was gently snoring. Flores, with the tip of his tongue protruding, Bump, and some of the other players were fast asleep. Pop looked on, absorbed.

Staring at the light gleaming on Pop's bald bean, Roy felt himself going off . . . way way down, drifting through the tides into golden water as he searched for this lady fish, or mermaid, or whatever you called her. His eyes grew big in the seeking, first fish eyes, then bulbous frog eyes. Sailing lower into the pale green sea, he sought everywhere for the reddish glint of her scales, until the water became dense and dark green and then everything gradually got so black he lost all sight of where he was. When he tried to rise up into the light he couldn't find it. He darted in all directions, and though there were times he saw flashes of her green tail, it was dark everywhere. He threshed up a storm of luminous bubbles but they gave out little light and he did not know where in all the glass to go.

Roy ripped open his lids and sprang up. He shoved his way out from between the benches.

The doctor was startled but made no attempt to stop him. Pop called out, "Hey, where do you think you're going?"

"Out."

"Sit down, dammit, you're on the team."

"I might be on the team but no medicine man is going to hypnotize me."

"You signed a contract to obey orders," Pop snapped shrilly.

"Yes, but not to let anybody monkey around in my mind."

As he headed into the tunnel he heard Pop swear by his eight-foot uncle that nobody by the name of Roy Hobbs would ever play ball for him as long as he lived.

He had waited before . . . and he waited now, on a spike-scuffed bench in the dugout, hidden from sky, wind and weather, from all but the dust that blew up from Knights Field and lodged dry in the throat, as the grass grew browner. And from time ticking off balls and strikes, batters up and out, halves and full innings, games won and (mostly) lost, days and nights, and the endless train miles from Philly, with in-between stops, along the arc to St. Louis, and circling back by way of Chi, Boston, Brooklyn . . . still waiting.

"C'mon, Roy," Red had urged, "apologize to Pop, then the next time Knobb comes around, join the boys and everything will be okay."

"Nix on that," said Roy, "I don't need a shyster quack to shoot me full of confidence juice. I want to go through on my own steam."

"He only wants everybody to relax and be able to do their best."

Roy shook his head. "I been a long time getting here and now that I am, I want to do it by myself, not with that kind of bunk."

"Do what?" Red asked.

"What I have to do."

Red shrugged and gave him up as too stubborn. Roy sat around, and though it said on his chest he was one of the team, he sat among them alone; at the train window, gazing at the moving trees, in front of his locker, absorbed in an untied shoe lace, in the dugout, squinting at the great glare of the game. He traveled in their company and dressed where they did but he joined them in nothing, except maybe batting practice, entering the cage with the lumber on his shoulder glistening like a leg bone in the sun and taking his chops at the pill. Almost always he hammered the swift, often murderous throws (the practice pitchers dumped their bag of tricks on him) deep into the stands, as the players watched and muttered at the swift flight of the balls, then forgot him when the game started. But there were days when the waiting got him. He could feel the strength draining from his bones, weakening him so he could hardly lift Wonderboy. He was unwilling to move then, for fear he would fall over on his puss and have to crawl away on all fours. Nobody noticed he did not bat when he felt this way except Pop; and Bump, seeing how white his face was, squirted contemptuous tobacco juice in the dust. Then when Roy's strength ebbed back, he would once again go into the batters' cage and do all sorts of marvelous things that made them watch in wonder.

He watched *them* and bad as he felt he had to laugh. They were a nutty bunch to begin with but when they were losing they were impossible. It was like some kind of sickness. They threw to the wrong bases, bumped heads together in the outfield, passed each other on the baselines, sometimes batted out of order, throwing both Pop and the ump into fits, and cussed everybody else for their mistakes. It was not uncommon to see them pile three men on a bag, or behold a catcher on the opposing team, in a single skip and jump, lay the tag on two of them as they came thundering together into home plate. Or watch Gabby Laslow, in a tight spot, freeze onto the ball, or Allie Stubbs get socked with it in the jaw, thrown by Olson on a steal as Allie admired a lady in the stands. Doc Knobb's hypnotism cut down their jitters but it didn't much help their coordination, yet when they were left unhypnotized for a few days, they were afflicted with more than the usual number of hexes and whammies and practiced all sorts of magic to undo them. To a man they crossed their fingers over spilled salt, or coffee or tea, or at the sight of a hearse. Emil Lajong did a backward flip whenever he located a crosseyed fan in the stands. Olson hated a woman who wore the same drab brown-feathered hat every time she showed up. He spat through two fingers whenever he spotted her in the crowd. Bump went through his ritual with the colored threads in his socks and shorts. Pop sometimes stroked a rabbit's foot. Red Blow never changed his clothes during a "winning streak," and Flores secretly touched his genitals whenever a bird flew over his head.

They were not much different from the fans in the patched and peeling stands. On weekdays the stadium usually looked like a haunted house but over the weekend crowds developed. The place often resembled a zoo full of oddballs, including gamblers, bums, drunks, and some ugly crackpots. Many of them came just to get a laugh out of the bonehead plays. Some, when the boys were losing, cursed and jeered, showering them—whenever they came close enough—with rotten cabbages, tomatoes, blackened bananas and occasionally an eggplant. Yet let the umpire call a close play against the Knights and he became a target for pop bottles, beer cans, old shoes or anything that happened to be lying around loose. Surprisingly, however, a few players were chosen for affection and even admiration by their fans. Sadie Sutter, a girl of sixty-plus, who wore large flowered hats, bobby sox, and short skirts, showed her undying love for Dave Olson every time he came up to the plate by banging with all her might on a Chinese gong she dragged into the stadium every day. A Hungarian cook, a hearty man with a hard yellow straw hat jammed tight on his skull, hopped up on his seat and crowed like a rooster whenever Emil Lajong originated a double play. And there was a girl named Gloria from Mississippi, a washed-out flower of the vestibules, who between innings when her eyes were not on the game, lined up a customer or two for a quickie later. She gave her heart to Gabby, yelling, "Get a move on, molasses," to set him in motion after a fly ball. Besides these, there had appeared early in the present season, a pompous Otto P. Zipp, whose peevish loudspeaker could be heard all over the park, his self-chosen mission to rout the critics of Bump Baily, most of whom razzed the big boy for short legging on the other fielders. The dwarf honked a loud horn at the end of a two-foot walking stick, and it sounded as if a flock of geese had been let loose at the offenders, driving them—his purple curses ringing in their ears—to seek shelter in some hidden hole in the stands or altogether out of the ballpark. Zipp was present at every home game, sitting at the rail in short left field, and Bump made it his much publicized business, as he trotted out to his position at the start of the game, to greet him with a loud kiss on the forehead, leaving Otto in a state of creamy bliss.

Roy got to know them all as he waited, all one if you looked long enough through the haze of cigarette smoke, except one . . . Memo Paris, Pop's redheaded niece, sad, spurned lady, who sat without wifehood in the wives' box behind third base. He could, if she would let him, find her with his eyes shut, with his hands alone as he had in the dark. Always in the act of love she lived in his mind, the only way he knew her, because she would not otherwise suffer his approach. *He* was to blame, she had wept one bitter midnight, so she hated his putrid guts. Since the team's return to the city (the phone banged in his ear and she ripped up his letters when they were delivered) whenever he got up from his seat in the hotel lobby as she stepped out of the elevator, to say how sorry he was for beginning at the wrong end, she tugged at her summer furpiece and breezed past him in greeneyed scorn, withering in the process Bump at the cigar stand, who had laughed aloud at Roy's rout. ("Honeybunch," he had explained, "it was out of the pity of my heart that I took that shmo into my room, because they didn't have one for him and I was intending to pass the night at the apartment of my he cousin from Mobile.

How'd I know you'd go in there when you said you weren't speaking to me?" He swore it hadn't been a gag—had he ever pulled one on her?—but Memo punished him in silence, punishing herself, and he knew it because she still came every day to see him play.) She walked out of the lobby, with her silver bracelets tinkling, swaying a little on her high heels, as if she had not too long ago learned to walk on them, and went with her beautiful body away, for which Roy everlastingly fried Bump Baily in the deep fat of his abomination.

It was for her he waited.

On the morning of the twenty-first of June Pop told Roy that as of tomorrow he was being shipped to a Class B team in the Great Lakes Association. Roy said he was quitting baseball anyway, but that same day, in answer to an angry question of Pop's as to why the team continued to flop, Doc Knobb said that the manager's hysterical behavior was undoing all the good he had done, and he offered to hypnotize Pop along with the others without hiking his fee. Pop shrilly told the psychologist he was too old for such bamboozlement, and Knobb retorted that his attitude was not only ridiculous but stupid. Pop got redfaced and told him to go to perdition with his hocus pocus and as of right then the doctor was canned.

That afternoon the Knights began a series with the second-place Phils. Instead of falling into a swoon when they learned there was to be no further hypnosis, the team played its best ball in weeks. Against superior pitching, in the sixth they bunched three singles for a run, and though Schultz had already given up five hits to the Phils, they were scattered and came to nothing. The Phils couldn't score till the top of the eighth, when with two out Schultz weakened, walking one man and handing the next a good enough throw to hit for a sharp single, so that there were now men on first and third. Up came Rogers, the Phils' slugger, and hit a fast curve for what looked like no more than a long fly ball, a routine catch, to left center. Now it happened that Bump was nearer to the ball than Flores, who was shifted to the right, but he was feeling horny in the sun and casting about in his mind for who to invite to his bed tonight, when he looked up and noticed this ball coming. He still had time to get under it but then saw

Flores going for it like a galloping horse, and the anguished look on the Mexican's face, his black eyes popping, neck like a thick rope, and mouth haunted, fascinated Bump so, he decided to let him have it if he wanted it that bad. At the last minute he tried to take it away from the Mex, risking a head-on collision, but the wind whipped the ball closer to the wall than he had bargained for, so Bump fell back to cover Flores in case he misplayed it.

The ball fell between them, good for a double, and scoring two of the Phils. Pop tore at what was left of his gray hair but couldn't grip it with his oily, bandaged fingers so he pulled at his ears till they were lit like red lamps. Luckily the next Phil smothered the fire by rolling to first, which kept the score at 2–1. When Bump returned to the dugout Pop cursed him from the cradle to the grave and for once Bump had no sassy answers. When it came his time to go out on deck, Pop snarled for him to stay where he was. Flores found a ripe one and landed on first but Pop stuck to his guns and looked down the line past Bump. His eye lit on Roy at the far end of the bench, and he called his name to go out there and hit. Bump turned purple. He grabbed a bat and headed for Roy but half the team jumped on him. Roy just sat there without moving and it looked to everyone like he wouldn't get up. The umpire roared in for a batter to come out, and after a while, as the players fidgeted and Pop fumed, Roy sighed and picked up Wonderboy. He slowly walked up the steps.

"Knock the cover off of it," Pop yelled.

"Attention, please," the P.A. man announced. "Roy Hobbs, number forty-five, batting for Baily."

A groan rose from the stands and turned into a roar of protest.

Otto Zipp jumped up and down on his seat, shaking his furious little fist at home plate.

"Throw him to the dogs," he shouted, and filled the air with his piercing curses.

Glancing at the wives' box, Roy saw that Memo had her head turned away. He set his jaw and advanced to the plate. His impulse was to knock the dirt out of his cleats but he refrained because he did not want to harm his bat in any way. Waiting for the pitcher to get set, Roy wiped his palms on his pants and twitched his cap. He lifted Wonderboy and waited rocklike for the throw.

He couldn't tell the color of the pitch that came at him. All he could think of was that he was sick to death of waiting, and tongue-out thirsty to begin. The ball was now a dew drop staring him in the eye so he stepped back and swung from the toes.

Wonderboy flashed in the sun. It caught the sphere where it was biggest. A noise like a twenty-one gun salute cracked the sky. There was a straining, ripping sound and a few drops of rain spattered to the ground. The ball screamed toward the pitcher and seemed suddenly to dive down at his feet. He grabbed it to throw to first and realized to his horror that he held only the cover. The rest of it, unraveling cotton thread as it rode, was headed into the outfield.

Roy was rounding first when the ball plummeted like a dead bird into center field. Attempting to retrieve and throw, the Philly fielder got tangled in thread. The second baseman rushed up, bit the cord and heaved the ball to the catcher but Roy had passed third and made home, standing. The umpire called him safe and immediately a rhubarb boiled. The Phils' manager and his players charged out of the dugout and were joined by the nine men on the field. At the same time, Pop, shouting in defense of the ump, rushed forth with all the Knights but Bump. The umpire, caught between both teams, had a troublesome time of it and was shoved this way and that. He tossed out two men on each side but by then came to the decision that the hit was a ground rules double. Flores had scored and the game was tied up. Roy was ordered back to second, and Pop announced he was finishing the game under protest. Somebody then shouted it was raining cats and dogs. The stands emptied like a yawn and the players piled into the dugouts. By the time Roy got in from second he was wading in water ankle deep. Pop sent him into the clubhouse for a change of uniform but he could have saved himself the trouble because it rained steadily for three days. The game was recorded as a 2–2 tie, to be replayed later in the season.

In the locker room Pop asked Roy to explain why he thought the cover had come off the ball.

"That's what you said to do, wasn't it?"

"That's right," said Pop, scratching his bean.

The next day he told Roy he was withdrawing his release and would hereafter use him as a pinch hitter and substitute fielder.

The rain had washed out the Phils' series but the Knights were starting another with the seventh-place Redbirds. In batting practice, Roy, who was exciting some curiosity for his freak hit of yesterday, looked tremendous but so did Bump. For the first time in a long while Roy went out to left field to limber up. Bump was out there too and Earl swatted fungos to both.

As they were changing into clean uniforms before the start of the game, Bump warned Roy in front of everybody, "Stay out of my way, busher, or you will get your head bashed."

Roy squirted spit on the floor.

When Pop later handed the batting order to Stuffy Briggs, the plate umpire, it had Bump's name scribbled on it as usual in the fourth slot, but Pop had already warned him that if he didn't hustle his behind when a ball was hit out to his field, he would rest it a long time on the bench.

Bump made no reply but it was obvious that he took Pop's words to heart, because he was a bang-up fielder that day. He accepted eight chances, twice chasing into center field to take them from Flores. He caught them to his left and right, dove for and came up with a breathtaking shoestringer, and running as if on fire, speared a fantastic catch over his shoulder. Still not satisfied, he pounded like a bull after his ninth try, again in Flores's territory, a smoking ball that sailed up high, headed for the wall. As Bump ran for it he could feel fear leaking through his stomach, and his legs unwillingly slowed down, but then he had this vision of himself as the league's best outfielder, acknowledged so by fans and players alike, even Pop, whom he'd be nothing less than forever respectful to, and in love with and married to Memo. Thinking this way he ran harder, though Zipp's geese honked madly at his back, and with a magnificent twisting jump, he trapped the ball in his iron fingers. Yet the wall continued to advance, and though the redheaded lady of his choice was on her feet shrieking, Bump bumped it with a skull-breaking bang, and the wall embraced his broken body.

*

Though Bump was on the critical list in the hospital, many newspapers continued to speculate about that ball whose cover Roy had knocked off. It was explained as everything from an optical illusion (neither the ball nor the cover was ever found, the remnant caught by the catcher disappeared, and it was thought some fan had snatched the cover) to a feat of prodigious strength. Baseball records and newspaper files were combed but no one could find any evidence that it had happened before, although some of the older scribes swore it had. Then it leaked out that Pop had ordered Roy to skin the ball and Roy had obliged, but no one took that very seriously. One of the sportswriters suggested that a hard downward chop could shear off the outer covering. He had tried it in his cellar and had split the horsehide. Another pointed out that such a blow would have produced an infield grounder, therefore maybe a tremendous upward slash? The first man proved that would have uncorked a sure pop fly whereas the ball, as everyone knew, had sailed straight out over the pitcher's head. So it had probably resulted from a very very forceful sock. But many a hitter had plastered the ball forcefully before, still another argued, and his idea was that it was defective to begin with, a fact the company that manufactured the ball vigorously denied. Max Mercy had his own theory. He wrote in his column, "My Eye in the Knot Hole" (the year he'd done the Broadway stint for his paper his eye was in the key hole), that Roy's bat was a suspicious one and hinted it might be filled with something a helluva lot stronger than wood. Red Blow publicly denied this. He said the bat had been examined by league authorities and was found to be less than forty-two inches long, less than two and three-quarters inches thick at its fattest part, and in weight less than two pounds, which made it a legal weapon. Mercy then demanded that the wood be X-rayed but Roy turned thumbs down on that proposition and kept Wonderboy hidden away when the sports columnist was nosing around in the clubhouse.

On the day after the accident Pop soberly gave Roy the nod to play in Bump's place. As Roy trotted out to left, Otto Zipp was in his usual seat but looking worn and aged. His face, tilted to the warming rays of the sun, was like a pancake with a cherry nose, and tears were streaming through slits where the eyes would be. He seemed to be waiting for his pre-game kiss on the brow but Roy passed without looking at him.

The long rain had turned the grass green and Roy romped in it like a happy calf in its pasture. The Redbirds, probing his armor, belted the ball to him whenever they could, which was often, because Hill was not too happy on the mound, but Roy took everything they aimed at him. He seemed to know the soft, hard, and bumpy places in the field and just how high a ball would bounce on them. From the flags on the stadium roof he noted the way the wind would blow the ball, and he was quick at fishing it out of the tricky undercurrents on the ground. Not sun, shadow, nor smoke-haze bothered him, and when a ball was knocked against the wall he estimated the angle of rebound and speared it as if its course had been plotted on a chart. He was good at gauging slices and knew when to charge the pill to save time on the throw. Once he put his head down and ran ahead of a shot going into the concrete. Though the crowd rose with a thunderous warning, he caught it with his back to the wall and did a little jig to show he was alive. Everyone laughed in relief, and they liked his long-legged loping and that he resembled an acrobat the way he tumbled and came up with the ball in his glove. For his performance that day there was much whistling and applause, except where he would have liked to hear it, an empty seat in the wives' box.

His batting was no less successful. He stood at the plate lean and loose, right-handed with an open stance, knees relaxed and shoulders squared. The bat he held in a curious position, lifted slightly above his head as if prepared to beat a rattlesnake to death, but it didn't harm his smooth stride into the pitch, nor the easy way he met the ball and slashed it out with a flick of the wrists. The pitchers tried something different every time he came up, sliders, sinkers, knucklers, but he swung and connected, spraying them to all fields. He was, Red Blow said to Pop, a natural, though somewhat less than perfect because he sometimes hit at bad ones, which caused Pop to frown.

"I mistrust a bad ball hitter."

"There are all kinds of hitters," Red answered. "Some are bucket foots, and some go for bad throws but none of them bother me as long as they naturally connect with anything that gets in their way."

Pop spat up over the dugout steps. "They sometimes make some harmful mistakes."

"Who don't?" Red asked.

Pop then muttered something about this bad ball hitter he knew who had reached for a lemon and cracked his spine.

But the only thing Roy cracked that day was the record for the number of triples hit in a major league debut and also the one for chances accepted in the outfield. Everybody agreed that in him the Knights had uncovered something special. One reporter wrote, "He can catch everything in creation," and Roy just about proved it. It happened that a woman who lived on the sixth floor of an apartment house overlooking the stadium was cleaning out her bird cage, near the end of the game, which the Knights took handily, when her canary flew out of the window and darted down across the field. Roy, who was waiting for the last out, saw something coming at him in the low rays of the sun, and leaping high, bagged it in his glove.

He got rid of the bloody mess in the clubhouse can.

WHEN BUMP died Memo went wild with grief. Bump, Bump, she wailed, pounding on the wall. Pop, who hovered over her at first, found her in bed clutching strands of red hair. Her cheeks were scratched where the tears rolled down. He was frightened and urged her to have the doctor but her piercing screams drove him away. She wept for days. Clad in black pajamas she lay across the white bed like a broken candle still lit. In her mind she planted kisses all over the corpse and when she kissed his mouthless mouth blew back the breath of life, her womb stirring at the image of his restoration. Yet she saw down a dark corridor that he was laid out dead, gripping in his fingers the glowing ball he had caught, and that there were too many locked doors to go through to return. She stopped trying to think of him alive and thought of him dead. Then she really hit the wall.

She could not stop weeping, as if the faucet were broken. Or she were a fountain they had forgotten to turn off. There was no end to her tears. They flowed on as if she had never wept before. Wherever she turned she cried, the world was wet. Her thoughts dripped on flowers, dark, stained ones in night fields. She moved among them, tasting their many darknesses, could not tell them from the rocks on the ground. His shade was there. She saw it drifting before her and recognized it by the broken places. Bump, oh Bump, but her voice was drowned in water. She heard a gurgle and the bubbles breaking and felt the tears go searing down a hurt face (hers) and though she wanted always to be with him she was (here) weeping.

After unnumbered days she dragged herself out of bed, disturbed by all the space, her bare feet with lacquered nails, her shaky presence among changeless things. She sought in the hollow closet souvenirs of him, an autographed baseball "to my Honey from her Bump" (tears), a cigarette lighter shaped like a bat, click-open-light. She blew it out and searching further found an old kewpie doll he had won for her and a pressed, yellowed gardenia, but couldn't with her wept-out nose detect the faintest odor; also a pair of purple shorts she herself had laundered and placed in the drawer among her soft (and useless) underthings. Going through her scrapbook, only rarely could she find menus (Sardi's, Toots Shor, and once the Diamond Horseshoe) or movie ticket stubs (Palace, Paramount, Capitol) and other such things of them both that one could paste in, but most were pictures she had clipped from the sports pages, showing Bump at bat, on the basepaths, and crossing the plate. She idly turned the pages, sighed deeply and put the book away, then picked up the old picture album, and here was her sadeyed mother, and the torn up, patched together one was of Daddy grinning, who with a grin had (forever) exited dancing with his dancing partner, and here she was herself, a little girl weeping, as if nothing ever changed . . . The heartbreak was always present—he had not been truly hers when he died (she tried not to think whose, in many cities, he had been) so that she now mourned someone who even before his death had made her a mourner. That was the thorn in her grief.

When the July stifle drove her out of her room she appeared in the hotel lobby in black, her hair turned a lighter, golden shade as though some of the fire had burned out of it, and Roy was moved by her appearance. He had imagined how she would look when he saw her again but both the black and red, though predictable, surprised him. They told him with thunderclap quickness what he wanted to be sure of, that she, despite green eyes brimming for Bump, was the one for him, the ever desirable only. Occasionally he reflected what if the red were black and ditto the other way? Here, for example, was this blackhaired dame in red and what about it? He could take her or leave her, though there was a time in his life when a red dress would excite his fancy, but with Memo, flaming above and dark below, there was no choice—he was chosen so why not admit it though it brought pain? He had tried lately to forget her but had a long memory for what he wanted so there was only this to do, wait till she came in out of the rain.

Sometimes it was tough to, even for one used to waiting. Once a hungry desire sent him down to knock at her door but she shut it in his face although he was standing there with his hat in his embarrassed hands. He thought of asking Pop to put in a good word for him—how long was life anyhow?—but something told him to wait. And from other cities, when the team was on the road, he sent her cards, candies, little presents, which were all stuffed in his mailbox when he returned. It took the heart out of him. Yet each morning when she came out of the elevator he would look up at her as she walked by on her high heels, although she never seemed to see him. Then one day she shed black and put on white but still looked as if she were wearing black, so he waited. Only, now, when he looked at her she sometimes glanced at him. He watched her dislike of him fade to something neutral which he slowly became confident he could beat.

"One thing I hafta tell you not to do, son," Pop said to Roy in the hotel lobby one rainy morning not long after Bump's funeral, "and that is to blame yourself about what happened to Bump. He had a tough break but it wasn't your fault."

"What do you mean my fault?"

Pop looked up. "All I mean to say was he did it himself."

"Never thought anything but."

"Some have said maybe it wouldn't happen if you didn't join the team, and maybe so, but I believe such things are outside of yours and my control and I wouldn't want you to worry that you had caused it in any way."

"I won't because I didn't. Bump didn't have to go to the wall for that shot, did he? We were ahead in runs and the bases were clear. He could've taken it when it came off the wall without losing a thing, couldn't he?"

Pop scratched his baldy. "I guess so."

"Who are the people who said I did it?"

"Well, nobody exactly. My niece said you coulda wanted it to happen but that don't mean a thing. She was hysterical then."

Roy felt uneasy. Had he arranged Bump's run into the wall? No. Had he wished the guy would drop dead? Only once, after the night with Memo. But he had never consciously hoped he would crack up against the wall. That was none of his doing and he told Pop to tell it to Memo. But Pop was embarrassed now and said to drop the whole thing, it was a lot of foolishness.

Though Roy denied wishing Bump's fate on him or having been in any way involved in it, he continued to be unwillingly concerned with him even after his death. He was conscious that he was filling Bump's shoes, not only because he batted in the clean-up slot and fielded in the sun field (often watched his shadow fly across the very spot Bump had dived into) and became, in no time to speak of, one of the leading hitters in the league and at present certainly the most sensational, but also because the crowds made no attempt to separate his identity from Bump's. To his annoyance, when he made a hot catch, the kind Bump in all his glory would have left alone, he could hear through the curtain of applause, "Nice work, Bumpsy, 'at's grabbin' th' old apple," or "Leave it to Bump, he will be where they drop." It was goddamn stupid. The same fans who a month ago were hissing Bump for short legging on the other fielders now praised his name so high Roy felt like painting up a sandwich sign to wear out on the field, that said, ROY HOBBS PLAYING.

Even Otto Zipp made no effort to distinguish him from his predecessor and used the honker to applaud his doings, though there were some who said the dwarf sounded half-hearted in his honking. And Roy also shared the limelight with Bump on the sports page, where the writers were constantly comparing them for everything under the sun. One of them went so far as to keep a tally of their batting averages—Roy's total after his first, second, and third weeks of play, as compared with Bump's at the beginning of the season. One paper even printed pictures showing the living and dead facing each other with bats held high, as white arrows pointed at various places in their anatomies to show how much alike their measurements and stances were.

All this irritated Roy no end until he happened to notice Memo walk into the lobby one night with a paper turned to the sports page. From having read the same paper he knew she had seen a column about Bump and him as batsmen, so he decided there might be some percentage to all these comparisons. He came to feel more kindly to the memory of Bump and thought he was not such a bad egg after all, even if he did go in for too many screwball gags. Thinking back on him, he could sort of understand why Memo had been interested in him, and he felt that, though he was superior to Bump as an athlete, they were both money players, both showmen in the game. He figured it was through these resemblances that

Memo would gradually get used to him and then come over all the way, although once she did, it would have to be for Hobbsie himself and not for some ghost by another name.

So he blazed away for her with his golden bat. It was not really golden, it was white, but in the sun it sometimes flashed gold and some of the opposing pitchers complained it shone in their eyes. Stuffy Briggs told Roy to put it away and use some other club but he stood on his rights and wouldn't. There was a hot rhubarb about that until Roy promised to rub some of the shine off Wonderboy. This he did with a hambone, and though the pitchers shut up, the bat still shone a dull gold. It brought him some wondrous averages in hits, runs, RBI's and total bases, and for the period of his few weeks in the game he led the league in homers and triples. (He was quoted in an interview as saying his singles were "mistakes." And he never bunted. "There is no percentage in bunts." Pop shook his head over that, but Red chuckled and said it was true for a wonderful hitter like Roy.) He also destroyed many short-term records, calling down on his performance tons of newspaper comment. However, his accomplishments were not entirely satisfying to him. He was gnawed by a nagging impatience—so much more to do, so much of the world to win for himself. He felt he had nothing of value yet to show for what he was accomplishing, and in his dreams he still sped over endless miles of monotonous rail toward something he desperately wanted. Memo, he sighed.

Pop couldn't believe his amazed eyes. "Beginner's luck," he muttered. Many a rookie had he seen come out blasting them in the breeze only to blow out in it with his tail between his legs. "The boy's having hisself a shower of luck. Usually they end up with a loud bust, so let's wait and see," he cautioned. Yet Roy continued on as before, by his own efforts winning many a ball game. The team too were doubtful he could go on like this, and doubtful of their doubt. They often discussed him when he wasn't around, compared him to Bump, and argued whether he was for the team or for himself. Olson said he was for the team. Cal Baker insisted no. When asked for a reason he could give none except to say, "Those big guys are always for themselves. They are not for the little guy. If he was for us why don't he come around more? Why does he hang out so much by himself?" "Yeah," answered Olson, "but we're outa the cellar now and who done that—the wind? That's what counts, not if he sits around chewin' his ass with us." Most of them agreed with Olson. Even if Roy wasn't actively interested in them he was a slick ballplayer and his example was having a good effect on them. In the course of three weeks they had achieved a coordination of fielding, hitting and pitching (Fowler and Schultz were whipping the opposition, and Hinkle and Hill, with an assist here and there from McGee, were at least breaking even) such as they had not for seasons known. Like a rusty locomotive pulling out of the roundhouse for the first time in years, they ground down the tracks, puffing, wheezing, belching smoke and shooting sparks. And before long they had dislodged the Reds, who had been living on the floor above them since the season started. When, near the end of July, they caught up with the Cubs and, twelve games behind the league-leading Pirates, took possession of sixth place, Pop rubbed his unbelieving eyes. The players thought now that the team is on its way up he will change his crabby ways and give us a smile once in a while, but Pop surprised them by growing sad, then actually melancholy at the thought that but for his keeping Roy out of the line-up for three weeks they might now be in first division.

A new day dawned on Knights Field. Looking down upon the crowds from his office in the curious tower he inhabited that rose on a slight tilt above the main entrance of the ball park, Judge Goodwill Banner was at first made uneasy by what he saw, for every rise in attendance would make it more difficult for him to get Pop to give up the managerial reins, a feat he hoped to accomplish by next season. However, the sound of the merry, clicking turnstiles was more than he could resist, so, although reluctantly, he put on extra help to sweep the stands and ramps and dust off seats that hadn't been sat in for years but were now almost always occupied.

The original Knights "fans," those who had come to see them suffer, were snowed under by this new breed here to cheer the boys on. Vegetables were abolished, even at the umps, and the crowd assisted the boys by working on the nerves of the visiting team with whammy words, catcalls, wisecracks, the kind of sustained jockeying that exhausted the rival pitchers and sometimes drove them out of the game. Now the old faithful were spouting steam—the Hungarian cook out-crowed a flock of healthy roosters, Gloria, the vestibule lady, acquired a better type customer, and Sadie Sutter gave up Dave Olson and now beat her hectic gong for the man of the hour. "Oh, you Roy," she screeched in her yolky cackle, "embracez moy," and the stands went wild with laughter. Victory was sweet, except for Otto Zipp, who no longer attended the games. Someone who met him waddling out of a subway station in Canarsie asked how come, but the dwarf only waved a pudgy palm in disgust. Nobody could guess what he meant by that and his honker lay dusty and silent on a shelf in the attic.

Even the weather was better, more temperate after the insulting early heat, with just enough rain to keep the grass a bright green and yet not pile up future double headers. Pop soon got into the spirit of winning, lowered the boom on his dismal thoughts, and showed he had a lighter side. He unwound the oily rags on his fingers and flushed them down the bowl. His hands healed and so did his heart, for even during the tensest struggle he looked a picture of contentment. And he was patient now, extraordinarily so, giving people the impression he had never been otherwise. Let a man bobble a hot one, opening the gate for a worrisome run, and he no longer jumped down his throat but wagged his head in silent sympathy. And sometimes he patted the offender on the surprised back. Formerly his strident yell was everywhere, on the field, in the dugout, clubhouse, players' duffel bags, also in their dreams, but now you never heard it because he no longer raised his voice, not even to Dizzy's cat when it wet on his shoes. Nobody teased him or played jokes on him any more and every tactic he ordered on the field was acted on, usually successfully. He was in the driver's seat. His muscles eased, the apoplexy went out of his system, and for his star fielder a lovelight shone in his eyes.

As Roy's fame grew, Bump was gradually forgotten. The fans no longer confused talent with genius. When they cheered, they cheered for Roy Hobbs alone. People wondered about him, wanted news of his life and career. Reporters kept after him for information and Max Mercy, who for some reason felt he ought to know a lot more about Roy than he did, worked a sharp pickax over his shadow but gathered no usable nugget. All that was known was that Roy had first played ball on an orphan asylum team, that his father was a restless itinerant worker and his mother rumored to have been a burlesque actress. Stingy with facts, Roy wouldn't confirm a thing. Mercy sent a questionnaire to one thousand country papers in the West but there were no towns or cities that claimed the hero as their own.

It came about that Roy discovered Memo at one of the home games, though not, as formerly, sitting in the wives' box. Happening to meet her later in the hotel elevator, where they were pressed close together because of the crowd, he got off at her floor. Taking her arm he said, "Memo, I don't know what more I can do to show you how sorry I am about that time and tell you how I feel in my heart for you now."

But Memo stared at him through a veil of tears and said, "I'm strictly a dead man's girl."

He figured she had to be made to forget. If she would go out with him he would give her a good time at the night clubs and musical shows. But to do that and buy her some decent presents a guy needed cash, and on the meager three thousand he got he had beans—barely enough to pay his hotel bill. He considered selling his name for endorsements and approached a sporting goods concern but they paid him only fifty dollars. Elsewhere he got a suit and a pair of shoes but no cash. An agent he consulted advised him that the companies were suspicious he might be a flash in the pan. "Lay low now," he advised. "By the end of the season, if you keep on like you're going, they'll be ready to talk turkey, then we'll put the heat on."

The newspaper boys supplied him with the cue for what to do next. They pointed out how he filled up Knights Field; and on the road, as soon as the Knights blew into town the game was a sellout and the customers weren't exactly coming to see a strip-tease. One of the columnists (not Mercy) wrote an open letter to the Judge, saying it was a crying shame that a man as good as Roy should get a rock-bottom salary when he was playing better ball than some of the so-called stars who drew up to a hundred grand. Roy was being gypped, the columnist wrote, and he called on the Judge to burn up his old contract and write a decent one instead. Why, even Bump had earned thirty-five thousand. That decided Roy. He figured for himself a flat forty-five thousand for the rest of the season, plus a guarantee of a percentage of the gate. He thought that if he got this sort of arrangement and really piled in the dough, it would do him no harm with Memo.

So one day after a long double header, both ends of which the Knights finally took, Roy climbed the slippery stairs up the tower to the Judge's office. The Judge's male secretary said he was busy but Roy sat down to wait so they soon let him in. The huge office was half dark, though lit on the double-windowed street side (the Judge counted the customers going in and from the opposite window he counted them in the stands) by the greenish evening sky. The Judge, a massive rumpled figure in a large chair before an empty mahogany desk, was wearing a black fedora with a round pot crown and smoking, under grizzled eyebrows, a fat, black King Oscar I. This always looked to be the same size in the rare newspaper photographs of the Judge, and many people maintained it was the same picture of him all the time, because it was a known fact that the Judge never left the tower and no photographer ever got in. Roy noted a shellacked half of stuffed shark, mounted on pine board on the faded green wall, and a framed motto piece that read:

> *"Be it ever so humble, there is no place like home"*
> *"Nihil nisi bonum"*
> *"All is not gold that glitters"*
> *"The dog is turned to his vomit again"*

The floor of the office was, of course, slanted—because of the way the tower, an addition to the stadium structure, had settled—and to level it the Judge had a rug made a quarter of an inch thick on one side and a good inch on the other, but the few visitors to the place noticed they were not standing strictly on keel so they quickly sat down, which was what Roy did too. He had heard that the door on the opposite side of the room led up to the Judge's apartment. Pop said that though the Judge was a sluggish man with a buck it was a lavish place, and the bathroom had a television set and a sunken bathtub inlaid with mother of pearl. It was also rumored that he kept in there two enormous medicine cabinets loaded with laxatives and cathartics.

The Judge looked Roy over, struck a match under the top of his desk and drew a flame into his dead King Oscar. He blew out a smelly cloud of yellow smoke that hid his face a full minute.

"Nice of you to come," he rumbled. "To what good cause may I attribute this pleasant surprise?"

"I guess you know, Judge," said Roy, trying to make himself comfortable.

The Judge rumbled in his belly.

"I'm reminded of a case that came before me once. 'What do you plead?' I asked the defendant. 'I leave it to you, Judge, take your choice,' he responded. I did and sent him to the penitentiary for twenty years."

The Judge coughed and cackled over that. Roy regarded him closely. Everybody had warned him he was a slick trader, especially Pop who had poured out a hot earful about his partner. "He will peel the skin off of your behind without you knowing it if you don't watch out." That was what had happened to him, he said, and he went on to tell Roy that not long after the Judge had bought into the club—after working up Charlie Gulch, Pop's old-time partner, against him and getting him to sell out—he had taken advantage of some financial troubles Pop was having with his two brothers who owned a paint factory, and also because of his own sickness that kept him in a hospital under expensive medical care all winter long, and the Judge put the squeeze on him to get ten per cent of his stock for a pittance, which had then looked like a life saver because Pop was overdrawn at the bank and they wouldn't lend him another cent on his share of the Knights. Later, when he realized how much of a say in things he had lost to the Judge he kicked himself all over the lot, for the Judge, as Red Blow had told Roy, drummed up all sorts of player deals to turn a buck, and though Pop fought him on these, he showed on paper that they were losing money at the gate and this was the only way to cover their losses and keep the team going, so Pop had to give in on most of them although he had fought the Judge to a standstill when he wanted to sell Bump and would do the same if he tried it with Roy. It beat Pop where

Goodie Banner, as he called him, had got the money to operate with in the first place. He had known him years ago as an impoverished shyster but once he got on the bench his fortunes improved. Yet his salary was only twelve thousand a year for the three years he had served so he must have had backing to buy into the club and later—the dratted nerve of the worm—to offer to buy Pop out altogether. He said he wouldn't exactly call the Judge a thief but he wouldn't exactly call him honest either. For instance, the Judge had once casually asked Pop if he wanted to go in for any sideline activities over what they had already contracted for, meaning concessions and the like. Pop said no, he was only interested in the game end of it, so the Judge drew up an agreement offering Pop five per cent of all receipts from enterprises initiated by himself, and he began to rent the place to miniature auto races, meetings, conventions, and dog races, making all sorts of money for himself, while things necessary to the team were being neglected. "When triple talk is invented," Pop said bitterly, "he will own the copyright."

It was dark in the office but the Judge made no attempt to switch on the lights. He sat there motionless, a lumpy figure aglow around the edges against the darkening sky.

Roy thought he better get down to brass tacks. "Well, Judge," he said, shifting in his chair, "I thought you might be expecting me to drop in and see you. You know what I am doing to the ball both here and on the road. The papers have been writing that you might be considering a new contract for me."

The Judge blew at the ash of his cigar.

Roy grew restless. "I figure forty-five thousand is a fair price for my work. That's only ten grand more than Bump was getting—and you can subtract off the three thousand in my contract now." This last was an afterthought and he had decided to leave out the percentage of the gate till next year.

The Judge rumbled, Roy couldn't tell if it was in his throat or belly.

"I was thinking of Olaf Jespersen." The Judge's eyes took on a faraway, slightly glazed look. "He was a farmer I knew in my youth—terrible life. Yet as farmers often do, he managed to live comfortably because he owned a plot of ground with a house on it and had come into possession of an extraordinary cow, Sieglinde. She was a splendid animal with soft and silky front and well-shaped hooves. Her milk yield was some nine gallons per diem, altogether exceptional. In a word she was a superior creature and had the nicest ways with children—her own of course; but Olaf was deeply disturbed by an ugly skin discoloration that ran across her rump. For a long while he had been eyeing Gussie, an albino cow of his neighbor down the road. One day he approached the man and asked if Gussie was for sale. The neighbor said yes, frankly admitting she gave very little milk although she consumed more than her share of fodder. Olaf said he was willing to trade Sieglinde for her and the neighbor readily agreed. Olaf went back for the cow but on the way to the neighbor's she stepped into a rut in the road and keeled over as if struck dead. Olaf suffered a heart attack. Thus they were found but Sieglinde recovered and became, before very long, her splendid nine-gallon self, whereas Olaf was incapacitated for the remainder of his days. I often drove past his place and saw him sitting on the moldy front porch, a doddering cripple starving to death with his tubercular albino cow."

Roy worked the fable around in his mind and got the point. It was not an impressive argument: be satisfied with what you have, and he said so to the Judge.

"'The love of money is the root of all evil,'" intoned the Judge.

"I do not love it, Judge. I have not been near enough to it to build up any affection to speak of."

"Think, on the one hand, of the almost indigent Abraham Lincoln, and on the other of Judas Iscariot. What I am saying is that emphasis upon money will pervert your values. One cannot begin to imagine how one's life may alter for the worse under the impetus of wealth-seeking."

Roy saw how the land lay. "I will drop it to thirty-five thousand, the same as Bump, but not a cent less."

The Judge struck a match, throwing shadows on the wall. It was now night. He sucked a flame into his cigar. It went in like a slug, out like a moth—in and out, then forever in and the match was out. The cigar glowed, the Judge blew out a black fog of smoke, then they were once more in the dark.

Lights on, you stingy bastard, Roy thought.

"Pardon the absence of light," the Judge said, almost making him jump. "As a youngster I was frightened of the dark—used to wake up sobbing in it, as if it were water and I were drowning—but you will observe that I have disciplined myself so thoroughly against that fear, that I much prefer a dark to a lit room, and water is my favorite beverage. Will you have some?"

"No."

"There is in the darkness a unity, if you will, that cannot be achieved in any other environment, a blending of self with what the self perceives, an exquisite mystical experience. I intend some day to write a disquisition 'On the Harmony of Darkness; Can Evil Exist in Harmony?' It may profit you to ponder the question."

"All I know about the dark is that you can't see in it."

"A pure canard. You know you can."

"Not good enough."

"You see me, don't you?"

"Maybe I do and maybe I don't."

"What do you mean?"

"I see somebody but I am not sure if it is you or a guy who sneaked in and took your chair."

The cigar glowed just enough to light up the Judge's rubbery lips. It was him all right.

"Twenty-five thousand," Roy said in a low voice. "Ten less than Bump."

The cigar lit for a long pull then went out. Its smell was giving Roy a headache. The Judge was silent so long Roy wasn't sure he would ever hear from him again. He wasn't even sure he was there any more but then he thought yes he is, I can smell him. He is here in the dark and if I come back tomorrow he will still be here and also the year after that.

"'He that maketh haste to be rich shall not be innocent,'" spoke the Judge.

"Judge," said Roy, "I am thirty-four, going on thirty-five. That's not haste, that's downright slow."

"I hear that you bet money on horse races?"

"In moderation, not more than a deuce on the daily double."

"Avoid gambling like a plague. It will cause your downfall.

And stay away from loose ladies. 'Put a knife to thy throat if thou be a man given to appetite.'"

Roy could hear him open a drawer and take something out. Handing it to him, he lit a match over it and Roy read: "The Curse of Venereal Disease."

He tossed the pamphlet on the desk.

"Yes or no?" he said.

"Yes or no what?" The Judge's voice was edged with anger.

"Fifteen thousand."

The Judge rose. "I shall have to ask you to fulfill the obligations of your contract."

Roy got up. "I wouldn't exactly say you were building up my good will for next year."

"I have learned to let the future take care of itself."

The Judge took some other papers out of the drawer. "I presume these are your signatures?" He scratched up another match.

"That's right."

"The first acknowledging the receipt of two uniforms and sundry articles?"

"Right."

"And the second indicating the receipt of a third uniform?"

"That's what it says."

"You were entitled to only two. I understand that some of the other clubs issue four, but that is an extravagance. Here, therefore, is a bill to the amount of fifty-one dollars for property destroyed. Will you remit or shall I deduct the sum from your next check?"

"I didn't destroy them, Bump did."

"They were your responsibility."

Roy picked up the receipts and bill and tore them to pieces. He did the same with the VD pamphlet, then blew the whole business over the Judge's head. The scraps of paper fluttered down like snow on his round hat.

"The interview is ended," snapped the Judge. He scratched up a match and with it led Roy to the stairs. He stood on the landing, his oily shadow dripping down the steps as Roy descended.

"Mr. Hobbs."

Roy stopped.

"Resist all evil—"

The match sputtered and went out. Roy went the rest of the way down in the pitch black.

"How'd you make out, kid?"

It was Max Mercy lurking under a foggy street lamp at the corner. He had tailed Roy from the dressing room and had spent a frustrated hour thinking I know the guy but who is he? It was on the tip of his tongue but he couldn't spit it out. He saw the face as he thought he had seen it before somewhere, but what team, where, in what league, and doing what that caused him to be remembered? The mystery was like an itch. The more he scratched the more he drew his own blood. At times the situation infuriated him. Once he dreamed he had the big s.o.b. by the throat and was forcing him to talk. Then he told the world Mercy knew.

The sight of the columnist did not calm Roy as he came out of the tower. Why does he haunt me? He thought he knew what Max sensed and he knew that he didn't want him to know. I don't want his dirty eyes peeking into my past. What luck for me that I had Sam's wallet in my pocket that night, and they wrote down his name. This creep will never find that out, or anything else about me unless I tell him, and the only time I'll do that is when I am dead.

"Listen, El Smearo," he said, "why don't you stay home in bed?"

Max laughed hollowly.

"Who has ever seen the like of it?" he said, trying to put some warmth into his voice. "Here's the public following everything a man does with their tongue hanging out and all he gives out with is little balls of nothing. What are you hiding? If it was something serious you woulda been caught long ago— your picture has been in the papers every day for weeks."

"I ain't hiding a thing."

"Who says you are? But what's all the mystery about? Where were you born? Why'd you stay out of the game so long? What was your life like before this? My paper will guarantee you five grand in cash for five three-thousand word articles on your past life. I'll help you write them. What do you say?"

"I say no. My life is my own business."

"Think of your public."

"All they're entitled to is to pay a buck and watch me play."

"Answer me this—is it true you once tried out with another major league team?"

"I got nothing to say."

"Then you don't deny it?"

"I got nothing to say."

"Were you once an acrobat or something in a circus?"

"Same answer as before."

Max scratched in his mustache. "Hobbs, the man nobody knows. Say, kid, you're not doing it on purpose, are you?"

"What do you mean?"

"To raise speculation and get publicity?"

"Nuts I am."

"I don't catch. You're a public figure. You got to give the fans something once in a while to keep up their good will to you."

Roy thought a second. "Okay, tell them my cheapskate of a boss has turned me down flat on a raise and I am still his slave for a lousy three thousand bucks."

Max wrote a hasty note in his black book.

"Listen, Roy, let's you and I have a little chin-chin. You'll like me better once you get to know me. Have you had your supper yet?"

"No."

"Then have a steak with me at the Pot of Fire. Know the place?"

"I have never been there."

"It's a night club with a nice girlie show. All the hot-shot celebrities like yourself hang out there. They have a good kitchen and a first class bar."

"Okay with me." He was in a mood for something for nothing.

In the cab Max said, "You know, I sometimes get the funny feeling that I have met you some place before. Is that right?"

Roy thrust his head forward. "Where?"

Max contemplated his eyes and solid chin.

"It musta been somebody else."

At the entrance to the Pot of Fire a beggar accosted them.

"Jesus," Max said, "can't I ever get rid of you?"

"All I ask is a buck."

"Go to hell."

The beggar was hurt. "You'll get yours," he said.

"You'll get yours," said Max. "I'll call a cop."

"You'll get yours," the beggar said. "You too," he said to Roy and spat on the sidewalk.

"Friend of yours?" Roy asked as they went down the stairs into the nightspot.

Max's face was inflamed. "I can't get rid of that scurvy bastard. Picks this place to hang around and they can't flush him outa here."

Inside the club the audience was in an uproar. The show was on and some screaming, half-naked girls were being chased by masked devils with tin pitchforks. Then the lights went out and the devils ran around poking at the customers. Roy was jabbed in the rear end. He grabbed at the devil but missed, then he heard a giggle and realized it was a girl. He grabbed for her again but the devil jabbed him and ran. When the lights went on all the girls and devils were gone. The customers guffawed and applauded.

"Come on," Max said.

The captain had recognized him and was beckoning them to a ringside table. Roy sat down. Max looked around and bounced up.

"See a party I know. Be right back."

The band struck up a number and the chorus wriggled out amid weaving spotlights for the finale. They were wearing red spangled briefs and brassieres and looked so pretty that Roy felt lonely.

Max was back.

"We're changing tables. Gus Sands wants us with him."

"Who's he?"

Max looked to see if Roy was kidding.

"You don't know Gus Sands?"

"Never heard of him."

"What d'ye read, the Podunk Pipsqueak? They call him the Supreme Bookie, he nets at least ten million a year. Awfully nice guy and he will give you the silk shirt off his back. Also somebody you know is with him."

"Who's that?"

"Memo Paris."

Roy got up. What's she doing here? He followed Max across the floor to Gus Sands's table. Memo was sitting there alone in a black strapless gown and wearing her hair up. The sight of her, so beautiful, hit him hard. He had been picturing her alone in her room nights. She said hello evasively. At first he thought she was still sore at him, but then he heard voices coming from the floor at the other side of the table and understood that was where she was looking.

A surprising semi-bald dome rose up above the table and Roy found himself staring into a pair of strange eyes, a mournful blue one and the other glowing weirdly golden. His scalp prickled as the bookie, a long stretch of bone, rose to his full height. The angle at which the spotlight had caught his glass eye, lighting it like a Christmas tree, changed, and the eye became just a ball of ice.

"S'matter, Gus?" Mercy said.

"Memo lost two bits." His voice was sugar soft. "Find it yet?" he asked the waiter, still down on all fours.

"Not yet, sir." He got up. "No, sir."

"Forget it." Sands flicked a deft fiver into the man's loose fist.

He shook hands with Roy. "Glad to meet you, slugger. Whyn't you sit down?"

"Tough luck, babyface," he said, giving Memo a smile. Roy sat down facing her but she barely glanced at him. Though dressed up, she was not entirely herself. The blue eye shadow she had on could not hide the dark circles around her eyes and she looked tired. Her chair was close to Gus's. Once he chucked her under the chin and she giggled. It sickened Roy because it didn't make sense.

The busboy cleaned up the remains of two lobsters. Gus slipped him a fiver.

"Nice kid," he said softly. Reaching for the menu, he handed it to Roy.

Roy read it and although he was hungry couldn't concentrate on food. What did this glass-eye bookie, a good fifty years if not more, mean to a lively girl like Memo, a girl who was, after all, just out of mourning for a young fellow like Bump? Over the top of the menu he noticed Gus's soft-boned hands and the thick, yellow-nailed fingers. He had pouches under both the good and fake eyes, and though he smiled a lot, his expression was melancholy. Roy disliked him right off. There was something wormy about him. He belonged in the dark with the Judge. Let them both haunt themselves there.

"Order, guys," Gus said.

Roy did just to have something to do.

The captain came over and asked was everything all right.

"Check and double check." Gus pressed two folded fives into his palm. Roy didn't like the way he threw out the bucks. He thought of the raise he didn't get and felt bad about it.

"Lemme buy you a drink, slugger," Gus said, pointing to his own Scotch.

"No, thanks."

"Clean living, eh?"

"The eyes," Roy said, pointing to his. "Got to keep 'em clear."

Gus smiled. "Nice goin', slugger."

"He needs a drink," Max said. "The Judge gave him nix on a raise."

Roy could have bopped him for telling it in front of Memo.

Gus was interested.

"Y'mean he didn't pull out his pouch and shake you out some rusty two-dollar gold pieces?"

Everybody laughed but Roy.

"I see you met him," Max said.

Gus winked the glass eye. "We had some dealings."

"How'd you make out?"

"No evidence. We were acquitted." He chuckled softly.

Max made a note in his book.

"Don't write that, Max," said Gus.

Max quickly tore out the page. "Whatever you say, Gus."

Gus beamed. He turned to Roy. "How'd it go today, slugger?"

"Fine," Roy said.

"He got five for five in the first, and four hits in the night-cap," Max explained.

"Say, what d'ye know?" Gus whistled softly. "That'll cost me a pretty penny." He focused his good eye on Roy. "I was betting against you today, slugger."

"You mean the Knights?"

"No, just you."

"Didn't know you bet on any special player."

"On anybody or anything. We bet on strikes, balls, hits, runs, innings, and full games. If a good team plays a lousy team we will bet on the spread of runs. We cover anything anyone wants to bet on. Once in a Series game I bet a hundred grand on three pitched balls."

"How'd you make out on that?"

"Guess."

"I guess you didn't."

"Right, I didn't." Gus chuckled. "But it don't matter. The next week I ruined the guy in a different deal. Sometimes we win, sometimes we don't but the percentage is for us. Today we lost on you, some other time we will clean up double."

"How'll you do that?"

"When you are not hitting so good."

"How'll you know when to bet on that?"

Gus pointed to his glass eye. "The Magic Eye," he said. "It sees everything and tells me."

The steaks came and Roy cut into his.

"Wanna see how it works, slugger? Let's you and I bet on something."

"I got nothing I want to bet on," Roy said, his mouth full of meat and potatoes.

"Bet on any old thing and I will come up with the opposite even though your luck is running high now."

"It's a helluva lot more than luck."

"I will bet anyway."

Memo looked interested. Roy decided to take a chance.

"How about that I will get four hits in tomorrow's game?"

Gus paused. "Don't bet on baseball now," he said. "Bet on something we can settle here."

"Well, you pick it and I'll bet against you."

"Done," said Gus. "Tell you what, see the bar over by the entrance?"

Roy nodded.

"We will bet on the next order. You see Harry there, don't you? He's just resting now. In a minute somebody's gonna order drinks and Harry will make them. We'll wait till a waiter goes over and gives him an order—any one of them in the joint any time you say, so nobody thinks it's rigged. Then I will name you one of the drinks that will go on the waiter's tray, before Harry makes them. If there is only one drink there I will have to name it exactly—for a grand."

Roy hesitated. "Make it a hundred."

Max tittered.

"A 'C' it is," Gus said. "Say when."

"Now."

Gus shut his eyes and rubbed his brow with his left hand. "One of the drinks on the tray will be a Pink Lady."

The way they were seated everybody but Mercy could see the bar, so he turned his chair around to watch.

"Your steak might get cold, Max."

"This I got to see."

Memo looked on, amused.

They waited a minute, then a waiter went over to the bar and said something to the bartender. Harry nodded and turned around for a bottle, but they couldn't see what he was mixing because a customer was standing in front of him. When he left, Roy saw a tall pink drink standing on the counter. He felt sick but then he thought maybe it's a sloe gin fizz. Harry poured a Scotch and soda for the same tray and the waiter came for it.

As he passed by, Gus called him over to the table.

"What is that red drink that you have got there?"

"This one?" said the waiter. "A Pink Lady, Mr. Sands."

Gus slipped him a fiver.

Everybody laughed.

"Nothing to it," said Gus.

"It never fails." Max had turned his chair and was eating. "Nice work, Gus."

Gus beamed. Memo patted his hand. Roy felt annoyed.

"That's a hundred," he said.

"It was a freak win," Gus said, "so we will write it off."

"No, I owe it to you but give me a chance to win it back."

He thought Memo was mocking him and it made him stubborn.

"Anything you say," Gus shrugged.

"You can say it," said Roy. "I'll cover you for two hundred."

Gus concentrated a minute. Everybody watched him, Roy tensely. It wasn't the money he was afraid of. He wanted to win in front of Memo.

"Let's play on some kind of a number," Gus said.

"What kind?"

"Of the amount of bills you are carrying on you."

A slow flush crept up Roy's cheeks.

"I will bet I can guess by one buck either way how much you have got on you now," Gus said.

"You're on." Roy's voice was husky.

Gus covered his good eye and pretended he was a mind reader trying to fathom the number. His glass eye stared unblinking.

"Ten bucks," he announced.

Roy's throat went dry. He drew his wallet out of his pants pocket. Max took it from him and loudly counted up a five and four single dollar bills. "Nine." He slapped the table and guffawed.

"Wonderful," Memo murmured.

"Three hundred I owe to you."

"Don't mention it."

"It was a bet. Will you take my IOU?"

"Wanna try again?"

"Sure."

"You'll lose your panties," Max warned.

"On what?" Gus asked.

Roy thought. "What about another number?"

"Righto. What kind?"

"I'll pick out a number from one to ten. You tell me what it is."

Gus considered. "For the three hundred?"

"Yes."

"Okay."

"Do you want me to write the number?"

"Keep it in your head."

"Go ahead."

"Got the number?"

"I have it."

Again Gus eclipsed his good eye and took a slow breath. He made it seem like a kind of magic he was doing. Memo was fascinated.

"Deuce," Gus quickly announced.

Roy felt as if he had been struck on the conk. He considered lying but knew they could tell if he did.

"That's right, how'd you do it?" He felt foolish.

Gus winked.

Max was all but coming apart with laughter. Memo looked away.

Gus swallowed his Scotch. "Two is a magic number," he crooned at Memo. "Two makes the world go around." She smiled slightly, watching Roy.

He tried to eat but felt numbed.

Max just couldn't stop cackling. Roy felt like busting him one in the snoot.

Gus put his long arm around Memo's bare shoulders. "I have lots of luck, don't I, babyface?"

She nodded and sipped her drink.

The lights went on. The m.c. bobbed up from a table he had been sitting at and went into his routine.

"Six hundred I owe to you," Roy said, throwing Max into another whoop of laughter.

"Forget it, slugger. Maybe some day you might be able to do me a favor."

They were all suddenly silent.

"What kind of favor?" Roy asked.

"When I am down and out you can buy me a cup o' coffee."

They laughed, except Roy.

"I'll pay you now." He left the table and disappeared.

In a few minutes he returned with a white tablecloth over his arm.

Roy flapped out the cloth and one of the spotlights happened to catch it in the air. It turned red, then gold.

"What's going on?" Max said.

Roy whisked the cloth over Gus's head.

"The first installment."

He grabbed the bookie's nose and yanked. A stream of silver dollars clattered into his plate.

Gus stared at the money. Memo looked at Roy in intense surprise.

People at the nearby tables turned to see what was going on.

Those in the rear craned and got up. The m.c. gave up his jokes and waved both spots to Roy.

"For Pete's sake, sit down," Max hissed.

Roy rippled the green cloth in front of Max's face and dragged out of his astonished mouth a dead herring.

Everybody in the place applauded.

From Memo's bosom, he plucked a duck egg.

Gus got red in the face. Roy grabbed his beak again and twisted—it shed more cartwheels.

"Second installment."

"What the hell is this?" Gus sputtered.

The color wheels spun. Roy turned purple, red, and yellow. From the glum Mercy's pocket he extracted a long salami. Gus's ears ran a third installment of silver. A whirl of the cloth and a white bunny hopped out of Memo's purse. From Max's size sixteen shirt collar, he teased out a pig's tail.

As the customers howled, Max pulled out his black book and furiously scribbled in it. Gus's blue, depressed eye hunted around for a way out but his glass one gleamed like a lamp in a graveyard. And Memo laughed and laughed till the tears streamed down her cheeks.

"**M**AYBE I might break my back while I am at it," Roy spoke into the microphone at home plate before a hushed sell-out crowd jampacked into Knights Field, "but I will do my best—the best I am able—to be the greatest there ever was in the game.

"I thank you." He finished with a gulp that echoed like an electric hiccup through the loudspeakers and sat down, not quite happy with himself despite the celebration, because when called on to speak he had meant to begin with a joke, then thank them for their favor and say what a good team the Knights were and how he enjoyed working for Pop Fisher, but it had come out this other way. On the other hand, so what the hell if they knew what was on his mind?

It was "Roy Hobbs Day," that had been in the making since two weeks ago, when Max Mercy printed in his column: "Roy Hobbs, El Swatto, has been ixnayed on a pay raise. Trying to kill the bird that lays the golden baseball, Judge?" A grass roots movement developed among the loyal fans to put the Judge to shame (if possible) and they had quickly arranged a Day for Roy, which was held after the Knights had bounced into third place, following a night game win over the Phils, who now led them by only four games, themselves two behind the first-place Pirates.

The whole thing was kept a surprise, and after batting practice was over on this particular Saturday afternoon in early August, the right field gate had swung open and a whole caravan of cars, led by a limousine full of officials and American Legionnaires, and followed by a gorgeous, under-slung white Mercedes-Benz and a lumbering warehouse van loaded with stuff, drove in and slowly circled the field to the music of a band playing "Yankee Doodle," while the crowd cheered shrilly. Someone then tapped Roy and said it was all for him.

"Who, me?" he said, rising . . .

When he had made his speech and retired to the dugout, after a quick, unbelieving glance at the mountain of gifts they were unpacking for him, the fans sat back in frozen silence, some quickly crossing their fingers, some spitting over their left shoulders, onto the steps so they wouldn't get anyone wet, almost all hoping he had not jinxed himself forever by saying what he had said. "The best there ever was in the game" might tempt the wrath of some mighty powerful ghosts. But they quickly recovered from the shock of his audacity and clapped up a thick thunder of applause.

It was everyman's party and they were determined to enjoy it. No one knew exactly who had supplied the big dough, but the loyal everyday fans had contributed all sorts of small change and single bucks to buy enough merchandise to furnish a fair-sized general store. When everything was unloaded from the van, Roy posed in front of it, fiddling with a gadget or two for the benefit of the photographers, though he later tipped off Dizzy to sell whatever he could to whoever had the cash. Mercy himself counted two television sets, a baby tractor, five hundred feet of pink plastic garden hose, a nanny goat, lifetime pass to the Paramount, one dozen hand-painted neckties offering different views of the Grand Canyon, six aluminum traveling cases, and a credit for seventy-five taxi rides in Philadelphia. Also three hundred pounds of a New Jersey brand Swiss cheese, a set of andirons and tongs, forty gallons of pistachio ice cream, six crates of lemons, a frozen side of hog, hunting knife, bearskin rug, snowshoes, four burner electric range, deed to a lot in Florida, twelve pairs of monogrammed blue shorts, movie camera and projector, a Chris-Craft motor boat—and, because everybody thought the Judge (unashamedly looking on from his window in the tower) was too cheap to live—a certified check for thirty-six hundred dollars. Although the committee had tried to keep out all oddball contributions, a few slipped in, including a smelly package of Limburger cheese, one human skull, bundle of comic books, can of rat exterminator, and a package of dull razor blades, this last with a card attached in the crabbed handwriting of Otto Zipp: "Here, cut your throat," but Roy did not take it to heart.

When he was told, to his amazement, that the Mercedes-Benz was his too, he could only say, "This is the happiest day of my life." Getting in, he drove around the park to the frenzied waving and whistling of the fans and whirring of movie cameras. The gleaming white job was light to the touch of

hand and foot and he felt he could float off in it over the stadium wall. But he stopped before Memo's box and asked if she
would go with him for a jaunt after the game, to which she,
lowering her eyes, replied she was agreeable.

Memo said she longed to see the ocean so they drove over the
bridge and down into Long Island toward Jones Beach, stopping when she was hungry, for charcoal-broiled steaks at a
roadside tavern. Afterwards it was night, lit up by a full moon
swimming in lemon juice, but at intervals eclipsed by rain
clouds that gathered in dark blots and shuttered the yellow
light off the fields and tree tops.

She spoke little, once remarking it looked like rain.

He didn't answer. Though he had started off riding high (he
had paid back the patrons of his Day by walloping a homer
that drove in the winning run) he now felt somewhat heavy
hearted. For the past two weeks he had been seeing Memo
most every day but had made little headway. There were times
when he thought yes, I am on my way up in her affections, but
no sooner did he think that when something she did or said, or
didn't do or didn't say, made him think no, I am not. It was a
confusing proposition to want a girl you'd already had and
couldn't get because you had; a situation common in his life,
of having first and then wanting what he had had, as if he
hadn't had it but just heard about it, and it had, in the hearing,
aroused his appetite. He even wished he had not had her that
night, and wondered—say he hadn't—whether he would be in
the least interested in her today.

In another sense it wasn't a bad evening. He was with her, at
least, and they were traveling together, relaxed, to the ocean.
He didn't exactly know where it was and though he liked the
water, tonight he did not much care if they never came to it.
He felt contentment in moving. It rested him by cutting down
the inside motion—that which got him nowhere, which was
where he was and she was not, or where his ambitions were
and he was chasing after. Sometimes he wished he had no
ambitions—often wondered where they had come from in his
life, because he remembered how satisfied he had been as a
youngster, and that with the little he had had—a dog, a stick,
an aloneness he loved (which did not bleed him like his later

loneliness), and he wished he could have lived longer in his boyhood. This was an old thought with him.

Hoping for a better fate in the future he stepped on the gas and was at once seized by an uneasy fear they were being followed. Since the mirror showed nobody behind them, he wondered at his suspicions and then recalled a black sedan that had been on their tail, he thought, all the way down from the city, only they had lost it a while back in turning off the highway. Yet he continued to watch in the mirror, though it showed only the lifeless moonlit road.

Memo said Jones Beach was too far and told him to stop the next time they came to a brook or pond where she could take off her shoes and go wading in the water. When he spied a small stream running along the edge of a wooded section between two towns, he slowed down. They parked across the shoulder of the asphalt and got out but as they crossed this wooden bridge to the grassy side of the stream, they were confronted by a sign: DANGER. POLLUTED WATER. NO SWIMMING. Roy was all for getting into the car to find another place, but Memo said no, they could watch the water from the bridge. She lit a cigarette, all in light, her hair and green summer dress, and her naked legs and even the slave bracelet around her left ankle gleaming in the light of the moon. Smoking, she watched the water flowing under the bridge, its movement reflected on her face.

After a while, seeing how silent she was, Roy said, "I bet I got enough today to furnish a house."

Memo said, "Bump was coming up for a Day just before he died."

He felt anger rise in his heart and asked coldly, "Well, Memo, what did he have that I haven't got?" He stood to his full height, strong and handsome.

Without looking at him she spoke Bump's name thoughtfully, then shook her head to snap out of it, as if it didn't pay to be thoughtful about Bump. "Oh," she answered, "he was carefree and full of life. He did the craziest things and always kept everybody in stitches. Even when he played ball, there was something carefree and playful about it. Maybe he went all the way after a fly ball or maybe he didn't, but once he made up his mind to catch it, it was exciting how he ran and exciting how he caught it. He made you think you had been wishing for a thing to happen for a long time and then he made it happen. And the same with his hitting. When you catch one, Roy, or go up to hit, everybody knows beforehand that it will land up in your glove, or be a hit. You work at it so—sometimes you even look desperate—but to him it was a playful game and so was his life. Nobody could ever tell what would happen next with Bump, and that was the wonderful thing of it."

Roy thought this is how she sees him now that he is dead. She forgets how hopping sore she was at him after that time in bed with me.

But Bump was dead, he thought, dead and buried in his new box, an inescapable six feet under, so he subtly changed the subject to Gus.

"Gus?" Memo said. At first her face was expressionless. "Oh, he's just like a daddy to me."

He asked her in what way but she laughed and said, "That was a funny business you did with him in the Pot of Fire. How did you do all those tricks?"

"Easy. They had a magic act all laid out to go on. I walked into the guy's dressing room and when they saw who I was they let me use his stuff just for the laughs."

"Who showed you how to use it?"

"Nobody. I have done some different things in my time, Memo."

"Such as what other ones?"

"You name it, I did it."

"What you did to Max was a scream."

A black cloud rolled like a slow wave across the moon.

"It's so strange," she murmured, looking at the moving water.

"What is?"

For a time she didn't speak, then she sighed and said she meant her life. "It's been strange ever since I can remember except for a year or two—mostly the part with Bump. That was the good part only it didn't last very long, not much of the good part ever did. When I was little my daddy walked out on us and I don't ever remember being happy again till the time I got to go to Hollywood when I was nineteen."

He waited.

"I won a beauty contest where they picked a winner from each state and she was sent to Hollywood to be a starlet. For a few weeks I felt like the Queen of the May, then they took a screen test and though I had the looks and figure my test did not come out so good in acting and they practically told me to go home. I couldn't stand the thought of that so I stayed there for three more years, doing night club work and going to an acting school besides, hoping that I would some day be a good enough actress but it didn't take. I knew what I was supposed to do but I couldn't make myself, in my thoughts, into somebody else. You're supposed to forget who you are but I couldn't. Then I came east and had some more bad times after my mother died, till I met Bump."

He thought she would cry but she didn't.

Memo watched the pebbles in the flowing water. "After Bump I realized I could never be happy any more."

"How do you know that?" Roy asked slowly.

"Oh, I know. I can tell from the way I feel. Sometimes in the morning I never want to wake up."

He felt a dreary emptiness at her words.

"What about yourself?" she asked, wanting to change the subject.

"What about me?" he said gloomily.

"Max says you are sort of a mystery."

"Max is a jerk. My past life is nobody's business."

"What was it like?"

"Like yours, for years I took it on the chin." He sounded as if he had caught a cold, took out his handkerchief and blew his nose.

"What happened?"

He wanted to tell her everything, match her story and go her a couple better but couldn't bring himself to. It wasn't, he thought, that he was afraid to tell her what had happened to him that first time (though the thought of doing that raised a hot blush on his pan, for he had never told anybody about it yet), but about the miserable years after that, when everything, everything he tried somehow went to pot as if that was its destiny in the first place, a thing he couldn't understand.

"What happened?" she asked again.

"The hell with it," he said.

"I told you about myself."

He watched the water.

"I have knocked around a lot and been hard hurt in plenty of ways," he said huskily. "There were times I thought I would never get anywhere and it made me eat my guts, but all that is gone now. I know I have the stuff and will get there."

"Get where?"

"Where I am going. Where I will be the champ and have what goes with it."

She drew back but he had caught her arm and tugged her to him.

"Don't."

"You got to live, Memo."

He trapped her lips, tasting of lemon drops, kissing hard. Happening to open his eyes, he saw her staring at him in the middle of the kiss. Shutting them, he dived deep down again. Then she caught his passion, opened her mouth for his tongue and went limp around the knees.

They swayed together and he turned his hand and slipped it through the top of her dress into her loose brassiere, cupping her warm small breast in his palm.

Her legs stiffened. She pushed at him, sobbing, "Don't touch it."

He was slow to react.

She wailed, "Don't, please don't."

He pulled his hand out, angrily disappointed.

She was crying now, rubbing her hand across her bosom.

"Did I hurt you?"

"Yes."

"How the hell did I do that? I was nice with it."

"It's sick," she wept.

He felt like he had had an icy shave and haircut. "Who says so?"

"It hurts. I know."

She could be lying, only her eyes were crisscrossed with fear and her arms goosefleshed.

"Did you go to a doctor?"

"I don't like them."

"You ought to go."

Memo ran off the bridge. He followed her to the car. She sat at the wheel and started the motor. Figuring she would calm down quicker this way he let her.

She backed the car onto the road and drove off. The moon sank into an enormous cloud-sea. Memo sped along the asphalt and turned at a fork down a hard dirt road.

"Put on the lights."

"I like it dark." Her white arms were stiff on the wheel.

He knew she didn't but figured she was still nervous.

Dripping dark cloud spray, the moon bobbed up and flooded the road ahead with bright light. Memo pressed her foot on the gas.

A thundering wind beat across his skull. Let her, he thought. Whatever she has got on her mind, let her get it off, especially if it is still Bump.

He thought about what she had said on the bridge about never being happy again and wondered what it meant. In a way he was tired of her—she was too complicated—but in a different way he desired her more than ever. He could not decide what to say or do next. Maybe wait, but he didn't want to any more. Yet what else was there to do?

The white moonlight shot through a stretch of woods ahead. He found himself wishing he could go back somewhere, go home, wherever that was. As he was thinking this, he looked up and saw in the moonlight a boy coming out of the woods, followed by his dog. Squinting through the windshield, he was unable to tell if the kid was an illusion thrown forth by the trees or someone really alive. After fifteen seconds he was still there. Roy yelled to Memo to slow down in case he wanted to cross the road. Instead, the car shot forward so fast the woods blurred, the trees racing along like shadows in weak light, then skipping into black and white, finally all black and the moon was gone.

"Lights!"

She sat there stiffly so he reached over and switched them on.

As the road flared up, Memo screamed and tugged at the wheel. He felt a thud and his heart sickened. It was a full minute before he realized they hadn't stopped.

"For Christ sake, stop—we hit somebody."

"No." Her face was bloodless.

He reached for the brake.

"Don't, it was just something on the road."

"I heard somebody groan."

"That was yourself."

He couldn't remember that he had.

"I want to go back and see."

"If you do, the cops will get us."

"What cops?"

"They have been after us since we started. I've been doing ninety."

He looked back and saw a black car with dimmed headlights speeding after them.

"Turn at the next bend," he ordered her, "and I will take over."

They were nearer to the Sound than he had suspected, and when a white pea-souper crawled in off the water Roy headed into it. Though the Mercedes showed no lights the whiteness of it was enough to keep it in the sedan's eye, so he welcomed the fog and within it easily ditched those who chased them.

On the way back he attempted to find the road along the woods to see if they had hit somebody. Memo had little patience with him. She was sure, despite Roy's insistence of an outside groan, that they had hit a rock or log in the road. If they went back the cops might be laying for them and they'd be arrested, which would cause no end of trouble.

He said he was going back anyway.

Roy had the feeling that the sedan was still at his shoulder—he could see it wasn't—as he tried to locate the bridge and then the road along the woods. He wasn't convinced they had not hit somebody and if he could do anything for the kid, even this late, he wanted to. So he turned the lights on bright, illuminating the swirling fog, and as they went by the fog-shrouded woods—he couldn't be sure it was the right woods—he searched the road intently for signs of a body or its blood but found nothing. Memo dozed off but was awakened when Roy, paying no heed to what lay ahead, ran off a low embankment, crashing the car into a tree. Though shaken up, neither of them was much hurt. Roy had a black eye and Memo bruised her sick breast. The car was a wreck.

*

Helping Memo out of a cab that same morning before dawn, Roy glanced into the hotel lobby just as Pop Fisher bounced up out of a couch and came charging at them like a runaway trolley. Memo said to run, so they raced down the street and ducked into the hotel by the side entrance, but they were barely to the stairs when Pop, who had doubled back on his tracks, came at them smoking with anger.

Memo sobbed she had taken all she could tonight and ran up the stairs. Roy had hoped to have another chance at a kiss but when Pop flew at him like a batty, loose-feathered fowl, killing the stillness of the place with his shrill crowing, he figured it best to keep him away from Memo.

He turned to Pop, who then got a closeup of Roy's rainbow eye and all but blew apart. He called him everything from a dadblamed sonovagun to a blankety blank Judas traitor for breaking training, hurting his eye, and blowing in at almost 5 A.M. on the day of an important twin bill with the Phils.

"You damn near drove me wild," he shouted. "I just about had heart failure when Red told me you weren't in your room at midnight."

He then and there fined Roy two hundred and fifty dollars, but reduced it to an even hundred when Roy sarcastically mentioned how much the Knights were paying him.

"And nothing is wrong with my eye," he said. "It don't hurt but a little and I can see out of it as clear as day, but if you want me to get some sleep before the game don't stand there jawing my head off."

Pop was quickly pacified. "I admit you are entitled to a good time on your Day but you have no idea of all that I have suffered in those hours I was waiting up for you. All kinds of terrible things ran through my mind. I don't hafta tell you it don't take much to kill off a man nowadays."

Roy laughed. "Nothing is going to kill me before my time. I am the type that will die a natural death."

Seeing the affectionate smile this raised up on Pop's puss, he felt sorry for the old man and said, "Even with one eye I will wow them for you today."

"I know you will, son," Pop almost purred. "You're the one I'm depending on to get us up there. We're hot now and I figure, barring any serious accidents, that we will catch up with the Pirates in less than two weeks. Then once we are first we should stay there till we take the flag. My God, when I think of that my legs get dizzy. I guess you know what that would mean to me after all of these years. Sometimes I feel I have been waiting for it my whole life. So take care of yourself. When all is said and done, you ain't a kid any more. At your age the body will often act up, so be wise and avoid any trouble."

"I am young in my mind and healthy in my body," Roy said. "You don't have to worry about me."

"Only be careful," Pop said.

Roy said good night but couldn't move because Pop had gripped his elbow. Leading him to the corner, he whispered to Roy not to have too much to do with Memo.

Roy stiffened.

"Don't get me wrong, son, she's not a bad girl—"

Roy glared.

Pop gulped. "I am the one who is really bad. It was me who introduced her to Bump." He looked sick. "I hoped she would straighten him out and sorta hold him in the team—but—well, you know how these things are. Bump was not the marrying kind and she sorta—well, you know what I mean."

"So what?" said Roy.

"Nothing," he answered brokenly. "Only I was wrong for encouraging them to get together with maybe in the back of my mind the idea of how they would do so—without getting married, that is—and I have suffered from it since."

Roy said nothing and Pop wouldn't look him in the eye. "What I started to say," he went on, "is that although she is not really a bad person, yet she is unlucky and always has been and I think that there is some kind of whammy in her that carries her luck to other people. That's why I would like you to watch out and not get too tied up with her."

"You're a lousy uncle."

"I am considering you."

"I will consider myself."

"Don't mistake me, son. She was my sister's girl and I do love her, but she is always dissatisfied and will snarl you up in her trouble in a way that will weaken your strength if you don't watch out."

"You might as well know that I love her."

Pop listened gloomily. "Does she feel the same to you?"

"Not yet but I think she will."

"Well, you are on your own." He looked so forlorn that Roy said, "Don't worry yourself about her. I will change her luck too."

"You might at that." Pop took out his billfold and extracted a pink paper that he handed to Roy.

Roy inspected it through his good eye. It was a check for two thousand dollars, made out to him. "What's it for?"

"The balance of your salary for the time you missed before you got here. I figure that you are entitled to at least the minimum pay for the year."

"Did the Judge send it?"

"That worm? He wouldn't send you his bad breath. It's my personal check." Pop was blushing.

Roy handed it back. "I am making out okay. If the Judge wants to raise my pay, all right, but I don't want your personal money."

"My boy, if you knew what you mean to me—"

"Don't say it." Roy's throat was thick with sentiment. "Wait till I get you the pennant."

He turned to go and bumped into Max Mercy at his elbow. Max's sleepy popeyes goggled when he saw Roy's shiner. He sped back into the lobby.

"That slob is up to no good," Roy said.

"He was sleeping on the couch next to where I was waiting for you to come home. He heard Red tell me you hadn't showed up. Kept a camera with him back there."

"He better not take a picture of my eye," Roy said.

He beat it up the back stairs with Max on his tail. Though the columnist carried a camera and a pocketful of flashbulbs he ran faster than Roy had expected, so to ditch him he shot through the second-floor door and sped down the corridor. Seeing over his shoulder that Max was still after him he ducked through a pair of open glass doors into an enormous black ballroom, strewn with chairs, potted palms, and music stands from a dance last night. The lingering odor of perfume mixed with cigarette smoke reminded him of the smell of Memo's hair and haunted him even now. He thought of hiding behind something but that would make him a ridiculous sitting duck for a chance shot of Max's, so since his good eye had become accustomed to the dark he nimbly picked his way among the obstacles, hoping the four-eyed monstrosity behind him would break his camera or maybe a leg. But Max seemed to smell his way around in the dark and hung tight. Reaching the glass doors at the other end of the ballroom, Roy sidestepped out just as a bulb lit in a wavering flash that would leave Max with a snapshot of nothing but a deserted ballroom. The columnist stuck like glue to Roy's shadow, spiraling after him up the stairs and through the long empty ninth-floor corridor (broad and soft-carpeted so that their footsteps were silent) which stretched ahead, it seemed to Roy, like an endless highway.

He felt he had been running for ages, then this blurred black forest slid past him, and as he slowed down, each black tree followed a white, and then all the trees were lit in somber light till the moon burst forth through the leaves and the woods glowed. Out of it appeared this boy and his dog, and Roy in his heart whispered him a confidential message: watch out when you cross the road, kid, but he had spoken too late, for the boy lay brokenboned and bleeding in a puddle of light, with no one to care for him or whisper a benediction upon his lost youth. A groan rose in Roy's throat (he holding a flashlight over the remains) for not having forced Memo to stop and go back to undo some of the harm. A sudden dark glare flashed over his head, eerily catapulting his shadow forward, and erasing in its incandescence the boy in the road. Roy felt a burning pain in his gut, yet simultaneously remembered there had been no sign of blood on the bumper or fender, and Memo said she had screamed because she saw in the mirror that they were being chased by cops. The black sedan that trailed them had not stopped either, which it would have done if there were cops in it and somebody was dying in the road. So Memo must've been right—either it was a rock, or maybe the kid's hound, probably not even that, for it did not appear there ever was any kid in those woods, except in his mind.

Ahead was his door. Max was panting after him. As Roy

shoved the key into the lock, poking his eye close to do the job quick, Max from fifteen feet away aimed the camera and snapped the shutter. The flashbulb burst in the reflector. The door slammed. Max swore blue bloody murder as Roy, inside, howled with laughing.

H<small>E HAD</small> a whopping good time at the ball game. Doc Casey had squeezed the swelling of his eye down and painted out the black with a flesh-tone color, and Roy led the attack against the Phils that sank them twice that afternoon, sweeping the series for the Knights and raising them into second place, only three games behind the Pirates. Pop was hilarious. The fans went wild. The newspapers called the Knights "the wonder team of the age" and said they were headed for the pennant.

On his way to Memo's after the game, Roy met her, wearing her summer furpiece, coming along the fourth-floor hall.

"I thought I would drop around and see how you are, Memo."

She continued her slightly swaying walk to the elevator.

"I am all right," she said.

He paused. "See the doctor yet?"

Memo blushed and said quickly, "He says it's neuritis—nothing serious."

She pressed the elevator button.

"Nothing serious?"

"That's what he said." She was looking up the elevator shaft and he sensed she had not been to the doctor. He guessed her breast was not sick. He guessed she had said that to get him to slow down. Though he did not care for her technique, he controlled his anger and asked her to go to the movies.

"Sorry. Gus is picking me up."

Back in his room he felt restless. He thought he'd be better off without her but the thought only made him bitter. Red Blow called him to go to the pictures but Roy said he had a headache. Later he went out by himself. That night he dreamed of her all night long. The sick breast had turned green yet he was anxious to have a feel of it.

The next day, against the Braves, Roy got exactly no hits. The Knights won, but against the Dodgers in Brooklyn on Tuesday he went hitless once more and they lost. Since he had never before gone without a hit more than six times in a row there was talk now of a slump. That made him uneasy but he tried not to think of it, concerning himself with Memo and continuing his search through the papers for news of a hit-and-run accident on Long Island. Finding no mention of one he blamed the whole thing on his imagination and thought he'd better forget it. And he told himself not to worry about the slump—it happened to the very best—but after a third day without even a bingle he couldn't help but worry.

As his hitlessness persisted everyone was astonished. It didn't seem possible this could happen to a miracle man like Roy. Enemy pitchers were the last to believe the news. They pitched him warily, fearing an eruption of his wrath, but before long they saw the worry in his eyes and would no longer yield those free and easy walks of yore. They straightened out their curves and whizzed them over the gut of the plate, counting on him either to top a slow roller to the infield or strike himself out. True, he was the same majestic-looking figure up there, well back in the box, legs spread wide, and with Wonderboy gleaming in the sun, raised over his shoulder (he had lowered it from his head). He swung with such power you could see a circle of dust lift off the ground as the bat passed over it, yet all it amounted to was breeze. It made many a pitcher feel like a pretty tough hombre to see Roy drag himself away from the plate and with lowered head enter the dugout.

"What's the matter with me?" he thought with irritation. He didn't feel himself (wondered if he could possibly be sick). He felt blunt and dull—all thumbs, muscles, and joints, Charley horse all over. He missed the sensation of the sock—the moment the stomach galloped just before the wood hit the ball, and the satisfying sting that sped through his arms and shoulders as he belted one. Though there was plenty of fielding to do—the Knights' pitchers were getting to be loose with the hits—he missed the special exercise of running the bases, whirling round them with the speed of a race horse as nine frantic men tried to cut him down. Most of all he missed the gloating that blew up his lungs when he crossed the plate and they ran up another tally opposite his name in the record book. A whole apparatus of physical and mental pleasures was on the kibosh and without them he felt like the Hobbs he thought he had left behind dead and buried.

"What am I doing that's wrong?" he asked himself. No one on the bench or in the clubhouse had offered any advice or information on the subject or even so much as mentioned slump. Not even Pop, also worried, but hoping it would fade as suddenly as it had appeared. Roy realized that he was over-anxious and pressing—either hitting impatiently in front of the ball or swinging too late—so that Wonderboy only got little bites of it or went hungry. Thinking he was maybe overstriding and getting his feet too far apart so that he could not pivot freely, he shifted his stride but that didn't help. He tried a new stance and attempted, by counting to himself, to alter his tim-ing. It did no good. To save his eyesight he cut out all reading and going to the pictures. At bat his expression was so dark and foreboding it gave the opposing pitchers the shakes, but still they had his number.

He spent hours fretting whether to ask for help or wait it out. Some day the slump was bound to go, but when? Not that he was ashamed to ask for help but once you had come this far you felt you had learned the game and could afford to give out with the advice instead of being forced to ask for it. He was, as they say, established and it was like breaking up the establishment to go around panhandling an earful. Like mak-ing a new beginning and he was sick up to here of new begin-nings. But as he continued to whiff he felt a little panicky. In the end he sought out Red Blow, drew him out to center field and asked in an embarrassed voice, "Red, what is the matter with me that I am not hitting them?" He gazed over the right field wall as he asked the question.

Red squirted tobacco juice into the grass.

"Well," he said, rubbing his freckled nose, "what's worrying your mind?"

Roy was slow to reply. "I am worrying that I am missing so many and can't get back in the groove."

"I mean besides that. You haven't knocked up a dame maybe?"

"No."

"Any financial worries about money?"

"Not right now."

"Are you doing something you don't like to do?"

"Such as what?"

"Once we had a guy here whose wife made him empty the garbage pail in the barrel every night and believe it or not it began to depress him. After that he fanned the breeze a whole month until one night he told her to take the damn garbage out herself, and the next day he hit again."

"No, nothing like that."

Red smiled. "Thought I'd get a laugh out of you, Roy. A good belly laugh has more than once broke up a slump."

"I would be glad to laugh but I don't feel much like it. I hate to say it but I feel more like crying."

Red was sympathetic. "I have seen lots of slumps in my time, Roy, and if I could tell you why they come I could make a fortune, buy a saloon and retire. All I know about them is you have to relax to beat 'em. I know how you feel now and I realize that every game we lose hurts us, but if you can take it easy and get rid of the nervousness that is for some reason in your system, you will soon snap into your form. From there on in you will hit like a house on fire."

"I might be dead by then," Roy said gloomily.

Red removed his cap and with the hand that held it scratched his head.

"All I can say is that you have got to figure this out for yourself, Roy."

Pop's advice was more practical. Roy visited the manager in his office after the next (fruitless) game. Pop was sitting at his roll top desk, compiling player averages in a looseleaf notebook. On the desk were a pair of sneakers, a picture of Ma Fisher, and an old clipping from the *Sporting News* saying how sensational the Knights were going. Pop closed the average book but not before Roy had seen a large red zero for the day's work opposite his name. The Knights had dropped back to third place, only a game higher than the Cardinals, and Pop's athlete's foot on his hands was acting up.

"What do I have to do to get out of this?" Roy asked moodily.

Pop looked at him over his half-moon specs.

"Nobody can tell you exactly, son, but I'd say right off stop climbing up after those bad balls."

Roy shook his head. "I don't think that's it. I can tell when they're bad but the reason I reach for them sometimes is that the pitchers don't throw me any good ones, which hasn't been so lately. Lately, they're almost all good but not for me."

"Danged if I know just what to tell you," Pop said, scratching at his reddened fingers. He too felt a little frightened. But he recommended bunting and trying to beat them out. He said Roy had a fast pair of legs and getting on base, in whichever way, might act to restore his confidence.

But Roy, who was not much of a bunter—never had his heart in letting the ball hit the bat and roll, when he could just as well lash out and send the same pitch over the fence—could not master the art of it overnight. He looked foolish trying to bunt, and soon gave it up.

Pop then recommended hitting at fast straight ones thrown by different pitchers for thirty minutes every morning, and to do this till he had got his timing back, because it was timing that was lost in a slump. Roy practiced diligently and got so he could connect, yet he couldn't seem to touch the same pitches during the game.

Then Pop advised him to drop all batting practice and to bat cold. That didn't help either.

"How is your eye that got hurt?" Pop asked.

"Doc tested it, he says I see perfect."

Pop looked grimly at Wonderboy. "Don't you think you ought to try another stick for a change? Sometimes that will end up a slump."

Roy wouldn't hear of it. "Wonderboy made all of my records with me and I am staying with him. Whatever is wrong is wrong with me and not my bat."

Pop looked miserable but didn't argue.

Only rarely he saw Memo. She was not around much, never at the games, though she had begun to come quite often a while back. Roy had the morbid feeling she couldn't stand him while he was in this slump. He knew that other people's worries bothered her and that she liked to be where everybody was merry. Maybe she thought the slump proved he was not as good a player as Bump. Whatever it was, she found excuses not to see him and he got only an occasional glimpse of her here and there in the building. One morning when he ran into her in the hotel grill room, Memo reddened and said she was sorry to read he was having a tough time.

Roy just nodded but she went on to say that Bump used to ease his nerves when he wasn't hitting by consulting a fortune-teller named Lola who lived in Jersey City.

"What for?" Roy asked.

"She used to tell him things that gave him a lift, like the time she said he was going to be left money by someone, and he felt so good it raised him clean out of his slump."

"Did he get the dough that she said?"

"Yes. Around Christmas his father died and left him a garage and a new Pontiac. Bump cleared nine thousand cash when he sold the property."

Roy thought it over afterwards. He had little faith that any fortuneteller could help him out of his trouble but the failure of each remedy he tried sank him deeper into the dumps and he was now clutching for any straw. Borrowing a car, he hunted up Lola in Jersey City, locating her in a two-story shack near the river. She was a fat woman of fifty, and wore black felt slippers broken at the seams, and a kitchen towel wrapped around her head.

"Step right inside the parlor," she said, holding aside the beaded curtain leading into a dark and smelly room, "and I will be with you in a jiffy, just as soon as I get rid of this loud mouth on the back porch."

Feeling ill at ease and foolish, Roy waited for her.

Lola finally came in with a Spanish shawl twisted around her. She lit up the crystal ball, passed her gnarled hands over it and peered nearsightedly into the glass. After watching for a minute she told Roy he would soon meet and fall in love with a darkhaired lady.

"Anything else?" he said impatiently.

Lola looked. A blank expression came over her face and she slowly shook her head. "Funny," she said, "there ain't a thing more."

"Nothing about me getting out of a slump in baseball?"

"Nothing. The future has closed down on me."

Roy stood up. "The trouble with what you said is that I am already in love with a swell-looking redhead."

Because of the shortness of the sitting Lola charged him a buck instead of the usual two.

After his visit to her, though Roy was as a rule not superstitious, he tried one or two things he had heard about to see how they would work. He put his socks on inside out, ran a red thread through his underpants, spat between two fingers when he met a black cat, and daily searched the stands for some crosseyed whammy who might be hexing him. He also ate less meat, though he was always hungry, and he arranged for a physical check-up. The doctor told him he was in good shape except for some high blood pressure that was caused by worrying and would diminish as soon as he relaxed. He practiced different grips on Wonderboy before his bureau mirror and sewed miraculous medals and evil-eye amulets of fish, goats, clenched fists, open scissors, and hunchbacks all over the inside of his clothes.

Little of this escaped the other Knights. While the going was good they had abandoned this sort of thing, but now that they were on the skids they felt the need of some extra assistance. So Dave Olson renewed his feud with the lady in the brown-feathered hat, Emil Lajong spun his protective backflips, and Flores revived the business with the birds. Clothes were put on from down up, gloves were arranged to point south when the players left the field to go to bat, and everybody, including Dizzy, owned at least one rabbit's foot. Despite these precautions the boys were once more afflicted by bonehead plays—failing to step on base on a simple force, walking off the field with two out as the winning run scored from first, attempting to stretch singles into triples, and fearing to leave first when the ball was good for at least two. And they were not ashamed to blame it all on Roy.

It didn't take the fans very long to grow disgusted with their antics. Some of them agreed it was Roy's fault, for jinxing himself and the team on his Day by promising the impossible out of his big mouth. Others, including a group of sportswriters, claimed the big boy had all the while been living on borrowed time, a large bag of wind burst by the law of averages. Sadie, dabbing at her eyes with the edge of her petticoat, kept her gong in storage, and Gloria disgustedly swore off men. And Otto Zipp had reappeared like a bad dream with his loud voice and pesky tooter venomously hooting Roy into oblivion. A few of the fans were ashamed that Otto was picking on somebody obviously down, but the majority approved his sentiments. The old-timers began once again to heave vegetables and oddments around, and following the dwarf's lead they heckled the players, especially Roy, calling him everything from a coward to a son of a bitch. Since Roy had always had rabbit ears, every taunt and barb hit its mark. He changed color and muttered at his tormentors. Once in a spasm of weakness he went slowly after a fly ball (lately he had to push himself to catch shots he had palmed with ease before), compelling Flores to rush into his territory to take it. The meatheads rose to a man and hissed. Roy shook his fist at their stupid faces. They booed. He thumbed his nose. "You'll get yours," they howled in chorus.

He had, a vile powerlessness seized him.

Seeing all this, Pop was darkly furious. He all but ripped the recently restored bandages off his pusing fingers. His temper flared wild and red, his voice tore, he ladled out fines like soup to breadline beggars, and he was vicious to Roy.

"It's that goshdamn bat," he roared one forenoon in the clubhouse. "When will you get rid of that danged Wonderboy and try some other stick?"

"Never," said Roy.

"Then rest your ass on the bench."

So Roy sat out the game on the far corner of the bench, from where he could watch Memo, lovelier than ever in a box up front, in the company of two undertakers, the smiling, one-eye Gus, and Mercy, catlike contented, whose lead that night would read: "Hobbs is benched. The All-American Out has sunk the Knights into second division."

He woke in the locker room, stretched out on a bench. He remembered lying down to dry out before dressing but he was still wet with sweat, and a lit match over his wristwatch told him it was past midnight. He sat up stiffly, groaned and rubbed his hard palms over his bearded face. The thinking started up and stunned him. He sat there paralyzed though his innards were in flight—the double-winged lungs, followed by the boat-shaped heart, trailing a long string of guts. He longed for a friend, a father, a home to return to—saw himself packing his duds in a suitcase, buying a ticket, and running for a train. Beyond the first station he'd fling Wonderboy out the window. (Years later, an old man returning to the city for a visit, he would scan the flats to see if it was there, glowing in the mud.) The train sped through the night across the country. In it he felt safe. He tittered.

The mousy laughter irritated him. "Am I outa my mind?" He fell to brooding and mumbled, "What am I doing that's wrong?" Now he shouted the question and it boomed back at him off the walls. Lighting matches, he hurriedly dressed. Before leaving, he remembered to wrap Wonderboy in flannel. In the street he breathed easier momentarily, till he suspected someone was following him. Stopping suddenly, he wheeled about. A woman, walking alone in the glare of the street lamp, noticed him. She went faster, her heels clicking down the street. He hugged the stadium wall, occasionally casting stealthy glances behind. In the tower burned a dark light, the Judge counting his shekels. He cursed him and dragged his carcass on.

A cabbie with a broken nose and cauliflower ear stared but did not recognize him. The hotel lobby was deserted. An old elevator man mumbled to himself. The ninth-floor hall was long and empty. Silent. He felt a driblet of fear . . . like a glug of water backing up the momentarily opened drain and polluting the bath with a dead spider, three lice, a rat turd, and things he couldn't stand to name or look at. For the first time in years he felt afraid to enter his room. The telephone rang. It rang and rang. He waited for it to stop. Finally it did. He warned himself he was acting like a crazy fool. Twisting the key in the lock, he pushed open the door. In the far corner of the room, something moved. His blood changed to falling snow.

Bracing himself to fight without strength he snapped on the light. A white shadow flew into the bathroom. Rushing in, he kicked the door open. An ancient hoary face stared at him. "Bump!" He groaned and shuddered. An age passed . . . His own face gazed back at him from the bathroom mirror, his past, his youth, the fleeting years. He all but blacked out in relief. His head, a jagged rock on aching shoulders, throbbed from its rocky interior. An oppressive sadness weighed like a live pain on his heart. Gasping for air, he stood at the open window and looked down at the dreary city till his legs and arms were drugged with heaviness. He shut the hall door and flopped into bed. In the dark he was lost in an overwhelming weakness . . . I am finished, he muttered. The pages of the record book fell apart and fluttered away in the wind. He slept and woke, finished. All night long he waited for the bloody silver bullet.

On the road Pop was in a foul mood. He cracked down on team privileges: no more traveling wives, no signing of food checks—Red dispensed the cash for meals every morning before breakfast—curfew at eleven and bed check every night. But Roy had discovered that the old boy had invited Memo to come along with them anyway. He went on the theory that Roy had taken to heart his advice to stay away from her and it was making a wreck out of him. Memo had declined the invitation and Pop guiltily kicked himself for asking her.

Roy was thinking about her the morning they came into Chicago and were on their way to the hotel in a cab—Pop, Red, and him. For a time he had succeeded in keeping her out of his thoughts but now, because of the renewed disappointment, she was back in again. He wondered whether Pop was right and she had maybe jinxed him into a slump. If so, would he do better out here, so far away from her?

The taxi turned up Michigan Avenue, where they had a clear view of the lake. Roy was silent. Red happened to glance out the back window. He stared at something and then said, "Have either of you guys noticed the black Cadillac that is following us around? I've seen that damn auto most everywhere we go."

Roy turned to see. His heart jumped. It looked like the car that had chased them halfway across Long Island.

"Drat 'em," Pop said. "I fired those guys a week ago. Guess they didn't get my postcard."

Red asked who they were.

"A private eye and his partner," Pop explained. "I hired them about a month back to watch the Great Man here and keep him outa trouble but it's a waste of good money now." He gazed back and fumed. "Those goshdarn saps."

Roy didn't say anything but he threw Pop a hard look and the manager was embarrassed.

As the cab pulled up before the hotel, a wild-eyed man in shirtsleeves, hairy-looking and frantic, rushed up to them.

"Any of you guys Roy Hobbs?"

"That's him," Pop said grimly, heading into the hotel with Red. He pointed back to where Roy was getting out of the cab.

"No autographs." Roy ducked past the man.

"Jesus God, Roy," he cried in a broken voice. He caught Roy's arm and held on to it. "Don't pass me by, for the love of God."

"What d'you want?" Roy stared, suspicious.

"Roy, you don't know me," the man sobbed. "My name's Mike Barney and I drive a truck for Cudahy's. I don't want a thing for myself, only a favor for my boy Pete. He was hurt in an accident, playin' in the street. They operated him for a broken skull a coupla days ago and he ain't doin' so good. The doctor says he ain't fightin' much."

Mike Barney's mouth twisted and he wept.

"What has that got to do with me?" Roy asked, white-faced.

The truck driver wiped his eyes on his sleeve. "Pete's a fan of yours, Roy. He got a scrapbook that thick fulla pictures of you. Yesterday they lemme go in and see him and I said to Pete you told me you'd sock a homer for him in the game tonight. After that he sorta smiled and looked better. They gonna let him listen a little tonight, and I know if you will hit one it will save him."

"Why did you say that for?" Roy said bitterly. "The way I am now I couldn't hit the side of a barn."

Holding to Roy's sleeve, Mike Barney fell to his knees. "Please, you gotta do it."

"Get up," Roy said. He pitied the guy and wanted to help him yet was afraid what would happen if he couldn't. He didn't want that responsibility.

Mike Barney stayed on his knees, sobbing. A crowd had collected and was watching them.

"I will do the best I can if I get the chance." Roy wrenched his sleeve free and hurried into the lobby.

"A father's blessing on you," the truck driver called after him in a cracked voice.

Dressing in the visitors' clubhouse for the game that night, Roy thought about the kid in the hospital. He had been thinking of him on and off and was anxious to do something for him. He could see himself walking up to the plate and clobbering a long one into the stands and then he imagined the boy, healed and whole, thanking him for saving his life. The picture was unusually vivid, and as he polished Wonderboy, his fingers itched to carry it into the batter's box and let go at a fat one.

But Pop had other plans. "You are still on the bench, Roy, unless you put that Wonderboy away and use a different stick."

Roy shook his head and Pop gave the line-up card to the ump without his name on it. When Mike Barney, sitting a few rows behind a box above third base, heard the announcement of the Knights' line-up without Roy in it, his face broke out in a sickish sweat.

The game began, Roy taking his non-playing position on the far corner of the bench and holding Wonderboy between his knees. It was a clear, warm night and the stands were just about full. The floods on the roof lit up the stadium brighter than day. Above the globe of light lay the dark night, and high in the sky the stars glittered. Though unhappy not to be playing, Roy, for no reason he could think of, felt better in his body than he had in a week. He had a hunch things could go well for him tonight, which was why he especially regretted not being in the game. Furthermore, Mike Barney was directly in his line of vision and sometimes stared at him. Roy's gaze went past him, farther down the stands, to where a young blackhaired woman, wearing a red dress, was sitting at an aisle seat in short left. He could clearly see the white flower she wore pinned on her bosom and that she seemed to spend more time craning to get a look into the Knights' dugout—at him, he could swear—than in watching the game. She interested him, in that red dress, and he would have liked a close gander at her but he couldn't get out there without arousing attention.

Pop was pitching Fowler, who had kept going pretty well during the two dismal weeks of Roy's slump, only he was very crabby at everybody—especially Roy—for not getting him any runs, and causing him to lose two well-pitched games. As a result Pop had to keep after him in the late innings, because when Fowler felt disgusted he wouldn't bear down on the opposing batters.

Up through the fifth he had kept the Cubs bottled up but he eased off the next inning and they reached him for two runs with only one out. Pop gave him a fierce glaring at and Fowler then tightened and finished off the side with a pop fly and strikeout. In the Knights' half of the seventh, Cal Baker came through with a stinging triple, scoring Stubbs, and was himself driven in by Flores's single. That tied the score but it became untied when, in their part of the inning, the Cubs placed two doubles back to back, to produce another run.

As the game went on Roy grew tense. He considered telling Pop about the kid and asking for a chance to hit. But Pop was a stubborn cuss and Roy knew he'd continue to insist on him laying Wonderboy aside. This he was afraid to do. Much as he wanted to help the boy—and it really troubled him now—he felt he didn't stand a Chinaman's chance at a hit without his own club. And if he once abandoned Wonderboy there was no telling what would happen to him. Probably it would finish his career for keeps, because never since he had made the bat had he swung at a ball with any other.

In the eighth on a double and sacrifice, Pop worked a runner around to third. The squeeze failed so he looked around anxiously for a pinch hitter. Catching Roy's eye, he said, as Roy had thought he would, "Take a decent stick and go on up there."

Roy didn't move. He was sweating heavily and it cost him a great effort to stay put. He could see the truck driver suffering in his seat, wiping his face, cracking his knuckles, and sighing. Roy averted his glance.

There was a commotion in the lower left field stands. This lady in the red dress, whoever she was, had risen, and standing in a sea of gaping faces, seemed to be searching for someone. Then she looked toward the Knights' dugout and sort of half bowed her head. A murmur went up from the crowd. Some of them explained it that she had got mixed up about the seventh inning stretch and others answered how could she when the scoreboard showed the seventh inning was over? As she stood there, so cleanly etched in light, as if trying to communicate something she couldn't express, some of the fans were embarrassed. And the stranger sitting next to her felt a strong sexual urge which he concealed behind an impatient cigarette. Roy scarcely noticed her because he was lost in worry, seriously considering whether he ought to give up on Wonderboy.

Pop of course had no idea what was going on in Roy's head, so he gave the nod to Ed Simmons, a substitute infielder. Ed picked a bat out of the rack and as he approached the plate the standing lady slowly sat down. Everyone seemed to forget her then. Ed flied out. Pop looked scornfully at Roy and shot a stream of snuff into the dust.

Fowler had a little more trouble in the Cubs' half of the eighth but a double play saved him, and the score was still 3–2. The ninth opened. Pop appeared worn out. Roy had his eyes shut. It was Fowler's turn to bat. The second guessers were certain Pop would yank him for a pinch hitter but Fowler was a pretty fair hitter for a pitcher, and if the Knights could tie the score, his pitching tonight was too good to waste. He swung at the first ball, connecting for a line drive single, to Pop's satisfaction. Allie Stubbs tried to lay one away but his hard-hit fly ball to center was caught. To everybody's surprise Fowler went down the white line on the next pitch and dove safe into second under a cloud of dust. A long single could tie the score, but Cal Baker, to his disgust, struck out and flung his bat away. Pop again searched the bench for a pinch hitter. He fastened his gaze on Roy but Roy was unapproachable. Pop turned bitterly away.

Mike Barney, a picture of despair, was doing exercises of grief. He stretched forth his long hairy arms, his knobby hands clasped, pleading. Roy felt as though they were reaching right into the dugout to throttle him.

He couldn't stand it any longer. "I give up." Placing Wonderboy on the bench he rose and stood abjectly in front of Pop.

Pop looked up at him sadly. "You win," he said. "Go on in."

Roy gulped. "With my own bat?"

Pop nodded and gazed away.

Roy got Wonderboy and walked out into the light. A roar of recognition drowned the announcement of his name but not the loud beating of his heart. Though he'd been at bat only three days ago, it felt like years—an ageless time. He almost wept at how long it had been.

Lon Toomey, the hulking Cub hurler, who had twice in the last two weeks handed Roy his lumps, smiled behind his glove. He shot a quick glance at Fowler on second, fingered the ball, reared and threw. Roy, at the plate, watched it streak by.

"Stuh-rike."

He toed in, his fears returning. What if the slump did not give way? How much longer could it go on without destroying him?

Toomey lifted his right leg high and threw. Roy swung from his heels at a bad ball and the umpire sneezed in the breeze.

"Strike two!"

Wonderboy resembled a sagging baloney. Pop cursed the bat and some of the Knights' rooters among the fans booed. Mike Barney's harrowed puss looked yellow.

Roy felt sick with remorse that he hadn't laid aside Wonderboy in the beginning and gone into the game with four licks at bat instead of only three miserable strikes, two of which he already used up. How could he explain to Barney that he had traded his kid's life away out of loyalty to a hunk of wood?

The lady in the stands hesitantly rose for the second time. A photographer who had stationed himself nearby snapped a clear shot of her. She was an attractive woman, around thirty, maybe more, and built solid but not too big. Her bosom was neat, and her dark hair, parted on the side, hung loose and soft. A reporter approached her and asked her name but she wouldn't give it to him, nor would she, blushing, say why she was standing now. The fans behind her hooted, "Down in front," but though her eyes showed she was troubled she remained standing.

Noticing Toomey watching her, Roy stole a quick look. He caught the red dress and a white rose, turned away, then came quickly back for another take, drawn by the feeling that her smile was for him. Now why would she do that for? She seemed to be wanting to say something, and then it flashed on him the reason she was standing was to show her confidence in him. He felt surprised that anybody would want to do that for him. At the same time he became aware that the night had spread out in all directions and was filled with an unbelievable fragrance.

A pitch streaked toward him. Toomey had pulled a fast one. With a sob Roy fell back and swung.

Part of the crowd broke for the exits. Mike Barney wept freely now, and the lady who had stood up for Roy absently pulled on her white gloves and left.

The ball shot through Toomey's astounded legs and began to climb. The second baseman, laying back on the grass on a hunch, stabbed high for it but it leaped over his straining fingers, sailed through the light and up into the dark, like a white star seeking an old constellation.

Toomey, shrunk to a pygmy, stared into the vast sky.

Roy circled the bases like a Mississippi steamboat, lights lit, flags fluttering, whistle banging, coming round the bend. The Knights poured out of their dugout to pound his back, and hundreds of their rooters hopped about in the field. He stood on the home base, lifting his cap to the lady's empty seat.

And though Fowler goose-egged the Cubs in the last of the ninth and got credit for the win, everybody knew it was Roy alone who had saved the boy's life.

IT SEEMED perfectly natural to Iris to be waiting for him, with her shoes off to ease her feet, here on the park grass. He had been in her mind so often in the past month she could not conceive of him as a stranger, though he certainly was. She remembered having fallen asleep thinking of him last night. She had been gazing at the stars through her window, unaware just when they dissolved into summer rain, although she remembered opening a brown eye in time to see the two-pronged lightning plunge through a cloud and spread its running fire in all directions. And though she was sometimes afraid she would be hurt by it (this was her particular fear) she did not get up to shut the window but watched the writhing flame roll across the sky, until it disappeared over the horizon. The night was drenched and fragrant. Without the others knowing, she had slipped on a dress and gone across the road to walk in a field of daisies whose white stars lit up her bare feet as she thought of tomorrow in much the way she had at sixteen.

Tonight was a high, free evening, still green and gold above the white fortress of buildings on Michigan Avenue, yet fading over the lake, from violet to the first blue of night. A breeze with a breath of autumn in it, despite that afternoon's heat in the city, blew at intervals through the trees. From time to time she caught herself glancing, sometimes frowning, at her wristwatch although it was her own fault she had come so early. Her arms showed gooseflesh and she wondered if she had been rash to wear a thin dress at night but that was silly because the night was warm. It did not take her long to comprehend that the gooseflesh was not for now but another time, long ago, a time she was, however, no longer afraid to remember.

Half her life ago, just out of childhood it seemed, but that couldn't be because she was too strangely ready for the irrevocable change that followed, she had one night alone in the movies met a man twice her age, with whom she had gone walking in the park. Sensing at once what he so unyieldingly desired, she felt instead of fright, amazement at her willingness to respond, considering she was not, like some she later met, starved of affection. But a mother's love was one thing, and his, when he embraced her under the thick-leaved tree that covered them, was something else again. She had all she could do to tear herself away from him, and rushed through the branches, scratching her face and arms in the bargain. But he would not let her go, leading her always into dark places, hidden from all but the light of the stars, and taught her with his kisses that she could race without running. All but bursting with motion she cried don't look, and when he restlessly turned away, undressed the bottom half of her. She offered herself in a white dress and bare feet and was considerably surprised when he pounced like a tiger.

A horn hooted.

It was Roy driving a hired car. He looked around for a parking place but she had slipped on her shoes and waved she was coming.

He had come across her picture in one of the morning papers the day after he had knocked out the homer for the kid. Slicing it out carefully with his knife, he folded it without creasing the face and kept it in his wallet. Whenever he had a minute to himself (he was a smashing success at bat—five for five, three home runs—and was lionized by all) he took the picture out and studied it, trying to figure out why she had done that for him; nobody else ever had. Usually when he was down he was down alone, without flowers or mourners. He suspected she might be batty or a grownup bobby soxer gone nuts over him for having his name and picture in the papers. But from the intelligent look of her it didn't seem likely. There were some players the ladies might fall for through seeing their pictures but not him—not that he was bad-looking or anything, just that he was no dream boy—nor was she the type to do it. In her wide eyes he saw something which caused him to believe she knew what life was like, though you really couldn't be sure.

He made up his mind and telephoned the photographer who had taken this shot of her, for any information he might have as to where she lived, but at his office they said he was covering a forest fire in Minnesota. During the game that afternoon Roy scanned the stands around him and in the fifth frame located her practically at his elbow in deep left. He got one of the ushers to take her a note saying could she meet him tonight? She wrote back not tonight but enclosed her phone number. After a shot of Scotch he called her. Her voice was interesting but she said frankly she wondered if their acquaintance ought to end now, because these things could be disillusioning when they dragged past their time. He said he didn't think she would disappoint him. After some coaxing she yielded, chiefly because Roy insisted he wanted to thank her in person for her support of him.

He held the door open and she stepped in.

"I'm Iris Lemon," she said with a blush.

"Roy Hobbs." He felt foolish for of course she knew his name. Despite his good intentions he was disappointed right off, because she was heavier than he had thought—the picture didn't show that so much or if it did he hadn't noticed—and she had lost something, in this soft brown dress, that she'd had in the red. He didn't like them hefty, yet on second thought it couldn't be said she really was. Big, yes, but shapely too. Her face and hair were pretty and her body—she knew what to wear on her feet—was well proportioned. He admitted she was attractive although as a rule he never thought so unless they were slim like Memo.

So he asked her right out was she married.

She seemed startled, then smiled and said, "No, are you?"

"Nope."

"How is it the girls missed you?"

Though tempted to go into a long explanation about that, he let it pass with a shrug. Neither of them was looking at the other. They both stared at the road ahead. The car hadn't moved.

Iris felt she had been mistaken to come. He seemed so big and bulky next to her, and close up looked disappointingly different from what she had expected. In street clothes he gained little and lost more, a warrior's quality he showed in his uniform. Now he looked like any big-muscled mechanic or bartender on his night off. Whatever difference could it have made to her that this particular one had slumped? She was amazed at her sentimentality.

Roy was thinking about Memo. If not for her he wouldn't be here trying to make himself at ease with this one. She hadn't treated him right. For a while things had looked good between them but no sooner had he gone into a slump when she began again to avoid him. Had she been nice to him instead, he'd have got out of his trouble sooner. However, he wasn't bitter, because Memo was remote, even unreal. Strange how quick he forgot what she was like, though he couldn't what she looked like. Yet with that thought even her image went up in smoke. Iris, a stranger, had done for him what the other wouldn't, in public view what's more. He felt for her a gratitude it was hard to hold in.

"When you get to know me better you will like me more." He surprised himself with that—the hoarse remark echoed within him—and she, sure she had misjudged him, felt a catch in her throat as she replied, "I like you now."

He stepped on the starter and they drove off in the lilac dusk. Where to? he had asked and she had said it made no difference, she liked to ride. He felt, once they started, as if he had been sprung from the coop, and only now, as the white moon popped into the sky, did he begin to appreciate how bad it had been with him during the time of his slump.

They drove so they could almost always see the lake. The new moon climbed higher in the blue night, shedding light like rain. They drove along the lit highway to where the lake turned up into Indiana and they could see the lumpy yellow dunes along the shore. Elsewhere the land was shadowless and flat except for a few trees here and there. Roy turned into a winding dirt road and before long they came to this deserted beach, enclosed in a broken arc of white birches. The wind here was balmy and the water lit on its surface.

He shut off the motor. In the silence—everything but the lapping of the lake water—they too were silent. He hesitated at what next move to make and she prayed it would be the right one although she was not quite sure what she meant.

Roy asked did she want to get out. She understood he wanted her to so she said yes. But she surprised him by saying she had been here before.

"How's the water?" he asked.

"Cold. The whole lake is, but you get used to it soon."

They walked along the shore and then to a cluster of birches. Iris sat on the ground under one of the trees and slipped off her shoes. Her movements were graceful, she made her big feet seem small.

He sat nearby, his eyes on her. She sensed he wanted to talk but now felt curiously unconcerned with his problems. She had not expected the night to be this beautiful. Since it was, she asked no more than to be allowed to enjoy it.

But Roy impatiently asked her why she had stood up for him the other night.

She did not immediately reply.

After a minute he asked again.

"I don't know," Iris sighed.

That was not the answer he had expected.

"How come?"

"I've been trying to explain it to myself." She lit a cigarette.

He was now a little in awe of her, something he had not foreseen, though he pretended not to be.

"You're a Knights' fan, ain't you?"

"No."

"Then how come—I don't get it."

"I'm not a baseball fan but I like to read about the different players. That's how I became interested in you—your career."

"You read about my slump?" His throat tightened at the word.

"Yes, and before that of your triumphs."

"Ever see me play—before the other night?"

She shook her head. "Once then and again yesterday."

"Why'd you come—the first time?"

She rubbed her cigarette into the dirt. "Because I hate to see a hero fail. There are so few of them."

She said it seriously and he felt she meant it.

"Without heroes we're all plain people and don't know how far we can go."

"You mean the big guys set the records and the little buggers try and bust them?"

"Yes, it's their function to be the best and for the rest of us to understand what they represent and guide ourselves accordingly."

He hadn't thought of it that way but it sounded all right.

"There are so many young boys you influence."

"That's right," said Roy.

"You've got to give them your best."

"I try to do that."

"I mean as a man too."

He nodded.

"I felt that if you knew people believed in you, you'd regain your power. That's why I stood up in the grandstand. I hadn't meant to before I came. It happened naturally. Of course I was embarrassed but I don't think you can do anything for anyone without giving up something of your own. What I gave up was my privacy among all those people. I hope you weren't ashamed of me?"

He shook his head. "Were you praying for me to smack one over the roof?"

"I hoped you might become yourself again."

"I was jinxed," Roy explained to her. "Something was keeping me out of my true form. Up at the plate I was blind as a bat and Wonderboy had the heebie jeebies. But when you stood up and I saw you with that red dress on and thought to myself she is with me even if nobody else is, it broke the whammy."

Iris laughed.

Roy crawled over to her and laid his head in her lap. She let him. Her dress was scented with lilac and clean laundry smell. Her thighs were firm under his head. He got a cigar out of his pocket and lit it but it stank up the night so he flung it away.

"I sure am glad you didn't stand me up," he sighed.

"Who would?" she smiled.

"You don't know the half of it."

She softly said she was willing to.

Roy struggled with himself. The urge to tell her was strong. On the other hand, talk about his inner self was always like plowing up a graveyard.

She saw the sweat gleaming on his brow. "Don't if you don't feel like it."

"Everything came out different than I thought." His eyes were clouded.

"In what sense?"

"Different."

"I don't understand."

He coughed, tore his voice clear and blurted, "My goddamn life didn't turn out like I wanted it to."

"Whose does?" she said cruelly. He looked up. Her expression was tender.

The sweat oozed out of him. "I wanted everything." His voice boomed out in the silence.

She waited.

"I had a lot to give to this game."

"Life?"

"Baseball. If I had started out fifteen years ago like I tried to, I'da been the king of them all by now."

"The king of what?"

"The best in the game," he said impatiently.

She sighed deeply. "You're so good now."

"I'da been better. I'da broke most every record there was."

"Does that mean so much to you?"

"Sure," he answered. "It's like what you said before. You break the records and everybody else tries to catch up with you if they can."

"Couldn't you be satisfied with just breaking a few?"

Her pinpricking was beginning to annoy him. "Not if I could break most of them," he insisted.

"But I don't understand why you should make so much of that. Are your values so—"

He heard a train hoot and went freezing cold.

"Where's that train?" he cried, jumping to his feet.

"What train?"

He stared into the night.

"The one I just heard."

"It must have been a bird cry. There are no trains here."

He gazed at her suspiciously but then relaxed and sat down.

"That way," he continued with what he had been saying, "if you leave all those records that nobody else can beat—they'll always remember you. You sorta never die."

"Are you afraid of death?"

Roy stared at her listening face. "Now what has that got to do with it?"

She didn't answer. Finally he laid his head back on her lap, his eyes shut.

She stroked his brow slowly with her fingers.

"What happened fifteen years ago, Roy?"

Roy felt like crying, yet he told her—the first one he ever had. "I was just a kid and I got shot by this batty dame on the night before my tryout, and after that I just couldn't get started again. I lost my confidence and everything I did flopped."

He said this was the shame in his life, that his fate, somehow, had always been the same (on the train going nowhere)—defeat in sight of his goal.

"Always?"

"Always the same."

"Always with a woman?"

He laughed harshly. "I sure met some honeys in my time. They burned me good."

"Why do you pick that type?"

"It's like I say—they picked me. It's the breaks."

"You could say no, couldn't you?"

"Not to that type dame I always fell for—they weren't like you."

She smiled.

"I mean you are a different kind."

"Does that finish me?"

"No," he said seriously.

"I won't ever hurt you, Roy."

"No."

"Don't ever hurt me."

"No."

"What beats me," he said with a trembling voice, "is why did it always have to happen to me? What did I do to deserve it?"

"Being stopped before you started?"

He nodded.

"Perhaps it was because you were a good person?"

"How's that?"

"Experience makes good people better."

She was staring at the lake.

"How does it do that?"

"Through their suffering."

"I had enough of that," he said in disgust.

"We have two lives, Roy, the life we learn with and the life we live with after that. Suffering is what brings us toward happiness."

"I had it up to here." He ran a finger across his windpipe.

"Had what?"

"What I suffered—and I don't want any more."

"It teaches us to want the right things."

"All it taught me is to stay away from it. I am sick of all I have suffered."

She shrank away a little.

He shut his eyes.

Afterwards, sighing, she began to rub his brow, and then his lips.

"And is that the mystery about you, Roy?"

"What mystery?"

"I don't know. Everyone seems to think there is one."

"I told you everything."

"Then there really isn't?"

"Nope."

Her cool fingers touched his eyelids. It was unaccountably sweet to him.

"You broke my jinx," he muttered.

"I'm thirty-three," she said, looking at the moonlit water.

He whistled but said, "I am no spring chicken either, honey."

"Iris."

"Iris, honey."

"That won't come between us?"

"What?"

"My age?"

"No."

"Nothing?"

"If you are not married?"

"No."

"Divorced?"

"No."

"A widow?"

"No," said Iris.

He opened his eyes. "How come with all your sex appeal you never got hitched?"

She gazed away.

Roy suddenly sat up and bounced to his feet. "Jesus, will you look at that water. What are we waiting for?" He tore at his tie.

Iris was saying that she had, however, brought a child into the world, a girl now grown, but Roy seemed not to hear, he was so busy getting out of his clothes. In no time to speak of he stood before her stripped to his shorts.

"Get undressed."

The thought of standing naked before him frightened her. She told herself not to be—she was no longer a child about the naked body. But she couldn't bring herself to remove her clothes in front of him so she went back to the car and undressed there. He waited impatiently, then before he expected her, she stepped out without a thing on and ran in the moonlight straight into the water, through the shallow part, and dived where it was deep.

Hopping high through the cold water, Roy plunged in after her. He dived neatly, kicked hard underwater and came up almost under her. Iris fell back out of his reach and swam away. He pursued her with less skill than she had but more strength. At first he damn near froze but as he swam his blood warmed. She would not stop and before long the white birches near the beach looked to be the size of match sticks.

Though they were only a dozen strokes apart she wouldn't let him gain, and after another fifty tiring yards he wondered how long this would go on. He called to her but she didn't answer and wouldn't stop. He was beginning to be winded and considered quitting, only he didn't want to give up. Then just about when his lungs were frying in live coals, she stopped swimming. As she trod water, the light on the surface hid all but her head from him.

He caught up with her at last and attempted to get his arms around her waist. "Give us a kiss, honey."

She was repelled and shoved him away.

He saw she meant it, realized he had made a mistake, and felt terrible.

Roy turned tail, kicking himself down into the dark water. As he sank lower it got darker and colder but he kept going down. Before long the water turned murky yet there was no bottom he could feel with his hands. Though his legs and arms were numb he continued to work his way down, filled with icy apprehensions and weird thoughts.

Iris couldn't believe it when he did not quickly rise. Before long she felt frightened. She looked everywhere but he was still under water. A sense of abandonment gripped her. She remembered standing up in the crowd that night, and said to herself that she had really stood up because he was a man whose life she wanted to share . . . a man who had suffered. She thought distractedly of a home, children, and him coming home every night to supper. But he had already left her . . .

. . . At last in the murk he touched the liquid mud at the bottom. He dimly thought he ought to feel proud to have done that but his mind was crammed with old memories flitting back and forth like ghostly sardines, and there wasn't a one of them that roused his pride or gave him any comfort.

So he forced himself, though sleepily, to somersault up and begin the slow task of climbing through all the iron bars of the currents . . . too slow, too tasteless, and he wondered was it worth it.

Opening his bloodshot eyes he was surprised how far down the moonlight had filtered. It dripped down like oil in the black water, and then, unexpectedly, there came into his sight this pair of golden arms searching, and a golden head with a frantic face. Even her hair sought him.

He felt relieved no end.

I am a lucky bastard.

He was climbing a long, slow ladder, broad at the base and narrowing on top, and she, trailing clusters of white bubbles, was weaving her way to him. She had golden breasts and when he looked to see, the hair between her legs was golden too.

With a watery howl bubbling from his blistered lungs he shot past her inverted eyes and bobbed up on the surface, inhaling the soothing coolness of the whole sky.

She rose beside him, gasping, her hair plastered to her naked skull, and kissed him full on the lips. He tore off his shorts and held her tight. She stayed in his arms.

"Why did you do it?" she wept.

"To see if I could touch the bottom."

They swam in together, taking their time. As they dragged themselves out of the water, she said, "Go make a fire, otherwise we will have nothing to dry ourselves with."

He covered her shoulders with his shirt and went hunting for wood. Under the trees he collected an armload of branches. Near the dunes he located some heavy boxwood. Then he came back to where she was sitting and began to build a fire. He set an even row of birch sticks down flat and with his knife shaved up a thick branch till he had a pile of dry shavings. These he lit with the only match he had. When they were burning he added some dry birch pieces he had cut up. He split the boxwood against a rock and when the fire was crackling added that, hunk by hunk, to the flames. Before long he had a roaring blaze going. The fire reddened the water and the lacy birches.

It reddened her naked body. Her thighs and rump were broad but her waist was narrow and virginal. Her breasts were hard, shapely. From above her hips she looked like a girl but the lower half of her looked like a woman.

Watching her, he thought he would wait for the fire to die down, when she was warm and dry and felt not rushed.

She was sitting close to the fire with her hair pulled over her head so the inside would dry first. She was thinking why did he go down? Did he touch the bottom of the lake out of pride, because he wants to make records, or did he do it in disappointment, because I wouldn't let him kiss me?

Roy was rubbing his hands before the fire. She looked up and said in a tremulous voice, "Roy, I have a confession to you. I was never married, but I am the mother of a grown girl."

He said he had heard her the first time.

She brushed her hair back with her fingers. "I don't often talk about it, but I want to tell you I made a mistake long ago and had a hard time afterwards. Anyway, the child meant everything to me and made me happy. I gave her a good upbringing and now she is grown and on her own, and I am free to think of myself and young enough to want to."

That was the end of it because Roy asked no questions.

He watched the fire. The flames sank low. When they had just about been sucked into the ashes he crept toward her and took her in his arms. Her breasts beat like hearts against him.

"You are really the first," she whispered.

He smiled, never so relaxed in sex.

But while he was in the middle of loving her she spoke: "I forgot to tell you I am a grandmother."

He stopped. Holy Jesus.

Then she remembered something else and tried, in fright, to raise herself.

"Roy, are you—"

But he shoved her back and went on from where he had left off.

AFTER A hilarious celebration in the dining car (which they roused to uproar by tossing baked potatoes and ketchup bottles around) and later in the Pullman, where a wild bunch led by Roy stripped the pajamas off players already sound asleep in their berths, peeled Red Blow out of his long underwear, and totally demolished the pants of a new summer suit of Pop's, who was anyway not sold on premature celebrations, Roy slept restlessly. In his sleep he knew he was restless and blamed it (in his sleep) on all he had eaten. The Knights had come out of Sportsman's Park after trouncing the Cards in a double header and making it an even dozen in a row without a loss, and the whole club had gone gay on the train, including, mildly, Pop himself, considerably thawed out now that the team had leapfrogged over the backs of the Dodgers and Cards into third place. They were again hot on the heels of the Phils and not too distant from the Pirates, with a whole month to go before the end of the season, and about sixty per cent of their remaining games on home grounds. Roy was of course in fine fettle, the acknowledged King of Klouters, whose sensational hitting, pulverizing every kind of pitching, more than made up for his slump. Yet no matter how many bangs he collected, he was ravenously hungry for more and all he could eat besides. The Knights had boarded the train at dinner time but he had stopped off at the station to devour half a dozen franks smothered in sauerkraut and he guzzled down six bottles of pop before his meal on the train, which consisted of two oversize sirloins, at least a dozen rolls, four orders of mashed, and three (some said five) slabs of apple pie. Still that didn't do the trick, for while they were all at cards that evening, he sneaked off the train as it was being hosed and oiled and hustled up another three wieners, and later secretly arranged with the steward for a midnight snack of a long T-bone with trimmings, although that did not keep him from waking several times during the night with pangs of hunger.

When the diner opened in the morning he put away an enormous breakfast and afterwards escaped those who were up, and found himself some privacy in a half-empty coach near the engine, where nobody bothered him because he was not too recognizable in gabardine, behind dark glasses. For a while he stared at the scattered outskirts of the city they were passing through, but in reality he was wondering whether to read the fat letter from Iris Lemon he had been carrying around in his suit pocket. Roy recalled the night on the lake shore, the long swim, the fire and after. The memory of all was not unpleasant, but what for the love of mud had made her take him for a sucker who would be interested in a grandmother? He found that still terrifying to think of, and although she was a nice enough girl, it had changed her in his mind from Iris more to lemon. To do her justice he concentrated on her good looks and the pleasures of her body but when her kid's kid came to mind, despite grandma's age of only thirty-three, that was asking too much and spoiled the appetizing part of her. It was simple enough to him: if he got serious with her it could only lead to one thing—him being a grandfather. God save him from that for he personally felt as young and frisky as a colt. That was what he told himself as the train sped east, and though he had a slight bellyache he fell into a sound sleep and dreamed how on frosty mornings when he was a kid the white grass stood up prickly stiff and the frozen air deep-cleaned his insides.

He awoke with Memo on his mind. To his wonder she turned up in his room in Boston the next night. It was after supper and he was sitting in a rocker near the window reading about himself in the paper when she knocked. He opened the door and she could have thrown him with a breath, so great was his surprise (and sadness) at seeing her. Memo laughingly said she had been visiting a girl friend's summer place on the Cape, and on her way back to New York had heard the boys were in town so she stopped off to say hello, and here she was. Her face and arms were tanned and she looked better than she had in a long while. He felt too that she had changed somehow in the weeks he hadn't seen her. That made him uneasy, as if any change in her would automatically be to his hurt. He searched her face but could not uncover anything new so explained it as the five pounds she said she had put on since he had seen her last.

He felt he still held it against her for giving him very little support at a time when he could use a lot, and also for turning Pop down when he had invited her to join them on the Western trip. Yet here, alone with her in his room, she so close and inevitably desirable—this struck him with the force of an unforgettable truth: the one he had had and always wanted—he thought it wouldn't do to put on a sourpuss and make complaints. True, there was something about her, like all the food he had lately been eating, that left him, after the having of it, unsatisfied, sometimes even with a greater hunger than before. Yet she was a truly beautiful doll with a form like Miss America, and despite the bumps and bruises he had taken, he was sure that once he got an armlock on her things would go better.

His face must have shown more than he intended, because she turned moodily to the window and said, "Roy, don't bawl me out for not seeing you for a while. There are some things I just can't take and one of them is being with people who are blue. I had too much of that in my life with my mother and it really makes me desperate." More tenderly she said, "That's why I had to stand off to the side, though I didn't like to, and wait till you had worked out of it, which I knew you would do. Now here I am the first chance I got and that is the way it used to be between Bump and me."

Roy said soberly, "When are you going to find out that I ain't Bump, Memo?"

"Don't be mad," she said, lifting her face to him. "All I meant to say is that I treat all my friends the same." She was close and warm-breathed. He caught her in his arms and she snuggled tight, and let him feel the "sick" breast without complaining. But when he tried to edge her to the bed, she broke for air and said no.

"Why not?" he demanded.

"I'm not well," said Memo.

He was suspicious. "What's wrong?"

Memo laughed. "Sometimes you are very innocent, Roy. When a girl says she is not well, does she have to draw you a map?"

Then he understood and was embarrassed for being so dimwitted. He did not insist on any more necking and thought it a good sign that she had talked to him so intimately.

*

The Knights took their three in Boston and the next day won a twi-night double header in Ebbets Field, making it seventeen straight wins on the comeback climb. Before Roy ended his slump they had fallen into fifth place, twelve games behind, then they slowly rose to third, and after this twin bill with Brooklyn, were within two of the Phils, who had been nip and tucking it all season with the Cards and Dodgers. The Pirates, though beaten three in a row by the Knights on their Western swing (the first Knight wins over them this season) were still in first place, two games ahead of the Phils in a tight National League race.

When the Knights returned to their home grounds for a three-game set with the cellar-dwelling Reds, the city awakened in a stampede. The fans, recovered from their stunned surprise at the brilliant progress of the team, turned out in droves. They piled into the stands with foolish smiles, for most of them had sworn off the Knights during the time of Roy's slump. Now for blocks around the field, the neighborhood was in an uproar as hordes fought their way out of subways, trolleys and buses, and along the packed streets to ticket windows that had been boarded up (to Judge Banner's heartfelt regret) from early that morning, while grunting lines of red-faced cops, reinforced by sweating mounties, tried to shove everybody back where they had come from. After many amused years at the expense of the laughingstock Knights, a scorching pennant fever blew through the city. Everywhere people were bent close to their radios or stretching their necks in bars to have a look at the miracle boys (so named by sportswriters from all over the U.S. who now crammed into the once deserted press boxes) whose every move aroused their fanatic supporters to a frenzy of excitement which whirled out of them in concentric rings around the figure of Roy Hobbs, hero and undeniable man of destiny. He, it was said by everyone, would lead the Knights to it.

The fans dearly loved Roy but Roy did not love the fans. He hadn't forgotten the dirty treatment they had dished out during the time of his trouble. Often he felt he would like to ram their cheers down their throats. Instead he took it out on the ball, pounding it to a pulp, as if the best way to get even with

the fans, the pitchers who had mocked him, and the statisti-
cians who had recorded (forever) the kind and quantity of his
failures, was to smash every conceivable record. He was like a
hunter stalking a bear, a whale, or maybe the sight of a single
fleeing star the way he went after that ball. He gave it no rest
(Wonderboy, after its long famine, chopping, chewing, devouring) and was not satisfied unless he lifted it (one eye cocked as
he swung) over the roof and spinning toward the horizon.
Often, for no accountable reason, he hated the pill, which
represented more of himself than he was willing to give away
for nothing to whoever found it one dull day in a dirty lot.
Sometimes as he watched the ball soar, it seemed to him all
circles, and he was mystified at his devotion to hacking at it,
for he had never really liked the sight of a circle. They got you
nowhere but back to the place you were to begin with, yet
here he stood banging them like smoke rings out of Wonderboy and everybody cheered like crazy. The more they cheered
the colder he got to them. He couldn't stop hitting and every
hit made him hungry for the next (a doctor said he had no
tapeworm but ate like that because he worked so hard), yet he
craved no cheers from the slobs in the stands. Only once he
momentarily forgave them—when reaching for a fly, he almost
cracked into the wall and they gasped their fright and shrieked
warnings. After he caught the ball he doffed his cap and they
rocked the rafters with their thunder.

The press, generally snotty to him during his slump, also
changed its tune. To a man (except one) they showered him
with praise, whooped him on, and in their columns unofficially
accoladed him Rookie of the Year (although they agreed he
resembled nothing so much as an old hand, a toughened veteran of baseball wars) and Most Valuable Player, and years before it was time talked of nominating him for a permanent
niche in the Cooperstown Hall of Fame. He belonged, they
wrote, with the other immortals, a giant in performance, who
resembled the burly boys of the eighties and nineties more
than the streamlined kids of today. He was a throwback to a
time of true heroes, not of the brittle, razzle dazzle boys that
had sprung up around the jack rabbit ball—a natural not seen
in a dog's age, and weren't they the lucky ones he had appeared
here and now to work his wonders before them? More than

one writer held his aching head when he speculated on all Roy might have accomplished had he come into the game at twenty.

The exception was of course Mercy, who continued to concern himself with Roy's past rather than his accomplishments. He spent hours in the morgue, trying to dredge up possible clues to possible crimes (What's he hiding from me?), wrote for information to prison wardens, sheriffs, county truant officers, heads of orphan asylums, and semipro managers in many cities in the West and Northwest, and by offering rewards, spurred all sorts of research on Roy by small-town sportswriters. His efforts proved fruitless until one day, to his surprise, he got a letter from a man who block printed on a sheet of notebook paper that for two hundred bucks he might be tempted to tell a thing or two about the new champ. Max hastily promised the dough and got his first break. Here was an old sideshow freak who swore that Roy had worked as a clown in a small traveling carnival. For proof he sent a poster showing the clown's face—in his white and red warpaint—bursting through a paper hoop. Roy was recognizable as the snubnose Bobo, who despite the painted laugh on his pan, seemed sadeyed and unhappy. Certain the picture would create a sensation, Max had it printed on the first page above the legend, "Roy Hobbs, Clown Prince of Baseball," but most of those who bought the paper refused to believe it was Roy and those who did, didn't give a hoot.

Roy was burned about the picture and vowed to kick the blabbermouth in the teeth. But he didn't exactly do that, for when they met the next evening, in the Midtown lobby, Max made a handsome apology. He said he had to hand it to Roy for beating everybody else in the game ten different ways, and he was sorry about the picture. Roy nodded but didn't show up on time at the chophouse down the block, where he was awaited by Pop, Red, and Max—to Pop's uneasiness, because Roy was prompt for his meals these days.

The waiter, a heavyset German with a schmaltzy accent and handlebar mustache, approached for their orders. He started the meal by spilling soup on Max's back, then serving him a steak that looked like the charcoal it had been broiled on. When Max loudly complained he brought him, after fifteen minutes, another, a bleeding beauty, but this the waiter snatched from under the columnist's knife because he had already collected Pop's and Roy's finished plates and wanted the third. Max let out a yawp, the frightened waiter dropped the dishes on his lap, and while stooping to collect the pieces, lurched against the table and spilled Max's beer all over his pants.

Pop sprang up and took an angry swipe at the man but Red hauled him down. Meanwhile the waiter was trying to wipe Max's pants with a wet towel and Max was swearing bloody murder at him. This got the waiter sore. Seizing the columnist by his coat collar he shook him and said he would teach him to talk like a "shentleman und nod a slob." He laid Max across his knee, and as the customers in the chophouse looked on in disbelief, smacked his rear with a heavy hand. Max managed to twist himself free. Slapping frantically at the German's face, he knocked off his mustache. In a minute everybody in the place was shrieking with laughter, and even Pop had to smile though he said to Red he was not at all surprised it had turned out to be Roy.

Roy had a Saturday date with Memo coming up but he was lonely for her that night so he went up to the fourth floor and rang her buzzer. She opened the door, dressed in black lounging pajamas with a black ribbon tied around her horsetail of red hair, which had a stunning effect on him.

Memo's face lit in a slow blush. "Why, Roy," she said, and seemed not to know what else to say.

"Shut the door," came a man's annoyed voice from inside, "or I might catch a cold."

"Gus is here," Memo quickly explained. "Come on in."

Roy entered, greatly disappointed.

Memo lived in a large and airy one-room apartment with a kitchenette, and a Murphy bed out of sight. Gus Sands, smoking a Between-the-Acts little cigar, was sitting at a table near the curtained window, examining a hand of double solitaire he and Memo had been playing. His coat was hanging on the chair and a hand-painted tie that Roy didn't like, showing a naked lady dancing with a red rose, hung like a tongue out of his unbuttoned vest, over a heavy gold watch chain.

Seeing who it was, Gus said, "Welcome home, slugger. I see you have climbed out of the hole that you were in."

"I suppose it cost you a couple of bucks," said Roy.

Gus was forced to laugh. He had extended his hand but Roy didn't shake. Memo glanced at Roy as if to say be nice to Gus.

Roy couldn't get rid of his irritation that he had found Gus here, and he felt doubly annoyed that she was still seeing him. He had heard nothing from her about Gus and had hoped the bookie was out of the picture, but here he was as shifty-eyed as ever. What she saw in this half-bald apology for a cigar store Indian had him beat, yet he was conscious of a fear in his chest that maybe Gus meant more to her than he had guessed. The thought of them sitting peacefully together playing cards gave him the uneasy feeling they might even be married or something. But that couldn't be because it didn't make sense. In the first place why would she marry a freak like Gus? Sure he had the bucks but Memo was a hot kid and she couldn't take them to bed with her. And how could she stand what he looked like in the morning without the glass eye in the slot? In the second place Gus wouldn't let *his* wife walk around without a potato-sized diamond, and the only piece of jewelry Memo wore was a ring with a small jade stone. Besides, what would they be doing here in this one-room box when Gus owned a penthouse apartment on Central Park West?

No. He blamed these fantastic thoughts on the fact that he was still not sure of her. And he kept wishing he could have her to himself tonight. Memo caught on because, when he looked at her, she shrugged.

Gus got suspicious. He stared at them with the baleful eye, the glass one frosty.

They were sitting around uncomfortably until Memo suggested they play cards. Gus cheered up at once.

"What'll it be, slugger?" he said, collecting the cards.

"Pinochle is the game for three."

"I hate pinochle," Memo said. "Let's play poker but not the open kind."

"Poker is not wise now," Gus said. "The one in the middle gets squeezed. Anybody like to shoot crap?"

He brought forth a pair of green dominoes. Roy said he was agreeable and Memo nodded. Gus wanted to roll on the table but Roy said the rug was better, with the dice bouncing against the wall.

They moved the table and squatted on the floor. Memo, kneeling, rolled first. Gus told her to fade high and in a few minutes she picked up two hundred dollars. Roy hit snake eyes right off, then sevened out after that. Gus shot, teasing Roy to cover the three one hundred dollar bills he had put down. Memo took twenty-five of it and Roy had the rest. Gus made his point and on the next roll took another two hundred from Roy. That was more than he was carrying in cash but Gus said he could play the rest of the game on credit. The bookie continued to roll passes. In no time he was twelve hundred in on Roy, not counting the cash he had lost. Roy was irritated because he didn't like to lose to Gus in front of Memo. He watched Gus's hands to make sure he wasn't palming another pair of dice. What made him suspicious was that Gus seemed to be uncomfortable. His glass eye was fastened on the dice but the good one roamed restlessly about. And he was now fading three hundred a throw and sidebetting high. Since Memo was taking only a ten spot here and there, Roy was covering the rest. By the end of Gus's second streak Roy was thirty-five hundred behind and his underwear was sweating. Gus finally went out, Memo quickly lost, then Roy, to his surprise, started off on a string of passes. Now he was hot and rolled the cubes for a long haul, growing merrier by the minute as Gus grew glummer. Before Roy was through, Gus had returned the cash he had taken from him and owed him eleven hundred besides. When Roy finally hit seven, Memo got up and said she had to make coffee. Gus and Roy played on but Roy was still the lucky one. Gus said that dice ought never to be played with less than four and gave up in disgust. He dusted off his knees.

"You sure had luck in your pants tonight, slugger."

"Some call it that."

Memo added the figures. She owed Roy two ten but Gus owed him twenty-one hundred. Roy laughed out loud.

Gus wrote out a check, his eye still restless.

Memo said she would write one too.

"Forget it," Roy said.

"I have covered hers in mine," said Gus, circling his pen around before signing.

Memo flushed. "I like to pay my own way."

Gus tore up the check and wrote another. Seeing how she

felt about it, Roy took Memo's, figuring he would return it in the form of some present or other.

Gus handed him a check for the twenty-one hundred. "Chicken feed," he said.

Roy gave the paper a loud smack with his lips. "I love it."

Gus dropped his guard and pinned his restless eye on Roy. "Say the word, slugger, and you can make yourself a nice pile of dough quick."

Roy wasn't sure he had heard right. Gus repeated the offer.

This time Roy was sure. "Say it again and I will spit in your good eye."

Gus's grayish complexion turned blue.

"Boys," Memo said uneasily.

Gus stalked into the bathroom.

Memo's face was pale. "Help me with the sandwiches, Roy."

"Did you hear what that bastard said to me?"

"Sometimes he talks through his hat."

"Why do you invite him here?"

She turned away. "He invited himself."

As she was slicing meat for the sandwiches Roy felt tender toward her. He slipped his arm around her waist. She looked up a little unhappily but when he kissed her she kissed back. They broke apart as Gus unlocked the bathroom door and came out glaring at them.

While they were all drinking coffee Roy was in good spirits and no longer minded that Gus was around. Memo kidded him about the way he wolfed the sandwiches, but she showed her affection by also serving him half a cold chicken which he picked to the bone. He demolished a large slab of chocolate cake and made a mental note for a hamburger or two before he went to bed. Though Gus had only had a cup of coffee he was thoughtfully picking his teeth. After a while he looked at his gold watch, buttoned his vest, and said he was going. Roy glanced at Memo but she yawned and said she had to get up very very early in the morning.

To everybody's disgust the Reds, as if contemptuous of the bums who had so long lived in the basement below them, snapped the Knights' streak at seventeen and the next day again beat them over a barrel. A great groan went up from the faithful. Stand back everybody, here they go again. Timber! As if by magic, attendance for a single game with the Phils sank to a handful. The Phils gave them another spanking. The press tipped their hats and turned their respectful attention to the Pirates, pointing out again how superb they were. It was beyond everybody how the half-baked Knights could ever hope to win the N.L. pennant. With twenty-one games left to play they were six behind the Pirates and four in back of the Phils. And to make matters worse, they'd fallen into a third-place tie with the Cards. Pop's boys still retained a mathematical chance all right but they were at best a first-rate third-place team, one writer put it, and ended his piece, "Wait till next year."

Pop held his suffering head. The players stole guilty looks at one another. Even the Great Man himself was in a rut, though not exactly a slump. Still, he was held by inferior pitching to three constipated singles in three days. Everyone on the team was conscious something drastic had to be done but none could say what. Time was after them with a bludgeon. Any game they lost was the last to lose. It was autumn almost. They saw leaves falling and shivered at the thought of the barren winds of winter.

The Pirates blew into town for their last games of the year with the Knights, a series of four. Thus far during the season they had trounced the Knights a fantastic 15–3 and despite the loss of their last three to the Knights (fool's luck) were prepared to blast them out of their field. Watching the way the Pirates cut up the pea patch with their merciless hitting and precision fielding, the New Yorkers grew more dejected. Here was a team that was really a team, not a Rube Goldberg contraption. Every man jack was a fine player and no one guy outstanding. The Knights' fans were embarrassed . . . Yet their boys managed to tease the first away from the Pirates. No one quite knew how, here a lucky bingle, there a lucky error. Opposite the first-place slickers they looked like hayseeds yet the harvest was theirs. But tomorrow was another day. Wait'll the boys from the smoky city had got the stiffness of the train ride out of their legs. Yet the Knights won again in the same inept way. Their own rooters, seeping back into the stands, whistled and cheered. By some freak of nature they took the third too. The last game was sold out before 10 A.M. Again the cops had trouble with the ticketless hordes that descended on them.

Walt Wickitt, the peerless Pirate manager, pitched his ace hurler, Dutch Vogelman, in that last game. Vogelman was a terrific pitcher, a twenty-three game winner, the only specimen in either league that season. He was poison to the Knights who had beat him only once in the past two years. Facing Roy in some six games, he had held him to a single in four, and crippled him altogether in the last two, during Roy's slump. Most everyone kissed this game goodbye, although Roy started with a homer his first time up. Schultz then gave up two runs to the Pirates. Roy hit another round tripper. Schultz made it three for the Pirates. Roy ended by slamming two more homers and that did it, 4–3. High and mighty to begin with, Vogelman looked like a drowned dog at the end, and the Pirates hurriedly packed their duffel bags and slunk out of the stadium. The Phils were now in first place by a game, the Pirates second, and the Knights were one behind them and coming up like a rocket. Again pennant fever raged through the city and there was cheering in the streets.

Now all that was left for the Knights in this nerve-racking race were four games in Brooklyn, including a Sunday double header, four with Boston and two more with the Reds, these at home. Then three away with the Phils, one of which was the playoff of the washed-out game in June when Roy had knocked the cover off the ball. Their schedule called for the wind-up in the last week of September, against the Reds in another three-game tilt at home, a soft finish, considering the fact that the Pirates and Phils had each other to contend with. If, God willing, the Knights made it (and were still functioning), the World Series was scheduled to begin on Tuesday, October first, at the Yankee Stadium, for the Yanks had already cinched the American League pennant.

The race went touch and go. To begin with the Knights dropped a squeaker (Roy went absolutely hitless) to the Dodgers as the Pirates won and the Phils lost—both now running neck and neck for first, the Knights two behind. Just as the boys were again despairing of themselves, Roy got after the ball again. He did not let on to anyone, but he had undergone a terrible day after his slaughter of the Pirates, a day of great physical weakness, a strange draining of strength from his arms and legs, followed by a splitting headache that whooshed in his ears. However, in the second game at Ebbets Field, he took hold of himself, gripped Wonderboy, and bashed the first pitch into the clock on the right field wall. The clock spattered minutes all over the place, and after that the Dodgers never knew what time it was. All they knew was that Roy Hobbs collected a phenomenal fourteen straight hits that shot them dead three times. Carried on by the momentum, the Knights ripped the Braves and brutally trounced the Reds, taking revenge on them for having ended their recent streak of seventeen.

With only six games to play, a triple first-place tie resulted. The Knights' fans beat themselves delirious, and it became almost unbearable when the Phils lost a heartbreaker to the Cards and dropped into second place, leaving the Pirates and Knights in the tie. Before the Phils could recover, the Knights descended upon Shibe Park, followed by wild trainloads of fans who had to be there to see. They saw their loveboys take the crucial playoff (Roy was terrific), squeak through the second game (he had a poor day), and thoroughly wipe the stunned Phils off the map in the last (again stupendous). At this point of highest tension the Pirate mechanism burst. To the insane cheering of the population of the City of New York, the Cubs pounded them twice, and the Reds came in with a surprise haymaker. A pall of silence descended upon Pennsylvania. Then a roar rose in Manhattan and leaped across the country. When the shouting stopped the Knights were undeniably on top by three over the Pirates, the Phils third by one more, and therefore mathematically out of the race. With three last ones to play against the lowly Reds, the Knights looked *in*. The worst that could possibly happen to them was a first-place tie with the Pirates—if the Pirates won their three from the Phils as the Knights lost theirs to the Reds—a fantastic impossibility the way Roy was mauling them.

The ride home from Philadelphia usually took a little more than an hour but it was a bughouse nightmare because of the way the fans on the train pummeled the players. Hearing that a mob had gathered at Penn Station to welcome the team, Pop ordered everyone off at Newark and into cabs. But as they approached the tunnel they were greeted by a deafening roar as every craft in the Hudson, and all the way down the bay, opened up with whistles and foghorns . . .

In their locker room after the last game at Philly, some of the boys had started chucking wet towels around but Pop, who had privately wept tears of joy, put the squelch on that.

"Cut out all that danged foolishness when we still need one more to win," he had sternly yelled.

When they protested that it looked at last that they were in, he turned lobster red and bellowed did they want to jinx themselves and cook their own gooses? As a result, despite all the attention they were receiving, the boys were a glum bunch going home. Some had secretly talked of celebrating once they had ditched the old fusspot but they were afraid to. Even Roy had fallen into low spirits, only he was thinking of Memo.

His heart ached the way he yearned for her (sometimes seeing her in a house they had bought, with a redheaded baby on her lap, and himself going fishing in a way that made it satisfying to fish, knowing that everything was all right behind him, and the home-cooked meal would be hot and plentiful, and the kid would carry the name of Roy Hobbs into generations his old man would never know. With this in mind he fished the stream in peace and later, sitting around the supper table, they ate the fish he had caught), yearning so deep that the depth ran through ever since he could remember, remembering the countless things he had wanted and missed out on, wondering, now that he was famous, if the intensity of his desires would ever go down. The only way that could happen (he relived that time in bed with her) was to have her always. That would end the dissatisfactions that ate him, no matter how great were his triumphs, and made his life still wanting and not having.

It later struck him that the picture he had drawn of Memo sitting domestically home wasn't exactly the girl she was. The kind he had in mind, though it bothered him to admit it, was more like Iris seemed to be, only she didn't suit him. Yet he could not help but wonder what was in her letter and he made up his mind he would read it once he got back in his room. Not that he would bother to answer, but he ought at least to know what she said.

He felt better, at the hotel, to find a note from Memo in his mailbox, saying to come up and celebrate with a drink. She greeted him at the door with a fresh kiss, her face flushed with how glad she was, saying, "Well, Roy, you've really done it. Everybody is talking about what a wonderful marvel you are."

"We still got this last one to take," he said modestly, though tickled at her praise. "I am not counting my onions till that."

"Oh, the Knights are sure to win. All the papers are saying it all depends what you do. You're the big boy, Roy."

He grabbed both her palms. "Bigger than Bump?"

Her eyelids fluttered but she said yes.

He pulled her close. She kissed for kiss with her warm wet mouth. Now is the time, he thought. Backing her against the wall, he slowly rubbed his hand up between her thighs.

She broke away, breathing heavily. He caught her and pressed his lips against her nippled blouse.

There were tears in her eyes.

He groaned, "Honey, we are the ones that are alive, not him."

"Don't say his name."

"You will forget him when I love you."

"Please let's not talk."

He lifted her in his arms and laid her down on the couch. She sat bolt upright.

"For Christ sakes, Memo, I am a grown guy and not a kid. When are you gonna be nice to me?"

"I am, Roy."

"Not the way I want it."

"I will." She was breathing quietly now.

"When?" he demanded.

She thought, distracted, then said, "Tomorrow—tomorrow night."

"That's too long."

"Later." She sighed, "Tonight."

"You are my sugar honey." He kissed her.

Her mood quickly changed. "Come on, let's celebrate."

"Celebrate what?"

"About the team."

Surprised she wanted to do that now, he said he was shaved and ready to go.

"I don't mean to go out." What she meant, she explained, was that she had prepared a snack in one of the party rooms upstairs. "They're bringing it all up from the kitchen—a buffet with cold meats and lots of other things. I thought it'd be fun to get some girls together with the boys and all enjoy ourselves."

Though he had on his mind what he was going to do to her later, and anything in between was a waste of time, still she had gone to all the trouble, and he wanted to please her. Nor was the mention of food exactly distasteful to him. He had made a double steak disappear on the train, but that was hours ago.

Memo served him a drink and finished telephoning the men she couldn't reach before. Though on the whole the players said they wanted to come, some, still remembering Pop, were doubtful they ought to, but Memo convinced them by saying that Roy and others were coming. She didn't ask the married players to bring their wives and they didn't mention the oversight to her.

At ten o'clock Memo went into the bathroom and put on a flaming yellow strapless gown. Roy got the idea that she was wearing nothing underneath and it gave him a tense pleasure. They rode up to the eighteenth floor. The party was already on. There were about a dozen men around but only four or five girls. Memo said more were coming later. Most of the players did not exactly look happy. A few were self-consciously talking to the girls, and the others were sitting on chairs gabbing among themselves. Flores stood in a corner with a melancholy expression on his phiz. Al Fowler, one of those having himself a fine time, called to him when was the wake.

Someone was pounding the keys of the upright piano against the wall. On the other side of the room, a brisk, pint-size chef with a tall puffed cap on, half again as big as him, stood behind a long, cloth-covered table, dishing out the delicatessen.

"Sure is some snack," Roy marveled. "You must've hocked your fur coat."

"Gus chipped in," Memo said absently.

He was immediately annoyed. "Is that ape coming up here?"

She looked hurt. "Don't call him dirty names. He is a fine, generous guy."

"Two bits he had the grub poisoned."

"That's not funny." Memo walked away but Roy went after

her and apologized, though her concern for the bookie—even on the night they were going to sleep together—unsettled and irritated him. Furthermore, he was now worried how Pop would take it if he found out about the players at this shindig despite his warning against celebrating too soon.

He asked Memo if the manager knew what was going on.

She was sweet again. "Don't worry about him, Roy. I'd've invited him but he wouldn't fit in at all here because we are all young people. Don't get anxious about the party, because Gus said not to serve any hard liquor."

"Nice kid, Gus. Must be laying his paper on us for a change."

Memo made no reply.

Everybody was there by then. Dave Olson had a cheerful blonde on his arm. Allie, Lajong, Hinkle, and Hill were harmonizing "Down by the Old Mill Stream." Fowler was showing some of the boys how to do a buck and wing. The cigar smoke was thick. To Roy things did still not sit just right. Everybody was watching everybody else, as if they were all waiting for a signal to get up and leave, and some of the players looked up nervously every time the door opened, as if they were expecting Doc Knobb, who used to hypnotize them before the games. Flores, from across the room, stared at Roy with black, mournful eyes, but Roy turned away. He couldn't walk out on Memo.

"Some blowout," Fowler said to him.

"Watch yourself, kid," Roy warned him in an undertone.

"Watch yourself yourself."

Roy threw him a hard look but Memo said, "Just let Roy head over to the table. He is dying for a bite."

It was true. Though the thought of having her tonight was on the top of his mind, he could not entirely forget the appetizing food. She led him to the table and he was surprised and slightly trembly at all there was of it—different kinds of delicatessen meat, appetizing fish, shrimp, crab and lobster, also caviar, salads, cheeses of all sorts, bread, rolls, and three flavors of ice cream. It made his belly ache, as if it had an existence apart from himself.

"What'll it be?" said the little chef. He had a large fork and plate poised but Roy took them from him, to his annoyance, and said he would fix what he wanted himself.

Memo helped. "Don't be stingy, Roy."

"Pile it on, honey."

"You sure are a scream the way you eat."

"I am a picnic." He kidded to ease the embarrassment his appetite caused him.

"Bump liked to shovel it down—" She caught herself.

After his plate was loaded, Memo placed a slice of ham and a roll on her own and they sat at a table in the far corner of the room—away from where Flores was standing—so Roy could concentrate on the food without having to bother with anybody.

Memo watched him, fascinated. She shredded the ham on her plate and nibbled on a roll.

"That all you're eating?" he asked.

"I guess I haven't got much appetite."

He was gobbling it down and it gave him a feeling of both having something and wanting it the same minute he was having it. And every mouthful seemed to have the effect of increasing his desire for her. He thought how satisfying it would be to lift that yellow dress over her bare thighs.

Roy didn't realize it till she mentioned it that his plate was empty. "Let me get you some more, hon."

"I will get it myself."

"Food is a woman's work." She took his plate to the table and the busy little chef heaped it high with corned beef, pastrami, turkey, potato salad, cheese, and pickles.

"You sure are nice to me," he said.

"You are a nice guy."

"Why did you get so much of it?"

"It's good for you, silly."

Roy laughed. "You sound like my grandma."

Memo was interested. "Weren't you brought up in an orphans' home, Roy?"

"I went there after grandma died."

"Didn't you ever live with your mother?"

He was suddenly thoughtful. "Seven years."

"What was she like? Do you remember?"

"A whore. She spoiled my old man's life. He was a good guy but died young."

A group of girls flocked through the door and Memo hastily excused herself. They were her showgirl friends from a Broadway musical that had just let out. She welcomed them and introduced them around. Dancing started and the party got livelier.

Roy polished his plate with a crust of bread. He felt as if he had hardly eaten anything—it was sliced so thin you could hardly chew your teeth into it.

Memo returned. "How about having something different now?" But Roy said no and got up. "Lemme say hello to some of the gals that came in."

"You are all alike." He thought she sounded jealous and it was all right if she was. The girls she brought him around to were tickled to meet him. They felt his muscles and wanted to know how he belted the ball so hard.

"Clean living," Roy told them.

The girls laughed out loud. He looked them over. The best of the bunch was a slightly chubby one with an appealing face, but in her body she did not compare to Memo.

When he told Memo she had more of what it took than the rest of them put together, she giggled nervously. He looked at her and felt she was different tonight in a way he could not figure out. He worried about Gus, but then he thought that after tonight he would be getting it steady, and then he would tell her he did not want that glass-eye monkey tailing her around.

Memo led him back to the table. She pointed out what she wanted for Roy and the chef ladled it into the plate. Her own came back with a slice of ham and a roll on it. He followed her to the corner table. He wondered if Flores was still standing in the opposite corner, watching, but he didn't look.

Gazing at the mountain of stuff Memo handed him, he said, "I am getting tired of eating."

Memo had returned to the subject of his mother. "But didn't you love her, Roy?"

He stared at her through one eye. "Who wants to know?"

"Just me."

"I don't remember." He helped himself to a forkful of food. "No."

"Didn't she love you?"

"She didn't love anybody."

Memo said, "Let's try some new combinations with the buffet. Sometimes when you eat things that you didn't know could mix together but they do, you satisfy your appetite all at once. Now let's mix this lobster meat with hidden treats of anchovies, and here we will lay it on this tasty pumpernickel and spread Greek salad over it, then smear this other slice of bread with nice sharp cheese and put it on top of the rest."

"All it needs now is a shovel of manure and a forest will grow out of it."

"Now don't be dirty, Roy."

"It looks like it could blow a man apart."

"All the food is very fresh."

After making the sandwich she went to the ladies' room. He felt depressed. Now why the hell did she have to go and ask him questions about his old lady? Thinking about her, he chewed on the sandwich. With the help of three bottles of lemon pop he downed it but had to guzzle three more of lime to get rid of the artificial lemon taste. He felt a little drunk and snickered because it was a food and pop drunk. He had the odd feeling he was down on his hands and knees searching for something that he couldn't find.

Flores stood at the table.

"If you tell them to go home," he hissed, "they weel."

Roy stared. "Tell who?"

"The players. They are afraid to stay here but they don't go because you stay."

"Go ahead and tell them to go."

"You tell them," Flores urged. "They weel leesten to your word."

"Right," said Roy.

Memo returned and Flores left him. Roy struggled to his feet, broke into a sweat, and sat down again. Fowler grabbed Memo and they whirled around. Roy didn't like them pressed so close together.

His face was damp. He reached into his pocket for a handkerchief and felt Iris's letter. For a second he thought he had found what he was looking for. More clearly than ever he remembered her pretty face and the brown eyes you could look into and see yourself as something more satisfying than you were, and he remembered telling her everything, the first time he had ever told anybody about it, and the relieved feeling he had afterward, and the long swim and Iris swimming down in the moonlit water searching for him, and the fire on the beach, she naked, and finally him banging her. For some reason this was the only thing he was ashamed of, though it couldn't be said she hadn't asked for it.

Fat girls write fat letters, he thought, and then he saw the little chef looking at him and was astonished at how hungry he felt.

Roy pushed himself up and headed for the table. The chef shined up a fast plate and with delight lifted the serving fork.

"I've had a snootful," Roy said.

The chef tittered. "It's all fresh food."

Roy looked into his button eyes. They were small pig's eyes. "Who says so?"

"It's the best there is."

"It stinks." He turned and walked stiffly to the door. Memo saw him. She waved gaily and kept on dancing.

He dragged his belly through the hall. When the elevator came it dropped him down in the lobby. He went along the corridor into the grill room. Carefully sitting down at the table, he ordered six hamburgers and two tall glasses of milk— clean food to kill the pangs of hunger.

The waiter told the cook the order, who got six red meat patties out of the refrigerator and pressed them on the grill. They softly sputtered. He thought he oughtn't to eat any more, but then he thought I am hungry. No, I am not hungry, I am hungry, whatever that means . . . What must I do not to be hungry? He considered fasting but he hadn't fasted since he was a kid. Besides, it made him hungry. He tried hard to recapture how it felt when he was hungry after a day of fishing and was sizzling lake bass over an open fire and boiling coffee in a tin can. All around his head were the sharp-pointed stars.

He was about to lift himself out of the chair but remembered his date with Memo and stayed put. There was time to kill before that so he might as well have a bite.

A hand whacked him across the shoulders.

It was Red Blow . . . Roy slowly sat down.

"Looked for a minute like you were gonna murder me," said Red.

"I thought it was somebody else."

"Who, for instance?"

Roy thought. "I am not sure. Maybe the Mex."

"Flores?"

"Sometimes he gets on my nerves."

"He is really a nice guy."

"I guess so."

Roy sat down. "Don't eat too much crap. We have a big day comin' up."

"I am just taking a bite."

"Better get to bed and have plenty of sleep."

"Yes."

Red looked glum. "Can't sleep myself. Don't know what's the matter with me." He yawned and twitched his shoulders. "You all right?"

"Fine and dandy. Have a hamburger."

"Not for me, thanks. Guess I will go for a little walk. Best thing when you can't sleep."

Roy nodded.

"Take care of yourself, feller. Tomorrow's our day. Pop'll dance a jig after tomorrow. You'll be his hero."

Roy didn't answer.

Red smiled a little sadly. "I'm gonna be sorry when it's over."

The waiter brought the six hamburgers. Red looked at them absently. "It's all up to you." He got up and left.

Through the window Roy watched him go down the street. "I'll be the hero."

The hamburgers looked like six dead birds. He took up the first one and gobbled it down. It was warm but dry. No more dead birds, he thought . . . not without ketchup. He poured a blop on three of the birds. Then he shuffled them up with the other two so as not to know which three had the ketchup and which two hadn't. Eating them, he could not tell the difference except that they all tasted like dead birds. They were not satisfying but the milk was. He made a mental note to drink more milk.

He paid and left. The elevator went up like a greased shot. As it stopped he felt a ripping pain on the floor of the stomach. The wax-faced elevator man watched him with big eyes. He stared at the old scarecrow, then stumbled out. He stood alone in the hall, trying to figure it out. Something was happening that he didn't understand. He roused himself to do battle, wishing for Wonderboy, but no enemy was visible. He rested and the pain left him.

The party was quiet. Flores had disappeared. The lights were dimmed and there was some preliminary sex work going on. Olson had his blonde backed into a corner. A group near the piano were passing a secret bottle around. In the center of the darkened room one of the girls held her dress over her pink panties and was doing bumps and grinds. A silent circle watched her.

Roy buttonholed Fowler. "Stay off the rotgut, kid."

"Stay away from the stuffin's, big shot."

Roy swiped at him but Fowler was gone. He wiped his sweaty face with his sleeve and searched for Memo to tell her it was time. He couldn't find her in the fog that had blown up, so he left the party and reeled down the stairs to the fourth floor. Feeling for her buzzer, he found the key left in the lock and softly turned it.

She was lying naked in bed, chewing a turkey drumstick as she looked at the pictures in a large scrapbook. Not till he was quite close did she see him. She let out a scream.

"You frightened me, Roy." Memo shut the scrapbook.

He had caught a glimpse of Bump's face. I'll take care of that bastard. He unzipped his fly.

Her green eyes closely watched him, her belly heaving above the red flame.

Undressing caused him great distress. Inside him they were tearing up a street. The sweat dripped from his face . . . Yet there was music, the sweetest piping he had ever heard. Dropping his pants he approached for the piping fulfillment.

She drew her legs back. Her expression puzzled him. It was not—the lights were wavering, blinking on and off. A thundering locomotive roared through the mountain. As it burst out of the rock with a whistle howl he felt on the verge of an extraordinary insight, but a bolt of shuddering lightning came at him from some unknown place. He threw up his arms for protection and it socked him, yowling, in the shattered gut. He lived a pain he could not believe existed. Agonized at the extent of it, Roy thudded to his knees as a picture he had long carried in his mind broke into pieces. He keeled over.

The raft with the singing green-eyed siren guarding the forbidden flame gave off into the rotting flood a scuttering one-eyed rat. In the distance though quite near, a toilet flushed, and though the hero braced himself against it, a rush of dirty water got a good grip and sucked him under.

Judge Banner had a money-saving contract with a small maternity hospital near Knights Field (it was there Bump had died) to treat all player emergencies, so that was where they had rushed Roy. The flustered obstetrician on duty decided to deliver the hero of his appendix. However, he fought them deliriously and his strength was too much for the surgeon, anesthetist, attendant, and two mild maternity nurses. They subdued him with a hypo only to uncover a scar snaking down his belly. Investigation showed he had no appendix—it had long ago been removed along with some other stuff. (All were surprised at his scarred and battered body.) The doctors considered cutting out the gall bladder or maybe part of the stomach but nobody wanted to be responsible for the effect of the operation upon the Knights and the general public. (The city was aghast. Crowds gathered outside the hospital, waiting for bulletins. The Japanese government issued an Edict of Sorrow.) So they used the stomach pump instead and dredged up unbelievable quantities of bilge. The patient moaned along with the ladies in labor on the floor, but the doctors adopted a policy of watchful waiting and held off anything drastic.

His belly racked his mind. Icy streams coursed through the fiery desert. He chattered and steamed, rarely conscious, tormented by his dreams. In them he waxed to gigantic heights then abruptly fell miles to be a little Roy dwarf (Hey, mister, you're stepping on my feet). He was caught in roaring gales amid loose, glaring lights, so bright they smothered the eyeballs. Iris's sad head topped Memo's dancing body, with Memo's vice versa upon the shimmying rest of Iris, a confused fusion that dizzied him. He hungered in nightmare for quantities of exotic food—wondrous fowl stuffed with fruit, and the multitudinous roe of tropical fish. When he bent his toothy head to devour, every last morsel vanished. So they served him a prime hunk of beef and he found it enormously delicious only to discover it was himself he was chewing. His thunderous roars sent nurses running from all directions. They were powerless before his flailing fists.

In delirium he hopped out of bed and hunted through the

corridors in a nightgown—frightening the newly delivered mothers—for a mop or broom that he snatched back to his aseptic chamber and practiced vicious cuts with before the dresser mirror . . . They found him on the floor . . . At dawn he warily rose and ferreted a plumber's plunger out of the utility closet but this time he was caught by three attendants and dragged back to bed. They strapped him down and there he lay a prisoner, as the frightened Knights dropped the third of three hot potatoes to the scarred and embittered last-place Reds. Since the resurgent Pirates had scattered the brains of the Phils, three in a bloody row, the season ended in a dead heat. A single playoff game in Knights Field was arranged for Monday next, the day before the World Series.

Late that afternoon the fever abated. He returned, unstrapped, to consciousness and recognized a harried Memo at his bedside. From her he learned what had happened to the team, and groaned in anguish. When she left, with a hankie pressed to her reddened nostrils, he discovered his troubles had only just begun. The specialist in the case, a tall stoop-shouldered man with a white mustache and sad eyes, who absently hefted a heavy gold watch as he spoke, gave Roy a bill of particulars. He began almost merrily by telling him there wasn't much doubt he would participate in the Monday playoff (Roy just about leaped out of the bed but the doctor held him back with a gesture). He could play, yes, though he'd not feel at his best, nor would he be able to extend himself so far as he would like, but he would certainly be present and in the game, which, as the doctor understood it, was the big thing for both Roy and his public. (Interest in the matter was so great, he said, that he had permitted release of this news to the press.) Public clamor had compelled his reluctant yielding, though it was his considered opinion that, ideally, Roy ought to rest a good deal longer before getting back to his—ah—normal activities. But someone had explained to him that baseball players were in a way like soldiers, and since he knew that the body's response to duty sometimes achieved many of the good results of prolonged care and medication, he had agreed to let him play.

However, all good news has its counterpart of bad, he almost sadly said, and to prove the point let it come out that it would be best for Roy to say goodbye forever to baseball—if he hoped to stay alive. His blood pressure—at times amazingly high—complicated by an athlete's heart—could conceivably cause his sudden death if he were to attempt to play next season, whereas if he worked at something light and relaxing, one might say he could go on for years, as many had. The doctor slipped the gold watch into his vest pocket, and nodding to the patient, departed. Roy felt that this giant hand holding a club had broken through the clouds and with a single blow crushed his skull.

The hours that followed were the most terrifying of his life (more so than fifteen years ago). He lived in the thought of death, would not move, speak, take food or receive visitors. Yet all the while he fanatically fought the doctor's revelation, wrestled it every waking second, though something in him said the old boy with the white mustache was right. He felt he had for years suspected something wrong, and this was it. Too much pressure in the pipes—blew your conk off. (He saw it blown sky high.) He was through—finished. Only he couldn't— just couldn't believe it. Me. I. Roy Hobbs forever out of the game? Inconceivable. He thought of the fantastic hundreds of records he had broken in so short a time, which had made him a hero to the people, and he thought of the thousands—tens of thousands—that he had pledged himself to break. A moan escaped him.

Still a doubt existed. Maybe white mustache was wrong? They could misjudge them too. Maybe there was a mite less wind behind the ball than he thought, and it would hit the ground at his feet rather than land in the glove. Mistakes could happen in everything. Wouldn't be the first time a sawbones was wrong. *Maybe he was a hundred per cent dead wrong.*

The next evening, amid a procession of fathers leaving the hospital at baby-feeding time, he sneaked out of the building. A cab got him to Knights Field, and Happy Pellers, the astonished groundskeeper, let him in. A phone call brought Dizzy to the scene. Roy changed into uniform (he almost wept to behold Wonderboy so forlorn in the locker) and Happy donned catcher's gear. Dizzy prepared to pitch. It was just to practice, Roy said, so he would have his eye and timing alert for the playoff Monday. Happy switched on the night floods to make things clearer. Dizzy practiced a few pitches and then with Roy standing at the plate, served one over the middle. As he swung, Roy felt a jet of steam blow through the center of his skull. They gathered him up, bundled him into a cab, and got him back to the hospital, where nobody had missed him.

It was a storm on and Roy out in it. Not exactly true, it was Sam Simpson who was lost and Roy outsearching him. He tracked up and down the hills, leaving his white tracks, till he come to this shack with the white on the roof.

Anybody in here? he calls.

Nope.

You don't know my friend Sam?

Nope.

He wept and try to go away.

Come on in, kiddo, I was only foolin'.

Roy dry his eyes and went in. Sam was settin' at the table under the open bulb, his collar and tie off, playing solitaire with all spades.

Roy sit by the fire till Sam finish. Sam looked up wearing his half-moon specs, glinting moonlight.

Well, son, said Sam, lightin' up on his cigar.

I swear I didn't do it, Sam.

Didn't do what?

Didn't do nothin'.

Who said you did?

Roy wouldn't answer, shut tight as a clam.

Sam stayed awhile, then he say to Roy, Take my advice, kiddo.

Yes, Sam.

Don't do it.

No, said Roy, I won't. He rose and stood headbent before Sam's chair.

Let's go back home, Sam, let's now.

Sam peered out the window.

I would like to, kiddo, honest, but we can't go out there now. Heck, it's snowin' baseballs.

When he came to, Roy made the specialist promise to tell no one about his condition just in case he had the slightest chance of improving enough to play for maybe another season. The specialist frankly said he didn't see that chance, but he was willing to keep mum because he believed in the principle of freedom of action. So he told no one and neither did Roy—not even Memo. (No one had even mentioned the subject of his playing in the Series but Roy had already privately decided to take his chances in that.)

But mostly his thoughts were dismal. That frightened feeling: bust before beginning. On the merry-go-round again about his failure to complete his mission in the game. About this he suffered most. He lay for hours staring at the window. Often the glass looked wet though it wasn't raining. A man who had been walking in bright sunshine limped away into a mist. This broke the heart . . . When the feeling passed, if it ever did, there was the necessity of making new choices. Since it was already the end of the season, he had about four months in which to cash in on testimonials, endorsements, ghost-written articles, personal appearances, and such like. But what after that, when spring training time came and he disappeared into the backwoods? He recalled a sickening procession of jobs—as cook, well-driller, mechanic, logger, bean-picker, and for whatever odd change, semipro ballplayer. He dared not think further.

And the loneliness too, from job to job, never some place in particular for any decent length of time because of the dissatisfaction that grew, after a short while, out of anything he did . . . But supposing he could collect around twenty-five G's—could that amount, to begin with, satisfy a girl like Memo if she married him? He tried to think of ways of investing twenty-five thousand—maybe in a restaurant or tavern—to build it up to fifty, and then somehow to double that. His mind skipped from money to Memo, the only one who came to see him every day. He remembered the excitement he felt for her in that strapless yellow dress the night of the party. And bad as he felt now he couldn't help but think how desirable she had looked, waiting for him naked in bed.

Such thoughts occupied him much of the time as he sat in the armchair, thumbing through old magazines, or resting in bed. He sometimes considered suicide but the thought was too oppressive to stay long in his mind. He dozed a good deal and usually woke feeling lonely. (Except for Red, once, nobody from the team had come to see him, though small knots of fans still gathered in the street and argued whether he would really be in Monday's game.) Saturday night he awoke from an after supper nap more gloomy than ever, so he reached under his pillow for Iris's letter. But just then Memo came into the room with an armful of flowers so he gladly let it lay where it was.

Despite how attractive she usually managed to keep herself (he could appreciate that in spite of a momentary return of the nausea) she appeared worn out now, with bluish shadows under her eyes. And he noticed, as she stuffed the flowers and red autumn leaves into the vase, that she was wearing the same black dress she had worn all week, a thing she never did before, and that her hair was lusterless and not well kept. She had days ago sorrowed it was her fault that this had happened to the team. How stupid not to have waited just a day or two more. (Pop, she wept, had called her filthy names.) She had despaired every minute—really despaired—up to the time she heard he was going to be in the playoff. At least she did not have it on her conscience that he would be out of that, so she felt better now. Not better enough, he worried, or she wouldn't be so lost and lonely-looking.

After she had arranged the flowers, Memo stood mutely at the open window, gazing down into the darkening street. When he least expected it, she sobbed out in a voice full of misery, "Oh, Roy, I can't stand it any longer, I can't."

He sat up. "What's wrong?"

Her voice was choked. "I can't go on with my life as it is." Memo dropped into the armchair and began to weep. In a minute everything around her was wet.

Tossing aside the blanket he swung his legs out of bed. She looked up, attempting to smile. "Don't get up, hon. I'll be all right."

Roy sat uneasily at the edge of the bed. He never knew what to do when they cried.

"It's just that I'm fed up," she wept. "Fed up. Pop is terrible to me and I don't want to go on living off him, even if he is my uncle. I have to get a job or something, or go somewhere."

"What did that bastard shrimp say to you?"

She found a handkerchief in her purse and blew her nose.

"It isn't his words," she said sadly. "Words can't kill. It's that I'm sick of this kind of life. I want to get away."

Then she let go again and looked like a little lost bird beating around in a cage. He was moved, and hovered over her like an old maid aunt trying to stop a leak.

"Don't cry, Memo. Just say the word and I will take care of you." In a cracked voice he said, "Just marry me."

She sobbed for the longest time. So long he grew jumpy with doubts about their future relations, but then she stopped crying and said in a damp voice, "Would you have me, Roy?"

He swayed with emotion as he got out thickly, "Would I?" To keep from hitting the ground he hopped into bed and sprawled out.

She came to him, her white hands clasped, her wet eyelids like sparkling flowers. "There's one thing you have to understand, Roy, and then maybe you won't want me. That is that I am afraid to be poor." She said it with intensity, her face turning dark at her words. "Maybe I am weak or spoiled, but I am the type who has to have somebody who can support her in a decent way. I'm sick of living like a slave. I got to have a house of my own, a maid to help me with the hard work, a decent car to shop with and a fur coat for winter time when it's cold. I don't want to have to worry every time a can of beans jumps a nickel. I suppose it's wrong to want all of that but I can't help it. I've been around too long and seen too much. I saw how my mother lived and I know it killed her. I made up my mind to have certain things. You understand that, don't you, Roy?"

He nodded.

"We have to face it," she said. "You're thirty-five now and that don't give you much time left as a ball player."

"What d'ye mean?" he asked, deadpan.

But it wasn't his blood pressure she was referring to. For a minute he was afraid she had found out.

"I'm sorry to say this, Roy, but I have to be practical. Suppose the next one is your last season, or that you will have one more after that? Sure, you'll probably get a good contract till then but it costs money to live, and then what'll we do for the rest of our lives?"

It was dark in the room now. He could scarcely see her.

"Turn on the lights."

She smeared powder over her nose and under her eyes, then pressed the button.

He stared at her.

She grew restless. "Roy—"

"I was just thinking, even if I had to quit right now I could still scrounge up about twenty-five grand in the next few months. That's a lotta dough."

She seemed doubtful. "What would you do with it?"

"We'd get hitched and I would invest in a business. Everybody does that. My name is famous already. We will make out okay. You will have what you want."

"What kind of business?" Memo asked.

"I can't say for sure—maybe a restaurant."

She made a face.

"What do you have in mind?" Roy asked.

"Oh, something big, Roy. I would like you to buy into a company where you could have an executive job and won't have to go poking your nose into the stew in a smelly restaurant."

A jet of nausea shot up from his gizzard. He admitted to himself he wanted nothing to do with restaurants.

"How much dough do we need to get in on one of those big companies?"

"I should think more than twenty-five thousand."

He gulped. "Around thirty-five?"

"More like fifty."

Roy frowned. Talk of that kind of dough gave him a bellyache. But Memo was right. It had to be something big or it wouldn't pay back enough. And if it was a big company he could take it a little easy, to protect his health, without anybody kicking. He pondered where to get another twenty-five thousand, and it had to be before the start of the next baseball season because as soon as everybody saw he wasn't playing, it wouldn't be easy to cash in on his name. People had no use for a has been. He had to be married and have the dough, both before next spring—in case he never did get to play. He thought of other means to earn some money fast—selling the story of his life to the papers, barnstorming a bit this fall and winter, not too strenuously. But neither of these things added up to much—not twenty-five grand. Roy lay back with his eyes shut.

Memo whispered something. His lids flew open. What was she doing with an old black dress on, her hair uncombed, looking like Lola, the Jersey City fortuneteller? Yet her voice was calm . . .

"Who sent you," he spoke harshly, "—that bastard Gus?"

She turned flame-faced but answered quietly, "The Judge."

"Banner?" Somebody inside of him—this nervous character lately hanging around—crashed a glass to the floor. Roy's pulses banged.

"He said he'd pay you fifteen thousand now and more next season. He says it would depend on you."

"I thought I smelled skunk."

"He asked me to deliver the message. I have nothing to do with it."

"Who else is in on this?"

"I don't know."

"Pop?"

"No."

He lay motionless for an age. She said no more, did not plead or prod. It grew late. An announcement was made for visitors to leave. She rose and tiredly put on her coat.

"I was thinking of all the years you would be out of the game."

"What does he want me to do?"

"It's something about the playoff—I don't know."

"They want me to drop it?"

She didn't answer.

"No," he said out loud.

She shrugged. "I told them you wouldn't."

She was thin and haggard-looking. Her shoulders drooped, her hands were bloodless. To refuse her just about broke his heart.

He fell into a deep slumber but had not slept very long before this rat-eyed vulture, black against the ceiling, began to flap around the room and dripping deep fat spiraled down toward his face. Wrestling together, they knocked over the tables and chairs, when the lights went on and waked him. Roy grabbed under the pillow for a gun he thought was there, only it wasn't. Awake, he saw through the glare that Judge Goodwill Banner, in dark glasses and hairy black fedora, was staring at him from the foot of the bed.

"What the hell do you want here?"

"Don't be alarmed," the Judge rumbled. "Miss Paris informed me you were not asleep, and the authorities granted me a few minutes to visit with you."

"I got nothing to say to you." The nightmare had weakened him. Not wanting the Judge to see that, he pulled himself into a sitting position.

The Judge, yellow-skinned in the electric light, and rumpled-looking, sat in the armchair with his potlike hat on. He sucked an unwilling flame into his King Oscar and tossed the burnt-out match on the floor.

"How is your health, young man?"

"Skip it. I am all right now."

The Judge scrutinized him.

"Wanna bet?" Roy said.

The Judge's rubbery lips tightened around his cigar. After a minute he removed it from his mouth and said cautiously, "I assume that Miss Paris has acquainted you with the terms of a certain proposal?"

"Leave her name out of it."

"An admirable suggestion—a proposal, you understand, made by persons unknown."

"Don't make me laugh. I got a good mind to sick the FBI on you."

The Judge examined his cigar. "I rely on your honor. You might consider, however, that there is no witness other than Miss Paris, and I assume you would be solicitous of her?"

"I said to leave her name out."

"Quite so. I believe she erred concerning the emolument offered—fifteen thousand, was it? My understanding is that twenty thousand, payable in cash in one sum, is closer to the correct amount. I'm sure you know the prevailing rate for this sort of thing is ten thousand dollars. We offer twice that. Any larger sum is unqualifiedly out of the question because it will impair the profitableness of the venture. I urge you to consider carefully. You know as well as I that you are in no condition to play."

"Then what are you offering me twenty thousand smackers for—to show your gratitude for how I have built up your bank account?"

"I see no reason for sarcasm. You were paid for your services as contracted. As for this offer, I frankly confess it is insurance. There is the possibility that you may get into the game and unexpectedly wreck it with a single blow. I personally doubt this will occur, but we prefer to take no chances."

"Don't kid yourself that I am too weak to play. You know that the doctor himself said I'll be in there Monday."

The Judge hesitated. "Twenty-five thousand," he finally said. "Absolutely my last offer."

"I hear the bookies collect ten million a day on baseball bets."

"Ridiculous."

"That's what I hear."

"It makes no difference, I am not a bookie. What is your answer?"

"I say no."

The Judge bit his lip.

Roy said, "Ain't you ashamed that you are selling a club down the river that hasn't won a pennant in twenty-five years and now they have a chance to?"

"We'll have substantially the same team next year," the Judge answered, "and I have no doubt that we will make a better job of the entire season, supported as we shall be by new players and possibly another manager. If we take on the Yankees now—that is, if we are foolish enough to win the playoff match—they will beat us a merciless four in a row, despite your presence. You are not strong enough to withstand the strain of a World Series, and you know it. We'd be ground to pulp, made the laughingstock of organized baseball, and your foolish friend, Pop Fisher, would this time destroy himself in his humiliation."

"What about all the jack you'd miss out on, even if we only played four Series games and lost every one?"

"I have calculated the amount and am certain I can do better, on the whole, in the way I suggest. I have reason to believe that, although we are considered to be the underdogs, certain gambling interests have been betting heavily on the Knights to win. Now it is my purpose, via the uncontested—so to speak—game, to teach these parasites a lesson they will never forget. After that they will not dare to infest our stands again."

"Pardon me while I throw up."

The Judge looked hurt.

"The odds favor us," Roy said. "I saw it in tonight's paper."

"In one only. The others quote odds against us."

Roy laughed out loud.

The Judge flushed through his yellow skin. "Honi soit qui mal y pense."

"Double to you," Roy said.

"Twenty-five thousand," said the Judge with an angry gesture. "The rest is silence."

Though Roy had a splitting headache he tried to think the situation out. The way he now felt, he wouldn't be able to stand at the plate with a feather duster on his shoulder, let alone a bat. Maybe the Judge's hunch was right, and he might not be able to do a single thing to help the Knights win their game. On the other hand—maybe he'd be himself, his real self. If he helped them win the playoff—no matter if they later dropped the Series four in a row—there would still be all sorts of endorsement offers and maybe even a contract to do a baseball movie. Then he'd have the dough to take care of Memo in proper style. Yet suppose he played and because of his weakness flopped as miserably as he had during his slump? That might sour the endorsements and everything else, and he'd end up with nothing—or very little. His mind went around in drunken circles.

All this time the Judge's voice was droning on. "I have observed," he was saying, "how one moral condition may lead to or become its opposite. I recall an occasion on the bench when out of the goodness of my heart and a warm belief in humanity I resolved to save a boy from serving a prison sentence. Though his guilt was clear, because of his age I suspended sentence and paroled him for a period of five years. That afternoon as I walked down the courthouse steps, I felt I could surely face my maker without a blush. However, not one week later the boy stood before me, arraigned as a most wicked parricide. I asked myself can any action—no matter what its origin or motive—which ends so evilly—can such an action possibly be designated as good?"

He took out a clotted handkerchief, spat into it, folded it and thrust it into his pocket. "Contrarily," he went on, "a deed of apparently evil significance may come to pure and beautiful flower. I have in mind a later case tried before me in which a physician swindled his patient, a paralytic, out of almost a quarter of a million dollars. So well did he contrive to hide the loot that it has till this day not been recovered. Nevertheless, the documentary evidence was strong enough to convict the embezzler and I sentenced him to a term of from forty to fifty years in prison, thus insuring he would not emerge from the penitentiary to enjoy his ill-gotten gains before he is eighty-three years of age. Yet, while testifying from his wheel chair at the trial, the paralytic astonished himself and all present by rising in righteous wrath against the malcontent and, indeed, tottered across the floor to wreak upon him his vengeance. Naturally the bailiff restrained him, but would you have guessed that he was, from that day on, sound in wind and limb, and as active as you or I? He wrote me afterwards that the return of his power of locomotion more than compensated him for the loss of his fortune."

Roy frowned. "Come out of the bushes."

The Judge paused. "I was trying to help you assess this action in terms of the future."

"You mean if I sell out?"

"Put it that way if you like."

"And that maybe some good might come out of it?"

"That is my assumption."

"For me, you mean?"

"For others too. It is impossible to predict who will be benefited."

"I thought you said you were doing this to get rid of the gamblers—that's good right off, ain't it?"

The Judge cleared his throat. "Indeed it is. However, one might consider, despite the difficulty of the personal situation —that is to say, within the context of one's own compunctions —that it is impossible to predict what further good may accrue to one, and others, in the future, as a result of an initially difficult decision."

Roy laughed. "You should be selling snake oil."

He had thought there might be something to the argument.

He was now sure there wasn't, for as the Judge had talked he recalled an experience he had had when he was a kid. He and his dog were following an old skid road into the heart of a spooky forest when the hound suddenly let out a yelp, ran on ahead, and got lost. It was late in the afternoon and he couldn't stand the thought of leaving the dog there alone all night, so he went into the wood after it. At first he could see daylight between the trees—to this minute he remembered how still the trunks were, as the tree tops circled around in the breeze— and in sight of daylight it wasn't so bad, nor a little deeper in, despite the green gloom, but just at about the time the darkness got so thick he was conscious of having to shove against it as he hallooed for the dog, he got this scared and lonely feeling that he was impossibly lost. With his heart whamming against his ribs he looked around but could recognize no direction in the darkness, let alone discover the right one. It was cold and he shivered. Only, the payoff of it was that the mutt found him and led him out of the woods. That was good out of good.

Roy pulled the covers over his head. "Go home."

The Judge didn't move. "There is also the matter of next season's contract."

Roy listened. Would there ever be a next season? He uncovered his head. "How much?"

"I shall offer—provided we agree on the other matter—a substantial raise."

"Talk figures."

"Forty-five thousand for the season. We might also work out some small percentage on the gate."

"Twenty-five thousand for dropping the game is not enough," said Roy. As he spoke an icicle of fright punctured his spine.

The Judge scowled and drew on his half-gone cigar. "Thirty," he said, "and no more."

"Thirty-five," Roy got out. "Don't forget I stand to lose a couple of thousand on the pay I could get in the Series."

"Utterly outrageous," snapped the Judge.

"Don't slam the door on your way out."

The Judge rose, brushed his wrinkled pants and left.

Roy stared at the ceiling—relieved.

The Judge returned. He removed his hat and wiped his

perspiring face with his dirty handkerchief. His head was covered with a thick black wig. You never got to the bottom of
that creep.

"You are impossible to deal with—but I accept." His voice
was flat. He covered his head with his hat.

But Roy said he had changed his mind when the Judge was
out of the room. He had thought it over and decided the boys
wanted to win that game and he wanted to help them. That
was good. He couldn't betray his own team and manager. That
was bad.

The Judge then hissed, "You may lose Miss Paris to someone else if you are not careful."

Roy bolted up. "To who for instance?"

"A better provider."

"You mean Gus Sands?"

The Judge did not directly reply. "A word to the wise—"

"That's none of your business," said Roy. He lay back. Then
he asked, "What if I couldn't lose the game by myself? The
Pirates ain't exactly world beaters. We roasted them the last
seven times. The boys might do it again even if I didn't hit a
thing."

The Judge rubbed his scaly hands. "The Knights are demor-
alized. Without you, I doubt they can win over a sandlot team,
contrary opinion notwithstanding. As for the contingency of
the flat failure of the opposing team, we have made the necessary arrangements to take care of that."

Roy was up again. "You mean there's somebody else in on
this deal?"

The Judge smiled around his cigar.

"Somebody on our team?"

"A key man."

"In that case—" Roy said slowly.

"The thirty-five thousand is final. There'll be no changing
that."

"With forty-five for the contract—"

"Agreed. You understand you are not under any circumstances to hit the ball safely?"

After a minute Roy said slowly, "I will take the pitch."

"I beg your pardon?"

"The fix is on."

The Judge caught on and said with a laugh, "I see you share my philological interests." He lit his dead King Oscar.

Through the nausea Roy remembered an old saying. He quoted, "Woe unto him who calls evil good and good evil."

The Judge glared at him.

Memo returned and covered his face with wet kisses. She tweaked his nose, mussed his hair, and called him wonderful. After she left he couldn't sleep so he reached under his pillow and got out Iris's letter.

". . . After my baby was born, the women of the home where my father had brought me to save himself further shame were after me to give it up. They said it would be bad for her to be brought up by an unmarried mother, and that I would have no time to myself or opportunity to take up my normal life. I tried, as they said, to be sensible and offer her for adoption, but I had been nursing her—although warned against it, nursing shrinks the breasts you know, and they were afraid for my figure—and the thought of tearing myself away from her forever was too much for me. Since Papa wouldn't have her in his house I decided to find a job and bring her up myself. That turned out to be a lot harder than I had expected, because I earned not very much and had to pay for baby's care all day, her things, the rent of course, and the clothes I had to have for work. At night I had supper to think of, bathing her, laundry, house cleaning, and preparing for the next day, which never changed from any other.

"Except for my baby I was nearly always alone, reading, mostly, to improve myself, although sometimes it was unbearable, especially before I was twenty and just after. It also took quite a while until I got rid of my guilt, or could look upon her as innocent of it, but eventually I did, and soon her loveliness and gaiety and all the tender feelings I had in my heart for her made up for a lot I had suffered. Yet I was tied to time—not so much to the past—nor to the expectations of the future, which was really too far away—only to here and now, day after day, until suddenly the years unrolled and a change came—more a reward of standing it so long than any sudden magic—and more quickly than I could believe, she had grown into a young woman, and almost as if I had wished it on her, fell in love with a wonderful boy and married him. Like me she was a mother before she was seventeen. Suddenly everywhere I looked seemed to be tomorrow, and I was at last free to take up my life where I had left it off one summer night when I went for a walk in the park with a stranger . . ."

He read down to the last page, where she once more mentioned herself as a grandmother. Roy crumpled the letter and pitched it against the wall.

ON THE morning of the game fist fights broke out all over the stands in Knights Field. Hats, bottles, apple cores, bananas, and the mushy contents of sack lunches were thrown around. A fan in one of the boxes had a rock bounced off his skull, opening a bleeding gash. Two special cops rushed up the steps and got hold of an innocent-looking guy with glasses, whose pockets were stuffed with odd-shaped rocks. They dragged him forth, although he was hollering he had collected them for his rock garden, and flung him headlong out of the park. He was from Pittsburgh and cursed the Knights into the ground. A disappointed truck driver who couldn't get in to see the game tackled him from behind, knocking the rock collector's head against the sidewalk and smashing his glasses. He spat out two bloody teeth and sat there sobbing till the ambulance came.

The sun hid behind the clouds for the most part. The day was chilly, football weather, but the stands were decorated with colored bunting, the flags on the grandstand roof rode high in the breeze and the crowd was raucous. The P.A. man tried to calm them but they were packed together too tight to be peaceful, for the Judge had sold hundreds of extra tickets and the standees raced for any seat that was vacant for a second. Besides, the Knights' fans were jumpy, their nerves ragged from following the ups and downs of the team. Some glum-face gents bitterly cursed Roy out, calling him welsher, fool, pig-horse for eating himself into that colossal bellyache. But he had his defenders, who claimed the Big Man's body burned food so fast he needed every bit he ate. They blamed the damage on ptomaine. The accusers wanted to know why no one else at the party had come down sick. They were answered where would the Knights be without Roy—at the bottom of the heap. The one who spoke got a rap on the ear for his trouble. The rapper was grabbed by a cop, run down the catwalk, and pitched into the rotunda. Yet though the fans were out of sorts and crabbing at each other, they presented a solid front when it came to laying bets. Many pessimistically shook their heads, but they counted up the seven straight wins over

the Pirates, figured in that Hobbs was back, and reached into
their pockets. Although there were not too many Pirate rooters around, the bets were quickly covered for every hard-
earned buck.

Otto Zipp was above all this. He sat like a small mountain
behind the rail in short left, reading the sports page of his
newspaper. He looked neither right nor left, and if somebody
tried to talk to him Otto gave him short shrift. Then when
they least expected it, he would honk his horn and cry out in
shrill tones, "Throw him to the hawks." After that he went
back to the sports page.

When the players began drifting into the clubhouse they were
surprised to see Roy there. He was wearing his uniform and
slowly polishing Wonderboy. The boys said hello and not
much more. Flores looked at his feet. Some of them were embarrassed that they hadn't gone to see him in the hospital. Secretly they were pleased he was here. Allie Stubbs even began
to kid around with Olson. Roy thought they would not act so
chipper if they knew he felt weak as piss and was dreading the
game. The Judge was absolutely crazy to pay him thirty-five
grand not to hit when he didn't feel able to even lift a stick. He
hoped Pop would guess how shaky he was and bench him.
What a laugh that would be on the Judge—serve the bastard
right. But when Pop came in, he didn't so much as glance in
Roy's direction. He walked straight into his office and slammed
the door, which suited Roy fine.

Pop had ordered everybody kept out of the clubhouse until
after the game but Mercy weaseled in. All smiles, he approached Roy, asking for the true story of what went on at the
party that night, but Red Blow saw him and told him to stay
outside. Max had tried the same act in the hospital last week.
The floor nurse caught him sneaking toward Roy's room and
had him dropped out on the front steps. After leaving the clubhouse Max sent in a note, inviting Roy to come out and make a
statement. People were calling him a filthy coward and what did
he intend to say to that? Roy gave out a one-word unprintable
reply. Mercy shot in a second note. "You'll get yours—M.M."
Roy tore it up and told the usher to take no more slop from
him.

Pop poked his baldy out of his door and called for Roy. The players looked around uneasily. Roy got up and finally went into the office. For an insufferable time Pop failed to speak. He was unshaven, his face exuding gray stubble that made him look eighty years old. His thin frame seemed shrunken and his left eye was a little crossed with fatigue. Pop leaned back in his creaking swivel chair, staring with tears in his eyes over his half moons at the picture of Ma on his desk. Roy examined his fingernails.

Pop sighed, "Roy, it's my own fault."

It made Roy edgy. "What is?"

"This mess that we are now in. I am not forgetting I kept you on the bench for three solid weeks in June. If I hadn't done that foolish thing we'da finished the season at least half a dozen games out in front."

Roy offered no reply.

"But your own mistake was a bad one too."

Roy nodded.

"A bad one, with the team right on top of hooking the pennant." Pop shook his head. Yet he said he wouldn't blame Roy too much because it wasn't entirely of his own doing. He then apologized for not coming to see him in the hospital. He had twice set out to but felt too grumpy to be fit company for a sick man, so he hadn't come. "It's not you that I am mad at, Roy—it's that blasted Memo. I shoulda pitched her out on her ass the first day she showed up at my door."

Roy got up.

"Sit down." Pop bent forward. "We can win today." His cold breath smelled bad. Roy drew his head back.

"Well, we can, can't we?"

He nodded.

"What's the matter with you?"

"I feel weak," Roy said, "and I am not betting how I will hit today."

Pop's voice got kindly again. "I say we can win it whichever way you feel. Once you begin to play you will feel stronger. And if the rest of those birds see you hustling they will break their backs to win. All they got to feel is there is somebody on this team who thinks they can."

Pop then related a story about a rookie third baseman he

once knew, a lad named Mulligan. He was a fine hitter and thrower but full of hard luck all his life. Once he was beaned at the plate and had his skull cracked. He returned for spring practice the following year and the first day out he crashed into another fielder and broke his arm. On the return from that he was on first running to second on a hit and run play and the batter smacked the ball straight at him, breaking two ribs and dislocating a disc in his spine. After that he quit baseball, to everybody's relief.

"He was just unlucky," Pop said, "and there wasn't a thing anybody could do to take the whammy off of him and change his hard luck. You know, Roy, I been lately thinking that a whole lot of people are like him, and for one reason or the other their lives will go the same way all the time, without them getting what they want, no matter what. I for one."

Then to Roy's surprise he said he never hoped to have a World Series flag. Pop swiveled his chair closer. "It ain't in the cards for me—that's all. I am wise to admit it to myself. It took a long time but I finally saw which way the arrow has been pointing." He sighed deeply. "But that don't hold true about our league pennant, Roy. That's the next best thing and I feel I am entitled to it. I feel if I win it just this once—I will be satisfied. I will be satisfied, and win or lose in the Series, I will quit baseball forever." He lowered his voice. "You see what it means to me, son?"

"I see."

"Roy, I would give my whole life to win this game and take the pennant. Promise me that you will go in there and do your damndest."

"I will go in," Roy sighed.

After the practice bell had rung, when he reluctantly climbed up out of the dugout and shoved himself toward the batting cage with his bat in his hand, as soon as the crowd got a look at him the boo birds opened up, alternating with shrill whistles and brassy catcalls. Roy hardened his jaws, but then a rumble erupted that sounded like bubbling tubfuls of people laughing and sobbing. The noise grew to a roar, boiled over, and to his astonishment, drowned out the disapprovers in an ovation of cheering. Men flung their hats into the air, scaling straws and limp felts, pounded each other's skulls, and cried themselves hoarse. Women screeched and ended up weeping. The shouting grew, piling reverberation upon reverberation, till it reached blast proportions. When it momentarily wore thin, Sadie Sutter's solemn gong could be heard, but as the roar rose again, the gonging grew faint and died in the distance. Roy felt feverish. The applause was about over when he removed his cap to clean the sweat off his brow, and once more thunder rolled across the field, continuing in waves as he entered the cage. With teeth clenched to stop the chattering, he took three swipes at the ball, driving each a decent distance. At Pop's urging he also went out onto the field to shag some flies. Again the cheers resounded, although he wished they wouldn't. He speared a few flies in his tracks, dropped his glove and walked to the dugout. The cheers trailed him in a foaming billow, but above the surflike roar and the renewed tolling of Sadie's gong, he could hear Otto Zipp's shrill curses. The dwarf drew down on his head a chorus of hisses but thumbed his cherry nose as Roy passed by. Roy paid him no heed whatsoever, infuriating Otto.

The Pirates flipped through their practice and the game began. Pop had picked Fowler to start for the Knights. Roy figured then that he knew who was in this deal with him. Leave it to the Judge to tie the bag in the most economical way— with the best hitter and pitcher. He had probably asked Pop who he was intending to pitch and then went out and bought him, though no doubt paying a good deal less than the price Roy was getting. What surprised and shocked him was that Fowler could be so corrupt though so young and in the best of health. If he only had half the promise of the future Fowler had, he would never have dirtied his paws in this business. However, as he watched Fowler pitch during the first inning he wasn't certain he was the one. His fast ball hopped today and he got rid of the first two Pirates with ease. Maybe he was playing it cagey first off, time would tell. Roy's thoughts were broken up by the sound, and echo behind him, of the crack of a bat. The third man up had taken hold of one and it was arcing into deep left. Already Flores was hot footing it in from center. It occurred to Roy that although he had promised the Judge he wouldn't hit, he had made no commitments as to catching them. Waving Flores aside, he ran several shaky steps and made a throbbing stab at the ball, spearing it on the half run for the third out. As he did so he noticed a movement up in the tower window and saw the Judge's stout figure pressed against the window. He then recollected he hadn't seen Memo since Saturday.

To nobody's surprise, Dutch Vogelman went to the mound for the Pirates. In a few minutes it was clear to all he was working with championship stuff, because he knocked the first three Knights off without half trying, including Flores, who was no easy victim. Roy had no chance to bat, for which he felt relieved. But after Fowler had also rubbed out the opposition, he was first up in the second inning. As he dragged Wonderboy up to the plate, the stands, after a short outburst, were hushed. Everybody remembered the four homers he had got off Vogelman the last time he had faced him. In the dugout Pop and the boys were peppering it up for him to give the ball a big ride, and so were Red Blow and Earl Wilson, on the baselines. What they didn't know was that Roy had been struck giddy with weakness. His heart whammed like a wheezing steam engine, his head felt nailed to a pole, his eardrums throbbed as if he were listening to the bottom of the sea, and his arms hung like dead weights. It was with the greatest effort that he raised Wonderboy. As he was slowly getting set, he sneaked a cautious glance up at the tower, and it did not exactly surprise him that Memo, still in black, was standing at the window next to the Judge, blankly gazing down at him. Anyway, he knew where she was now.

Vogelman had been taking his time. For a pitcher he was a comparatively short duck, with a long beak, powerful arms and legs, red sleeves leaking out of a battered jersey, and a nervous delivery. Despite the fact that he had ended the regular season as a twenty-five game winner, he worried to bursting beads of sweat at the thought of pitching to Roy. Every time he recalled those four gopher balls, one after the other landing in the stands, he cringed with embarrassment. And he knew, although there was nobody on base at the moment, that if he served one of them up now, it could conceivably ice the game for the Knights and louse up the very peak of his year of triumph. So Vogelman delayed by wiping the shine off the ball, inspecting the stitches, fumbling for the resin bag, scuffing his cleats in the dirt, and removing his cap to rub away the sweat he had worked up. When the boos of the crowd got good and loud, Stuffy Briggs bellowed for him to throw and Vogelman reluctantly let go with a pitch.

The ball was a whizzer but dripping lard. Weak as he felt, Roy had to smile at what he could really do to that baby if he had his heart set on it, but he swung the slightest bit too late, grunting as the ball shot past Wonderboy—which almost broke his wrists to get at it—and plunked in the pocket of the catcher's glove.

. . . Where had she been since Saturday? Sunday was the first day she hadn't come to the hospital, the day she knew he was getting out of the joint. He had left alone, followed by some reporters he wouldn't talk to, and had taken a cab to the hotel. Once in his room he got into pajamas, and wondering why she hadn't at least called him, fell asleep. He had then had this dream of her—seeing her in some city, it looked like Boston—and she didn't recognize him when they passed but walked on fast in her swaying walk. He chased after her and she was (he remembered) swallowed up in the crowd. But he saw the red hair and followed after that, only it turned out to be a dyed redhead with a mean mouth and dirty eyes. Where's Memo? he called, and woke thinking she was here in the room, but she wasn't, and he hadn't seen her till he located her up there in the tower.

Roy gazed at the empty bases. Striking out with nobody on was the least harm he could do the team, yet his fingers itched to sock it a little. He couldn't trust himself to because—who could tell?—it might go over the fence, the way Wonderboy was tugging at his muscles. Vogelman then tried a low-breaking curve that Roy had to "take" for ball one. The pitcher came back with a foolish floater that he pretended to almost break his back reaching after.

Strike two. There were only three.

. . . He was remembering the time his old lady drowned the black tom cat in the tub. It had gotten into the bathroom with her and bit at her bare ankles. She once and for all grabbed the cursed thing and dropped it into the hot tub. The cat fought to get out, but she shrilly beat it back and though it yowled mournfully, gave it no mercy. Yet it managed in its hysterical cat-way to stay afloat in the scalding water that she bathed in to cut her weight down, until she shoved its dirty biting head under, from which her hand bled all over. But when the water was drained, and the cat, all glossy wet, with its pink tongue caught between its teeth, lay there dead, the whole thing got to be too much for her and she couldn't lift it out of the tub.

He closed his eyes before the next pitch in the hope it would be quickly called against him, but it curved out for a ripe ball two. Opening his lids, he saw Mercy in a nearby seat, gazing at him with a malevolent sneer. You too, Max, Roy thought, tightening his hold on the bat. Vogelman was beginning to act more confident. You too, Vogelman, and he shut his eyes again, thinking how, after that time with Iris on the beach, when they were driving home, she rested her head against his arm. She was frightened, wanted him to comfort her but he wouldn't. "When will you grow up, Roy?" she said.

Vogelman blistered across a hot, somewhat high one, not too bad to miss, and that made it three and out. Otto Zipp held his nose and pulled the chain, and Roy, quivering, remained for a few seconds with the stick raised over his head, shriveling the dwarf into the silence and immobility that prevailed elsewhere. He threw Wonderboy aside—some in the front boxes let out a gasp—and returned empty-handed to the bench. The Judge and Memo had gone from the tower window.

As the Pirates came to bat for their half of the third (there were no Knight hits after Roy struck out) a breeze blew dust all over the place. Some of the fans with nothing better to do were shoveling the rotten fruit and slices of buttered sandwich bread into paper sacks, or kicking it under their seats. Nobody seemed to be hungry and the Stevens boys, despite all their barking, sold only a few hot coffees. Nor was there much talk of the past half inning. A few complained that Roy had never looked so bad—like a sloppy walrus. Others reminded them the game was young yet.

Neither team scored in either the third or fourth. The way the Knights fanned made Roy wonder if they had all been bought off by the Judge. Yet it didn't seem likely. He was too stingy. In the fifth came his next turn, again first up, a small break.

The stands awoke and began a rhythmic clapping. "Lift 'at pill, Roy. Bust its guts. Make it bleed. You can do it, kid."

"You can do it," Pop hollered from the dugout steps.

With a heavy heart Roy pulled himself up to the plate. He had shooting pains in back muscles that had never bothered him before and a crick in his neck. He couldn't comfortably straighten up and the weight of Wonderboy crouched him further. But Vogelman, despite Roy's strikeout, was burdened with worry over what he still *might* do. He wiped his face with his red sleeve but failed to calm down. By wide margins his first two throws were balls. To help him out, Roy swung under the third pitch. Otto Zipp then let out a string of boos, bahs, and bums, Roy thought he better foul the next one for strike two but Vogelman wouldn't let him, throwing almost over his head. Remembering he could walk if he wanted to, Roy waited. There was no harm to anybody in that and it would look better for him. The next pitch came in too close, and that was how he got to first and the Judge again to the window. But it made no difference one way or the other, for though Lajong sacrificed him to second, Gabby slashed a high one across the diamond which the second baseman jumped for, and he tagged Roy for an unassisted double play. Nobody could blame *him* for that, Roy thought, as he headed out to the field. He stole a look back at Pop and the manager was muttering to himself out of loose lips in a bony face. It seemed to Roy he had known the old man all his life long.

He found himself thinking of maybe quitting the deal with the Judge. He could send a note up there saying the fix was off. But he couldn't think what to write Memo. He tried to imagine what it would be like living without her and couldn't stand the thought of the loneliness.

Dave Olson opened the sixth with the Knights' first hit, a thumping double. The stands sounded like a gigantic drawerful of voices that had suddenly been pulled open. But Benz went down swinging, then Fowler bunted into another quick d.p. and the drawerful of voices was shut. Roy wondered about that bunt. He had a notion Fowler would commit himself soon because time was on the go. But Fowler didn't, making it another sweep of three Pirates. He had thus far given up only two safeties. In the seventh, the Knights, sensing Vogelman was tiring, found their way to him. Allie Stubbs chopped a grass cutter through a hole in the infield for a single. Baker, attempting to lay down a bunt, was overanxious and struck out. Then Flores lifted one just above the first baseman's frantic fingers, and Stubbs, running with his head down, sprang safely into third. Roy was on deck but with two on base his heart misgave him. The crowd jumped to its feet, roaring for him to come through.

As he approached the plate, the sun, that had been plumbing the clouds since the game began, at last broke through and bathed the stadium in a golden glow that caused the crowd to murmur. As the warmth fell upon him, Roy felt a sob break in his throat. The weakness left his legs, his heart beat steadily, his giddy gut tightened, and he stood firm and strong upon the earth. Though it startled him to find it so, he had regained a sense of his own well-being. A thousand springlike thoughts crowded through his mind, blotting out the dark diagnosis of the white-mustached specialist. He felt almost happy, and that he could do anything he wanted, if he wanted. His eyes scanned the forward rows in left field but stopped at Zipp's surly face. He felt suddenly anguished at what he had promised the Judge.

On his first swing—at a bad pitch—Otto let out a stream of jeers, oaths, and horn hoots that burned Roy to his bones. I will get that little ass-faced bastard. On the next pitch he shortened his hold on Wonderboy, stepped in front of the ball, and pulled it sharply foul. The ball whizzed past Otto's nose and boomed down an entrance way. The dwarf turned into flour, then as the blood rushed back to his face, grew furious. He jumped up and down on his seat, shook his fist, and screeched curses.

"Carrion, offal, turd—flush the bowl."

Roy tried to send the next ball through his teeth. It hit the rail with a bong and bounced into the air. A fan behind Otto caught it in his straw hat. Though the crowd laughed, the boos at Roy grew louder. Red Blow held up two warning fingers. Roy chopped a third foul at the dwarf. With a shriek he covered his face with his arms and ducked.

Several rows up from Otto, a dark-haired woman in a white dress had risen and was standing alone amid the crowd. Christ, another one, Roy thought. At the last split second he had tried to hold his swing but couldn't. The ball spun like a shot at Otto, struck his hard skull with a thud, and was deflected upward. It caught the lady in the face, and to the crowd's horror, she went soundlessly down.

A commotion rose in the stands. Fans by the hundreds piled out of their seats to get at her but the cops and ushers blocked their way, warning them not to crush her to death. Stuffy Briggs called time. Roy dropped his bat, hopped into the boxes and ran up the stairs—his clacking cleats shooting sparks—and along the aisle to where she lay. Many of the fans were standing on their seats to see and there was a crowd pressed around her. Murmuring lynch threats, they let Roy through. A doctor was attending her but she was stretched out unconscious.

Roy already knew who it was. "Iris," he groaned.

Iris woke, opened her good eye and sighed, "Roy."

Lifting her in his arms, he carried her to the clubhouse. Doc Casey and Dizzy kept everybody out. Max Mercy, hot for news, jammed his foot in the door but Dizzy crushed it hard, and Max danced as he cursed.

Roy gently laid her on the trainer's table. The left side of her face was hurt, bruised and rainbow-colored. Her eye was black and the lid thick. But the right side was still calm and lovely.

What have I done, he thought, and why did I do it? And he thought of all the wrong things he had done in his life and tried to undo them but who could?

The doctor went out to call an ambulance. Roy closed the door after him.

"Oh, Roy," sighed Iris.

"Iris, I am sorry."

"Roy, you must win—"

He groaned. "Why didn't you come here before?"

"My letter—you never answered."

He bowed his head.

The doctor entered. "Contusions and lacerations. Not much

to worry about, but to be on the safe side she ought to be X-rayed."

"Don't spare any expenses," Roy said.

"She'll be fine. You can go back to the game now."

"You must win, Roy," said Iris.

Seeing there was more to this than he had thought, the doctor left.

Roy turned to her trying to keep in mind that she was a grandmother but when he scanned the fine shape of her body, he couldn't. Instead there rose in him an odd disgust for Memo. It came quickly, nauseating him.

"Darling," whispered Iris, "win for our boy."

He stared at her. "What boy?"

"I am pregnant." There were tears in her eyes.

Her belly was slender . . . then the impact hit him.

"Holy Jesus."

Iris smiled with quivering lips.

Bending over, he kissed her mouth and tasted blood. He kissed her breasts, they smelled of roses. He kissed her hard belly, wild with love for her and the child.

"Win for us, you were meant to."

She took his head in her hands and drew it to her bosom. How like the one who jumped me in the park that night he looks, she thought, and to drive the thought away pressed his head deeper into her breasts, thinking, this will be different. Oh, Roy, be my love and protect me. But by then the ambulance had come so they took her away.

In the dugout Pop confronted him with withering curses. "Get in there and attend to business. No more monkey shines or I will pitch you out on your banana."

Roy nodded. Climbing out of the dugout, to his dismay he found Wonderboy lying near the water fountain, in the mud. He tenderly wiped it dry. Stuffy called time in and the Pirates, furious at the long delay (Wickitt had demanded the forfeit of the game, but Pop had scared Stuffy into waiting for Roy by threatening to go to court), returned to their positions, Allie and Flores to third and first, and Roy stepped into the batter's box to face a storm of Bronx cheers. They came in wind-driven sheets until Vogelman reared and threw, then they stopped.

It was 0 and 2 on him because, except for the one he had purposely missed, Roy had turned each pitch into a foul. He watched Vogelman with burning eyes. Vogelman was almost hypnotized. He saw a different man and didn't like what he saw. His next throw was wide of the plate. Ball one. Then a quick ball two, and the pitcher was nervous again. He took a very long time with the next throw but to his horror the pellet slipped away from him and hit the dirt just short of the plate. Allie broke for home but the catcher quickly trapped it and threw to third. Flopping back, Allie made it with his fingers. Flores, in the meantime, had taken second.

And that was ball three. Roy now prayed for a decent throw.

Vogelman glanced at Allie edging into a lead again, kicked, and threw almost in desperation. Roy swung from his cleats.

Thunder crashed. The pitcher stuffed his maimed fingers into his ears. His eyes were blinded. Pop rose and crowed himself hoarse. Otto Zipp, carrying a dark lump on his noodle, cowered beneath the ledge. Some of the fans had seen lightning, thought it was going to rain, and raised their coat collars. Most of them were on their feet, raving at the flight of the ball. Allie had raced in to score, so had Flores, and Roy was heading into second, when the umpire waved them all back. The ball had landed clearly foul. The fans groaned in shuddering tones.

Wonderboy lay on the ground split lengthwise, one half pointing to first, the other to third.

The Knights' bat boy nervously collected both the pieces and thrust a Louisville Slugger into Roy's limp hand. The crowd sat in raw silence as the nerveless Vogelman delivered his next pitch. It floated in, perfect for pickling, but Roy failed to lift the bat.

Lajong, who followed, also struck out.

With the Knights back in the field, Fowler quickly gave up a whacking triple to the first Pirate hitter. This was followed by a hard double, and almost before any of the stunned fans could realize it, the first run of the game was in. Pop bounced off the bench as if electrocuted and signaled the bullpen into hot activity. Red Blow sauntered out to the mound to quiet Fowler down but Fowler said he was all right so Red left.

The next Pirate laced a long hopper to left. The shouting of the crowd woke Roy out of his grief for Wonderboy. He tore in for the ball, made a running jab for it and held it. With an effort he heaved to third, holding both runners to one bag. He knew now he was right about Fowler. The pitcher had pulled the plug. Roy signaled time and drifted in to talk to him. Both Red and Dave Olson also walked forward for a mound conference but Roy waved them back. As he approached the dark-faced Fowler, he saw the Judge up at the window, puffing his cigar.

Roy spoke in a low voice. "Watch out, kid, we don't want to lose the game."

Fowler studied him craftily. "Cut the crap, big shot. A lotta winning you been doing."

"Throw the ball good," Roy advised him.

"I will, when you start hitting it."

"Listen," Roy said patiently. "This might be my last season in the game for I am already thirty-five. You want it to be yours?"

Fowler paled. "You wouldn't dare open your trap."

"Try something funny again and you will see."

Fowler turned angrily away. The fans began to whistle and stamp. "Set 'em up," called Stuffy Briggs. Roy returned to left but after that, Fowler somehow managed to keep the next two men from connecting, and everybody said too bad that Roy hadn't given him that pep talk after the first hit. Some of the fans remarked had anybody noticed that Roy had thumbed his nose up to the tower at the end of the inning?

Every time Vogelman put Roy away, he felt infinitely better, consequently his pitching improved as the game progressed. Though he was surprised in the eighth to have Gabby Laslow touch him for a sharp single, he forced Olson to pop to short, Benz to line to him, and Fowler obliged by biting at three gamey ones for the last out. Counting up who he would have to throw to in the ninth, Vogelman discovered that if he got Stubbs, Baker, and the more difficult Flores out, there would be no Roy Hobbs to pitch to. The idea so excited him he determined to beat his brains out trying. Fowler, on the other hand, despite Roy's good advice to him, got sloppier in his throwing, although subtly, so that nobody could be sure why, only his support was a whole lot better than he had hoped for, and neither of the first two Pirates up in the ninth, though they had walloped the ball hard, could land on base. Flores, the Mexican jumping bean, had nailed both shots. The third Pirate then caught a juicy pitch and poled out a high looping beauty to left, but Roy, running back—back—back, speared it against the wall. Though he was winded and cursed Fowler through his teeth, he couldn't help but smile, picturing the pitcher's disgust. And he felt confident that the boys would hold him a turn at bat and he would destroy Vogelman and save the game, the most important thing he ever had to do in his life.

Pop, on the other hand, was losing hope. His hands trembled and his false teeth felt like rocks in his mouth, so he plucked them out and dropped them into his shirt pocket. Instead of Allie, he called Ed Simmons to pinch hit, but Vogelman, working with renewed speed and canniness, got Ed to hit a soft one to center field. Pop swayed on the bench, drooling a little out of the corners of his puckered mouth. Red was a ghost, even his freckles were pale. The stands were shrouded in darkening silence. Baker spat and approached the plate. Remembering he hadn't once hit safely today, Pop called him back and substituted Hank Kelly, another pinch hitter.

Vogelman struck him out. He dried his mouth on his sleeve, smiling faintly to himself for the first time since the game began. One more—the Mex. To finish him meant slamming the door on Hobbs, a clean shut-out, and tomorrow the World Series. The sun fell back in the sky and a hush hung like a smell in the air. Flores, with a crazed look in his eye, faced the pitcher. Fouling the first throw, he took for a ball, and swung savagely at the third pitch. He missed. Two strikes, there were only three . . . Roy felt himself slowly dying. You died alone. At least if he were up there batting . . . The Mexican's face was lit in anguish. With bulging eyes he rushed at the next throw, and cursing in Spanish, swung. The ball wobbled crazily in the air, took off, and leaped for the right field wall. Running as though death dogged him, Flores made it, sliding headlong into third. Vogelman, drained of his heart's blood, stared at him through glazed eyes.

The silence shattered into insane, raucous noise.

Roy rose from the bench. When he saw Pop searching

among the other faces, his heart flopped and froze. He would gladly get down on his knees and kiss the old man's skinny, crooked feet, do anything to get up there this last time. Pop's haunted gleam settled on him, wavered, traveled down the line of grim faces . . . and came back to Roy. He called his name.

Up close he had black rings around his eyes, and when he spoke his voice broke.

"See what we have come to, Roy."

Roy stared at the dugout floor. "Let me go in."

"What would you expect to do?"

"Murder it."

"Murder which?"

"The ball—I swear."

Pop's eyes wavered to the men on the bench. Reluctantly his gaze returned to Roy. "If you weren't so damn busy gunning fouls into the stands that last time, you woulda straightened out that big one, and with three scoring, that woulda been the game."

"Now I understand why they call them fouls."

"Go on in," Pop said. He added in afterthought, "Keep us alive."

Roy selected out of the rack a bat that looked something like Wonderboy. He swung it once and advanced to the plate. Flores was dancing on the bag, beating his body as if it were burning, and jabbering in Spanish that if by the mercy of St. Christopher he was allowed to make the voyage home from third, he would forever after light candles before the saint.

The blank-faced crowd was almost hidden by the darkness crouching in the stands. Home plate lay under a deepening dusty shadow but Roy saw things with more light than he ever had before. A hit, tying up the game, would cure what ailed him. Only a homer, with himself scoring the winning run, would truly redeem him.

Vogelman was contemplating how close he had come to paradise. If the Mex had missed that pitch, the game would now be over. All night long he'd've felt eight foot tall, and when he got into bed with his wife, she'd've given it to him the way they do to heroes.

The sight of his nemesis crouched low in the brooding darkness around the plate filled him with fear.

Sighing, he brought himself, without conviction, to throw.

"Bo-ool one."

The staring faces in the stands broke into a cry that stayed till the end of the game.

Vogelman was drenched in sweat. He could have thrown a spitter without half trying but didn't know how and was afraid to monkey with them.

The next went in cap high.

"Eee bo-ool."

Wickitt, the Pirate manager, ambled out to the mound.

"S'matter, Dutch?"

"Take me outa here," Vogelman moaned.

"What the hell for? You got that bastard three times so far and you can do it again."

"He gives me the shits, Walt. Look at him standing there like a goddamn gorilla. Look at his burning eyes. He ain't human."

Wickitt talked low as he studied Roy. "That ain't what I see. He looks old and beat up. Last week he had a mile-high belly-ache in a ladies' hospital. They say he could drop dead any minute. Bear up and curve 'em low. I don't think he can bend to his knees. Get one strike on him and he will be your nookie."

He left the mound.

Vogelman threw the next ball with his flesh screaming.

"Bo-ool three."

He sought for Wickitt but the manager kept his face hidden.

In that case, the pitcher thought, I will walk him. They could yank him after that—he was a sick man.

Roy was also considering a walk. It would relieve him of re-sponsibility but not make up for all the harm he had done. He discarded the idea. Vogelman made a bony steeple with his arms. Gazing at the plate, he found his eyes were misty and he couldn't read the catcher's sign. He looked again and saw Roy, in full armor, mounted on a black charger. Vogelman stared hard, his arms held high so as not to balk. Yes, there he was coming at him with a long lance as thick as a young tree. He rubbed his arm across his eyes and keeled over in a dead faint.

A roar ascended skywards.

The sun slid behind the clouds. It got cold again. Wickitt,

leaning darkly out of the dugout, raised his arm aloft to the
center field bullpen. The boy who had been pitching flipped
the ball to the bullpen catcher, straightened his cap, and began
the long trek in. He was twenty, a scrawny youth with light
eyes.

"Herman Youngberry, number sixty-six, pitching for the
Pirates."

Few in the stands had heard of him, but before his long trek
to the mound was finished his life was common knowledge.
He was a six-footer but weighed a skinny one fifty-eight. One
day about two years ago a Pirate scout watching him pitching
for his home town team had written on a card, "This boy has a
fluid delivery of a blinding fast ball and an exploding curve."
Though he offered him a contract then and there, Youngberry
refused to sign because it was his lifelong ambition to be a
farmer. Everybody, including the girl he was engaged to, argued him into signing. He didn't say so but he had it in mind
to earn enough money to buy a three hundred acre farm and
then quit baseball forever. Sometimes when he pitched, he saw
fields of golden wheat gleaming in the sun.

He had come to the Pirates on the first of September from
one of their class A clubs, to help in the pennant drive. Since
then he'd worked up a three won, two lost record. He'd seen
what Roy had done to Vogelman the day he hit the four homers, and just now, and wasn't anxious to face him. After throwing his warm-ups he stepped off the mound and looked away
as Roy got back into the box.

Despite the rest he had had, Roy's armpits were creepy with
sweat. He felt a bulk of heaviness around his middle and that
the individual hairs on his legs and chest were bristling.

Youngberry gazed around to see how they were playing
Roy. It was straightaway and deep, with the infield pulled back
too. Flores, though hopping about, was on the bag. The
pitcher took a full wind-up and became aware the Knights
were yelling dirty names to rattle him.

Roy had considered and decided against a surprise bunt. As
things were, it was best to take three good swings.

He felt the shadow of the Judge and Memo fouling the air
around him and turned to shake his fist at them but they had
left the window.

The ball lit its own path.

The speed of the pitch surprised Stuffy Briggs and it was a little time before he could work his tongue free.

"Stuh-rike."

Roy's nose was full of the dust he had raised.

"Throw him to the pigs," shrilled Otto Zipp.

If he bunted, the surprise could get him to first, and Flores home for the tying run. The only trouble was he had not much confidence in his ability to bunt. Roy stared at the kid, trying to hook his eye, but Youngberry wouldn't look at him. As Roy stared a fog blew up around the young pitcher, full of old ghosts and snowy scenes. The fog shot forth a snaky finger and Roy carefully searched under it for the ball but it was already in the catcher's mitt.

"Strike two."

"Off with his head," Otto shrieked.

It felt like winter. He wished for fire to warm his frozen fingers. Too late for the bunt now. He wished he had tried it. It would have caught them flatfooted.

Pop ran out with a rabbit's foot but Roy wouldn't take it. He would never give up, he swore. Flores had fallen to his knees on third and was imploring the sky.

Roy caught the pitcher's eye. His own had blood in them. Youngberry shuddered. He threw—a bad ball—but the batter leaped at it.

He struck out with a roar.

Bump Baily's form glowed red on the wall. There was a wail in the wind. He feared the mob would swarm all over him, tear him apart, and strew his polluted remains over the field, but they had vanished. Only O. Zipp climbed down out of his seat. He waddled to the plate, picked up the bat and took a vicious cut at something. He must've connected, because his dumpy bow legs went like pistons around the bases. Thundering down from third he slid into the plate and called himself safe.

Otto dusted himself off, lit a cigar and went home.

WHEN IT was night he dragged the two halves of the bat into left field, and with his jackknife cut a long rectangular slash into the turf and dug out the earth. With his hands he deepened the grave in the dry earth and packed the sides tight. He then placed the broken bat in it. He couldn't stand seeing it in two pieces so he removed them and tried squeezing them together in the hope they would stick but the split was smooth, as if the bat had willed its own brokenness, and the two parts would not stay together. Roy undid his shoelaces and wound one around the slender handle of the bat, and the other he tied around the hitting part of the wood, so that except for the knotted laces and the split he knew was there it looked like a whole bat. And this was the way he buried it, wishing it would take root and become a tree. He poured back the earth, carefully pressing it down, and replaced the grass. He trod on it in his stocking feet, and after a last long look around, walked off the field. At the fountain he considered whether to carry out a few handfuls of water to wet the earth above Wonderboy but they would only leak through his fingers before he got there, and since he doubted he could find the exact spot in the dark he went down the dugout steps and into the tunnel.

He felt afraid to go in the clubhouse and so was glad the lights were left on with nobody there. From the looks of things everybody had got their clothes on and torn out. All was silence except the drip drop of the shower and he did not want to go in there. He got rid of his uniform in the soiled clothes can, then dressed in street clothes. He felt something thick against his chest and brought out a sealed envelope. Tearing it open, he discovered a package of thousand dollar bills. He had never seen one before and here were thirty-five. In with the bills was a typewritten note: "The contract will have to wait. There are grave doubts that your cooperation was wholehearted." Roy burned the paper with a match. He considered burning the bills but didn't. He tried to stuff them into his wallet. The wad was too thick so he put them back in the envelope and slipped it into his pocket.

The street was chill and its swaying lights, dark. He shivered as he went to the corner. At the tower he pulled himself up the unlit stairs.

The Judge's secretary was gone but his private door was unlocked so Roy let himself in. The office was pitch black. He located the apartment door and stumbled up the narrow stairs. When he came into the Judge's overstuffed apartment, they were all sitting around a table, the redheaded Memo, the Judge with a green eyeshade over his black wig, and the Supreme Bookie, enjoying a little cigar. They were counting piles of betting slips and a mass of bills. Memo was adding the figures with an adding machine.

Gus got up quickly when he saw Roy. "Nice goin', slugger," he said softly. Smiling, he advanced with his arm extended. "That was some fine show you put on today."

Roy slugged the slug and he went down in open-mouthed wonder. His head hit the floor and the glass eye dropped out and rolled into a mousehole.

Memo was furious. "Don't touch him, you big bastard. He's worth a million of your kind."

Roy said, "You act all right, Memo, but only like a whore."

"Tut," said the Judge.

She ran to him and tried to scratch his eyes but he pushed her aside and she fell over Gus. With a cry she lifted the bookie's head on her lap and made mothering noises over him.

Roy took the envelope out of his pocket. He slapped the Judge's wig and eyeshade off and showered the thousand dollar bills on his wormy head.

The Judge raised a revolver.

"That will do, Hobbs. Another move and I shall be forced to defend myself."

Roy snatched the gun and dropped it in the wastebasket. He twisted the Judge's nose till he screamed. Then he lifted him onto the table and pounded his back with his fists. The Judge made groans and pig squeals. With his foot Roy shoved the carcass off the table. He hit the floor with a crash and had a bowel movement in his pants. He lay moaning amid the betting slips and bills.

Memo had let Gus's head fall and ran around the table to the basket. Raising the pistol, she shot at Roy's back. The bullet grazed his shoulder and broke the Judge's bathroom mirror. The glass clattered to the floor.

Roy turned to her.

"Don't come any nearer or I'll shoot."

He slowly moved forward.

"You filthy scum, I hate your guts and always have since the day you murdered Bump."

Her finger tightened on the trigger but when he came very close she sobbed aloud and thrust the muzzle into her mouth. He gently took the gun from her, opened the cylinder, and shook the cartridges into his palm. He pocketed them and again dumped the gun into the basket.

She was sobbing hysterically as he left.

Going down the tower stairs he fought his overwhelming self-hatred. In each stinking wave of it he remembered some disgusting happening of his life.

He thought, I never did learn anything out of my past life, now I have to suffer again.

When he hit the street he was exhausted. He had not shaved, and a black beard gripped his face. He felt old and grimy.

He stared into faces of people he passed along the street but nobody recognized him.

"He coulda been a king," a woman remarked to a man.

At the corner near some stores he watched the comings and goings of the night traffic. He felt the insides of him beginning to take off (chug chug choo choo . . .). Pretty soon they were in fast flight. A boy thrust a newspaper at him. He wanted to say no but had no voice. The headline screamed, "Suspicion of Hobbs's Sellout—Max Mercy." Under this was a photo Mercy had triumphantly discovered, showing Roy on his back, an obscene bullet imbedded in his gut. Around him danced a naked lady: "Hobbs at nineteen."

And there was also a statement by the baseball commissioner. "If this alleged report is true, that is the last of Roy Hobbs in organized baseball. He will be excluded from the game and all his records forever destroyed."

Roy handed the paper back to the kid.

"Say it ain't true, Roy."

When Roy looked into the boy's eyes he wanted to say it wasn't but couldn't, and he lifted his hands to his face and wept many bitter tears.

THE ASSISTANT

For Ann with love

THE EARLY November street was dark though night had ended, but the wind, to the grocer's surprise, already clawed. It flung his apron into his face as he bent for the two milk cases at the curb. Morris Bober dragged the heavy boxes to the door, panting. A large brown bag of hard rolls stood in the doorway along with the sour-faced, gray-haired Poilisheh huddled there, who wanted one.

"What's the matter so late?"

"Ten after six," said the grocer.

"Is cold," she complained.

Turning the key in the lock he let her in. Usually he lugged in the milk and lit the gas radiators, but the Polish woman was impatient. Morris poured the bag of rolls into a wire basket on the counter and found an unseeded one for her. Slicing it in halves, he wrapped it in white store paper. She tucked the roll into her cord market bag and left three pennies on the counter. He rang up the sale on an old noisy cash register, smoothed and put away the bag the rolls had come in, finished pulling in the milk, and stored the bottles at the bottom of the refrigerator. He lit the gas radiator at the front of the store and went into the back to light the one there.

He boiled up coffee in a blackened enamel pot and sipped it, chewing on a roll, not tasting what he was eating. After he had cleaned up he waited; he waited for Nick Fuso, the upstairs tenant, a young mechanic who worked in a garage in the neighborhood. Nick came in every morning around seven for twenty cents' worth of ham and a loaf of bread.

But the front door opened and a girl of ten entered, her face pinched and eyes excited. His heart held no welcome for her.

"My mother says," she said quickly, "can you trust her till tomorrow for a pound of butter, loaf of rye bread and a small bottle of cider vinegar?"

He knew the mother. "No more trust."

The girl burst into tears.

Morris gave her a quarter-pound of butter, the bread and vinegar. He found a penciled spot on the worn counter, near the cash register, and wrote a sum under "Drunk Woman."

The total now came to $2.03, which he never hoped to see. But Ida would nag if she noticed a new figure, so he reduced the amount to $1.61. His peace—the little he lived with—was worth forty-two cents.

He sat in a chair at the round wooden table in the rear of the store and scanned, with raised brows, yesterday's Jewish paper that he had already thoroughly read. From time to time he looked absently through the square windowless window cut through the wall, to see if anybody had by chance come into the store. Sometimes when he looked up from his newspaper, he was startled to see a customer standing silently at the counter.

Now the store looked like a long dark tunnel.

The grocer sighed and waited. Waiting he thought he did poorly. When times were bad time was bad. It died as he waited, stinking in his nose.

A workman came in for a fifteen-cent can of King Oscar Norwegian sardines.

Morris went back to waiting. In twenty-one years the store had changed little. Twice he had painted all over, once added new shelving. The old-fashioned double windows at the front a carpenter had made into a large single one. Ten years ago the sign hanging outside fell to the ground but he had never replaced it. Once, when business hit a long good spell, he had had the wooden icebox ripped out and a new white refrigerated showcase put in. The showcase stood at the front in line with the old counter and he often leaned against it as he stared out of the window. Otherwise the store was the same. Years ago it was more a delicatessen; now, though he still sold a little delicatessen, it was more a poor grocery.

A half-hour passed. When Nick Fuso failed to appear, Morris got up and stationed himself at the front window, behind a large cardboard display sign the beer people had rigged up in an otherwise empty window. After a while the hall door opened, and Nick came out in a thick, hand-knitted green sweater. He trotted around the corner and soon returned carrying a bag of groceries. Morris was now visible at the window. Nick saw the look on his face but didn't look long. He ran into the house, trying to make it seem it was the wind that was chasing him. The door slammed behind him, a loud door.

The grocer gazed into the street. He wished fleetingly that he could once more be out in the open, as when he was a boy—never in the house, but the sound of the blustery wind frightened him. He thought again of selling the store but who would buy? Ida still hoped to sell. Every day she hoped. The thought caused him grimly to smile, although he did not feel like smiling. It was an impossible idea so he tried to put it out of his mind. Still, there were times when he went into the back, poured himself a spout of coffee and pleasantly thought of selling. Yet if he miraculously did, where would he go, where? He had a moment of uneasiness as he pictured himself without a roof over his head. There he stood in all kinds of weather, drenched in rain, and the snow froze on his head. No, not for an age had he lived a whole day in the open. As a boy, always running in the muddy, rutted streets of the village, or across the fields, or bathing with the other boys in the river; but as a man, in America, he rarely saw the sky. In the early days when he drove a horse and wagon, yes, but not since his first store. In a store you were entombed.

The milkman drove up to the door in his truck and hurried in, a bull, for his empties. He lugged out a caseful and returned with two half-pints of light cream. Then Otto Vogel, the meat provisions man, entered, a bushy-mustached German carrying a smoked liverwurst and string of wieners in his oily meat basket. Morris paid cash for the liverwurst; from a German he wanted no favors. Otto left with the wieners. The bread driver, new on the route, exchanged three fresh loaves for three stale and walked out without a word. Leo, the cake man, glanced hastily at the package cake on top of the refrigerator and called, "See you Monday, Morris."

Morris didn't answer.

Leo hesitated. "Bad all over, Morris."

"Here is the worst."

"See you Monday."

A young housewife from close by bought sixty-three cents' worth; another came in for forty-one cents'. He had earned his first cash dollar for the day.

Breitbart, the bulb peddler, laid down his two enormous cartons of light bulbs and diffidently entered the back.

"Go in," Morris urged. He boiled up some tea and served it in a thick glass, with a slice of lemon. The peddler eased himself into a chair, derby hat and coat on, and gulped the hot tea, his Adam's apple bobbing.

"So how goes now?" asked the grocer.

"Slow," shrugged Breitbart.

Morris sighed. "How is your boy?"

Breitbart nodded absently, then picked up the Jewish paper and read. After ten minutes he got up, scratched all over, lifted across his thin shoulders the two large cartons tied together with clothesline and left.

Morris watched him go.

The world suffers. *He* felt every schmerz.

At lunchtime Ida came down. She had cleaned the whole house.

Morris was standing before the faded couch, looking out of the rear window at the back yards. He had been thinking of Ephraim.

His wife saw his wet eyes.

"So stop sometime, please." Her own grew wet.

He went to the sink, caught cold water in his cupped palms and dipped his face into it.

"The Italyener," he said, drying himself, "bought this morning across the street."

She was irritated. "Give him for twenty-nine dollars five rooms so he should spit in your face."

"A cold water flat," he reminded her.

"You put in gas radiators."

"Who says he spits? This I didn't say."

"You said something to him not nice?"

"Me?"

"Then why he went across the street?"

"Why? Go ask him," he said angrily.

"How much you took in till now?"

"Dirt."

She turned away.

He absent-mindedly scratched a match and lit a cigarette.

"Stop with the smoking," she nagged.

He took a quick drag, clipped the butt with his thumb nail and quickly thrust it under his apron into his pants pocket.

The smoke made him cough. He coughed harshly, his face lit like a tomato. Ida held her hands over her ears. Finally he brought up a gob of phlegm and wiped his mouth with his handkerchief, then his eyes.

"Cigarettes," she said bitterly. "Why don't you listen what the doctor tells you?"

"Doctors," he remarked.

Afterward he noticed the dress she was wearing. "What is the picnic?"

Ida said, embarrassed, "I thought to myself maybe will come today the buyer."

She was fifty-one, nine years younger than he, her thick hair still almost all black. But her face was lined, and her legs hurt when she stood too long on them, although she now wore shoes with arch supports. She had waked that morning resenting the grocer for having dragged her, so many years ago, out of a Jewish neighborhood into this. She missed to this day their old friends and landsleit—lost for parnusseh unrealized. That was bad enough, but on top of their isolation, the endless worry about money embittered her. She shared unwillingly the grocer's fate though she did not show it and her dissatisfaction went no farther than nagging—her guilt that she had talked him into a grocery store when he was in the first year of evening high school, preparing, he had said, for pharmacy. He was, through the years, a hard man to move. In the past she could sometimes resist him, but the weight of his endurance was too much for her now.

"A buyer," Morris grunted, "will come next Purim."

"Don't be so smart. Karp telephoned him."

"Karp," he said in disgust. "Where he telephoned—the cheapskate?"

"Here."

"When?"

"Yesterday. You were sleeping."

"What did he told him?"

"For sale a store—yours, cheap."

"What do you mean cheap?"

"The key is worth now nothing. For the stock and the fixtures that they are worth also nothing, maybe three thousand, maybe less."

"I paid four."

"Twenty-one years ago," she said irritably. "So don't sell, go in auction."

"He wants the house too?"

"Karp don't know. Maybe."

"Big mouth. Imagine a man that they held him up four times in the last three years and he still don't take in a telephone. What he says ain't worth a cent. He promised me he wouldn't put in a grocery around the corner, but what did he put?— a grocery. Why does he bring me buyers? Why didn't he keep out the German around the corner?"

She sighed. "He tries to help you now because he feels sorry for you."

"Who needs his sorrow?" Morris said. "Who needs him?"

"So why *you* didn't have the sense to make out of your grocery a wine and liquor store when came out the licenses?"

"Who had cash for stock?"

"So if you don't have, don't talk."

"A business for drunken bums."

"A business is a business. What Julius Karp takes in next door in a day we don't take in in two weeks."

But Ida saw he was annoyed and changed the subject.

"I told you to oil the floor."

"I forgot."

"I asked you special. By now would be dry."

"I will do later."

"Later the customers will walk in the oil and make everything dirty."

"What customers?" he shouted. "Who customers? Who comes in here?"

"Go," she said quietly. "Go upstairs and sleep. I will oil myself."

But he got out the oil can and mop and oiled the floor until the wood shone darkly. No one had come in.

She had prepared his soup. "Helen left this morning without breakfast."

"She wasn't hungry."

"Something worries her."

He said with sarcasm, "What worries her?" Meaning: the store, his health, that most of her meager wages went to keep up payments on the house; that she had wanted a college education but had got instead a job she disliked. Her father's daughter, no wonder she didn't feel like eating.

"If she will only get married," Ida murmured.

"She will get."

"Soon." She was on the verge of tears.

He grunted.

"I don't understand why she don't see Nat Pearl anymore. All summer they went together like lovers."

"A showoff."

"He'll be someday a rich lawyer."

"I don't like him."

"Louis Karp also likes her. I wish she will give him a chance."

"A stupe," Morris said, "like the father."

"Everybody is a stupe but not Morris Bober."

He was staring out at the back yards.

"Eat already and go to sleep," she said impatiently.

He finished the soup and went upstairs. The going up was easier than coming down. In the bedroom, sighing, he drew down the black window shades. He was half asleep, so pleasant was the anticipation. Sleep was his one true refreshment; it excited him to go to sleep. Morris took off his apron, tie and trousers, and laid them on a chair. Sitting at the edge of the sagging wide bed, he unlaced his misshapen shoes and slid under the cold covers in shirt, long underwear and white socks. He nudged his eye into the pillow and waited to grow warm. He crawled toward sleep. But upstairs Tessie Fuso was running the vacuum cleaner, and though the grocer tried to blot the incident out of his mind, he remembered Nick's visit to the German and on the verge of sleep felt bad.

He recalled the bad times he had lived through, but now times were worse than in the past; now they were impossible. His store was always a marginal one, up today, down tomorrow— as the wind blew. Overnight business could go down enough to hurt; yet as a rule it slowly recovered—sometimes it seemed to take forever—went up, not high enough to be really *up*, only not down. When he had first bought the grocery it was all right for the neighborhood; it had got worse as the neighborhood had. Yet even a year ago, staying open seven days a week, sixteen hours a day, he could still eke out a living. What kind of

living?—a living; you lived. Now, though he toiled the same
hard hours, he was close to bankruptcy, his patience torn.
In the past when bad times came he had somehow lived
through them, and when good times returned, they more
or less returned to him. But now, since the appearance of H.
Schmitz across the street ten months ago, all times were
bad.

Last year a broken tailor, a poor man with a sick wife, had
locked up his shop and gone away, and from the minute of the
store's emptiness Morris had felt a gnawing anxiety. He went
with hesitation to Karp, who owned the building, and asked
him to please keep out another grocery. In this kind of neighborhood one was more than enough. If another squeezed in
they would both starve. Karp answered that the neighborhood
was better than Morris gave it credit (for schnapps, thought
the grocer), but he promised he would look for another tailor
or maybe a shoemaker, to rent to. He said so but the grocer
didn't believe him. Yet weeks went by and the store stayed
empty. Though Ida pooh-poohed his worries, Morris could
not overcome his underlying dread. Then one day, as he daily
expected, there appeared a sign in the empty store window,
announcing the coming of a new fancy delicatessen and
grocery.

Morris ran to Karp. "What did you do to me?"

The liquor dealer said with a one-shouldered shrug, "You
saw how long stayed empty the store. Who will pay my taxes?
But don't worry," he added, "he'll sell more delicatessen but
you'll sell more groceries. Wait, you'll see he'll bring you in
customers."

Morris groaned; he knew his fate.

Yet as the days went by, the store still sitting empty—
emptier, he found himself thinking maybe the new business
would never materialize. Maybe the man had changed his
mind. It was possible he had seen how poor the neighborhood
was and would not attempt to open the new place. Morris
wanted to ask Karp if he had guessed right but could not bear
to humiliate himself further.

Often after he had locked his grocery at night, he would go
secretly around the corner and cross the quiet street. The
empty store, dark and deserted, was one door to the left of the

corner drugstore; and if no one was looking the grocer would peer through its dusty window, trying to see through shadows whether the emptiness had changed. For two months it stayed the same, and every night he went away reprieved. Then one time—after he saw that Karp was, for once, avoiding him—he spied a web of shelves sprouting from the rear wall, and that shattered the hope he had climbed into.

In a few days the shelves stretched many arms along the other walls, and soon the whole tiered and layered place glowed with new paint. Morris told himself to stay away but he could not help coming nightly to inspect, appraise, then guess the damage, in dollars, to himself. Each night as he looked, in his mind he destroyed what had been built, tried to make of it nothing, but the growth was too quick. Every day the place flowered with new fixtures—streamlined counters, the latest refrigerator, fluorescent lights, a fruit stall, a chromium cash register; then from the wholesalers arrived a mountain of cartons and wooden boxes of all sizes, and one night there appeared in the white light a stranger, a gaunt German with a German pompadour, who spent the silent night hours, a dead cigar stuck in his teeth, packing out symmetrical rows of brightly labeled cans, jars, gleaming bottles. Though Morris hated the new store, in a curious way he loved it too, so that sometimes as he entered his own old-fashioned place of business, he could not stand the sight of it; and now he understood why Nick Fuso had that morning run around the corner and crossed the street—to taste the newness of the place and be waited on by Heinrich Schmitz, an energetic German dressed like a doctor, in a white duck jacket. And that was where many of his other customers had gone, and stayed, so that his own poor living was cut in impossible half.

Morris tried hard to sleep but couldn't and grew restless in bed. After another quarter of an hour he decided to dress and go downstairs, but there drifted into his mind, with ease and no sorrow, the form and image of his boy Ephraim, gone so long from him, and he fell deeply and calmly asleep.

Helen Bober squeezed into a subway seat between two women and was on the last page of a chapter when a man dissolved in front of her and another appeared; she knew without looking that Nat Pearl was standing there. She thought she would go on reading, but couldn't, and shut her book.

"Hello, Helen." Nat touched a gloved hand to a new hat. He was cordial but as usual held back something—his future. He carried a fat law book, so she was glad to be protected with a book of her own. But not enough protected, for her hat and coat felt suddenly shabby, a trick of the mind, because on her they would still do.

"*Don Quixote?*"

She nodded.

He seemed respectful, then said in an undertone, "I haven't seen you a long time. Where've you been keeping yourself?"

She blushed under her clothes.

"Did I offend you in some way or other?"

Both of the women beside her seemed stolidly deaf. One held a rosary in her heavy hand.

"No." The offense was hers against herself.

"So what's the score?" Nat's voice was low, his gray eyes annoyed.

"No score," she murmured.

"How so?"

"You're you, I'm me."

This he considered a minute, then remarked, "I haven't much of a head for oracles."

But she felt she had said enough.

He tried another way. "Betty asks for you."

"Give her my best." She had not meant it but this sounded funny because they all lived on the same block, separated by one house.

Tight-jawed, he opened his book. She returned to hers, hiding her thoughts behind the antics of a madman until memory overthrew him and she found herself ensnared in scenes of summer that she would gladly undo, although she loved the season; but how could you undo what you had done again in the fall, unwillingly willing? Virginity she thought she had parted with without sorrow, yet was surprised by torments of conscience, or was it disappointment at being valued under her expectations? Nat Pearl, handsome, cleft-chinned, gifted, ambitious, had wanted without too much trouble a lay and she, half in love, had obliged and regretted. Not the loving, but that it had taken her so long to realize how little he wanted. Not her, Helen Bober.

Why should he?—magna cum laude, Columbia, now in his second year at law school, she only a high school graduate with a year's evening college credit mostly in lit; he with first-rate prospects, also rich friends he had never bothered to introduce her to; she as poor as her name sounded, with little promise of a better future. She had more than once asked herself if she had meant by her favors to work up a claim on him. Always she denied it. She had wanted, admittedly, satisfaction, but more than that—respect for the giver of what she had to give, had hoped desire would become more than just that. She wanted, simply, a future in love. Enjoyment she had somehow had, felt very moving the freedom of fundamental intimacy with a man. Though she wished for more of the same, she wanted it without aftermath of conscience, or pride, or sense of waste. So she promised herself next time it would go the other way; first mutual love, then loving, harder maybe on the nerves, but easier in memory. Thus she had reasoned, until one night in September, when coming up to see his sister Betty, she had found herself alone in the house with Nat and had done again what she had promised herself she wouldn't. Afterward she fought self-hatred. Since then, to this day, without telling him why, she had avoided Nat Pearl.

Two stations before their stop, Helen shut her book, got up in silence and left the train. On the platform, as the train moved away, she caught a glimpse of Nat standing before her empty seat, calmly reading. She walked on, lacking, wanting, not wanting, not happy.

Coming up the subway steps, she went into the park by a side entrance, and despite the sharp wind and her threadbare coat, took the long way home. The leafless trees left her with un-earned sadness. She mourned the long age before spring and feared loneliness in winter. Wishing she hadn't come, she left the park, searching the faces of strangers although she couldn't stand their stares. She went quickly along the Parkway, glancing with envy into the lighted depths of private houses that were, for no reason she could give, except experience, not for her. She promised herself she would save every cent possible and register next fall for a full program at NYU, night.

When she reached her block, a row of faded yellow brick houses, two stories squatting on ancient stores, Sam Pearl, stifling a yawn, was reaching into his corner candy store window to put on the lamp. He snapped the string and the dull glow from the fly-specked globe fell upon her. Helen quickened her step. Sam, always sociable, a former cabbie, bulky, wearing bifocals and chewing gum, beamed at her but she pretended no see. Most of the day he sat hunched over dope sheets spread out on the soda fountain counter, smoking as he chewed gum, making smeary marks with a pencil stub under horses' names. He neglected the store; his wife Goldie was the broad-backed one, yet she did not much complain, because Sam's luck with the nags was exceptional and he had nicely supported Nat in college until the scholarships started rolling in.

Around the corner, through the many-bottled window that blinked in neon "KARP wines and liquors," she glimpsed paunchy Julius Karp, with bushy eyebrows and an ambitious mouth, blowing imaginary dust off a bottle as he slipped a deft fifth of something into a paper bag, while Louis, slightly popeyed son and heir, looking up from clipping to the quick his poor fingernails, smiled amiably upon a sale. The Karps, Pearls and Bobers, representing attached houses and stores, but otherwise detachment, made up the small Jewish segment of this gentile community. They had somehow, her father first, then Karp, later Pearl, drifted together here where no other Jews dwelt, except on the far fringes of the neighborhood. None of them did well and were too poor to move elsewhere until Karp, who with a shoe store that barely made him a living, got the brilliant idea after Prohibition gurgled down the drain and liquor licenses were offered to the public, to borrow cash from a white-bearded rich uncle and put in for one. To everybody's surprise he got the license, though Karp, when asked how, winked a heavy-lidded eye and answered nothing. Within a short time after cheap shoes had become expensive bottles, in spite of the poor neighborhood—or maybe because of it, Helen supposed—he became astonishingly successful and retired his overweight wife from the meager railroad flat above the store to a big house on the Parkway—from which she hardly ever stepped forth—the house complete with two-car garage and Mercury; and at the same time as Karp changed his luck—to hear her father tell it—he became wise without brains.

The grocer, on the other hand, had never altered his fortune, unless degrees of poverty meant alteration, for luck and he were, if not natural enemies, not good friends. He labored long hours, was the soul of honesty—he could not escape his honesty, it was bedrock; to cheat would cause an explosion in him, yet he trusted cheaters—coveted nobody's nothing and always got poorer. The harder he worked—his toil was a form of time devouring time—the less he seemed to have. He was Morris Bober and could be nobody more fortunate. With that name you had no sure sense of property, as if it were in your blood and history not to possess, or if by some miracle to own something, to do so on the verge of loss. At the end you were sixty and had less than at thirty. It was, she thought, surely a talent.

Helen removed her hat as she entered the grocery. "Me," she called, as she had from childhood. It meant that whoever was sitting in the back should sit and not suddenly think he was going to get rich.

Morris awoke, soured by the long afternoon sleep. He dressed, combed his hair with a broken comb and trudged downstairs, a heavy-bodied man with sloping shoulders and bushy gray hair in need of a haircut. He came down with his apron on. Although he felt chilly he poured out a cup of cold coffee, and backed against the radiator, slowly sipped it. Ida sat at the table, reading.

"Why you let me sleep so long?" the grocer complained.

She didn't answer.

"Yesterday or today's paper?"

"Yesterday."

He rinsed the cup and set it on the top of the gas range. In the store he rang up "no sale" and took a nickel out of the drawer. Morris lifted the lid of the cash register, struck a match on the underside of the counter, and holding the flame cupped in his palm, peered at the figure of his earnings. Ida had taken in three dollars. Who could afford a paper?

Nevertheless he went for one, doubting the small pleasure

he would get from it. What was so worth reading about the world? Through Karp's window, as he passed, he saw Louis waiting on a customer while four others crowded the counter. Der oilem iz a goilem. Morris took the *Forward* from the newsstand and dropped a nickel into the cigar box. Sam Pearl, working over a green racing sheet, gave him a wave of his hammy hand. They never bothered to talk. What did he know about race horses? What did the other know of the tragic quality of life? Wisdom flew over his hard head.

The grocer returned to the rear of his store and sat on the couch, letting the diminishing light in the yard fall upon the paper. He read nearsightedly, with eyes stretched wide, but his thoughts would not let him read long. He put down the newspaper.

"So where is your buyer?" he asked Ida.

Looking absently into the store she did not reply.

"You should sell long ago the store," she remarked after a minute.

"When the store was good, who wanted to sell? After came bad times, who wanted to buy?"

"Everything we did too late. The store we didn't sell in time. I said, 'Morris, sell now the store.' You said, 'Wait.' What for? The house we bought too late, so we have still a big mortgage that it's hard to pay every month. 'Don't buy,' I said, 'times are bad.' 'Buy,' you said, 'will get better. We will save rent.'"

He answered nothing. If you had failed to do the right thing, talk was useless.

When Helen entered, she asked if the buyer had come. She had forgotten about him but remembered when she saw her mother's dress.

Opening her purse, she took out her pay check and handed it to her father. The grocer, without a word, slipped it under his apron into his pants pocket.

"Not yet," Ida answered, also embarrassed. "Maybe later."

"Nobody goes in the night to buy a store," Morris said. "The time to go is in the day to see how many customers. If this man comes here he will see with one eye the store is dead, then he will run home."

"Did you eat lunch?" Ida asked Helen.

"Yes."

"What did you eat?"

"I don't save menus, Mama."

"Your supper is ready." Ida lit the flame under the pot on the gas range.

"What makes you think he'll come today?" Helen asked her.

"Karp told me yesterday. He knows a refugee that he looks to buy a grocery. He works in the Bronx, so he will be here late."

Morris shook his head.

"He's a young man," Ida went on, "maybe thirty—thirty-two. Karp says he saved a little cash. He can make alterations, buy new goods, fix up modern, advertise a little and make here a nice business."

"Karp should live so long," the grocer said.

"Let's eat." Helen sat at the table.

Ida said she would eat later.

"What about you, Papa?"

"I am not hungry." He picked up his paper.

She ate alone. It would be wonderful to sell out and move but the possibility struck her as remote. If you had lived so long in one place, all but two years of your life, you didn't move out overnight.

Afterward she got up to help with the dishes but Ida wouldn't let her. "Go rest," she said.

Helen took her things and went upstairs.

She hated the drab five-room flat; a gray kitchen she used for breakfast so she could quickly get out to work in the morning. The living room was colorless and cramped; for all its overstuffed furniture of twenty years ago it seemed barren because it was lived in so little, her parents being seven days out of seven in the store; even their rare visitors, when invited upstairs, preferred to remain in the back. Sometimes Helen asked a friend up, but she went to other people's houses if she had a choice. Her bedroom was another impossibility, tiny, dark, despite the two by three foot opening in the wall, through which she could see the living room windows; and at night Morris and Ida had to pass through her room to get to theirs, and from their bedroom back to the bathroom. They had several times talked of giving her the big room, the only comfortable one in the house, but there was no place else that would hold their double bed. The fifth room was a small icebox off the second floor stairs, in which Ida stored a few odds and ends of clothes and furniture. Such was home. Helen had once in anger remarked that the place was awful to live in, and it had made her feel bad that her father had felt so bad.

She heard Morris's slow footsteps on the stairs. He came aimlessly into the living room and tried to relax in a stiff armchair. He sat with sad eyes, saying nothing, which was how he began when he wanted to say something.

When she and her brother were kids, at least on Jewish holidays Morris would close the store and venture forth to Second Avenue to see a Yiddish play, or take the family visiting; but after Ephraim died he rarely went beyond the corner. Thinking about his life always left her with a sense of the waste of her own.

She looks like a little bird, Morris thought. Why should she be lonely? Look how pretty she looks. Whoever saw such blue eyes?

He reached into his pants pocket and took out a five-dollar bill.

"Take," he said, rising and embarrassedly handing her the money. "You will need for shoes."

"You just gave me five dollars downstairs."

"Here is five more."

"Wednesday was the first of the month, Pa."

"I can't take away from you all your pay."

"You're not taking, I'm giving."

She made him put the five away. He did, with renewed shame. "What did I ever give you? Even your college education I took away."

"It was my own decision not to go, yet maybe I will yet. You can never tell."

"How can you go? You are twenty-three years old."

"Aren't you always saying a person's never too old to go to school?"

"My child," he sighed, "for myself I don't care, for you I want the best but what did I give you?"

"I'll give myself," she smiled. "There's hope."

With this he had to be satisfied. He still conceded her a future.

But before he went down, he said gently, "What's the matter you stay home so much lately? You had a fight with Nat?"

"No." Blushing, she answered, "I don't think we see things in the same way."

He hadn't the heart to ask more.

Going down, he met Ida on the stairs and knew she would cover the same ground.

In the evening there was a flurry of business. Morris's mood quickened and he exchanged pleasantries with the customers. Carl Johnsen, the Swedish painter, whom he hadn't seen in weeks, came in with a wet smile and bought two dollars' worth of beer, cold cuts and sliced Swiss cheese. The grocer was at first worried he would ask to charge—he had never paid what he owed on the books before Morris had stopped giving trust—but the painter had the cash. Mrs. Anderson, an old loyal customer, bought for a dollar. A stranger then came in and left eighty-eight cents. After him two more customers appeared. Morris felt a little surge of hope. Maybe things were picking up. But after half past eight his hands grew heavy with nothing to do. For years he had been the only one for miles around who stayed open at night and had just about made a living from it, but now Schmitz matched him hour for hour. Morris sneaked a little smoke, then began to cough. Ida pounded on the floor upstairs, so he clipped the butt and put it away. He felt restless and stood at the front window, watching the street. He watched a trolley go by. Mr. Lawler, formerly a customer, good for at least a fiver on Friday nights, passed the store. Morris hadn't seen him for months but knew where he was going. Mr. Lawler averted his gaze and hurried along. Morris watched him disappear around the corner. He lit a match and again checked the register—nine and a half dollars, not even expenses.

Julius Karp opened the front door and poked his foolish head in.

"Podolsky came?"

"Who Podolsky?"

"The refugee."

Morris said in annoyance, "What refugee?"

With a grunt Karp shut the door behind him. He was short,

pompous, a natty dresser in his advanced age. In the past, like
Morris, he had toiled long hours in his shoe store, now he
stayed all day in silk pajamas until it came time to relieve Louis
before supper. Though the little man was insensitive and a
blunderer, Morris had got along fairly well with him, but since
Karp had rented the tailor shop to another grocer, sometimes
they did not speak. Years ago Karp had spent much time in the
back of the grocery, complaining of his poverty as if it were a
new invention and he its first victim. Since his success with
wines and liquors he came in less often, but he still visited
Morris more than his welcome entitled him to, usually to run
down the grocery and spout unwanted advice. His ticket of
admission was his luck, which he gathered wherever he reached,
at a loss, Morris thought, to somebody else. Once a drunk had
heaved a rock at Karp's window, but it had shattered his. Another time, Sam Pearl gave the liquor dealer a tip on a horse,
then forgot to place a bet himself. Karp collected five hundred
for his ten-dollar bill. For years the grocer had escaped resenting the man's good luck, but lately he had caught himself
wishing on him some small misfortune.

"Podolsky is the one I called up to take a look at your
gesheft," Karp answered.

"Who is this refugee, tell me, an enemy yours?"

Karp stared at him unpleasantly.

"Does a man," Morris insisted, "send a friend he should buy
such a store that you yourself took away from it the best
business?"

"Podolsky ain't you," the liquor dealer replied. "I told him
about this place. I said, 'The neighborhood is improving. You
can buy cheap and build up this store. It's run down for years,
nobody changed anything there for twenty years.'"

"You should live so long how much I changed—" Morris
began but he didn't finish, for Karp was at the window, peering
nervously into the dark street.

"You saw that gray car that just passed," the liquor dealer
said. "This is the third time I saw it in the last twenty minutes."
His eyes were restless.

Morris knew what worried him. "Put in a telephone in your
store," he advised, "so you will feel better."

Karp watched the street for another minute and worriedly

replied, "Not for a liquor store in this neighborhood. If I had a telephone, every drunken bum would call me to make deliveries, and when you go there they don't have a cent."

He opened the door but shut it in afterthought. "Listen, Morris," he said, lowering his voice, "if they come back again, I will lock my front door and put out my lights. Then I will call you from the back window so you can telephone the police."

"This will cost you five cents," Morris said grimly.

"My credit is class A."

Karp left the grocery, disturbed.

God bless Julius Karp, the grocer thought. Without him I would have my life too easy. God made Karp so a poor grocery man will not forget his life is hard. For Karp, he thought, it was miraculously not so hard, but what was there to envy? He would allow the liquor dealer his bottles and gelt just not to be him. Life was bad enough.

At nine-thirty a stranger came in for a box of matches. Fifteen minutes later Morris put out the lights in his window. The street was deserted except for an automobile parked in front of the laundry across the car tracks. Morris peered at it sharply but could see nobody in it. He considered locking up and going to bed, then decided to stay open the last few minutes. Sometimes a person came in at a minute to ten. A dime was a dime.

A noise at the side door which led into the hall frightened him.

"Ida?"

The door opened slowly. Tessie Fuso came in in her housecoat, a homely Italian girl with a big face.

"Are you closed, Mr. Bober?" she asked embarrassedly.

"Come in," said Morris.

"I'm sorry I came through the back way but I was undressed and didn't want to go out in the street."

"Don't worry."

"Please give me twenty cents' ham for Nick's lunch tomorrow."

He understood. She was making amends for Nick's trip around the corner that morning. He cut her an extra slice of ham.

Tessie bought also a quart of milk, package of paper napkins and loaf of bread. When she had gone he lifted the register lid. Ten dollars. He thought he had long ago touched bottom but now knew there was none.

I slaved my whole life for nothing, he thought.

Then he heard Karp calling him from the rear. The grocer went inside, worn out.

Raising the window he called harshly, "What's the matter there?"

"Telephone the police," cried Karp. "The car is parked across the street."

"What car?"

"The holdupniks."

"There is nobody in this car, I saw myself."

"For God's sake, I tell you call the police. I will pay for the telephone."

Morris shut the window. He looked up the phone number and was about to dial the police when the store door opened and he hurried inside.

Two men were standing at the other side of the counter, with handkerchiefs over their faces. One wore a dirty yellow clotted one, the other's was white. The one with the white one began pulling out the store lights. It took the grocer a half-minute to comprehend that he, not Karp, was their victim.

Morris sat at the table, the dark light of the dusty bulb falling on his head, gazing dully at the few crumpled bills before him, including Helen's check, and the small pile of silver. The gunman with the dirty handkerchief, fleshy, wearing a fuzzy black hat, waved a pistol at the grocer's head. His pimply brow was thick with sweat; from time to time with furtive eyes he glanced into the darkened store. The other, a taller man in an old cap and torn sneakers, to control his trembling leaned against the sink, cleaning his fingernails with a matchstick. A cracked mirror hung behind him on the wall above the sink and every so often he turned to stare into it.

"I know damn well this ain't everything you took in," said the heavy one to Morris, in a hoarse, unnatural voice. "Where've you got the rest hid?"

Morris, sick to his stomach, couldn't speak.

"Tell the goddam truth." He aimed the gun at the grocer's mouth.

"Times are bad," Morris muttered.

"You're a Jew liar."

The man at the sink fluttered his hand, catching the other's attention. They met in the center of the room, the other with the cap hunched awkwardly over the one in the fuzzy hat, whispering into his ear.

"No," snapped the heavy one sullenly.

His partner bent lower, whispering earnestly through his handkerchief.

"I say he hid it," the heavy one snarled, "and I'm gonna get it if I have to crack his goddam head."

At the table he whacked the grocer across the face.

Morris moaned.

The one at the sink hastily rinsed a cup and filled it with water. He brought it to the grocer, spilling some on his apron as he raised the cup to his lips.

Morris tried to swallow but managed only a dry sip. His frightened eyes sought the man's but he was looking elsewhere.

"Please," murmured the grocer.

"Hurry up," warned the one with the gun.

The tall one straightened up and gulped down the water. He rinsed the cup and placed it on a cupboard shelf.

He then began to hunt among the cups and dishes there and pulled out the pots on the bottom. Next, he went hurriedly through the drawers of an old bureau in the room, and on hands and knees searched under the couch. He ducked into the store, removed the empty cash drawer from the register and thrust his hand into the slot, but came up with nothing.

Returning to the kitchen he took the other by the arm and whispered to him urgently.

The heavy one elbowed him aside.

"We better scram out of here."

"Are you gonna go chicken on me?"

"That's all the dough he has, let's beat it."

"Business is bad," Morris muttered.

"Your Jew ass is bad, you understand?"

"Don't hurt me."

"I will give you your last chance. Where have you got it hid?"

"I am a poor man." He spoke through cracked lips.

The one in the dirty handkerchief raised his gun. The other, staring into the mirror, waved frantically, his black eyes bulging, but Morris saw the blow descend and felt sick of himself, of soured expectations, endless frustration, the years gone up in smoke, he could not begin to count how many. He had hoped for much in America and got little. And because of him Helen and Ida had less. He had defrauded them, he and the bloodsucking store.

He fell without a cry. The end fitted the day. It was his luck, others had better.

DURING THE week that Morris lay in bed with a thickly bandaged head, Ida tended the store fitfully. She went up and down twenty times a day until her bones ached and her head hurt with all her worries. Helen stayed home Saturday, a half-day in her place, and Monday, to help her mother, but she could not risk longer than that, so Ida, who ate in snatches and had worked up a massive nervousness, had to shut the store for a full day, although Morris angrily protested. He needed no attention, he insisted, and urged her to keep open at least half the day or he would lose his remaining few customers; but Ida, short of breath, said she hadn't the strength, her legs hurt. The grocer attempted to get up and pull on his pants but was struck by a violent headache and had to drag himself back to bed.

On the Tuesday the store was closed a man appeared in the neighborhood, a stranger who spent much of his time standing on Sam Pearl's corner with a toothpick in his teeth, intently observing the people who passed by; or he would drift down the long block of stores, some empty, from Pearl's to the bar at the far end of the street. Beyond that was a freight yard, and in the distance, a bulky warehouse. After an occasional slow beer in the tavern, the stranger turned the corner and wandered past the high-fenced coal yard; he would go around the block until he got back to Sam's candy store. Once in a while the man would walk over to Morris's closed grocery, and with both hands shading his brow, stare through the window; sighing, he went back to Sam's. When he had as much as he could take of the corner he walked around the block again, or elsewhere in the neighborhood.

Helen had pasted a paper on the window of the front door, that said her father wasn't well but the store would open on Wednesday. The man spent a good deal of time studying this paper. He was young, dark-bearded, wore an old brown rain-stained hat, cracked patent leather shoes and a long black overcoat that looked as if it had been lived in. He was tall and not bad looking, except for a nose that had been broken and badly set, unbalancing his face. His eyes were melancholy. Sometimes he sat at the fountain with Sam Pearl, lost in his thoughts, smoking from a crumpled pack of cigarettes he had bought with pennies. Sam, who was used to all kinds of people, and had in his time seen many strangers appear in the neighborhood and as quickly disappear, showed no special concern for the man, though Goldie, after a full day of his presence, complained that too much was too much; he didn't pay rent. Sam did notice that the stranger sometimes seemed to be under stress, sighed much and muttered inaudibly to himself. However, he paid the man scant attention—everybody to their own troubles. Other times the stranger, as if he had somehow squared himself with himself, seemed relaxed, even satisfied with his existence. He read through Sam's magazines, strolled around in the neighborhood and when he returned, lit a fresh cigarette as he opened a paperbound book from the rack in the store. Sam served him coffee when he asked for it, and the stranger, squinting from the smoke of the butt in his mouth, carefully counted out five pennies to pay. Though nobody had asked him he said his name was Frank Alpine and he had lately come from the West, looking for a better opportunity. Sam advised if he could qualify for a chauffeur's license, to try for work as a hack driver. It wasn't a bad life. The man agreed but stayed around as if he was expecting something else to open up. Sam put him down as a moody gink.

The day Ida reopened the grocery the stranger disappeared but he returned to the candy store the next morning, and seating himself at the fountain, asked for coffee. He looked bleary, unhappy, his beard hard, dark, contrasting with the pallor of his face; his nostrils were inflamed and his voice was husky. He looks half in his grave, Sam thought. God knows what hole he slept in last night.

As Frank Alpine was stirring his coffee, with his free hand he opened a magazine lying on the counter, and his eye was caught by a picture in color of a monk. He lifted the coffee cup to drink but had to put it down, and he stared at the picture for five minutes.

Sam, out of curiosity, went behind him with a broom, to see what he was looking at. The picture was of a thin-faced, dark-bearded monk in a coarse brown garment, standing barefooted on a sunny country road. His skinny, hairy arms were raised to a flock of birds that dipped over his head. In the background was a grove of leafy trees; and in the far distance a church in sunlight.

"He looks like some kind of a priest," Sam said cautiously.

"No, it's St. Francis of Assisi. You can tell from that brown robe he's wearing and all those birds in the air. That's the time he was preaching to them. When I was a kid, an old priest used to come to the orphans' home where I was raised, and every time he came he read us a different story about St. Francis. They are clear in my mind to this day."

"Stories are stories," Sam said.

"Don't ask me why I never forgot them."

Sam took a closer squint at the picture. "Talking to the birds? What was he—crazy? I don't say this out of any harm."

The stranger smiled at the Jew. "He was a great man. The way I look at it, it takes a certain kind of a nerve to preach to birds."

"That makes him great, because he talked to birds?"

"Also for other things. For instance, he gave everything away that he owned, every cent, all his clothes off his back. He enjoyed to be poor. He said poverty was a queen and he loved her like she was a beautiful woman."

Sam shook his head. "It ain't beautiful, kiddo. To be poor is dirty work."

"He took a fresh view of things."

The candy store owner glanced again at St. Francis, then poked his broom into a dirty corner. Frank, as he drank his coffee, continued to study the picture. He said to Sam, "Every time I read about somebody like him I get a feeling inside of me I have to fight to keep from crying. He was born good, which is a talent if you have it."

He spoke with embarrassment, embarrassing Sam.

Frank drained his cup and left.

That night as he was wandering past Morris's store he glanced through the door and saw Helen inside, relieving her mother. She looked up and noticed him staring at her through the plate glass. His appearance startled her; his eyes were haunted, hungry, sad; she got the impression he would come in and ask for a handout and had made up her mind to give him a dime, but instead he disappeared.

On Friday Morris weakly descended the stairs at six A.M., and Ida, nagging, came after him. She had been opening at eight o'clock and had begged him to stay in bed until then, but he had refused, saying he had to give the Poilisheh her roll.

"Why does three cents for a lousy roll mean more to you than another hour sleep?" Ida complained.

"Who can sleep?"

"You need rest, the doctor said."

"Rest I will take in my grave."

She shuddered. Morris said, "For fifteen years she gets here her roll, so let her get."

"All right, but let me open up. I will give her and you go back to bed."

"I stayed in bed too long. Makes me feel weak."

But the woman wasn't there and Morris feared he had lost her to the German. Ida insisted on dragging in the milk boxes, threatening to shout if he made a move for them. She packed the bottles into the refrigerator. After Nick Fuso they waited hours for another customer. Morris sat at the table, reading the paper, occasionally raising his hand gently to feel the bandage around his head. When he shut his eyes he still experienced moments of weakness. By noon he was glad to go upstairs and crawl into bed and he didn't get up until Helen came home.

The next morning he insisted on opening alone. The Poilisheh was there. He did not know her name. She worked somewhere in a laundry and had a little dog called Polaschaya. When she came home at night she took the little Polish dog for a walk around the block. He liked to run loose in the coal yard. She lived in one of the stucco houses nearby. Ida called her die antisemitke, but that part of her didn't bother Morris. She had come with it from the old country, a different kind of anti-Semitism from in America. Sometimes he suspected she needled him a little by asking for a "Jewish roll," and once or twice, with an odd smile, she wanted a "Jewish pickle." Generally she said nothing at all. This morning Morris handed her her roll and she said nothing. She didn't ask him about his bandaged head though her quick beady eyes stared at it, nor why he had not been there for a week; but she put six pennies on the counter instead of three. He figured she had taken a roll from the bag one of the days the store hadn't opened on time. He rang up the six-cent sale.

Morris went outside to pull in the two milk cases. He gripped the boxes but they were like rocks, so he let one go and tugged at the other. A storm cloud formed in his head and blew up to the size of a house. Morris reeled and almost fell into the gutter, but he was caught by Frank Alpine, in his long coat, steadied and led back into the store. Frank then hauled in the milk cases and refrigerated the bottles. He quickly swept up behind the counter and went into the back. Morris, recovered, warmly thanked him.

Frank said huskily, his eyes on his scarred and heavy hands, that he was new to the neighborhood but living here now with a married sister. He had lately come from the West and was looking for a better job.

The grocer offered him a cup of coffee, which he at once accepted. As he sat down Frank placed his hat on the floor at his feet, and he drank the coffee with three heaping spoonfuls of sugar, to get warm quick, he said. When Morris offered him a seeded hard roll, he bit into it hungrily. "Jesus, this is good bread." After he had finished he wiped his mouth with his handkerchief, then swept the crumbs off the table with one hand into the other, and though Morris protested, he rinsed the cup and saucer at the sink, dried them and set them on top of the gas range, where the grocer had got them.

"Much obliged for everything." He had picked up his hat but made no move to leave.

"Once in San Francisco I worked in a grocery for a couple of months," he remarked after a minute, "only it was one of those supermarket chain store deals."

"The chain store kills the small man."

"Personally I like a small store myself. I might someday have one."

"A store is a prison. Look for something better."

"At least you're your own boss."

"To be a boss of nothing is nothing."

"Still and all, the idea of it appeals to me. The only thing is I would need experience on what goods to order. I mean about brand names, and et cetera. I guess I ought to look for a job in a store and get more experience."

"Try the A&P," advised the grocer.

"I might."

Morris dropped the subject. The man put on his hat.

"What's the matter," he said, staring at the grocer's bandage, "did you have some kind of an accident to your head?"

Morris nodded. He didn't care to talk about it, so the stranger, somehow disappointed, left.

He happened to be in the street very early on Monday when Morris was again struggling with the milk cases. The stranger tipped his hat and said he was off to the city to find a job but he had time to help him pull in the milk. This he did and quickly left. However, the grocer thought he saw him pass by in the other direction about an hour later. That afternoon when he went for his *Forward* he noticed him sitting at the fountain with Sam Pearl. The next morning, just after six, Frank was there to help him haul in the milk bottles and he willingly accepted when Morris, who knew a poor man when he saw one, invited him for coffee.

"How is going now the job?" Morris asked as they were eating.

"So-so," said Frank, his glance shifting. He seemed preoccupied, nervous. Every few minutes he would set down his cup and uneasily look around. His lips parted as if to speak, his eyes took on a tormented expression, but then he shut his jaw as if he had decided it was better never to say what he intended. He seemed to need to talk, broke into sweat—his brow gleamed with it—his pupils widening as he struggled. He looked to Morris like someone who had to retch—no matter where; but after a brutal interval his eyes grew dull. He sighed heavily and gulped down the last of his coffee. After, he brought up a belch. This for a moment satisfied him.

Whatever he wants to say, Morris thought, let him say it to somebody else. I am only a grocer. He shifted in his chair, fearing to catch some illness.

Again the tall man leaned forward, drew a breath and once more was at the point of speaking, but now a shudder passed through him, followed by a fit of shivering.

The grocer hastened to the stove and poured out a cup of steaming coffee. Frank swallowed it in two terrible gulps. He soon stopped shaking, but looked defeated, humiliated, like somebody, the grocer felt, who had lost out on something he had wanted badly.

"You caught a cold?" he asked sympathetically.

The stranger nodded, scratched up a match on the sole of his cracked shoe, lit a cigarette and sat there, listless.

"I had a rough life," he muttered, and lapsed into silence.

Neither of them spoke. Then the grocer, to ease the other's mood, casually inquired, "Where in the neighborhood lives your sister? Maybe I know her."

Frank answered in a monotone. "I forget the exact address. Near the park somewheres."

"What is her name?"

"Mrs. Garibaldi."

"What kind name is this?"

"What do you mean?" Frank stared at him.

"I mean the nationality?"

"Italian. I am of Italian extraction. My name is Frank Alpine—Alpino in Italian."

The smell of Frank Alpine's cigarette compelled Morris to light his butt. He thought he could control his cough and tried but couldn't. He coughed till he feared his head would pop off. Frank watched with interest. Ida banged on the floor upstairs, and the grocer ashamedly pinched his cigarette and dropped it into the garbage pail.

"She don't like me to smoke," he explained between coughs. "My lungs ain't so healthy."

"Who don't?"

"My wife. It's a catarrh some kind. My mother had it all her life and lived till eighty-four. But they took a picture of my chest last year and found two dried spots. This frightened my wife."

Frank slowly put out his cigarette. "What I started out to say before about my life," he said heavily, "is that I have had a funny one, only I don't mean funny. I mean I've been through a lot. I've been close to some wonderful things—jobs, for instance, education, women, but close is as far as I go." His hands were tightly clasped between his knees. "Don't ask me why, but sooner or later everything I think is worth having gets away from me in some way or other. I work like a mule for what I want, and just when it looks like I am going to get it I make some kind of a stupid move, and everything that is just about nailed down tight blows up in my face."

"Don't throw away your chance for education," Morris advised. "It's the best thing for a young man."

"I could've been a college graduate by now, but when the time came to start going, I missed out because something else turned up that I took instead. With me one wrong thing leads to another and it ends in a trap. I want the moon so all I get is cheese."

"You are young yet."

"Twenty-five," he said bitterly.

"You look older."

"I feel old—damn old."

Morris shook his head.

"Sometimes I think your life keeps going the way it starts out on you," Frank went on. "The week after I was born my mother was dead and buried. I never saw her face, not even a picture. When I was five years old, one day my old man leaves this furnished room where we were staying, to get a pack of butts. He takes off and that was the last I ever saw of him. They traced him years later but by then he was dead. I was raised in an orphans' home and when I was eight they farmed me out to a tough family. I ran away ten times, also from the next people I lived with. I think about my life a lot. I say to myself, 'What do you expect to happen after all of that?' Of course, every now and again, you understand, I hit some nice good spots in between, but they are few and far, and usually I end up like I started out, with nothing."

The grocer was moved. Poor boy.

"I've often tried to change the way things work out for me but I don't know how, even when I think I do. I have it in my heart to do more than I can remember." He paused, cleared his throat and said, "That makes me sound stupid but it's not as easy as that. What I mean to say is that when I need it most something is missing in me, in me or on account of me. I always have this dream where I want to tell somebody something on the telephone so bad it hurts, but then when I am in the booth, instead of a phone being there, a bunch of bananas is hanging on a hook."

He gazed at the grocer then at the floor. "All my life I wanted to accomplish something worthwhile—a thing people will say took a little doing, but I don't. I am too restless—six months in any one place is too much for me. Also I grab at everything too quick—too impatient. I don't do what I have to—that's what I mean. The result is I move into a place with nothing, and I move out with nothing. You understand me?"

"Yes," said Morris.

Frank fell into silence. After a while he said, "I don't under-stand myself. I don't really know what I'm saying to you or why I am saying it."

"Rest yourself," said Morris.

"What kind of a life is that for a man my age?"

He waited for the grocer to reply—to tell him how to live his life, but Morris was thinking, I am sixty and he talks like me.

"Take some more coffee," he said.

"No, thanks." Frank lit another cigarette and smoked it to the tip. He seemed eased yet not eased, as though he had ac-complished something (What? wondered the grocer) yet had not. His face was relaxed, almost sleepy, but he cracked the knuckles of both hands and silently sighed.

Why don't he go home? the grocer thought. I am a working man.

"I'm going." Frank got up but stayed.

"What happened to your head?" he asked again.

Morris felt the bandage. "This Friday before last I had here a holdup."

"You mean they slugged you?"

The grocer nodded.

"Bastards like that ought to die." Frank spoke vehemently.

Morris stared at him.

Frank brushed his sleeve. "You people are Jews, aren't you?"

"Yes," said the grocer, still watching him.

"I always liked Jews." His eyes were downcast.

Morris did not speak.

"I suppose you have some kids?" Frank asked.

"Me?"

"Excuse me for being curious."

"A girl." Morris sighed. "I had once a wonderful boy but he died from an ear sickness that they had in those days."

"Too bad." Frank blew his nose.

A gentleman, Morris thought with a watery eye.

"Is the girl the one that was here behind the counter a couple of nights last week?"

"Yes," the grocer replied, a little uneasily.

"Well, thanks for all the coffee."

"Let me make you a sandwich. Maybe you'll be hungry later."

"No thanks."

The Jew insisted, but Frank felt he had all he wanted from him at the moment.

Left alone, Morris began to worry about his health. He felt dizzy at times, often headachy. Murderers, he thought. Standing before the cracked and faded mirror at the sink he unwound the bandage from his head. He wanted to leave it off but the scar was still ugly, not nice for the customers, so he tied a fresh bandage around his skull. As he did this he thought of that night with bitterness, recalling the buyer who hadn't come, nor had since then, nor ever would. Since his recovery, Morris had not spoken to Karp. Against words the liquor dealer had other words, but silence silenced him.

Afterward the grocer looked up from his paper and was startled to see somebody out front washing his window with a brush on a stick. He ran out with a roar to drive the intruder away, for there were nervy window cleaners who did the job without asking permission, then held out their palms to collect. But when Morris came out of the store he saw the window washer was Frank Alpine.

"Just to show my thanks and appreciation." Frank explained he had borrowed the pail from Sam Pearl and the brush and squeegee from the butcher next door.

Ida then entered the store by the inside door, and seeing the window being washed, hurried outside.

"You got rich all of a sudden?" she asked Morris, her face inflamed.

"He does me a favor," the grocer replied.

"That's right," said Frank, bearing down on the squeegee.

"Come inside, it's cold." In the store Ida asked, "Who is this goy?"

"A poor boy, an Italyener he looks for a job. He gives me a help in the morning with the cases milk."

"If you sold containers like I told you a thousand times, you wouldn't need help."

"Containers leak. I like bottles."

"Talk to the wind," Ida said.

Frank came in blowing his breath on water-reddened fists. "How's it look now, folks, though you can't really tell till I do the inside."

Ida remarked under her breath, "Pay now for your favor."

"Fine," Morris said to Frank. He went to the register and rang up "no sale."

"No, thanks," Frank said, holding up his hand. "For services already rendered."

Ida reddened.

"Another cup coffee?" Morris asked.

"Thanks. Not as of now."

"Let me make you a sandwich?"

"I just ate."

He walked out, threw the dirty water into the gutter, returned the pail and brush, then came back to the grocery. He went behind the counter and into the rear, pausing to rap on the doorjamb.

"How do you like the clean window?" he asked Ida.

"Clean is clean." She was cool.

"I don't want to intrude here but your husband was nice to me, so I just thought maybe I could ask for one more small favor. I am looking for work and I want to try some kind of a grocery job just for size. Maybe I might like it, who knows? It happens I forgot some of the things about cutting and weighing and such, so I am wondering if you would mind me working around here for a couple-three weeks without wages just so I could learn again? It won't cost you a red cent. I know I am a stranger but I am an honest guy. Whoever keeps an eye on me will find that out in no time. That's fair enough, isn't it?"

Ida said, "Mister, isn't here a school."

"What do you say, pop?" Frank asked Morris.

"Because somebody is a stranger don't mean they ain't honest," answered the grocer. "This subject don't interest me. Interests me what you can learn here. Only one thing"—he pressed his hand to his chest—"a heartache."

"You got nothing to lose on my proposition, has he now, Mrs?" Frank said. "I understand he don't feel so hot yet, and if I helped him out a short week or two it would be good for his health, wouldn't it?"

Ida didn't answer.

But Morris said flatly, "No. It's a small, poor store. Three people would be too much."

Frank flipped an apron off a hook behind the door and

before either of them could say a word, removed his hat and dropped the loop over his head. He tied the apron strings around him.

"How's that for fit?"

Ida flushed, and Morris ordered him to take it off and put it back on the hook.

"No bad feelings, I hope," Frank said on his way out.

Helen Bober and Louis Karp walked, no hands touching, in the windy dark on the Coney Island boardwalk.

Louis had, on his way home for supper that evening, stopped her in front of the liquor store, on her way in from work.

"How's about a ride in the Mercury, Helen? I never see you much anymore. Things were better in the bygone days in high school."

Helen smiled. "Honestly, Louis, that's so far away." A sense of mourning at once oppressed her, which she fought to a practiced draw.

"Near or far, it's all the same for me." He was built with broad back and narrow head, and despite prominent eyes was presentable. In high school, before he quit, he had worn his wet hair slicked straight back. One day, after studying a picture of a movie actor in the *Daily News*, he had run a part across his head. This was as much change as she had known in him. If Nat Pearl was ambitious, Louis made a relaxed living letting the fruit of his father's investment fall into his lap.

"Anyway," he said, "why not a ride for old-times' sake?"

She thought a minute, a gloved finger pressed into her cheek; but it was a fake gesture because she was lonely.

"For old-times' sake, where?"

"Name your scenery—continuous performance."

"The Island?"

He raised his coat collar. "Brr, it's a cold, windy night. You wanna freeze?"

Seeing her hesitation, he said, "But I'll die game. When'll I pick you up?"

"Ring my bell after eight and I'll come down."

"Check," Louis said. "Eight bells."

They walked to Seagate, where the boardwalk ended. She gazed with envy through a wire fence at the large lit houses fronting the ocean. The Island was deserted, except here and there an open hamburger joint or pinball machine concession. Gone from the sky was the umbrella of rosy light that glowed over the place in summertime. A few cold stars gleamed down. In the distance a dark Ferris wheel looked like a stopped clock. They stood at the rail of the boardwalk, watching the black, restless sea.

All during their walk she had been thinking about her life, the difference between her aloneness now and the fun when she was young and spending every day of summer in a lively crowd of kids on the beach. But as her high school friends had got married, she had one by one given them up; and as others of them graduated from college, envious, ashamed of how little she was accomplishing, she stopped seeing them too. At first it hurt to drop people but after a time it became a not too difficult habit. Now she saw almost no one, occasionally Betty Pearl, who understood, but not enough to make much difference.

Louis, his face reddened by the wind, sensed her mood.

"What's got in you, Helen?" he said, putting his arm around her.

"I can't really explain it. All night I've been thinking of the swell times we had on this beach when we were kids. And do you remember the parties? I suppose I'm blue that I'm no longer seventeen."

"What's so wrong about twenty-three?"

"It's old, Louis. Our lives change so quickly. You know what youth means?"

"Sure I know. You don't catch me giving away nothing for nothing. I got my youth yet."

"When a person is young he's privileged," Helen said, "with all kinds of possibilities. Wonderful things might happen, and when you get up in the morning you feel they will. That's what youth means, and that's what I've lost. Nowadays I feel that every day is like the day before, and what's worse, like the day after."

"So now you're a grandmother?"

"The world has shrunk for me."

"What do you wanna be—Miss Rheingold?"

"I want a larger and better life. I want the return of my possibilities."

"Such as which ones?"

She clutched the rail, cold through her gloves. "Education," she said, "prospects. Things I've wanted but never had."

"Also a man?"

"Also a man."

His arm tightened around her waist. "Talk is too cold, baby, how's about a kiss?"

She brushed his cold lips, then averted her head. He did not press her.

"Louis," she said, watching a far-off light on the water, "what do you want out of your life?"

He kept his arm around her. "The same thing I got—plus."

"Plus what?"

"Plus more, so my wife and family can have also."

"What if she wanted something different than you do?"

"Whatever she wanted I would gladly give her."

"But what if she wanted to make herself a better person, have bigger ideas, live a more worthwhile life? We die so quickly, so helplessly. Life *has* to have some meaning."

"I ain't gonna stop anybody from being better," Louis said. "That's up to them."

"I suppose," she said.

"Say, baby, let's drop this deep philosophy and go trap a hamburger. My stomach complains."

"Just a little longer. It's been ages since I came here this late in the year."

He pumped his arms. "Jesus, this wind, it flies up my pants. At least gimme another kiss." He unbuttoned his overcoat.

She let him kiss her. He felt her breast. Helen stepped back out of his embrace. "Don't, Louis."

"Why not?" He stood there awkwardly, annoyed.

"It gives me no pleasure."

"I suppose I'm the first guy that ever gave it a nip?"

"Are you collecting statistics?"

"Okay," he said, "I'm sorry. You know I ain't a bad guy, Helen."

"I know you're not, but please don't do what I don't like."

"There was a time you treated me a whole lot better."

"That was the past, we were kids."

It's funny, she remembered, how necking made glorious dreams.

"We were older than that, up till the time Nat Pearl started in college, then you got interested in him. I suppose you got him in mind for the future?"

"If I do, I don't know it."

"But he's the one you want, ain't he? I like to know what that stuck up has got beside a college education? I work for my living."

"No, I don't want him, Louis." But she thought, Suppose Nat said I love you? For magic words a girl might do magic tricks.

"So if that's so, what's wrong with me?"

"Nothing. We're friends."

"Friends I got all I need."

"What do you need, Louis?"

"Cut out the wisecracks, Helen. Would it interest you that I would honestly like to marry you?" He paled at his nerve.

She was surprised, touched.

"Thank you," she murmured.

"Thank you ain't good enough. Give me yes or no."

"No, Louis."

"That's what I thought." He gazed blankly at the ocean.

"I never guessed you were at all remotely interested. You go with girls who are so different from me."

"Please, when I go with them you can't see my thoughts."

"No," she admitted.

"I can give you a whole lot better than you got."

"I know you can, but I want a different life from mine now, or yours. I don't want a storekeeper for a husband."

"Wines and liquors ain't exactly pisher groceries."

"I know."

"It ain't because your old man don't like mine?"

"No."

She listened to the wind-driven, sobbing surf. Louis said, "Let's go get the hamburgers."

"Gladly." She took his arm but could tell from the stiff way he walked that he was hurt.

As they drove home on the Parkway, Louis said, "If you

can't have everything you want, at least take something. Don't be so goddam proud."

Touché. "What shall I take, Louis?"

He paused. "Take less."

"Less I'll never take."

"People got to compromise."

"I won't with my ideals."

"So what'll you be then, a dried-up prune of an old maid? What's the percentage of that?"

"None."

"So what'll you do?"

"I'll wait. I'll dream. Something will happen."

"Nuts," he said.

He let her off in front of the grocery.

"Thanks for everything."

"You'll make me laugh." Louis drove off.

The store was closed, upstairs dark. She pictured her father asleep after his long day, dreaming of Ephraim. What am I saving myself for? she asked herself. What unhappy Bober fate?

It snowed lightly the next day—too early in the year, complained Ida, and when the snow had melted it snowed again. The grocer remarked, as he was dressing in the dark, that he would shovel after he had opened the store. He enjoyed shoveling snow. It reminded him that he had practically lived in it in his boyhood; but Ida forbade him to exert himself because he still complained of dizziness. Later, when he tried to lug the milk cases through the snow, he found it all but impossible. And there was no Frank Alpine to help him, for he had disappeared after washing the window.

Ida came down shortly after her husband, in a heavy cloth coat, a woolen scarf pinned around her head and wearing galoshes. She shoveled a path through the snow and together they pulled in the milk. Only then did Morris notice that a quart bottle was missing from one of the cases.

"Who took it?" Ida cried.

"How do I know?"

"Did you count yet the rolls?"

"No."

"I told you always to count right away."

"The baker will steal from me? I know him twenty years."

"Count what everybody delivers, I told you a thousand times."

He dumped the rolls out of the basket and counted them. Three were missing and he had sold only one to the Poilisheh. To appease Ida he said they were all there.

The next morning another quart of milk and two rolls were gone. He was worried but didn't tell Ida the truth when she asked him if anything else was missing. He often hid unpleasant news from her because she made it worse. He mentioned the missing bottle to the milkman, who answered, "Morris, I swear I left every bottle in that case. Am I responsible for this lousy neighborhood?"

He promised to cart the milk cases into the vestibule for a few days. Maybe whoever was stealing the bottles would be afraid to go in there. Morris considered asking the milk company for a storage box. Years ago he had had one at the curb, a large wooden box in which the milk was padlocked; but he had given it up after developing a hernia lifting the heavy cases out, so he decided against a box.

On the third day, when a quart of milk and two rolls had again been taken, the grocer, much disturbed, considered calling the police. It wasn't the first time he had lost milk and rolls in this neighborhood. That had happened more than once—usually some poor person stealing a breakfast. For this reason Morris preferred not to call the police but to get rid of the thief by himself. To do it, he would usually wake up very early and wait at his bedroom window in the dark. Then when the man—sometimes it was a woman—showed up and was helping himself to the milk, Morris would quickly raise the window and shout down, "Get outa here, you thief you." The thief, startled—sometimes it was a customer who could afford to buy the milk he was stealing—would drop the bottle and run. Usually he never appeared again—a lost customer cut another way—and the next goniff was somebody else.

So this morning Morris arose at four-thirty, a little before the milk was delivered, and sat in the cold in his long underwear, to wait. The street was heavy with darkness as he peered down. Soon the milk truck came, and the milkman, his breath foggy, lugged the two cases of milk into the vestibule. Then the street was silent again, the night dark, the snow white. One or two people trudged by. An hour later, Witzig, the baker, delivered the rolls, but no one else stopped at the door. Just before six Morris dressed hastily and went downstairs. A bottle of milk was gone, and when he counted the rolls, so were two of them.

He still kept the truth from Ida. The next night she awoke and found him at the window in the dark.

"What's the matter?" she asked, sitting up in bed.

"I can't sleep."

"So don't sit in your underwear in the cold. Come back to bed."

He did as she said. Later, the milk and rolls were missing.

In the store he asked the Poilisheh whether she had seen anyone sneak into the vestibule and steal a quart of milk. She stared at him with small eyes, grabbed the sliced roll and slammed the door.

Morris had a theory that the thief lived on the block. Nick Fuso wouldn't do such a thing; if he did Morris would have heard him going down the stairs, then coming up again. The thief was somebody from outside. He sneaked along the street close to the houses, where Morris couldn't see him because of the cornice that hung over the store; then he softly opened the hall door, took the milk, two rolls from the bag, and stole away, hugging the house fronts.

The grocer suspected Mike Papadopolous, the Greek boy who lived on the floor above Karp's store. He had served a reformatory sentence at eighteen. A year later he had in the dead of night climbed down the fire escape overhanging Karp's back yard, boosted himself up on the fence and forced a window into the grocery. There he stole three cartons of cigarettes, and a roll of dimes that Morris had left in the cash register. In the morning, as the grocer was opening the store, Mike's mother, a thin, old-looking woman, returned the cigarettes and dimes to him. She had caught her son coming in with them and had walloped his head with a shoe. She clawed his face, making him confess what he had done. Returning the cigarettes and dimes, she had begged Morris not to have the boy arrested and he had assured her he wouldn't do such a thing.

On this day that he had guessed it might be Mike taking the milk and rolls, shortly after eight A.M., Morris went up the stairs and knocked reluctantly on Mrs. Papadopolous's door.

"Excuse me that I bother you," he said, and told her what had been happening to his milk and rolls.

"Mike work all nights in restaurants," she said. "No come home till nine o'clock in mornings. Sleep all days." Her eyes smoldered. The grocer left.

Now he was greatly troubled. Should he tell Ida and let her call the police? They were bothering him at least once a week with questions about the holdup but had produced nobody. Still, maybe it would be best to call them, for this stealing had gone on for almost a week. Who could afford it? Yet he waited, and that night as he was leaving the store by the side door, which he always padlocked after shutting the front door from inside, he flicked on the cellar light and as he peered down the stairs, his nightly habit, his heart tightened with foreboding that somebody was down there. Morris unlocked the lock, went back into the store and got a hatchet. Forcing his courage, he slowly descended the wooden steps. The cellar was empty. He searched in the dusty storage bins, poked around all over, but there was no sign of anybody.

In the morning he told Ida what was going on and she, calling him big fool, telephoned the police. A stocky, red-faced detective came, Mr. Minogue, from a nearby precinct, who was in charge of investigating Morris's holdup. He was a soft-spoken, unsmiling man, bald, a widower who had once lived in this neighborhood. He had a son Ward, who had gone to Helen's junior high school, a wild boy, always in trouble for manhandling girls. When he saw one he knew playing in front of her house, or on the stoop, he would come swooping down and chase her into the hall. There, no matter how desperately the girl struggled, or tenderly begged him to stop, Ward forced his hand down her dress and squeezed her breast till she screamed. Then by the time her mother came running down the stairs he had ducked out of the hall, leaving the girl sobbing. The detective, when he heard of these happenings, regularly beat up his son, but it didn't do much good. Then one day, about eight years ago, Ward was canned from his job for stealing from the company. His father beat him sick and bloody with his billy and drove him out of the neighborhood. After that, Ward disappeared and nobody knew where he had gone. People felt sorry for the detective, for he was a strict man and they knew what it meant to him to have such a son.

Mr. Minogue seated himself at the table in the rear and listened to Ida's complaint. He slipped on his glasses and wrote in a little black notebook. The detective said he would have a cop watch the store mornings after the milk was delivered, and if there was any more trouble to let him know.

As he was leaving, he said, "Morris, would you recognize Ward Minogue if you happened to see him again? I hear he's been seen around but whereabouts I don't know."

"I don't know," said Morris. "Maybe yes or maybe no. I didn't see him for years."

"If I ever meet up with him," said the detective, "I might bring him in to you for identification."

"What for?"

"I don't know myself—just for possible identification."

Ida said afterward that if Morris had called the police in the first place, he might have saved himself a few bottles of milk that they could hardly afford to lose.

That night, on an impulse, the grocer closed the store an hour later than usual. He snapped on the cellar light and cautiously descended the stairs, gripping his hatchet. Near the bottom he uttered a cry and the hatchet fell from his hands. A man's drawn and haggard face stared up at him in dismay. It was Frank Alpine, gray and unshaven. He had been asleep with his hat and coat on, sitting on a box against the wall. The light had awakened him.

"What do you want here?" Morris cried out.

"Nothing," Frank said dully. "I have just been sleeping in the cellar. No harm done."

"Did you steal from me my milk and rolls?"

"Yes," he confessed. "On account of I was hungry."

"Why didn't you ask me?"

Frank got up. "Nobody has any responsibility to take care of me but myself. I couldn't find any job. I used up every last cent I had. My coat is too thin for this cold and lousy climate. The snow and the rain get in my shoes so I am always shivering. Also, I had no place to sleep. That's why I came down here."

"Don't you stay any more with your sister?"

"I have no sister. That was a lie I told you. I am alone by myself."

"Why you told me you had a sister?"

"I didn't want you to think I was a bum."

Morris regarded the man silently. "Were you ever in prison sometimes?"

"Never, I swear to Christ."

"How you came to me in my cellar?"

"By accident. One night I was walking around in the snow so I tried the cellar door and found out you left it unlocked, then I started coming down at night about an hour after you closed the store. In the morning, when they delivered the milk and rolls, I sneaked up through the hall, opened the door and took what I needed for breakfast. That's practically all I ate all day. After you came down and got busy with some customer or a salesman, I left by the hallway with the empty milk bottle under my coat. Later I threw it away in a lot. That's all there is to it. Tonight I took a chance and came in while you were still in the back of the store, because I have a cold and don't feel too good."

"How can you sleep in such a cold and drafty cellar?"

"I slept in worse."

"Are you hungry now?"

"I'm always hungry."

"Come upstairs."

Morris picked up his hatchet, and Frank, blowing his nose in his damp handkerchief, followed him up the stairs.

Morris lit a light in the store and made two fat liverwurst sandwiches with mustard, and in the back heated up a can of bean soup. Frank sat at the table in his coat, his hat lying at his feet. He ate with great hunger, his hand trembling as he brought the spoon to his mouth. The grocer had to look away.

As the man was finishing his meal, with coffee and cupcakes, Ida came down in felt slippers and bathrobe.

"What happened?" she asked in fright, when she saw Frank Alpine.

"He's hungry," Morris said.

She guessed at once. "He stole the milk!"

"He was hungry," explained Morris. "He slept in the cellar."

"I was practically starving," said Frank.

"Why didn't you look for a job?" Ida asked.

"I looked all over."

After, Ida said to Frank, "When you finish, please go someplace else." She turned to her husband. "Morris, tell him to go someplace else. We are poor people."

"This he knows."

"I'll go away," Frank said, "as the lady wishes."

"Tonight is already too late," Morris said. "Who wants he should walk all night in the streets?"

"I don't want him here." She was tense.

"Where you want him to go?"

Frank set his coffee cup on the saucer and listened with interest.

"This ain't my business," Ida answered.

"Don't anybody worry," said Frank. "I'll leave in ten minutes' time. You got a cigarette, Morris?"

The grocer went to the bureau and took out of the drawer a crumpled pack of cigarettes.

"It's stale," he apologized.

"Don't make any difference." Frank lit a stale cigarette, inhaling with pleasure.

"I'll go after a short while," he said to Ida.

"I don't like trouble," she explained.

"I won't make any. I might look like a bum in these clothes, but I am not. All my life I lived with good people."

"Let him stay here tonight on the couch," Morris said to Ida.

"No. Give him better a dollar he should go someplace else."

"The cellar would be fine," Frank remarked.

"It's too damp. Also rats."

"If you let me stay there one more night I promise I will get out the first thing in the morning. You don't have to be afraid to trust me. I am an honest man."

"You can sleep here," Morris said.

"Morris, you crazy," shouted Ida.

"I'll work it off for you," Frank said. "Whatever I cost you I'll pay you back. Anything you want me to do, I'll do it."

"We will see," Morris said.

"No," insisted Ida.

But Morris won out, and they went up, leaving Frank in the back, the gas radiator left lit.

"He will clean out the store," Ida said wrathfully.

"Where is his truck?" Morris asked, smiling. Seriously he said, "He's a poor boy. I feel sorry for him."

They went to bed. Ida slept badly. Sometimes she was racked by awful dreams. Then she awoke and sat up in bed, straining to hear noises in the store—of Frank packing huge bags of groceries to steal. But there was no sound. She dreamed she came down in the morning and all the stock was gone, the shelves as barren as the picked bones of dead birds. She dreamed, too, that the Italyener had sneaked up into the house and was peeking through the keyhole of Helen's door. Only when Morris got up to open the store did Ida fall fitfully asleep.

The grocer trudged down the stairs with a dull pain in his head. His legs felt weak. His sleep had not been refreshing.

The snow was gone from the streets and the milk boxes were again lying on the sidewalk near the curb. None of the bottles were missing. The grocer was about to drag in the milk cases when the Poilisheh came by. She went inside and placed three pennies on the counter. He entered with the brown bag of rolls, cut up one and wrapped it. She took it wordlessly and left.

Morris looked through the window in the wall. Frank was asleep on the couch in his clothes, his coat covering him. His beard was black, his mouth loosely open.

The grocer went out into the street, grabbed both milk boxes and yanked. The shape of a black hat blew up in his head, flared into hissing light, and exploded. He thought he was rising but felt himself fall.

Frank dragged him in and laid him on the couch. He ran upstairs and banged on the door. Helen, holding a housecoat over her nightdress, opened it. She suppressed a cry.

"Tell your mother your father just passed out. I called the ambulance."

She screamed. As he ran down the stairs he could hear Ida moaning. Frank hurried into the back of the store. The Jew lay white and motionless on the couch. Frank gently removed his apron. Draping the loop over his own head, he tied the tapes around him.

"I need the experience," he muttered.

MORRIS HAD reopened the wound on his head. The ambulance doctor, the same who had treated him after the holdup, said he had got up too soon last time and worn himself out. He again bandaged the grocer's head, saying to Ida, "This time let him lay in bed a good couple of weeks till his strength comes back." "You tell him, doctor," she begged, "he don't listen to me." So the doctor told Morris, and Morris weakly nodded. Ida, in a gray state of collapse, remained with the patient all day. So did Helen, after calling the ladies' underthings concern where she worked. Frank Alpine stayed competently downstairs in the store. At noon Ida remembered him and came down to tell him to leave. Recalling her dreams, she connected him with their new misfortune. She felt that if he had not stayed the night, this might not have happened.

Frank was clean-shaven in the back, having borrowed Morris's safety razor, his thick hair neatly combed, and when she appeared he hopped up to ring open the cash register, showing her a pile of puffy bills.

"Fifteen," he said, "count every one."

She was astonished. "How is so much?"

He explained, "We had a busy morning. A lot of people stopped in to ask about Morris's accident."

Ida had planned to replace him with Helen for the time being, until she herself could take over, but she was now of two minds.

"Maybe you can stay," she faltered, "if you want to, till tomorrow."

"I'll sleep in the cellar, Mrs. You don't have to worry about me. I am as honest as the day."

"Don't sleep in the cellar," she said with a tremble to her voice, "my husband said on the couch. What can anybody steal here? We have nothing."

"How is he now?" Frank asked in a low voice.

She blew her nose.

The next morning Helen went reluctantly to work. Ida came down at ten to see how things were. This time there were only eight dollars in the drawer, but still better than lately. He apologized, "Not so good today, but I wrote down every article I sold so you'll know nothing stuck to my fingers." He produced a list of goods sold, written on wrapping paper. She happened to notice that it began with three cents for a roll. Glancing around, Ida saw he had packed out the few cartons delivered yesterday, swept up, washed the window from the inside and had straightened the cans on the shelves. The place looked a little less dreary.

During the day he also kept himself busy with odd jobs. He cleaned the trap of the kitchen sink, which swallowed water slowly, and in the store fixed a light whose chain wouldn't pull, making useless one lamp. Neither of them mentioned his leaving. Ida, still uneasy, wanted to tell him to go but she couldn't ask Helen to stay home any more, and the prospect of two weeks alone in the store, with her feet and a sick man in the bargain to attend upstairs, was too much for her. Maybe she would let the Italian stay ten days or so. With Morris fairly well recovered there would be no reason to keep him after that. In the meantime he would have three good meals a day and a bed, for being little more than a watchman. What business, after all, did they do here? And while Morris was not around she would change a thing or two she should have done before. So when the milkman stopped by for yesterday's empties, she ordered containers brought from now on. Frank Alpine heartily approved. "Why should we bother with bottles?" he said.

Despite all she had to do upstairs, and her recent good impressions of him, Ida haunted the store, watching his every move. She was worried because, now, not Morris but she was responsible for the man's presence in the store. If something bad happened, it would be her fault. Therefore, though she climbed the stairs often to tend to her husband's needs, she hurried back down, arriving pale and breathless to see what Frank was up to. But anything he happened to be doing was helpful. Her suspicions died slowly, though they never wholly died.

She tried not to be too friendly to him, to make him feel that a distant relationship meant a short one. When they were in the back or for a few minutes together behind the counter she discouraged conversation, took up something to do, or clean, or her paper to read. And in the matter of teaching him the business there was also little to say. Morris had price tags displayed under all items on the shelves, and Ida supplied Frank with a list of prices for meats and salads and for the miscellaneous unmarked things like loose coffee, rice or beans. She taught him how to wrap neatly and efficiently, as Morris had long ago taught her, how to read the scale and to set and handle the electric meat slicer. He caught on quickly; she suspected he knew more than he said he did. He added rapidly and accurately, did not overcut meats or overload the scale on bulk items, as she had urged him not to do, and judged well the length of paper needed to wrap with, and what number bag to pack goods into, conserving the larger bags which cost more money. Since he learned so fast, and since she had seen in him not the least evidence of dishonesty (a hungry man who took milk and rolls, though not above suspicion, was not the same as a thief), Ida forced herself to remain upstairs with more calm, in order to give Morris his medicine, bathe her aching feet and keep up the house, which was always dusty from the coal yard. Yet she felt, whenever she thought of it, always a little troubled at the thought of a stranger's presence below, a goy, after all, and she looked forward to the time when he was gone.

Although his hours were long—six to six, at which time she served him his supper—Frank was content. In the store he was quits with the outside world, safe from cold, hunger and a damp bed. He had cigarettes when he wanted them and was comfortable in clean clothes Morris had sent down, even a pair of pants that fitted him after Ida lengthened and pressed the cuffs. The store was fixed, a cave, motionless. He had all his life been on the move, no matter where he was; here he somehow couldn't be. Here he could stand at the window and watch the world go by, content to be here.

It wasn't a bad life. He woke before dawn. The Polish dame was planted at the door like a statue, distrusting him with beady eyes to open the place in time for her to get to work. Her he didn't like; he would gladly have slept longer. To get up in the middle of the night for three lousy cents was a joke but he did it for the Jew. After packing away the milk containers, turning bottomside up the occasional one that leaked, he swept the store and then the sidewalk. In the back he washed, shaved, had coffee and a sandwich, at first made with meat from a ham or roast pork butt, then after a few days, from the best cut. As he smoked after coffee he thought of everything he could do to improve this dump if it were his. When somebody came into the store he was up with a bound, offering service with a smile. Nick Fuso, on Frank's first day, was surprised to see him there, knowing Morris could not afford a clerk. But Frank said that though the pay was scarce there were other advantages. They spoke about this and that, and when the upstairs tenant learned Frank Alpine was a paisan, he told him to come up and meet Tessie. She cordially invited him for macaroni that same night, and he said he would come if they let him bring the macs.

Ida, after the first few days, began to go down at her regular hour, around ten, after she had finished the housework; and she busied herself with writing in a notebook which bills they had got and which paid. She also wrote out, in a halting hand, a few meager special-account checks for bills that could not be paid in cash directly to the drivers, mopped the kitchen floor, emptied the garbage pail into the metal can on the curb outside and prepared salad if it was needed. Frank watched her shred cabbage on the meat slicer for coleslaw, which she made in careful quantity, because if it turned sour it had to be dumped into the garbage. Potato salad was a bigger job, and she cooked up a large pot of new potatoes, which Frank helped her peel hot in their steaming jackets. Every Friday she prepared fish cakes and a panful of homemade baked beans, first soaking the little beans overnight, pouring out the water, then spreading brown sugar on top before baking. Her expression as she dipped in among the soggy beans pieces of ham from a butt she had cut up caught his eye, and he felt for her repugnance for hating to touch the ham, and some for himself because he had never lived this close to Jews before. At lunchtime there was a little "rush," which meant that a few dirty-faced laborers from the coal yard and a couple of store clerks from on the block wanted sandwiches and containers of hot coffee. But the "rush," for which they both went behind the counter, petered out in a matter of minutes and then came the dead hours of the afternoon. Ida said he ought to take some time off, but he answered that he had nowhere special to go and stayed in the back, reading the *Daily News* on the couch, or flipping through some magazines that he had got out of the public library, which he had discovered during one of his solitary walks in the neighborhood.

At three, when Ida departed for an hour or so to see if Morris needed something, and to rest, Frank felt relieved. Alone, he did a lot of casual eating, sometimes with unexpected pleasure. He sampled nuts, raisins, and small boxes of stale dates or dried figs, which he liked anyway; he also opened packages of crackers, macaroons, cupcakes and doughnuts, tearing up their wrappers into small pieces and flushing them down the toilet. Sometimes in the middle of eating sweets he would get very hungry for something more substantial, so he made a thick meat and Swiss cheese sandwich on a seeded hard roll spread with mustard, and swallowed it down with a bottle of ice-cold beer. Satisfied, he stopped roaming in the store.

Now and then there were sudden unlooked-for flurries of customers, mostly women, whom he waited on attentively, talking to them about all kinds of things. The drivers, too, liked his sociability and cheery manner and stayed to chew the fat. Otto Vogel, once when he was weighing a ham, warned him in a low voice, "Don't work for a Yid, kiddo. They will steal your ass while you are sitting on it." Frank, though he said he didn't expect to stay long, felt embarrassed for being there; then, to his surprise, he got another warning, from an apologetic Jew salesman of paper products, Al Marcus, a prosperous, yet very sick and solemn character who wouldn't stop working. "This kind of a store is a death tomb, positive," Al Marcus said. "Run out while you can. Take my word, if you stay six months, you'll stay forever."

"Don't worry about that," answered Frank.

Alone afterward, he stood at the window, thinking thoughts about his past, and wanting a new life. Would he ever get what he wanted? Sometimes he stared out of the back yard window at nothing at all, or at the clothesline above, moving idly in the wind, flying Morris's scarecrow union suits, Ida's hefty bloomers, modestly folded lengthwise, and her housedresses guarding her daughter's flower-like panties and restless brassieres.

In the evening, whether he wanted to or not, he was "off." Ida insisted, fair was fair. She fed him a quick supper and allowed him, with apologies because she couldn't afford more, fifty cents' spending money. He occasionally passed the time upstairs with the Fusos or went with them to a picture at the local movie house. Sometimes he walked, in spite of the cold, and stopped off at a poolroom he knew, about a mile and a half from the grocery store. When he got back, always before closing, for Ida wouldn't let him keep a key to the store in his pocket, she counted up the day's receipts, put most of the cash into a small paper bag and took it with her, leaving Frank five dollars to open up with in the morning. After she had gone, he turned the key in the front door lock, hooked the side door through which she had left, put out the store lights and sat in his undershirt in the rear, reading tomorrow's pink-sheeted paper that he had picked off Sam Pearl's stand on his way home. Then he undressed and went restlessly to bed in a pair of Morris's bulky, rarely used, flannel pajamas.

The old dame, he thought with disgust, always hurried him out of the joint before her daughter came down for supper.

The girl was in his mind a lot. He couldn't help it, imagined seeing her in the things that were hanging on the line—he had always had a good imagination. He pictured her as she came down the stairs in the morning; also saw himself standing in the hall after she came home, watching her skirts go flying as she ran up the stairs. He rarely saw her around, had never spoken to her but twice, on the day her father had passed out. She had kept her distance—who could blame her, dressed as he was and what he looked like then? He had the feeling as he spoke to her, a few hurried words, that he knew more about her than anybody would give him credit for. He had got this thought the first time he had ever laid eyes on her, that night he saw her through the grocery window. When she had looked at him he was at once aware of something starved about her, a hunger in her eyes he couldn't forget because it made him remember his own, so he knew how wide open she must be. But he wouldn't try to push anything, for he had heard that these Jewish babes could be troublemakers and he was not looking for any of that now—at least no more than usual; besides, he didn't want to spoil anything before it got started. There were some dames you had to wait for—for them to come to you.

His desire grew to get to know her, he supposed because she had never once come into the store in all the time he was there except after he left at night. There was no way to see and talk to her to her face, and this increased his curiosity. He felt they were both lonely but her old lady kept her away from him as if he had a dirty disease; the result was he grew more impatient to find out what she was like, get to be friends with her for whatever it was worth. So, since she was never around, he listened and watched for her. When he heard her walking down the stairs he went to the front window and stood there waiting for her to come out; he tried to look casual, as if he weren't watching, just in case she happened to glance back and see him; but she never did, as if she liked nothing about the place enough to look back on. She had a pretty face and a good figure, small-breasted, neat, as if she had meant herself to look that way. He liked to watch her brisk, awkward walk till she turned the corner. It was a sexy walk, with a wobble in it, a strange movement, as though she might dart sideways although she was walking forward. Her legs were just a bit bowed, and maybe that was the sexy part of it. She stayed in his mind after she had turned the corner; her legs and small breasts and the pink brassieres that covered them. He would be reading something or lying on his back on the couch, smoking, and she would appear in his mind, walking to the corner. He did not have to shut his eyes to see her. Turn around, he said out loud, but in his thoughts she wouldn't.

To see her coming toward him he stood at the lit grocery window at night, but often before he could catch sight of her she was on her way upstairs, or already changing her dress in her room, and his chance was over for the day. She came home about a quarter to six, sometimes a little earlier, so he tried to be at the window around then, which wasn't so easy because that was the time for Morris's few supper customers to come in. So he rarely saw her come home from work, though he always heard her on the stairs. One day things were slower than usual in the store, it was dead at five-thirty, and Frank said to himself, Today I will see her. He combed his hair in the toilet so that Ida wouldn't notice, changed into a clean apron, lit a cigarette, and stood at the window, visible in its light. At twenty to six, just after he had practically shoved a woman out of the joint, a dame who had happened to walk in off the trolley, he saw Helen turn Sam Pearl's corner. Her face was prettier than he had remembered and his throat tightened as she walked to within a couple of feet of him, her eyes blue, her hair, which she wore fairly long, brown, and she had an absentminded way of smoothing it back off the side of her face. He thought she didn't look Jewish, which was all to the good. But her expression was discontented, and her mouth a little drawn. She seemed to be thinking of something she had no hope of ever getting. This moved him, so that when she glanced up and saw his eyes on her, his face plainly showed his emotion. It must have bothered her because she quickly walked, without noticing him further, to the hall and disappeared inside.

The next morning he didn't see her—as if she had sneaked out on him—and at night he was waiting on somebody when she returned from work; regretfully he heard the door slam behind her. Afterward he felt downhearted; every sight lost to a guy who lived with his eyes was lost for all time. He thought up different ways to meet her and exchange a few words. What he had on his mind to say to her about himself was beginning to weigh on him, though he hadn't clearly figured out the words. Once he thought of coming in on her unexpectedly while she was eating her supper, but then he would have Ida to deal with. He also had the idea of opening the door the next time he saw her and calling her into the store; he could say that some guy had telephoned her, and after that talk about something else, but nobody did call her. She was in her way a lone bird, which suited him fine, though why she should be with her looks he couldn't figure out. He got the feeling that she wanted something big out of life, and this scared him. Still, he tried to think of schemes of getting her inside the store, even planning to ask her something like did she know where her old man kept his saw; only she mightn't like that, her mother being around all day to tell him. He had to watch out not to scare her any farther away than the old dame had done.

For a couple of nights after work he stood in a hallway next door to the laundry across the street in the hope that she would come out to do some errand, then he would cross over, tip his hat and ask if he could keep her company to where she was going. But this did not pay off either, because she didn't leave the house. The second night he waited fruitlessly until Ida put out the lights in the grocery window.

One evening toward the end of the second week after Morris's accident, Frank's loneliness burdened him to the point of irritation. He was eating his supper a few minutes after Helen had returned from work, while Ida happened to be upstairs with Morris. He had seen Helen come round the corner and had nodded to her as she approached the house. Caught by surprise, she half-smiled, then entered the hall. It was then the lonely feeling gripped him. While he was eating, he felt he had to get her into the store before her old lady came down and it was time for him to leave. The only excuse he could think of was to call Helen to answer the phone and after he would say that the guy must've hung up. It was a trick but he had to do it. He warned himself not to, because it would be starting out the wrong way with her and he might someday regret it. He tried to think of a better way but time was pressing him and he couldn't.

Frank got up, went over to the bureau, and took the phone off its cradle. He then walked out into the hall, opened the vestibule door, and holding his breath, pressed the Bober bell.

Ida looked over the banister. "What's the matter?"

"Telephone for Helen."

He could see her hesitate, so he returned quickly to the store. He sat down, pretending to be eating, his heart whamming so hard it hurt. All he wanted, he told himself, was to talk to her a minute so the next time would be easier.

Helen eagerly entered the kitchen. On the stairs she had noticed the excitement that flowed through her. My God, it's gotten to be that a phone call is an event.

If it's Nat, she thought, I might give him another chance.

Frank half-rose as she entered, then sat down.

"Thanks," she said to him as she picked up the phone.

"Hello." While she waited he could hear the buzz in the receiver.

"There's nobody there," she said, mystified.

He laid down his fork. "This girl called you," he said gently.

But when he saw the disappointment in her eyes, how bad she felt, he felt bad.

"You must've been cut off."

She gave him a long look. She was wearing a white blouse that showed the firmness of her small breasts. He wet his dry lips, trying to figure out some quick way to square himself, but his mind, usually crowded with all sorts of schemes, had gone blank. He felt very bad, as he had known he would, that he had done what he had. If he had it to do over he wouldn't do it this way.

"Did she leave you her name?" Helen asked.

"No."

"It wasn't Betty Pearl?"

"No."

She absently brushed back her hair. "Did she say anything to you?"

"Only to call you." He paused. "Her voice was nice—like yours. Maybe she didn't get me straight when I said you were upstairs but I would ring your doorbell, and that's why she hung up."

"I don't know why anybody would do that."

Neither did he. He wanted to step clear of his mess but saw no way other than to keep on lying. But lying made their talk useless. When he lied he was somebody else lying to somebody else. It wasn't the two of them as they were. He should have kept that in his mind.

She stood at the bureau, holding the telephone in her hand as if still expecting the buzz to become a voice; so he waited for the same thing, a voice to speak and say he had been telling the truth, that he was a man of fine character. Only that didn't happen either.

He gazed at her with dignity as he considered saying the simple truth, starting from there, come what would, but the thought of confessing what he had done almost panicked him.

"I'm sorry," he said brokenly, but by then she was gone, and he was attempting to fix in his memory what she had looked like so close.

Helen too was troubled. Not only could she not explain why she believed yet did not fully believe him, nor why she had lately become so conscious of his presence among them, though he never strayed from the store, but she was also disturbed by her mother's efforts to keep her away from him.

"Eat when he leaves," Ida had said. "I am not used to goyim in my house." This annoyed Helen because of the assumption that she would keel over for somebody just because he happened to be a gentile. It meant, obviously, her mother didn't trust her. If she had been casual about him, Helen doubted she would have paid him any attention to speak of. He was interesting looking, true, but what except a poor grocery clerk? Out of nothing Ida was trying to make something.

Though Ida was still concerned at having the young Italian around the place, she observed with pleased surprise how, practically from the day of his appearance, the store had improved. During the first week there were days when they had taken in from five to seven dollars more than they were averaging daily in the months since summer. And the same held for the second week. The store was of course still a poor store, but with this forty to fifty a week more they might at least limp along until a buyer appeared. She could at first not understand why more people were coming in, why more goods were being sold. True, the same thing had happened before. Without warning, after a long season of dearth, three or four customers, lost faces, straggled in one day, as if they had been let out of their poor rooms with a few pennies in their pockets. And others, who had skimped on food, began to buy more. A storekeeper could tell almost at once when times were getting better. People seemed less worried and irritable, less in competition for the little sunlight in the world. Yet the curious thing was that business, according to most of the drivers, had not very much improved anywhere. One of them said that Schmitz around the corner was having his troubles too; furthermore he wasn't feeling so good. So the sudden pickup of business in the store, Ida thought, would not have happened without Frank Alpine. It took her a while to admit this to herself.

The customers seemed to like him. He talked a lot as he waited on them, sometimes saying things that embarrassed Ida but made the customers, the gentile housewives, laugh. He somehow drew in people she had never before seen in the neighborhood, not only women, men too. Frank tried things that Morris and she could never do, such as attempting to sell people more than they asked for, and usually he succeeded.

"What can you do with a quarter of a pound?" he would say. "A quarter is for the birds—not even a mouthful. Better make it a half." So they would make it a half. Or he would say, "Here's a new brand of mustard that we just got in today. It weighs two ounces more than the stuff they sell you in the supermarkets for the same price. Why don't you give it a try? If you don't like it, bring it back and I will gargle it." And they laughed and bought it. This made Ida wonder if Morris and she were really suited to the grocery business. They had never been salesmen.

One of the women customers called Frank a supersalesman, a word that brought a pleased smile to his lips. He was clever and worked hard. Ida's respect for him reluctantly grew; gradually she became more relaxed in his presence. Morris was right in recognizing that he was not a bum but a boy who had gone through bad times. She pitied him for having lived in an orphan asylum. He did his work quickly, never complained, kept himself neat and clean now that he had soap and water around, and answered her politely. The one or two times, just lately, that he had briefly talked to Helen in her presence, he had spoken like a gentleman and didn't try to stretch a word into a mouthful. Ida discussed the situation with Morris and they raised his "spending money" from fifty cents a day to five dollars for the week. Despite her good will to him, this worried Ida, but, after all, he was bringing more money into the store, the place looked spic and span—let him keep five dollars of their poor profit. Bad as things still were, he willingly did so much extra around the store—how could they not pay him a little something? Besides, she thought, he would soon be leaving.

Frank accepted the little raise with an embarrassed smile. "You don't have to pay me anything more, Mrs, I said I would work for nothing to make up for past favors from your husband and also to learn the business. Besides that, you give me my bed and board, so you don't owe me a thing."

"Take," she said, handing him a crumpled five-dollar bill. He let the money lie on the counter till she urged him to put it into his pocket. Frank felt troubled about the raise because he was earning something for his labor that Ida knew nothing of, for business was a little better than she thought. During the day, while she was not around, he sold at least a buck's worth, or a buck and a half, that he made no attempt to ring up on the register. Ida guessed nothing; the list of sold items he had supplied her with in the beginning they had discontinued as impractical. It wasn't hard for him to scrape up here a bit of change, there a bit. At the end of the second week he had ten dollars in his pocket. With this and the five she gave him he bought a shaving kit, a pair of cheap brown suede shoes, a couple of shirts and a tie or two; he figured that if he stayed around two more weeks he would own an inexpensive suit. He had nothing to be ashamed of, he thought—it was practically his own dough he was taking. The grocer and his wife wouldn't miss it because they didn't know they had it, and they wouldn't have it if it wasn't for his hard work. If he weren't working there, they would have less than they had with him taking what he took.

Thus he settled it in his mind only to find himself remorseful. He groaned, scratching the backs of his hands with his thick nails. Sometimes he felt short of breath and sweated profusely. He talked aloud to himself when he was alone, usually when he was shaving or in the toilet, exhorted himself to be honest. Yet he felt a curious pleasure in his misery, as he had at times in the past when he was doing something he knew he oughtn't to, so he kept on dropping quarters into his pants pocket.

One night he felt very bad about all the wrong he was doing and vowed to set himself straight. If I could do one right thing, he thought, maybe that would start me off; then he thought if he could get the gun and get rid of it he would at least feel better. He left the grocery after supper and wandered restlessly in the foggy streets, feeling cramped in the chest from his long days in the store and because his life hadn't changed much since he had come here. As he passed by the cemetery, he tried to keep out of his mind the memory of the holdup but it kept coming back in. He saw himself sitting with Ward Minogue in the parked car, waiting for Karp to come out of the grocery, but when he did his store lights went out and he hid in the back among the bottles. Ward said to drive quick around the block so they would flush the Jew out, and he would slug him on the sidewalk and take his fat wallet away; but when they got back, Karp's car was gone with him in it, and Ward cursed him into an early grave. Frank said Karp had beat it, so they ought to scram, but Ward sat there with heartburn, watching, with his small eyes, the grocery store, the one lit place on the block besides the candy store on the corner.

"No," Frank urged, "it's just a little joint, I got my doubts if they took in thirty bucks today."

"Thirty is thirty," Ward said. "I don't care if it's Karp or Bober, a Jew is a Jew."

"Why not the candy store?"

Ward made a face. "I can't stand penny candy."

"How do you know his name?" asked Frank.

"Who?"

"The Jew grocer."

"I used to go to school with his daughter. She has a nice ass."

"Then if that's so, he will recognize you."

"Not with a rag around my snoot, and I will rough up my voice. He ain't seen me for eight or nine years. I was a skinny kid then."

"Have it your way. I will keep the car running."

"Come in with me," Ward said. "The block is dead. Nobody will expect a stickup in this dump."

But Frank hesitated. "I thought you said Karp was the one you were out after?"

"I will take Karp some other time. Come on."

Frank put on his cap and crossed the car tracks with Ward Minogue. "It's your funeral," he said, but it was really his own.

He remembered thinking as they went into the store, a Jew is a Jew, what difference does it make? Now he thought, I held him up because he was a Jew. What the hell are they to me so that I gave them credit for it?

But he didn't know the answer and walked faster, from time to time glancing through the spiked iron fence at the shrouded gravestones. Once he felt he was being followed and his heart picked up a hard beat. He hurried past the cemetery and turned right on the first street after it, hugging the stoops of the stone houses as he went quickly down the dark street. When he reached the poolroom he felt relieved.

Pop's poolroom was a dreary four-table joint, owned by a glum old Italian with a blue-veined bald head and droopy hands, who sat close to his cash register.

"Seen Ward yet?" Frank said.

Pop pointed to the rear where Ward Minogue, in his fuzzy black hat and a bulky overcoat, was practicing shots alone at a table. Frank watched him place a black ball at a corner pocket and aim a white at it. Ward leaned tensely forward, his face strained, a dead butt hanging from his sick mouth. He shot but missed. He banged his cue on the floor.

Frank had drifted past the players at the other tables. When Ward looked up and saw him, his eyes lit with fear. The fear drained after he recognized who it was. But his pimply face was covered with sweat.

He spat his butt to the floor. "What have you got on your feet, you bastard, gumshoes?"

"I didn't want to spoil your shot."

"Anyway you did."

"I've been looking for you about a week."

"I was on my vacation." Ward smiled in the corner of his mouth.

"On a drunk?"

Ward put his hand to his chest and brought up a belch. "I wish to hell it was. Somebody tipped my old man I was around here, so I hid out for a while. I had a rough time. My heartburn is acting up." He hung up his cue, then wiped his face with a dirty handkerchief.

"Why don't you go to a doctor?" Frank said.

"The hell with them."

"Some medicine might help you."

"What will help me is if my goddam father drops dead."

"I want to talk to you, Ward," Frank said in a low voice.

"So talk."

Frank nodded toward the players at the next table.

"Come out in the yard," Ward said. "I got something I want to say to you."

Frank followed him out the rear door into a small enclosed back yard with a wooden bench against the building. A weak bulb shone down on them from the top of the doorjamb.

Ward sat down on the bench and lit a cigarette. Frank did

the same, from his own pack. He puffed but got no pleasure from the butt, so he threw it away.

"Sit down," said Ward.

Frank sat on the bench. Even in the fog he stinks, he thought.

"What do you want me for?" Ward asked, his small eyes restless.

"I want my gun, Ward. Where is it?"

"What for?"

"I want to throw it in the ocean."

Ward snickered. "Cat got your nuts?"

"I don't want some dick coming around and asking me do I own it."

"I thought you said you bought the rod off a fence."

"That's right."

"Then nobody's got a record of it, so what are you scared of?"

"If you lost it," Frank said, "they trace them even without a record."

"I won't lose it," Ward said. After a minute he ground his cigarette into the dirt. "I will give it back to you after we do this job I have on my mind."

Frank looked at him. "What kind of a job?"

"Karp. I want to stick him up."

"Why Karp?—there are bigger liquor stores."

"I hate that Jew son of a bitch and his popeyed Louis. When I was a kid all I had to do was go near banjo eyes and they would complain to my old man and get me beat up."

"They would recognize you if you go in there."

"Bober didn't. I will use a handkerchief and wear some different clothes. Tomorrow I will go out and pick up a car. All you got to do is drive and I will make the heist."

"You better stay away from that block," Frank warned. "Somebody might recognize you."

Ward moodily rubbed his chest. "All right, you sold me. We will go somewheres else."

"Not with me," Frank said.

"Think it over."

"I've had all I want."

Ward showed his disgust. "The minute I saw you I knew you would puke all over."

Frank didn't answer.

"Don't act so innocent," Ward said angrily. "You're hot, the same as me."

"I know," Frank said.

"I slugged him because he was lying where he hid the rest of the dough," Ward argued.

"He didn't hide it. It's a poor, lousy store."

"I guess you know all about that."

"What do you mean?"

"Can the crud. I know you been working there."

Frank drew a breath. "You following me again, Ward?"

Ward smiled. "I followed you one night after you left the poolroom. I found out you were working for a Jew and living on bird crap."

Frank slowly got up. "I felt sorry for him after you slugged him, so I went back to give him a hand while he was in a weak condition. But I won't be staying there long."

"That was real sweet of you. I suppose you gave him back the lousy seven and a half bucks that was your part of the take?"

"I put it back in the cash register. I told the Mrs the business was getting better."

"I never thought I would meet up with a goddam Salvation Army soldier."

"I did it to quiet my conscience," Frank said.

Ward rose. "That ain't your conscience you are worried about."

"No?"

"It's something else. I hear those Jew girls make nice ripe lays."

Frank went back without his gun.

Helen was with her mother as Ida counted the cash.

Frank stood behind the counter, cleaning his fingernails with his jackknife blade, waiting for them to leave so he could close up.

"I think I'll take a hot shower before I go to bed," Helen said to her mother. "I've felt chilled all night."

"Good night," Ida said to Frank. "I left five dollars change for the morning."

"Good night," said Frank.

They left by the rear door and he heard them go up the stairs. Frank closed the store and went into the back. He thumbed through tomorrow's *News*, then got restless.

After a while he went into the store and listened at the side door; he unlatched the lock, snapped on the cellar light, closed the cellar door behind him so no light would leak out into the hall, then quietly descended the stairs.

He found the air shaft where an old unused dumb-waiter stood, pushed the dusty box back and gazed up the vertical shaft. It was pitch-dark. Neither the Bobers' bathroom window nor the Fusos' showed any light.

Frank struggled against himself but not for long. Shoving the dumb-waiter back as far as it would go, he squeezed into the shaft and then boosted himself up on top of the box. His heart shook him with its beating.

When his eyes got used to the dark he saw that her bathroom window was only a couple of feet above his head. He felt along the wall as high as he could reach and touched a narrow ledge around the air shaft. He thought he could anchor himself on it and see into the bathroom.

But if you do it, he told himself, you will suffer.

Though his throat hurt and his clothes were drenched in sweat, the excitement of what he might see forced him to go up.

Crossing himself, Frank grabbed both of the dumb-waiter ropes and slowly pulled himself up, praying the pulley at the skylight wouldn't squeak too much.

A light went on over his head.

Holding his breath, he crouched motionless, clinging to the swaying ropes. Then the bathroom window was shut with a bang. For a while he couldn't move, the strength gone out of him. He thought he might lose his grip and fall, and he thought of her opening the bathroom window and seeing him lying at the bottom of the shaft in a broken, filthy heap.

It was a mistake to do it, he thought.

But she might be in the shower before he could get a look at her, so, trembling, he began again to pull himself up. In a few minutes he was straddling the ledge, holding onto the ropes to steady himself yet keep his full weight off the wood.

Leaning forward, though not too far, he could see through the uncurtained crossed sash window into the old-fashioned bathroom. Helen was there looking with sad eyes at herself in the mirror. He thought she would stand there forever, but at last she unzippered her housecoat, stepping out of it.

He felt a throb of pain at her nakedness, an overwhelming desire to love her, at the same time an awareness of loss, of never having had what he had wanted most, and other such memories he didn't care to recall.

Her body was young, soft, lovely, the breasts like small birds in flight, her ass like a flower. Yet it was a lonely body in spite of its lovely form, lonelier. Bodies are lonely, he thought, but in bed she wouldn't be. She seemed realer to him now than she had been, revealed without clothes, personal, possible. He felt greedy as he gazed, all eyes at a banquet, hungry so long as he must look. But in looking he was forcing her out of reach, making her into a thing only of his seeing, her eyes reflecting his sins, rotten past, spoiled ideals, his passion poisoned by his shame.

Frank's eyes grew moist and he wiped them with one hand. When he gazed up again she seemed, to his horror, to be staring at him through the window, a mocking smile on her lips, her eyes filled with scorn, pitiless. He thought wildly of jumping, bolting, broken-boned, out of the house; but she turned on the shower and stepped into the tub, drawing the flowered plastic curtain around her.

The window was quickly covered with steam. For this he was relieved, grateful. He let himself down silently. In the cellar, instead of the grinding remorse he had expected to suffer, he felt a moving joy.

O N A Saturday morning in December, Morris, after a little more than two impatient weeks upstairs, came down with his head healed. The night before, Ida told Frank he would have to leave in the morning, but when Morris later learned this they had an argument. Although he hadn't said so to Ida, the grocer, after his long layoff, was depressed at the prospect of having to take up his dreary existence in the store. He dreaded the deadweight of hours, mostly sad memories of his lost years of youth. That business was better gave him some comfort but not enough, for he was convinced from all Ida had told him that business was better only because of their assistant, whom he remembered as a stranger with hungry eyes, a man to be pitied. Yet the why of it was simple enough—the store had improved not because this cellar dweller was a magician, but because he was not Jewish. The goyim in the neighborhood were happier with one of their own. A Jew stuck in their throats. Yes, they had, on and off, patronized his store, called him by his first name and asked for credit as if he were obliged to give it, which he had, in the past, often foolishly done; but in their hearts they hated him. If it weren't so, Frank's presence could not have made such a quick difference in income. He was afraid that the extra forty-five dollars weekly would melt away overnight if the Italian left and he vehemently said so to Ida. She, though she feared he was right, still argued that Frank must be let go. How could they, she asked, keep him working seven days a week, twelve hours a day, for a miserable five dollars? It was unjust. The grocer agreed, but why push the boy into the street if he wanted to stay longer? The five dollars, he admitted, was nothing, but what of the bed and board, the free packs of cigarettes, the bottles of beer she said he guzzled in the store? If things went on well, he would offer him more, maybe even a small commission, very small—maybe on all they took in over a hundred and fifty a week, a sum they had not realized since Schmitz had opened up around the corner; meantime he would give him his Sundays off and otherwise reduce his hours. Since Morris was now able to open the store, Frank could stay in bed till nine. This proposition was no great bargain but the grocer insisted that the man have the chance to take or refuse it.

Ida, a red flush spreading on her neck, said, "Are you crazy, Morris? Even with the forty more that comes in, which we give him away five dollars, our little profit, who can afford to keep him here? Look what he eats. It's impossible."

"We can't afford to keep him but we can't afford to lose him, on account he might improve more the business if he stays," Morris answered.

"How can three people work in such a small store?" she cried.

"Rest your sick feet," he answered. "Sleep longer in the morning and stay more upstairs in the house. Who needs you should be so tired every night?"

"Also," Ida argued, "who wants him in the back all night so we can't go inside after the store is closed when we forget something?"

"This I thought about also. I think I will take off from Nick's rent upstairs a couple dollars and tell him he should give Frank the little room to sleep in. They don't use it for nothing, only storage. There, with plenty blankets he will be comfortable, with a door which it goes right in the hall so he can come in and go out with his own key without bothering anybody. He can wash himself here in the store."

"A couple dollars less from the rent comes also from our poor pocket," Ida replied, pressing her clasped hands to her bosom. "But the most important is I don't want him here on account of Helen. I don't like the way he looks on her."

Morris gazed at her. "So you like maybe how Nat looks on her, or Louis Karp? That's the way they look, the boys. Tell me better, how does she look on him?"

She shrugged stiffly.

"This is what I thought. You know yourself Helen wouldn't be interested in such a boy. A grocery clerk don't interest her. Does she go out with the salesmen where she works, that they ask her? No. She wants better—so let her have better."

"Will be trouble," she murmured.

He belittled her fears, and when he came down on Saturday morning, spoke to Frank about staying on for a while. Frank had arisen before six and was sitting dejectedly on the couch when the grocer came in. He agreed at once to continue on in the store under the conditions Morris offered.

More animated now, the clerk said he liked the idea of living upstairs near Nick and Tessie; and Morris that day arranged it, in spite of Ida's misgivings, by promising three dollars off their rent. Tessie lugged out of the room a trunk, garment bags and a few odds and ends of furniture; after, she dusted and vacuumed. Between what she offered, and what Morris got out of his bin in the cellar, they supplied a bed with a fairly good mattress, a usable chest of drawers, chair, small table, electric heater and even an old radio Nick had around. Although the room was cold, because it had no radiator and was locked off from the Fusos' gas-heated bedroom, Frank was satisfied. Tessie worried about what would happen if he had to go to the bathroom at night, and Nick talked the matter over with Frank, saying apologetically that she was ashamed to have him go through their bedroom, but Frank said he never woke up at night. Anyway, Nick had a key made to the front door patent lock. He said if Frank ever had to get up he could walk across the hall and let himself in through the front without waking them. And he could also use their bathtub, just so long as he told them when he would want it.

This arrangement suited Tessie. Everyone was satisfied but Ida, who was unhappy with herself for having kept Frank on. She made the grocer promise he would send the clerk away before the summer. Business was always more active in the summertime, so Morris agreed. She asked him to tell Frank at once that he would be let go then, and when the grocer did, the clerk smiled amiably and said the summer was a long ways off but anyway it was all right with him.

The grocer felt his mood change. It was a better mood than he had expected. A few of his old customers had returned. One woman told him that Schmitz was not giving as good service as he once did; he was having trouble with his health and was thinking of selling the store. Let him sell, thought Morris. He thought, let him die, then severely struck his chest.

Ida stayed upstairs most of the day, reluctantly at first, less so as time went by. She came down to prepare lunch and supper—Frank still ate before Helen—or to make a salad when it was needed. She attended to little else in the store; Frank did the cleaning and mopping. Upstairs, Ida took care of the house, read a bit, listened to the Jewish programs on the radio and knitted. Helen bought some wool and Ida knitted her a sweater. In the night, after Frank had gone, Ida spent her time in the store, added up the accounts in her notebook and left with Morris when he closed up.

The grocer got along well with his assistant. They divided tasks and waited on alternate customers, though the waiting in between was still much too long. Morris went up for naps to forget the store. He too urged Frank to take some time off in the afternoon, to break the monotony of the day. Frank, somewhat restless, finally began to. Sometimes he went up to his room and lay on the bed, listening to the radio. Usually he put his coat on over his apron and visited one of the other stores on the block. He liked Giannola, the Italian barber across the street, an old man who had recently lost his wife and sat in the shop all day, even when it was long past time to go home; the old barber gave a fine haircut. Occasionally Frank dropped in on Louis Karp and gassed with him, but generally Louis bored him. Sometimes he went into the butcher store, next door to Morris, and talked in the back room with Artie, the butcher's son, a blond fellow with a bad complexion who was interested in riding horses. Frank said he might go riding with him sometime but he never did though Artie invited him. Once in a while he drank a beer in the bar on the corner, where he liked Earl, the bartender. Yet when the clerk got back to the grocery he was glad to go in.

When he and Morris were together in the back they spent a lot of time talking. Morris liked Frank's company; he liked to hear about strange places, and Frank told him about some of the cities he had been to, in his long wandering, and some of the different jobs he had worked at. He had passed part of his early life in Oakland, California, but most of it across the bay in a home in San Francisco. He told Morris stories about his hard times as a kid. In this second family the home had sent him to, the man used to work him hard in his machine shop. "I wasn't twelve," Frank said, "and he kept me out of school as long as he could get away with."

After staying with that family for three years, he took off.

"Then began my long period of travels." The clerk fell silent, and the ticking clock, on the shelf above the sink, sounded flat and heavy. "I am mostly self-educated," he ended.

Morris told Frank about life in the old country. They were poor and there were pogroms. So when he was about to be conscripted into the czar's army his father said, "Run to America." A landsman, a friend of his father, had sent money for his passage. But he waited for the Russians to call him up, because if you left the district before they had conscripted you, then your father was arrested, fined and imprisoned. If the son got away after induction, then the father could not be blamed; it was the army's responsibility. Morris and his father, a peddler in butter and eggs, planned that he would try to get away on his first day in the barracks.

So on that day, Morris said, he told the sergeant, a peasant with red eyes and a bushy mustache which smelled of tobacco, that he wanted to buy some cigarettes in the town. He felt scared but was doing what his father had advised him to do. The half-drunk sergeant agreed he could go, but since Morris was not yet in uniform he would have to go along with him. It was a September day and had just rained. They walked along a muddy road till they reached the town. There, in an inn, Morris bought cigarettes for himself and the sergeant; then, as he had planned it with his father, he invited the soldier to drink some vodka with him. His stomach became rigid at the chance he was taking. He had never drunk in an inn before, and he had never before tried to deceive anybody to this extent. The sergeant, filling his glass often, told Morris the story of his life, crying when he came to the part where, through forgetfulness, he had not attended his mother's funeral. Then he blew his nose, and wagging a thick finger in Morris's face, warned him if he had any plans to skip, he had better forget them if he expected to live. A dead Jew was of less consequence than a live one. Morris felt a heavy gloom descend on him. In his heart he surrendered his freedom for years to come. Yet once they had left the inn and were trudging in the mud back to the barracks, his hopes rose as the sergeant, in his stupor, kept falling behind. Morris walked slowly on, then the sergeant would cup his hands to his mouth, and cursing, haloo for him to wait. Morris waited. They would go on together, the sergeant muttering to himself, Morris uncertain what would happen next. Then the soldier stopped to urinate into a ditch in the road. Morris pretended to wait but he walked on, every minute expecting a bullet to crash through his shoulders and leave him lying in the dirt, his future with the worms. But then, as if seized by his fate, he began to run. The halooing and cursing grew louder as the red-faced sergeant, waving a revolver, stumbled after him; but when he reached the bend of the tree-lined road where he had last seen Morris, nobody was there but a yellow-bearded peasant driving a nag pulling a load of hay.

Telling this story excited the grocer. He lit a cigarette and smoked without coughing. But when he had finished, when there was no more to say, a sadness settled on him. Sitting in his chair, he seemed a small, lonely man. All the time he had been upstairs his hair had grown bushier and he wore a thick pelt of it at the back of his neck. His face was thinner than before.

Frank thought about the story Morris had just told him. That was the big jig in his life but where had it got him? He had escaped out of the Russian Army to the U.S.A., but once in a store he was like a fish fried in deep fat.

"After I came here I wanted to be a druggist," Morris said. "I went for a year in night school. I took algebra, also German and English. '"Come," said the wind to the leaves one day, "come over the meadow with me and play."' This is a poem I learned. But I didn't have the patience to stay in night school, so when I met my wife I gave up my chances." Sighing, he said, "Without education you are lost."

Frank nodded.

"You're still young," Morris said. "A young man without a family is free. Don't do what I did."

"I won't," Frank said.

But the grocer didn't seem to believe him. It made the clerk uncomfortable to see the wet-eyed old bird brooding over him. His pity leaks out of his pants, he thought, but he would get used to it.

When they were behind the counter together, Morris kept an eye on Frank and tried to improve some of the things Ida had taught him. The clerk did very well what he was supposed to.

As if ashamed somebody could learn the business so easily, Morris explained to him how different it had been to be a grocer only a few years ago. In those days one was more of a macher, a craftsman. Who was ever called on nowadays to slice up a loaf of bread for a customer, or ladle out a quart of milk?

"Now is everything in containers, jars, or packages. Even hard cheeses that they cut them for hundreds of years by hand come now sliced up in cellophane packages. Nobody has to know anything any more."

"I remember the family milk cans," Frank said, "only my family sent me out to get beer in them."

But Morris said it was a good idea that milk wasn't sold loose any more. "I used to know grocers that they took out a quart or two cream from the top of the can, then they put in water. This water-milk they sold at the regular price."

He told Frank about some other tricks he had seen. "In some stores they bought two kinds loose coffee and two kinds tub butter. One was low grade, the other was medium, but the medium they put half in the medium bin and half in the best. So if you bought the best coffee or the best butter you got medium—nothing else."

Frank laughed. "I'll bet some of the customers came back saying that the best butter tasted better than the medium."

"It's easy to fool people," said Morris.

"Why don't you try a couple of those tricks yourself, Morris? Your amount of profit is small."

Morris looked at him in surprise. "Why should I steal from my customers? Do they steal from me?"

"They would if they could."

"When a man is honest he don't worry when he sleeps. This is more important than to steal a nickel."

Frank nodded.

But he continued to steal. He would stop for a few days then almost with relief go back to it. There were times stealing made him feel good. It felt good to have some change in his pocket, and it felt good to pluck a buck from under the Jew's nose. He would slip it into his pants pocket so deftly that he had to keep himself from laughing. With this money, and what he earned, he bought a suit and hat, and got new tubes for Nick's radio. Now and then, through Sam Pearl, who telephoned it in for him, he laid a two-buck bet on a horse, but as a rule he was careful with the dough. He opened a small savings account in a bank near the library and hid the bankbook under his mattress. The money was for future use.

When he felt pepped up about stealing, it was also because he felt he had brought them luck. If he stopped stealing he bet business would fall off again. He was doing them a favor, at the same time making it a little worth his while to stay on and give them a hand. Taking this small cut was his way of showing himself he had something to give. Besides, he planned to return everything sometime or why would he be marking down the figure of what he took? He kept it on a small card in his shoe. He might someday plunk down a tenner or so on some longshot and then have enough to pay back every lousy cent of what he had taken.

For this reason he could not explain why, from one day to another, he should begin to feel bad about snitching the bucks from Morris, but he did. Sometimes he went around with a quiet grief in him, as if he had just buried a friend and was carrying the fresh grave within himself. This was an old feeling of his. He remembered having had something like it for years back. On days he felt this way he sometimes got headaches and went around muttering to himself. He was afraid to look into the mirror for fear it would split apart and drop into the sink. He was wound up so tight he would spin for a week if the spring snapped. He was full of sudden rages at himself. These were his worst days and he suffered trying to hide his feelings. Yet they had a curious way of ending. The rage he felt disappeared like a windstorm that quietly pooped out, and he felt a sort of gentleness creeping in. He felt gentle to the people who came into the store, especially the kids, whom he gave penny crackers to for nothing. He was gentle to Morris, and the Jew was gentle to him. And he was filled with a quiet gentleness for Helen and no longer climbed the air shaft to spy on her, naked in the bathroom.

And there were days when he was sick to death of everything. He had had it, up to here. Going downstairs in the morning he thought he would gladly help the store burn if it caught on fire. Thinking of Morris waiting on the same lousy customers day after day throughout the years, as they picked out with dirty fingers the same cheap items they ate every day of their flea-bitten lives, then when they were gone, waiting for them to come back again, he felt like leaning over the banister and throwing up. What kind of a man did you have to be born to shut yourself up in an overgrown coffin and never once during the day, so help you, outside of going for your Yiddish newspaper, poke your beak out of the door for a snootful of air? The answer wasn't hard to say—you had to be a Jew. They were born prisoners. That was what Morris was, with his deadly patience, or endurance, or whatever the hell it was; and it explained Al Marcus, the paper products salesman, and that skinny rooster Breitbart, who dragged from store to store his two heavy cartons full of bulbs.

Al Marcus, who had once, with an apologetic smile, warned the clerk not to trap himself in a grocery, was a well-dressed man of forty-six, but he looked, whenever you saw him, as if he had just lapped up cyanide. His face was the whitest Frank had ever seen, and what anybody saw in his eyes if he took a good look, would not help his appetite. The truth of it was, the grocer had confided to Frank, that Al had cancer and was supposed to be dead in his grave a year ago, but he fooled the doctors; he stayed alive if you could call it that. Although he had a comfortable pile, he wouldn't quit working and showed up regularly once a month to take orders for paper bags, wrapping paper and containers. No matter how bad business was, Morris tried to have some kind of little order waiting for him. Al would suck on an unlit cigar, scribble an item or two on a pink page in his metal-covered salesbook, then stand around a few minutes, making small talk, his eyes far away from what he was saying; and after that, tip his hat and take off for the next place. Everybody knew how sick he was, and a couple of the storekeepers earnestly advised him to quit working, but Al, smiling apologetically, took his cigar out of his mouth and said, "If I stay home, somebody in a high hat is gonna walk up the stairs and put a knock on my door. This way let him at least move his bony ass around and try and find me."

As for Breitbart, according to Morris, nine years ago he had owned a good business, but his brother ran it into the ground, gambling, then he took off with what was left of the bank account, persuading Breitbart's wife to come along and keep it company. That left him with a drawerful of bills and no credit; also a not too bright five-year-old boy. Breitbart went bankrupt; his creditors plucked every feather. For months he and the boy lived in a small, dirty furnished room, Breitbart not having the heart to go out to look for work. Times were bad. He went on relief and later took to peddling. He was now in his fifties but his hair had turned white and he acted like an old man. He bought electric bulbs at wholesale and carried two cartons of them slung, with clothesline rope, over his shoulder. Every day, in his crooked shoes, he walked miles, looking into stores and calling out in a mournful voice, "Lights for sale." At night he went home and cooked supper for his Hymie, who played hooky whenever he could from the vocational school where they were making him into a shoemaker.

When Breitbart first came to Morris's neighborhood and dropped into the store, the grocer, seeing his fatigue, offered him a glass of tea with lemon. The peddler eased the rope off his shoulder and set his boxes on the floor. In the back he gulped the hot tea in silence, warming both hands on the glass. And though he had, besides his other troubles, the seven-year itch, which kept him awake half the night, he never complained. After ten minutes he got up, thanked the grocer, fitted the rope onto his lean and itchy shoulder and left. One day he told Morris the story of his life and they both wept.

That's what they live for, Frank thought, to suffer. And the one that has got the biggest pain in the gut and can hold onto it the longest without running to the toilet is the best Jew. No wonder they got on his nerves.

Winter tormented Helen. She ran from it, hid in the house. In the house she revenged herself on December by crossing off the calendar all its days. If Nat would only call, she thought endlessly, but the telephone was deaf and dumb. She dreamed of him nightly, felt deeply in love, famished for him; would gladly have danced into his warm white bed if only he nodded, or she dared ask him to ask her; but Nat never called. She hadn't for a minute glimpsed him since running into him on the subway early in November. He lived around the corner but it might as well be Paradise. So with a sharp-pointed pencil she scratched out each dead day while it still lived.

Though Frank hungered for her company he rarely spoke to her. Now and then he passed her on the street. She murmured hello and walked on with her books, conscious of his eyes following her. Sometimes in the store, as if in defiance of her mother, she stopped to talk for a minute with the clerk. Once he startled her by abruptly mentioning this book he was reading. He longed to ask her to go out with him, but never dared; the old lady's eyes showed distrust of the goings on. So he waited. Mostly he watched for her at the window. He studied her hidden face, sensed her lacks, which deepened his own, but didn't know what to do about it.

December yielded nothing to spring. She awoke to each frozen, lonely day with dulled feeling. Then one Sunday afternoon winter leaned backward for an hour and she went walking. Suddenly she forgave everyone everything. A warmish breath of air was enough to inspire; she was again grateful for living. But the sun soon sank and it snowed pellets. She returned home, leaden. Frank was standing at Sam Pearl's deserted corner but she seemed not to see him though she brushed by. He felt very bad. He wanted her but the facts made a terrible construction. They were Jews and he was not. If he started going out with Helen her mother would throw a double fit and Morris another. And Helen made him feel, from the way she carried herself, even when she seemed most lonely, that she had plans for something big in her life—nobody like F. Alpine. He had nothing, a backbreaking past, had committed a crime against her old man, and in spite of his touchy conscience, was stealing from him too. How complicated could impossible get?

He saw only one way of squeezing through the stone knot; start by shoveling out the load he was carrying around in his mind by admitting to Morris that he was one of the guys that had held him up. It was a funny thing about that; he wasn't really sorry they had stuck up a Jew but he hadn't expected to be sorry that they had picked on this particular one, Bober; yet now he was. He had not minded, if by mind you meant in expectation, but what he hadn't minded no longer seemed to matter. The matter was how he now felt, and he now felt bad he had done it. And when Helen was around he felt worse.

So the confession had to come first—this stuck like a bone through the neck. From the minute he had tailed Ward Minogue into the grocery that night, he had got this sick feeling that he might someday have to vomit up in words, no matter how hard or disgusting it was to do, the thing he was then engaged in doing. He felt he had known this, in some frightful way, a long time before he went into the store, before he had met Minogue, or even come east; that he had really known all his life he would sometime, through throat blistered with shame, his eyes in the dirt, have to tell some poor son of a bitch that he was the one who had hurt or betrayed him. This thought had lived in him with claws; or like a thirst he could never spit out, a repulsive need to get out of his system all that had happened—for whatever had happened had happened wrong; to clean it out of his self and bring in a little peace, a little order; to change the beginning, beginning with the past that always stupendously stank up the now—to change his life before the smell of it suffocated him.

Yet when the chance came to say it, when he was alone with Morris that November morning in the back of the store, as they were drinking the coffee that the Jew had served him, and the impulse came on him to spill everything now, *now*, he had strained to heave it up, but it was like tearing up your whole life, with the broken roots and blood; and a fear burned in his gut that once he had got started saying the wrongs he had done he would never leave off until he had turned black; so instead he had told him a few hurried things about how ass-backward his life had gone, which didn't even begin to say what he wanted. He had worked on Morris's pity and left halfway satisfied, but not for long, because soon the need to say it returned and he heard himself groaning, but groans weren't words.

He argued with himself that he was smart in not revealing to the grocer more than he had. Enough was enough; besides, how much of a confession was the Jew entitled to for the seven and a half bucks he had taken, then put back into his cash register drawer, and for the knock on the head he had got from Ward, whom he himself had come with unwillingly?

Maybe willing, but not to do what had finally been done. That deserved some consideration, didn't it? Furthermore, he had begged the creep not to hurt anybody, and had later turned him down when he cooked up another scheme of stickup against Karp, who they were out to get in the first place. That showed his good intentions for the future, didn't it? And who was it, after all was said and done, that had waited around shivering in his pants in the dark cold, to pull in Morris's milk boxes, and had worked his ass to a frazzle twelve hours a day while the Jew lay upstairs resting in his bed? And was even now keeping him from starvation in his little rat hole? All that added up to something too.

That was how he argued with himself, but it didn't help for long, and he was soon again fighting out how to jump free of what he had done. He would someday confess it all—he promised himself. If Morris accepted his explanation and solemn apology, it would clear the rocks out of the road for the next move. As for his present stealing from the cash register, he had decided that once he had told the grocer all there was to say about the holdup, he would at the same time start paying back into the drawer, out of his little salary and the few bucks he had put away in the bank, what he had taken, and that would fix that. It wouldn't necessarily mean that Helen Bober would then and there fall for him—the opposite could happen—but if she *did*, he wouldn't feel bad about it.

He knew by heart what he would say to the grocer once he got to say it. One day while they were talking in the back, he would begin, as he had once done, about how his life was mostly made up of lost chances, some so promising he could still not stand to remember them. Well, after certain bad breaks through various causes, mostly his own mistakes—he was piled high with regrets—after many such failures, though he tried every which way to free himself from them, usually he failed; so after a time he gave up and let himself be a bum. He lived in gutters, cellars if he was lucky, slept in lots, ate what the dogs wouldn't, or couldn't, and what he scrounged out of garbage cans. He wore what he found, slept where he flopped and guzzled anything.

By rights this should have killed him, but he lived on, bearded, smelly, dragging himself through the seasons without

a hope to go by. How many months he had existed this way he
would never know. Nobody kept the score of it. But one day
while he lay in some hole he had crawled into, he had this
terrific idea that he was really an important guy, and was torn
out of his reverie with the thought that he was living this kind
of life only because he hadn't known he was meant for something a whole lot better—to do something big, different. He
had not till that minute understood this. In the past he had
usually thought of himself as an average guy, but there in this
cellar it came to him he was wrong. That was why his luck had
so often curdled, because he had the wrong idea of what he
really was and had spent all his energy trying to do the wrong
things. Then when he had asked himself what should he be
doing, he had another powerful idea, that he was meant for
crime. He had at times teased himself with this thought, but
now it wouldn't let go of him. At crime he would change his
luck, make adventure, live like a prince. He shivered with
pleasure as he conceived robberies, assaults—murders if it had
to be—each violent act helping to satisfy a craving that somebody suffer as his own fortune improved. He felt infinitely relieved, believing that if a person figured for himself something
big, something different in his life, he had a better chance to
get it than some poor jerk who couldn't think that high up.

So he gave up his outhouse existence. He began to work
again, got himself a room, saved and bought a gun. Then he
headed east, where he figured he could live the way he
wanted—where there was money, nightclubs, babes. After a
week of prowling around in Boston, not sure where he ought
to start off, he hopped a freight to Brooklyn and a couple of
days after he got there met Ward Minogue. As they were
shooting pool one night, Ward cannily detected the gun on
him and made him the proposition that they do a holdup together. Frank welcomed the idea of some kind of start but said
he wanted to think about it more. He went to Coney Island,
and while sitting on the boardwalk, worrying about what he
ought to do, got this oppressive feeling he was being watched.
When he turned around it was Ward Minogue. Ward sat down
and told him that it was a Jew he planned to rob, so Frank
agreed to go with him.

But on the night of the holdup he found himself nervous. In

the car Ward sensed it and cursed him. Frank felt he had to stick it out, but the minute they were both in the grocery and tying handkerchiefs around their mouths, the whole idea seemed senseless. He could feel it poop out in his mind. His plans of crime lay down and died. He could hardly breathe in his unhappiness, wanted to rush out into the street and be swallowed up out of existence, but he couldn't let Ward stay there alone. In the back, nauseated by the sight of the Jew's bloodied head, he realized he had made the worst mistake yet, the hardest to wipe out. And that ended his short life of violent crime, another pipe dream, and he was trapped tighter in the tangle of his failures. All this he thought he would someday tell Morris. He knew the Jew well enough to feel sure of his mercy.

Yet there were times when he imagined himself, instead, telling it all to Helen. He wanted to do something that would open her eyes to his true self, but who could be a hero in a grocery store? Telling her would take guts and guts was something. He continued to feel he deserved a better fate, and he would find it if he only once—*once*—did the right thing—the thing to do at the right time. Maybe if they were ever together for any decent amount of time, he would ask her to listen. At first she might be embarrassed, but when he started telling her about his life, he knew she would hear him to the end. After that—who knew? With a dame all you needed was a beginning.

But when the clerk caught himself coldly and saw the sentimentality of his thinking—he was a sentimental wop at heart—he knew he was having another of his hopped-up dreams. What kind of a chance did he think he would have with her after he had admitted the stickup of her old man? So he figured the best thing was to keep quiet. At the same time a foreboding crept into him that if he said nothing now, he would someday soon have a dirtier past to reveal.

A few days after Christmas, on the night of a full moon, Frank, dressed in his new clothes, hurried to the library, about a dozen blocks from the grocery. The library was an enlarged store, well lit, with bulging shelves of books that smelled warm on winter nights. In the rear there were a few large reading tables. It was a pleasant place to come to out of the cold. His guess was good, soon Helen arrived. She wore a red woolen scarf on her head, one end thrown over her shoulder. He was at a table reading. She noticed him as she closed the door behind her; he knew it. They had met here, briefly, before. She had wondered what he read at the table, and once in passing, glanced quickly over his shoulder. She had guessed *Popular Mechanics*, but it was the life of somebody or other. Tonight, as usual, she was aware of his eyes on her as she moved about from shelf to shelf. When, after an hour, she left, he caught a tight hidden glance in his direction. Frank got up and checked out a book. She was halfway down the street before he caught up with her.

"Big moon." He reached up to tip his hat and awkwardly discovered he wasn't wearing any.

"It feels like snow," Helen answered.

He glanced at her to see if she was kidding, then at the sky. It was cloudless, flooded with moonlight.

"Maybe." As they approached the street corner, he remarked, "We could take a walk in the park if it's okay with you."

She shivered at the suggestion, yet turned with a nervous laugh at the corner, and walked by his side. She had said almost nothing to him since the night he had called her to answer the empty phone. Who it had been she would never know; the incident still puzzled her.

Helen felt for him, as they walked, an irritation bordering on something worse. She knew what caused it—her mother, in making every gentile, by definition, dangerous; therefore he and she, together, represented some potential evil. She was also annoyed that his eating eyes were always on her, for he saw, she felt, more than his occasionally trapped gaze revealed. She fought her dislike of him, reasoning it wasn't his fault if her mother had made him into an enemy; and if he was always looking at her, it meant at least he saw something attractive or why would he look? Considering her lonely life, for that she owed him gratitude.

The unpleasant feeling passed and she glanced guardedly up at him. He was walking unmarked in moonlight, innocent of her reaction to him. She felt then—this thought had come to her before—that there might be more to him than she had imagined. She felt ashamed she had never thanked him for the help he had given her father.

In the park the moon was smaller, a wanderer in the white sky. He was talking about winter. "It's funny you mentioned snow before," Frank said. "I was reading about the life of St. Francis in the library, and when you mentioned the snow it made me think about this story where he wakes up one winter night, asking himself did he do the right thing to be a monk. My God, he thought, supposing I met some nice young girl and got married to her and by now I had a wife and a family? That made him feel bad so he couldn't sleep. He got out of his straw bed and went outside of the church or monastery or wherever he was staying. The ground was all covered with snow. Out of it he made this snow woman, and he said, 'There, that's my wife.' Then he made two or three kids out of the snow. After, he kissed them all and went inside and laid down in the straw. He felt a whole lot better and fell asleep."

The story surprised and touched her.

"Did you just read that?"

"No. I remember it from the time I was a kid. My head is full of those stories, don't ask me why. A priest used to read them to the orphans in this home I was in, and I guess I never forgot them. They come into my thoughts for no reason at all."

He had had a haircut and in his new clothes was hardly recognizable as her father's baggy-pants assistant who had slept a week in their cellar. Tonight he looked like somebody she had never seen before. His clothes showed taste, and he was, in his way, interesting looking. Without an apron on he seemed younger.

They passed an empty bench. "What do you say if we sit down?" Frank said.

"I'd rather walk."

"Smoke?"

"No."

He lit a cigarette, then caught up with her.

"Sure is some night."

"I want to say thanks for helping my father," Helen said. "You've been very kind. I should have mentioned it before."

"Nobody has to thank me. Your father did me some good favors." He felt uncomfortable.

"Anyway, don't make a career of a grocery," she said. "There's no future in it."

He puffed with a smile on his lips. "Everybody warns me. Don't worry, my imagination is too big for me to get stuck in a grocery. It's only temporary work."

"It isn't what you usually do?"

"No." He set himself to be honest. "I'm just taking a breather, you could call it. I started out wrong and have to change my direction where I am going. The way it happened I landed up in your father's store, but I'm only staying there till I figure out what's my next move."

He remembered the confession he had considered making to her, but the time wasn't ready yet. You could confess as a stranger, and you could confess as a friend.

"I've tried about everything," he said, "now I got to choose one thing and stick with it. I'm tired of being on the move all the time."

"Isn't it a little late for you to be getting started?"

"I'm twenty-five. There are plenty of guys who start that late and some I have read about started later. Age don't mean a thing. It doesn't make you less than anybody else."

"I never said so." At the next empty bench she paused. "We could sit here for a few minutes if you like."

"Sure." Frank wiped the seat with his handkerchief before she sat down. He offered her his cigarettes.

"I said I don't smoke."

"Sorry, I thought you didn't want to smoke while you were walking. Some girls don't like to." He put his pack away.

She noticed the book he was carrying. "What are you reading?"

He showed it to her.

"The Life of Napoleon?"

"That's right."

"Why him?"

"Why not—he was great, wasn't he?"

"Others were in better ways."

"I'll read about them too," Frank said.

"Do you read a lot?"

"Sure. I am a curious guy. I like to know why people tick. I like to know the reason they do the things they do, if you know what I mean."

She said she did.

He asked her what book she was reading.

"*The Idiot*. Do you know it?"

"No. What's it about?"

"It's a novel."

"I'd rather read the truth," he said.

"It is the truth."

Helen asked, "Are you a high school graduate?"

He laughed. "Sure I am. Education is free in this country."

She blushed. "It was a silly question."

"I didn't mean any wisecrack," he said quickly.

"I didn't take it as such."

"I went to high school in three different states and finally got finished up at night—in a night school. I planned on going to college but this job came along that I couldn't turn down, so I changed my mind, but it was a mistake."

"I had to help my mother and father out," Helen said, "so I couldn't go either. I've taken courses in NYU at night—mostly lit courses—and I've added up about a year's credit, but it's very hard at night. My work doesn't satisfy me. I would still like to go full time in the day."

He flipped his butt away. "I've been thinking about starting in college lately, even if I am this age. I know a guy who did it."

"Would you go at night?" she asked.

"Maybe, maybe in the day if I could get the right kind of a job—in an all-night cafeteria or something like that, for instance. This guy I just mentioned did that—assistant manager or something. After five or six years he graduated an engineer. Now he's making his pile, working all over the country."

"It's hard doing it that way—very hard."

"The hours are rough but you get used to it. When you got something good to do, sleep is a waste of time."

"It takes years at night."

"Time don't mean anything to me."

"It does to me."

"The way I figure, anything is possible. I always think about the different kinds of chances I have. This has stuck in my mind—don't get yourself trapped in one thing, because maybe you can do something else a whole lot better. That's why I guess I never settled down so far. I've been exploring conditions. I still have some very good ambitions which I would like to see come true. The first step to that, I know for sure now, is to get a good education. I didn't use to think like that, but the more I live the more I do. Now it's always on my mind."

"I've always felt that way," Helen said.

He lit another cigarette, throwing the burnt match away. "What kind of work do you do?"

"I'm a secretary."

"You like it?" He smoked with half-closed eyes. She sensed he knew she didn't care for her job and suspected he had heard her father or mother say so.

After a while, she answered, "No, I don't. The job never changes. And I could live happily without seeing some of those characters I have to deal with all day long, the salesmen, I mean."

"They get fresh?"

"They talk a lot. I'd like to be doing something that feels useful—some kind of social work or maybe teaching. I have no sense of accomplishment in what I'm doing now. Five o'clock comes and at last I go home. That's about all I live for, I guess."

She spoke of her daily routine, but after a minute saw he was only half-listening. He was staring at the moon-drenched trees in the distance, his face drawn, his lit eyes elsewhere.

Helen sneezed, unwound her scarf and wrapped it tightly around her head.

"Shall we go now?"

"Just till I finish my cigarette."

Some fat nerve, she thought.

Yet his face, even with the broken nose, was sensitive in the dark light. What makes me so irritable? She had had the wrong idea of him but it was her own fault, the result of staying so long apart from people.

He drew a long jagged breath.

"Is something the matter?" she asked.

Frank cleared his throat but his voice was hoarse. "No, just something popped into my mind when I was looking at the moon. You know how your thoughts are."

"Nature sets you thinking?"

"I like scenery."

"I walk a lot for that reason."

"I like the sky at night, but you see more of it in the West. Out here the sky is too high, there are too many big buildings."

He squashed his cigarette with his heel and wearily rose, looking now like someone who had parted with his youth.

She got up and walked with him, curious about him. The moon moved above them in the homeless sky.

After a long silence, he said as they were walking, "I'd like to tell you what I was thinking about."

"Please, you don't have to."

"I feel like talking," he said. "I got to thinking about this carnie outfit I worked for one time when I was about twenty-one. Right after I got the job I fell for a girl in an acrobatic act. She was built something like you—on the slim side, I would say. At first I don't think I rated with her. I think she thought I wasn't a serious type of guy. She was kind of a complicated girl, you know, moody, with lots of problems in her mind that she kept to herself. Well, one day we got to talking and she told me she wanted to be a nun. I said, 'I don't think it will suit you.' 'What do you know about me?' she said. I didn't tell her, although I know people pretty well, don't ask me why, I guess you are born with certain things. Anyway, the whole summer long I was nuts about her but she wouldn't give me another look though there was nobody else around that I saw she went with. 'Is it my age?' I asked her. 'No, but you haven't lived,' she answered me. 'If you only could see in my heart all I have lived through,' I said, but I have my doubts if she believed me. All we ever did was talk like that. Once in a while I would ask her for a date, not thinking I would ever get one, and I never did. 'Give up,' I said to myself, 'all she is interested in is herself.'

"Then one morning, when it was getting to be around fall and you could smell the season changing, I said to her I was taking off when the show closed. 'Where are you going?' she asked me. I said I was going to look for a better life. She didn't answer anything to that. I said, 'Do you still want to be a nun?' She got red and looked away, then she answered she wasn't sure about that any more. I could see she had changed but I wasn't fool enough to think it was account of me. But I guess it really was, because by accident our hands sort of touched, and when I saw the way she looked at me, it was hard to breathe. My God, I thought, we are both in love. I said to her, 'Honey, meet me here after the show tonight and let's go where we will be alone.' She said yes. Before she left she gave me a quick kiss.

"Anyway, that same afternoon she took off in her old man's jalopy to buy a blouse she had seen in some store window in the last town, but on the way back it started to rain. Exactly what happened I don't know. I guess she misjudged a curve or something and went flying off the road. The jalopy bounced down the hill, and her neck was broken. . . . That's how it ended."

They walked in silence. Helen was moved. But why, she thought, all the sad music?

"I'm awfully sorry."

"It was years ago."

"It was a tragic thing to happen."

"I couldn't expect better," he said.

"Life renews itself."

"My luck stays the same."

"Go on with your plans for an education."

"That's about it," Frank said. "That's what I got to do."

Their eyes met, she felt her scalp prickle.

Then they left the park and went home.

Outside the dark grocery store she quickly said good night.

"I'll stay out a little longer," Frank said. "I like to see the moon."

She went upstairs.

In bed she thought of their walk, wondering how much to believe of what he had told her about his ambitions and plans for college. He could not have said anything to make a better impression on her. And what was the purpose of the sad tale of the carnival girl "built something like you"? Who was he mixing up with his carnival girls? Yet he had told the story simply, without any visible attempt to work on her sympathy. Probably it was a true memory, recalled because he happened to be feeling lonely. She had had her own moonlit memories to contend with. Thinking about Frank, she tried to see him straight but came up with a confusing image: the grocery clerk with the greedy eyes, on top of the ex-carnival hand and future serious college student, a man of possibilities.

On the verge of sleep she sensed a desire on his part to involve her in his life. The aversion she felt for him before returned but she succeeded without too much effort in dispelling it. Thoroughly awake now, she regretted she could not see the sky from her window in the wall, or look down into the street. Who was he making into a wife out of snowy moonlight?

EARNINGS IN the grocery, especially around Christmas and New Year's, continued to rise. For the last two weeks in December Morris averaged an unusual one hundred and ninety. Ida had a new theory to explain the spurt of business: an apartment house had opened for rentals a few blocks away; furthermore, she had heard that Schmitz was not so attentive to his store as he was before. An unmarried storekeeper was sometimes erratic. Morris didn't deny these things but he still attributed their good fortune mostly to his clerk. For reasons that were clear to him the customers liked Frank, so they brought in their friends. As a result, the grocer could once more meet his running expenses, and with pinching and scrimping, even pay off some outstanding bills. Grateful to Frank—who seemed to take for granted the upswing of business—he planned to pay him more than the measly five dollars they shamefacedly gave him, but cautiously decided to see if the added income would continue in January, when business usually slackened off. Even if he regularly took in two hundred a week, with the slight profit he made he could hardly afford a clerk. Before things were easier they had to take in a minimum of two-fifty or three hundred, an impossibility.

Since, though, the situation was better, Morris told Helen that he wanted her to keep more of her hard-earned twenty-five dollars; he said she must now keep fifteen, and if business stayed as it was maybe he would not need her assistance any more. He hoped so. Helen was overwhelmed at having fifteen a week to spend on herself. She needed shoes badly and could use a new coat—hers was little better than a rag—and a dress or two. And she wanted to put away a few dollars for future tuition at NYU. She felt like her father about Frank—he had changed their luck. Remembering what he had said in the park that night about his ambitions and desire for education, she felt he someday would get what he wanted because he was obviously more than just an ordinary person.

He was often at the library. Almost every time Helen went there she saw him sitting over an open book at one of the tables; she wondered if all he did in his spare time was come here and read. She respected him for it. She herself averaged two weekly visits, each time checking out only a book or two, because it was one of her few pleasures to return for another. Even at her loneliest she liked being among books, although she was sometimes depressed to see how much there was to read that she hadn't. Meeting Frank so often, she was at first uneasy: he haunted the place, for what? But, a library was a library; he came here, as she did, to satisfy certain needs. Like her he read a lot because he was lonely, Helen thought. She thought this after he had told her about the carnival girl. Gradually her uneasiness left her.

Although he left, as a rule, when she did, if she wanted to walk home alone, he did not intrude. Sometimes he rode back on the trolley while she walked. Sometimes she was on the trolley and saw him walking. But generally, so long as the weather was not too bad, they went home together, a couple of times turning off into the park. He told her more about himself. He had lived a different life from most people she had known, and she envied him all the places he had been to. Her own life, she thought, was much like her father's, restricted by his store, his habits, hers. Morris hardly ever journeyed past the corner, except on rare occasions, usually to return something a customer had left on the counter. When Ephraim was alive, when they were kids, her father liked to go bathing Sunday afternoons at Coney Island; and on Jewish holidays they would sometimes see a Yiddish play, or ride on the subway to the Bronx to call on landsleit. But after Ephraim died Morris had for years gone nowhere. Neither had she, for other reasons. Where could she go without a cent? She read with eagerness of far-off places but spent her life close to home. She would have given much to visit Charleston, New Orleans, San Francisco, cities she had heard so much about, but she hardly ever got beyond the borough of Manhattan. Hearing Frank talk of Mexico, Texas, California, other such places, she realized anew the meagerness of her movements: every day but Sunday on the BMT to Thirty-fourth Street and back. Add to that a twice-weekly visit to the library at night. In summer, the same as before, except a few times—usually during her vacation—to Manhattan Beach; also, if she were lucky, to a concert or two at Lewisohn Stadium. Once when she was twenty and worn out, her mother had insisted she go for a week to an inexpensive adult camp in New Jersey. Before that, while in high school, she had traveled to Washington, D.C., with her American history class for a week end of visiting government buildings. So far and no further in the open world. To stick so close to where she had lived her whole life was a crime. His stories made her impatient—she wanted to travel, experience, live.

One night as they were sitting on a bench in an enclosed part of the park beyond the tree-lined plaza, Frank said he had definitely made up his mind to start college in the fall. This excited her, and for hours afterward Helen couldn't stop thinking about it. She imagined all the interesting courses he could take, envied him the worthwhile people he'd meet in his classes, the fun he'd have studying. She pictured him in nice clothes, his hair cut shorter, maybe his nose straightened, speaking a more careful English, interested in music and literature, learning about politics, psychology, philosophy; wanting to know more the more he knew, in this way growing in value to himself and others. She imagined herself invited by him to a campus concert or play, where she would meet his college friends, people of promise. Afterward as they crossed the campus in the dark, Frank would point out the buildings his classes met in, classes taught by distinguished professors. And maybe if she closed h\er eyes she could see a time—miracle of miracles—when Helen Bober was enrolled here, not just a stranger on the run, pecking at a course or two at night, and tomorrow morning back at Levenspiel's Louisville Panties and Bras. At least he made her dream.

To help him prepare for college Helen said he ought to read some good novels, some of the great ones. She wanted Frank to like novels, to enjoy in them what she did. So she checked out *Madame Bovary, Anna Karenina* and *Crime and Punishment,* all by writers he had barely heard of, but they were very satisfying books, she said. He noticed she handled each yellow-paged volume as though she were holding in her respectful hands the works of God Almighty. As if—according to her— you could read in them everything you couldn't afford not to know—the Truth about Life. Frank carried the three books up to his room, and huddled in a blanket to escape the cold that seeped in through the loose window frames, had rough going.

The stories were hard to get into because the people and places were strange to him, their crazy names difficult to hold in his mind and some of the sentences were so godawful complicated he forgot the beginning before he got to the end. The opening pages irritated him as he pushed through forests of odd facts and actions. Though he stared for hours at the words, starting one book, then another, then the third—in the end, in exasperation, he flung them aside.

But because Helen had read and respected these books, it shamed him that he hadn't, so he picked one up from the floor and went back to it. As he dragged himself through the first chapters, gradually the reading became easier and he got interested in the people—their lives in one way or another wounded—some to death. Frank read, at the start, in snatches, then in bursts of strange hunger, and before too long he had managed to finish the books. He had started *Madame Bovary* with some curiosity, but in the end he felt disgusted, wearied, left cold. He did not know why people would want to write about that kind of a dame. Yet he felt a little sorry for her and the way things had happened, till there was no way out of it but her death. *Anna Karenina* was better; she was more interesting and better in bed. He didn't want her to kill herself under the train in the end. Still, although Frank felt he could also take the book or leave it, he was moved at the deep change that came over Levin in the woods just after he had thought of hanging himself. At least he wanted to live. *Crime and Punishment* repelled yet fascinated him, with everybody in the joint confessing to something every time he opened his yap—to some weakness, or sickness, or crime. Raskolnikov, the student, gave him a pain, with all his miseries. Frank first had the idea he must be a Jew and was surprised when he found he wasn't. He felt, in places in the book, even when it excited him, as if his face had been shoved into dirty water in the gutter; in other places, as if he had been on a drunk for a month. He was glad when he was finished with the book, although he liked Sonia, the prostitute, and thought of her for days after he had read it.

Afterward Helen suggested other novels by the same writers, so he would know them better, but Frank balked, saying he wasn't sure that he had understood those he had read. "I'm sure you have," she answered, "if you got to know the people."

"I know them," he muttered. But to please her he worked through two more thick books, sometimes tasting nausea on his tongue, his face strained as he read, eyes bright black, frowning, although he usually felt some relief at the end of the book. He wondered what Helen found so satisfying in all this goddamned human misery, and suspected her of knowing he had spied on her in the bathroom and was using the books to punish him for it. But then he thought it was an unlikely idea. Anyway, he could not get out of his thoughts how quick some people's lives went to pot when they couldn't make up their minds what to do when they had to do it; and he was troubled by the thought of how easy it was for a man to wreck his whole life in a single wrong act. After that the guy suffered forever, no matter what he did to make up for the wrong. At times, as the clerk had sat in his room late at night, a book held stiffly in his reddened hands, his head numb although he wore a hat, he felt a strange falling away from the printed page and had this crazy sensation that he was reading about himself. At first this picked him up but then it deeply depressed him.

One rainy night, as Helen was about to go up to Frank's room to ask him to take back something he had given her that she didn't want, before she could go the phone rang, and Ida hastened out into the hall to call her. Frank, lying on his bed in his room, watching the rainy window, heard her go downstairs. Morris was in the store waiting on someone as Helen came in, but her mother sat in the back over a cup of tea.

"It's Nat," Ida whispered, not moving.

She'll tell herself she isn't listening, thought Helen.

Her first feeling was that she didn't want to talk to the law student, but his voice was warm, which for him meant extended effort, and a warm voice on a wet night was a warm voice. She could easily picture what he looked like as he spoke into the phone. Yet she wished he had called her in December, when she had so desperately wanted him, for now she was again aware of a detachment in herself that she couldn't account for.

"Nobody sees you any more, Helen," Nat began. "Where've you disappeared to?"

"Oh, I've been around," she said, trying to hide a slight tremble in her voice. "And you?"

"Is somebody there where you're talking that you sound so restrained?"

"That's right."

"I thought so. So let me make it quick and clean. Helen, it's been a long time. I want to see you. What do you say if we take in a play this Saturday night? I can stop off for tickets on my way uptown tomorrow."

"Thanks, Nat. I don't think so." She heard her mother sigh.

Nat cleared his throat. "Helen, I honestly want to know how somebody's supposed to defend himself when he hasn't any idea what's in the indictment against him? What kind of a crime have I committed? Yield the details."

"I'm not a lawyer—I don't make indictments."

"So call it a cause—what's the cause? One day we're close to each other, the next I'm alone on an island, holding my hat. What did I do, please tell me?"

"Let's drop this subject."

Here Ida rose and went into the store, softly closing the door behind her. Thanks, thought Helen. She kept her voice low so they wouldn't hear her through the window in the wall.

"You're a funny kid," Nat was saying. "You've got some old-fashioned values about some things. I always told you you punish yourself too much. Why should anybody have such a hot and heavy conscience in these times? People are freer in the twentieth century. Pardon me for saying it but it's true."

She blushed. His insight was to his credit. "My values are my values," she replied.

"What," Nat argued, "would people's lives be like if every-body regretted every beautiful minute of all that happened? Where's the poetry of living?"

"I hope you're alone," she said angrily, "where you're so blithely discussing this subject."

He sounded weary, hurt. "Of course I'm alone. My God, Helen, how low have I fallen in your opinion?"

"I told you what was going on at this end. Up to a minute ago my mother was still in the room."

"I'm sorry, I forgot."

"It's all right now."

"Look, girl," he said affectionately, "the telephone is no place to hash out our personal relations. What do you say if I run upstairs and see you right away? We got to come to some kind of a sensible understanding. I'm not exactly a pig, Helen. What you don't want is your privilege, if I may be so frank. So you don't want, but at least let's be friends and go out once in a while. Let me come up and talk to you."

"Some other time, Nat, I have to do something now."

"For instance?"

"Some other time," she said.

"Why not?" Nat answered amiably.

When he had hung up, Helen stood at the phone, wondering if she had done right. She felt she hadn't.

Ida entered the kitchen. "What did he want—Nat?"

"Just to talk."

"He asked you to go out?"

She admitted it.

"What did you answer him?"

"I said I would some other time."

"What do you mean 'some other time'?" Ida said sharply. "What are you already, Helen, an old lady? What good is it to sit so many nights alone upstairs? Who gets rich from reading? What's the matter with you?"

"Nothing's the matter, Mama." She left the store and went into the hall.

"Don't forget you're twenty-three years old," Ida called after her.

"I won't."

Upstairs her nervousness grew. When she thought what she had to do she didn't want to, yet felt she must.

They had met, she and Frank, last night at the library, the third time in eight days. Helen noticed as they were leaving that he clumsily carried a package she took to contain some shirts or underwear, but on the way home Frank flung away his cigarette, and under a street lamp handed it to her. "Here, this is for you."

"For me? What is it?"

"You'll find out."

She took it half-willingly, and thanked him. Helen carried it awkwardly the rest of the way home, neither of them saying much. She had been caught by surprise. If she had given herself a minute to think, she would have refused it on grounds that it was wise just to stay friends; because, she thought, neither of them really knew the other. But once she had the thing in her hands she hadn't the nerve to ask him to take it back. It was a medium-sized box of some sort with something heavy in it—she guessed a book; yet it seemed too big for a book. As she held it against her breast, she felt a throb of desire for Frank and this disturbed her. About a block from the grocery, nervously saying good night, she went on ahead. This was how they parted when the store window was still lit.

Ida was downstairs with Morris when Helen came into the house, so no questions were asked. She shivered a little as she unwrapped the box on her bed, ready to hide it the minute she heard a footstep on the stairs. Lifting the carton lid, she found two packages in it, each wrapped in white tissue paper and tied with red ribbons with uneven bows, obviously by Frank. When she had untied the first present, Helen gasped at the sight of a long, hand-woven scarf—rich black wool interlaced with gold thread. She was startled to discover that the second present was a red leather copy of Shakespeare's plays. There was no card.

She sat weakly down on the bed. I can't, she told herself. They were expensive things, probably had cost him every penny of the hard-earned money he was saving for college. Even supposing he had enough for that, she still couldn't take his gifts. It wasn't right, and coming from him, it was, somehow, less than not right.

She wanted then and there to go up to his room and leave them at the door with a note, but hadn't the heart to the very night he had given them to her.

The next evening, after a day of worry, she felt she must return them; and now she wished she had done it before Nat had called, then she might have been more relaxed on the phone.

Helen got down on her hands and knees and reached under the bed for the carton with Frank's scarf and book in it. It touched her that he had given her such lovely things—so much nicer than anyone else ever had. Nat, at his best, had produced a half-dozen small pink roses.

For gifts you pay, Helen thought. She drew a deep breath, and taking the box went quietly up the stairs. She tapped hesitantly on Frank's door. He had recognized her step and was waiting behind the door. His fists were clenched, the nails cutting his palms.

When he opened the door and his glance fell on what she was carrying, he frowned as though struck in the face.

Helen stepped awkwardly into the little room, quickly shutting the door behind her. She suppressed a shudder at the smallness and barrenness of the place. On his unmade bed lay a sock he had been trying to mend.

"Are the Fusos home?" she asked in a low voice.

"They went out." He spoke dully, his eyes hopelessly stuck to the things he had given her.

Helen handed him the box with the presents. "Thanks so much, Frank," she said, trying to smile, "but I really don't think I ought to take them. You'll need every cent for your college tuition in the fall."

"That's not the reason you mean," he said.

Her face reddened. She was about to explain that her mother would surely make a scene if she saw his gifts, but instead said, "I can't keep them."

"Why not?"

It wasn't easy to answer and he didn't make it easier, just held the rejected presents in his big hands as if they were living things that had suddenly died.

"I can't," she got out. "Your taste is so nice, I'm sorry."

"Okay," he said wearily. He tossed the box on the bed and the Shakespeare fell to the floor. She stooped quickly to pick it up and was unnerved to see it had opened to "Romeo and Juliet."

"Good night." She left his room and went hastily downstairs. In her room she thought she heard the distant sound of a man crying. She listened tensely, her hand on her throbbing throat, but no longer heard it.

Helen took a shower to relax, then got into a nightgown and housecoat. She picked up a book but couldn't read. She had noticed before signs he might be in love with her, but now she was almost sure of it. Carrying his package as he had walked with her last night, he had been somebody different, though the hat and overcoat were the same. There seemed to be about him a size and potentiality she had not seen before. He did not say love but love was in him. When the insight came to her, at almost the minute he was handing her the package, she had reacted with gooseflesh. That it had gone this far was her own fault. She had warned herself not to get mixed up with him but hadn't obeyed her warning. Out of loneliness she had encouraged him. What else, going so often to the library, knowing he would be there? And she had stopped off with him, on their walks, for pizzas and coffee; had listened to his stories, discussed with him plans for college, talked at length about books he was reading; at the same time she had been concealing these meetings from her father and mother. He knew it, no wonder he had built up hopes.

The strange thing was there were times she felt she liked him very much. He was, in many ways, a worthwhile person, and where a man gave off honest feeling, was she a machine to shut off her own? Yet she knew she mustn't become seriously attracted to him because there would be trouble in buckets. Trouble, thank you, she had had enough of. She wanted now a peaceful life without worry—any more worries. Friends they could be, in a minor key; she might on a moonlit night even hold hands with him, but beyond that nothing. She should have said something of the sort; he would have saved his presents for a better prospect and she would not now be feeling guilt at having hurt him. Yet in a way he had surprised her by his apparent depth of affection. She had not expected anything to happen so quickly, because, for her, things had happened in reverse order. Usually she fell in love first, then the man, if he wasn't Nat Pearl, responded. So the other way around was nice for a change, and she wished it would happen more often, but with the right one. She must go, she decided, less to the library; he would then understand, if he didn't already, and give up any idea of having her love. When he realized what was what he would get over his pain, if he really felt any. But her thoughts gave her no peace, and though she tried often, she could still not concentrate on her books. When Morris and Ida trudged through her room, her light was out and she seemed to be sleeping.

As she left the house for work the next morning, to her

dismay she spied the carton containing his presents on top of some greasy garbage bags in the stuffed rubbish can at the curb. The cover of the can apparently had been squeezed down on the box but had fallen off and now lay on the sidewalk. Lifting the carton cover, Helen saw the two gifts, loosely covered with the tissue paper. Angered by the waste, she plucked the scarf and book out of the crushed cardboard box and went quickly into the hall with them. If she took them upstairs Ida would want to know what she had, so she decided to hide them in the cellar. She turned on the light and went quietly down, trying to keep her high heels from clicking on the stairs. Then she removed the tissue paper and hid the presents, neither of which had been harmed, in the bottom drawer of a broken chiffonier in their bin. The dirty tissue paper and red ribbons she rolled up in a sheet of old newspaper, then went upstairs and pressed it into the garbage can. Helen noticed her father at the window, idly watching her. She passed into the store, said good morning, washed her hands and left for work. On the subway she felt despondent.

After supper that night, while Ida was washing dishes, Helen sneaked down into the cellar, got the scarf and book and carried them up to Frank's room. She knocked and nobody answered. She considered leaving them at the door but felt he would throw them away again unless she spoke to him first.

Tessie opened her door. "I heard him go out a while before, Helen." Her eyes were on the things in her hands.

Helen blushed. "Thanks, Tessie."

"Any message?"

"No." She returned to her floor and once more pushed the gifts under her bed. Changing her mind, she put the book and scarf in different bureau drawers, hiding them under her underwear. When her mother came up she was listening to the radio.

"You going someplace tonight, Helen?"

"Maybe, I don't know. Maybe to the library."

"Why so much to the library? You went a couple days ago."

"I go to meet Clark Gable, Mama."

"Helen, don't get fresh."

Sighing, she said she was sorry.

Ida sighed too. "Some people want their children to read more. I want you to read less."

"That won't get me married any faster."

Ida knitted but soon grew restless and went down to the store again. Helen got out Frank's things, packed them in heavy paper she had bought on her way home, tied the bundle with cord, and took the trolley to the library. He wasn't there.

The next night she tried first his room, then when she was able to slip out of the house, again the library, but found him in neither place.

"Does Frank still work here?" she asked Morris in the morning.

"Of course he works."

"I haven't seen him for a while," she said. "I thought he might be gone."

"In the summer he leaves."

"Did he say that?"

"Mama says."

"Does he know?"

"He knows. Why you ask me?"

She said she was just curious.

As Helen came into the hall that evening she heard the clerk descending the stairs and waited for him at the landing. Lifting his hat, he was about to pass when she spoke.

"Frank, why did you throw your two presents into the garbage?"

"What good were they to me?"

"It was a terrible waste. You should have got your money back."

He smiled in the corners of his mouth. "Easy come, easy go."

"Don't joke. I took them out of the rubbish and have them in my room for you. They weren't damaged."

"Thanks."

"Please give them back and get your money. You'll need every penny for the fall."

"Since I was a kid I hate to go back with stuff I bought."

"Then let me have the sales checks and I'll return them during my lunch hour."

"I lost them," he answered.

She said gently, "Frank, sometimes things turn out other than we plan. Don't feel hurt."

"When I don't feel hurt, I hope they bury me."

He left the house, she walked up the stairs.

Over the week end Helen went back to crossing off the days on the calendar. She found she had crossed nothing since New Year's. She fixed that. On Sunday the weather turned fair and she grew restless. She wished again for Nat to call her; instead his sister did and they walked, in the early afternoon, on the Parkway.

Betty was twenty-seven and resembled Sam Pearl. She was large-boned and on the plain side but made good use of reddish hair and a nice nature. She was in her ideas, Helen thought, somewhat dull. They had not too much in common and saw each other infrequently, but liked to talk once in a while, or go to a movie together. Recently Betty had become engaged to a CPA in her office and was with him most of the time. Now she sported a prosperous diamond ring on her stylish finger. Helen, for once, envied her, and Betty, as if she had guessed, wished her the same good luck.

"And it should happen soon," she said.

"Many thanks, Betty."

After they had gone a few blocks, Betty said, "Helen, I don't like to butt in somebody else's private business but for a long time I wanted to ask you what happened between you and my brother Nat. I once asked him and he gave me double talk."

"You know how such things go."

"I thought you liked him?"

"I did."

"Then why don't you see him any more? Did you have some kind of a fight?"

"No fights. We didn't have the same things in mind."

Betty asked no more. Later, she remarked, "Sometime give him another chance, Helen. Nat really has the makings of a good person. Shep, my boy friend, thinks so too. His worst fault is he thinks his brains entitle him to certain privileges. You'll see, in time he'll get over it."

"I may," Helen said. "We'll see sometime."

They returned to the candy store, where Shep Hirsch, Betty's stout, eyeglassed, future husband was waiting to take her for a drive in his Pontiac.

"Come along, Helen," said Betty.

"With pleasure." Shep tipped his hat.

"Go, Helen," advised Goldie Pearl.

"Thanks, all, from the bottom of my heart," said Helen, "but I have some of my underthings to iron."

Upstairs, she stood at the window, looking out at the back yards. The remnants of last week's dirty snow. No single blade of green, or flower to light the eye or lift the heart. She felt as if she were made of knots and in desperation got on her coat, tied a yellow kerchief around her head and left the house again, not knowing which way to go. She wandered toward the leafless park.

At the approach to the park's main entrance there was a small island in the street, a concrete triangle formed by intersecting avenues. Here people sat on benches during the day and tossed peanuts or pieces of bread to the noisy pigeons that haunted the place. Coming up the block, Helen saw a man squatting by one of the benches, feeding the birds. Otherwise, the island was deserted. When the man rose, the pigeons fluttered up with him, a few landing on his arms and shoulders, one perched on his fingers, pecking peanuts from his cupped palm. Another fat bird sat on his hat. The man clapped his hands when the peanuts were gone and the birds, beating their wings, scattered.

When she recognized Frank Alpine, Helen hesitated. She felt in no mood to see him, but remembering the package hidden in her bureau drawer, determined once and for all to get rid of it. Reaching the corner, she crossed over to the island.

Frank saw her coming and wasn't sure he cared one way or the other. The return of his presents had collapsed his hopes. He had thought that if she ever fell for him it would change his life in the way he wanted it to happen, although at times the very thought of another change, even in this sense of it, made him miserable. Yet what was the payoff, for instance, of marrying a dame like her and having to do with Jews the rest of his life? So he told himself he didn't care one way or the other.

"Hi," Helen said.

He touched his hat. His face looked tired but his eyes were clear and his gaze steady, as if he had been through something and had beat it. She felt sorry if she had caused him any trouble.

"I had a cold," Frank remarked.

"You should get more sun."

Helen sat down on the edge of the bench, as if she were afraid, he thought, she would be asked to take a lease on it; and he sat a little apart from her. One of the pigeons began to chase another running in circles and landed on its back. Helen looked away but Frank idly watched the birds until they flew off.

"Frank," she said, "I hate to sound like a pest on this subject, but if there's anything I can't stand it's waste. I know you're not Rockefeller, so would you mind giving me the names of the stores where you bought your kind presents so that I can return them? I think I can without the sales checks."

Her eyes, he noticed, were a hard blue, and though he thought it ridiculous, he was a little scared of her, as if she were far too determined, too dead serious for him. At the same time he felt he still liked her. He had not thought so, but with them sitting together like this he thought again that he did. It was in a way a hopeless feeling, yet it was more than that because he did not exactly feel hopeless. He felt, as he sat next to her and saw her worn, unhappy face, that he still had a chance.

Frank cracked his knuckles one by one. He turned to her. "Look, Helen, maybe I try to work too fast. If so, I am sorry. I am the type of a person, who if he likes somebody, has to show it. I like to give her things, if you understand that, though I do know that not everybody likes to take. That's their business. My nature is to give and I couldn't change it even if I wanted. So okay. I am also sorry I got sore and dumped your presents in the can and you had to take them out. But what I want to say is this. Why don't you just go ahead and keep one of those things that I got for you? Let it be a little memory of a guy you once knew that wants to thank you for the good books you told him to read. You don't have to worry that I expect anything for what I give you."

"Frank . . ." she said, reddening.

"Just let me finish. How's this for a deal? If you keep one of those things, I will take the other back to the store and get what I paid for it. What do you say?"

She was not sure what to say, but since she wanted to be finished with it, nodded at his proposal.

"Fine," Frank said. "Now what do you want the most?"

"Well, the scarf is awfully nice, but I'd rather keep the book."

"So keep the book then," he said. "You can give me the scarf anytime you want and I promise I will bring it back."

He lit a cigarette and inhaled deeply.

She considered whether to say good-by, now that the matter had been settled, and go on with her walk.

"You busy now?" he asked.

She guessed a short stroll. "No."

"How about a movie?"

It took her a minute to reply. Was he starting up once more? She felt she must quickly set limits to keep him from again creeping too close. Yet out of respect for his already hurt feelings, she thought it best that she think out exactly what to say and tactfully say it, later on.

"I'll have to be back early."

"So let's go," he said, getting up.

Helen slowly untied her kerchief, then knotted it, and they went off together.

As they walked she kept wondering if she hadn't made a mistake in accepting the book. In spite of what he had said about expecting nothing she felt a gift was a claim, and she wanted none on her. Yet, when, almost without noticing, she once more asked herself if she liked him at all, she had to admit she did a little. But not enough to get worried about; she liked him but not with an eye to the possibility of any deeper feeling. He was not the kind of man she wanted to be in love with. She made that very clear to herself, for among his other disadvantages there was something about him, evasive, hidden. He sometimes appeared to be more than he was, sometimes less. His aspirations, she sensed, were somehow apart from the self he presented normally when he wasn't trying, though he was always more or less trying; therefore when he was trying less. She could not quite explain this to herself, for if he could make himself seem better, broader, wiser when he tried, then he had these things in him because you couldn't make them out of nothing. There was more to him than his appearance. Still, he hid what he had and he hid what he hadn't. With one hand the magician showed his cards, with the other he turned them into smoke. At the very minute he was revealing himself, saying who he was, he made you wonder if it was true. You looked into mirrors and saw mirrors and didn't know what was right or real or important. She had gradually got the feeling that he only pretended to be frank about himself, that in telling so much about his experiences, his trick was to hide his true self. Maybe not purposely—maybe he had no idea he was doing it. She asked herself whether he might have been married already. He had once said he never was. And was there more to the story of the once-kissed, tragic carnival girl? He had said no. If not, what made her feel he had done something—committed himself in a way she couldn't guess?

As they were approaching the movie theater, a thought of her mother crossed her mind and she heard herself say, "Don't forget I'm Jewish."

"So what?" Frank said.

Inside in the dark, recalling what he had answered her, he felt this elated feeling, as if he had crashed head on through a brick wall but hadn't bruised himself.

She had bitten her tongue but made no reply.

Anyway, by summer he'd be gone.

Ida was very unhappy that she had kept Frank on when she could have got rid of him so easily. She was to blame and she actively worried. Though she had no evidence, she suspected Helen was interested in the clerk. *Something* was going on between them. She did not ask her daughter what, because a denial would shame her. And though she had tried she felt she could not really trust Frank. Yes, he had helped the business, but how much would they have to pay for it? Sometimes when she came upon him alone in the store, his expression, she told herself, was sneaky. He sighed often, muttered to himself, and if he saw he was observed, pretended he hadn't. Whatever he did there was more in it than he was doing. He was like a man with two minds. With one he was here, with the other someplace else. Even while he read he was doing more than reading. And his silence spoke a language she couldn't understand. Something bothered him and Ida suspected it was her daughter. Only when Helen happened to come into the store or the back while he was there, did he seem to relax, become one person. Ida was troubled, although she could not discover in Helen any response to him. Helen was quiet in his presence, detached, almost cold to the clerk. She gave him for his restless eyes, nothing—her back. Yet for this reason, too, Ida worried.

One night, after Helen had left the house, when her mother heard the clerk's footsteps going down the stairs, she quickly got into a coat, wrapped a shawl around her head and trudged through a sprinkle of snow after him. He walked to the movie house several blocks away, paid his money, and passed in. Ida was almost certain that Helen was inside, waiting for him. She returned home with nails in her heart and found her daughter upstairs, ironing. Another night she followed Helen to the library. Ida waited across the street, shivering for almost an hour in the cold, until Helen emerged, then followed her home. She chided herself for her suspicions but they would not fly from her mind. Once, listening from the back, she heard her daughter and the clerk talking about a book. This annoyed her. And when Helen later happened to mention that Frank had plans to begin college in the autumn, Ida felt he was saying that only to get her interested in him.

She spoke to Morris and cautiously asked if he had noticed anything developing between Helen and the clerk.

"Don't be foolish," the grocer replied. He had thought about the possibility, at times felt concerned, but after pondering how different they were, had put the idea out of his head.

"Morris, I am afraid."

"You are afraid of everything, even which it don't exist."

"Tell him to leave now—business is better."

"So is better," he muttered, "but who knows how will be next week. We decided he will stay till summer."

"Morris, he will make trouble."

"What kind trouble will he make?"

"Wait," she said, clasping her hands, "a tragedy will happen."

Her remark at first annoyed, then worried him.

The next morning the grocer and his clerk were sitting at the table, peeling hot potatoes. The pot had been drained of water and dumped on its side; they sat close to the steaming pile of potatoes, hunched over, ripping off the salt-stained skins with small knives. Frank seemed ill at ease. He hadn't shaved and had dark blobs under his eyes. Morris wondered if he had been drinking but there was never any smell of liquor about him. They worked without speaking, each lost in his thoughts.

After a half-hour, Frank, squirming restlessly in his chair, remarked, "Say, Morris, suppose somebody asked you what do the Jews believe in, what would you tell them?"

The grocer stopped peeling, unable at once to reply.

"What I like to know is what is a Jew anyway?"

Because he was ashamed of his meager education Morris was never comfortable with such questions, yet he felt he must answer.

"My father used to say to be a Jew all you need is a good heart."

"What do you say?"

"The important thing is the Torah. This is the Law—a Jew must believe in the Law."

"Let me ask you this," Frank went on. "Do you consider yourself a real Jew?"

Morris was startled. "What do you mean if I am a real Jew?"

"Don't get sore about this," Frank said, "but I can give you an argument that you aren't. First thing, you don't go to the synagogue—not that I have ever seen. You don't keep your kitchen kosher and you don't eat kosher. You don't even wear one of those little black hats like this tailor I knew in South Chicago. He prayed three times a day. I even hear the Mrs say you kept the store open on Jewish holidays, it makes no difference if she yells her head off."

"Sometimes," Morris answered, flushing, "to have to eat, you must keep open on holidays. On Yom Kippur I don't keep open. But I don't worry about kosher, which is to me old-fashioned. What I worry is to follow the Jewish Law."

"But all those things are the Law, aren't they? And don't the Law say you can't eat any pig, but I have seen you taste ham."

"This is not important to me if I taste pig or if I don't. To some Jews is this important but not to me. Nobody will tell me that I am not Jewish because I put in my mouth once in a while, when my tongue is dry, a piece ham. But they will tell me, and I will believe them, if I forget the Law. This means to do what is right, to be honest, to be good. This means to other people. Our life is hard enough. Why should we hurt somebody else? For everybody should be the best, not only for you or me. We ain't animals. This is why we need the Law. This is what a Jew believes."

"I think other religions have those ideas too," Frank said. "But tell me why it is that the Jews suffer so damn much, Morris? It seems to me that they like to suffer, don't they?"

"Do you like to suffer? They suffer because they are Jews."

"That's what I mean, they suffer more than they have to."

"If you live, you suffer. Some people suffer more, but not because they want. But I think if a Jew don't suffer for the Law, he will suffer for nothing."

"What do you suffer for, Morris?" Frank said.

"I suffer for you," Morris said calmly.

Frank laid his knife down on the table. His mouth ached. "What do you mean?"

"I mean you suffer for me."

The clerk let it go at that.

"If a Jew forgets the Law," Morris ended, "he is not a good Jew, and not a good man."

Frank picked up his knife and began to tear the skins off the potatoes. The grocer peeled his pile in silence. The clerk asked nothing more.

When the potatoes were cooling, Morris, troubled by their talk, asked himself why Frank had brought up this subject. A thought of Helen, for some reason, crossed his mind.

"Tell me the truth," he said, "why did you ask me such questions?"

Frank shifted in his chair. He answered slowly, "To be truthful to you, Morris, once I didn't have much use for the Jews."

Morris looked at him without moving.

"But that was long ago," said Frank, "before I got to know what they were like. I don't think I understood much about them."

His brow was covered with sweat.

"Happens like this many times," Morris said.

But his confession had not made the clerk any happier.

One afternoon, shortly after lunch, happening to glance at himself in the mirror, Morris saw how bushy his hair was and how thick the pelt on his neck; he felt ashamed. So he said to Frank he was going across the street to the barber. The clerk, studying the racing page of the *Mirror*, nodded. Morris hung up his apron and went into the store to get some change from the cash register. After he took a few quarters out of the drawer, he checked the receipts for the day and was pleased. He left the grocery and crossed the car tracks to the barber shop.

The chair was empty and he didn't have to wait. As Mr. Giannola, who smelled of olive oil, worked on him and they talked, Morris, though embarrassed at all the hair that had to be cut by the barber, found himself thinking mostly of his store. If it would only stay like this—no Karp's paradise, but at least livable, not the terrible misery of only a few months ago—he would be satisfied. Ida had again been nagging him to sell, but what was the use of selling until things all over got better and he could find a place he would have confidence in? Al Marcus, Breitbart, all the drivers he talked to, still complained about business. The best thing was not to look for trouble but stay where he was. Maybe in the summer, after Frank left, he would sell out and search for a new place.

As he rested in the barber's chair, the grocer, watching through the window his own store, saw with satisfaction that at least three customers had been in since he had sat down. One man left with a large lumpy bag, in which Morris imagined at least six bottles of beer. Also, two women had come out with heavy packages, one carrying a loaded market bag. Figuring, let's say, at least two dollars apiece for the women, he estimated he had taken in a nice fiver and earned his haircut. When the barber unpinned the sheet around him and Morris returned to the grocery, he struck a match over the cash register and peered with anticipation at the figures. To his great surprise he saw that only a little more than three dollars had been added to the sum he had noted on leaving the store. He was stunned. How could it be only three if the bags had been packed tight with groceries? Could it be they contained maybe a couple of boxes of some large item like cornflakes, that came to nothing? He could hardly believe this and felt upset to the point of illness.

In the back he hung up his overcoat, and with fumbling fingers tied his apron strings.

Frank glanced up from the racing page with a smile. "You look different without all the kelp on you, Morris. You look like a sheep that had the wool clipped off it."

The grocer, ashen, nodded.

"What's the matter your face is so pale?"

"I don't feel so good."

"Whyn't you go up then and take your snooze?"

"After."

He shakily poured himself a cup of coffee.

"How's business?" he asked, his back to the clerk.

"So-so," said Frank.

"How many customers you had since I went to the barber?"

"Two or three."

Unable to meet Frank's eye, Morris went into the store and stood at the window, staring at the barber shop, his thoughts in a turmoil, tormented by anxiety. Was the Italyener stealing from the cash register? The customers had come out with stuffed bags, what was there to show for it? Could he have given things on credit? They had told him never to. So what then?

A man entered and Morris waited on him. The man spent forty-one cents. When Morris rang up the sale, he saw it added correctly to the previous total. So the register was not broken. He was now almost certain that Frank had been stealing, and when he asked himself how long, he was numbed.

Frank went into the store and saw the dazed grocer at the window.

"Don't you feel any better, Morris?"

"It will go away."

"Take care of yourself. You don't want to get sick any more."

Morris wet his lips but made no reply. All day he went around, dragging his heart. He had said nothing to Ida, he didn't dare.

For the next few days he carefully watched the clerk. He had decided to give him the benefit of doubt yet not rest till he knew the truth. Sometimes he sat at the table inside, pretending to be reading, but he was carefully listening to each item the customer ordered. He jotted down the prices and when Frank packed the groceries, quickly calculated the approximate sum. After the customer had gone he went idly to the register and secretly examined the amount the clerk had rung up. Always it was near the figure he had figured, a few pennies more or less. So Morris said he would go upstairs for a few minutes, but instead stationed himself in the hall, behind the back door. Peering through a crack in the wood, he could see into the store. Standing here, he added in his head the prices of the items ordered, and later, about fifteen minutes, casually checked the receipts and found totaled there the sum he had estimated. He began to doubt his suspicions. He may have wrongly guessed the contents of the customers' bags when he was at the barber's. Yet he could still not believe they had spent only three dollars; maybe Frank had caught on and was being wary.

Morris then thought, yes, the clerk could have been stealing, but if so it was more his fault than Frank's. He was a grown man with a man's needs and all he was paying him, including his meager commission, was about six or seven dollars a week. True, he got his room and meals free, plus cigarettes, but what was six or seven dollars to anybody in times like these, when a decent pair of shoes cost eight to ten? The fault was therefore his for paying slave wages for a workman's services, including the extra things Frank did, like last week cleaning out the stopped sewer pipe in the cellar with a long wire and so saving five or ten dollars that would surely have gone to the plumber, not to mention how his presence alone had improved the store.

So although he worked on a slim markup, one late afternoon when he and Frank were packing out some cartons of goods that had just been delivered, Morris said to his assistant standing on the stepladder, "Frank, I think from now on till it comes summer I will raise you your wages to straight fifteen dollars without any commission. I would like to pay you more, but you know how much we do here business."

Frank looked down at the grocer. "What for, Morris? The store can't afford to pay me any more than I am getting. If I take fifteen your profit will be shot. Let it go the way it is now. I am satisfied."

"A young man needs more and he spends more."

"I got all I want."

"Let it be like I said."

"I don't want it," said the clerk, annoyed.

"Take," insisted the grocer.

Frank finished his packing then got down, saying he was going to Sam Pearl's. His eyes were averted as he went past the grocer.

Morris continued to pack the cans on the shelves. Rather than admit Frank's raise to Ida and start a fuss, he decided to withhold from the register the money he would need to pay him, a little every day so it would not be noticed. He would privately give it to the clerk sometime on Saturday, before Ida handed him his regular wages.

HELEN FELT herself, despite the strongest doubts, falling in love with Frank. It was a dizzying dance, she didn't want to. The month was cold—it often snowed—she had a rough time, fighting hesitancies, fears of a disastrous mistake. One night she dreamed their house had burned down and her poor parents had nowhere to go. They stood on the sidewalk, wailing in their underwear. Waking, she fought an old distrust of the broken-faced stranger, without success. The stranger had changed, grown unstrange. That was the clue to what was happening to her. One day he seemed unknown, lurking at the far end of an unlit cellar; the next he was standing in sunlight, a smile on his face, as if all she knew of him and all she didn't, had fused into a healed and easily remembered whole. If he was hiding anything, she thought, it was his past pain, his orphanhood and consequent suffering. His eyes were quieter, wiser. His crooked nose fitted his face and his face fitted him. It stayed on straight. He was gentle, waiting for whatever he awaited with a grace she respected. She felt she had changed him and this affected her. That she had willed to stay free of him made little difference now. She felt tender to him, wanted him close by. She had, she thought, changed in changing him.

After she had accepted his gift of a book their relationship had subtly altered. What else, if whenever she read in her Shakespeare, she thought of Frank Alpine, even heard his voice in the plays? Whatever she read, he crept into her thoughts; in every book he haunted the words, a character in a plot somebody else had invented, as if all associations had only one end. He was, to begin with, everywhere. So, without speaking of it, they met again in the library. That they were meeting among books relieved her doubt, as if she believed, what possible wrong can I do among books, what possible harm can come to me here?

In the library he too seemed surer of himself—though once they were on their way home he became almost remote, strangely watchful, looking back from time to time as though they were being followed, but who or what would follow them? He never took her as far as the store; as before, by mutual consent, she went on ahead, then he walked around the block and entered the hall from the other way so he wouldn't have to go past the grocery window and possibly be seen coming from the direction she had come from. Helen interpreted his caution to mean he sensed victory and didn't want to endanger it. It meant he valued her more than she was altogether sure she wanted to be.

Then one night they walked across a field in the park and turned to one another. She tried to awaken in herself a feeling of danger, but danger was dulled, beyond her, in his arms. Pressed against him, responsive to his touch, she felt the cold ebb out of the night, and a warmth come over her. Her lips parted—she drew from his impassioned kiss all she had long desired. Yet at the moment of sweetest joy she felt again the presence of doubt, almost a touch of illness. This made her sad. The fault was her. It meant she still could not fully accept him. There were still signals signaling no. She had only to think of them and they would work in her, pinching the nerves. On their way home she could not forget the first happiness of their kiss. But why should a kiss become anxiety? Then she saw that his eyes were sad, and she wept when he wasn't looking. Would it never come spring?

She stalled love with arguments, only to be surprised at their swift dissolution; found it difficult to keep her reasons securely nailed down, as they were before. They flew up in the mind, shifted, changed, as if something had altered familiar weights, values, even experience. He wasn't, for instance, Jewish. Not too long ago this was the greatest barrier, her protection against ever taking him seriously; now it no longer seemed such an urgently important thing—how could it in times like these? How could anything be important but love and fulfill-ment? It had lately come to her that her worry he was a gentile was less for her own sake than for her mother and father. Al-though she had only loosely been brought up as Jewish she felt loyal to the Jews, more for what they had gone through than what she knew of their history or theology—loved them as a people, thought with pride of herself as one of them; she had never imagined she would marry anybody but a Jew. But she had recently come to think that in such unhappy times—when the odds were so high against personal happiness—to find love was miraculous, and to fulfill it as best two people could was what really mattered. Was it more important to insist a man's religious beliefs be exactly hers (if it was a question of religion), or that the two of them have in common ideals, a desire to keep love in their lives, and to preserve in every possible way what was best in themselves? The less difference among people, the better; thus she settled it for herself yet was dissatisfied for those for whom she hadn't settled it.

But her logic, if it was logic, wouldn't decide a thing for her unhappy parents once they found out what was going on. With Frank enrolled in college maybe some of Ida's doubts of his worth as a person might wither away, but college was not the synagogue, a B.A. not a bar mitzvah; and her mother and even her father with his liberal ideas would insist that Frank had to be what he wasn't. Helen wasn't at all sure she could handle them if it ever came to a showdown. She dreaded the arguments, their tear-stained pleas and her own misery for taking from the small sum of peace they had in the world, adding to the portion of their unhappiness. God knows they had had enough of that. Still, there was just so much time to live, so little of youth among the years; one had to make certain heartbreaking choices. She foresaw the necessity of upholding her own, enduring pain yet keeping to her decisions. Morris and Ida would be grievously hurt, but before too long their pain would grow less and perhaps leave them; yet she could not help but hope her own children would someday marry Jews.

And if she married Frank, her first job would be to help him realize his wish to be somebody. Nat Pearl wanted to be "somebody," but to him this meant making money to lead the life of some of his well-to-do friends at law school. Frank, on the other hand, was struggling to realize himself as a person, a more worthwhile ambition. Though Nat had an excellent formal education, Frank knew more about life and gave the impression of greater potential depth. She wanted him to become what he might, and conceived a plan to support him through college. Maybe she could even see him through a master's degree, once he knew what he wanted to do. She realized this would mean the end of her own vague plans for going to day college, but that was really lost long ago, and she thought she would at last accept the fact once Frank had got what she hadn't. Maybe after he was working, perhaps as an engineer or chemist, she could take a year of college just to slake her thirst. By then she would be almost thirty, but it would be worth postponing having a family to give him a good start and herself a taste of what she had always wanted. She also hoped they would be able to leave New York. She wanted to see more of the country. And if things eventually worked out, maybe Ida and Morris would someday sell the store and come to live near them. They might all live in California, her parents in a little house of their own where they could take life easy and be near their grandchildren. The future offered more in the way of realizable possibilities, Helen thought, if a person dared take a chance with it. The question was, did she?

She postponed making any important decision. She feared most of all the great compromise—she had seen so many of the people she knew settle for so much less than they had always wanted. She feared to be forced to choose beyond a certain point, to accept less of the good life than she had hungered for, appreciably less—to tie up with a fate far short of her ideals. That she mustn't do, whether it meant taking Frank or letting him go. Her constant fear, underlying all others, was that her life would not turn out as she had hoped, or would turn out vastly different. She was willing to change, make substitutions, but she would not part with the substance of her dreams. Well, she would know by summertime what to do. In the meantime Frank went every third night to the library and there she was. But when the old-maid librarian smiled knowingly upon them, Helen felt embarrassed, so they met elsewhere. They met in cafeterias, movie houses, the pizza place—where it was impossible to say much, or hold him or be held. To talk they walked, to kiss they hid.

Frank said he was getting the college bulletins he had written for, and around May he would have a transcript of his high school record sent to whichever place they picked for him to go. He showed he knew she had plans for him. He didn't say much more, for he was always afraid the old jinx would grab hold of him if he opened his mouth a little too wide.

At first he waited patiently. What else was there to do? He had waited and was still waiting. He had been born waiting. But before long, though he tried not to show it, he was beginning to be fed up with his physical loneliness. He grew tired of the frustrations of kissing in doorways, a cold feel on a bench in the park. He thought of her as he had seen her in the bathroom, and the memory became a burden. He was the victim of the sharp edge of his hunger. So he wanted her to the point where he thought up schemes for getting her into his room and in bed. He wanted satisfaction, relief, a stake in the future. She's not yours till she gives it to you, he thought. That's the way they all are. It wasn't always true, but it was true enough. He wanted an end to the torment of coming to a boil, then thank you, no more. He wanted to take her completely.

They met more often now. At a bench on the Parkway, on street corners—in the wide windy world. When it rained or snowed, they stepped into doorways, or went home.

He complained one night, "What a joke. We leave the same warm house to meet out in the cold here."

She said nothing.

"Forget it," Frank said, looking into her troubled eyes, "we will take it the way it is."

"This is our youth," she said bitterly.

He wanted then to ask her to come to his room but felt she wouldn't, so he didn't ask.

One cold, starry night she led him through the trees in the park near where they usually sat, onto a broad meadow where on summer nights lovers lay in the grass.

"Come on and sit down on the ground for a minute," Frank urged, "there's nobody here now."

But Helen wouldn't.

"Why not?" he asked.

"Not now," she said.

She realized, though he later denied it, that the situation had made him impatient. Sometimes he was moody for hours. She worried, wondering what rusty wound their homelessness had opened in him.

One evening they sat alone on a bench on the Parkway, Frank with his arm around her; but because they were so close to home Helen was jumpy and moved away whenever somebody passed by.

After the third time Frank said, "Listen, Helen, this is no

good. Some night we will have to go where we can be inside."

"Where?" she asked.

"Where do you say?"

"I can't say anything, Frank. I don't know."

"How long is this going to keep up like this?"

"As long as we like," she said, smiling faintly, "or as long as we like each other."

"I don't mean it that way. What I am talking about is not having any place private to go to."

She answered nothing.

"Maybe some night we ought to sneak up to my room," he suggested. "We could do it easy enough—I don't mean tonight but maybe Friday, after Nick and Tessie go to the show and your mother is down in the store. I bought a new heater and the room keeps warm. Nobody will know you are there. We would be alone for once. We have never been alone that way."

"I couldn't," Helen said.

"Why?"

"Frank, I can't."

"When will I get a chance to put my arms around you without being an acrobat?"

"Frank," said Helen, "there's one thing I wish to make clear to you. I won't sleep with you now, if that's what you mean. It'll have to wait till I am really sure I love you, maybe till we're married, if we ever are."

"I never asked you to," Frank said. "All I said was for you to come up to my room so we could spend the time more comfortable, not you bucking away from me every time a shadow passes."

He lit a cigarette and smoked in silence.

"I'm sorry." After a minute she said, "I thought I ought to tell you how I feel on this subject. I was going to sometime anyway."

They got up and walked, Frank gnawing his wound.

A cold rain washed the yellow slush out of the gutters. It rained drearily for two days. Helen had promised to see Frank on Friday night but she didn't like the thought of going out in the wet. When she came home from work, and got the chance, she slipped a note under his door, then went down. The note said that if Nick and Tessie did go to the movies, she would try to come up to his room for a while.

At half past seven Nick knocked on Frank's door and asked him if he wanted to go to the pictures. Frank said no, he thought he had seen the picture that was playing. Nick said good-by and he and Tessie, bundled in raincoats and carrying umbrellas, left the house. Helen waited for her mother to go down to Morris, but Ida complained that her feet hurt, and said she would rest. Helen then went down herself, knowing Frank would hear her on the stairs and figure something had gone wrong. He would understand she could not go up to see him so long as anyone might hear her.

But a few minutes later, Ida came down, saying she felt restless upstairs. Helen then said she intended to drop in on Betty Pearl and might go along with her to the dressmaker who was making her wedding things.

"It's raining," said Ida.

"I know, Mama," Helen answered, hating her deceit.

She went up to her room, got her hat and coat, rubbers and an umbrella; then walked down, letting the door bang, as if she had just left the house. She quietly opened it and went on tiptoe up the stairs.

Frank had guessed what was going on and opened his door to her quick tap. She was pale, obviously troubled, but very lovely. He held her hard and could feel her heartbeat against his chest.

She will let me tonight, he told himself.

Helen was still uneasy. It took her a while to quiet her conscience for having lied to her mother. Frank had put out the light and tuned in the radio to soft dance music; now he lay on the bed, smoking. For a time she sat awkwardly in his chair, watching the glow of his cigarette, and when not that, the drops of lit rain on the window, reflecting the street light. But after he had rubbed his butt into an ash tray on the floor, Helen stepped out of her shoes and lay down beside him on the narrow bed, Frank moving over to the wall.

"This is more like it," he sighed.

She lay with closed eyes in his arms, feeling the warmth of

the heater like a hand on her back. For a minute she half-dozed, then woke to his kisses. She lay motionless, a little tense, but when he stopped kissing her, relaxed. She listened to the quiet sound of the rain in the street, making it in her mind into spring rain, though spring was weeks away; and within the rain grew all sorts of flowers; and amid the spring flowers, in this flowering dark—a sweet spring night—she lay with him in the open under new stars and a cry rose to her throat. When he kissed her again, she responded with passion.

"Darling."

"I love you, Helen, you are my girl."

They kissed breathlessly, then he undid the buttons of her blouse. She sat up to unhook her brassiere but as she was doing it, felt his fingers under her skirt.

Helen grabbed his hand. "Please, Frank. Let's not get that hot and bothered."

"What are we waiting for, honey?" He tried to move his hand but her legs tightened and she swung her feet off the bed.

He pulled her back, pressing her shoulders down. She felt his body trembling on hers and for a fleeting minute thought he might hurt her; but he didn't.

She lay stiff, unresponsive on the bed. When he kissed her again she didn't move. It took a while before he lay back. She saw by the reflected glow of the heater how unhappy he looked.

Helen sat on the edge of the bed, buttoning her blouse.

His hands covered his face. He said nothing but she could feel his body shivering on the bed.

"Christ," he muttered.

"I'm sorry," she said softly. "I told you I wouldn't."

Five minutes passed. Frank slowly sat up. "Are you a virgin, is that what's eating you?"

"I'm not," she said.

"I thought you were," he said, surprised. "You act like one."

"I said I wasn't."

"Then why do you act like one? Don't you know what it does to people?"

"I'm people."

"Then why do you do it for?"

"Because I believe in what I'm doing."

"I thought you said you weren't a virgin?"

"You don't have to be a virgin to have ideals in sex."

"What I don't understand is if you did it before, what's the difference if we do it now?"

"We can't, just because I did," she said, brushing her hair back. "That's the point. I did it and that's why I can't with you now. I said I wouldn't, that night on the Parkway."

"I don't get it," Frank said.

"Loving should come with love."

"I said I love you, Helen, you heard me say it."

"I mean I have to love you too. I think I do but sometimes I'm not sure."

He fell again into silence. She listened absent-mindedly to the radio but nobody was dancing now.

"Don't be hurt, Frank."

"I'm tired of that," he said harshly.

"Frank," said Helen, "I said I slept with somebody before and the truth of it is, if you want to know, I'm sorry I did. I admit I had some pleasure, but after, I thought it wasn't worth it, only I didn't know at the time I would feel that way, because at the time I didn't know what I wanted. I suppose I felt I wanted to be free, so I settled for sex. But if you're not in love sex isn't being free, so I made a promise to myself that I never would any more unless I really fell in love with somebody. I don't want to dislike myself. I want to be disciplined, and you have to be too if I ask it. I ask it so I might someday love you without reservations."

"Crap," Frank said, but then, to his surprise, the idea seized him. He thought of himself as disciplined, then wished he were. This seemed to him like an old and faraway thought, and he remembered with regret and strange sadness how often he had wished for better control over himself, and how little of it he had achieved.

He said, "I didn't mean to say what I just now did, Helen."

"I know," she answered.

"Helen," he said huskily, "I want you to know I am a very good guy in my heart."

"I don't think otherwise."

"Even when I am bad I am good."

She said she thought she knew what he meant.

They kissed, again and again. He thought there were a whole lot worse things than waiting for something that was going to be good once he got it.

Helen lay back on the bed and dozed, awaking when Nick and Tessie came into their bedroom, talking about the movie they had seen. It was a love story and Tessie had liked it very much. After they undressed and got into bed their double bed creaked. Helen felt bad for Frank but Frank did not seem to feel bad. Nick and Tessie soon fell asleep. Helen, breathing lightly, listened to their heavy breathing, worrying how she was going to get down to her floor, because if Ida was awake she would hear her on the stairs. But Frank said in a low voice that he would carry her to the vestibule, then she could go up after a few minutes, as if she had just come home from some place.

She put on her coat, hat and rubbers, and was careful to remember her umbrella. Frank carried her down the stairs. There were only his slow, heavy steps going down. And not long after they had kissed good night and he had gone for a walk in the rain, Helen opened the hall door and went up.

Then Ida fell asleep.

Thereafter Helen and Frank met outside the house.

It was snowing in the afternoon, when the front door opened and in came Detective Minogue, pushing before him this stocky handcuffed guy, unshaven, and wearing a faded green wind-breaker and denim slacks. He was about twenty-seven, with tired eyes and no hat. In the store he lifted his manacled hands to wipe the snow off his wet hair.

"Where's Morris?" the detective asked the clerk.

"In the back."

"Go on in," said Detective Minogue to the handcuffed man.

They went into the back. Morris was sitting on the couch, stealing a smoke. He hurriedly put out the butt and dropped it into the garbage pail.

"Morris," said the detective, "I think I have got the one who hit you on the head."

The grocer's face turned white as flour. He stared at the man but didn't approach him.

After a minute he muttered, "I don't know if it's him. He had his face covered with a handkerchief."

"He's a big son of a bitch," the detective said. "The one that hit you was big, wasn't he?"

"Heavy," said Morris. "The other was big."

Frank was standing in the doorway, watching.

Detective Minogue turned to him. "Who're you?"

"He's my clerk," explained Morris.

The detective unbuttoned his overcoat and took a clean handkerchief out of his suit pocket. "Do me a favor," he said to Frank. "Tie this around his puss."

"I would rather not," Frank answered.

"As a favor. To save me the trouble of getting hit on the head with his cuffs."

Frank took the handkerchief, and though not liking to, tied it around the man's face, the suspect holding himself stiffly erect.

"How about it now, Morris?"

"I can't tell you," Morris said, embarrassed. He had to sit down.

"You want some water, Morris?" Frank asked.

"No."

"Take your time," said Detective Minogue, "look him over good."

"I don't recognize him. The other acted more rough. He had a rough voice—not nice."

"Say something, son," the detective said.

"I didn't hold this guy up," said the suspect in a dead voice.

"Is that the voice, Morris?"

"No."

"Does he look like the other one—the heavy guy's partner?"

"No, this is a different man."

"How are you so sure?"

"The helper was a nervous man. He was bigger than this one. Also this one has got small hands. The helper had big heavy hands."

"Are you positive? We grabbed him on a job last night. He held up a grocery with another guy who got away."

The detective pulled the handkerchief off the man's face.

"I don't know him," Morris said with finality.

Detective Minogue folded the handkerchief and tucked it into his pocket. He slipped his eyeglasses into a leather case. "Morris, I think I asked you already if you saw my son Ward Minogue around here. Have you yet?"

"No," said the grocer.

Frank went over to the sink and rinsed his mouth with a cup of water.

"Maybe you know him?" the detective asked him.

"No," said the clerk.

"O.K., then." The detective unbuttoned his overcoat. "By the way, Morris, did you ever find out who was stealing your milk that time?"

"Nobody steals any more," said Morris.

"Come on, son," said the detective to the suspect.

The handcuffed man went out of the store into the snow, the detective following him.

Frank watched them get into the police car, sorry for the guy. What if they arrested me now, he thought, although I am not the same guy I once was?

Morris, thinking of the stolen milk bottles, gazed guiltily at his assistant.

Frank happened to notice the size of his hands, then had to go to the toilet.

As he was lying in his bed after supper, thinking about his life, Frank heard footsteps coming up the stairs and someone banged on his door. For a minute his heart hammered with fear, but he got up and forced himself to open the door. Grinning at him from under his fuzzy hat stood Ward Minogue, his eyes small and smeary. He had lost weight and looked worse.

Frank let him in and turned on the radio. Ward sat on the bed, his shoes dripping from the snow.

"Who told you I lived here?" Frank asked.

"I watched you go in the hall, opened the door and heard you go up the stairs," Ward said.

How am I ever going to get rid of this bastard, Frank thought.

"You better stay away from here," he said with a heavy heart. "If Morris recognizes you in that goddamned hat, we will both go to jail."

"I came to visit my popeyed friend, Louis Karp," said Ward. "I wanted a bottle but he wouldn't give it to me because I am short on cash, so I thought my good-looking friend Frank Alpine will lend me some. He's an honest, hard-working bastard."

"You picked the wrong guy. I am poor."

Ward eyed him craftily. "I was sure you'd have saved up a pile by now, stealing from the Jew."

Frank stared at him but didn't answer.

Ward's glance shifted. "Even if you are stealing his chicken feed, it ain't any skin off me. Why I came is this. I got a new job that we can do without any trouble."

"I told you I am not interested in your jobs, Ward."

"I thought you would like to get your gun back, otherwise it might accidentally get lost with your name on it."

Frank rubbed his hands.

"All you got to do is drive," Ward said amiably. "The job is a cinch, a big liquor joint in Bay Ridge. After nine o'clock they only keep one man on. The take will be over three hundred."

"Ward, you don't look to me in any kind of condition to do a stickup. You look more like you need to be in a hospital."

"All I got is a bad heartburn."

"You better take care of yourself."

"You are making me cry."

"Why don't you start going straight?"

"Why don't you?"

"I am trying to."

"Your Jew girl must be some inspiration."

"Don't talk about her, Ward."

"I tailed you last week when you took her in the park. She's a nice piece. How often do you get it?"

"Get the hell out of here."

Ward got up unsteadily. "Hand over fifty bucks or I will fix you good with your Jew boss and your Jew girl. I will write them a letter who did the stickup last November."

Frank rose, his face hard. Taking his wallet out of his pocket, he emptied it on the bed. There were eight single dollar bills. "That's all I have got."

Ward snatched up the money. "I'll be back for more."

"Ward," Frank said through tight teeth, "if you drag your

ass up here any more to make trouble, or if you ever follow me and my girl again, or tell Morris anything, the first thing I will do is telephone your old man at the police station and tell him under which rock he can find you. He was in the grocery asking about you today, and if he ever meets up with you, he looks like he will bust your head off."

Ward with a moan spat at the clerk and missed, the gob of spit trickling down the wall.

"You stinking kike," he snarled. Rushing out into the hall, he all but fell down two flights of stairs.

The grocer and Ida ran out to see who was making the racket, but by then Ward was gone.

Frank lay in bed, his eyes closed.

One dark and windy night when Helen left the house late, Ida followed her through the cold streets and across the plaza into the interior of the deserted park, and saw her meet Frank Alpine. There, in an opening between a semicircle of tall lilac shrubs and a grove of dark maples, were a few benches, dimly lit and private, where they liked to come to be alone. Ida watched them sitting together on one of the benches, kissing. She dragged herself home and went upstairs, half-dead. Morris was asleep and she didn't want to wake him, so she sat in the kitchen, sobbing.

When Helen returned and saw her mother weeping at the kitchen table, she knew Ida knew, and Helen was both moved and frightened.

Out of pity she asked, "Mama, why are you crying?"

Ida at last raised her tear-stained face and said in despair, "Why do I cry? I cry for the world. I cry for my life that it went away wasted. I cry for you."

"What have I done?"

"You have killed me in my heart."

"I've done nothing that's wrong, nothing I'm ashamed of."

"You are not ashamed that you kissed a goy?"

Helen gasped. "Did you follow me, Mama?"

"Yes," Ida wept.

"How could you?"

"How could you kiss a goy?"

"I'm not ashamed that we kissed."

She still hoped to avoid an argument. Everything was unsettled, premature.

Ida said, "If you marry such a man your whole life will be poisoned."

"Mama, you'll have to be satisfied with what I now say. I have no plans to marry anybody."

"What kind plans you got then with a man that he kisses you alone in a place where nobody can find you in the park?"

"I've been kissed before."

"But a goy, Helen, an Italyener."

"A man, a human being like us."

"A man is not good enough. For a Jewish girl must be a Jew."

"Mama, it's very late. I don't wish to argue. Let's not wake Papa."

"Frank is not for you. I don't like him. His eyes don't look at a person when he talks to them."

"His eyes are sad. He's had a hard life."

"Let him go and find someplace a shikse that he likes, not a Jewish girl."

"I have to work in the morning. I'm going to bed."

Ida quieted down. When Helen was undressing she came into her room. "Helen," she said, holding back her tears, "the only thing I want for you is the best. Don't make my mistake. Don't make worse and spoil your whole life, with a poor man that he is only a grocery clerk which we don't know about him nothing. Marry somebody who can give you a better life, a nice professional boy with a college education. Don't mix up now with a stranger. Helen, I know what I'm talking. Believe me, I know." She was crying again.

"I'll try my best," Helen said.

Ida dabbed at her eyes with a handkerchief. "Helen, darling, do me one favor."

"What is it? I am very tired."

"Please call up Nat tomorrow. Just to speak to him. Say hello, and if he asks you to go out with him, tell him yes. Give him a chance."

"I gave him one."

"Last summer you enjoyed so much with him. You went to the beach, to concerts. What happened?"

"Our tastes are different," Helen said wearily.

"In the summer you said your tastes were the same."

"I learned otherwise."

"He is a Jewish boy, Helen, a college graduate. Give him another chance."

"All right," said Helen, "now will you go to sleep?"

"Also don't go no more with Frank. Don't let him kiss you, it's not nice."

"I can't promise."

"Please, Helen."

"I said I'd call Nat. Let that be an end of it now. Good night, Mama."

"Good night," Ida said sadly.

Though her mother's suggestion depressed her, Helen called Nat from her office the next day. He was cordial, said he had bought a secondhand car from his future brother-in-law and invited her to go for a drive.

She said she would sometime.

"How about Friday night?" Nat asked.

She was seeing Frank on Friday. "Could you make it Saturday?"

"I happen to have an engagement Saturday, also Thursday—something doing at the law school."

"Then Friday is all right." She agreed reluctantly, thinking it would be best to change the date with Frank, to satisfy her mother.

When Morris came up for his nap that afternoon Ida desperately begged him to send Frank away at once.

"Leave me alone on this subject ten minutes."

"Morris," she said, "last night I went out when Helen went, and I saw she met Frank in the park, and they kissed each the other."

Morris frowned. "He kissed her?"

"Yes."

"She kissed him?"

"I saw with my eyes."

But the grocer, after thinking about it, said wearily, "So what is a kiss? A kiss is nothing."

Ida said furiously, "Are you crazy?"

"He will go away soon," he reminded her. "In the summer."

Tears sprang into her eyes. "By summer could happen here ten times a tragedy."

"What kind tragedy you expecting—murder?"

"Worse," she cried.

His heart turned cold, he lost his temper. "Leave me alone on this subject, for God's sakes."

"Wait," Ida bitterly warned.

On Thursday of that week Julius Karp left Louis in the liquor store and stepped outside to peek through the grocery window to see if Morris was alone. Karp had not set foot in Morris's store since the night of the holdup, and he uneasily considered the reception he might meet if he were to go in now. Usually, after a time of not speaking to one another, it was Morris Bober, by nature unable to hold a grudge, who gave in and spoke to Karp; but this time he had put out of his mind the possibility of seeking out the liquor dealer and re-establishing their fruitless relationship. While in bed during his last convalescence he had thought much of Karp—an unwilling and distasteful thinking—and had discovered he disliked him more than he had imagined. He resented him as a crass and stupid person who had fallen through luck into flowing prosperity. His every good fortune spattered others with misfortune, as if there was just so much luck in the world and what Karp left over wasn't fit to eat. Morris was incensed by thoughts of the long years he had toiled without just reward. Though this was not Karp's fault, it *was* that a delicatessen had moved in across the street to make a poor man poorer. Nor could the grocer forgive him the blow he had taken on the head in his place, who could in health and wealth better afford it. Therefore it gave him a certain satisfaction not to have anything to do with the liquor dealer, though he was every day next door.

Karp, on the other hand, had been content to wait for Morris to loosen up first. He pictured the grocer yielding his aloof silence while he enjoyed the signs of its dissolution, meanwhile pitying the poor Jew his hard luck life—in capital letters. Some were born that way. Whereas Karp in whatever he touched now coined pure gold, if Morris Bober found a rotten egg in the street, it was already cracked and leaking. Such a one needed someone with experience to advise him when to stay out of the rain. But Morris, whether he knew how Karp felt, or not, remained rigidly uncommunicative—offering not so much as a flicker of recognition when on his way to the corner for his daily *Forward*, he passed the liquor dealer standing in front of his store or caught his eye peeking into his front window. As a month passed, now, quickly, almost four, Karp came to the uncomfortable conclusion that although Ida was still friendly to him, he would this time get nothing for free from Morris; he wasn't going to give in. He reacted coldly to this insight, would give back what he got—so let it be indifference. But indifference was not a commodity he was pleased to exchange. For some reason that was not clear to him Karp liked Morris to like him, and it soon rankled that his down-at-the-heels neighbor continued to remain distant. So he had been hit on the head in a holdup, but was the fault Karp's? *He* had taken care—why hadn't Morris, the shlimozel? Why, when he had warned him there were two holdupniks across the street, hadn't he like a sensible person gone first to lock his door, then telephoned the police? Why?—because he was inept, unfortunate.

And because he was, his troubles grew like bananas in bunches. First, in another accident to his hard head, then through employing Frank Alpine. Karp, no fool, knew the makings of a bad situation when he saw it. Frank, whom he had got acquainted with and considered a fly-by-night rolling stone, would soon make trouble—of that he was certain. Morris's fly-specked, worm-eaten shop did not earn half enough to pay for a full-time helper, and it was idiotic extravagance for the grocer, after he was better, to keep the clerk working for him. Karp soon learned from Louis that his estimate of a bad situation was correct. He found out that Frank every so often invested in a bottle of the best stuff, paying, naturally, cash—but whose? Furthermore Sam Pearl, another waster, had mentioned that the clerk would now and then paste a two-dollar bill on some nag's useless nose, from which it blew off in the breeze. This done by a man who was no doubt paid in peanuts added up to only one thing—he stole. Who did he steal from? Naturally from M. Bober, who had anyway nothing—who else? Rockefeller knew how to take care of his millions, but if Morris earned a dime he lost it before he could put it into his torn pocket. It was the nature of clerks to steal from those they

were working for. Karp had, as a young man, privately pecu-
lated from his employer, a half-blind shoe wholesaler; and
Louis, he knew, snitched from him, but by Louis he was not
bothered. He was, after all, a son; he worked in the business
and would someday—it shouldn't be too soon—own it. Also,
by strict warnings and occasional surprise inventories he held
Louis down to a bare minimum—beans. A stranger stealing
money was another matter—slimy. It gave Karp gooseflesh to
think of the Italian working for him.

And since misfortune was the grocer's lot, the stranger
would shovel on more, not less, for it was always dangerous to
have a young goy around where there was a Jewish girl. This
worked out by an unchangeable law that Karp would gladly
have explained to Morris had they been speaking, and saved
him serious trouble. That *this* trouble, too, existed he had
confirmed twice in the last week. Once he saw Helen and
Frank walking on the Parkway under the trees, and another
time while driving home past the local movie house, he had
glimpsed them coming out after a show, holding hands. Since
then he had often thought about them, indeed with anxiety,
and felt he would in some way like to assist the luckless Bober.

Without doubt Morris kept Frank on to make his life easier,
and probably, being Bober, he had no idea what was happening behind his back. Well, Julius Karp would warn him of his
daughter's danger. Tactfully he would explain him what was
what. After, he would put in a plug for Louis, who, Karp was
aware, had long liked Helen but was not sure enough of himself to be successful with her. Swat Louis down and he retreated
to tenderize his fingernails with his teeth. In some things he
needed a push. Karp felt he could ease his son's way to Helen
by making Morris a proposition he had had in the back of his
head for almost a year. He would describe Louis' prospects
after marriage in terms of cold cash and other advantages, and
suggest that Morris speak to Helen on the subject of going
with him seriously. If they went together a couple of months—
Louis would give her an extravagant good time—and the
combination worked out, it would benefit not only the daughter, but the grocer as well, for then Karp would take over
Morris's sad gesheft and renovate and enlarge it into a self-
service market with the latest fixtures and goods. His tenant

around the corner he would eliminate when his lease expired—
a sacrifice, but worthwhile. After that, with himself as the silent
partner giving practical advice, it would take a marvelous ca-
tastrophe to keep the grocer from earning a decent living in
his old age.

Karp foresaw that the main problem of this matter would be
Helen, whom he knew as a strictly independent yet not unworthy girl, even if she had pretensions to marriage with a
professional—although she had got no place with Nat Pearl.
To be successful, Nat needed what Louis Karp would have
plenty of, not a poor girl. So he had acted in his best interests
in gently shooing Helen away when her thoughts got too
warm—a fact Karp had picked up from Sam Pearl. Louis, on
the other hand, could afford a girl like Helen, and Helen, independent and intelligent, would be good for Louis. The liquor store owner decided that when the opportunity came he
would talk turkey to her like a Dutch uncle. He would patiently
explain that her only future with Frank would be as an outcast,
poorer even than her father and sharing his foolish fate;
whereas with Louis she could have what she wanted and
more—leave it to her father-in-law. Karp felt that once Frank
had gone she would listen to reason and appreciate the good
life he was offering her. Twenty-three or -four was a dangerous
age for a single girl. At that age she would not get younger; at
that age even a goy looked good.

Having observed that Frank had gone into Sam Pearl's
place, and that Morris was for the moment alone in the back of
his store, Karp coughed clear his throat and stepped inside the
grocery. When Morris, emerging from the rear, saw who it
after all was, he experienced a moment of vindictive triumph,
but this was followed by annoyance that the pest was once
more present, and at the same time by an uncomfortable remembrance that Karp never entered unaccompanied by bad
news. Therefore he stayed silent, waiting for the liquor dealer,
in prosperous sport jacket and gabardine slacks which could
not camouflage his protrusive belly nor subtract from the
foolishness of his face, to speak; but for once Karp's active
tongue lay flat on its back as, embarrassed in recalling the results of his very last visit here, he stared at the visible scar on
Morris's head.

In pity for him, the grocer spoke, his tone friendlier than he would have guessed. "So how are you, Karp?"

"Thanks. What have I got to complain?" Beaming, he thrust a pudgy hand across the counter and Morris found himself unwillingly weighing the heavy diamond ring that pressed his fingers.

Since it did not seem sensible to Karp, one minute after their reconciliation, to blurt out news of a calamity concerning Morris's daughter, he fiddled around for words to say and came up with, "How's business?"

Morris had hoped he would ask. "Fine, and every day gets better."

Karp contracted his brows; yet it occurred to him that Morris's business might have improved more than he had guessed, when peering at odd moments through the grocery window, he had discovered a customer or two instead of the usual dense emptiness. Now on the inside after several months, he noticed the store seemed better taken care of, the shelves solidly packed with stock. But if business was better he at once knew why.

Yet he casually asked, "How is this possible? You are maybe advertising in the paper?"

Morris smiled at the sad joke. Where there was no wit money couldn't buy it. "By word of mouth," he remarked, "is the best advertising."

"This is according to what the mouth says."

"It says," Morris answered without shame, "that I got a fine clerk who has pepped me up the business. Instead going down in the winter, every day goes up."

"Your clerk did this?" Karp said, thoughtfully scratching under one buttock.

"The customers like him. A goy brings in goyim."

"New customers?"

"New, old."

"Something else helps you also?"

"Also helps a little the new apartment house that it opened in December."

"Hmm," said Karp, "nothing more?"

Morris shrugged. "I don't think so. I hear your Schmitz don't feel so good and he don't give service like he used to give. Came back a few customers from him, but the most important help to me is Frank."

Karp was astonished. Could it be that the man didn't know what had happened practically under his nose? He then and there saw a God-given opportunity to boot the clerk out of the place forever. "That wasn't Frank Alpine who improved you your business," he said decisively. "That was something else."

Morris smiled slightly. As usual the sage knew every reason for every happening.

But Karp persisted. "How long does he work here?"

"You know when he came—in November."

"And right away the business started to pick up?"

"Little by little."

"This happened," Karp announced with excitement, "not because this goy came here. What did he know about the grocery business? Nothing. Your store improved because my tenant Schmitz got sick and had to close his store part of the day. Didn't you know that?"

"I heard he was sick," Morris answered, his throat tightening, "but the drivers said his old father came to give him a help."

"That's right," Karp said, "but in the middle December he went every morning to the hospital for treatments. First the father stayed in the store, then he got too tired so Schmitz didn't open till maybe nine, ten o'clock, instead of seven. And instead of closing ten o'clock at night, he closed eight. This went on like this till last month, then he couldn't open till eleven o'clock in the morning, and so he lost half a day's business. He tried to sell the store but nobody would buy then. Yesterday he closed up altogether. Didn't somebody mention that to you?"

"One of the customers said," Morris answered, distressed, "but I thought it was temporary."

"He's very sick," said Karp solemnly. "He won't open again."

My God, thought Morris. For months he had watched the store when it was empty and while it was being altered, but never since its opening had he gone past Sam Pearl's corner to look at it. He hadn't the heart to. But why had no one told him that the place had been closing part of the day for more than two months—Ida, Helen? Probably they had gone past it without noticing the door was sometimes closed. In their minds, as in his, it was always open for *his* business.

"I don't say," Karp was saying, "that your clerk didn't help your income, but the real reason things got better is when Schmitz couldn't stay open, some of his customers came here. Naturally, Frank wouldn't tell you that."

Filled with foreboding, Morris reflected on what the liquor dealer had said. "What happened to Schmitz?"

"He has a bad blood disease and lays now in the hospital."

"Poor man," the grocer sighed. Hope wrestled shame as he asked, "Will he give the store in auction?"

Karp was devastating. "What do you mean give in auction? It's a good store. He sold it Wednesday to two up-to-date Norwegian partners and they will open next week a modern fancy grocery and delicatessen. You will see where your business will go."

Morris, with clouded eyes, died slowly.

Karp, to his horror, realized he had shot at the clerk and wounded the grocer. He remarked hastily, "What could I do? I couldn't tell him to go in auction if he had a chance to sell."

The grocer wasn't listening. He was thinking of Frank with a violent sense of outrage, of having been deceived.

"Listen, Morris," Karp said quickly, "I got a proposition for you about your gesheft. Throw out first on his ass this Italyener that he fooled you, then tell Helen that my Louis—"

But when the ghost behind the counter cursed him in a strange tongue for the tidings he had brought, Karp backed out of the store and was swallowed in his own.

After a perilous night at the hands of ancient enemies, Morris escaped from his bed and appeared in the store at five A.M. There he faced the burdensome day alone. The grocer had struggled all night with Karp's terrible news—had tossed around like a red coal why nobody had told him before how sick the German was—maybe one of the salesmen, or Breitbart, or a customer. Probably no one had thought it too important, seeing that Schmitz's store was until yesterday open daily. Sure he was sick, but somebody had already mentioned that, and why should they tell him again if they figured that people got sick but then they got better? Hadn't he himself been sick, but who had talked of it in the neighborhood? Probably nobody. People had their own worries to worry about. As for the news that Schmitz had sold his store, the grocer felt that here he had nothing to complain of—he had been informed at once, like a rock dropped on his skull.

As for what he would do with Frank, after long pondering the situation, thinking how the clerk had acted concerning their increase in business—as if he alone had created their better times—Morris at length decided that Frank had not—as he had assumed when Karp told him the news—tried to trick him into believing that he was responsible for the store's change for the better. The grocer supposed that the clerk, like himself, was probably ignorant of the true reason for their change of luck. Maybe he shouldn't have been, since he at least got out during the day, visited other places on the block, heard news, gossip—maybe he should have known, but Morris felt he didn't, possibly because he wanted to believe he was their benefactor. Maybe that was why he had been too blind to see what he should have seen, too deaf to have heard what he had heard. It was possible.

After his first confusion and fright, Morris had decided he must sell the store—he had by eight o'clock already told a couple of drivers to pass the word around—but he must under no circumstances part with Frank and must keep him here to do all he could to prevent the Norwegian partners, after they had reopened the store, from quickly calling back the customers of Schmitz who were with him now. He couldn't believe that Frank hadn't helped. It had not been proved in the Supreme Court that the German's sickness was the only source of their recent good fortune. Karp said so but since when did Karp speak the word of God? Of course Frank had helped the business—only not so much as they had thought. Ida was not so wrong about that. But maybe Frank could hold onto a few people; the grocer doubted he himself could. He hadn't the energy, the nerve to be alone in the store during another time of change for the worse. The years had eaten away his strength.

When Frank came down he at once noticed that the grocer was not himself, but the clerk was too concerned with his own problems to ask Morris what ailed him. Often since the time

Helen had been in his room he had recalled her remark that he must discipline himself and wondered why he had been so moved by the word, why it should now bang around in his head like a stick against a drum. With the idea of self-control came the feeling of the beauty of it—the beauty of a person being able to do things the way he wanted to, to do good if he wanted; and this feeling was followed by regret—of the slow dribbling away, starting long ago, of his character, without him lifting a finger to stop it. But today, as he scraped at his hard beard with a safety razor, he made up his mind to return, bit by bit until all paid up, the hundred and forty-odd bucks he had filched from Morris in the months he had worked for him, the figure of which he had kept for this very purpose written on a card hidden in his shoe.

To clean up the slate in a single swipe, he thought again of telling Morris about his part in the holdup. A week ago he was on the point of getting it past his teeth, had even spoken aloud the grocer's name, but when Morris looked up Frank felt it was useless and said never mind. He was born, he thought, with a worrisome conscience that had never done him too much good, although at times he had liked having the acid weight of it in him because it had made him feel he was at least that different from other people. It made him want to set himself straight so he could build his love for Helen right, so it would stay right.

But when he pictured himself confessing, the Jew listening with a fat ear, he still could not stand the thought of it. Why should he make more trouble for himself than he could now handle, and end by defeating his purpose to fix things up and have a better life? The past was the past and the hell with it. He had unwillingly taken part in a holdup, but he was, like Morris, more of a victim of Ward Minogue. If alone, he wouldn't have done it. That didn't excuse him that he did, but it at least showed his true feelings. So what was there to confess if the whole thing had been sort of an accident? Let bygones be gone. He had no control over the past—could only shine it up here and there and shut up as to the rest. From now on he would keep his mind on tomorrow, and tomorrow take up the kind of life that he saw he valued more than how he had been living. He would change and live in a worthwhile way.

Impatient to begin, he waited to empty the contents of his wallet into the cash drawer. He thought he could try it when Morris was napping; but then for some cockeyed reason, although there was nothing for her to do in the store today, Ida came down and sat in the back with him. She was heavy-faced, dispirited; she sighed often but said nothing, although she acted as if she couldn't stand the sight of him. He knew why, Helen had told him, and he felt uncomfortable, as if he were wearing wet clothes she wouldn't let him take off; but the best thing was to keep his trap shut and let Helen handle her end of it.

Ida wouldn't leave, so he couldn't put the dough back although his itch to do so had grown into impatience. Whenever somebody went into the store Ida insisted on waiting on them, but this last time after she came back she said to Frank, stretched out on the couch with a butt in his mouth, that she wasn't feeling so well and was going up.

"Feel better," he said sitting up, but she didn't reply and at last left. He went quickly into the store, once he was sure she was upstairs. His wallet contained a five-dollar bill and a single, and he planned to put it all back in the register, which would leave him only with a few coins in his pocket but tomorrow was payday anyway. After ringing up the six bucks, to erase the evidence of an unlikely sale he rang up "no sale." Frank then felt a surge of joy at what he had done and his eyes misted. In the back he drew off his shoe, got out the card, and subtracted six dollars from the total amount he owed. He figured he could pay it all up in a couple-three months, by taking out of the bank the money—about eighty bucks—that was left there, returning it bit by bit, and when that was all used up, giving back part of his weekly salary till he had the debt squared. The trick was to get the money back without arousing anybody's suspicion he was putting in the drawer more than the business was earning.

While he was still in a good mood over what he had done, Helen called up.

"Frank," she said, "are you alone? If not say wrong number and hang up."

"I am alone."

"Have you seen how nice it is today? I went for a walk at lunchtime and it feels like spring has arrived."

"It's still in February. Don't take your coat off too soon."

"After Washington's Birthday winter loses its heart. Do you smell the wonderful air?"

"Not right now."

"Get outside in the sun," she said, "it's warm and wonderful."

"Why did you call me for?" he asked.

"Must I have an excuse to call?" she said softly.

"You never do."

"I called because I wished I were seeing you tonight instead of Nat."

"You don't have to go out with him if you don't want to."

"I'd better, because of my mother."

"Change it to some other time."

She thought a minute then said she had better to get it over with.

"Do it any way you like."

"Frank, do you think we could meet after I see Nat—maybe at half past eleven, or twelve at the latest? Would you like to meet me then?"

"Sure, but what's it all about?"

"I'll tell you when I see you," she said with a little laugh. "Should we meet on the Parkway or our regular place in front of the lilac trees?"

"Wherever you say. The park is okay."

"I really hate to go there since my mother followed us."

"Don't worry about that, honey." He said, "Have you got something nice to tell me?"

"Very nice," Helen said.

He thought he knew what it was. He thought he would carry her like a bride up to his room, then when it was over carry her down so she could go up alone without fear her mother suspected where she had been.

Just then Morris came into the store so he hung up.

The grocer inspected the figure in the cash register and the satisfying sum there set him sighing. By Saturday they would surely have two-forty or fifty, but it wouldn't be that high any more once the Norwegians opened up.

Noticing Morris peering at the register under the yellow flame of his match, Frank remembered that all he had left on him was about seventy cents. He wished Helen had called him before he had put back the six bucks in the drawer. If it rained tonight they might need a cab to get home from the park, or maybe if they went up in his room she would be hungry after and want a pizza or something. Anyway, he could borrow a buck from her if he needed it. He also thought of asking Louis Karp for a little loan but didn't like to.

Morris went out for his *Forward* and spread it before him on the table, but he wasn't reading. He was thinking how distracted he was about the future. While he was upstairs, he had lain in bed trying to think of ways to cut down his expenses. He had thought of the fifteen dollars weekly he paid Frank and had worried over how large the sum was. He had also thought of Helen being kissed by the clerk, and of Ida's warnings, and all this had worked on his nerves. He seriously considered telling Frank to go but couldn't make the decision to. He wished he had let him go long ago.

Frank had decided he didn't like to ask Helen for any money—it wasn't a nice thing to do with a girl you liked. He thought it was better to take a buck out of the register drawer, out of the amount he had just put back. He wished he had paid back the five and kept himself the one-buck bill.

Morris sneaked a glance at his clerk sitting on the couch. Recalling the time he had sat in the barber's chair, watching the customers coming out of the grocery with big bags, he felt uneasy. I wonder if he steals from me, he thought. The question filled him with dread because he had asked it of himself many times yet had never answered it with certainty.

He saw through the window in the wall that a woman had come into the store. Frank got up from the couch. "I'll take this one, Morris."

Morris spoke to his newspaper. "I got anyway something to clean up in the cellar."

"What have you got there?"

"Something."

When Frank walked behind the counter, Morris went down into the cellar but didn't stay there. He stole up the stairs and stationed himself behind the hall door. Peering through a crack in the wood, he clearly saw the woman and heard her ordering. He added up the prices of the items as she ordered them.

The bill came to $1.81. When Frank rang up the money, the grocer held his breath for a painful second, then stepped inside the store.

The customer, hugging her bag of groceries, was on her way out of the front door. Frank had his hand under his apron, in his pants pocket. He gazed at the grocer with a startled expression. The amount rung up on the cash register was eighty-one cents.

Morris groaned within himself.

Frank, though tense with shame, pretended nothing was wrong. This enraged Morris. "The bill was a dollar more, why did you ring a dollar less?"

The clerk, after a time of long agony, heard himself say, "It's just a mistake, Morris."

"No," thundered the grocer. "I heard behind the hall door how much you sold her. Don't think I don't know you did many times the same thing before."

Frank could say nothing.

"Give it here the dollar," Morris ordered, extending his trembling hand.

Anguished, the clerk tried lying. "You're making a mistake. The register owes me a buck. I ran short on nickels so I got twenty from Sam Pearl with my own dough. After, I accidentally rang up one buck instead of 'no sale.' That's why I took it back this way. No harm done, I tell you."

"This is a lie," cried Morris. "I left inside a roll nickels in case anybody needed." He strode behind the counter, rang "no sale" and held up the roll of nickels. "Tell the truth."

Frank thought, This shouldn't be happening to me, for I am a different person now.

"I was short, Morris," he admitted, "that's the truth of it. I figured I would pay you back tomorrow after I got my pay." He took the crumpled dollar out of his pants pocket and Morris snatched it from his hand.

"Why didn't you ask me to lend you a dollar instead to steal it?"

The clerk realized it hadn't occurred to him to borrow from the grocer. The reason was simple—he had never borrowed, he had always stolen.

"I didn't think about it. I made a mistake."

"Always mistakes," the grocer said wrathfully.

"All my life," sighed Frank.

"You stole from me since the day I saw you."

"I confess to it," Frank said, "but for God's sake, Morris, I swear I was paying it back to you. Even today I put back six bucks. That's why you got so much in the drawer from the time you went up to snooze until now. Ask the Mrs if we took in more than two bucks while you were upstairs. The rest I put in."

He thought of taking off his shoe and showing Morris how carefully he had kept track of the money he had taken, but he didn't want to do that because the amount was so large it might anger the grocer more.

"You put it in," Morris cried, "but it belongs to me. I don't want a thief here." He counted fifteen dollars out of the register. "Here's your week's pay—the last. Please leave now the store."

His anger was gone. He spoke in sadness and fear of tomorrow.

"Give me one last chance," Frank begged, "Morris, please." His face was gaunt, his eyes haunted, his beard like night.

Morris, though moved by the man, thought of Helen.

"No."

Frank stared at the gray and broken Jew and seeing, despite tears in his eyes, that he would not yield, hung up his apron on a hook and left.

The night's new beauty struck Helen with the anguish of loss as she hurried into the lamplit park a half-hour after midnight. That morning as she had stepped into the street, wearing a new dress under her old coat, the fragrant day had moved her to tears and she felt then she was truly in love with Frank. Whatever the future held it couldn't deny her the sense of release and fulfillment she had felt then. Hours later, when she was with Nat Pearl, as they stopped off for a drink at a roadside tavern, then at his insistence drove into Long Island, her thoughts were still on Frank and she was impatient to be with him.

Nat was Nat. He exerted himself tonight, giving out with charm. He talked with charm and was hurt with charm. Unchanged after all the months she hadn't been with him, as they were parked on the dark shore overlooking the starlit Sound, after a few charming preliminaries he had put his arms around her. "Helen, how can we forget what pleasure we had in the past?"

She pushed him away, angered. "It's gone, I've forgotten. If you're so much of a gentleman, Nat, you ought to forget it too. Was a couple of times in bed a mortgage on my future?"

"Helen, don't talk like a stranger. For Pete's sake, be human."

"I *am* human, please remember."

"We were once good friends. My plea is for friendship again."

"Why don't you admit by friendship you mean something different?"

"Helen . . ."

"No."

He sat back at the wheel. "Christ, you have become a suspicious character."

She said, "Things have changed—you must realize."

"Who have they changed for," he asked sullenly, "that dago I hear you go with?"

Her answer was ice.

On the way home he tried to unsay what he had said, but Helen yielded him only a quick good-by. She left him with relief and a poignant sense of all she had wasted of the night.

Worried that Frank had had to wait so long, she hurried across the lit plaza and along a gravel path bordered by tall lilac shrubs, toward their meeting place. As she approached their bench, although she was troubled by a foreboding he would not be there, she couldn't believe it, then was painfully disappointed to find that though others were present—it was true, he wasn't.

Could he have been and gone already? It didn't seem possible; he had always waited before, no matter how late she was. And since she had told him she had something important to say, nothing less than that she now knew she loved him, surely he would want to hear what. She sat down, fearing he had had an accident.

Usually they were alone at this spot, but the almost warmish late-February night had brought out company. On a bench diagonally opposite Helen, in the dark under budding branches, sat two young lovers locked in a long kiss. The bench at her left was empty, but on the one beyond that a man was sleeping under a dim lamp. A cat nosed at his shadow and departed. The man woke with a grunt, squinted at Helen, yawned and went back to sleep. The lovers at last broke apart and left in silence, the boy awkwardly trailing the happy girl. Helen deeply envied her, an awful feeling to end the day with.

Glancing at her watch she saw it was already past one. Shivering, she rose, then sat down to wait five last minutes. She felt the stars clustered like a distant weight above her head. Utterly lonely, she regretted the spring-like loveliness of the night; it had gone, in her hands, to waste. She was tired of anticipation, of waiting for nothing.

A man was standing unsteadily before her, heavy, dirty, stinking of whiskey. Helen half-rose, struck with fright.

He flipped off his hat and said huskily, "Don't be afraid of me, Helen. I'm personally a fine guy—son of a cop. You remember me, don't you—Ward Minogue that went to your school? My old man beat me up once in the girls' yard."

Though it was years since she had seen him she recognized Ward, at once recalling the incident of his following a girl into a lavatory. Instinctively Helen raised her arm to protect herself. She kept herself from screaming, or he might grab her. How stupid, she thought, to wait for this.

"I remember you, Ward."

"Could I sit down?"

She hesitated. "All right."

Helen edged as far away from him as she could. He looked half-stupefied. If he made a move she would run, screaming.

"How did you recognize me in the dark?" she asked, pretending to be casual as she glanced stealthily around to see how best to escape. If she could get past the trees, it was then another twenty feet along the shrub-lined path before she could be out in the open. Once on the plaza there would be people around she could appeal to.

God only help me, she thought.

"I saw you a couple of times lately," Ward answered, rubbing his hand slowly across his chest.

"Where?"

"Around. Once I saw you come out of your old man's

grocery and I figured it was you. You have still kept your looks," he grinned.

"Thanks. Don't you feel so well?"

"I got gas pains in my chest and a goddam headache."

"In case you want one I have a box of aspirins in my purse."

"No, they make me puke." She noticed that he was glancing toward the trees. She grew more anxious, thought of offering him her purse if he only wouldn't touch her.

"How's your boy friend, Frank Alpine?" Ward asked, with a wet wink.

She said in surprise, "Do you know Frank?"

"He's an old friend of mine," he answered. "He was here lookin' for you."

"Is—he all right?"

"Not so hot," said Ward. "He had to go home."

She got up. "I have to leave now."

But he was standing.

"Good night." Helen walked away from him.

"He told me to give you this paper." Ward thrust his hand into his coat pocket.

She didn't believe him but paused long enough for him to move forward. He grabbed her with astonishing swiftness, smothering her scream with his smelly hand, as he dragged her toward the trees.

"All I want is what you give that wop," Ward grunted.

She kicked, clawed, bit his hand, broke loose. He caught her by her coat collar, ripped it off. She screamed again and ran forward but he pounced upon her and got his arm over her mouth. Ward shoved her hard against a tree, knocking the breath out of her. He held her tightly by the throat as with his other hand he ripped open her coat and tore her dress off the shoulder, exposing her brassiere.

Struggling, kicking wildly, she caught him between the legs with her knee. He cried out and cracked her across the face. She felt the strength go out of her and fought not to faint. She screamed but heard no sound.

Helen felt his body shuddering against her. I am disgraced, she thought, yet felt curiously freed of his stinking presence, as if he had dissolved into a can of filth and she had kicked it away. Her legs buckled and she slid to the ground. I've fainted, went through her mind, although she felt she was still fighting him.

Dimly she realized that a struggle was going on near her. She heard the noise of a blow, and Ward Minogue cried out in great pain and staggered away.

Frank, she thought with tremulous joy. Helen felt herself gently lifted and knew she was in his arms. She sobbed in relief. He kissed her eyes and lips and he kissed her half-naked breast. She held him tightly with both arms, weeping, laughing, murmuring she had come to tell him she loved him.

He put her down and they kissed under the dark trees. She tasted whiskey on his tongue and was momentarily afraid.

"I love you, Helen," he murmured, attempting clumsily to cover her breast with the torn dress as he drew her deeper into the dark, and from under the trees onto the star-dark field.

They sank to their knees on the winter earth, Helen urgently whispering, "Please not now, darling," but he spoke of his starved and passionate love, and all the endless heartbreaking waiting. Even as he spoke he thought of her as beyond his reach, forever in the bathroom as he spied, so he stopped her pleas with kisses. . . .

Afterward, she cried, "Dog—uncircumcised dog!"

WHILE MORRIS was sitting alone in the back the next morning, a boy brought in a pink handbill and left it on the counter. When the grocer picked it up he saw it announced the change of management and reopening on Monday, by Taast and Pederson, of the grocery and fancy delicatessen around the corner. There followed, in large print, a list of specials they were offering during their first week, bargains Morris could never hope to match, because he couldn't afford the loss the Norwegians were planning to take. The grocer felt he was standing in an icy draft blowing from some hidden hole in the store. In the kitchen, though he stood with his legs and buttocks pressed against the gas radiator, it took an age to diminish the chill that had penetrated his bones.

All morning he scanned the crumpled handbill, muttering to himself; he sipped cold coffee, thinking of the future, and off and on, of Frank Alpine. The clerk had left last night without taking his fifteen dollars' wages. Morris thought he would come in for it this morning but, as the hours passed, knew he wouldn't, maybe having left it to make up some of the money he had stolen; yet maybe not. For the thousandth time the grocer wondered if he had done right in ordering Frank to go. True, he had stolen from him, but also true, he was paying it back. His story that he had put six dollars into the register and then found he had left himself without a penny in his pocket was probably the truth, because the sum in the register, when Morris counted it, was more than they usually took in during the dead part of the afternoon when he napped. The clerk was an unfortunate man; yet the grocer was alternately glad and sorry the incident had occurred. He was glad he had finally let him go. For Helen's sake it had had to be done, and for Ida's peace of mind, as well as his own. Still, he felt unhappy to lose his assistant and be by himself when the Norwegians opened up.

Ida came down, puffy-eyed from poor sleep. She felt a hopeless rage against the world. What will become of Helen? she asked herself, and cracked her knuckles against her chest. But when Morris looked up to listen to her complaints, she was afraid to say anything. A half-hour later, aware that something had changed in the store, she thought of the clerk.

"Where is he?" she asked.

"He left," Morris answered.

"Where did he leave?" she said in astonishment.

"He left for good."

She gazed at him. "Morris, what happened, tell me?"

"Nothing," he said, embarrassed. "I told him to leave."

"Why, all of a sudden?"

"Didn't you say you didn't want him here no more?"

"From the first day I saw him, but you always said no."

"Now I said yes."

"A stone falls off my heart." But she was not satisfied. "Did he move out of the house yet?"

"I don't know."

"I will go and ask the upstairske."

"Leave her alone. We will know when he moves."

"When did you tell him to leave?"

"Last night."

"So why didn't you tell me last night?" she said angrily. "Why you told me he went early to the movies?"

"I was nervous."

"Morris," she asked in fright, "did something else happen? Did Helen—"

"Nothing happened."

"Does she know he left?"

"I didn't tell her. Why she went so early to work this morning?"

"She went early?"

"Yes."

"I don't know," Ida said uneasily.

He produced the handbill. "This is why I feel bad."

She glanced at it, not comprehending.

"The German," he explained. "They bought him out, two Norwegians."

She gasped. "When?"

"This week. Schmitz is sick. He lays now in the hospital."

"I told you," Ida said.

"You told me?"

"Vey is mir. I told you after Christmas—when improved

more the business. I told you the drivers said the German was losing customers. You said no, Frank improved the business. A goy brings in goyim, you said. How much strength I had to argue with you?"

"Did you tell me he kept closed in the morning his store?"

"Who said? I didn't know this."

"Karp told me."

"Karp was here?"

"He came on Thursday to tell me the good news."

"What good news?"

"That Schmitz sold out."

"Is this good news?" she asked.

"Maybe to him but not to me."

"You didn't tell me he came."

"I tell you now," he said irritably. "Schmitz sold out. Monday will open two Norwegians. Our business will go to hell again. We will starve here."

"Some helper you had," she said with bitterness. "Why didn't you listen to me when I said let him go?"

"I listened," he said wearily.

She was silent, then asked, "So when Karp told you Schmitz sold his store you told Frank to leave?"

"The next day."

"Thank God."

"See if you say next week 'Thank God.'"

"What is this got to do with Frank? Did he help us?"

"I don't know."

"You don't know," she said shrilly. "You just told me you said he should leave when you found out where came our business."

"I don't know," he said miserably, "I don't know where it came."

"It didn't come from him."

"Where it came I don't worry any more. Where will it come next week I worry." He read aloud the specials the Norwegians were offering.

She squeezed her hands white. "Morris, we must sell the store."

"So sell." Sighing, Morris removed his apron. "I will take my rest."

"It's only half past eleven."

"I feel cold." He looked depressed.

"Eat something first—your soup."

"Who can eat?"

"Drink a hot glass tea."

"No."

"Morris," she said quietly, "don't worry so much. Something will happen. We will always have to eat."

He made no reply, folded the handbill into a small square and took it upstairs with him.

The rooms were cold. Ida always shut off the radiators when she went down and lit them again in the late afternoon about an hour before Helen returned. Now the house was too cold. Morris turned on the stopcock of the bedroom radiator, then found he had no match in his pocket. He got one in the kitchen.

Under the covers he felt shivery. He lay under two blankets and a quilt yet shivered. He wondered if he was sick but soon fell asleep. He was glad when he felt sleep come over him, although it brought night too quickly. But if you slept it was night, that's how things were. Looking, that same night, from the street into his store, he beheld Taast and Pederson—one with a small blond mustache, the other half-bald, a light shining on his head—standing behind *his* counter, poking into *his* cash register. The grocer rushed in but they were gabbing in German and paid no attention to his gibbering Yiddish. At that moment Frank came out of the back with Helen. Though the clerk spoke a musical Italian, Morris recognized a dirty word. He struck his assistant across the face and they wrestled furiously on the floor, Helen screaming mutely. Frank dumped him heavily on his back and sat on his poor chest. He thought his lungs would burst. He tried hard to cry out but his voice cracked his throat and no one would help. He considered the possibility of dying and would have liked to.

Tessie Fuso dreamed of a tree hit by thunder and knocked over; she dreamed she heard someone groan terribly and awoke in fright, listened, then went back to sleep. Frank Alpine, at the dirty end of a long night, awoke groaning. He awoke with a shout—awake, he thought, forever. His impulse was to leap out of bed and rush down to the store; then he remembered that Morris had thrown him out. It was a gray, dreary winter morning. Nick had gone to work and Tessie, in her bathrobe, was sitting in the kitchen, drinking coffee. She heard Frank cry out again but had just discovered that she was pregnant, so did nothing more than wonder at his nightmare.

He lay in bed with the blankets pulled over his head, trying to smother his thoughts but they escaped and stank. The more he smothered them the more they stank. He smelled garbage in the bed and couldn't move out of it. He couldn't because he was it—the stink in his own broken nose. What you did was how bad you smelled. Unable to stand it he flung the covers aside and struggled to dress but couldn't make it. The sight of his bare feet utterly disgusted him. He thirsted for a cigarette but couldn't light one for fear of seeing his hand. He shut his eyes and lit a match. The match burned his nose. He stepped on the lit match with his bare feet and danced in pain.

Oh my God, why did I do it? Why did I ever do it? Why did I do it?

His thoughts were killing him. He couldn't stand them. He sat on the edge of the twisted bed, his thoughtful head ready to bust in his hands. He wanted to run. Part of him was already in flight, he didn't know where. He just wanted to run. But while he was running, he wanted to be back. He wanted to be back with Helen, to be forgiven. It wasn't asking too much. People forgave people—who else? He could explain if she would listen. Explaining was a way of getting close to somebody you had hurt; as if in hurting them you were giving them a reason to love you. He had come, he would say, to the park to wait for her, to hear what she had to tell him. He felt he knew she would say she loved him; it meant they would soon sleep together. This stayed in his mind and he sat there waiting to hear her say it, at the same time in an agony that she never would, that he would lose her the minute she found out why her father had kicked him out of the grocery. What could he tell her about that? He sat for hours trying to think what to say, at last growing famished. At midnight he left to get a pizza but stopped instead in a bar. Then when he saw his face in the mirror he felt a nose-thumbing revulsion. Where have you ever been, he asked the one in the glass, except on the inside of a circle? What have you ever done but always the wrong thing?

When he returned to the park, there was Ward Minogue hurting her. He just about killed Ward. Then when he had Helen in his arms, crying, saying at last that she loved him, he had this hopeless feeling it was the end and now he would never see her again. He thought he must love her before she was lost to him. She said no, not to, but he couldn't believe it the same minute she was saying she loved him. He thought, Once I start she will come along with me. So then he did it. He loved her with his love. She should have known that. She should not have gone wild, beat his face with her fists, called him dirty names, run from him, his apologies, pleadings, sorrow.

Oh Jesus, what did I do?

He moaned; had got instead of a happy ending, a bad smell. If he could root out what he had done, smash and destroy it; but it was done, beyond him to undo. It was where he could never lay hands on it any more—in his stinking mind. His thoughts would forever suffocate him. He had failed once too often. He should somewhere have stopped and changed the way he was going, his luck, himself, stopped hating the world, got a decent education, a job, a nice girl. He had lived without will, betrayed every good intention. Had he ever confessed the holdup to Morris? Hadn't he stolen from the cash register till the minute he was canned? In a single terrible act in the park hadn't he murdered the last of his good hopes, the love he had so long waited for—his chance at a future? His goddamned life had pushed him wherever it went; he had led it nowhere. He was blown around in any breath that blew, owned nothing, not even experience to show for the years he had lived. If you had experience you knew at least when to start and where to quit; all he knew was how to mangle himself more. The self he had secretly considered valuable was, for all he could make of it, a dead rat. He stank.

This time his shout frightened Tessie. Frank got up on the run but he had run everywhere. There was no place left to escape to. The room shrank. The bed was flying up at him. He felt trapped—sick, wanted to cry but couldn't. He planned to kill himself, at the same minute had a terrifying insight: that all the while he was acting like he wasn't, he was really a man of stern morality.

*

Ida had awakened in the night and heard her daughter crying. Nat did something to her, she thought wildly, but was ashamed to go to Helen and beg her to say what. She guessed he had acted like a lout—it was no wonder Helen had stopped seeing him. All night she blamed herself for having urged her to go out with the law student. She fell into an unhappy sleep.

It was growing light when Morris left the flat. Helen dragged herself out of bed and sat with reddened eyes in the bathroom, sewing on her coat collar. Once near the office she would give it to a tailor to fix so the tear couldn't be seen. With her new dress she could do nothing. Rolling it into a hopeless ball, she hid it under some things in her bottom bureau drawer. Monday she would buy one exactly like it and hang it in her closet. Undressing for a shower—her third in hours—she burst into tears at the sight of her body. Every man she drew to her dirtied her. How could she have encouraged him? She felt a violent self-hatred for trusting him, when from the very beginning she had sensed he was untrustable. How could she have allowed herself to fall in love with anybody like him? She was filled with loathing at the fantasy she had created, of making him into what he couldn't be—educable, promising, kind and good, when he was no more than a bum. Where were her wits, her sense of elemental self-preservation?

Under the shower she soaped herself heavily, crying as she washed. At seven, before her mother awakened, she dressed and left the house, too sickened to eat. She would gladly have forgotten her life, in sleep, but dared not stay home, dared not be questioned. When she returned from her half-day of work, if he was still there, she would order him to leave or would scream him out of the house.

Coming home from the garage, Nick smelled gas in the hall. He inspected the radiators in his flat, saw they were both lit, then knocked on Frank's door.

After a minute the door opened a crack.

"Do you smell anything?" Nick said, staring at the eye in the crack.

"Mind your goddamned business."

"Are you nuts? I smell gas in the house, it's dangerous."

"Gas?" Frank flung open the door. He was in pajamas, haggard.

"What's the matter, you sick?"

"Where do you smell the gas?"

"Don't tell me you can't smell it."

"I got a bad cold," Frank said hoarsely.

"Maybe it's comin' from the cellar," said Nick.

They ran down a flight and then the odor hit Frank, an acrid stench thick enough to wade through.

"It's coming from this floor," Nick said.

Frank pounded on the door. "Helen, there's gas here, let me in. Helen," he cried.

"Shove it," said Nick.

Frank pushed his shoulder against the door. It was unlocked and he fell in. Nick quickly opened the kitchen window while Frank, in his bare feet, roamed through the house. Helen was not there but he found Morris in bed.

The clerk, coughing, dragged the grocer out of bed and carrying him to the living room, laid him on the floor. Nick closed the stopcock of the bedroom radiator and threw open every window. Frank got down on his knees, bent over Morris, clamped his hands to his sides and pumped.

Tessie ran in in fright, and Nick shouted to her to call Ida.

Ida came stumbling up the stairs, moaning, "Oh, my God, oh, my God."

Seeing Morris lying on the floor, his underwear soaked, his face the color of a cooked beet, flecks of foam in the corners of his mouth, she let out a piercing shriek.

Helen, coming dully into the hall, heard her mother's cry. She smelled the gas and ran in terror up the stairs, expecting death.

When she saw Frank in his pajamas bent over her father's back, her throat thickened in disgust. She screamed in fear and hatred.

Frank couldn't look at her, frightened to.

"His eyes just moved," Nick said.

Morris awoke with a massive ache in his chest. His head felt like corroded metal, his mouth horribly dry, his stomach crawling with pain. He was ashamed to find himself stretched out in his long underwear on the floor.

"Morris," cried Ida.

Frank got up, embarrassed at his bare feet and pajamas.

"Papa, Papa." Helen was on her knees.

"Why did you do it for?" Ida yelled in the grocer's ear.

"What happened?" he gasped.

"Why did you do it for?" she wept.

"Are you crazy?" he muttered. "I forgot to light the gas. A mistake."

Helen broke into sobbing, her lips twisted. Frank had to turn his head.

"The only thing that saved him was he got some air," Nick said. "You're lucky this flat ain't windproof, Morris."

Tessie shivered. "It's cold. Cover him, he's sweating."

"Put him in bed," Ida said.

Frank and Nick lifted the grocer and carried him in to his bed. Ida and Helen covered him with blankets and quilt.

"Thanks," Morris said to them. He stared at Frank. Frank looked at the floor.

"Shut the windows," Tessie said. "The smell is gone."

"Wait a little longer," said Frank. He glanced at Helen but her back was to him. She was still crying.

"Why did he do it?" Ida moaned.

Morris gazed long at her, then shut his eyes.

"Leave him rest," Nick advised.

"Don't light any matches for another hour," Frank told Ida.

Tessie closed all but one window and they left. Ida and Helen remained with Morris in the bedroom.

Frank lingered in Helen's room but nothing welcomed him there.

Later he dressed and went down to the store. Business was brisk. Ida came down, and though he begged her not to, shut the store.

That afternoon Morris developed a fever and the doctor said he had to go to the hospital. An ambulance came and took the grocer away, his wife and daughter riding with him.

From his window upstairs, Frank watched them go.

Sunday morning the store was still shut tight. Though he feared to, Frank considered knocking on Ida's door and asking for the key. But Helen might open the door, and since he would not know what to say to her over the doorsill, he went instead down the cellar, and mounting the dumb-waiter, wriggled through the little window in the air shaft, into the store toilet. Once in the back, the clerk shaved and had his coffee. He thought he would stay in the store till somebody told him to scram; and even if they did, he would try in some way to stay longer. That was his only hope left, if there was any. Turning the front door lock, he carried in the milk and rolls and was ready for business. The register was empty, so he borrowed five dollars in change from Sam Pearl, saying he would pay it back from what he took in. Sam wanted to know how Morris was and Frank said he didn't know.

Shortly after half past eight, the clerk was standing at the front window when Ida and her daughter left the house. Helen looked like last year's flower. Observing her, he felt a pang of loss, shame, regret. He felt an unbearable deprivation—that yesterday he had almost had some wonderful thing but today it was gone, all but the misery of remembering it was. Whenever he thought of what he had almost had it made him frantic. He felt like rushing outside, drawing her into a doorway, and declaring the stupendous value of his love for her. But he did nothing. He didn't exactly hide but he didn't show himself, and they soon went away to the subway.

Later he thought he would also go and see Morris in the hospital, as soon as he knew which one he was in—after they got home; but they didn't return till midnight. The store was closed and he saw them from his room, two dark figures getting out of a cab. Monday, the day the Norwegians opened their store, Ida came down at seven A.M. to paste a piece of paper on the door saying Morris Bober was sick and the grocery would be closed till Tuesday or Wednesday. To her amazement, Frank Alpine was standing, in his apron, behind the counter. She entered in anger.

Frank was miserably nervous that Morris or Helen, either or both, had told her all the wrong he had done them, because if they had, he was finished.

"How did you get in here?" Ida asked wrathfully.

He said through the air shaft window. "Thinking of your trouble, I didn't want to bother you about the key, Mrs."

She vigorously forbade him ever to come in that way again. Her face was deeply lined, her eyes weary, mouth bitter, but he could tell that for some miraculous reason she didn't know what he had done.

Frank pulled a handful of dollar bills out of his pants pocket and a little bag of change, laying it all on the counter. "I took in forty-one bucks yesterday."

"You were here yesterday?"

"I got in how I explained you. There was a nice rush around four till about six. We are all out of potato salad."

Her eyes grew tears. He asked how Morris felt.

She touched her wet lids with a handkerchief. "Morris has pneumonia."

"Ah, too bad. Give him my sorrow if you can. How's he coming along out of it?"

"He's a very sick man, he has weak lungs."

"I think I'll go to see him in the hospital."

"Not now," Ida said.

"When he's better. How long do you think he'll be there?"

"I don't know. The doctor will telephone today."

"Look, Mrs," Frank said. "Why don't you stop worrying about the store while Morris is sick and let me take care of it? You know I make no demands."

"My husband told you to go out from the store."

He furtively studied her face but there was no sign of accusation.

"I won't stay very long," he answered. "You don't have to worry about that. I'll stay here till Morris gets better. You'll need every cent for the hospital bills. I don't ask a thing for myself."

"Did Morris tell you why you must leave?"

His heart galloped. Did she or didn't she know? If yes, he would say it was a mistake—deny he had touched a red cent in the register. Wasn't the proof of that in the pile of dough that lay right in front of her eyes on the counter? But he answered, "Sure, he didn't want me to hang around Helen any more."

"Yes, she is a Jewish girl. You should look for somebody else. But he also found out that Schmitz was sick since December and kept closed his store in the mornings, also earlier in the night. This was what improved our income, not you."

She then told Frank that the German had sold out and two Norwegians were opening up today.

Frank flushed. "I knew that Schmitz was sick and kept his store closed sometimes, but that isn't what made your business get better. What did that was how hard I worked building up the trade. And I bet I can keep this place in the same shape it is, even with two Norwegians around the corner or three Greeks. What's more, I bet I can raise the take-in higher."

Though she was half-inclined to believe him, she couldn't.

"Wait, you'll see how smart you are."

"Then let me have a chance to show you. Don't pay me anything, the room and meals are enough."

"What," she asked in desperation, "do you want from us?"

"Just to help out. I have my debt to Morris."

"You have no debt. He has a debt to you that you saved him from the gas."

"Nick smelled it first. Anyway I feel I have a debt to him for all the things he has done for me. That's my nature, when I'm thankful, I'm thankful."

"Please don't bother Helen. She is not for you."

"I won't."

She let him stay. If you were so poor where was your choice?

Taast and Pederson opened up with a horseshoe of spring flowers in their window. Their pink handbills brought them steady business and Frank had plenty of time on his hands. During the day only a few of the regulars came into the grocery. At night, after the Norwegians had closed, the grocery had a spurt of activity, but when Frank pulled the strings of the window lights around eleven, he had only fifteen dollars in the register. He didn't worry too much. Monday was a slow day anyway, and besides, people were entitled to grab off a few specials while they could get them. He figured nobody could tell what difference the Norwegians would make to the business until a couple of weeks had gone by, when the neighborhood was used to them and things settled back to normal. Nobody was going to give specials away that cheap every day. A store wasn't a charity, and when they stopped giving something for nothing, he would match them in service and also prices and get his customers back.

Tuesday was slow, also as usual. Wednesday picked up a little, but Thursday was slow again. Friday was better. Saturday was the best day of the week, although not so good as Saturdays lately. At the end of the week the grocery was close to a hundred short of its recent weekly average. Expecting something like this, Frank had closed up for a half-hour on Thursday and taken the trolley to the bank. He withdrew twenty-five dollars from his savings account and put the money into the register, five on Thursday, ten on Friday and ten on Saturday, so that when Ida wrote the figures down in her book each night she wouldn't feel too bad. Seventy-five less for the week wasn't as bad as a hundred.

Morris, better after ten days in the hospital, was brought home in a cab by Ida and Helen and laid to bed to convalesce. Frank, gripping his courage, thought of going up to see him and this time starting out right, right off. He thought of bringing him some fresh baked goods to eat, maybe a piece of cheesecake that he knew the grocer liked, or some apple strudel; but the clerk was afraid it was still too soon and Morris might ask him where he had got the money to buy the cake. He might yell, "You thief, you, the only reason you stay here still is because I am sick upstairs." Yet if Morris felt this way he would already have told Ida what Frank had done. The clerk now was sure he hadn't mentioned it, because she wouldn't have waited this long to pitch him out on his ear. He thought a lot about the way Morris kept things to himself. It was a way a person had if he figured he could be wrong about how he sized up a situation. It could be that he might take a different view of Frank in time. The clerk tried to invent reasons why it might be worth the grocer's while, after he got on his feet again, to keep him on in the grocery. Frank felt he would promise anything to stay there. "Don't worry that I ever will steal from you or anybody else any more, Morris. If I do, I hope I drop dead on the spot." He hoped that this promise, and the favor he was doing him by keeping the store open, would convince Morris of his sincerity. Yet he thought he would wait a while longer before going up to see him.

Helen hadn't said anything to anybody about him either and it wasn't hard to understand why. The wrong he had done her was never out of his mind. He hadn't intended wrong but he had done it; now he intended right. He would do anything she wanted, and if she wanted nothing he would do something, what he should do; and he would do it all on his own will, nobody pushing him but himself. He would do it with discipline and with love.

All this time he had snatched only glimpses of her, though his heart was heavy with all he hoped to say. He saw her through the plate glass window—she on the undersea side. Through the green glass she looked drowned, yet never, God help him, lovelier. He felt a tender pity for her, mixed with shame for having made her pitiable. Once, as she came home from work, her eyes happened to look into his and showed disgust. Now I am finished, he thought, she will come in here and tell me to go die some place; but when she looked away she was never there. He was agonized to be so completely apart from her, left apologizing to her shadow, to the floral fragrance she left in the air. To himself he confessed his deed, but not to her. That was the curse of it, to have it to make but who would listen? At times he felt like crying but it made him feel too much like a kid to cry. He didn't like to, did it badly.

Once he met her in the hall. She was gone before he could move his lips. He felt for her a rush of love. He felt, after she had left, that hopelessness was his punishment. He had expected that punishment to be drastic, swift; instead it came slowly—it never came, yet was there.

There was no approach to her. What had happened had put her in another world, no way in.

Early one morning, he stood in the hall till she came down the stairs.

"Helen," he said, snatching off the cloth cap he now wore in the store, "my heart is sorrowful. I want to apologize."

Her lips quivered. "Don't speak to me," she said, in a voice choked with contempt. "I don't want your apologies. I don't want to see you, and I don't want to know you. As soon as my father is better, please leave. You've helped him and my mother and I thank you for that, but you're no help to me. You make me sick."

The door banged behind her.

That night he dreamed he was standing in the snow outside her window. His feet were bare yet not cold. He had waited a long time in the falling snow, and some of it lay on his head and had all but frozen his face; but he waited longer until, moved by pity, she opened the window and flung something out. It floated down; he thought it was a piece of paper with writing on it but saw that it was a white flower, surprising to see in wintertime. Frank caught it in his hand. As she had tossed the flower out through the partly opened window he had glimpsed her fingers only, yet he saw the light of her room and even felt the warmth of it. Then when he looked again the window was shut tight, sealed with ice. Even as he dreamed, he knew it had never been open. There was no such window. He gazed down at his hand for the flower and before he could see it wasn't there, felt himself wake.

The next day he waited for her at the foot of the stairs, bareheaded in the light that fell on his head from the lamp.

She came down, her frozen face averted.

"Helen, nothing can kill the love I feel for you."

"In your mouth it's a dirty word."

"If a guy did wrong, must he suffer forever?"

"I personally don't care what happens to you."

Whenever he waited at the stairs, she passed without a word, as if he didn't exist. He didn't.

If the store blows away some dark night I might as well be dead, Frank thought. He tried every way to hang on. Business was terrible. He wasn't sure how long the grocery could last or how long the grocer and his wife would let him try to keep it alive. If the store collapsed everything would be gone. But if he kept it going there was always the chance that something might change, and if it did, maybe something else might. If he kept the grocery on its feet till Morris came down, at least he would have a couple of weeks to change how things were. Weeks were nothing but it might as well be nothing because to do what he had to do he needed years.

Taast and Pederson had the specials going week after week. They thought of one come-on after another to keep the customers buying. Frank's customers were disappearing. Some of them now passed him in the street without saying hello. One or two crossed the trolley tracks and walked on the other side of the street, not to have to see his stricken face at the window. He withdrew all he had left in the bank and each week padded the income a little, but Ida saw how bad things were. She was despondent and talked of giving the place over to the auctioneer. This made him frantic. He felt he had to try harder.

He tried out all sorts of schemes. He got specials on credit and sold half the stuff, but then the Norwegians began to sell it cheaper, and the rest remained on his shelves. He stayed open all night for a couple of nights but did not take in enough to pay for the light. Having nothing much to do, he thought he would fix up the store. With all but the last five dollars from the bank account, he bought a few gallons of cheap paint. Then removing the goods from one section of the shelves, he scraped away the mildewed paper on the walls and painted them a nice light yellow. When one section was painted he went to work on the next. After he had finished the walls he borrowed a tall ladder, scraped the ceiling bit by bit and painted it white. He also replaced a few shelves and neatly finished them in dime store varnish. In the end he had to admit that all his work hadn't brought back a single customer.

Though it seemed impossible the store got worse.

"What are you telling Morris about the business?" Frank asked Ida.

"He don't ask me so I don't tell him," she said dully.

"How is he now?"

"Weak yet. The doctor says his lungs are like paper. He reads or he sleeps. Sometimes he listens to the radio."

"Let him rest. It's good for him."

She said again, "Why do you work so hard for nothing? What do you stay here for?"

For love, he wanted to say, but hadn't the nerve. "For Morris."

But he didn't fool her. She would even then have told him to pack and go, although he kept them for the moment off the street, had she not known for a fact that Helen no longer bothered with him. He had probably through some stupidity fallen out of her good graces. Possibly her father's illness had made her more considerate of them. She had been a fool to worry. Yet she now worried because Helen, at her age, showed so little interest in men. Nat had called but she wouldn't go near the phone.

Frank scraped down on expenses. With Ida's permission he had the telephone removed. He hated to do it because he thought Helen might sometime come down to answer it. He also reduced the gas bill by lighting only one of the two radiators downstairs. He kept the one in the front lit so the customers wouldn't feel the cold, but he no longer used the one in the kitchen. He wore a heavy sweater, a vest and a flannel shirt under his apron, and his cap on his head. But Ida, even with her coat on, when she could no longer stand the emptiness of the front, or the freezing back, escaped upstairs. One day she came into the kitchen, and seeing him salting up a soup plate of boiled potatoes for lunch, began to cry.

He thought always of Helen. How could she know what was going on in him? If she ever looked at him again she would see the same guy on the outside. He could see out but nobody could see in.

When Betty Pearl got married Helen didn't go to the wedding. The day before she apologized embarrassedly, said she wasn't feeling too well—blamed her father's illness. Betty said she understood, thinking it had something to do with her brother. "Next time," she remarked with a little laugh, but Helen, seeing she was hurt, felt bad. She reconsidered facing the ceremony, rigmarole, relatives, Nat or no Nat—maybe she could still go; but couldn't bring herself to. She was no fixture for a wedding. They might say to her, "With such a face, go better to a funeral." Though she had many a night wept herself out, her memories kept a hard hold in her mind. Crazy woman, how could she have brought herself to love such a man? How could she have considered marrying someone not Jewish? A total, worthless stranger. Only God had saved her from a disastrous mistake. With such thoughts she lost all feeling for weddings.

Her sleep suffered. Every day she dreaded every night. From bedtime to dawn she eked out only a few wearisome unconscious hours. She dreamed she would soon awake and soon awoke. Awake, she felt sorry for herself, and sorrow, no soporific, induced sorrow. Her mind stamped out endless worries: her father's health, for instance; he showed little interest in recovery. The store, as ever. Ida wept in whispers in the kitchen. "Don't tell Papa." But they would sometime soon have to. She cursed all grocery stores. And worried at seeing nobody, planning no future. Each morning she crossed off the calendar the sleepless day to be. God forbid such days.

Though Helen turned over all but four dollars of her check to her mother and it went into the register, they were always hard up for cash to meet expenses. One day Frank got an idea about how he might lay hold of some dough. He thought he would collect an old bill from Carl, the Swedish painter. He knew the painter owed Morris over seventy bucks. He looked for the housepainter every day but Carl did not come in.

One morning Frank was standing at the window when he saw him leave Karp's with a wrapped bottle in his pocket.

Frank ran out and reminded Carl of his old bill. He asked him to pay something on the account.

"This is all fixed up with me and Morris," the painter answered. "Don't stick your dirty nose in."

"Morris is sick, he needs the dough," Frank said.

Carl shoved the clerk aside and went on his way.

Frank was sore. "I'll collect from that drunk bastard."

Ida was in the store, so Frank said he would be back soon. He hung up his apron, got his overcoat and followed Carl to his house. After getting the address, he returned to the grocery. He was still angered at the painter for the way he had acted when he had asked him to pay his bill.

That evening he returned to the shabby four-story tenement and climbed the creaking staircase to the top floor. A thin, dark-haired woman came wearily to the door. She was old until his eyes got used to her face, then he realized she was young but looked old.

"Are you Carl the painter's wife?"

"That's right."

"Could I talk to him?"

"On a job?" she said hopefully.

"No. Something different."

She looked old again. "He hasn't worked for months."

"I just want to talk to him."

She let him into a large room which was a kitchen and living room combined, the two halves separated by an undrawn curtain. In the middle of the living room part stood a kerosene heater that stank. This smell mixed with the sour smell of cabbage cooking. The four kids, a boy about twelve and three younger girls, were in the room, drawing on paper, cutting and pasting. They stared at Frank but silently went on with what they were doing. The clerk didn't feel comfortable. He stood at the window, looking down on the dreary lamplit street. He now figured he would cut the bill in half if the painter would pay up the rest.

The painter's wife covered the sizzling frying pan with a pot lid and went into the bedroom. She came back and said her husband was sleeping.

"I'll wait a while," said Frank.

She went back to her frying. The oldest girl set the table, and they all sat down to eat. He noticed they had left a place for their old man. He would soon have to crawl out of his hole. The mother didn't sit down. Paying no attention to Frank, she poured skim milk out of a container into the kids' glasses, then served each one a frankfurter fried in dough. She also gave everybody a forkful of hot sauerkraut.

The kids ate hungrily, not talking. The oldest girl glanced at Frank then stared at her plate when he looked at her.

When the plates were empty she said, "Is there any more, Mama?"

"Go to bed," said the painter's wife.

Frank had a bad headache from the stink of the heater.

"I'll see Carl some other time," he said. His spit tasted like brass.

"I'm sorry he didn't wake up."

He ran back to the store. Under the mattress of his bed he had his last three bucks hidden. He took the bills and ran back to Carl's house. But on the way he met Ward Minogue. His face was yellow and shrunken, as if he had escaped out of a morgue.

"I been looking for you," said Ward. He pulled Frank's revolver out of a paper bag. "How much is this worth to you?"

"Shit."

"I'm sick," sobbed Ward.

Frank gave the three bucks to him and later dropped the gun into a sewer.

*

He read a book about the Jews, a short history. He had many times seen this book on one of the library shelves and had never taken it down, but one day he checked it out to satisfy his curiosity. He read the first part with interest, but after the Crusades and the Inquisition, when the Jews were having it tough, he had to force himself to keep reading. He skimmed the bloody chapters but read slowly the ones about their civilization and accomplishments. He also read about the ghettos, where the half-starved, bearded prisoners spent their lives trying to figure out why they were the Chosen People. He tried to figure out why but couldn't. He couldn't finish the book and brought it back to the library.

Some nights he spied on the Norwegians. He would go around the corner without his apron and stand on the step of Sam Pearl's hallway, looking across the street at the grocery and fancy delicatessen. The window was loaded with all kinds of shiny cans. Inside, the store was lit as bright as day. The shelves were tightly packed with appetizing goods that made him feel hungry. And there were always customers inside, although his place was generally empty. Sometimes after the partners locked up and went home, Frank crossed to their side of the street and peered through the window into the dark store, as if he might learn from what he saw in it the secret of all good fortune and so change his luck and his life.

One night after he had closed the store, he took a long walk and stepped into the Coffee Pot, an all-night joint he had been in once or twice.

Frank asked the owner if he needed a man for night work.

"I need a counterman for coffee, short orders, and to wash the few dishes," the owner answered.

"I am your boy," said Frank.

The work was from ten to six A.M. and paid thirty-five dollars. When he got home in the morning, Frank opened the grocery. At the end of a week's working, without ringing it up, he put the thirty-five into the cash register. This, and Helen's wages, kept them from going under.

The clerk slept on the couch in the back of the store during the day. He had rigged up a buzzer that waked him when somebody opened the front door. He did not suffer from lack of sleep.

He lived in his prison in a climate of regret that he had turned a good thing into a bad, and this thought, though ancient, renewed the pain in his heart. His dreams were bad, taking place in the park at night. The garbage smell stank in his nose. He groaned his life away, his mouth crammed with words he couldn't speak. Mornings, standing at the store window, he watched Helen go off to work. He was there when she came home. She walked, slightly bowlegged, toward the door, her eyes cast down, blind to his presence. A million things to say, some extraordinary, welled up in him, choked his throat; daily they died. He thought endlessly of escape, but that would be what he always did last—beat it. This time he would stay. They would carry him out in a box. When the walls caved in they could dig for him with shovels.

Once he found a two-by-four pine board in the cellar, sawed off a hunk, and with his jackknife began to carve it into something. To his surprise it turned into a bird flying. It was shaped off balance but with a certain beauty. He thought of offering it to Helen but it seemed too rough a thing—the first he had ever made. So he tried his hand at something else. He set out to carve her a flower and it came out a rose starting to bloom. When it was done it was delicate in the way its petals were opening yet firm as a real flower. He thought about painting it red and giving it to her but decided to leave off the paint. He wrapped the wooden flower in store paper, printed Helen's name on the outside, and a few minutes before she came home from work, taped the package onto the outside of the mailbox in the vestibule. He saw her enter, then heard her go up the stairs. Looking into the vestibule, he saw she had taken his flower.

The wooden flower reminded Helen of her unhappiness. She lived in hatred of herself for having loved the clerk against her better judgment. She had fallen in love, she thought, to escape her predicament. More than ever she felt herself a victim of circumstance—in a bad dream symbolized by the nightmarish store below, and the relentless, scheming presence in it of the clerk, whom she should have shouted out of the house but had selfishly spared.

In the morning, as he aimed a pail of garbage into the can at the curb, Frank saw at the bottom of it his wooden flower.

O N THE day he had returned from the hospital Morris felt the urge to jump into his pants and run down to the store, but the doctor, after listening to his lungs, then tapping his hairy knuckles across the grocer's chest, said, "You're coming along fine, so what's your big hurry?" To Ida he privately said, "He has to rest, I don't mean maybe." Seeing her fright he explained, "Sixty isn't sixteen." Morris, after arguing a bit, lay back in bed and after that didn't care if he ever stepped into the store again. His recovery was slow.

With reservations, spring was on its way. There was at least more light in the day; it burst through the bedroom windows. But a cold wind roared in the streets, giving him goose pimples in bed; and sometimes, after half a day of pure sunshine, the sky darkened and some rags of snow fell. He was filled with melancholy and spent hours dreaming of his boyhood. He remembered the green fields. Where a boy runs he never forgets. His father, his mother, his only sister whom he hadn't seen in years, gottenyu. The wailing wind cried to him. . . .

The awning flapping below in the street awoke his dread of the grocery. He had not for a long time asked Ida what went on downstairs but he knew without thinking. He knew in his blood. When he consciously thought of it he remembered that the register rang rarely, so he knew again. He heard heavy silence below. What else can you hear from a graveyard whose noiseless tombstones hold down the sick earth? The smell of death seeped up through the cracks in the floor. He understood why Ida did not dare go downstairs but sought anything to do here. Who could stay in such a place but a goy whose heart was stone? The fate of his store floated like a black-feathered bird dimly in his mind; but as soon as he began to feel stronger, the thing grew lit eyes, worrying him no end. One morning as he sat up against a pillow, scanning yesterday's *Forward*, his thoughts grew so wretched that he broke into sweat and his heart beat erratically. Morris heaved aside his covers, strode crookedly out of bed and began hurriedly to dress.

Ida hastened into the bedroom. "What are you doing, Morris—a sick man?"

"I must go down."

"Who needs you? There is nothing there. Go rest some more."

He fought a greedy desire to get back into bed and live there but could not quiet his anxiety.

"I must go."

She begged him not to but he wouldn't listen.

"How much he takes in now?" Morris asked as he belted his trousers.

"Nothing. Maybe seventy-five."

"A week?"

"What else?"

It was terrible but he had feared worse. His head buzzed with schemes for saving the store. Once he was downstairs he felt he could make things better. His fear came from being here, not where he was needed.

"He keeps open all day?"

"From morning till night—why I don't know."

"Why he stays here?" he asked with sudden irritation.

"He stays," she shrugged.

"What do you pay him?"

"Nothing—he says he don't want."

"So what he wants—my bitter blood?"

"He says he wants to help you."

He muttered something to himself. "You watch him sometimes?"

"Why should I watch him?" she said, worried. "He took something from you?"

"I don't want him here no more. I don't want him near Helen."

"Helen don't talk to him."

He gazed at Ida. "What happened?"

"Go ask her. What happened with Nat? She's like you, she don't tell me anything."

"He's got to leave today. I don't want him here."

"Morris," she said hesitantly, "he gave you good help, believe me. Keep him one more week till you feel stronger."

"No." He buttoned his sweater and despite her pleading went shakily down the stairs.

*

Frank heard him coming and grew cold.

The clerk had for weeks feared the time the grocer would leave his bed, although in a curious way he had also looked forward to it. He had spent many fruitless hours trying to construct a story that would make Morris relent and keep him on. He had planned to say, "Didn't I starve rather than to spend the money from the holdup, so I could put it back in the register—which I did, though I admit I took a couple of rolls and some milk to keep myself alive?" But he had no confidence in that. He could also proclaim his long service to the grocer, his long patient labor in the store; but the fact that he had stolen from him during all this time spoiled his claim. He might mention that he had saved Morris after he had swallowed a bellyful of gas, but it was Nick who had saved him as much as he. The clerk felt he was without any good appeal to the grocer—that he had used up all his credit with him, but then he was struck by a strange and exciting idea, a possible if impossible ace in the hole. He figured that if he finally sincerely revealed his part in the holdup, he might in the telling of it arouse in Morris a true understanding of his nature, and a sympathy for his great struggle to overcome his past. Understanding his clerk's plight—the meaning of his long service to him—might make the grocer keep him on, so he would again have the chance to square everything with all concerned. As he pondered this idea, Frank realized it was a wild chance that might doom rather than redeem him. Yet he felt he would try it if Morris insisted he had to leave. What could he lose after that? But when the clerk pictured himself saying what he had done and had been forgiven by the grocer, and he tried to imagine the relief he would feel, he couldn't, because his overdue confession wouldn't be complete or satisfying so long as he kept hidden what he had done to his daughter. About that he knew he could never open his mouth, so he felt that no matter what he did manage to say there would always be some disgusting thing left unsaid, some further sin to confess, and this he found utterly depressing.

Frank was standing behind the counter near the cash register, paring his fingernails with his knife blade when the grocer, his face pale, the skin of it loose, his neck swimming in his shirt collar, his dark eyes unfriendly, entered the store through the hall door.

The clerk tipped his cap and edged away from the cash register.

"Glad to see you back again, Morris," he said, regretting he hadn't once gone up to see him in all the days the grocer had been upstairs. Morris nodded coldly and went into the rear. Frank followed him in, fell on one knee, and lit the radiator.

"It's pretty cold here, so I better light this up. I've been keeping it shut off to save on the gas bill."

"Frank," Morris said firmly, "I thank you that you helped me when I took in my lungs so much gas, also that you kept the store open when I was sick, but now you got to go."

"Morris," answered Frank, heavy-hearted, "I swear I never stole another red cent after that last time, and I hope God will strike me dead right here if it isn't the truth."

"This ain't why I want you to go," Morris answered.

"Then why do you?" asked the clerk, flushing.

"You know," the grocer said, his eyes downcast.

"Morris," Frank said, at agonizing last, "I have something important I want to tell you. I tried to tell you before only I couldn't work my nerve up. Morris, don't blame me now for what I once did, because I am now a changed man, but I was one of the guys that held you up that night. I swear to God I didn't want to once I got in here, but I couldn't get out of it. I tried to tell you about it—that's why I came back here in the first place, and the first chance I got I put my share of the money back in the register—but I didn't have the guts to say it. I couldn't look you in the eye. Even now I feel sick about what I am saying, but I'm telling it to you so you will know how much I suffered on account of what I did, and that I am very sorry you were hurt on your head—even though not by me. The thing you got to understand is I am not the same person I once was. I might look so to you, but if you could see what's been going on in my heart you would know I have changed. You can trust me now, I swear it, and that's why I am asking you to let me stay and help you."

Having said this, the clerk experienced a moment of extraordinary relief—a treeful of birds broke into song; but the song was silenced when Morris, his eyes heavy, said, "This I already know, you don't tell me nothing new."

The clerk groaned. "How do you know it?"

"I figured out when I was laying upstairs in bed. I had once a bad dream that you hurt me, then I remembered—"

"But I didn't hurt you," the clerk broke in emotionally. "I was the one that gave you the water to drink. Remember?"

"I remember. I remember your hands. I remember your eyes. This day when the detective brought in here the hold-upnik that he didn't hold me up I saw in your eyes that you did something wrong. Then when I stayed behind the hall door and you stole from me a dollar and put it in your pocket, I thought I saw you before in some place but I didn't know where. That day you saved me from the gas I almost recognized you; then when I was laying in bed I had nothing to think about, only my worries and how I threw away my life in this store, then I remembered when you first came here, when we sat at this table, you told me you always did the wrong thing in your life; this minute when I remembered this I said to myself, 'Frank is the one that made on me the holdup.'"

"Morris," Frank said hoarsely, "I am sorry."

Morris was too unhappy to speak. Though he pitied the clerk, he did not want a confessed criminal around. Even if he had reformed, what good would it do to keep him here—another mouth to feed, another pair of eyes to the death watch?

"Did you tell Helen what I did?" sighed Frank.

"Helen ain't interested in you."

"One last chance, Morris," the clerk pleaded.

"Who was the antisimeet that he hit me on the head?"

"Ward Minogue," Frank said after a minute. "He's sick now."

"Ah," sighed Morris, "the poor father."

"We meant to hold Karp up, not you. Please let me stay one more month. I'll pay for my own food and also my rent."

"With what will you pay if I don't pay you—with my debts?"

"I have a little job at night after the store closes. I make a few odd bucks."

"No," said the grocer.

"Morris, you need my help here. You don't know how bad everything is."

But the grocer had set his heart against his assistant and would not let him stay.

Frank hung up his apron and left the store. Later, he bought a suitcase and packed his few things. When he returned Nick's radio, he said good-by to Tessie.

"Where are you going now, Frank?"

"I don't know."

"Are you ever coming back?"

"I don't know. Say good-by to Nick."

Before leaving, Frank wrote a note to Helen, once more saying he was sorry for the wrong he had done her. He wrote she was the finest girl he had ever met. He had bitched up his life. Helen wept over the note but had no thought of answering.

Although Morris liked the improvements Frank had made in the store he saw at once that they had not the least effect on business. Business was terrible. And with Frank's going the income shrank impossibly lower, a loss of ten terrible dollars from the previous week. He thought he had seen the store at its worst but this brought him close to fainting.

"What will we do?" he desperately asked his wife and daughter, huddled in their overcoats one Sunday night in the unheated back of the store.

"What else?" Ida said, "give right away in auction."

"The best thing is to sell even if we have to give away," Morris argued. "If we sell the store we can also make something on the house. Then I can pay my debts and have maybe a couple thousand dollars. But if we give in auction how can I sell the house?"

"So if we sell who will buy?" Ida snapped.

"Can't we auction off the store without going into bankruptcy?" Helen asked.

"If we auction we will get nothing. Then when the store is empty and it stays for rent, nobody will buy the house. There are already two places for rent on this block. If the wholesalers hear I went in auction they will force me in bankruptcy and take away the house also. But if we sell the store, then we can get a better price for the house."

"Nobody will buy," Ida said. "I told you when to sell but you wouldn't listen."

"Suppose you did sell the house and store," Helen asked, "what would you do then?"

"Maybe I could find a small place, maybe a candy store. If I could find a partner we could open up a store in a nice neighborhood."

Ida groaned. "Penny candy I won't sell. Also a partner we had already, he should drop dead."

"Couldn't you look for a job?" Helen said.

"Who will give me at my age a job?" Morris asked.

"You're acquainted with some people in the business," she answered. "Maybe somebody could get you a cashier's job in a supermarket."

"You want your father to stand all day on his feet with his varicose veins?" Ida asked.

"It would be better than sitting in the freezing back of an empty store."

"So what will we do?" Morris asked, but nobody answered.

Upstairs, Ida told Helen that things would be better if she got married.

"Who should I marry, Mama?"

"Louis Karp," said Ida.

The next evening she visited Karp when he was alone in the liquor store and told him their troubles. The liquor dealer whistled through his teeth.

Ida said, "You remember last November you wanted to send us a man by the name Podolsky, a refugee he was interested to go in the grocery business?"

"Yes. He said he would come here but he caught a cold in his chest."

"Did he buy some place a store?"

"Not yet," Karp said cautiously.

"He still wants to buy?"

"Maybe. But how could I recommend him a store like yours?"

"Don't recommend him the store, recommend him the price. Morris will sell now for two thousand cash. If he wants the house we will give him a good price. The refugee is young, he can fix up the business and give the goyim a good competition."

"Maybe I'll call him sometime," Karp remarked. He casually inquired about Helen. Surely she would be getting married soon?

Ida faced the way she hoped the wind was blowing. "Tell Louis not to be so bashful. Helen is lonely and wants to go out with somebody."

Karp coughed into his fist. "I don't see your clerk any more. How is that?" He spoke offhandedly, walking carefully, knowing the size of his big feet.

"Frank," Ida said solemnly, "don't work for us any more. Morris told him to leave, so he left last week."

Karp raised bushy brows. "Maybe," he said slowly, "I will call Podolsky and tell him to come tomorrow night. He works in the day."

"In the morning is the best time. Comes in then a few Morris's old customers."

"I will tell him to take off Wednesday morning," Karp said.

He later told Louis what Ida had said about Helen, but Louis, looking up from clipping his fingernails, said she wasn't his type.

"When you got gelt in your pocket any woman is your type," Karp said.

"Not her."

"We will see."

The next afternoon Karp came into Morris's and speaking as if they were the happiest of friends, advised the grocer: "Let Podolsky look around here but not too long. Also keep your mouth shut about the business. Don't try to sell him anything. When he finishes in here he will come to my house and I will explain him what's what."

Morris, hiding his feelings, nodded. He felt he had to get away from the store, from Karp, before he collapsed. Reluctantly he agreed to do as the liquor dealer suggested.

Early Wednesday morning Podolsky arrived, a shy young man in a thick greenish suit that looked as if it had been made out of a horse blanket. He wore a small foreign-looking hat and carried a loose umbrella. His face was innocent and his eyes glistened with good will.

Morris, uneasy at what he was engaged in, invited Podolsky into the back, where Ida nervously awaited him, but the refugee tipped his hat and said he would stay in the store. He slid into the corner near the door and nothing could drag him out.

Luckily, a few customers dribbled in, and Podolsky watched with interest as Morris professionally handled them.

When the store was empty, the grocer tried to make casual talk from behind the counter, but Podolsky, though constantly clearing his throat, had little to say. Overwhelmed by pity for the poor refugee, at what he had in all probability lived through, a man who had sweated blood to save a few brutal dollars, Morris, unable to stand the planned dishonesty, came from behind the counter, and taking Podolsky by the coat lapels, told him earnestly that the store was run down but that a boy with his health and strength, with modern methods and a little cash, could build it up in a reasonable time and make a decent living out of it.

Ida shrilly called from the kitchen she needed the grocer to help her peel potatoes, but Morris kept on talking till he was swimming in his sea of woes; then he recalled Karp's warning, and though he felt more than ever that the liquor dealer was thoroughly an ass, abruptly broke off the story he was telling. Yet before he could tear himself away from the refugee, he remarked, "I could sell for two thousand, but for fifteen-sixteen cash, anybody who wants it can take the store. The house we will talk about later. Is this reasonable?"

"Why not?" Podolsky murmured, then again clammed up.

Morris retreated into the kitchen. Ida looked at him as if he had committed murder but did not speak. Two or three more people appeared, then after ten-thirty the dry trickle of customers stopped. Ida grew fidgety and tried to think of ways to get Podolsky out of the place but he stayed on. She asked him to come into the back for a glass of tea; he courteously refused. She remarked that Karp must now be anxious to see him; Podolsky bobbed his head and stayed. He tightened the cloth around his umbrella stick. Not knowing what else to say she absently promised to leave him all her recipes for salads. He thanked her, to her surprise, profusely.

From half past ten to twelve nobody approached the store. Morris went down to the cellar and hid. Ida sat dully in the back. Podolsky waited in his corner. Nobody saw as he eased himself and his black umbrella out of the grocery and fled.

On Thursday morning Morris spat on his shoebrush and polished his shoes. He was wearing his suit. He rang the hall bell for Ida to come down, then put on his hat and coat, old but neat because he rarely used them. Dressed, he rang up "no sale" and hesitantly pocketed eight quarters.

He was on his way to Charlie Sobeloff, an old partner. Years ago, Charlie, a cross-eyed but clever conniver, had come to the grocer with a meager thousand dollars in his pocket, borrowed money, and offered to go into partnership with him—Morris to furnish four thousand—to buy a grocery Charlie had in mind. The grocer disliked Charlie's nervousness and pale cross-eyes, one avoiding what the other looked at; but he was persuaded by the man's nagging enthusiasm and they bought the store. It was a good business, Morris thought, and he was satisfied. But Charlie, who had taken accountancy in night school, said he would handle the books, and Morris, in spite of Ida's warnings, consented, because, the grocer argued, the books were always in front of his eyes for inspection. But Charlie's talented nose had sniffed the right sucker. Morris never looked at the books until, two years after they had bought the place, the business collapsed.

The grocer, stunned, heartbroken, could not at first understand what had happened, but Charlie had figures to prove that the calamity had been bound to occur. The overhead was too high—they had paid themselves too high wages—his fault, Charlie admitted; also profits were low, the price of goods increasing. Morris now knew that his partner had, behind his back, cheated, manipulated, stolen whatever lay loose. They sold the place for a miserable price, Morris going out dazed, cleaned out, whereas Charlie in a short time was able to raise the cash to repurchase and restock the store, which he gradually worked into a thriving self-service business. For years the two had not met, but within the last four or five years, the ex-partner, when he returned from his winters in Miami, for reasons unknown to Morris, sought out the grocer and sat with him in the back, his eyes roving, his ringed fingers drumming on the table as he talked on about old times when they were young. Morris, through the years, had lost his hatred of the man, though Ida still could not stand him, and it was to Charlie Sobeloff that the grocer, with a growing sense of panic, had decided to run for help, a job—anything.

When Ida came down and saw Morris, in his hat and coat,

standing moodily by the door, she said in surprise, "Morris, where you going?"

"I go to my grave," the grocer said.

Seeing he was overwrought, she cried out, clasping her hands to her bosom, "Where do you go, tell me?"

He had the door open. "I go for a job."

"Come back," she cried in anger. "Who will give you?"

But he knew what she would say and was already in the street.

As he went quickly past Karp's he noticed that Louis had five customers—drunkards all—lined up at the counter and was doing a thriving business in brown bottles. *He* had sold only two quarts of milk in four hours. Although it shamed him, Morris wished the liquor store would burn to the ground.

At the corner he paused, overwhelmed by the necessity of choosing a direction. He hadn't remembered that space provided so many ways to go. He chose without joy. The day, though breezy, was not bad—it promised better, but he had little love left for nature. It gave nothing to a Jew. The March wind hastened him along, prodding the shoulders. He felt weightless, unmanned, the victim in motion of whatever blew at his back; wind, worries, debts, Karp, holdupniks, ruin. He did not go, he was pushed. He had the will of a victim, no will to speak of.

"For what I worked so hard for? Where is my youth, where did it go?"

The years had passed without profit or pity. Who could he blame? What fate didn't do to him he had done to himself. The right thing was to make the right choice but he made the wrong. Even when it was right it was wrong. To understand why, you needed an education but he had none. All he knew was he wanted better but had not after all these years learned how to get it. Luck was a gift. Karp had it, a few of his old friends had it, well-to-do men with grandchildren already, while his poor daughter, made in his image, faced—if not actively sought—old-maidhood. Life was meager, the world changed for the worse. America had become too complicated. One man counted for nothing. There were too many stores, depressions, anxieties. What had he escaped to here?

The subway was crowded and he had to stand till a pregnant woman, getting off, signaled him to her seat. He was ashamed to take it but nobody else moved, so he sat down. After a while he began to feel at ease, thought he would be satisfied to ride on like this, provided he never got to where he was going. But he did. At Myrtle Avenue he groaned softly, and left the train.

Arriving at Sobeloff's Self-Service Market, Morris, although he had heard of the growth of the place from Al Marcus, was amazed at its size. Charlie had tripled the original space by buying the building next door and knocking out the wall between the stores, later running an extension three-quarters of the way into the back yards. The result was a huge market with a large number of stalls and shelved sections loaded with groceries. The supermarket was so crowded with people that to Morris, as he peered half-scared through the window, it looked like a department store. He felt a pang, thinking that part of this might now be his if he had taken care of what he had once owned. He would not envy Charlie Sobeloff his dishonest wealth, but when he thought of what he could do for Helen with a little money his regret deepened that he had nothing.

He spied Charlie standing near the fruit stalls, the balabos, surveying the busy scene with satisfaction. He wore a gray Homburg and blue serge suit, but under the unbuttoned suit jacket he had tied a folded apron around his silk-shirted paunch, and wandered around, thus attired, overseeing. The grocer, looking through the window, saw himself opening the door and walking the long half block to where Charlie was standing.

He tried to speak but was unable to, until after so much silence the boss said he was busy, so say it.

"You got for me, Charlie," muttered the grocer, "a job? Maybe a cashier or something? My business is bad, I am going in auction."

Charlie, still unable to look straight at him, smiled. "I got five steady cashiers but maybe I can use you part time. Hang up your coat in the locker downstairs and I'll give you directions what to do."

Morris saw himself putting on a white duck jacket with "Sobeloff's Self-Service" stitched in red over the region of the heart. He would stand several hours a day at the checking counter, packing, adding, ringing up the cash into one of Charlie's massive chromium registers. At quitting time, the boss would come over to check his money.

"You're short a dollar, Morris," Charlie said with a little chuckle, "but we will let it go."

"No," the grocer heard himself say. "I am short a dollar, so I will pay a dollar."

He took several quarters out of his pants pocket, counted four, and dropped them into his ex-partner's palm. Then he announced he was through, hung up his starched jacket, slipped on his coat and walked with dignity to the door. He joined the one at the window and soon went away.

Morris clung to the edge of a silent knot of men who drifted along Sixth Avenue, stopping at the employment agency doors to read impassively the list of jobs chalked up on the blackboard signs. There were openings for cooks, bakers, waiters, porters, handymen. Once in a while one of the men would secretly detach himself from the others and go into the agency. Morris followed along with them to Forty-fourth Street, where he noted a job listed for countermen behind a steam counter in a cafeteria. He went one flight up a narrow staircase and into a room that smelled of tobacco smoke. The grocer stood there, uncomfortable, until the big-faced owner of the agency happened to look up over the roll-top desk he was sitting at.

"You looking for something, mister?"

"Counterman," Morris said.

"You got experience?"

"Thirty years."

The owner laughed. "You're the champ but they want a kid they can pay twenty a week."

"You got something for a man my experience?"

"Can you slice sandwich meat nice and thin?"

"The best."

"Come back next week, I might have something for you."

The grocer continued along with the crowd. At Forty-seventh Street he applied for a waiter's job in a kosher restaurant but the agency had filled the job and forgotten to erase it from their sign.

"So what else you got for me?" Morris asked the manager.

"What work do you do?"

"I had my own store, grocery and delicatessen."

"So why do you ask for waiter?"

"I didn't see for counterman anything."

"How old are you?"

"Fifty-five."

"I should live so long till you see fifty-five again," said the manager. As Morris turned to go the man offered him a cigarette but the grocer said his cough kept him from smoking.

At Fiftieth he went up a dark staircase and sat on a wooden bench at the far end of a long room.

The boss of the agency, a man with a broad back and a fat rear, holding a dead cigar butt between stubby fingers, had his heavy foot on a chair as he talked in a low voice to two gray-hatted Filipinos.

Seeing Morris on the bench he called out, "Whaddye want, pop?"

"Nothing. I sit on account I am tired."

"Go home," said the boss.

He went downstairs and had coffee at a dish-laden table in the Automat.

America.

Morris rode the bus to East Thirteenth Street, where Breitbart lived. He hoped the peddler would be home but only his son Hymie was. The boy was sitting in the kitchen, eating corn-flakes with milk and reading the comics.

"What time comes home Papa?" Morris asked.

"About seven, maybe eight," Hymie mumbled.

Morris sat down to rest. Hymie ate, and read the comics. He had big restless eyes.

"How old are you?"

"Fourteen."

The grocer got up. He found two quarters in his pocket and left them on the table. "Be a good boy. Your father loves you."

He got into the subway at Union Square and rode to the Bronx, to the apartment house where Al Marcus lived. He felt sure Al would help him find something. He would be satisfied, he thought, with little, maybe a night watchman's job.

When he rang Al's bell, a well-dressed woman with sad eyes came to the door.

"Excuse me," said Morris. "My name is Mr. Bober. I am an old-time customer Al Marcus's. I came to see him."

"I am Mrs. Margolies, his sister-in-law."

"If he ain't home I will wait."

"You'll wait a long time," she said, "they took him to the hospital yesterday."

Though he knew why he couldn't help asking.

"Can you go on living if you're already dead?"

When the grocer got home in the cold twilight Ida took one look at him and began to cry.

"What did I tell you?"

That night Morris, alone in the store after Ida had gone up to soak her poor feet, felt an uncontrollable craving for some heavy sweet cream. He remembered the delicious taste of bread dipped in rich milk when he was a boy. He found a half-pint bottle of whipping cream in the refrigerator and took it, guiltily, with a loaf of stale white bread, into the back. Pouring some cream into a saucer, he soaked it up with bread, greedily wolfing the cream-laden bread.

A noise in the store startled him. He hid the cream and bread in the gas range.

At the counter stood a skinny man in an old hat and a dark overcoat down to his ankles. His nose was long, throat gaunt, and he wore a wisp of red beard on his bony chin.

"A gut shabos," said the scarecrow.

"A gut shabos," Morris answered, though shabos was a day away.

"It smells here," said the skinny stranger, his small eyes shrewd, "like a open grave."

"Business is bad."

The man wet his lips and whispered, "Insurinks you got—fire insurinks?"

Morris was frightened. "What is your business?"

"How much?"

"How much what?"

"A smart man hears one word but he understand two. How much you got insurinks?"

"Two thousand for the store."

"Feh."

"Five thousand for the house."

"A shame. Should be ten."

"Who needs ten for this house?"

"Nobody knows."

"What do you want here?" Morris asked, irritated.

The man rubbed his skinny, red-haired hands. "What does a macher want?"

"What kind of a macher? What do you make?"

He shrugged slyly. "I make a living." The macher spoke soundlessly. "I make fires."

Morris drew back.

The macher waited with downcast eyes. "We are poor people," he murmured.

"What do you want from me?"

"We are poor people," the macher said, apologetically. "God loves the poor people but he helps the rich. The insurinks companies are rich. They take away your money and what they give you? Nothing. Don't feel sorry for the insurinks companies."

He proposed a fire. He would make it swiftly, safely, economically—guaranteed to collect.

From his coat pocket he produced a strip of celluloid. "You know what is this?"

Morris, staring at it, preferred not to say.

"Celluloy," hissed the macher. He struck a large yellow match and lit the celluloid. It flared instantly. He held it a second then let it fall to the counter, where it quickly burned itself out. With a *poof* he blew away nothing. Only the stench remained, floating in air.

"Magic," he hoarsely announced. "No ashes. This is why we use celluloy, not paper, not rags. You push a piece in a crack, and the fire burns in a minute. Then when comes the fire marshal and insurinks investigator, what they find?—nothing. For nothing they pay cash—two thousand for the store, five for the house." A smile crawled over his face.

Morris shivered. "You want me I should burn down my house and my store to collect the insurance?"

"I want," said the macher slyly, "tsu you want?"

The grocer fell silent.

"Take," said the macher persuasively, "your family and go

for a ride to Cunyiland. When you come back is the job finished. Cost—five hundred." He lightly dusted his fingers.

"Upstairs lives two people," muttered the grocer.

"When they go out?"

"Sometimes to the movies, Friday night." He spoke dully, not sure why he was revealing secrets to a total stranger.

"So let be Friday night. I am not kosher."

"But who's got five hundred dollars?"

The macher's face fell. He sighed deeply. "I will make for two hundred. I will do a good job. You will get six—seven thousand. After, pay me another three hundred."

But Morris had decided. "Impossible."

"You don't like the price?"

"I don't like fires. I don't like monkey business."

The macher argued another half-hour and departed reluctantly.

The next night a car pulled up in front of the door, and the grocer watched Nick and Tessie, dressed for a party, get in and drive off. Twenty minutes later Ida and Helen came down to go to a movie. Helen had asked her mother to go with her, and Ida said yes, seeing how restless her daughter was. When he realized that the house was deserted, Morris felt suddenly agitated.

After ten minutes, he went up the stairs, and searched in a camphor-smelling trunk in the small room for a celluloid collar he had once worn. Ida saved everything, but he couldn't locate it. He searched in Helen's bureau drawer and found an envelope full of picture negatives. Discarding several of her as a school girl, Morris took some of boys in bathing suits, nobody he recognized. Hurrying down, he found matches and went into the cellar. He thought that one of the bins would be a good place to start the fire but settled instead on the air shaft. The flames would shoot up in an instant, and through the open toilet window into the store. Gooseflesh crept over him. He figured he could start the fire and wait in the hall. Once the flames had got a good start, he would rush into the street and ring the alarm. He could later say he had fallen asleep on the couch and had been awakened by the smoke. By the time the fire engines came, the house would be badly damaged. The hoses and axes would do the rest.

Morris inserted the celluloid strips into a crack between two boards, on the inside of the dumb-waiter. His hand shook and he whispered to himself as he touched the match to the negatives. Then the flame shot up in a stupefying stench and at once crawled up the wall of the dumb-waiter. Morris watched, hypnotized, then let out a terrible cry. Slapping frantically at the burning negatives, he knocked them to the cellar floor. As he hunted for something with which to beat out the fire in the dumb-waiter, he discovered that the bottom of his apron was burning. He smacked the flames with both hands and then his sweater sleeves began to blaze. He sobbed for God's mercy, and was at once roughly seized from behind and flung to the ground.

Frank Alpine smothered the grocer's burning clothes with his overcoat. He banged out the fire in the dumb-waiter with his shoe.

Morris moaned.

"For Christ's sake," Frank pleaded, "take me back here."

But the grocer ordered him out of the house.

SATURDAY NIGHT, about one A.M., Karp's store began to burn.

In the early evening, Ward Minogue had knocked on Frank's door and learned from Tessie that the clerk had moved.

"Where to?"

"I don't know. Ask Mr. Bober," Tessie said, anxious to get rid of him.

Downstairs, Ward peered through the grocery window and seeing Morris, hurriedly withdrew. Though alcohol nauseated him lately, his thirst for a drink was killing him. He thought if he could get a couple of swigs past the nausea he would feel better. But all he had in his pocket was a dime, so he went into Karp's and begged Louis to trust him to a cheap fifth of anything.

"I wouldn't trust you for a fifth of sewer water," Louis said.

Ward grabbed a bottle of wine from the counter and flung it at Louis' head. He ducked but the wine smashed some bottles on the shelf. As Louis, yelling murder, rushed into the street, Ward snatched a bottle of whiskey and ran out of the store and up the block. He had gone past the butcher's when the bottle slipped from under his arm and broke on the sidewalk. Ward looked back with anguish but kept on running.

By the time the cops came Ward had disappeared. After supper that night, Detective Minogue, roaming the cold streets, saw his son in Earl's bar, standing over a beer. The detective went in by the side door but Ward saw him in the mirror and bolted out the front. Although short of breath, driven by great fear, he ran toward the coal yard. Hearing his father behind him, Ward leaped across the rusted chain stretched in front of the loading platform and sped over the cobblestones toward the back of the yard. He scrambled under one of the trucks in the shed.

The detective, calling him filthy names, hunted him in the dark for fifteen minutes. Then he took out his pistol and fired a shot into the shed. Ward, thinking he would be killed, crawled out from under the truck and ran into his father's arms.

Though he pleaded with the detective not to hurt him, crying he had diabetes and would surely get gangrene, his father beat him mercilessly with his billy until Ward collapsed.

Bending over him, the detective yelled, "I told you to stay the hell out of this neighborhood. This is my last warning to you. If I ever see you again, I'll murder you." He dusted his coat and left the coal yard.

Ward lay on the cobblestones. His nose had been gushing blood but it soon stopped. Getting up, he felt so dizzy he wept. He staggered into the shed and climbed into the cab of one of the coal trucks, thinking he would sleep there. But when he lit a cigarette he was overcome with nausea. Ward threw the butt out and waited for the nausea to leave him. When it did he was thirsty again. If he could climb the coal yard fence, then some of the smaller ones beyond it, he would land up in Karp's back yard. He knew from having cased the place once that the liquor store had a barred window in the back, but that the rusty iron bars were old and loose. He thought that if he got his strength back he could force them apart.

He dragged himself over the coal yard fence, then more slowly over the others until he stood at last in Karp's weedy back yard. The liquor store had been closed since midnight and there were no lights burning in the house. Above the dark grocery one of Bober's windows was lit, so he had to be careful or the Jew might hear him.

Twice, at intervals of ten minutes, he tried to bend the bars but failed. The third time, straining till he shook, he slowly forced the inside two apart. The window was unlocked. Ward got his fingertips under it and lifted it with care because it squeaked. When it was open, he squeezed through the bent bars, squirming into the back of the liquor store. Once in there he laughed a little to himself and moved around freely, knowing Karp was too cheap to have a burglar alarm. From the stock in the rear Ward sampled and spat out three different brands of whiskey. Forcing himself, he gurgled down a third of a bottle of gin. In a couple of minutes he forgot his aches and pains and lost the sorrow he had been feeling for himself. He snickered when he imagined Louis' comic puss as he found the empty bottles all over the floor in the morning. Remembering the cash register, Ward staggered out front and rang it open. It was empty. He angrily smashed a whiskey bottle on it. A feeling of nausea gagged him and with a croak he threw up over Karp's counter. Feeling better, he began by the light of the street lamp to smash the whiskey bottles against the cash register.

Mike Papadopolous, whose bedroom was right above the front part of the liquor store, was awakened by the noise. After five minutes he figured something was wrong so he got up and dressed. Ward had, in the meantime, destroyed a whole shelf of bottles, when he felt a hunger to smoke. It took him two minutes to get a match struck and the light touching his butt. He tasted the smoke with pleasure as the flame briefly lit his face, then he shook the match and flipped it over his shoulder. It landed, still burning, in a puddle of alcohol. The fire flew up with a zoom. Ward, lit like a flaming tree, flailed at himself. Screaming, he ran through the back and tried to get out of the window but was caught between the bars and, exhausted, died.

Smelling smoke, Mike came down in a rush and seeing fire in the store, raced to the drugstore corner to turn in the alarm. As he was running back, the plate glass window of the liquor store exploded and a roaring flame boiled up in the place. After Mike had got his mother and the upstairs tenants out of the house, he ran into Bober's hall, shouting there was a fire next door. They were all up—Helen, who had been reading when the window crashed, had run up to call Nick and Tessie. They left the house, bundled in sweaters and overcoats, and stood across the street, huddled together with some passers-by, watching the fire destroy Karp's once prosperous business, then devour the house. Despite the heavy streams of water the firemen poured into the flames, the fire, fed by the blazing alcohol, rose to the roof, and when it was at last smothered, all that was left of Karp's property was a gutted, dripping shell.

As the firemen began with grappling hooks to tear out the burned fixtures and heave them onto the sidewalk, everybody fell silent. Ida moaned softly, with shut eyes thinking of Morris's burned sweater that she had found in the cellar, and the singed hair she had noticed on his hands. Sam Pearl, lost without his bifocals, mumbled to himself. Nat, hatless, an overcoat on over pajamas, edged close to Helen until he stood by her side. Morris was fighting a tormenting emotion.

A car drew up and parked beyond the drugstore. Karp got out with Louis and they crossed the hose-filled street to their store. Karp took one unbearable look at his former gesheft, and though it was for the most part insured, tottered forward and collapsed. Louis yelled at him to wake up. Two of the firemen carried the stricken liquor dealer to his car, and Louis frantically drove him home.

Afterward Morris couldn't sleep. He stood at his bedroom window in his long underwear, looking down at the pile of burned and broken fixtures on the sidewalk. With a frozen hand the grocer clawed at a live pain in his breast. He felt an overwhelming hatred of himself. He had wished it on Karp— just this. His anguish was terrible.

Sunday, the last of March, was overcast at eight A.M., and there were snow flurries in the air. Winter still spits in my face, thought the weary grocer. He watched the fat wet flakes melt as they touched the ground. It's too warm for snow, he thought, tomorrow will come April. Maybe. He had awakened with a wound, a gap in his side, a hole in the ground he might fall through if he stepped outside where the liquor store had been. But the earth held him up and the odd feeling wore off. It went as he reflected it was no use mourning Karp's loss; his pocketbook would protect him from too much pain. Pain was for poor people. For Karp's tenants the fire was a tragedy, and for Ward Minogue, dead young; maybe also for the detective, but not for Julius Karp. Morris could have used the fire, so Karp had got it for free. Everything to him who has.

As the grocer was thinking this, the liquor dealer, apparently the victim of a sleepless night, appeared in the falling snow and entered the grocery. He wore a narrow-brimmed hat with a foolish little feather in the band and a double-breasted overcoat, but despite his stylish appearance, his eyes, with dark bags under them, were filled with gloom, his complexion pasty, lips blue. Where his forehead had smacked the sidewalk last night he wore a plaster patch—an unhappy figure, the loss of his business the worst that could happen to him. He couldn't stand the vision of dollars he might be taking in, flying daily away. Karp seemed embarrassed, ill. The grocer, his shame awakened, invited him into the back for tea. Ida, also up early, made a fuss over him.

Karp took a hot sip or two of tea, but after setting the cup down, hadn't the strength to lift it from the saucer. After a fidgety silence he spoke. "Morris, I want to buy your house. Also the store." He drew a deep, trembly breath.

Ida let out a stifled cry. Morris was stupefied.

"What for? The business is terrible."

"Not so terrible," cried Ida.

"Don't interest me the grocery business," Karp gloomily replied. "Only the location. Next door," he said, but couldn't go on.

They understood.

He explained it would take months to rebuild his house and place of business. But if he took over Morris's store he could have it refixtured, painted, stocked in a couple of weeks, thus keeping to a minimum his loss of trade.

Morris couldn't believe his ears. He was filled with excitement and dread that somebody would tell him he had just dreamed a dream, or that Karp, fat fish, would turn into a fat bird and fly away, screeching, "Don't you believe me," or in some heartbreaking way change his mind.

So he put his foot on anticipation and kept his mouth shut, but when Karp asked him to name his price the grocer had one ready. "Nine thousand for the house—three down, my equity— and for the store twenty-five hundred cash." After all, bad as it was, the grocery was a going business, and for the refrigerator alone he had paid nine hundred dollars. With trepidation he figured a fair fifty-five hundred in cash in his hands, enough after he had paid his debts to look for a new business. Seeing Ida's astonished expression, he was surprised at his nerve and thought Karp would surely laugh him in the face and offer less—which he would grab anyway; but the liquor dealer listlessly nodded. "I will give you twenty-five hundred for the store, less the auction price of stock and fixtures."

"This is your business," Morris replied.

Karp could not bear to discuss the terms any further. "My lawyer will draw the contract."

When he left the grocery, the liquor dealer vanished in the

swirling snow. Ida wept joyfully, while Morris, still stunned, reflected that his luck had changed. So had Karp's, for what Karp had lost he had in a sense gained, as if to make up for the misery the man had caused him in the past. Yesterday he wouldn't have believed how things would balance out today.

The spring snow moved Morris profoundly. He watched it falling, seeing in it scenes of his childhood, remembering things he thought he had forgotten. All morning he watched the shifting snow. He thought of himself, a boy running in it, whooping at blackbirds as they flew from the snowy trees; he felt an irresistible thirst to be out in the open.

"I think I will shovel the snow," he told Ida at lunchtime.

"Go better to sleep."

"It ain't nice for the customers."

"What customers—who needs them?"

"People can't walk in such high snow," he argued.

"Wait, tomorrow it will be melted."

"It's Sunday, it don't look so nice for the goyim that they go to church."

Her voice had an edge to it. "You want to catch pneumonia, Morris?"

"It's spring," he murmured.

"It's winter."

"I will wear my hat and coat."

"Your feet will get wet. You have no galoshes."

"Only five minutes."

"No," she said flatly.

Later, he thought.

All afternoon the snow came softly down and by evening it had reached a depth of six inches. When the snowing stopped, a wind rose and blew clouds of it through the streets. He watched at the front window.

Ida hung over him all day. He didn't get out till late. After closing he had sat relentlessly over a piece of store paper, writing a long list, until she grew impatient.

"Why do you stay so late?"

"I figure the stock for the auctioneer."

"This is Karp's business."

"I must help, he don't know the prices."

Talk of the store's sale relieved her. "Come up soon," she yawned.

He waited until he felt she was asleep, then went down to the cellar for the shovel. He put on his hat and a pair of old gloves and stepped out into the street. To his surprise the wind wrapped him in an icy jacket, his apron flapping noisily. He had expected, the last of March, a milder night. The surprise lingered in his mind but the shoveling warmed him. He kept his back to Karp's burned hole, though with the black turned white it wasn't too hard to look at.

Scooping up a shovelful of snow he heaved it into the street. It turned to dust in mid-air and whirled whitely away.

He recalled the hard winters when he had first come to America. After about fifteen years they turned mild but now they were hard again. It had been a hard life, but now with God's help he would have an easier time.

He flung another load of snow into the street. "A better life," he muttered.

Nick and Tessie came home from somewhere.

"At least put something warm on, Mr. Bober," advised Tessie.

"I'm almost finished," Morris grunted.

"It's your health," said Nick.

The first floor window shot up. Ida stood there in her flannel nightgown, her hair down.

"Are you crazy?" she shouted to the grocer.

"Finished," he answered.

"Without a coat—are you crazy?"

"Took me ten minutes."

Nick and Tessie went into the house.

"Come up now," Ida shouted.

"Finished," Morris cried. He heaved a last angry shovelful into the gutter. A little of the sidewalk remained to be cleaned but now that she was nagging he felt too tired to do it.

Morris dragged the wet shovel into the store. The warmth struck him across the head. He felt himself reeling and had a momentary fright but after a glass of hot tea with lemon felt rested.

As he was drinking the tea it began to snow again. He watched a thousand flakes push at the window, as if they wanted to snow through the glass and in the kitchen. He saw the snow as a moving curtain, and then he saw it in lit single flakes, not touching each other.

Ida banged hard on the floor, so he finally closed and went upstairs.

She was sitting in her bathrobe with Helen in the living room, her eyes dark with anger. "Are you a baby you had to go out in the snow? What's the matter with such a man?"

"I had my hat on. What am I, tissue paper?"

"You had pneumonia," she shouted.

"Mama, lower your voice," Helen said, "they'll hear upstairs."

"Who asked him to shovel snow, for God's sakes?"

"For twenty-two years stinks in my nose this store. I wanted to smell in my lungs some fresh air."

"Not in the ice cold."

"Tomorrow is April."

"Anyway," Helen said, "don't tempt fate, Papa."

"What kind of winter can be in April?"

"Come to sleep." Ida marched off to bed.

He sat with Helen on the couch. Since hearing of Karp's visit that morning she had lost her moodiness, looked again like a happy girl. He thought with sadness how pretty she was. He wanted to give her something—only good.

"How do you feel that I am selling the house and store?" he asked her.

"You know how I feel."

"Tell me anyway."

"Refreshed."

"We will move to a better neighborhood like you like. I will find a better parnusseh. You will keep your wages."

She smiled at him.

"I remember when you were a little baby," Morris said.

She kissed his hand.

"I want the most you should be happy."

"I will be." Her eyes grew wet. "If you only knew all the good things I'd like to give you, Papa."

"You gave me."

"I'll give you better."

"Look how it snows," said Morris.

They watched the snow through the moving windows, then Morris said good night.

"Sleep well," Helen said.

But he lay in bed restless, almost dejected. There was so much to do, so many changes to make and get used to. To-morrow was the day Karp would bring the deposit. Tuesday the auctioneer would come and they would go over the goods and fixtures. Wednesday they could hold the auction. Thursday, for the first time in almost a generation, he would be without a place of business. Such a long time. After so many years in one place he hated the thought of having to get used to another. He disliked leaving the neighborhood though he hadn't liked it. It made him uncomfortable to be in a strange place. He thought uneasily of having to locate, appraise, and buy a new store. He would prefer to live above the store, but Helen wanted them to take a small apartment, so let it be a small apartment. Once he had the store he would let them look for a place to live. But the store he would have to find himself. What he feared most was that he would make another mistake and again settle in a prison. The possibility of this worried him intensely. Why would the owner want to sell? Would he be an honest man or, underneath, a thief? And once he had bought the place, would business keep up or go down? Would times stay good? Would he make a living? His thoughts exhausted him. He could feel his poor heart running a race against the merciless future.

He fell heavily asleep but awoke in a couple of hours, drenched in hot sweat. Yet his feet were freezing and he knew that if he kept his thoughts on them he would break into shivering. Then his right shoulder began to hurt, and when he forced himself to take a deep breath, his left side pained him. He knew he was sick and was miserably disappointed. He lay in the dark, trying not to think how stupid it had been to shovel the snow. He must have caught a chill. He thought he would not. He thought he was entitled, after twenty-two years, to a few minutes of freedom. Now his plans would have to wait, although Ida could finish the business with Karp and make arrangements with the auctioneer. Gradually he accepted the thought that he had a cold—maybe flu. He considered waking her to call a doctor but who could they call without a telephone? And if Helen got dressed and used Sam Pearl's phone, what an embarrassment that would be, waking up a whole family when she rang their bell; also arousing a doctor out of his precious sleep, who would say after examining him, "Mister, what's all the excitement? You got the flu, so stay in bed." For such advice he didn't need to call a doctor in his nightshirt. He could wait a few hours till morning. Morris dozed but felt fever shake him in his sleep. He awoke with his hair stiff. Maybe he had pneumonia? After a while he grew calmer. He was sick but sickness was nothing new to him. Probably if he hadn't shoveled snow he would have got sick anyway. In the last few days he hadn't felt so well—headachy, weak in the knees. Yet though he tried to resign himself to what had happened, he felt enormously bitter that he had become ill. So he had shoveled snow in the street, but did it have to snow in April? And if it did, did he have to get sick the minute he stepped out into the open air? It frustrated him hopelessly that every move he made seemed to turn into an inevitable thing.

He dreamed of Ephraim. He had recognized him when the dream began by his brown eyes, clearly his father's. Ephraim wore a beanie cut from the crown of an old hat of Morris's, covered with buttons and shiny pins, but the rest of him was in rags. Though he did not for some reason expect otherwise, this and that the boy looked hungry shocked the grocer.

"I gave you to eat three times a day, Ephraim," he explained, "so why did you leave so soon your father?"

Ephraim was too shy to answer, but Morris, in a rush of love for him—a child was so small at that age—promised him a good start in life.

"Don't worry, I'll give you a fine college education."

Ephraim—a gentleman—averted his face as he snickered.

"I give you my word . . ."

The boy disappeared in the wake of laughter.

"Stay alive," his father cried after him.

When the grocer felt himself awaking, he tried to get back into the dream but it easily evaded him. His eyes were wet. He thought of his life with sadness. For his family he had not provided, the poor man's disgrace. Ida was asleep at his side.

He wanted to awaken her and apologize. He thought of
Helen. It would be terrible if she became an old maid. He
moaned a little, thinking of Frank. His mood was of regret. I
gave away my life for nothing. It was the thunderous truth.

Was the snow still falling?

Morris died in the hospital, three days later, and was buried
the day after in an enormous cemetery—it went on for miles—
in Queens. He had been a member of a burial society since
coming to America and the services took place in the Society's
funeral parlor on the Lower East Side, where the grocer had
lived as a young man. At noon in the chapel's antechamber,
Ida, gray-faced and in mourning, every minute on the edge of
fainting, sat in a high-backed tapestried chair, rocking her
head. At her side, wasted, red-eyed from weeping, sat Helen.
Landsleit, old friends, drawn by funeral notices in the Jewish
morning papers, lamented aloud as they bent to kiss her, dropping pulpy tears on her hands. They sat on folding chairs facing
the bereaved and talked in whispers. Frank Alpine stood for a
moment, his hat uncomfortably on, in a corner of the room.
When the place grew crowded he left and seated himself
among the handful of mourners already assembled in the long
narrow chapel, dimly lit by thick, yellow wall lamps. The rows
of benches were dark and heavy. In the front of the chapel, on
a metal stand, lay the grocer's plain wooden coffin.

At one P.M., the gray-haired undertaker, breathing heavily,
escorted the widow and her daughter to the front row on the
left, not far from the coffin. A wailing began among the
mourners. The chapel was a little more than half-full of old
friends of the grocer, a few distant relatives, burial society ac-
quaintances, and one or two customers. Breitbart, the bulb
peddler, sat, stricken, against the right wall. Charlie Sobeloff,
grown heavy-faced and stout, appeared, with Florida tan and
sad crossed eye, together with his stylish wife, who sat staring
at Ida. The entire Pearl family was present, Betty with her new
husband, and Nat, sober, concerned for Helen, wearing a
black skull cap. A few rows behind them was Louis Karp, alone
and ill at ease among strangers. Also Witzig, the baker, who
had served Morris bread and rolls for twenty years. And Mr.
Giannola, the barber, and Nick and Tessie Fuso, behind whom

Frank Alpine sat. When the bearded rabbi entered the chapel through a side door, Frank took off his hat but quickly put it on again.

The secretary of the Society appeared, a soft-voiced man with little hair, his glasses lit with reflections of the wall lamps, and read from a handwritten paper praise for Morris Bober and lamentation for his loss. When he announced the body could be seen, the undertaker and his assistant, a man in a chauffeur's cap, lifted the coffin lid and a few people came forward. Helen wept profusely at her father's waxen, berouged image, the head wrapped in a prayer shawl, the thin mouth slightly twisted.

Ida flung up both arms, crying in Yiddish at the corpse, "Morris, why didn't you listen to me? You went away and left me with a child, alone in the world. Why did you do it?" She broke into racking sobs and was gently escorted by Helen and the breathless undertaker to her seat, where she pressed her wet face against her daughter's shoulder. Frank went up last. He could see, where the prayer shawl fell back a little, the scar on the grocer's head, but outside of that it wasn't Morris. He felt a loss but it was an old one.

The rabbi then prayed, a stocky man with a pointed black beard. He stood on the podium near the coffin, wearing an old Homburg, a faded black frock coat over brown trousers, and bulbous shoes. After his prayer in Hebrew, when the mourners were seated, in a voice laden with sorrow he spoke of the dead man.

"My dear friends, I never had the pleasure to meet this good grocery man that he now lays in his coffin. He lived in a neighborhood where I didn't come in. Still and all I talked this morning to people that knew him and I am now sorry I didn't know him also. I would enjoy to speak to such a man. I talked to the bereaved widow, who lost her dear husband. I talked to his poor beloved daughter Helen, who is now without a father to guide her. To them I talked, also to landsleit and old friends, and each and all told me the same, that Morris Bober, who passed away so untimely—he caught double pneumonia from shoveling snow in front of his place of business so people could pass by on the sidewalk—was a man who couldn't be more honest. Such a person I am sorry I didn't meet sometime in my life. If I met him somewhere, maybe when he went to visit in a Jewish neighborhood—maybe at Rosh Hashana or Pesach— I would say to him, 'God bless you, Morris Bober.' Helen, his dear daughter, remembers from when she was a small girl that her father ran two blocks in the snow to give back to a poor Italian lady a nickel that she forgot on the counter. Who runs in wintertime without hat or coat, without rubbers to protect his feet, two blocks in the snow to give back five cents that a customer forgot? Couldn't he wait till she comes in tomorrow? Not Morris Bober, let him rest in peace. He didn't want the poor woman to worry, so he ran after her in the snow. This is why the grocer had so many friends who admi-red him."

The rabbi paused and gazed over the heads of the mourners.

"He was also a very hard worker, a man that never stopped working. How many mornings he got up in the dark and dressed himself in the cold, I can't count. After, he went downstairs to stay all day in the grocery. He worked long long hours. Six o'clock every morning he opened and he closed after ten every night, sometimes later. Fifteen, sixteen hours a day he was in the store, seven days a week, to make a living for his family. His dear wife Ida told me she will never forget his steps going down the stairs each morning, and also in the night when he came up so tired for his few hours' sleep before he will open again the next day the store. This went on for twenty-two years in this store alone, day after day, except the few days when he was too sick. And for this reason that he worked so hard and bitter, in his house, on his table, was always something to eat. So besides honest he was a good provider."

The rabbi gazed down at his prayer book, then looked up.

"When a Jew dies, who asks if he is a Jew? He is a Jew, we don't ask. There are many ways to be a Jew. So if somebody comes to me and says, 'Rabbi, shall we call such a man Jewish who lived and worked among the gentiles and sold them pig meat, trayfe, that we don't eat it, and not once in twenty years comes inside a synagogue, is such a man a Jew, rabbi?' To him I will say, 'Yes, Morris Bober was to me a true Jew because he lived in the Jewish experience, which he remembered, and with the Jewish heart.' Maybe not to our formal tradition—for

this I don't excuse him—but he was true to the spirit of our
life—to want for others that which he wants also for himself.
He followed the Law which God gave to Moses on Sinai and
told him to bring to the people. He suffered, he endu-red, but
with hope. Who told me this? I know. He asked for himself
little—nothing, but he wanted for his beloved child a better
existence than he had. For such reasons he was a Jew. What
more does our sweet God ask his poor people? So let Him now
take care of the widow, to comfort and protect her, and give to
the fatherless child what her father wanted her to have. 'Yaskadal v'yiskadash shmey, rabo. B'olmo divro . . .'"

The mourners rose and prayed with the rabbi.

Helen, in her grief, grew restless. He's overdone it, she
thought. I said Papa was honest but what was the good of such
honesty if he couldn't exist in this world? Yes, he ran after this
poor woman to give her back a nickel but he also trusted cheaters who took away what belonged to him. Poor Papa; being
naturally honest, he didn't believe that others come by their
dishonesty naturally. And he couldn't hold onto those things he
had worked so hard to get. He gave away, in a sense, more than
he owned. He was no saint; he was in a way weak; his only true
strength in his sweet nature and his understanding. He knew, at
least, what was good. And I didn't say he had many friends who
admired him. That's the rabbi's invention. People liked him, but
who can admire a man passing his life in such a store? He buried
himself in it; he didn't have the imagination to know what he
was missing. He made himself a victim. He could, with a little
more courage, have been more than he was.

Helen prayed for peace on the soul of her dead father.

Ida, holding a wet handkerchief to her eyes, thought, So
what if we had to eat? When you eat you don't want to worry
whose money you are eating—yours or the wholesalers'. If he
had money he had bills; and when he had more money he had
more bills. A person doesn't always want to worry if she will
be in the street tomorrow. She wants sometimes a minute's
peace. But maybe it's my fault, because I didn't let him be a
druggist.

She wept because her judgment of the grocer was harsh although she loved him. Helen, she thought, must marry a
professional.

When the prayer was done the rabbi left the chapel through the side door, and the coffin was lifted by some of the Society members and the undertaker's assistant, carried on their shoulders outside, and placed in the hearse. The people in the chapel filed out and went home, except Frank Alpine, who sat alone in the funeral parlor.

Suffering, he thought, is like a piece of goods. I bet the Jews could make a suit of clothes out of it. The other funny thing is that there are more of them around than anybody knows about.

In the cemetery it was spring. The snow had melted on all but a few graves, the air was warm, fragrant. The small group of mourners following the grocer's coffin were hot in their overcoats. At the Society's plot, crowded with tombstones, two gravediggers had dug a fresh pit in the earth and were standing back, holding their shovels. As the rabbi prayed over the empty grave—from up close his beard was thick with gray—Helen rested her head against the coffin held by the pallbearers.

"Good-by, Papa."

Then the rabbi prayed aloud over the coffin as the gravediggers lowered it to the bottom of the grave.

"Gently . . . gently."

Ida, supported by Sam Pearl and the secretary of the Society, sobbed uncontrollably. She bent forward, shouting into the grave, "Morris, take care of Helen, you hear me, Morris?"

The rabbi, blessing it, tossed in the first shovelful of earth.

"Gently."

Then the diggers began to push in the loose earth around the grave and as it fell on the coffin the mourners wept aloud.

Helen tossed in a rose.

Frank, standing close to the edge of the grave, leaned forward to see where the flower fell. He lost his balance, and though flailing his arms, landed feet first on the coffin.

Helen turned her head away.

Ida wailed.

"Get the hell out of there," Nat Pearl said.

Frank scrambled out of the grave, helped by the diggers. I spoiled the funeral, he thought. He felt pity on the world for harboring him.

At last the coffin was covered, the grave full, running over. The rabbi said a last short Kaddish. Nat took Helen by the arm and led her away.

She gazed back once, with grief, then went with him.

Louis Karp was waiting for them in the dark hallway when Ida and Helen returned from the cemetery.

"Excuse me for bothering you on this sad occasion," he said, holding his hat in his hand, "but I wanna tell you why my father couldn't get to the funeral. He's sick and has to lay flat on his back for the next six weeks or so. The other night when he passed out at the fire, we found out later he had a heart attack. He's lucky he's still alive."

"Vey is mir," muttered Ida.

"The doctor says he's gonna have to retire from here on in," Louis said, with a shrug, "so I don't think he'll wanna buy your house any more. Myself," he added, "I got a job of salesman for a liquor concern."

He said good-by and left them.

"Your father is better off dead," said Ida.

As they toiled up the stairs they heard the dull cling of the register in the store and knew the grocer was the one who had danced on the grocer's coffin.

FRANK LIVED in the back, his clothes hung in a bought closet, sleeping under his overcoat on the couch. He had used their week of mourning, when mother and daughter were confined upstairs, to get the store going. Staying open kept it breathing, but beyond that things were rocky. If not for his thirty-five weekly dollars in the register he would have had to close up. Seeing he paid his little bills, the wholesalers extended credit. People stopped in to say they were sorry Morris was dead. One man said the grocer was the only storekeeper that had ever trusted him for anything. He paid Frank back eleven dollars that he owed Morris. Frank told anybody who asked that he was keeping the business going for the widow. They approved of that.

He gave Ida twelve dollars a week rent and promised her more when times got better. He said when they did, he might buy the store from her, but it would have to be on small installments because he had no money for a down payment. She didn't answer him. She was worried about the future and feared she might starve. She lived on the rent he paid her, plus Nick's rent, and Helen's salary. Ida now had a little job sewing epaulettes for military uniforms, a bag of which Abe Rubin, a landsman of Morris's, delivered in his car every Monday morning. That brought in another twenty-eight to thirty a month. She rarely went down to the store. To speak to her, Frank had to go upstairs and knock on her door. Once, through Rubin, someone came to look at the grocery and Frank was worried, but the man soon left.

He lived in the future, to be forgiven. On the stairs one morning he said to Helen, "Things are changed. I am not the same guy I was."

"Always," she answered, "you remind me of everything I want to forget."

"Those books you once gave me to read," he said, "did you understand them yourself?"

Helen waked from a bad dream. In the dream she had got up to leave the house in the middle of the night to escape Frank waiting on the stairs; but there he stood under the yellow lamp, fondling his lascivious cap. As she approached, his lips formed, "I love you."

"I'll scream if you say it."

She screamed and woke.

At a quarter to seven she forced herself out of bed, shut off the alarm before it rang and drew off her nightgown. The sight of her body mortified her. What a waste, she thought. She wanted to be a virgin again and at the same time a mother.

Ida was still asleep in the half-empty bed that had for a life-time served two. Helen brushed her hair, washed, and put on coffee. Standing at the kitchen window, she gazed out at the back yards in flower, feeling sorrow for her father lying in his immovable grave. What had she ever given him, ever done to make his poor life better? She wept for Morris, thinking of his compromises and surrenders. She felt she must do something for herself, accomplish some worthwhile thing or suffer his fate. Only by growing in value as a person could she make Morris's life meaningful, in the sense that she was of him. She must, she thought, in some way eventually earn her degree. It would take years—but was the only way.

Frank stopped waiting for her in the hall. She had cried out one morning, "Why do you force yourself on me?" and it had struck him that his penitence was a hammer, so he withdrew. But he watched her when he could, through an opening in the tissue paper backing of the store window. He watched as if he were seeing for the first time her slender figure, high small breasts, the slim roundness of her hips and the exciting quality of her slightly bowed legs. She always looked lonely. He tried to think what he could ever do for her and all he could think of was to give her something she had no use for, that would end up in the garbage.

The idea of doing something for her seemed as futile as his other thoughts till one day, the tissue paper held a little aside as he watched her impassively entering the house, he had a thought so extraordinary it made the hair on the back of his neck stiffen. He figured the best thing he could do was help her get the college education she had always wanted. There was nothing she wanted more. But where, if she agreed to let him—he doubted it every minute it was in his mind—could he get the money unless he stole it? The more he pondered this plan, the more it excited him until he couldn't stand the possibility it might be impossible.

He carried in his wallet the note Helen had once written him, that she would come up to his room if Nick and Tessie went to the movies, and he read it often.

One day he got another idea. He pasted a sign in the window: "Hot Sandwiches And Hot Soups To Go." He figured he could use his short-order cooking experience to advantage in the grocery. He had some handbills printed, advertising these new things and paid a kid half a buck to deliver them to places where there were working men. He followed the boy for a couple of blocks to see that he didn't dump the papers into a sewer. Before the end of the week a few new people were coming in at lunch and suppertime. They said this was the first time you could get any hot food to take out in the neighborhood. Frank also tried his hand at ravioli and lasagna once a week, making them from recipes he got out of a cookbook in the library. He experimented with baking small pizzas in the gas stove, which he sold for two bits apiece. The pasta and pizzas sold better than the hot sandwiches. People came in for them. He considered putting a table or two in the grocery but there was no room, so all the food had to go.

He got another little break. The milkman told him the two Norwegians had taken to yelling at each other in front of their customers. He said they were making less than they had expected. The store was fine for one man but not for two, so they each wanted to buy the other out. Pederson's nerves couldn't stand the fighting, and Taast bought him out at the end of May and had the place all to himself. But he found that the long hours alone were killing his feet. His wife came in to help out around suppertime; however Taast couldn't stand being away from his family every night, when everyone else was free and at home, so he decided to close at seven-thirty and stop fighting Frank until almost ten. These couple of hours all to himself at night helped Frank. He got back some of the customers who came home from work late, and also the housewives who at the last minute needed something for breakfast. And Frank noticed, from peering into Taast's window after he was closed, that he was no longer so generous with the specials.

The weather turned hot in July. People cooked less, lived more on delicatessen, canned goods, bottled drinks. He sold a lot of beer. His pastas and pizzas went very well. He heard that Taast had tried making pizzas but they were too doughy. Also, instead of using canned soups, Frank made a minestrone of his own that everybody praised; it took time to cook up, but the profit was better. And the new things he was selling pushed other goods along. He now paid Ida ninety a month for rent and the use of her store. She was earning more money on her epaulettes, and did not think so often that she would starve.

"Why do you give me so much?" she asked him when he raised the money to ninety.

"Maybe Helen could keep some of her wages?" he suggested.

"Helen isn't interested any more in you," she said sternly.

He didn't answer her.

But that night after supper—he had treated himself to ham and eggs and now smoked a cigar—Frank cleared the table and sat down to figure out how much it would cost to support Helen in college if she would quit her job and give all her time to education. When he had figured out the tuition from the college catalogues he had collected, he saw he couldn't do it. His heart was heavy. Later he thought maybe he could work it if she went to a free college. He could give her enough for her daily expenses and also to make up whatever money she now gave her mother. He figured that to do it would be a rocky load on his head, but he *had* to do it, it was his only hope; he could think of no other. All he asked for himself was the privilege of giving her something she couldn't give back.

The big thing, exciting yet frightening, was to talk to her, say what he hoped to do. He always had it in mind to say but found it very hard. To speak to her, after all that had happened to them, seemed impossible—opening on peril, disgrace, physical pain. What was the magic word to begin with? He despaired he could ever convince her. She was remote, sinned against, unfeeling, or if she felt, it was disgust of him. He cursed himself for having conceived this mess he couldn't now bring himself to speak of.

One August night after he had seen her come home from work in the company of Nat Pearl, sick of the misery of unmotion, Frank made himself move. He was standing behind the counter piling bottles of beer into a woman's market bag when he caught sight of Helen going by with some books on her arm. She was wearing a new summer dress, red trimmed with black, and the sight of her struck him with renewed hunger. All summer she had wandered at night alone in the neighborhood, trying to outwalk her loneliness. He had been tempted to close up and follow her, but until he had his new idea he could not think what he dared say that she wouldn't run from. Hurrying the customer out of the store, Frank washed, slicked back his hair and quickly changed into a fresh sport shirt. He locked the store and hurried in the direction Helen had gone. The day had been hot but was cooling now and still. The sky was golden green, though below the light was dark. After running a block he remembered something and trudged back to the store. He sat in the back listening to his heart hammering in his ears. In ten minutes he lit a lamp in the store window. The globe drew a ragged moth. Knowing how long she lingered among books, he shaved. Then locking the front door again, he went toward the library. He figured he would wait across the street till she came out. He would cross over and catch up with her on her way home. Before she could even see him, he would speak his piece and be done with it. Yes or no, she could say, and if no, he would shut the joint tomorrow and skiddoo.

He was nearing the library when he glanced up and saw her. She was about half a block away and walking toward him. He stood there not knowing which way to go, dreading to be met by her as lovely as she looked, standing like a crippled dog as she passed him. He thought of running back the way he had come, but she saw him, turned and went in haste the other way; so, reviving an old habit, he was after her, and before she could deny him, had touched her arm. They shivered. Giving her no time to focus her contempt, he blurted out what he had so long saved to say but could not now stand to hear himself speak.

When Helen realized what he was offering her, her heart moved violently. She had known he would follow and speak, but she could never in a thousand years have guessed he would say *this*. Considering the conditions of his existence, she was startled by his continuing ability to surprise her, make God-knows-what-next-move. His staying power mystified and frightened her, because she felt in herself, since the death of Ward Minogue, a waning of outrage. Although she detested the memory of her experience in the park, lately it had come back to her how she had desired that night to give herself to Frank, and might have if Ward hadn't touched her. She had wanted him. If there had been no Ward Minogue, there would have been no assault. If he had made his starved leap in bed she would have returned passion. She had hated him, she thought, to divert hatred from herself.

But her response to his offer was an instantaneous no. She said it almost savagely, to escape any possibility of being directly obligated to him, of another entrapment, nausea.

"I couldn't think of it."

He was astonished to have got this far, to be walking at her side—only it was a night in a different season, and her summer face was gentler than her winter one, her body more womanly; yet it all added up to loss, the more he wanted her the more he had lost.

"In your father's name," he said. "If not for you, then for him."

"What has my father got to do with it?"

"It's his store. Let it support you to go to college like he wanted you to."

"It can't without you. I don't want your help."

"Morris did me a big favor. I can't return it to him but I might to you. Also because I lost myself that night—"

"For God's sake, don't say it."

He didn't, was dumb. They walked dumbly on. To her horror they were coming to the park. Abruptly she went the other way.

He caught up with her. "You could graduate in three years. You wouldn't have any worry about expenses. You could study all you want."

"What would you expect to get from this—virtue?"

"I already said why—I owe something to Morris."

"For what? Taking you into his stinking store and making a prisoner out of you?"

What more could he say? To his misery, what he had done to her father rose in his mind. He had often imagined he would someday tell her, but not now. Yet the wish to say it overwhelmed him. He tried wildly to escape it. His throat hurt, his stomach heaved. He clamped his teeth tight but the words came up in blobs, in a repulsive stream.

He spoke with pain. "I was the one that held him up that time. Minogue and me. Ward picked on him after Karp ran away, but it was my fault too on account of I went in with him."

She screamed and might have gone on screaming but strangers were staring.

"Helen, I swear—"

"You criminal. How could you hit such a gentle person? What harm did he ever do you?"

"I didn't hit him, Ward did. I gave him a drink of water. He saw I didn't want to hurt him. After, I came to work for him to square up what I did wrong. For Christ's sake, Helen, try to understand me."

With contorted face she ran from him.

"I confessed it to him," he shouted after her.

He had managed well in the summer and fall, but after Christmas business dragged, and though his night salary had been raised five bucks, he found it impossible to meet all his expenses. Every penny looked as big as the moon. Once he spent an hour searching for a two-bit piece he had dropped behind the counter. He tore up a loose floor board and was elated to recover more than three dollars in green and grimy coins that Morris had lost during the years.

For himself he spent only for the barest necessities, though his clothes were falling apart. When he could no longer sew up the holes in his undershirts he threw them away and wore none. He soaked his laundry in the sink and hung it to dry in the kitchen. He was, as a rule, prompt in his payment of jobbers and wholesalers, but during the winter he kept them waiting. One man he held off his neck by threatening to go bankrupt. Another he promised tomorrow. He slipped a couple of bucks to his most important salesman, to calm them at the office. Thus he kept going. But he never missed a payment of rent to Ida. He valued his payments to her because Helen had returned to night college in the fall, and if he didn't give the ninety to Ida, Helen wouldn't have enough for her own needs.

He was always tired. His spine ached as if it had been twisted like a cat's tail. On his night off from the Coffee Pot he slept without moving, dreaming of sleep. In the dead hours at the Coffee Pot, he sat with his head on his arms at the counter, and during the day in the grocery he took catnaps whenever he could, trusting the buzzer to rouse him, although other noises did not. When he awoke, his eyes were hot and watery, his head like porous lead. He grew thin, his neck scrawny, face bones prominent, his broken nose sharp. He saw life from a continual wet-eyed yawn. He drank black coffee till his stomach turned sour. In the evening he did nothing—read a little. Or he sat in the back with the lights out, smoking, listening to the blues on the radio.

He had other worries, had noticed Nat was hanging around Helen more. A couple of times a week the law student drove her home from work. Now and then, over the week end, they went for a ride at night. Nat would toot his horn in front of the door and she came out dressed up and smiling, neither of them noticing Frank, in open sight. And she had had a new telephone put in upstairs, and once or twice a week he heard it ring. The phone made him jumpy, jealous of Nat. Once on his night off from the Coffee Pot, Frank woke abruptly when Helen and somebody came into the hall. Sneaking into the store and listening at the side door, he could hear them whispering; then they were quiet and he imagined them necking. For hours after, he couldn't get back to sleep, desiring her so. The next week, listening at the door, he discovered the guy she was kissing was Nat. His jealousy ate him good.

She never entered the store. To see her he had to stand at the front window.

"Jesus," he said, "why am I killing myself so?" He gave himself many unhappy answers, the best being that while he was doing this he was doing nothing worse.

But then he took to doing things he had promised himself

he never would again. He did them with dread of what he would do next. He climbed up the air shaft to spy on Helen in the bathroom. Twice he saw her disrobe. He ached for her, for the flesh he had lived in a moment. Yet he hated her for having loved him, for to desire what he had once had, and hadn't now, was torture. He swore to himself that he would never spy on her again, but he did. And in the store he took to cheating customers. When they weren't watching the scale he short-weighted them. A couple of times he shortchanged an old dame who never knew how much she had in her purse.

Then one day, for no reason he could give, though the reason felt familiar, he stopped climbing up the air shaft to peek at Helen, and he was honest in the store.

One night in January Helen was waiting at the curb for a trolley. She had been studying with a girl in her class and afterward had listened to some records, so she had left later than she had planned. The trolley was late in coming, and though she was cold, she was considering walking home, when she began to feel she was being watched. Looking into the store before which she was standing, she saw nobody there but the counterman resting his head on his arms. As she observed him, trying to figure out why she felt so strange, he raised his sleepy head and she saw in surprise that it was Frank Alpine. He gazed with burning eyes in a bony face, with sad regret, at his reflection in the window, then went drunkenly back to sleep. It took her a minute to realize he hadn't seen her. She felt the momentary return of an old misery, yet the winter night seemed clear and beautiful.

When the trolley came, she took a seat in the rear. Her thoughts were heavy. She remembered Ida saying Frank worked some place at night but the news had meant nothing to her. Now that she had seen him there, groggy from overwork, thin, unhappy, a burden lay on her, because it was no mystery who he was working for. He had kept them alive. Because of him she had enough to go to school at night.

In bed, half-asleep, she watched the watcher. It came to her that he had changed. It's true, he's not the same man, she said to herself. I should have known by now. She had despised him for the evil he had done, without understanding the why or aftermath, or admitting there could be an end to the bad and a beginning of good.

It was a strange thing about people—they could look the same but be different. He had been one thing, low, dirty, but because of something in himself—something she couldn't define, a memory perhaps, an ideal he might have forgotten and then remembered—he had changed into somebody else, no longer what he had been. She should have recognized it before. What he did to me he did wrong, she thought, but since he has changed in his heart he owes me nothing.

On her way to work one morning a week later, Helen, carrying her brief case, entered the grocery and found Frank hidden behind the tissue paper of the window, watching her. He was embarrassed, and she was curiously moved by the sight of his face.

"I came in to thank you for the help you're giving us," she explained.

"Don't thank me," he said.

"You owe us nothing."

"It's just my way."

They were silent, then he mentioned his idea of her going to day college. It would be more satisfying to her than at night.

"No, thank you," Helen said, blushing. "I couldn't think of it, especially not with you working so hard."

"It's no extra trouble."

"No, please."

"Maybe the store might get better, then I could do it on what we take in here?"

"I'd rather not."

"Think about it," Frank said.

She hesitated, then answered she would.

He wanted to ask her if he still had any chance with her but decided to let that wait till a later time.

Before she left, Helen, balancing the brief case on her knee, unsnapped it and took out a leather-bound book. "I wanted you to know I'm still using your Shakespeare."

He watched her walk to the corner, a good-looking girl, carrying his book in her brief case. She was wearing flat-heeled shoes, making her legs slightly more bowed, which for some reason he found satisfying.

The next night, listening at the side door, he heard a scuffle in the hall and wanted to break in and assist her but held himself back. He heard Nat say something harsh, then Helen slapped him and he heard her run upstairs.

"You bitch," Nat called after her.

One morning in the middle of March the grocer was sleeping heavily after a night off from the Coffee Pot, when he was awakened by a pounding on the front door. It was the Polish nut wanting her three-cent roll. She came later these days but still too early. The hell with all that, he thought, I need my sleep. But after a few minutes he grew restless and began to dress. Business still wasn't so hot. Frank washed his face before the cracked mirror. His thick hair needed cutting but it could wait one more week. He thought of growing himself a beard but was afraid it would scare some of the customers away, so he settled for a mustache. He had been letting one grow for two weeks and was surprised at the amount of red in it. He sometimes wondered if his old lady had been a redhead.

Unlocking the door, he let her in. The Polish dame complained he had kept her waiting too long in the cold. He sliced a roll for her, wrapped it, and rang up three cents.

At seven, standing by the window, he saw Nick, a new father, come out of the hall and run around the corner. Frank hid behind the paper and soon saw him return, carrying a bag of groceries he had bought in Taast's store. Nick ducked into the hallway and Frank felt bad.

"I think I will make this joint into a restaurant."

After he had mopped the kitchen floor and swept the store, Breitbart appeared, dragging his heavy boxes. Lowering the cartons of bulbs to the floor, the peddler took off his derby and wiped his brow with a yellowed handkerchief.

"How's it going?" Frank asked.

"Schwer."

Breitbart drank the tea and lemon that Frank cooked up for him, meanwhile reading his *Forward*. After about ten minutes he folded the newspaper into a small, thick square and pushed it into his coat pocket. He lifted the bulbs onto his itchy shoulders and left.

Frank had only six customers all morning. To keep from

getting nervous he took out a book he was reading. It was the Bible and he sometimes thought there were parts of it he could have written himself.

As he was reading he had this pleasant thought. He saw St. Francis come dancing out of the woods in his brown rags, a couple of scrawny birds flying around over his head. St. F. stopped in front of the grocery, and reaching into the garbage can, plucked the wooden rose out of it. He tossed it into the air and it turned into a real flower that he caught in his hand. With a bow he gave it to Helen, who had just come out of the house. "Little sister, here is your little sister the rose." From him she took it, although it was with the love and best wishes of Frank Alpine.

One day in April Frank went to the hospital and had himself circumcised. For a couple of days he dragged himself around with a pain between his legs. The pain enraged and inspired him. After Passover he became a Jew.

A Note to My Norwegian Readers on The Assistant

AFTER COMPLETING my first novel, *The Natural*, in essence mythic, I wanted to do a more serious, deeper perhaps, realistic piece of work. The apprentice character interested me, as he has in much of my fiction, the man, who as much as he can in the modern world, is in the process of changing his fate, his life. This sort of person, not at all complicated, appears for the first time in my writing in the short story, "The First Seven Years" (included in my first story collection, *The Magic Barrel*), and I thought I would like to develop the possibilities of his type. The refugee shoemaker in the story becomes the Italo-American assistant, Frank Alpine, whose way of achieving his spiritual freedom is to adopt the burdens of a Jew. The grocery story background came from "The Cost of Living," another short story written in the early fifties, and now reprinted in my most recent story collection, *Idiots First*. Morris Bober resembles Sam Thomashevsky, though his fate, I should think, is more moving, because he helps call it down upon himself, whereas Sam is the victim mostly of economic circumstances. Thus from these two stories came the store background, and characters who were to become Frank Alpine, Morris Bober, and Ida and Helen Bober.

What sort of Jew is Frank? Not much of one, I am sometimes told, because his beliefs are not explicitly stated; certainly they do not seem to be Orthodox beliefs. I admit that Frank sees the Jew a good deal as a symbol, and that there is perhaps an element of Christianity in his Judaism. However, I doubt that his view of the Jew is limited only to the man who has suffered. I think he has begun to understand the meaning of the Law, and since he is engaged, at the end of the book, in reading the Old Testament, perhaps he will appreciate the Prophetic quality of the Jewish religion. As for the Christian elements in Judaism, ideas flow backwards and forwards, and it is ridiculous to define love, charity, endurance, as the particular quality or province of one religion over another. I would want Frank to continue to love St. Francis as much as he may love Isaiah. If it is possible to wish a fate upon a character one has created, I would hope that his making a Jew of himself, however envisioned or achieved, will lead him into a richer humanity.

TWENTY STORIES

Benefit Performance

MAURICE ROSENFELD was conscious of himself as he took the key from his pocket and inserted it into the door of his small apartment. The Jewish actor saw his graying hair, the thick black eyebrows, the hunch of disappointment in his shoulders, and the sardonic grimness of his face accentuated by the twisted line of the lips. Rosenfeld turned the key in the lock, aware that he was playing his role well. Tragedy in the twisting of a key, he thought.

"Who's there?" said a voice from inside the apartment.

Surprised, Rosenfeld pushed open the door and saw that it was his daughter who had called out. Sophie was lying in her bed, which became the couch when it was folded together, and her bedroom became the living room. There was one other room, a small one, where Rosenfeld and his wife slept, and an alcove for the kitchen. When her father was working and came home late after the performance, Sophie would set up three screens around her bed so that she would not be awakened by the light which he put on while heating up some milk for himself before going to bed. The screens served another purpose. Whenever Sophie and her father quarreled, she set them up and let him rant outside. Deprived of her presence, he became silent and sulked. She sat on her sofa, reading a magazine by the light of her own lamp and blessing the screens for giving her privacy and preserving her dignity.

The screens were stacked up in the corner, and Rosenfeld was surprised to see his daughter in bed.

"What's the matter?" he said.

"I'm not well," she answered.

"Where's Momma?"

"She went to work."

"Today she's working?"

"She had half a day off. She's working from five to ten."

Rosenfeld looked around. The table in the alcove was not set and it was nearly suppertime.

"She left me to eat, something?"

417

"No, she thought you were going to eat with Markowitz. Is there anything doing?"

"No," he said bitterly, "nothing is doing. The Jewish theayter is deep in hell. Since the war, the Jews stay home. Everybody else goes out for a good time to forget their troubles, but Jews stay home and worry. Second Avenue is like a tomb."

"What did Markowitz want to see you for?" Sophie asked.

"A benefit, something. I should act in a benefit for Isaac Levin."

"Don't worry," she said, "you had a good season last year."

"I'm too young to live on memories," he said.

Sophie had no answer to that.

"If you want me to make you something, I'll get up," she said.

He walked into the kitchen and looked into the pots on the gas range.

"No, I'll make for myself. Here is some potatoes and carrots left over. I'll warm them up."

"Warm up the hamburger in the oven. Momma made one for me, but I couldn't eat it."

Rosenfeld pulled down the door of the broiler and glanced distastefully at the hamburger on the wire grill. "No, it burns me my stomach when I eat chopmeat," he said, closing the broiler door.

"How is your stomach?" she asked.

He placed his hand underneath his heart. "Today I got gas." He was moved by her solicitousness.

"How are you feeling?" he asked her.

"Like always. The first day is bad."

"It will go away."

"Yes, I know," she said.

He lit the flame under the vegetables and began to stir the mashed potatoes. They were lumpy. The remnants of his appetite disappeared. Sophie saw the look on his face and said, "Put some butter in the potatoes." For a moment Rosenfeld did not move, but when Sophie repeated her suggestion, he opened the icebox.

"What butter?" he said, looking among the bottles and the fruit. "Here is no butter."

Sophie reached for her housecoat, drew it on over her head, and pulled up the zipper. Then she stepped into her slippers.

"I'll put some milk in," she said.

Without wanting to, he was beginning to grow angry.

"Who wants you to? Stay in bed. I'll take care myself of the—the supper," he ended sarcastically.

"Poppa," she said, "don't be stubborn. I've got to get up anyway."

"For me you don't have to get up."

"I said I have to get up anyway."

"What's the matter?"

"Someone is coming."

He turned toward her. "Who's coming?"

"Pa, let's not start that."

"Who's coming?"

"I don't want to fight. I'm sick today."

"Who's coming, answer me."

"Ephraim."

"The plum-ber?" He was sarcastic.

"Please, Pa, don't fight."

"*I* should fight with a plum-ber?"

"You always insult him."

"*I* insult a plum-ber? He insults *me* to come here."

"He's not coming to see you. He's coming to see me."

"He insults *you* to come here. What does a plum-ber, who didn't even finish high school, want with you? You don't need a plum-ber."

"I don't care what I need, Poppa, I'm twenty-eight years old," she said.

"But a plum-ber!"

"He's a good boy. I've known him for twelve years, since we were in high school. He's honest and he makes a nice steady living."

"All right," Rosenfeld said angrily. "So *I* don't make a steady living. So go on, spill some more salt on my bleeding wounds."

"Poppa, don't act, please. I only said *he* made a steady living. I didn't say anything about you."

"Who's acting?" he shouted, banging the icebox door shut and turning quickly. "Even if I didn't support you and your mother steady, at least I showed you the world and brought you in company with the greatest Jewish actors of our times. Adler, Schwartz, Ben-Ami, Goldenburg, all of them have been in my house. You heard the best conversation about life, about books and music and all kinds art. You toured with me everywhere. You were in South America. You were in England. You were in Chicago, Boston, Detroit. You got a father whose Shylock in Yiddish even the American critics came to see and raved about it. *This* is living. *This* is life. Not with a plum-ber. So who is he going to bring into your house, some more plum-bers, they should sit in the kitchen and talk about pipes and how to fix a leak in the toilet? This is living? This is conversation? When he comes here, does he open his mouth? The only thing he says is yes and no, yes and no—like a machine. This is not for you."

Sophie had listened to her father in silence.

"Poppa, that's not fair," she said quietly, "you make him afraid to talk to you."

The answer seemed to satisfy him.

"Don't be so much in the hurry," he said more calmly. "You can get better."

"Please drop the subject."

The bell rang. Sophie pressed the buzzer.

"Poppa, for godsake, please be nice to him."

He said nothing but turned to his cooking, and she went into the bathroom.

Ephraim knocked on the door.

"Come in!"

The door opened and he walked in. He was tall, very well built and neatly dressed. His hair was carefully slicked back, but his hands were beefy and red from constant washing in hot water, which did not remove the calluses on his palms or the grease pockets underneath his nails. He was embarrassed to find only Sophie's father in.

"Is Sophie here?" he asked.

"Good evening," said Rosenfeld sarcastically.

Ephraim blushed.

"Good evening," he said. "Is Sophie here?"

"She will be here in a minute."

"Thank you very much." He remained standing.

Rosenfeld poured some milk into the potatoes and stirred them with a fork. "So you working now in the project houses?" he asked.

Ephraim was surprised to be addressed so politely. "No," he said. "We're working in the Brooklyn Navy Yard on the new ships."

"Hmm, must be a lot of toilets on the battleships?" Rosenfeld asked.

Ephraim did not answer him. Sophie came out of the bathroom with her hair neatly combed and a small blue ribbon in it to match the blue in her housecoat.

"Hello, Eph," she said.

He nodded.

"Sit down," she said, placing a chair near her bed. "I'll get back into bed." She lifted her feet out of the slippers, fixed the pillow so she could sit up, and covered herself with her blanket. Ephraim was facing her. Over his shoulder she could see her father scooping out the vegetables onto a plate. Then he sat down at the table and began to mash them.

"What's new, Eph?" she asked.

He sat with his elbows resting on his knees, the fingers of both hands interlocked.

"Nothing new," he said.

"Did you work today?"

"Only half a day. I got three weeks' overtime."

"What else is new?"

He shrugged his shoulders.

"Did you hear about Edith and Mortie?" she asked.

"No," he said. Rosenfeld lowered his fork.

"They got married Sunday."

"That's good," he said.

"Oh, another thing, I bought tickets for the Russian War Relief at Madison Square Garden. Can you go Friday night?"

"Yes," he said. Rosenfeld banged his fork down on his plate. Ephraim did not turn and Sophie did not look up. They were silent for a moment, and then Sophie began again.

"Oh, I forgot," she said, "I wrote to Washington for those civil-service requirements for you. Did your mother tell you?"

"Yes," he said.

Rosenfeld banged his fist on the table. "Yes and no, yes and no," he shouted. "Don't you know no other words?"

Ephraim did not turn around.

"Poppa, *please*," begged Sophie.

"Yes and no," shouted her father, "yes and no. Is this the way to talk to an educated girl?"

Ephraim turned around and said with dignity, "I'm not talking to you. I'm talking to your daughter."

"You not *talking* to her. You *insulting* her with yes and no. This is not talk."

"I'm not an actor," said Ephraim. "I work with my hands."

"Don't open your mouth to insult me."

Ephraim's jaw was trembling. "You insulted me first."

"Please, please," cried Sophie. "Poppa, if you don't stop, I'm going to put up the screens."

"So put up the screens to hide the plum-ber," her father taunted.

"At least a plumber can support a wife and don't have to send her out to work for him," cried Ephraim, his voice full of emotion.

"Oh, Ephraim, don't," moaned Sophie.

For a moment Rosenfeld was stunned. Then his face reddened and he began to stutter, "You nothing, you. You nothing," he cried. His lips moved noiselessly as he tried to find words to say. Suddenly he caught himself and paused. He rose slowly. Rosenfeld crossed his arms over his breast, then raised them ceilingward and began to speak deliberately in fluent Yiddish.

"Hear me earnestly, great and good God. Hear the story of the afflictions of a second Job. Hear how the years have poured misery upon me, so that in my age, when most men are gathering their harvest of sweet flowers, I cull nothing but weeds.

"I have a daughter, O God, upon whom I have lavished my deepest affection, whom I have given every opportunity for growth and education, who has become so mad in her desire for carnal satisfaction that she is ready to bestow herself upon a man unworthy to touch the hem of her garment, to a common, ordinary, wordless, plum-ber, who has neither ideals nor—"

"Poppa," screamed Sophie, "Poppa, stop it!"

Rosenfeld stopped and a look of unutterable woe appeared on his face. He lowered his arms and turned his head toward Ephraim, his nostrils raised in scorn.

"Plum-ber," he said bitterly.

Ephraim looked at him with hatred. He tried to move, but couldn't.

"You cheap actor," he cried suddenly, with venomous fury. "You can go straight to hell!" He strode over to the door, tore it open, and banged it so furiously that the room seemed to shake.

By degrees Rosenfeld lowered his head. His shoulders hunched in disappointment, and he saw himself, with his graying hair, a tragic figure. Again he raised his head slowly and looked in Sophie's direction. She was already setting up the screens. Rosenfeld moved toward the table in the alcove and glanced down at the vegetables on the plate. They bored him. He went over to the gas range, carefully lit the flame under the broiler, and pulled down the door to see whether the hamburger was cooking. It was. He closed the door, lowered the flame a bit, and said quietly:

"Tonight I will eat chopmeat."

1943

The Place Is Different Now

LATE ONE warm night in July, a week after they had let
Wally Mullane out of the hospital on Welfare Island, he
was back in his old neighborhood, searching for a place to
sleep. He tried the stores on the avenue first, but they were
closed, even the candy store on the corner. The hall doors
were all shut, and the cellars padlocked. He peered into the
barbershop window and cursed his luck for getting there so
late, because Mr. Davido would have let him sleep on one of
the barber chairs.

He walked for a block along the avenue, past the stores, and
turned in on Third Street, where the rows of frame houses
began. In the middle of the block, he crossed the street and
slipped into an alley between two old-fashioned frame houses.
He tried the garage doors, but they were locked too. As he
came out of the alley, he spotted a white-topped prowl car
with shaded lights moving slowly down the street, close to the
curb, under the trees. Ducking back into the alley, he hid behind a tree in the back yard and waited there nervously for the
police car to go by. If the car stopped, he would run. He would
climb the fences and come out in his mother's yard on Fourth
Street, but he didn't like the idea. The lights moved by. In five
minutes Wally sneaked out of the alley and walked quickly up
the street. He wanted to try the cellars of the private houses
but was afraid to because someone might wake and take him
for a burglar. They would call the police, and it would be just
his luck if his brother Jimmy was driving one of the radio cars.

All night long Wally hunted through the neighborhood, up
Fourth, then Fifth Street, then along the parkway, all the way
from the cemetery to the railroad cut, which was a block from
the avenue and ran parallel to it. He thought of sleeping in the
BMT elevated station but didn't have a nickel, so that was out.
The coal yard near the railroad cut was out too, because they
kept a watchman there. At five o'clock, tired from wandering,
he turned into Fourth Street again and stood under a tree,
across the street from his mother's house. He wanted to go

into the cellar and sleep there, but he thought of Jimmy and his sister Agnes and said to hell with that.

Wally walked slowly down the avenue to the El station and stood on the corner watching it grow light. Gray light seeped into the morning sky, and the quiet streets were full of thinning warm darkness. It made Wally feel sad. The neighborhood looked the same but wasn't. He thought of the fellows who were gone now and he thought of his friend Vincent Davido, the barber's son, who had been gone since before the war. He thought of himself not having set foot in his own house for years, and it made him feel like crying.

There was an empty milk box in front of the delicatessen. Wally dragged it across the sidewalk and placed it against the El pillar to have a backrest. He was tired but didn't want to fall asleep, because soon the people would be going up the station and he wanted to see if there was anyone he knew. He thought if he saw two or three people he knew, maybe they would give him about fifty cents and he would have enough for a beer and some ham and eggs.

Just before the sun came up, Wally fell asleep. The people buying their papers at the newsstand looked at him before they went upstairs to the station. Not many of them knew him. A fat man in a gray suit who recognized him stood on the corner with a disgusted look on his face, watching Wally sleep. Wally sat heavy-bellied on the milk box, with his head leaning back against the pillar and his mouth open. His straw-colored hair was slicked back. His face, red and smudged, was unshaven and thick with loose flesh. He had on a brown suit, oily with filth, black shoes, and a soiled shirt, with a rag of a brown tie knotted at the collar.

"The bastard's always drunk," said the fat man to the man from the candy store who had come out to collect the pennies on the newsstand. The storekeeper nodded.

At eight o'clock, a water truck turned the corner of Second Street and rumbled along the avenue toward the El, shooting two fanlike sprays of water out of its iron belly. The water foamed white where it hit the sizzling asphalt and shot up a powdery mist into the air. As the truck turned under the El, the floating cool mist settled upon Wally's sweating face and he woke up. He looked around wildly, but it wasn't Jimmy and the feeling of fright went away.

The day was heavy with wet, blistering heat, and Wally had a headache. His stomach rumbled and his tongue was sour. He wanted to eat but he didn't have a cent.

Several people walked past him on their way to work, and Wally looked at their faces but saw no one he knew. He didn't like to ask strangers for money. It was different if you knew them. Looking into the candy-store window to see the time, he was annoyed that it was eight-twenty-five. From long experience Wally knew that he had missed his best chances. The factory workers and those who worked in the stores had passed by very early in the morning, and the white-collar employees who followed them about an hour or so later were also gone. Only the stragglers and the women shoppers were left. You couldn't get much out of them. Wally thought he would wait awhile, and if no one came along soon, he'd go over to the fruit store and ask them if they had any spoiled fruit.

At half past eight, Mr. Davido, who lived on the top floor above the delicatessen, came out of the house to open his barbershop across the street. He was shocked when he saw Wally standing on the corner. How strange it is, he thought, when you see something that looks as if it was always there and everything seems the same once more.

The barber was a small, dark-skinned man nearing sixty. His fuzzy hair was gray, and he wore old-fashioned pince-nez with a black ribbon attached to them. His arms were short and heavy, and his fingers were stubby, but he maneuvered them well when he was shaving someone or cutting his hair. The customers knew how quickly and surely those short fingers moved when a man was in a hurry to get out of the shop. When there was no hurry, Mr. Davido worked slowly. Sometimes, as he was cutting a man's hair, the man would happen to look into the mirror and see the barber staring absently out the window, his lips pursed and his eyes filled with quiet sadness. Then, in a minute, he would raise his brows and begin cutting again, his short, stubby fingers snipping quickly to make up for time he had lost.

"Hey, Wally," he said, "where you keep yourself? You don't come aroun for a long time."

"I was sick," Wally said. "I was in a hospital."

"Whatsamatter, Wally, you still drinkin poison whiskey?"

"Nah, I ain't allowed to drink anymore. I got diabetes. They took a blood test an it showed diabetes."

Mr. Davido frowned and shook his head. "Take care of yourself," he said.

"I had a bad time. I almost got gangrene. When you get that, they amputate your legs off."

"How you get that, Wally?"

"From my brother Jimmy when he beat me up. My whole legs was swollen. The doctor said it was a miracle I didn't get gangrene."

Wally looked up the avenue as he talked. The barber followed his glance.

"You better keep away from your brother."

"I'm watchin out."

"You better leave this neighborhood, Wally. Your brother told you he don't like you in this neighborhood. There's a lot of jobs nowadays, Wally. Why don't you get some kind of a job and get a furnish room to live?"

"Yeah, I'm thinkin of gettin a job."

"Look every day," said the barber.

"I'll look," said Wally.

"You better look now. Go to the employment agency."

"I'll go," said Wally. "First I'm lookin for somebody. There's a lot of strange faces here. The neighborhood is changed."

"That's right," said the barber, "a lot of the young single fellows is gone. I can tell in the shop. The married men don't come in for shaves like the single fellows, only haircuts. They buy electric razors. The single fellows was sports."

"I guess everyone is gone or they got married," said Wally.

"They went to the war but some never came back, and a lot of them moved away to other places."

"Did you ever hear from Vincent?" Wally asked.

"No."

"I just thought I'd ask you."

"No," said the barber. There was silence for a minute; then he said, "Come over later, Wally. I shave you."

"When?"

"Later."

Wally watched Mr. Davido cross the avenue and go past the drugstore and laundry to his barbershop. Before he went in, he took a key from his vest pocket and wound up the barber pole. The red spiral, followed by the white and blue spirals, went round and round.

A man and a woman walked by, and Wally thought he recognized the man, but whoever he was lowered his eyes and passed by. Wally looked after him contemptuously.

He became tired of watching the stragglers and drifted over to the newsstand to read the headlines. Mr. Margolies, the owner of the candy store, came out again and picked up the pennies on the stand.

Wally was sore. "What's the matter, you think I'm gonna steal your lousy pennies?"

"Please," said Mr. Margolies, "to you I don't have to explain my business."

"I'm sorry I ever spent a cent in your joint."

Mr. Margolies's face grew red. "Go way, you troublemaker, you. Go way from here," he cried, flipping his hand.

"Aw, screwball."

A strong hand grasped Wally's shoulder and swung him around. For an instant he went blind with fear and his body sagged, but when he saw it was his oldest sister, Agnes, standing there with his mother, he straightened, pretending he hadn't been afraid.

"What'd you do now, you drunken slob?" said Agnes in her thick voice.

"I didn't do anything."

Mr. Margolies had seen the look on Wally's face. "He didn't do anything," he said. "He was only blocking the stand so the customers couldn't get near the papers."

Then he retreated into the store.

"You were told to stay out of this neighborhood," rasped Agnes. She was a tall, redheaded woman, very strongly built. Her shoulders were broad, and her thick breasts hung heavily against her yellow dress.

"I was just standin here."

"Who is that, Agnes?" asked his mother, peering through thick glasses.

"It's Wallace," Agnes said disgustedly.

"Hello, Ma," Wally said in a soft voice.

"Wallace, where have you been?" Mrs. Mullane was a stout woman, big-bellied and stoop-shouldered. Her pink scalp shone through her thin white hair, which she kept up with two amber-colored combs. Her eyes blinked under her thick glasses and she clung tightly to her daughter's arm for fear she would walk into something she couldn't see.

"I was in the hospital, Ma. Jimmy beat me up."

"And rightly so, you drunken bum," said Agnes. "You had your chances. Jimmy used to give you money to go to the agencies for a job, and the minute he had his back turned, you hit the bottle."

"It was the Depression. I couldn't get a job."

"You mean nobody would take you after the BMT canned you for spendin the nickel collections on the racehorses."

"Aw, shut up."

"You're a disgrace to your mother and your family. The least you could do is to get out of here and stay out. We suffered enough on account of you."

Wally changed his tone. "I'm sick. The doctor said I got diabetes."

Agnes said nothing.

"Wallace," his mother asked, "did you take a shower?"

"No, Ma."

"You ought to take one."

"I have no place."

Agnes grasped her mother's arm. "I'm takin your mother to the eye hospital."

"Wait awhile, Agnes," said Mrs. Mullane pettishly. "Wallace, are you wearing a clean shirt?"

"No, I ain't, Ma."

"Well, you come home for one."

"Jimmy'd break his back."

"He needs a clean shirt," insisted Mrs. Mullane.

"I got one in the laundry," said Wally.

"Well, then take it out, Wallace."

"I ain't got the money."

"Ma, don't give any money to him. He'll only throw it away on drink."

"He ought to have a clean shirt."

She opened her pocketbook and fumbled in her change purse.

"A shirt is twenty cents," said Agnes.

Mrs. Mullane peered at the coin she held in her hand. "Is this a dime, Agnes?"

"No, it's a penny. Let me get it for you." Agnes took two dimes from the change purse and dropped them into Wally's outstretched palm.

"Here, bum."

He let it go by. "Do you think I could have a little something to eat with, Ma?"

"No," said Agnes. She gripped her mother's elbow and walked forward.

"Change your shirt, Wallace," Mrs. Mullane called to him from the El steps. Wally watched them go upstairs and disappear into the station.

He felt weak, his legs unsteady. Thinking it was because his stomach was empty, he decided to get some pretzels and beer with the dimes. Later, he could get some spoiled fruit from the fruit store and would ask Mr. Davido for some bread. Wally walked along under the El to McCafferty's tavern, near the railroad cut.

Opening the screen door, he glanced along the bar and was almost paralyzed with fright. His brother Jimmy, in uniform, was standing at the rear of the bar drinking a beer. Wally's heart banged hard as he stepped back and closed the screen door. It slipped from his hand and slammed shut. The men at the bar looked up, and Jimmy saw Wally through the door.

"Jesus Christ!"

Wally was already running. He heard the door slam and knew Jimmy was coming after him. Though he strained every muscle in his heavy, jouncing body, he could hear Jimmy's footsteps coming nearer. Wally sped down the block, across the tracks of the railroad siding, and into the coal yard. He ran past some men loading a coal truck and crossed the cobblestoned yard, with his brother coming after him. Wally's lungs hurt. He wanted to run inside the coal loft and hide, but he knew he would be cornered there. He looked around wildly, then made for the hill of coal near the fence. He scrambled up. Jimmy came up after him, but Wally kicked down the coal and it hit Jimmy on the face and chest. He slipped and cursed, but gripped his club and came up again. At the top of the coal pile, Wally boosted himself up on the fence and dropped heavily to the other side. As he hit the earth his legs shook, but fear would not let him stop. He ran across a back yard and thumped up the inclined wooden cellar door, jumping clumsily over a picket fence. Out of the corner of his eye he saw Jimmy hoisting himself over the coal-yard fence. Wally wanted to get into the delicatessen man's back yard so he could go down to the cellar and come out on the avenue. Mr. Davido would let him hide in the toilet of the barbershop.

Wally ran across the flower bed in the next back yard and lifted himself over the picket fence. His sweaty palms slipped and he pitched forward, his pants cuff caught on one of the pointed boards. His hands were in the soft earth of an iris bed, and he dangled from the picket fence by one leg. He wriggled his leg and pulled frantically. The cuff tore away and he fell into the flower bed. He pushed himself up, but before he could move, Jimmy had hurdled the fence and tackled him. Wally fell on the ground, the breath knocked out of him. He lay there whimpering.

"You dirty bastard," Jimmy said. "I'll break your goddamn back."

He swung his club down on Wally's legs. Wally shrieked and tried to pull in his legs, but Jimmy held him down and whacked him across the thighs and buttocks. Wally tried to shield his legs with his arms, but Jimmy beat him harder.

"Oh, please, please, please," cried Wally, wriggling under his brother's blows, "please, Jimmy, my legs, my legs. Don't hit my legs!"

"You scum."

"My legs," screamed Wally, "my legs, I'll get gangrene, my legs, my legs!"

The pain burned through his body. He felt nauseated. "My legs," he moaned.

Jimmy let up. He wiped his wet face and said, "I told you to stay the hell outta this neighborhood. If I see you here again, I'll murder you."

Looking up, Wally saw two frightened women gazing at them out of their windows. Jimmy brushed off his uniform and went over to the cellar door. He pulled it open and walked downstairs.

Wally lay still among the trampled flowers.

"Why didn't the policeman arrest him?" asked Mrs. Werner, the delicatessen man's wife.

"It's the policeman's brother," explained Mrs. Margolies.

He lay on his stomach, arms outstretched, and his cheek pressed against the ground. His nose was bleeding, but he was too exhausted to move. The sweat ran down his arms and the back of his coat was stained dark with it. For a long while he had no thoughts; then the nausea subsided a little, and bits of things floated through his mind. He recalled how he used to play in the coal yard with Jimmy when they were kids. He thought of the Fourth Street boys coasting down the snow-covered sides of the railroad cut in the winter. Then he thought of standing in front of the candy store on quiet summer evenings, with his shirtsleeves rolled up, smoking and fooling around with Vincent and the guys, talking about women, good times, and ball players, while they all waited for the late papers to come in. He thought about Vincent, and he remembered the day Vincent went away. It was during the Depression, and the unemployed guys stood on the corner, smoking and chewing gum and making remarks to the girls who passed by. Like Wally, Vincent had quit going to the agencies, and he stayed on the corner with the rest of them, smoking and spitting around. A girl passed by and Vincent said something to her which made the guys laugh. Mr. Davido was looking out the window of the barbershop across the street. He slammed down the scissors and left the customer sitting in the chair. His face was red as he crossed the street. He grabbed Vincent by the arm and struck him hard across the face, shouting, "You bum, why don't you go look for a job?" Vincent's face turned gray. He didn't say anything, but walked away, and they never saw him again. That's how it was.

Mrs. Margolies said, "He's laying there for a long time. Do you think he's dead?"

"No," said Mrs. Werner, "I just saw him move."

Wally pushed himself up and stumbled down the stone steps of the cellar. Groping his way along the wall, he came up the stairs in front of the delicatessen. He searched through his pockets for the twenty cents his mother had given him but couldn't find them. The nausea came back and he wanted a place to sit down and rest. He crossed the street, walking unsteadily toward the barbershop.

Mr. Davido was standing near the window, sharpening a straight razor on a piece of sandstone. The sight of Wally that morning had brought up old memories, and he was thinking about Vincent. As he rubbed the razor round and round on the lathered sandstone, he glanced up and saw Wally staggering across the street. His pants were torn and covered with dirt, and his face was bloody. Wally opened the screen door, but Mr. Davido said sharply, "Stay outta here now, you're drunk."

"Honest I ain't," said Wally. "I didn't have a drop."

"Why you look like that?"

"Jimmy caught me and almost killed me. My legs must be black and blue." Wally lowered himself into a chair.

"I'm sorry, Wally." Mr. Davido got him some water, and Wally swallowed a little.

"Come on, Wally, on the chair," the barber said heartily. "I shave you an you rest an feel cooler."

He helped Wally onto the barber's chair; then he lowered the back and raised the front so that Wally lay stretched out as if he were on a bed. The barber swung a towel around his neck and began to rub a blob of hot lather into his beard. It was a tough beard and hadn't been shaved for a week. Mr. Davido rubbed the lather in deeply with his gentle, stubby fingers.

As he was rubbing Wally's beard, the barber looked at him in the mirror and thought how he had changed. The barber's eyes grew sad as he recalled how things used to be, and he turned away to look out the window. He thought about his son Vincent. How wonderful it would be if Vincent came home someday, he would put his arms around his boy and kiss him on the cheek . . .

Wally was also thinking how it used to be. He remembered how it was when he looked in the mirror before going out on Saturday night. He had a yellow mustache and wore a green hat. He remembered his expensive suits and the white carnation in his buttonhole and a good cigar to smoke.

He opened his eyes.

"You know," he said, "the place is different now."

"Yes," said the barber, looking out the window.

Wally closed his eyes.

Mr. Davido looked down at him. Wally was breathing quietly. His lips were pulled together tightly, and the tears were rolling down his cheeks. The barber slowly raised the lather until it mixed with the tears.

1943

Steady Customer

THE TWO lunch waitresses had heard the sad news from Mr. Mollendorf when they came in at ten-thirty, and for the rest of the day their eyes were red and swollen from crying. After lunch, when things grew slow, they sat on the bench in front of the wall mirror in the rear of the restaurant and they would look at Eileen's empty tables, and then they would begin to cry again. At four o'clock, after the two girls for the evening meal had hung up their raincoats and umbrellas and had changed into their uniforms, Gracie and Clara told them, and the four of them began to cry.

"She was only twenty-eight," wept Mary, and the sobs grew louder as the girls thought of Eileen lying dead in the hospital after her gallbladder operation.

At four-fifteen, Mr. Mollendorf, the chef and owner of the restaurant, came out of the kitchen in his apron and chef's cap and asked them please to control themselves and set the tables for the evening meal. It was a sad thing that had happened, but this was a business establishment from which they all drew their living, and it wasn't good for the customers to be served by a bunch of crying women. As he turned to go into the kitchen, something occurred to Mr. Mollendorf and he said, "Which one of you girls wants to serve Eileen's station tonight?"

No one spoke. They were almost horrified at the thought.

"The one who serves it tonight can serve it all the time from now on," said Mr. Mollendorf.

No one answered him. They knew Eileen's station was the best in the restaurant, good for at least a dollar more each night, but no one spoke.

"Well, what about you, Gracie? You were her best friend," said the boss.

"No, please, no, Mr. Mollendorf. Honest, I just couldn't."

"Clara? You could use a little extra money."

"No, thanks, Mr. Mollendorf."

"Mary?"

"No, sir."

"Elsie?"

"No, thank you."

Mr. Mollendorf shrugged his shoulders. "In that case, okay," he said. "Now I just got to call the agency for a new girl and give her the best station."

The girls, neatly attired in their trim black-and-white uniforms, were silent. They all looked so frightened Mr. Mollendorf felt sorry for them.

"Okay, girls," he said in a kind voice, "don't worry. I'm hurt too. She was a very fine person, very fine, and only twenty-eight years." He wiped his eye with the back of his hand and then went back into the kitchen.

"He ain't so bad," said Mary. They all agreed Mr. Mollendorf was all right. They set the tables for the evening meal. The afternoon dragged on and it began to rain harder outside.

"Even the heavens are crying," said Mary.

"I guess the supper will be spoiled," said Clara.

"Let it," Elsie said. "I don't feel like working anyway, when I think of her laying there dead in the hospital."

"You know what?" said Gracie quietly.

"What?"

"Her—her steady customer—"

The girls had forgotten him. In spite of themselves, the tears came once more.

"When he comes in, I'm not gonna let any new girl wait on him," Gracie told them, "I'm gonna wait on him myself."

"That's right, Gracie," Clara agreed. "You couldn't let a stranger tell him. It just—well, it wouldn't be right."

At five-thirty, the new girl came from the agency. She carried her uniform in a cardboard dress box from Klein's. Mr. Mollendorf told Gracie to take her downstairs to change, then give her the bill of fare and show her where things were. Gracie took the new waitress, whose name was Rose, downstairs to the lockers. Then she told Rose about Eileen and her operation.

"I'm very sorry to hear that," said Rose, "truly I am. I don't want to enrich myself on the dead."

"No, nobody does."

"Leastways not I."

Gracie told her about Eileen's steady customer. "When he comes in, will you mind if I serve him?" she asked. "You know, it's more personal."

"I understand perfectly," Rose said. "Anything I can do, I will gladly do it."

"Thanks."

"Were they goin together?"

"Well—not exactly, but they woulda soon. He's been coming here every night for the past two years and he always sits at Eileen's table. She knew exactly what he wanted. All he does is give the meat order, everything else is the same. First, he has fruit cup, then green-pea soup with croutons or vegetable soup—it's all according what we're serving—then he has his meat order—medium, with string beans and mashed potatoes, and then homemade apple pie or blueberry pie, if blueberries are in season, and coffee with two creams, because he likes it light. Eileen knew exactly what he wanted. He didn't have to say two words."

"He musta been used to her."

"Yeah, and he liked her. At first he was shy and didn't talk to her much, but after about five or six months she sorta won him around with her smile and her nice ways and he began to talk to her. Eileen always said he was very smart. He used to know everything about current events and the war and stuff like that."

"Do you think he'll take it bad?"

"Yeah," said Gracie, "I think so—that's why I want to tell him myself. You know how it is."

"Yes I know," Rose said sentimentally.

Rose had changed into her uniform, which was also black with a white collar and cuffs and a white apron. A customer could tell that she hadn't worked there before, because her shoes were black whereas the other girls wore white shoes.

Gracie introduced Rose to the girls and showed her Eileen's section. "He sits in this seat here," she said, pointing to the third table along the wall. "You can recognize him because he's thin and sorta blond and he always reads the *World-Telegram*."

"If I see him, I'll call you," said Rose.

"That's right."

They went back to the bench near the mirror and the girls sat there talking in quiet tones. They told Rose stories of Eileen's goodness—how she never got married because she was supporting her old mother, whom her two married brothers had neglected, and how pretty and good-natured she was, never getting angry at a girl who cut in ahead of her in the kitchen, and how she was always smiling so that everyone liked her.

The girls watched the rain streaming down the windows. The restaurant was empty and seemed emptier still when they looked at each of the tables so neatly set with silverware and white napkins and tablecloths. At the front of the store the cashier read a book, and the waitresses sat at the back in the half darkness, thinking about the things people think when somebody has just died.

"What time does this guy come in?" Rose asked Gracie while they were getting desserts in the kitchen.

"Usually half past seven."

Rose looked at her wristwatch. "It's ten to eight."

"Sometimes he don't come in. Maybe on account of the rain he won't come in tonight," Gracie said.

"I hope he does."

When Gracie went outside again, she saw him hanging up his coat near his regular table and her heart skipped a beat. She served her desserts and caught Rose's eye. Rose looked and saw him reading the *World-Telegram*. She smiled knowingly. The other waitresses saw the interchange of glances and the atmosphere grew tense.

Gracie straightened her apron and tried to calm herself. She decided to say nothing and let him ask. She went over to the table in Eileen's section and poured a glass of water for the man. He looked up from his newspaper. His eyes were a kind of dull blue and his hair was dry and thinning on top. He was mildly surprised at seeing Gracie.

"Shall—shall I give you the order?"

"Yes, sir." She would tell him when he asked her where Eileen was. Gracie girded herself for the moment. The girls were at their tasks, looking up to see what was going on.

"Well," he said, lightly rubbing his cheek with his long, bony fingers, "I usually take a fruit cup, and green-pea soup with croutons. Then tonight I'll have chopped steak—medium, please, and string beans and mashed potatoes."

Gracie wrote quickly.

"I usually take blueberry pie and coffee with two creams for dessert."

She closed her book and stood there for a minute, waiting for him to ask about Eileen, but he turned to his paper. She was disappointed. He looked up again.

"Did I—is something wrong?"

"No, sir." She walked hurriedly into the kitchen, her face set hard.

Two of the girls gathered around her in the kitchen.

"Did you tell him?" asked Mary.

"No, he didn't even ask where she was."

Mary's face fell. "Oh," she exclaimed, disappointed.

"That's the way they are," said Clara philosophically. "They don't know whether you're dead or alive and they don't care."

"Yeah," said Gracie.

"Maybe he thinks she's off tonight," Mary suggested.

Gracie brightened. "You got somethin'," she said, "except he knew she was off Thursdays, and this is Tuesday."

"Yes, but maybe he forgot."

"Tell him outright," said Clara, "tell him outright and see what he says."

"Yes, maybe I'll do that."

Gracie got the bread and butter, some salad, and a fruit cup. She set the food down on his table, and he lowered his newspaper.

"Sir," she said.

He looked up, almost frightened.

"Being you're a steady customer," she said, "I thought you might be interested to know that Eileen, the girl who usually serves here—well, she's—she passed away this morning in the hospital from a gallbladder operation."

Gracie wasn't able to control herself. Her mouth was distorted and the tears began to roll down her cheeks. The girls knew that she had told him.

He didn't know what to say. He swallowed and was embarrassed, and he looked around nervously at the other tables.

"I—I see," he said, his voice curiously uncontrolled. "I'm sorry." His eyes dropped to the paper. Gracie blinked the tears out of her eyes and pressed her lips tightly together. She walked quickly away.

"The hell with him," she said to Clara in the kitchen. "The hell with him. I only hope he croaks."

"He deserves it," Clara said.

Gracie called Rose over. She tore out his check from her order book. "Here," she said, "serve him. I can't stand his guts."

"Did you tell him?" asked Rose.

"I told him all right, but nothing to what I'd like to tell him."

"They're all alike," said Clara.

The word went around to the other girls, and they looked at him scornfully as they walked past his table with their loaded trays. Rose served him mechanically. She removed his fruit dish and shoved down the soup. He seemed not to notice. His eyes were on his paper.

The girls were angry and talked about him in the kitchen.

"You'd think he'd show a little loyalty," said Mary.

"Didn't he ask more about it?"

"No, he just said, 'I see. I'm sorry'—cold like, and he didn't say another word."

"I'd like to ram this chopped steak down his throat," Rose said vehemently.

"Me too," said Clara.

They went out again, but they could not control their glances. Before long, the customers were staring in the direction of the man. From the scornful faces of the waitresses they knew that something was wrong.

Once, he glanced up and he saw the people looking at him. His eyes fell quickly, and his hand trembled as he cut his meat. Then suddenly he wiped his lips and laid his napkin on the table. He picked up his check and took his hat and coat from the hook on the wall. His face was very white. He quickly paid his check and left.

The girls were stunned. They stood frozen, their serving

suspended. When the door closed behind him, they gathered together some soiled dishes and hurried into the kitchen.

"Did you see that?" asked Clara. "He left right in the middle of the meal."

"He must've felt sick about Eileen," said Mary.

"Maybe he saw how we felt about him," Gracie said.

"No, I don't think so. I think Mary's right," Clara said. "Some guys are like that. They don't talk much, but inside they eat their heart out."

"I don't know," said Gracie.

"For godsakes, girls," called Mr. Mollendorf, "I'm running a restaurant here, not a meeting hall. Go back to your tables."

The group broke up. They filed out into the restaurant through the swinging doors.

"I'm convinced," Clara said to Gracie, "I'm convinced he really and truly loved her."

1943

The Literary Life of Laban Goldman

COMING UPSTAIRS, Laban Goldman was rehearsing arguments against taking his wife to the movies so that he could attend his regular classes in night school, when he met Mrs. Campbell, his neighbor, who lived in the apartment next door.

"Look, Mrs. Campbell," said Laban, holding up a newspaper. "Again! This time in *The Brooklyn Eagle*."

"Another letter?" Mrs. Campbell said. "How do you do it?"

"They like the way I express myself on the subject of divorce." He pointed to his letter in the newspaper.

"I'll read it over later," Mrs. Campbell said. "Joe brings home the *Eagle*. He cuts out your letters. You know, he showed everyone the one about tolerance. Everyone thought the sentiments were very excellent."

"You mean my *New York Times* letter?" Laban beamed.

"Yes, it had excellent sentiments," said Mrs. Campbell, continuing downstairs. "Maybe someday you ought to write a book."

A tremor of bittersweet joy shook Laban Goldman. "With all my heart, I concur with your hope," he called down after her.

"Nobody can tell," Mrs. Campbell said.

Laban opened the door of his apartment and stepped into the hallway. The meeting with Mrs. Campbell had given him confidence. He felt that his arguments would take on added eloquence. As he was hanging up his hat and coat on the clothes tree in the hall, he heard his wife talking on the telephone.

"Laban?" she called.

"Yes." He tried to make it sound cold.

Emma came into the hallway. She was a small woman, heavily built.

"Sylvia is calling," she said.

He held up the paper. "The editor printed a letter," he said quickly. "It means I will have to go to school tonight."

Emma clutched her hands and pressed them to her bosom. "Laban," she cried, "you promised me."

"Tomorrow night."

"No, tonight!"

"Tomorrow night."

"Laban!" she screamed.

He held his ground. "Don't make an issue," he said. "To-morrow is the same picture."

Emma bounded over to the telephone. "Sylvia," she cried, "you see, now he doesn't go."

Laban tried to duck into his room, but she was too quick for him.

"Telephone," she announced coldly. Wearily he walked over to the phone.

"Poppa," said Sylvia, "why have you broken your promise that you gave to Momma?"

"Listen, Sylvia, for a minute, without talking. I didn't break my promise. All I want to do is to delay or postpone it till to-morrow, and she jumps to conclusions."

"You promised me today," cried Emma, who was standing there, listening.

"Please," he said, "have the common decency to refrain from talking when I'm talking to someone else."

"You are talking to my daughter," she declared with dignity.

"I am well aware and conscious that your daughter is your daughter."

"All the time big words," she taunted.

"Poppa, don't fight," said Sylvia over the telephone. "You promised you would take Momma to the movies tonight."

"It just so happens that my presence is required in school tonight. *The Brooklyn Eagle* printed a vital letter I wrote, and Mr. Taub, my English teacher, likes to discuss them in class."

"Can't it wait till tomorrow?"

"The issue is alive and pertinent today. Tomorrow, today's paper will be yesterday's."

"What is the letter about?"

"It's a sociological subject of import. You will read it."

"Poppa, this can't go on," said Sylvia sharply. "I have two young children to take care of. I can't keep tearing myself away from my family every other night to take Momma to the movies. It's your duty to take her out."

"I have no alternative."

"What do you mean, Poppa?"

"My education comes first."

"You can get just as much education four nights a week as you can five."

"That will not hold water mathematically," he said.

"Poppa, you're a pretty smart man. Couldn't you stay home just one night a week, say on Wednesdays, and take Momma out?"

"To me, the movies are not worth it."

"You mean your wife is not worth it," broke in Emma again.

"I wasn't talking to you," said Laban.

"Don't fight, *please*," said Sylvia. "Poppa, try to be considerate."

"I'm *too* considerate," Laban said. "That's why I didn't advance in my whole life up to now. It's about time I showed some consideration for myself."

"I'm not going to argue with you about that anymore, but I warn you, Poppa, you will have to take more responsibility about Momma. It isn't fair to let her stay home all alone at night."

"That's her problem."

"It's yours," broke in Emma.

Laban lost his temper. "It's yours," he shouted.

"Goodbye, Poppa," said Sylvia hastily. "Tell Momma I'll come over at eight o'clock."

Laban hung up the receiver. His wife's face was red. Her whole body was heaving with indignation.

"To who you married," she asked bitterly, "to the night school?"

"Twenty-seven years I have been married to you in a life which I got nothing from it," he said.

"You got to eat," she said, "you got to sleep, and you got a nice house. From your wife who brought up your child, I will say nothing."

"This is ancient history," sneered Laban. "Tell me, please, have I got understanding? Did I get encouragement to study to take civil-service examinations so I am now a government clerk who is making twenty-six hundred dollars a year and always well provided for his family? Did I get encouragement to study subjects in high school? Did I get praise when I wrote letters to the editor which the best papers in New York saw fit to print them? Answer me this."

"Hear thou me, Laban—" began Emma in Yiddish.

"Talk English, please," Laban shouted. "When in Rome, do what the Romans do."

"I don't express myself so good in English."

"So go to school and learn."

Emma completely lost her temper. "Big words I need to clean the house? School I need to cook for you?" she shouted.

"You don't have to cook for me!"

"I don't have to cook?" she asked sarcastically. "So good!" Emma drew herself up. "So tonight, cook your own supper!" She stomped angrily into the hall and turned at the door of her room. "And when you'll get an ulcer from your cooking," she said, "so write a letter to the editor." She banged the door of her room shut.

Laban went into his room and stuffed his books and newspaper into his briefcase. "She makes my whole life disagreeable," he muttered. He put on his hat and coat and went downstairs. His first impulse had been to go to the restaurant, but his appetite was gone, so he went to the cafeteria on the corner of the avenue near the school. The quarrel had depressed him because he had counted on avoiding it. He ate half a sandwich, drank his coffee, and hurried off to school.

He went through his biology and geometry classes without paying much attention to the discussions, but his interest picked up in his Spanish class when Miss Moscowitz, who was also in his English class, came into the room. Laban nodded to her. She was a tall, thin young woman in her early thirties. Except for her glasses and a few pockmarks on her cheek, almost entirely hidden by the careful use of rouge, she wasn't bad-looking. She and Laban were the shining lights of their English class, and it thrilled him to think how he would impress her with his letter. He debated with himself on the procedure of introducing the letter into the discussion. Should he ask Mr. Taub for permission to read the letter to the class, or should he wait for a favorable moment and surprise the class by reading the letter then? He decided to wait. When he thought how dramatic the scene would be, Laban's excitement grew. The bell rang. He gathered up his books and, without waiting for Miss Moscowitz, walked toward his English room.

Mr. Taub began the lesson with a discussion on the element of fate in *Romeo and Juliet*, the play the class had just read. The class, adults and young people, both American and foreign-born, gave their opinions on the subject as Laban nervously sought for an opening. He was usually very active in this type of discussion, but he decided not to participate too much tonight in order to give his full attention to discovering a subject relevant to the letter. Miss Moscowitz was particularly effective in her answers. She analyzed the various elements of the plot with such impressive clarity that the class held its breath as she talked. Laban squirmed uncomfortably in his seat as the period grew shorter. He knew that he would feel miserable if he had not read his letter, especially since he had not even participated in the discussion. Mr. Taub brought up another question: "How did the lovers themselves contribute to their tragedy?"

Again Miss Moscowitz's hand shot up. The teacher looked around, but no hands were raised so he nodded to her.

"Their passion was the cause of the tragedy," said Miss Moscowitz, rising from her seat; but before she could go on, Laban Goldman's hand was waving in the air.

"Ah, Mr. Goldman," said the teacher, "we haven't heard from you tonight. Suppose we let him go on, Miss Moscowitz?"

"Gladly," she said, resuming her seat.

Laban rose and nodded to Miss Moscowitz. He tried to appear at ease, but his whole body was throbbing with excitement. He stepped into the aisle, thrust his right hand into his trouser pocket, and cleared his throat.

"A young woman like Miss Moscowitz should be complimented on her very clear and visionary answers. There was once a poet who quoted 'Passions spin the plot,' and Miss Moscowitz saw that this quotation is also true in this play. The youthful lovers, Romeo and Juliet, both of them were so overwhelmed and disturbed by their youthful ardor for each other that they could not discern or see clearly what their problems would be. This is not true only of these Shakespeare lovers, but also of all people in particular. When a man is young, he is carried away by his ardor and passion for a woman with the obvious and apparent result that he don't take into consideration his wife's real characteristics—whether she is suited to be his mate in mind as well as in the body. The result of this incongruence is very frequently tragedy or, nowadays, divorce. On this subject I would like to quote you some words of mine which were printed in a newspaper, *The Brooklyn Eagle*, today."

He paused and looked at the teacher.

"Please do," said Mr. Taub. The class buzzed with interest.

Laban's hands trembled as he took the paper from his briefcase. He cleared his throat again.

To the Editor of *The Brooklyn Eagle*:

I would like to point out to your attention that there are many important problems that we are forgetting on account of the war. It is not my purpose or intention to disavow the war, but it is my purpose to say a few words on the subject of divorce.

New York State is back in the dark ages where this problem is concerned. Many a man of unstained reputation has his life filled with the darkness of tragedy because he will not allow his reputation to be defiled or soiled. I refer to adultery, which, outside of desertion, which takes too long, is the only practicable means of securing a divorce in this state. When will we become enlightened enough to learn that incompatibility "breeds contempt," and that such a condition festers in the mind the way adultery festers in the body?

In view of this fact, there is only one conclusion—that we ought to have a law here to provide us with divorce on the grounds of incompatibility. I consider this to be *Quod Erat Demonstrandum*.

Laban Goldman
Brooklyn, January 28, 1942

Laban lowered his paper, and in the pause that ensued he said, "I don't have to explain to the people in this class who are taking Geometry 1 or 2 what this Latin quotation means."

The class was deeply impressed. They applauded as Laban sat down. His legs trembled, but he was filled with the great happiness of triumph.

"Thank you, Mr. Goldman," said Mr. Taub. "It pleases me to see that you are continuing your literary pursuits, and I should like the class to note that there was a definite Introduction,

Body, and Conclusion in Mr. Goldman's composition—that is to say—his letter. Without having seen the paper, I feel sure that there are three paragraphs in the letter he read to us. Isn't that so, Mr. Goldman?"

"Absolutely!" said Laban. "I invite all to inspect the evidence."

Miss Moscowitz's hand shot up. The teacher nodded.

"I don't know how the class feels, but I for one am honored to be in a class with a man of Mr. Goldman's obvious experience and literary talent. I thought that the gist of the letter was definitely very excellent."

The class applauded as she sat down. The bell rang, and school was over for the night.

Laban caught up with Miss Moscowitz in the hall and walked downstairs with her. "The bell rang too soon before I could reciprocate the way you felt about me," he said.

"Oh, thank you," said Miss Moscowitz, her face lighting with happiness. "That makes it mutual."

"Without doubt," said Laban, as they were continuing downstairs. He felt very good.

The students poured out into the street and began to disperse in many directions, but Laban did not feel like going home. The glow of triumph was warm within him, and he felt that he wanted to talk. He tipped his hat and said, "Miss Moscowitz, I realize I am a middle-aged man and you are a young woman, but I am young in my mind so I would like to continue our conversation. Would you care to accompany me to the cafeteria, we should have some coffee?"

"Gladly," said Miss Moscowitz, "and I am not such a young woman. Besides, I get along better with a more mature man."

Very much pleased, he took her arm and led her up the block to the cafeteria on the corner. Miss Moscowitz arranged the silverware and the paper napkins on the table while he went for the coffee and cake.

As they sipped their coffee, Laban felt twenty years younger, and a sense of gladness filled his heart. It seemed to him that his past was like a soiled garment which he had cast off. Now his vision was sharp and he saw things clearly. When he looked at Miss Moscowitz, he was surprised and pleased to see how pretty she was. Within him, a great torrent of words was fighting for release.

"You know, Miss Moscowitz—" he began.

"Please call me Ruth," she said.

"Ah, Ruth, ever faithful in the Bible," Laban mused. "My name is Laban."

"Laban, that's a distinguished name."

"It's also a biblical name. What I started out to say," he went on, "was to tell you the background of my letter which they printed today."

"Oh, please do, I am definitely interested."

"Well, that letter is true and autobiographical," he said impressively.

"Without meaning to be personal, how?" she asked.

"Well, I'll tell you in a nutshell," Laban said. "You are a woman of intelligence and you will understand. What I meant," he went on, acknowledging her smile with a nod, "what I meant was that I was the main character in the letter." He sought carefully for his words. "Like Romeo and Juliet, I was influenced by passion when I was a young man, and the result was I married a woman who was incompatible with my mind."

"I'm very sorry," said Miss Moscowitz.

Laban grew moody. "She has no interest in the subjects I'm interested in. She don't read much and she don't know the elementary facts about psychology and the world."

Miss Moscowitz was silent.

"If I had married someone with my own interests when I was young," he mused, "—someone like you, why I can assure you that this day I would be a writer. I had great dreams for writing, and with my experience and understanding of life, I can assure you that I would write some very fine books."

"I believe you," she said. "I really do."

He sighed and looked out of the window.

Miss Moscowitz glanced over his shoulder and saw a short, stout woman with a red, angry face bearing down upon them. She held a cup of coffee in her hand and was trying to keep it from spilling as she pushed her way toward Laban's table. A young woman was trying to restrain her. Miss Moscowitz sized up the situation at once.

"Mr. Goldman," she said in a tight voice, "your wife is coming."

He was startled and half rose, but Emma was already upon them.

"So this is night school!" she cried angrily, banging the half-spilled cup of coffee on the table. "This is education every night?"

"Momma, please," begged Sylvia, "everyone is looking."

"He is a married man, you housebreaker!" Emma shouted at Miss Moscowitz.

Miss Moscowitz rose. Her face had grown pale, and the pockmarks were quite visible.

"I can assure you that the only relationship that I have had with Mr. Goldman is purely platonic. He is a member of my English class," she said with dignity.

"Big words," sneered Emma.

"Be still," Laban cried. He turned to Miss Moscowitz. "I apologize to you, Miss Moscowitz. This is my cross I bear," he said bitterly.

"Poppa, please," begged Sylvia.

Miss Moscowitz picked up her books.

"Wait," called Laban, "I will pay your check."

"Over my dead body," cried Emma.

"That will not be necessary," said Miss Moscowitz. "Good night."

She paid her check and went out through the revolving door.

"You ignoramus, you," shouted Laban, "look what you did!"

"Oh, he's cursing me," Emma wailed, bursting into tears.

"Oh, Poppa, this is so mortifying," said Sylvia. "Everyone is staring at us."

"Let them look," he said. "Let them see what a man of sensitivity and understanding has to suffer because of incompatible ignorance." He snatched up his briefcase, thrust his hat on his head, and strode over to the door. He tossed a coin on the counter and pushed through the revolving door into the street. Emma was still sobbing at the table, and Sylvia was trying to comfort her.

Laban turned at the corner and walked down the avenue in

the direction away from his home. The good feeling was gone and a mood of depression settled upon him as he thought about the scene in the cafeteria. To his surprise he saw things clearly, more clearly than he ever had before. He thought about his life with quiet objectivity and he enjoyed the calmness that came to him as he did so. The events of the day flowed into his thoughts, and Laban remembered his triumph in the classroom. The feeling of depression lifted.

"Ah," he sighed, as he walked along, "with my experience, what a book I could really write!"

1943

The Cost of Living

WINTER HAD fled the city streets but Sam Tomashevsky's face, when he stumbled into the back room of his grocery store, was a blizzard. Sura, sitting at the round table eating bread and a salted tomato, looked up in fright, and the tomato turned a deeper red. She gulped the bite she had bitten and with pudgy fist socked her chest to make it go down. The gesture already was one of mourning, for she knew from the wordless sight of him there was trouble.

"My God," Sam croaked.

She screamed, making him shudder, and he fell wearily into a chair. Sura was standing, enraged and frightened.

"Speak, for God's sake."

"Next door," Sam muttered.

"What happened next door?"—upping her voice.

"Comes a store!"

"What kind of a store?" The cry was piercing.

He waved his arms in rage. "A grocery comes next door."

"Oi." She bit her knuckle and sank down moaning. It could not have been worse.

They had, all winter, been haunted by the empty store. An Italian shoemaker had owned it for years, and then a streamlined shoe-repair shop had opened up next block where they had two men in red smocks hammering away in the window and everyone stopped to look. Pellegrino's business had slackened off as if someone was shutting a faucet, and one day he had looked at his workbench, and when everything stopped jumping, it loomed up ugly and empty. All morning he had sat motionless, but in the afternoon he put down the hammer he had been clutching and got his jacket and an old darkened Panama hat a customer had never called for when he used to do hat cleaning and blocking; then he went into the neighborhood, asking among his former customers for work they might want done. He collected two pairs of shoes, a man's brown and white ones for summertime and a pair of ladies' dancing slippers. At the same time, Sam found his own soles and heels had been worn paper thin for being so many hours on his feet—he could feel the cold floorboards under him as he walked—and that made three pairs all together, which was what Mr. Pellegrino had that week—and another pair the week after. When the time came for him to pay next month's rent he sold everything to a junkman and bought candy to peddle with in the streets, but after a while no one saw the shoemaker any more, a stocky man with round eyeglasses and a bristling mustache, wearing a summer hat in wintertime.

When they tore up the counters and other fixtures and moved them out, when the store was empty except for the sink glowing in the rear, Sam would occasionally stand there at night, everyone on the block but him closed, peering into the window exuding darkness. Often while gazing through the dusty plate glass, which gave him back the image of a grocer gazing out, he felt as he had when he was a boy in Kamenets-Podolski and going—the three of them—to the river; they would, as they passed, swoop a frightened glance into a tall wooden house, eerily narrow, topped by a strange double-steepled roof, where there had once been a ghastly murder and now the place was haunted. Returning late, at times in early moonlight, they walked a distance away, speechless, listening to the ravenous silence of the house, room after room fallen into deeper stillness, and in the midmost a pit of churning quiet from which, if you thought about it, evil erupted. And so it seemed in the dark recesses of the empty store, where so many shoes had been leathered and hammered into life, and so many people had left something of themselves in the coming and going, that even in emptiness the store contained some memory of their presences, unspoken echoes in declining tiers, and that in a sense was what was so frightening. Afterwards when Sam went by the store, even in daylight he was afraid to look, and quickly walked past, as they had the haunted house when he was a boy.

But whenever he shut his eyes the empty store was stuck in his mind, a long black hole eternally revolving so that while he slept he was not asleep but within, revolving: what if it should happen to me? What if after twenty-seven years of toil (he should years ago have got out), what if after all of that, your own store, a place of business . . . after all the years, the years, the thousands of cans he had wiped off and packed away, the milk cases dragged in like rocks from the street before dawn in freeze or heat; insults, petty thievery, doling of credit to the impoverished by the poor; the peeling ceiling, fly-specked shelves, puffed cans, dirt, swollen veins, the back-breaking sixteen-hour day like a heavy hand slapping, upon awaking, the skull, pushing the head down to bend the body's bones; the hours; the work, the years, my God, and where is my life now? Who will save me now, and where will I go, where? Often he had thought these thoughts, subdued after months; and the garish FOR RENT sign had yellowed and fallen in the window so how could anyone know the place was to let? But they did. Today when he had all but laid the ghost of fear, a streamer in red cracked him across the eyes: National Grocery Will Open Another of Its Bargain Price Stores On These Premises, and the woe went into him and his heart bled.

At last Sam raised his head and told her, "I will go to the landlord next door."

Sura looked at him through puffy eyelids. "So what will you say?"

"I will talk to him."

Ordinarily she would have said, "Sam, don't be a fool," but she let him go.

Averting his head from the glare of the new red sign in the window, he entered the hall next door. As he labored up the steps the bleak light of the skylight fell on him and grew heavier as he ascended. He went unwillingly, not knowing what he would say to the landlord. Reaching the top floor, he paused before the door at the jabbering in Italian of a woman bewailing her fate. Sam already had one foot on the top stair, ready to descend, when he heard the coffee advertisement and realized it had been a radio play. Now the radio was off, the hallway oppressively silent. He listened and at first heard no voices inside, so he knocked without allowing himself to think any more. He was a little frightened and lived in suspense until the slow heavy steps of the landlord, who was also the barber across the street, reached the door, and it was—after some impatient fumbling with the lock—opened.

When the barber saw Sam in the hall he was disturbed, and Sam at once knew why he had not been in the grocery store even once in the past two weeks. However, the barber, becoming cordial, invited Sam to step into the kitchen where his wife and a stranger were seated at the table eating from piled-high plates of spaghetti.

"Thanks," said Sam shyly. "I just ate."

The barber came out into the hall, shutting the door behind him. He glanced vaguely down the stairway and turned to Sam. His movements were unresolved. Since the death of his son in the war he had become absentminded; and sometimes when he walked one had the impression he was dragging something.

"Is it true?" Sam asked in embarrassment. "What it says downstairs on the sign?"

"Sam," the barber began heavily. He stopped to wipe his mouth with a paper napkin he held in his hand and said, "Sam, you know this store I had no rent for it for seven months?"

"I know."

"I can't afford. I was waiting for maybe a liquor store or a hardware, but I don't have no offers from them. Last month this chain store make me an offer and then I wait five weeks for something else. I had to take it, I couldn't help myself."

Shadows thickened in the darkness. In a sense Pellegrino was present, standing with them at the top of the stairs.

"When will they move in?" Sam sighed.

"Not till May."

The grocer was too faint to say anything. They stared at each other, not knowing what to suggest. But the barber forced a laugh and said the chain store wouldn't hurt Sam's business.

"Why not?"

"Because you carry different brands of goods and when the customers want those brands they go to you."

"Why should they go to me if my prices are higher?"

"A chain store brings more customers and they might like things that you got."

Sam felt ashamed. He did not doubt the barber's sincerity, but his stock was meager and he could not imagine chain store customers interested in what he had to sell.

Holding Sam by the arm, the barber told him in confidential tones of a friend who had a meat store next to an A&P supermarket and was making out very well.

Sam tried hard to believe he would make out well but couldn't.

"So did you sign with them the lease yet?" he asked.

"Friday," said the barber.

"Friday?" Sam had a wild hope. "Maybe," he said, trying to hold it down, "maybe I could find you, before Friday, a new tenant?"

"What kind of a tenant?"

"A tenant," Sam said.

"What kind of store is he interested?"

Sam tried to think. "A shoe store," he said.

"Shoemaker?"

"No, a shoe store where they sell shoes."

The barber pondered it. At last he said if Sam could get a tenant he wouldn't sign the lease with the chain store.

As Sam descended the stairs the light from the top-floor bulb diminished on his shoulders but not the heaviness, for he had no one in mind to take the store.

However, before Friday he thought of two people. One was the red-haired salesman for a wholesale grocery jobber, who had lately been recounting his investments in new stores; but when Sam spoke to him on the phone he said he was only interested in high-income grocery stores, which was no solution to the problem. The other man he hesitated to call, because he didn't like him. That was I. Kaufman, a former dry-goods merchant, with a wart under his left eyebrow. Kaufman had made some fortunate real estate deals and had become quite wealthy. Years ago he and Sam had stores next to one another on Marcy Avenue in Williamsburg. Sam took him for a lout and was not above saying so, for which Sura often ridiculed him, seeing how Kaufman had prospered, and where Sam was. Yet they stayed on comparatively good terms, perhaps because the grocer never asked for favors. When Kaufman happened to be around in the Buick, he usually dropped in, which Sam increasingly disliked, for Kaufman gave advice without stint and Sura sandpapered it in when he had left.

Despite qualms he telephoned him. Kaufman was pontifically surprised and said yes he would see what he could do. On Friday morning the barber took the red sign out of the window so as not to prejudice a possible deal. When Kaufman marched in with his cane that forenoon, Sam, who for once, at Sura's request, had dispensed with his apron, explained to him they had thought of the empty store next door as perfect for a shoe store because the neighborhood had none and the rent was reasonable. And since Kaufman was always investing in one project or another they thought he might be interested in this. The barber came over from across the street and unlocked the door. Kaufman clomped into the empty store, appraised the structure of the place, tested the floor, peered through the barred window into the back yard, and squinting, totaled with moving lips how much shelving was necessary and at what cost. Then he asked the barber how much rent and the barber named a modest figure.

Kaufman nodded sagely and said nothing to either of them there, but in the grocery store he vehemently berated Sam for wasting his time.

"I didn't want to make you ashamed in front of the goy," he said in anger, even his wart red, "but who do you think, if he is in his right mind, will open a shoe store in this stinky neighborhood?"

Before departing, he gave good advice the way a tube bloops toothpaste, and ended by saying to Sam, "If a chain store grocery comes in you're finished. Get out of here before the birds pick the meat out of your bones."

Then he drove off in his Buick. Sura was about to begin a commentary, but Sam pounded his fist on the table and that ended it. That evening the barber pasted the red sign back on the window, for he had signed the lease.

Lying awake nights, Sam knew what was going on inside the store, though he never went near it. He could see carpenters sawing the sweet-smelling pine that willingly yielded to the sharp blade and became in tiers the shelves rising almost to the ceiling. The painters arrived, a long man and a short one he was positive he knew, their faces covered with paint drops. They thickly calcimined the ceiling and painted everything in bright colors, impractical for a grocery but pleasing to the eye. Electricians appeared with fluorescent lamps which obliterated the yellow darkness of globed bulbs; and then the fixture men hauled down from their vans the long marble-top counters and gleaming enameled three-windowed refrigerator, for cooking, medium, and best butter; and a case for frozen foods, creamy white, the latest thing. As he was admiring it all, he turned to see if anyone was watching him, and when he had reassured himself, and turned again to look through the window, it had been whitened so he could see nothing more. He had to get up then to smoke a cigarette and was tempted to put on his pants and go in slippers quietly down the stairs to see if the window was really soaped up. That it might be kept him there, so he returned to bed, and being still unable to sleep he worked until he had polished, with a bit of rag, a small hole in the center of the white window, and enlarged that till he could make out everything clearly. The store was assembled now, spic-and-span, roomy, ready to receive the goods; it was a pleasure to come in. He whispered to himself this would be good if it was mine, but then the alarm banged in his ear and he had to get up and drag in the milk cases. At 8 A.M. three enormous trucks rolled down the block and six young men in white duck jackets jumped off and packed the store in seven hours. All day Sam's heart beat so hard he sometimes fondled it with his hand as though trying to calm a bird that wanted to fly off.

When the chain store opened in the middle of May, with a horseshoe wreath of roses in the window, Sura counted up that night and proclaimed they were ten dollars short; which wasn't so bad, Sam said, till she reminded him ten times six was sixty. She openly wept, sobbing they must do *something*, driving Sam to a thorough wiping of the shelves with wet cloths she handed him, oiling the floor, and washing, inside and out, the front window, which she redecorated with white tissue paper from the five-and-ten. Then she told him to call the wholesaler, who read off this week's specials; and when they were delivered, Sam packed three cases of cans in a towering pyramid in the window. Only no one seemed to buy. They were fifty dollars short the next week and Sam thought, if it stays like this we can exist, and he cut the price of beer, lettering with black crayon on wrapping paper a sign for the window that beer was reduced in price, thus selling fully five cases more that day, though Sura nagged what was the good of it if they made no profit—lost on paper bags—and the customers who came in for beer went next door for bread and canned goods?

Yet Sam still hoped, but the next week they were seventy-two behind, and in two weeks a clean hundred. The chain store, with a manager and two clerks, was busy all day, but with Sam there was never, any more, anything resembling a rush. Then he discovered that they carried, next door, every brand he had and many he hadn't, and he felt for the barber a furious anger.

That summer, usually better for his business, was bad, and the fall was worse. The store was so silent it got to be a piercing pleasure when someone opened the door. They sat long hours under the unshaded bulb in the rear, reading and re-reading the newspaper, and looking up hopefully when anyone passed by in the street, though trying not to look when they could tell he was going next door. Sam now kept open an hour longer, till midnight, although that wearied him greatly, but he was able, during the extra hour, to pick up a dollar or two among the housewives who had run out of milk, or needed a last-minute loaf of bread for school sandwiches. To cut expenses he put out one of the two lights in the window and a lamp in the store. He had the phone removed, bought his paper bags from peddlers, shaved every second day and, although he would not admit it, ate less. Then in an unexpected burst of optimism he ordered eighteen cases of goods from the jobber and filled the empty sections of his shelves with low-priced items clearly marked, but as Sura said, who saw them if nobody came in? People he had seen every day for ten, fifteen, even twenty years disappeared as if they had moved or died. Sometimes when he was delivering a small order somewhere he saw a former customer who either quickly crossed the street, or ducked the other way and walked around the block. The barber, too, avoided him and he avoided the barber. Sam schemed to give short weight on loose items but couldn't bring himself to. He considered canvassing the neighborhood from house to house for orders he would personally deliver but then remembered Mr. Pellegrino and gave up the idea. Sura, who had all their married life nagged him, now sat silent in the back. When Sam counted the receipts for the first week in December he knew he could no longer hope. The wind blew outside and the store was cold. He offered it for sale but no one would take it.

One morning Sura got up and slowly ripped her cheeks with

her fingernails. Sam went across the street for a haircut. He had formerly had his hair cut once a month, but now it had grown ten weeks and was thickly pelted at the back of the neck. The barber cut it with his eyes shut. Then Sam called an auctioneer, who moved in with two lively assistants and a red auction flag that flapped and furled in the icy breeze as though it were a holiday. The money they got was not a quarter of the sum needed to pay the creditors. Sam and Sura closed the store and moved away. So long as he lived he would not return to the old neighborhood, afraid his store was standing empty, and he dreaded to look through the window.

1949

The Prison

THOUGH HE tried not to think of it, at twenty-nine Tommy Castelli's life was a screaming bore. It wasn't just Rosa or the store they tended for profits counted in pennies, or the unendurably slow hours and endless drivel that went with selling candy, cigarettes, and soda water; it was this sick-in-the-stomach feeling of being trapped in old mistakes, even some he had made before Rosa changed Tony into Tommy. He had been as Tony a kid of many dreams and schemes, especially getting out of this tenement-crowded, kid-squawking neighborhood, with its lousy poverty, but everything had fouled up against him before he could. When he was sixteen he quit the vocational school where they were making him into a shoemaker, and began to hang out with the gray-hatted, thick-soled-shoe boys, who had the spare time and the mazuma and showed it in fat wonderful rolls down in the cellar clubs to all who would look, and everybody did, popeyed. They were the ones who had bought the silver caffe espresso urn and later the television, and they arranged the pizza parties and had the girls down; but it was getting in with them and their cars, leading to the holdup of a liquor store, that had started all the present trouble. Lucky for him the coal-and-ice man who was their landlord knew the leader in the district, and they arranged something so nobody bothered him after that. Then before he knew what was going on—he had been frightened sick by the whole mess—there was his father cooking up a deal with Rosa Agnello's old man that Tony would marry her and the father-in-law would, out of his savings, open a candy store for him to make an honest living. He wouldn't spit on a candy store, and Rosa was too plain and lank a chick for his personal taste, so he beat it off to Texas and bummed around in too much space, and when he came back everybody said it was for Rosa and the candy store, and it was all arranged again and he, without saying no, was in it.

That was how he had landed on Prince Street in the Village, working from eight in the morning to almost midnight every day, except for an hour off each afternoon when he went upstairs to sleep, and on Tuesdays, when the store was closed and he slept some more and went at night alone to the movies. He was too tired always for schemes now, but once he tried to make a little cash on the side by secretly taking in punchboards some syndicate was distributing in the neighborhood, on which he collected a nice cut and in this way saved fifty-five bucks that Rosa didn't know about; but then the syndicate was written up by a newspaper, and the punchboards all disappeared. Another time, when Rosa was at her mother's house, he took a chance and let them put in a slot machine that could guarantee a nice piece of change if he kept it long enough. He knew of course he couldn't hide it from her, so when she came and screamed when she saw it, he was ready and patient, for once not yelling back when she yelled, and he explained it was not the same as gambling because anybody who played it got a roll of mints every time he put in a nickel. Also the machine would supply them a few extra dollars cash they could use to buy a television so he could see the fights without going to a bar; but Rosa wouldn't let up screaming, and later her father came in shouting that he was a criminal and chopped the machine apart with a plumber's hammer. The next day the cops raided for slot machines and gave out summonses wherever they found them, and though Tommy's place was practically the only candy store in the neighborhood that didn't have one, he felt bad about the machine for a long time.

Mornings had been his best time of day because Rosa stayed upstairs cleaning, and since few people came into the store till noon, he could sit around alone, a toothpick in his teeth, looking over the *News* and *Mirror* on the fountain counter, or maybe gab with one of the old cellar-club guys who had happened to come by for a pack of butts, about a horse that was running that day or how the numbers were paying lately; or just sit there, drinking coffee and thinking how far away he could get on the fifty-five he had stashed away in the cellar. Generally the mornings were this way, but after the slot machine, usually the whole day stank and he along with it. Time rotted in him, and all he could think of the whole morning, was going to sleep in the afternoon, and he would wake up with the sour remembrance of the long night in the store ahead of him, while everybody else was doing as he damn pleased. He cursed the candy store and Rosa, and cursed, from its beginning, his unhappy life.

It was on one of these bad mornings that a ten-year-old girl from around the block came in and asked for two rolls of colored tissue paper, one red and one yellow. He wanted to tell her to go to hell and stop bothering, but instead went with bad grace to the rear, where Rosa, whose bright idea it was to keep the stuff, had put it. He went from force of habit, for the girl had been coming in every Monday since the summer for the same thing, because her rock-faced mother, who looked as if she arranged her own widowhood, took care of some small kids after school and gave them the paper to cut out dolls and such things. The girl, whose name he didn't know, resembled her mother, except her features were not quite so sharp and she had very light skin with dark eyes; but she was a plain kid and would be more so at twenty. He had noticed, when he went to get the paper, that she always hung back as if afraid to go where it was dark, though he kept the comics there and most of the other kids had to be slapped away from them; and that when he brought her the tissue paper her skin seemed to grow whiter and her eyes shone. She always handed him two hot dimes and went out without glancing back.

It happened that Rosa, who trusted nobody, had just hung a mirror on the back wall, and as Tommy opened the drawer to get the girl her paper this Monday morning that he felt so bad, he looked up and saw in the glass something that made it seem as if he were dreaming. The girl had disappeared, but he saw a white hand reach into the candy case for a chocolate bar and for another, then she came forth from behind the counter and stood there, innocently waiting for him. He felt at first like grabbing her by the neck and socking till she threw up, but he had been caught, as he sometimes was, by this thought of how his Uncle Dom, years ago before he went away, used to take with him Tony alone of all the kids, when he went crabbing to Sheepshead Bay. Once they went at night and threw the baited wire traps into the water and after a while pulled them up and they had this green lobster in one, and just then this fat-faced cop came along and said they had to throw it back unless it was nine inches. Dom said it was nine inches, but the cop said not to be a wise guy so Dom measured it and it was ten, and they laughed about that lobster all night. Then he remembered how he had felt after Dom was gone, and tears filled his eyes. He found himself thinking about the way his life had turned out, and then about this girl, moved that she was so young and a thief. He felt he ought to do something for her, warn her to cut it out before she got trapped and fouled up her life before it got started. His urge to do this was strong, but when he went forward she looked up frightened because he had taken so long. The fear in her eyes bothered him and he didn't say anything. She thrust out the dimes, grabbed at the tissue rolls and ran out of the store.

He had to sit down. He kept trying to make the desire to speak to her go away, but it came back stronger than ever. He asked himself what difference does it make if she swipes candy— so she swipes it; and the role of reformer was strange and distasteful to him, yet he could not convince himself that what he felt he must do was unimportant. But he worried he would not know what to say to her. Always he had trouble speaking right, stumbled over words, especially in new situations. He was afraid he would sound like a jerk and she would not take him seriously. He had to tell her in a sure way so that even if it scared her, she would understand he had done it to set her straight. He mentioned her to no one but often thought about her, always looking around whenever he went outside to raise the awning or wash the window, to see if any of the girls playing in the street was her, but they never were. The following Monday, an hour after opening the store he had smoked a full pack of butts. He thought he had found what he wanted to say but was afraid for some reason she wouldn't come in, or if she did, this time she would be afraid to take the candy. He wasn't sure he wanted that to happen until he had said what he had to say. But at about eleven, while he was reading the *News*, she appeared, asking for the tissue paper, her eyes shining so he had to look away. He knew she meant to steal. Going to the rear he slowly opened the drawer, keeping his head lowered as he sneaked a look into the glass and saw her slide behind the counter. His heart beat hard and his feet felt nailed to the floor. He tried to remember what he had intended to do, but his mind was like a dark, empty room so he let her, in the end, slip away and stood tongue-tied, the dimes burning his palm.

Afterwards, he told himself that he hadn't spoken to her because it was while she still had the candy on her, and she would have been scared worse than he wanted. When he went upstairs, instead of sleeping, he sat at the kitchen window, looking out into the back yard. He blamed himself for being too soft, too chicken, but then he thought, no there was a better way to do it. He would do it indirectly, slip her a hint he knew, and he was pretty sure that would stop her. Sometime after, he would explain her why it was good she had stopped. So next time he cleaned out this candy platter she helped herself from, thinking she might get wise he was on to her, but she seemed not to, only hesitated with her hand before she took two candy bars from the next plate and dropped them into the black patent leather purse she always had with her. The time after that he cleaned out the whole top shelf, and still she was not suspicious, and reached down to the next and took something different. One Monday he put some loose change, nickels and dimes, on the candy plate, but she left them there, only taking the candy, which bothered him a little. Rosa asked him what he was mooning about so much and why was he eating chocolate lately. He didn't answer her, and she began to look suspiciously at the women who came in, not excluding the little girls; and he would have been glad to rap her in the teeth, but it didn't matter as long as she didn't know what he had on his mind. At the same time he figured he would have to do something sure soon, or it would get harder for the girl to stop her stealing. He had to be strong about it. Then he thought of a plan that satisfied him. He would leave two bars on the plate and put in the wrapper of one a note she could read when she was alone. He tried out on paper many messages to her, and the one that seemed best he cleanly printed on a strip of cardboard and slipped it under the wrapper of one chocolate bar. It said, "Don't do this any more or you will suffer your whole life." He puzzled whether to sign it A Friend or Your Friend and finally chose Your Friend.

This was Friday, and he could not hold his impatience for Monday. But on Monday she did not appear. He waited for a long time, until Rosa came down, then he had to go up and the girl still hadn't come. He was greatly disappointed because she had never failed to come before. He lay on the bed, his shoes on, staring at the ceiling. He felt hurt, the sucker she had played him for and was now finished with because she probably had another on her hook. The more he thought about it the worse he felt. He worked up a splitting headache that kept him from sleeping, then he suddenly slept and woke without it. But he had awaked depressed, saddened. He thought about Dom getting out of jail and going away God knows where. He wondered whether he would ever meet up with him somewhere, if he took the fifty-five bucks and left. Then he remembered Dom was a pretty old guy now, and he might not know him if they did meet. He thought about life. You never really got what you wanted. No matter how hard you tried you made mistakes and couldn't get past them. You could never see the sky outside or the ocean because you were in a prison, except nobody called it a prison, and if you did they didn't know what you were talking about, or they said they didn't. A pall settled on him. He lay motionless, without thought or sympathy for himself or anybody.

But when he finally went downstairs, ironically amused that Rosa had allowed him so long a time off without bitching, there were people in the store and he could hear her screeching. Shoving his way through the crowd he saw in one sickening look that she had caught the girl with the candy bars and was shaking her so hard the kid's head bounced back and forth like a balloon on a stick. With a curse he tore her away from the girl, whose sickly face showed the depth of her fright.

"Whatsamatter," he shouted at Rosa, "you want her blood?"

"She's a thief," cried Rosa.

"Shut your face."

To stop her yowling he slapped her across her mouth, but it was a harder crack than he had intended. Rosa fell back with a gasp. She did not cry but looked around dazedly at everybody, and tried to smile, and everybody there could see her teeth were flecked with blood.

"Go home," Tommy ordered the girl, but then there was a movement near the door and her mother came into the store.

"What happened?" she said.

"She stole my candy," Rosa cried.

"I let her take it," said Tommy.

Rosa stared at him as if she had been hit again, then with mouth distorted began to sob.

"One was for you, Mother," said the girl.

Her mother socked her hard across the face. "You little thief, this time you'll get your hands burned good."

She pawed at the girl, grabbed her arm and yanked it. The girl, like a grotesque dancer, half ran, half fell forward, but at the door she managed to turn her white face and thrust out at him her red tongue.

1949

The First Seven Years

FELD, THE shoemaker, was annoyed that his helper, Sobel, was so insensitive to his reverie that he wouldn't for a minute cease his fanatic pounding at the other bench. He gave him a look, but Sobel's bald head was bent over the last as he worked, and he didn't notice. The shoemaker shrugged and continued to peer through the partly frosted window at the nearsighted haze of falling February snow. Neither the shifting white blur outside, nor the sudden deep remembrance of the snowy Polish village where he had wasted his youth, could turn his thoughts from Max the college boy (a constant visitor in the mind since early that morning when Feld saw him trudging through the snowdrifts on his way to school), whom he so much respected because of the sacrifices he had made throughout the years—in winter or direst heat—to further his education. An old wish returned to haunt the shoemaker: that he had had a son instead of a daughter, but this blew away in the snow, for Feld, if anything, was a practical man. Yet he could not help but contrast the diligence of the boy, who was a peddler's son, with Miriam's unconcern for an education. True, she was always with a book in her hand, yet when the opportunity arose for a college education, she had said no she would rather find a job. He had begged her to go, pointing out how many fathers could not afford to send their children to college, but she said she wanted to be independent. As for education, what was it, she asked, but books, which Sobel, who diligently read the classics, would as usual advise her on. Her answer greatly grieved her father.

A figure emerged from the snow and the door opened. At the counter the man withdrew from a wet paper bag a pair of battered shoes for repair. Who he was the shoemaker for a moment had no idea, then his heart trembled as he realized, before he had thoroughly discerned the face, that Max himself was standing there, embarrassedly explaining what he wanted done to his old shoes. Though Feld listened eagerly, he couldn't hear a word, for the opportunity that had burst upon him was deafening.

He couldn't exactly recall when the thought had occurred to him, because it was clear he had more than once considered suggesting to the boy that he go out with Miriam. But he had not dared speak, for if Max said no, how would he face him again? Or suppose Miriam, who harped so often on independence, blew up in anger and shouted at him for his meddling? Still, the chance was too good to let by: all it meant was an introduction. They might long ago have become friends had they happened to meet somewhere, therefore was it not his duty—an obligation—to bring them together, nothing more, a harmless connivance to replace an accidental encounter in the subway, let's say, or a mutual friend's introduction in the street? Just let him once see and talk to her and he would for sure be interested. As for Miriam, what possible harm for a working girl in an office, who met only loudmouthed salesmen and illiterate shipping clerks, to make the acquaintance of a fine scholarly boy? Maybe he would awaken in her a desire to go to college; if not—the shoemaker's mind at last came to grips with the truth—let her marry an educated man and live a better life.

When Max finished describing what he wanted done to his shoes, Feld marked them, both with enormous holes in the soles which he pretended not to notice, with large white-chalk X's and the rubber heels, thinned to the nails, he marked with O's, though it troubled him he might have mixed up the letters. Max inquired the price, and the shoemaker cleared his throat and asked the boy, above Sobel's insistent hammering, would he please step through the side door there into the hall. Though surprised, Max did as the shoemaker requested, and Feld went in after him. For a minute they were both silent, because Sobel had stopped banging, and it seemed they understood neither was to say anything until the noise began again. When it did, loudly, the shoemaker quickly told Max why he had asked to talk to him.

"Ever since you went to high school," he said, in the dimly lit hallway, "I watched you in the morning go to the subway to school, and I said always to myself, this is a fine boy that he wants so much an education."

"Thanks," Max said, nervously alert. He was tall and grotesquely thin, with sharply cut features, particularly a beak-like nose. He was wearing a loose, long, slushy overcoat that hung down to his ankles, looking like a rug draped over his bony shoulders, and a soggy old brown hat, as battered as the shoes he had brought in.

"I am a businessman," the shoemaker abruptly said to conceal his embarrassment, "so I will explain you right away why I talk to you. I have a girl, my daughter Miriam—she is nineteen—a very nice girl and also so pretty that everybody looks on her when she passes by in the street. She is smart, always with a book, and I thought to myself that a boy like you, an educated boy—I thought maybe you will be interested sometime to meet a girl like this." He laughed a bit when he had finished and was tempted to say more but had the good sense not to.

Max stared down like a hawk. For an uncomfortable second he was silent, then he asked, "Did you say nineteen?"

"Yes."

"Would it be all right to inquire if you have a picture of her?"

"Just a minute." The shoemaker went into the store and hastily returned with a snapshot that Max held up to the light.

"She's all right," he said.

Feld waited.

"And is she sensible—not the flighty kind?"

"She is very sensible."

After another short pause, Max said it was okay with him if he met her.

"Here is my telephone," said the shoemaker, hurriedly handing him a slip of paper. "Call her up. She comes home from work six o'clock."

Max folded the paper and tucked it away into his worn leather wallet.

"About the shoes," he said. "How much did you say they will cost me?"

"Don't worry about the price."

"I just like to have an idea."

"A dollar—dollar fifty. A dollar fifty," the shoemaker said.

At once he felt bad, for he usually charged $2.25 for this kind of job. Either he should have asked the regular price or done the work for nothing.

Later, as he entered the store, he was startled by a violent clanging and looked up to see Sobel pounding upon the naked last. It broke, the iron striking the floor and jumping with a thump against the wall, but before the enraged shoemaker could cry out, the assistant had torn his hat and coat off the hook and rushed out into the snow.

So Feld, who had looked forward to anticipating how it would go with his daughter and Max, instead had a great worry on his mind. Without his temperamental helper he was a lost man, especially as it was years now since he had carried the store alone. The shoemaker had for an age suffered from a heart condition that threatened collapse if he dared exert himself. Five years ago, after an attack, it had appeared as though he would have either to sacrifice his business on the auction block and live on a pittance thereafter, or put himself at the mercy of some unscrupulous employee who would in the end probably ruin him. But just at the moment of his darkest despair, this Polish refugee, Sobel, had appeared one night out of the street and begged for work. He was a stocky man, poorly dressed, with a bald head that had once been blond, a severely plain face, and soft blue eyes prone to tears over the sad books he read, a young man but old—no one would have guessed thirty. Though he confessed he knew nothing of shoemaking, he said he was apt and would work for very little if Feld taught him the trade. Thinking that with, after all, a landsman, he would have less to fear than from a complete stranger, Feld took him on and within six weeks the refugee rebuilt as good a shoe as he, and not long thereafter expertly ran the business for the thoroughly relieved shoemaker.

Feld could trust him with anything and did, frequently going home after an hour or two at the store, leaving all the money in the till, knowing Sobel would guard every cent of it. The amazing thing was that he demanded so little. His wants were few; in money he wasn't interested—in nothing but books, it seemed—which he one by one lent to Miriam, together with his profuse, queer written comments, manufactured during his lonely rooming house evenings, thick pads of commentary which the shoemaker peered at and twitched his shoulders over as his daughter, from her fourteenth year, read page by sanctified page, as if the word of God were inscribed on them. To protect Sobel, Feld himself had to see that he received more than he asked for. Yet his conscience bothered him for not insisting that the assistant accept a better wage than he was getting, though Feld had honestly told him he could earn a handsome salary if he worked elsewhere, or maybe opened a place of his own. But the assistant answered, somewhat ungraciously, that he was not interested in going elsewhere, and though Feld frequently asked himself, What keeps him here? why does he stay? he finally answered it that the man, no doubt because of his terrible experiences as a refugee, was afraid of the world.

After the incident with the broken last, angered by Sobel's behavior, the shoemaker decided to let him stew for a week in the rooming house, although his own strength was taxed dangerously and the business suffered. However, after several sharp nagging warnings from both his wife and daughter, he went finally in search of Sobel, as he had once before, quite recently, when over some fancied slight—Feld had merely asked him not to give Miriam so many books to read because her eyes were strained and red—the assistant had left the place in a huff, an incident which, as usual, came to nothing, for he had returned after the shoemaker had talked to him, and taken his seat at the bench. But this time, after Feld had plodded through the snow to Sobel's house—he had thought of sending Miriam but the idea became repugnant to him—the burly landlady at the door informed him in a nasal voice that Sobel was not at home, and though Feld knew this was a nasty lie, for where had the refugee to go? still for some reason he was not completely sure of—it may have been the cold and his fatigue—he decided not to insist on seeing him. Instead he went home and hired a new helper.

Thus he settled the matter, though not entirely to his satisfaction, for he had much more to do than before, and so, for example, could no longer lie late in bed mornings because he had to get up to open the store for the new assistant, a speechless, dark man with an irritating rasp as he worked, whom he would not trust with the key as he had Sobel. Furthermore, this one, though able to do a fair repair job, knew nothing of grades of leather or prices, so Feld had to make his own purchases; and every night at closing time it was necessary to count the money in the till and lock up. However, he was not dissatisfied, for he lived much in his thoughts of Max and Miriam. The college boy had called her, and they had arranged a meeting for this coming Friday night. The shoemaker would personally have preferred Saturday, which he felt would make it a date of the first magnitude, but he learned Friday was Miriam's choice, so he said nothing. The day of the week did not matter. What mattered was the aftermath. Would they like each other and want to be friends? He sighed at all the time that would have to go by before he knew for sure. Often he was tempted to talk to Miriam about the boy, to ask whether she thought she would like his type—he had told her only that he considered Max a nice boy and had suggested he call her— but the one time he tried she snapped at him—justly—how should she know?

At last Friday came. Feld was not feeling particularly well so he stayed in bed, and Mrs. Feld thought it better to remain in the bedroom with him when Max called. Miriam received the boy, and her parents could hear their voices, his throaty one, as they talked. Just before leaving, Miriam brought Max to the bedroom door and he stood there a minute, a tall, slightly hunched figure wearing a thick, droopy suit, and apparently at ease as he greeted the shoemaker and his wife, which was surely a good sign. And Miriam, although she had worked all day, looked fresh and pretty. She was a large-framed girl with a well-shaped body, and she had a fine open face and soft hair. They made, Feld thought, a first-class couple.

Miriam returned after 11:30. Her mother was already asleep, but the shoemaker got out of bed and after locating his bathrobe went into the kitchen, where Miriam, to his surprise, sat at the table, reading.

"So where did you go?" Feld asked pleasantly.

"For a walk," she said, not looking up.

"I advised him," Feld said, clearing his throat, "he shouldn't spend so much money."

"I didn't care."

The shoemaker boiled up some water for tea and sat down at the table with a cupful and a thick slice of lemon.

"So how," he sighed after a sip, "did you enjoy?"

"It was all right."

He was silent. She must have sensed his disappointment, for she added, "You can't really tell much the first time."

"You will see him again?"

Turning a page, she said that Max had asked for another date.

"For when?"

"Saturday."

"So what did you say?"

"What did I say?" she asked, delaying for a moment—"I said yes."

Afterwards she inquired about Sobel, and Feld, without exactly knowing why, said the assistant had got another job. Miriam said nothing more and went on reading. The shoemaker's conscience did not trouble him; he was satisfied with the Saturday date.

During the week, by placing here and there a deft question, he managed to get from Miriam some information about Max. It surprised him to learn that the boy was not studying to be either a doctor or lawyer but was taking a business course leading to a degree in accountancy. Feld was a little disappointed because he thought of accountants as bookkeepers and would have preferred "a higher profession." However, it was not long before he had investigated the subject and discovered that Certified Public Accountants were highly respected people, so he was thoroughly content as Saturday approached. But because Saturday was a busy day, he was much in the store and therefore did not see Max when he came to call for Miriam. From his wife he learned there had been nothing especially revealing about their greeting. Max had rung the bell and Miriam had got her coat and left with him—nothing more. Feld did not probe, for his wife was not particularly observant. Instead, he waited up for Miriam with a newspaper on his lap, which he scarcely looked at so lost was he in thinking of the future. He awoke to find her in the room with him, tiredly removing her hat. Greeting her, he was suddenly inexplicably afraid to ask anything about the evening. But since she volunteered nothing he was at last forced to inquire how she had enjoyed herself. Miriam began something noncommittal, but apparently changed her mind, for she said after a minute, "I was bored."

When Feld had sufficiently recovered from his anguished disappointment to ask why, she answered without hesitation, "Because he's nothing more than a materialist."

"What means this word?"

"He has no soul. He's only interested in things."

He considered her statement for a long time, then asked, "Will you see him again?"

"He didn't ask."

"Suppose he will ask you?"

"I won't see him."

He did not argue; however, as the days went by he hoped increasingly she would change her mind. He wished the boy would telephone, because he was sure there was more to him than Miriam, with her inexperienced eye, could discern. But Max didn't call. As a matter of fact he took a different route to school, no longer passing the shoemaker's store, and Feld was deeply hurt.

Then one afternoon Max came in and asked for his shoes. The shoemaker took them down from the shelf where he had placed them, apart from the other pairs. He had done the work himself and the soles and heels were well built and firm. The shoes had been highly polished and somehow looked better than new. Max's Adam's apple went up once when he saw them, and his eyes had little lights in them.

"How much?" he asked, without directly looking at the shoemaker.

"Like I told you before," Feld answered sadly. "One dollar fifty cents."

Max handed him two crumpled bills and received in return a newly minted silver half dollar.

He left. Miriam had not been mentioned. That night the shoemaker discovered that his new assistant had been all the while stealing from him, and he suffered a heart attack.

Though the attack was very mild, he lay in bed for three weeks. Miriam spoke of going for Sobel, but sick as he was Feld rose in wrath against the idea. Yet in his heart he knew there was no other way, and the first weary day back in the shop thoroughly convinced him, so that night after supper he dragged himself to Sobel's rooming house.

He toiled up the stairs, though he knew it was bad for him, and at the top knocked at the door. Sobel opened it and the shoemaker entered. The room was a small, poor one, with a single window facing the street. It contained a narrow cot, a low table, and several stacks of books piled haphazardly around on the floor along the wall, which made him think how queer Sobel was, to be uneducated and read so much. He had once asked him, Sobel, why you read so much? and the assistant could not answer him. Did you ever study in a college someplace? he had asked, but Sobel shook his head. He read, he said, to know. But to know what, the shoemaker demanded, and to know, why? Sobel never explained, which proved he read so much because he was queer.

Feld sat down to recover his breath. The assistant was resting on his bed with his heavy back to the wall. His shirt and trousers were clean, and his stubby fingers, away from the shoemaker's bench, were strangely pallid. His face was thin and pale, as if he had been shut in this room since the day he had bolted from the store.

"So when you will come back to work?" Feld asked him.

To his surprise, Sobel burst out, "Never."

Jumping up, he strode over to the window that looked out upon the miserable street. "Why should I come back?" he cried.

"I will raise your wages."

"Who cares for your wages!"

The shoemaker, knowing he didn't care, was at a loss what else to say.

"What do you want from me, Sobel?"

"Nothing."

"I always treated you like you was my son."

Sobel vehemently denied it. "So why you look for strange boys in the street they should go out with Miriam? Why you don't think of me?"

The shoemaker's hands and feet turned freezing cold. His voice became so hoarse he couldn't speak. At last he cleared his throat and croaked, "So what has my daughter got to do with a shoemaker thirty-five years old who works for me?"

"Why do you think I worked so long for you?" Sobel cried out. "For the stingy wages I sacrificed five years of my life so you could have to eat and drink and where to sleep?"

"Then for what?" shouted the shoemaker.

"For Miriam," he blurted—"for her."

The shoemaker, after a time, managed to say, "I pay wages in cash, Sobel," and lapsed into silence. Though he was seething with excitement, his mind was coldly clear, and he had to admit to himself he had sensed all along that Sobel felt this way. He had never so much as thought it consciously, but he had felt it and was afraid.

"Miriam knows?" he muttered hoarsely.

"She knows."

"You told her?"

"No."

"Then how does she know?"

"How does she know?" Sobel said. "Because she knows. She knows who I am and what is in my heart."

Feld had a sudden insight. In some devious way, with his books and commentary, Sobel had given Miriam to understand that he loved her. The shoemaker felt a terrible anger at him for his deceit.

"Sobel, you are crazy," he said bitterly. "She will never marry a man so old and ugly like you."

Sobel turned black with rage. He cursed the shoemaker, but then, though he trembled to hold it in, his eyes filled with tears and he broke into deep sobs. With his back to Feld, he stood at the window, fists clenched, and his shoulders shook with his choked sobbing.

Watching him, the shoemaker's anger diminished. His teeth were on edge with pity for the man, and his eyes grew moist. How strange and sad that a refugee, a grown man, bald and old with his miseries, who had by the skin of his teeth escaped Hitler's incinerators, should fall in love, when he had got to America, with a girl less than half his age. Day after day, for five years he had sat at his bench, cutting and hammering away, waiting for the girl to become a woman, unable to ease his heart with speech, knowing no protest but desperation.

"Ugly I didn't mean," he said half aloud.

Then he realized that what he had called ugly was not Sobel but Miriam's life if she married him. He felt for his daughter a strange and gripping sorrow, as if she were already Sobel's bride, the wife, after all, of a shoemaker, and had in her life no more than her mother had had. And all his dreams for her—why he had slaved and destroyed his heart with anxiety and labor—all these dreams of a better life were dead.

The room was quiet. Sobel was standing by the window reading, and it was curious that when he read he looked young.

"She is only nineteen," Feld said brokenly. "This is too young yet to get married. Don't ask her for two years more, till she is twenty-one, then you can talk to her."

Sobel didn't answer. Feld rose and left. He went slowly down the stairs but once outside, though it was an icy night and the crisp falling snow whitened the street, he walked with a stronger stride.

But the next morning, when the shoemaker arrived, heavy-hearted, to open the store, he saw he needn't have come, for his assistant was already seated at the last, pounding leather for his love.

1950

The Death of Me

MARCUS WAS a tailor, long ago before the war, a buoyant man with a bushy head of graying hair, fine fragile brows, and benevolent hands, who comparatively late in life had become a clothier. Because he had prospered, so to say, into ill health, he had to employ an assistant tailor in the rear room, who made alterations on garments but could not, when the work piled high, handle the pressing, so that it became necessary to put on a presser; therefore though the store did well, it did not do too well.

It might have done better but the presser, Josip Bruzak, a heavy, beery, perspiring Pole, who worked in undershirt and felt slippers, his pants loose on his beefy hips, the legs crumpling around his ankles, conceived a violent dislike for Emilio Vizo, the tailor—or it worked the other way, Marcus wasn't sure—a thin, dry, pigeon-chested Sicilian, who bore or returned the Pole a steely malice. Because of their quarrels the business suffered.

Why they should fight as they did, fluttering and snarling like angry cocks, and using, in the bargain, terrible language, loud coarse words that affronted the customers and sometimes made the embarrassed Marcus feel dizzy to the point of fainting, mystified the clothier, who knew their troubles and felt they were, as people, much alike. Bruzak, who lived in a half-ruined rooming house near the East River, constantly guzzled beer at work and kept a dozen bottles in a rusty pan full of ice. When Marcus, in the beginning, objected, Josip, always respectful to the clothier, locked away the pan and disappeared through the back door into the tavern down the block where he had his glass, in the process wasting so much precious time it paid Marcus to tell him to go back to the pan. Every day at lunch Josip pulled out of the drawer a small sharp knife and cut chunks of the hard garlic salami he ate with puffy lumps of white bread, washing it all down with beer and then black coffee brewed on the one-burner gas stove for the tailor's iron. Sometimes he cooked up a soupy mess of cabbage which stank up the store, but on the whole neither the salami nor the cabbage interested him, and for days he seemed weary and uneasy until the mailman brought him, about every third week, a letter from the other side. When the letters came, he more than once tore them in half with his bumbling fingers; he forgot his work, and sitting on a backless chair, fished out of the same drawer where he kept his salami a pair of cracked eyeglasses which he attached to his ears by means of looped cords he had tied on in place of the broken sidepieces. Then he read the tissue sheets he held in his fist, a crabbed Polish writing in faded brown ink whose every word he uttered aloud so that Marcus, who understood the language but preferred not to hear, heard. Before the presser had dipped two sentences into the letter, his face dissolved and he cried, tears smearing his cheeks and chin so that it looked as though he had been sprayed with something to kill flies. At the end he fell into a roar of sobbing, a terrible thing to behold, which incapacitated him for hours and wasted the morning.

Marcus had often thought of telling him to read his letters at home, but the news in them wrung his heart and he could not bring himself to scold Josip, who was, by the way, a master presser. Once he began on a pile of suits, the steaming machine hissed without letup, and every garment came out neat, without puff or excessive crease, and the arms, legs, and pleats were as sharp as knives. As for the news in the letters it was always the same, concerning the sad experiences of his tubercular wife and unfortunate fourteen-year-old son, whom Josip, except in pictures, had never seen, a boy who lived, literally, in the mud with the pigs, and was also sick, so that even if his father saved up money for his passage to America, and the boy could obtain a visa, he would never get past the immigration doctors. Marcus more than once gave the presser a suit of clothes to send to his son, and occasionally some cash, but he wondered if these things ever got to him. He had the uncomfortable thought that Josip, in the last fourteen years, might have brought the boy over had he wanted, his wife too, before she had contracted tuberculosis, but for some reason he preferred to weep over them where they were.

Emilio, the tailor, was another lone wolf. Every day he had a forty-cent lunch in the diner about three blocks away but returned early to read his *Corriere*. His strangeness was that he was always whispering to himself. No one could understand what he said, but it was sibilant and insistent, and wherever he stood, one could hear his hissing voice urging something, or moaning softly though he never wept. He whispered when he sewed a button on, or shortened a sleeve, or when he used the iron. Whispering when he hung up his coat in the morning, he was still whispering when he put on his black hat, wriggled his sparse shoulders into his coat, and left, in loneliness, the store at night. Only once did he hint what the whispering was about; when the clothier, noticing his pallor one morning, brought him a cup of coffee, in gratitude the tailor confided that his wife, who had returned last week, had left him again this, and he held up the outstretched fingers of one bony hand to show she had five times run out on him. Marcus offered the man his sympathy, and thereafter when he heard the tailor whispering in the rear of the store, could always picture the wife coming back to him from wherever she had been, saying she was this time—she swore—going to stay for good, but at night when they were in bed and he was whispering about her in the dark, she would think to herself she was sick of this and in the morning was gone. And so the man's ceaseless whisper irritated Marcus; he had to leave the store to hear silence, yet he kept Emilio on because he was a fine tailor, a demon with a needle, who could sew up a perfect cuff in less time than it takes an ordinary workman to take measurements, the kind of tailor who, when you were looking for one, was very rare.

For more than a year, despite the fact that they both made noises in the rear room, neither the presser nor the tailor seemed to notice one another; then one day, as though an invisible wall between them had fallen, they were at each other's throat. Marcus, it appeared, walked in at the very birth of their venom, when, leaving a customer in the store one afternoon, he went back to get a piece of marking chalk and came on a sight that froze him. There they were in the afternoon sunlight that flooded the rear of the shop, momentarily blinding the clothier so that he had time to think he couldn't possibly be seeing what he saw—the two at opposite corners staring stilly at one another—a live, almost hairy staring of intense hatred. The sneering Pole in one trembling hand squeezed a heavy wooden pressing block, while the livid tailor, his back like a cat's against the wall, held aloft in his rigid fingers a pair of cutter's shears.

"What is it?" Marcus shouted when he had recovered his voice, but neither of them would break the stone silence and remained as when he had discovered them, glaring across the shop at the other, the tailor's lips moving, and the presser breathing like a dog in heat, an eeriness about them that Marcus had never suspected.

"My God," he cried, his body drenched in cold creeping wetness, "tell me what happened here." But neither uttered a sound, so he shrieked through the constriction in his throat, which made the words grate awfully, "Go back to work—" hardly believing they would obey; and when they did, Bruzak turning like a lump back to the machine, and the tailor stiffly to his hot iron, Marcus was softened by their compliance and, speaking as if to children, said with tears in his eyes, "Boys, remember, don't fight."

Afterwards the clothier stood alone in the shade of the store, staring through the glass of the front door at nothing at all; lost, in thinking of them at his very back, in a horrid world of gray grass and mottled sunlight, of moaning and blood-smell. They had made him dizzy. He lowered himself into the leather chair, praying no customer would enter until he had sufficiently recovered from his nausea. So sighing, he shut his eyes and felt his skull liven with new terror to see them both engaged in round pursuit in his mind. One ran hot after the other, lumbering but in flight, who had stolen his box of broken buttons. Skirting the lit and smoking sands, they scrambled high up a craggy cliff, locked in two-handed struggle, teetering on the ledge, till one slipped in slime and pulled the other with him. Reaching forth empty hands, they clutched nothing in stiffened fingers, as Marcus, the watcher, shrieked without sound at their evanescence.

He sat dizzily until these thoughts had left him.

When he was again himself, remembrance made it a kind of dream. He denied any untoward incident had happened; yet knowing it had, called it a triviality—hadn't he, in the factory he had worked in on coming to America, often seen such fights among the men?—trivial things they all forgot, no matter how momentarily fierce.

However, on the very next day, and thereafter without skipping a day, the two in the back broke out of their hatred into thunderous quarreling that did damage to the business; in ugly voices they called each other dirty names, embarrassing the clothier so that he threw the measuring tape he wore like a garment on his shoulders once around his neck. Customer and clothier glanced nervously at each other, and Marcus quickly ran through the measurements; the customer, who as a rule liked to linger in talk of his new clothes, left hurriedly after paying cash, to escape the drone of disgusting names hurled about in the back yet clearly heard in front so that no one had privacy.

Not only would they curse and heap destruction on each other but they muttered in their respective tongues other dreadful things. The clothier understood Josip shouting he would tear off someone's genitals and rub the bloody mess in salt; so he guessed Emilio was shrieking the same things, and was saddened and maddened at once.

He went many times to the rear, pleading with them, and they listened to his every word with interest and tolerance, because the clothier, besides being a kind man—this showed in his eyes—was also eloquent, which they both enjoyed. Yet, whatever his words, they did no good, for the minute he had finished and turned his back on them they began again. Embittered, Marcus withdrew into the store and sat nursing his misery under the yellow-faced clock ticking away yellow minutes, till it was time to stop—it was amazing they got anything done—and go home.

His urge was to bounce them out on their behinds but he couldn't conceive where to find two others who were such skilled and, in essence, proficient workers, without having to pay a fortune in gold. Therefore, with reform uppermost in his mind, he caught Emilio one noon as he was leaving for lunch, whispered him into a corner and said, "Listen, Emilio, you're the smart one, tell me why do you fight? Why do you hate him and why does he hate you, and why do you use such bad words?"

Though he enjoyed the whispering and was soft in the clothier's palms, the tailor, who liked these little attentions, lowered his eyes and blushed darkly, but either would not or could not reply.

So Marcus sat under the clock all afternoon with his fingers in his ears. And he caught the presser on his way out that evening and said to him, "Please, Josip, tell me what he did to you? Josip, why do you fight, you have a sick wife and boy?" But Josip, who also felt an affection for the clothier—he was, despite Polish, no anti-Semite—merely caught him in his hammy arms, and though he had to clutch at his trousers which were falling and impeding his movements, hugged Marcus in a ponderous polka, then with a cackle pushed him aside, and in his beer jag, danced away.

When they began the same dirty hullabaloo the next morning and drove a customer out at once, the clothier stormed into the rear and they turned from their cursing—both fatigued and green-gray to the gills—and listened to Marcus begging, shaming, weeping, but especially paid heed when he, who found screeching unsuited to him, dropped it and gave advice and little preachments in a low becoming tone. He was a tall man, and because of his illness, quite thin. What flesh remained had wasted further in these troublesome months, and his hair was white now so that, as he stood before them, expostulating, exhorting, he was in appearance like an old hermit, if not a saint, and the workers showed respect and keen interest as he spoke.

It was a homily about his long-dead dear father, when they were all children living in a rutted village of small huts, a gaunt family of ten—nine boys and an undersized girl. Oh, they were marvelously poor: on occasion he had chewed bark and even grass, bloating his belly, and often the boys bit one another, including the sister, upon the arms and neck in rage at their hunger.

"So my poor father, who had a long beard down to here"— he stooped reaching his hand to his knee and at once tears sprang up in Josip's eyes—"my father said, 'Children, we are poor people and strangers wherever we go, let us at least live in peace, or if not—'"

But the clothier was not able to finish because the presser, plumped down on the backless chair, where he read his letters, swaying a little, had begun to whimper and then bawl, and the tailor, who was making odd clicking noises in his throat, had to turn away.

"Promise," Marcus begged, "that you won't fight any more."

Josip wept his promise, and Emilio, with wet eyes, gravely nodded.

This, the clothier exulted, was fellowship, and with a blessing on both their heads, departed, but even before he was altogether gone the air behind him was greased with their fury.

Twenty-four hours later he fenced them in. A carpenter came and built a thick partition, halving the presser's and tailor's work space, and for once there was astonished quiet between them. They were, in fact, absolutely silent for a full week. Marcus, had he had the energy, would have jumped in joy, and kicked his heels together. He noticed, of course, that the presser occasionally stopped pressing and came befuddled to the new door to see if the tailor was still there, and though the tailor did the same, it went no further than that. Thereafter Emilio Vizo no longer whispered to himself and Josip Bruzak touched no beer; and when the emaciated letters arrived from the other side, he took them home to read by the dirty window of his dark room; when night came, though there was electricity, he preferred to read by candlelight.

One Monday morning he opened his table drawer to get at his garlic salami and found it had been roughly broken in two. With his pointed knife, he rushed at the tailor, who, at that very moment, because someone had battered his black hat, was coming at him with his burning iron. He caught the presser along the calf of the arm and opened a smelly purple wound, just as Josip stuck him in the groin, and the knife hung there for a minute.

Roaring, wailing, the clothier ran in, and, despite their wounds, sent them packing. When he left, they locked themselves together and choked necks.

Marcus rushed in again, shouting, "No, no, please, *please*," flailing his withered arms, nauseated, enervated (all he could hear in the uproar was the thundering clock), and his heart, like a fragile pitcher, toppled from the shelf and bump-bumped down the stairs, cracking at the bottom, the shards flying everywhere.

Although the old Jew's eyes were glazed as he crumpled, the assassins could plainly read in them, What did I tell you? *You see?*

1951

The Bill

THOUGH THE street was somewhere near a river, it was landlocked and narrow, a crooked row of aged brick tenement buildings. A child throwing a ball straight up saw a bit of pale sky. On the corner, opposite the blackened tenement where Schlegel worked as janitor, stood another like it except that this included the only store on the street—going down five stone steps into the basement, a small, dark delicatessen owned by Mr. and Mrs. F. Panessa, really a hole in the wall.

They had just bought it with the last of their money, Mrs. Panessa told the janitor's wife, so as not to have to depend on either of their daughters, both of whom, Mrs. Schlegel understood, were married to selfish men who had badly affected their characters. To be completely independent of them, Panessa, a retired factory worker, withdrew his three thousand of savings and bought this little delicatessen store. When Mrs. Schlegel, looking around—though she knew the delicatessen quite well for the many years she and Willy had been janitors across the way—when she asked, "Why did you buy this one?" Mrs. Panessa cheerfully replied because it was a small place and they would not have to overwork; Panessa was sixty-three. They were not here to coin money but to support themselves without working too hard. After talking it over many nights and days, they had decided that the store would at least give them a living. She gazed into Etta Schlegel's gaunt eyes and Etta said she hoped so.

She told Willy about the new people across the street who had bought out the Jew, and said to buy there if there was a chance; she meant by that they would continue to shop at the self-service, but when they had forgotten to buy something, they could go to Panessa's. Willy did as he was told. He was tall and broad-backed, with a heavy face seamed dark from the coal and ashes he shoveled around all winter, and his hair often looked gray from the dust the wind whirled up at him out of the ashcans, when he was lining them up for the sanitation truck. Always in overalls—he complained he never stopped working—he would drift across the street and down the steps when something was needed, and lighting his pipe, would stand around talking to Mrs. Panessa as her husband, a small bent man with a fitful smile, stood behind the counter waiting for the janitor after a long interval of talk to ask, upon reflection, for a dime's worth of this or that, the whole business never amounting to more than half a dollar. Then one day Willy got to talking about how the tenants goaded him all the time, and what the cruel and stingy landlord could think up for him to do in that smelly five-floor dungeon. He was absorbed by what he was saying and before he knew it had run up a three-dollar order, though all he had on him was fifty cents. Willy looked like a dog that had just had a licking, but Mr. Panessa, after clearing his throat, chirped up it didn't matter, he could pay the rest whenever he wanted. He said that everything was run on credit, business and everything else, because after all what was credit but the fact that people were human beings, and if you were really a human being you gave credit to somebody else and he gave credit to you. That surprised Willy because he had never heard a storekeeper say it before. After a couple of days he paid the two-fifty, but when Panessa said he could trust whenever he felt like it, Willy sucked a flame into his pipe, then began to order all sorts of things.

When he brought home two large bagfuls of stuff, Etta shouted he must be crazy. Willy answered he had charged everything and paid no cash.

"But we have to pay sometime, don't we?" Etta shouted. "And we have to pay higher prices than in the self-service." She said then what she always said, "We're poor people, Willy. We can't afford too much."

Though Willy saw the justice of her remarks, despite her scolding he still went across the street and trusted. Once he had a crumpled ten-dollar bill in his pants pocket and the amount came to less than four, but he didn't offer to pay, and let Panessa write it in the book. Etta knew he had the money so she screamed when he admitted he had bought on credit.

"Why are you doing it for? Why don't you pay if you have the money?"

He didn't answer but after a time he said there were other things he had to buy once in a while. He went into the furnace room and came out with a wrapped package which he opened, and it contained a beaded black dress.

Etta cried over the dress and said she would never wear it because the only time he ever brought her anything was when he had done something wrong. Thereafter she let him do all the grocery shopping and she did not speak when he bought on trust.

Willy continued to buy at Panessa's. It seemed they were always waiting for him to come in. They lived in three tiny rooms on the floor above the store, and when Mrs. Panessa saw him out of her window, she ran down to the store. Willy came up from his basement, crossed the street, and went down the steps into the delicatessen, looming large as he opened the door. Every time he bought, it was never less than two dollars' worth, and sometimes it would go as high as five. Mrs. Panessa would pack everything into a deep double bag, after Panessa had called off each item and written the price with a smeary black pencil into his looseleaf notebook. Whenever Willy walked in, Panessa would open the book, wet his fingertip, and flip through a number of blank pages till he found Willy's account in the center of the book. After the order was packed and tied up, Panessa added the amount, touching each figure with his pencil, hissing to himself as he added, and Mrs. Panessa's bird eyes would follow the figuring until Panessa wrote down a sum, and the new total sum (after Panessa had glanced up at Willy and saw that Willy was looking) was twice underscored and then Panessa shut the book. Willy, with his loose unlit pipe in his mouth, did not move until the book was put away under the counter; then he roused himself and embracing the bundles—with which they offered to help him across the street though he always refused—plunged out of the store.

One day when the sum total came to eighty-three dollars and some cents, Panessa, lifting his head and smiling, asked Willy when he could pay something on the account. The very next day Willy stopped buying at Panessa's and after that Etta, with her cord market bag, began to shop again at the self-service, and neither of them went across the street for as much as a pound of prunes or a box of salt they had meant to buy but had forgotten.

Etta, when she returned from shopping at the self-service, scraped the wall on her side of the street to get as far away as possible from Panessa's.

Later she asked Willy if he had paid them anything.

He said no.

"When will you?"

He said he didn't know.

A month went by, then Etta met Mrs. Panessa around the corner, and though Mrs. Panessa, looking unhappy, said nothing about the bill, Etta came home and reminded Willy.

"Leave me alone," he said, "I got enough trouble of my own."

"What kind of trouble have you got, Willy?"

"The goddamn tenants and the goddamn landlord," he shouted and slammed the door.

When he returned he said, "What have I got that I can pay? Ain't I a poor man every day of my life?"

She was sitting at the table and lowered her arms and put her head down on them and wept.

"With what?" he shouted, his face lit dark and webbed. "With the meat off of my bones? With the ashes in my eyes. With the piss I mop up on the floors. With the cold in my lungs when I sleep."

He felt for Panessa and his wife a grating hatred and vowed never to pay because he hated them so much, especially the humpback behind the counter. If he ever smiled at him again with those goddamn eyes he would lift him off the floor and crack his bent bones.

That night he went out and got drunk and lay till morning in the gutter. When he returned, with filthy clothes and bloodied eyes, Etta held up to him the picture of their four-year-old son who had died of diphtheria, and Willy, weeping splashy tears, swore he would never touch another drop.

Each morning he went out to line up the ashcans he never looked the full way across the street.

"Give credit," he mimicked, "give credit."

Hard times set in. The landlord ordered cut down on heat, cut down on hot water. He cut down on Willy's expense money and wages. The tenants were angered. All day they pestered Willy like clusters of flies and he told them what the landlord had ordered. Then they cursed Willy and Willy cursed them. They telephoned the Board of Health, but when the inspectors arrived they said the temperature was within the legal minimum though the house was drafty. However, the tenants still complained they were cold and goaded Willy about it all day, but he said he was cold too. He said he was freezing but no one believed him.

One day he looked up from lining up four ashcans for the sanitation truck to remove and saw Mr. and Mrs. Panessa staring at him from the store. They were staring up through the glass front door and when he looked at them at first his eyes blurred, and they appeared to be two scrawny, loose-feathered birds.

He went down the block to get a wrench from another janitor, and when he got back they then reminded him of two skinny leafless bushes sprouting up through the wooden floor. He could see through the bushes to the empty shelves.

In the spring, when the grass shoots were sticking up in the cracks in the sidewalk, he told Etta, "I'm only waiting till I can pay it all."

"How, Willy?"

"We can save up."

"How?"

"How much do we save a month?"

"Nothing."

"How much have you got hid away?"

"Nothing any more."

"I'll pay them bit by bit. I will, by Jesus."

The trouble was there was no place they could get the money. Sometimes when he was trying to think of the different ways there were to get money his thoughts ran ahead and he saw what it would be like when he paid. He would wrap the wad of bills with a thick rubber band and then go up the stairs and cross the street and go down the five steps into the store. He would say to Panessa, "Here it is, little old man, and I bet you didn't think I would do it, and I don't suppose nobody else did and sometimes me myself, but here it is in bucks all held together by a fat rubber band." After hefting the wad a little, he placed it, like making a move on a checkerboard, squarely in the center of the counter, and the diminutive man and his wife both unpeeled it, squeaking and squealing over each blackened buck, and marveling that so many ones had been put together into such a small pack.

Such was the dream Willy dreamed but he could never make it come true.

He worked hard to. He got up early and scrubbed the stairs from cellar to roof with soap and a hard brush, then went over that with a wet mop. He cleaned the woodwork too and oiled the bannister till it shone the whole zigzag way down, and rubbed the mailboxes in the vestibule with metal polish and a soft rag until you could see your face in them. He saw his own heavy face with a surprising yellow mustache he had recently grown and the tan felt cap he wore that a tenant had left behind in a closetful of junk when he had moved. Etta helped him and they cleaned the whole cellar and the dark courtyard under the crisscrossed clotheslines, and they were quick to respond to any kind of request, even from tenants they didn't like, for sink or toilet repairs. Both worked themselves to exhaustion every day, but as they knew from the beginning, no extra money came in.

One morning when Willy was shining up the mailboxes, he found in his own a letter for him. Removing his cap, he opened the envelope and held the paper to the light as he read the trembling writing. It was from Mrs. Panessa, who wrote her husband was sick across the street, and she had no money in the house so could he pay her just ten dollars and the rest could wait for later.

He tore the letter to bits and hid all day in the cellar. That night, Etta, who had been searching for him in the streets, found him behind the furnace amid the pipes, and she asked him what he was doing there.

He explained about the letter.

"Hiding won't do you any good at all," she said hopelessly.

"What should I do then?"

"Go to sleep, I guess."

He went to sleep but the next morning burst out of his covers, pulled on his overalls, and ran out of the house with an overcoat flung over his shoulders. Around the corner he found a pawnshop, where he got ten dollars for the coat and was gleeful.

But when he ran back, there was a hearse or something across the street and two men in black were carrying this small and narrow pine box out of the house.

"Who's dead, a child?" he asked one of the tenants.

"No, a man named Mr. Panessa."

Willy couldn't speak. His throat had turned to bone.

After the pine box was squeezed through the vestibule doors, Mrs. Panessa, grieved all over, tottered out alone. Willy turned his head away although he thought she wouldn't recognize him because of his new mustache and tan cap.

"What'd he die of?" he whispered to the tenant.

"I really couldn't say."

But Mrs. Panessa, walking behind the box, had heard.

"Old age," she shrilly called back.

He tried to say some sweet thing but his tongue hung in his mouth like dead fruit on a tree, and his heart was a black-painted window.

Mrs. Panessa moved away to live first with one stone-faced daughter, then with the other. And the bill was never paid.

1951

An Apology

E ARLY ONE morning, during a wearying hot spell in the city, a police car that happened to be cruising along Canal Street drew over to the curb and one of the two policemen in the car leaned out of the window and fingered a come-here to an old man wearing a black derby hat, who carried a large carton on his back, held by clothesline rope to his shoulder, and dragged a smaller carton with his other hand.

"Hey, Mac."

But the peddler, either not hearing or paying no attention, went on. At that, the policeman, the younger of the two, pushed open the door and sprang out. He strode over to the peddler and, shoving the large carton on his back, swung him around as if he were straw. The peddler stared at him in frightened astonishment. He was a gaunt, shriveled man with very large eyes which at the moment gave the effect of turning lights, so that the policeman was a little surprised, though not for long.

"Are you deaf?" he said.

The peddler's lips moved in a way that suggested he might be, but at last he cried out, "Why do you push me?" and again surprised the policeman with the amount of wail that rang in his voice.

"Why didn't you stop when I called you?"

"So who knows you called me? Did you say my name?"

"What is your name?"

The peddler clamped his sparse yellow teeth rigidly together.

"And where's your license?"

"What license?—who license?"

"None of your wisecracks—your license to peddle. We saw you peddle."

The peddler did not deny it.

"What's in the big box?"

"Hundred watt."

"Hundred what?"

"Lights."

493

"What's in the other?"

"Sixty watt."

"Don't you know it's against the law to peddle without a license?"

Without answering, the peddler looked around, but there was no one in sight except the other policeman in the car and his eyes were shut as if he was catching a little lost sleep.

The policeman on the sidewalk opened his black summons book.

"Spill it, Pop, where do you live?"

The peddler stared down at the cracked sidewalk.

"Hurry up, Lou," called the policeman from the car. He was an older man, though not so old as the peddler.

"Just a second, Walter, this old guy here is balky."

With his pencil he prodded the peddler, who was still staring at the sidewalk but who then spoke, saying he had no money to buy a license.

"But you have the money to buy bulbs. Don't you know you're cheating the city when you don't pay the legitimate fees?"

". . ."

"Talk, will you?"

"Come on, Lou."

"Come on yourself, this nanny goat won't talk."

The other policeman slowly got out of the car, a heavy man with gray hair and a red face shiny with perspiration.

"You better give him the information he wants, mister."

The peddler, holding himself stiff, stared between them. By this time some people had gathered and were looking on, but Lou scattered them with a wave of his arm.

"All right, Walter, give me a hand. This bird goes to the station house."

Walter looked at him with some doubt, but Lou said, "Resisting an officer in the performance of his duty."

He took the peddler's arm and urged him forward. The carton of bulbs slipped off his shoulder, pulling him to his knees.

"Veh is mir."

Walter helped him up and they lifted him into the car. The young cop hauled the large carton to the rear of the car, opened the trunk, and shoved it in sideways. As they drove off, a man in front of one of the stores held up a box and shouted, "Hey, you forgot this one," but neither of them turned to look back, and the peddler didn't seem to be listening.

On their way to the station house they passed the Brooklyn Bridge.

"Just a second, Lou," said Walter. "Could you drive across the bridge now and stop at my house? My feet are perspiring and I'd like to change my shirt."

"After we get this character booked."

But Walter querulously insisted it would take too long, and though Lou didn't want to drive him home he finally gave in. Neither of them spoke on the way to Walter's house, which was not far from the bridge, on a nice quiet street of three-story brownstone houses with young trees in front of them, newly planted not far from the curb.

When Walter got out, he said to the peddler, "If you were in Germany they would have killed you. All we were trying to do was give you a summons that would maybe cost you a buck fine." Then he went up the stone steps.

After a while Lou became impatient waiting for him and honked the horn. A window shade on the second floor slid up and Walter in his underwear called down, "Just five minutes, Lou—I'm just drying my feet."

He came down all spry and they drove back several blocks and onto the bridge. Midway across, they had to slow down in a long traffic line, and to their astonishment the peddler pushed open the door and reeled out upon the bridge, miraculously ducking out of the way of the trailers and trucks coming from the other direction. He scooted across the pedestrians' walk and clambered with ferocious strength up on the railing of the bridge.

But Lou, who was very quick, immediately pursued him and managed to get his hand on the peddler's coattails as he stood poised on the railing for the jump.

With a yank Lou pulled him to the ground. The back of his head struck against the sidewalk and his derby hat bounced up, twirled, and landed at his feet. However, he did not lose consciousness. He lay on the ground moaning and tearing with clawlike fingers at his chest and arms.

Both the policemen stood there looking down at him, not sure what to do since there was absolutely no bleeding. As they were talking it over, a fat woman with moist eyes who, despite the heat, was wearing a white shawl over her head and carrying, with the handle over her pudgy arm, a large basket of salted five-cent pretzels passed by and stopped out of curiosity to see what had happened.

Seeing the man on the ground she called out, "Bloostein!" but he did not look at her and continued tearing at his arms.

"Do you know him?" Lou asked her.

"It's Bloostein. I know him from the neighborhood."

"Where does he live?"

She thought for a minute but didn't know. "My father said he used to own a store on Second Avenue but he lost it. Then his missus died and also his daughter was killed in a fire. Now he's got the seven years' itch and they can't cure it in the clinic. They say he peddles with light bulbs."

"Don't you know his address?"

"Not me. What did he do?"

"It doesn't matter what he tried to do," said Walter.

"Goodbye, Bloostein, I have to go to the schoolyard," the fat lady apologized. She picked up the basket and went with her pretzels down the bridge.

By now Bloostein had stopped his frantic scratching and lay quietly on the sidewalk. The sun shone straight into his eyes but he did nothing to shield them.

Lou, who was quite pale, looked at Walter and Walter said, "Let him go."

They got him up on his feet, dusted his coat, and placed his dented hat on his head. Lou said he would get the bulbs out of the car, but Walter said, "Not here, down at the foot of the bridge."

They helped Bloostein back to the car and in a few minutes let him go with his carton of bulbs at the foot of the bridge, not far from the place where they had first chanced to see him.

But that night, after their tour of duty, when Lou drove him home, Walter got out of the car and saw, after a moment of disbelief, that Bloostein himself was waiting for him in front of his house.

"Hey, Lou," he called, but Lou had already driven off so he had to face the peddler alone. Bloostein looked, with his carton of bulbs, much as he had that morning, except for the smudge where the dent on his derby hat had been, and his eyes were fleshy with fatigue.

"What do you want here?" Walter said to him.

The peddler parted his lips, then pointed to his carton. "My little box lights."

"What about it?"

"What did you do with them?"

Walter thought a few seconds and remembered the other box of bulbs.

"You sure you haven't gone back and hid them somewhere?" he asked sternly.

Bloostein wouldn't look at him.

The policeman felt very hot. "All right, we'll try and locate them, but first I have to have my supper. I'm hungry."

He went up the steps and turned to say something more, but a woman came out of the house and he raised his hat to her and went in.

After supper he would have liked very much to relax in front of the radio, but instead he changed out of his uniform, said he was going to the corner, and walked, conscious of his heavy disappointment, down the stairs.

Bloostein was planted where he had left him.

"My car's in the garage." Walter went slowly up the street, Bloostein following with his carton of bulbs on his back.

At the garage Walter motioned him into the car. Bloostein lifted the carton into the back seat and got in with it. Walter drove out and over the bridge to Canal Street, to the place where they had taken the peddler into the car.

He parked and went into three of the stores there, flashing his badge and asking if anyone knew who had got the bulbs they had forgotten. No one knew for sure, but the clerk in the third store thought it might be someone next door whose name and address he gave to Walter.

Before returning to the car Walter went into a tavern and had a few beers. Over the fourth he had a hunch and called the police property clerk, who said he had taken in no electric bulbs that day. Walter walked out and asked Bloostein how many bulbs he had had in the carton.

"Five dozen."

"At how much—wholesale?"

"Eight cents."

"That's four-eighty," he figured. Taking a five-dollar bill from his wallet, he handed it to Bloostein, who wouldn't accept it.

"What do you want, the purple heart?"

"My little box lights."

Walter then kidded, "Now you're gonna take a little ride."

They then rode to the address he had been given but no one knew where the one who had the bulbs was. Finally a bald-headed, stocky man in an undershirt came down from the top floor and said he was the man's uncle and what did Walter want.

Walter convinced him it wasn't serious. "It's just that he happens to know where these bulbs are that we left behind by mistake after an arrest."

The uncle said if it wasn't really serious he would give him the address of the social club where he could find his nephew. The address was a lot farther uptown and on the East Side.

"This is foolish," Walter said to himself as he came out of the house. He thought maybe he could take his time and Bloostein might go away, so he stopped at another beer parlor and had several more as he watched a ten-round fight on television.

He came out sweaty from the beers.

But Bloostein was there.

Walter scratched under his arm. "What's good for an itch?" he said. When he got into the car he thought he was a little bit drunk but it didn't bother him and he drove to the social club on the East Side where a dance was going on. He asked the ticket taker in a tuxedo if this nephew was around.

The ticket taker, whose right eye was very crossed, assured him that nobody by the name mentioned was there.

"It's really not very important," Walter said. "Just about a small carton of bulbs he happens to be holding for this old geezer outside."

"I wouldn't know anything about it."

"It's nothing to worry about."

Walter stood by the door a few minutes and watched the dancers, but there was no one whose face he could recognize.

"He's really not there."

"I don't doubt your word."

Afterward he said it was a nice dance but he had to leave.

"Stay awhile," said the ticket taker.

"I have to go," said Walter. "I have a date with a backseat driver." The ticket taker winked with his good eye, which had a comical effect, but Walter didn't smile and soon he left.

"Still here, kid?" he asked Bloostein.

He started the car and drove back to Sixth Avenue, where he stopped at a liquor store and bought himself a fifth of whiskey. In the car he tore the wrapper off the bottle and took a long pull.

"Drink?" He offered the bottle to Bloostein.

Bloostein was perched like a skinny owl on the back seat gazing at him.

Walter capped the bottle but did not start the car. He sat for a long time at the wheel, moodily meditating. At the point where he was beginning to feel down in the dumps, he got a sudden idea. The idea was so simple and good he quickly started the motor and drove downtown straight to Canal, where there was a hardware store that stayed open to midnight. He almost ran into the place and in ten minutes came out with a wrapped carton containing five dozen 60-watt bulbs.

"The joyride's finished, my friend."

The peddler got out and Walter unloaded the large carton and left it standing on the sidewalk near the smaller one.

He drove off quickly.

Going over the bridge he felt relieved, yet at the same time a little anxious to get to sleep because he had to be up at six. He garaged the car and then walked home and upstairs, taking care to move about softly in the bathroom so as not to waken his son, a light sleeper, or his wife, who slept heavily but couldn't get back to sleep once she had been waked up. Undressing, he got into bed with her, but though the night was hot he felt like a cake of ice covered with a sheet. After a while he got up, raised the shade, and stood by the window.

The quiet street was drenched in moonlight, and warm dark shadows fell from the tender trees. But in the tree shadow in front of the house were two strange oblongs and a gnarled, grotesque-hatted silhouette that stretched a tormented distance down the block. Walter's heart pounded heavily, for he knew it was Bloostein.

He put on his robe and straw slippers and ran down the stairs.

"What's wrong?"

Bloostein stared at the moonlit sidewalk.

"What do you want?"

". . ."

"You better go, Bloostein. This is too late for monkey business. You got your bulbs. Now you better just go home and leave me alone. I hate to have to call the police. Just go home."

Then he lumbered up the stone steps and the flight of carpeted stairs. Inside the bedroom he could hear his son moan in his sleep. Walter lay down and slept, but was awakened by the sound of soft rain. Getting up, he stared out. There was the peddler in the rain, with his white upraised face looking at the window, so near he might be standing on stilts.

Hastening into the hall, Walter rummaged in a closet for an umbrella but couldn't find one. Then his wife woke and called in a loud whisper, "Who's there?" He stood motionless and she listened a minute and evidently went back to sleep. Then because he couldn't find the umbrella he got out a light summer blanket, brought it into the little storage room next to the bedroom, and, taking the screen out of the window, threw the blanket out to Bloostein so he wouldn't get too wet. The white blanket seemed to float down.

He returned to bed, by an effort of the will keeping himself there for hours. Then he noticed that the rain had stopped and he got up to make sure. The blanket lay heaped where it had fallen on the sidewalk. Bloostein was standing away from it, under the tree.

Walter's straw slippers squeaked as he walked down the

stairs. The heat had broken and now a breeze came through the street, shivering the leaves in summer cold.

In the doorway he thought, What's my hurry? I can wait him out till six, then just let the mummy try to follow me into the station house.

"Bloostein," he said, going down the steps, but as the old man looked up, he felt a sickening emptiness.

Staring down at the sidewalk he thought about everything. At last he raised his head and slowly said, "Bloostein, I owe you an apology. I'm really sorry the whole thing happened. I haven't been able to sleep. From my heart I'm truly sorry."

Bloostein gazed at him with enormous eyes reflecting the moon. He answered nothing, but it seemed he had shrunk and so had his shadow.

Walter said good night. He went up and lay down under the sheet.

"What's the matter?" said his wife.

"Nothing."

She turned over on her side. "Don't wake Sonny."

"No."

He rose and went to the window. Raising the shade, he stared out. Yes, gone. He, his boxes of lights and soft summer blanket. He looked again, but the long, moon-whitened street had never been so empty.

1951

The Loan

THE SWEET, the heady smell of Lieb's white bread drew customers in droves long before the loaves were baked. Alert behind the counter, Bessie, Lieb's second wife, discerned a stranger among them, a frail, gnarled man with a hard hat who hung, disjoined, at the edge of the crowd. Though the stranger looked harmless enough among the aggressive purchasers of baked goods, she was at once concerned. Her glance questioned him but he signaled with a deprecatory nod of his hatted head that he would wait—glad to (forever)—though his face glittered with misery. If suffering had marked him, he no longer sought to conceal the sign; the shining was his own—him—now. So he frightened Bessie.

She made quick hash of the customers, and when they, after her annihilating service, were gone, she returned him her stare.

He tipped his hat. "Pardon me—Kobotsky. Is Lieb the baker here?"

"Who Kobotsky?"

"An old friend"—frightening her further.

"From where?"

"From long ago."

"What do you want to see him?"

The question insulted, so Kobotsky was reluctant to say.

As if drawn into the shop by the magic of a voice the baker, shirtless, appeared from the rear. His pink fleshy arms had been deep in dough. For a hat he wore jauntily a flour-covered brown paper sack. His peering glasses were dusty with flour, and the inquisitive face white with it, so that he resembled a paunchy ghost; but the ghost, through the glasses, was Kobotsky, not he.

"Kobotsky," the baker cried almost with a sob, for it was so many years gone Kobotsky reminded him of, when they were both at least young, and circumstances were—ah, different. Unable, for sentimental reasons, to refrain from smarting tears, he jabbed them away with a thrust of the hand.

Kobotsky removed his hat—he had grown all but bald

where Lieb was gray—and patted his flushed forehead with an immaculate handkerchief.

Lieb sprang forward with a stool. "Sit, Kobotsky."

"Not here," Bessie murmured.

"Customers," she explained to Kobotsky. "Soon comes the supper rush."

"Better in the back," nodded Kobotsky.

So that was where they went, happier for the privacy. But it happened that no customers came so Bessie went in to hear.

Kobotsky sat enthroned on a tall stool in a corner of the room, stoop-shouldered, his black coat and hat on, the stiff, gray-veined hands drooping over thin thighs. Lieb, peering through full moons, eased his bones on a flour sack. Bessie lent an attentive ear, but the visitor was dumb. Embarrassed, Lieb did the talking: ah, of old times. The world was new. We were, Kobotsky, young. Do you remember how both together, immigrants out of steerage, we registered in night school?

"Haben, hatte, gehabt." He cackled at the sound of it.

No word from the gaunt one on the stool. Bessie fluttered around an impatient duster. She shot a glance into the shop: empty.

Lieb, acting the life of the party, recited, to cheer his friend: "'Come,' said the wind to the trees one day, 'Come over the meadow with me and play.' Remember, Kobotsky?"

Bessie sniffed aloud. "Lieb, the bread!"

The baker bounced up, strode over to the gas oven, and pulled one of the tiered doors down. Just in time he yanked out the trays of brown breads in hot pans, and set them on the tin-top worktable.

Bessie clucked at the narrow escape.

Lieb peered into the shop. "Customers," he said triumphantly. Flushed, she went in. Kobotsky, with wetted lips, watched her go. Lieb set to work molding the risen dough in a huge bowl into two trays of pans. Soon the bread was baking, but Bessie was back.

The honey odor of the new loaves distracted Kobotsky. He breathed the fragrance as if this were the first air he was tasting, and even beat his fist against his chest at the delicious smell.

"Oh, my God," he all but wept. "Wonderful."

"With tears," Lieb said humbly, pointing to the large bowl of dough.

Kobotsky nodded.

For thirty years, the baker explained, he was never with a penny to his name. One day, out of misery, he had wept into the dough. Thereafter his bread was such it brought customers in from everywhere.

"My cakes they don't like so much, but my bread and rolls they run miles to buy."

Kobotsky blew his nose, then peeked into the shop: three customers.

"Lieb"—a whisper.

Despite himself the baker stiffened.

The visitor's eyes swept back to Bessie out front, then under raised brows, questioned the baker.

Lieb, however, remained mute.

Kobotsky coughed clear his throat. "Lieb, I need two hundred dollars." His voice broke.

Lieb slowly sank onto the sack. He knew—had known. From the minute of Kobotsky's appearance he had weighed in his thoughts the possibility of this against the remembrance of the lost and bitter hundred, fifteen years ago. Kobotsky swore he had repaid it, Lieb said no. Afterwards a broken friendship. It took years to blot out of the system the memoried outrage.

Kobotsky bowed his head.

At least admit you were wrong, Lieb thought, waiting a cruelly long time.

Kobotsky stared at his crippled hands. Once a cutter of furs, driven by arthritis out of the business.

Lieb gazed too. The bottom of a truss bit into his belly. Both eyes were cloudy with cataracts. Though the doctor swore he would see after the operation, he feared otherwise.

He sighed. The wrong was in the past. Forgiven: forgiven at the dim sight of him.

"For myself, positively, but she"—Lieb nodded toward the shop—"is a second wife. Everything is in her name." He held up empty hands.

Kobotsky's eyes were shut.

"But I will ask her—" Lieb looked doubtful.

"My wife needs—"

The baker raised a palm. "Don't speak."

"Tell her—"

"Leave it to me."

He seized the broom and circled the room, raising clouds of white dust.

When Bessie, breathless, got back she threw one look at them, and with tightened lips waited adamant.

Lieb hastily scoured the pots in the iron sink, stored the bread pans under the table, and stacked the fragrant loaves. He put one eye to the slot of the oven: baking, all baking.

Facing Bessie, he broke into a sweat so hot it momentarily stunned him.

Kobotsky squirmed atop the stool.

"Bessie," said the baker at last, "this is my old friend."

She nodded gravely.

Kobotsky lifted his hat.

"His mother—God bless her—gave me many times a plate hot soup. Also when I came to this country, for years I ate at his table. His wife is a very fine person—Dora—you will some-day meet her—"

Kobotsky softly groaned.

"So why I didn't meet her yet?" Bessie said, after a dozen years still jealous of the first wife's prerogatives.

"You will."

"Why didn't I?"

"Lieb—" pleaded Kobotsky.

"Because I didn't see her myself fifteen years," Lieb admitted.

"Why not?" she pounced.

Lieb paused. "A mistake."

Kobotsky turned away.

"My fault," said Lieb.

"Because you never go anyplace," Bessie spat out. "Because you live always in the shop. Because it means nothing to you to have friends."

Lieb solemnly agreed.

"Now she is sick," he announced. "The doctor must operate. This will cost two hundred dollars. I promised Kobotsky—"

Bessie screamed.

Hat in hand, Kobotsky got off the stool.

Pressing a palm to her bosom, Bessie lifted her arm to her eyes. She tottered. They both ran forward to steady her but she did not fall. Kobotsky retreated quickly to the stool and Lieb returned to the sink.

Bessie, her face like the inside of a loaf, quietly addressed the visitor. "I have pity for your wife but we can't help you. I am sorry, Mr. Kobotsky, we are poor people, we don't have the money."

"A mistake," Lieb cried, enraged.

Bessie strode over to the shelf and tore out a bill box. She dumped its contents on the table, the papers flying everywhere.

"Bills," she shouted.

Kobotsky hunched his shoulders.

"Bessie, we have in the bank—"

"No—"

"I saw the bankbook."

"So what if you saved a few dollars, so have you got life insurance?"

He made no answer.

"Can you get?" she taunted.

The front door banged. It banged often. The shop was crowded with customers clamoring for bread. Bessie stomped out to wait on them.

In the rear the wounded stirred. Kobotsky, with bony fingers, buttoned his overcoat.

"Sit," sighed the baker.

"Lieb, I am sorry—"

Kobotsky sat, his face lit with sadness.

When Bessie finally was rid of the rush, Lieb went into the shop. He spoke to her quietly, almost in a whisper, and she answered as quietly, but it took only a minute to start them quarreling.

Kobotsky slipped off the stool. He went to the sink, wet half his handkerchief, and held it to his dry eyes. Folding the damp handkerchief, he thrust it into his overcoat pocket, then took out a small penknife and quickly pared his fingernails.

As he entered the shop, Lieb was pleading with Bessie, reciting the embittered hours of his toil, the enduring drudgery. And now that he had a penny to his name, what was there to live for if he could not share it with a dear friend? But Bessie had her back to him.

"Please," Kobotsky said, "don't fight. I will go away now."

Lieb gazed at him in exasperation. Bessie stayed with head averted.

"Yes," Kobotsky sighed, "the money I wanted for Dora, but she is not sick, Lieb, she is dead."

"Ai," Lieb cried, wringing his hands.

Bessie faced the visitor, pallid.

"Not now," he spoke kindly, "five years ago."

Lieb groaned.

"The money I need for a stone on her grave. She never had a stone. Next Sunday is five years that she is dead and every year I promise her, 'Dora, this year I will give you your stone,' and every year I gave her nothing."

The grave, to his everlasting shame, lay uncovered before all eyes. He had long ago paid a fifty-dollar deposit for a head-stone with her name on it in clearly chiseled letters, but had never got the rest of the money. If there wasn't one thing to do with it there was always another: first an operation; the second year he couldn't work, imprisoned again by arthritis; the third a widowed sister lost her only son and the little Kobotsky earned had to help support her; the fourth incapacitated by boils that made him ashamed to walk out into the street. This year he was at least working, but only for just enough to eat and sleep, so Dora still lay without a stone, and for aught he knew he would someday return to the cemetery and find her grave gone.

Tears sprang into the baker's eyes. One gaze at Bessie's face—and the odd looseness of her neck and shoulders—told him that she too was moved. Ah, he had won out. She would now say yes, give the money, and they would then all sit down at the table and eat together.

But Bessie, though weeping, shook her head, and before they could guess what, had blurted out the story of her afflictions: how the Bolsheviki came when she was a little girl and dragged her beloved father into the snowy fields without his shoes; the shots scattered the blackbirds in the trees and the snow oozed blood; how, when she was married a year, her husband, a sweet and gentle man, an educated accountant—rare in those days and that place—died of typhus in Warsaw; and how she, abandoned in her grief, years later found sanctuary in the home of an older brother in Germany, who sacrificed his own chances to send her, before the war, to America, and himself ended, with wife and daughter, in one of Hitler's incinerators.

"So I came to America and met here a poor baker, a poor man—who was always in his life poor—without a cent and without enjoyment, and I married him, God knows why, and with my both hands, working day and night, I fixed up for him his piece of business and we make now, after twelve years, a little living. But Lieb is not a healthy man, also with eyes that he needs an operation, and this is not yet everything. Suppose, God forbid, that he died, what will I do alone by myself? Where will I go, where, and who will take care of me if I have nothing?"

The baker, who had often heard this tale, munched, as he listened, chunks of bread.

When she had finished he tossed the shell of a loaf away. Kobotsky, at the end of the story, held his hands over his ears.

Tears streaming from her eyes, Bessie raised her head and suspiciously sniffed the air. Screeching suddenly, she ran into the rear and with a cry wrenched open the oven door. A cloud of smoke billowed out at her. The loaves in the trays were blackened bricks—charred corpses.

Kobotsky and the baker embraced and sighed over their lost youth. They pressed mouths together and parted forever.

1952

The Girl of My Dreams

AFTER MITKA had burned the manuscript of his heart-broken novel in the blackened bottom of Mrs. Lutz's rusty trash can in her back yard, although the emotional land-lady tried all sorts of bait and schemes to lure him forth, and he could tell as he lay abed, from the new sounds on the floor and her penetrating perfume, that there was an unattached fe-male loose on the premises (wondrous possibility of yore), he resisted all and with a twist of the key had locked himself a prisoner in his room, only venturing out after midnight for crackers and tea and an occasional can of fruit; and this went on for too many weeks to count.

In the late fall, after a long year and a half of voyaging among more than twenty publishers, the novel had returned to stay and he had hurled it into a barrel burning autumn leaves, stir-ring the mess with a long length of pipe, to get the inner sheets afire. Overhead a few dead apples hung like forgotten Christmas ornaments upon the leafless tree. The sparks, as he stirred, flew to the apples, the withered fruit representing not only creation gone for nothing (three long years), but all his hopes, and the proud ideas he had given his book; and Mitka, al-though not a sentimentalist, felt as if he had burned (it took a thick two hours) an everlasting hollow in himself.

Into the fire also went a sheaf of odd-size papers (why he had saved them he would never know): copies of letters to lit-erary agents and their replies; mostly, however, printed rejec-tion forms, with perhaps three typed notes from lady editors, saying they were returning the MS of his novel, among other reasons—but this prevailed—because of the symbolism, the fact that it was obscure. Only one of the ladies had written let's hear from you again. Though he cursed them to damnation it did not cause the acceptance of his book. Yet for a year Mitka labored over a new one, up to the time of the return of the old manuscript, when, upon rereading that, then the new work, he discovered the same symbolism, more obscure than ever; so he shoved the second book aside. True, at odd moments he sneaked out of bed to try a new thought with his pen, but the words refused to budge; besides he had lost the belief that anything he said could make significant meaning, and if it perhaps did, that it could be conveyed in all its truth and drama to some publisher's reader in his aseptic office high above Madison Avenue; so he wrote nothing for months—although Mrs. Lutz actively mourned—and vowed never to write again though he felt the vow was worthless, because he couldn't write anyway whether he had vowed or no.

So Mitka sat alone and still in his faded yellow-papered room, the badly colored Orozco reproduction he had picked up, showing Mexican peasants bent and suffering, thumbtacked above the peeling mantelpiece, and stared through sore eyes at the antics of pigeons on the roof across the street; or aimlessly followed traffic—not people—in the street; he slept for good or ill a great deal, had bad dreams, some horrific, and awaking, looked long at the ceiling, which never represented the sky although he imagined it snowing; listened to music if it came from the distance, and occasionally attempted to read some historical or philosophical work but shut it with a bang if it lit the imagination and made him think of writing. At times he cautioned himself, Mitka, this will have to end or you will, but the warning did not change his ways. He grew wan and thin, and once when he beheld his meager thighs as he dressed, if he were a weeper he would have wept.

Now Mrs. Lutz, herself a writer—a bad one but always interested in writers and had them in her house whenever she could fish one up (her introductory inquisition masterfully sniffed this fact among the first) even when she could ill afford it—Mrs. Lutz knew all this about Mitka and she daily attempted some unsuccessful ministration. She tried tempting him down to her kitchen with spry descriptions of lunch: steaming soup, Mitka, with soft white rolls, calf's foot jelly, rice with tomato sauce, celery hearts, delicious breast of chicken—beef if he preferred—and his choice of satisfying sweets; also with fat notes slipped under his door in sealed envelopes, describing when she was a little girl, and the intimate details of her sad life since with Mr. Lutz, imploring a better fate on Mitka; or she left at the door all sorts of books fished out of her ancient library that he never looked at, magazines with stories marked, "You can do better," and when it arrived, her own copy, for him to read first, of the *Writer's Journal*. All these attempts having this day failed—his door shut (Mitka voiceless) though she had hid in the hall an hour to await its opening—Mrs. Lutz dropped to one horsy knee and with her keyhole eye peeked in: he lay outstretched in bed.

"Mitka," she wailed, "how thin you have grown—a skeleton—it frightens me. Come downstairs and eat."

He remained motionless, so she enticed him otherwise: "Here are clean sheets on my arm, let me refresh your bed and air the room."

He groaned for her to go away.

Mrs. Lutz groped a minute. "We have with us a new guest on your floor, girl by the name of Beatrice—a real beauty, Mitka, and a writer too."

He was silent but, she knew, listening.

"I'd say a tender twenty-one or -two, pinched waist, firm breasts, pretty face, and you should see her little panties hanging on the line—like flowers all."

"What does she write?" he solemnly inquired.

Mrs. Lutz found herself coughing.

"Advertising copy, as I understand, but she would like to write verse."

He turned away, wordless.

She left a tray in the hall—a bowl of hot soup whose odor nearly drove him mad, two folded sheets, pillow case, fresh towels, and a copy of that morning's *Globe*.

After he had ravished the soup and all but chewed the linen, he tore open the *Globe* to confirm that he was missing nothing. The headlines told him: correct. He was about to crumple the paper and pitch it out the window when he recalled "The Open Globe" on the editorial page, a column he hadn't looked at in years. In the past he had reached for the paper with five cents and trembling fingers, for "The Open Globe," come-one, come-all to the public, to every writer under a rock, inviting contributions in the form of stories at five bucks the thousand-word throw. Though he now hated the memory of it, it was his repeated acceptance here—a dozen stories in less than half a year (he had bought a blue suit and a two-pound jar of jam)—that had started him writing the novel (requies-cat); from that to the second abortion, to the impotence and murderous self-hatred that had descended upon him after-wards. Open Globe, indeed. He gnashed his teeth but the holes in them hurt. Yet the not unsweet remembrance of past triumphs—the quarter of a million potential readers every time he appeared in print, all within a single city so that *every-body* knew when he was in (people reading him in buses, at cafeteria tables, park benches, as Mitka the Magician lurked around, watching for smiles and tears); also flattering letters from publishers' editors, fan letters too, from the most unlikely people—fame is the purr, the yip the yay. Remembering, he cast a momentarily dewy eye upon the column, and having done so, devoured the print.

The story socked in the belly. This girl, Madeleine Thorn, who wrote the piece as "I"—though she only traced herself here and there she came at once alive to him—he pictured her as maybe twenty-three, slim yet soft-bodied, the face whip-lashed with understanding—that Thorn was not for nothing; anyway, there she was that day, running up and down the stairs in joy and terror. She too lived in a rooming house, at work on her novel, bit by bit, nights, after a depleting secretarial grind each day; page by page, each neatly typed and slipped into the carton under her bed. At the very end of the book a last chap-ter to go of the first draft, she had one night got out the carton and lay on the bed, rereading, to see if the book was any good. Page after page she dropped on the floor, at last falling asleep, worried she hadn't got it right, wearied at how much rewriting (this sank in by degrees) she would have to do, when the light of the risen sun struck her eyes and she pounced up, realizing she had forgotten to set the alarm. With a sweep of the hand she shot the typewritten sheets under the bed, washed, slipped on a fresh dress, and ran a comb through her hair. Down the stairs she ran and out of the house.

At work, strangely a good day. The novel again came to-gether in the mind and she memo'd what she'd have to do—not very much really, to make it the decent book she had hoped to write. Home, happy, holding flowers, to be met on the first floor by the landlady, flouncing and all smiles: guess what I've gone and done for you today; describing new curtains, matching bedspread, a rug no less, to keep your tootsies warm, and surprise! the room spring-cleaned from top to bottom. Oh my God. The girl tore up the stairs. Falling on her hands and knees in her room she searched under the bed: an empty carton. Downstairs like dark light. Where, landlady, are the typewritten papers that were under my bed? She spoke with her hand to her throat. "Oh, those that I found on the floor, honey? I thought you meant for me to sweep the mess out and so I did." Madeleine, controlling her voice: "Are they perhaps in the garbage? I—don't believe they collect it till Thursday." "No, love, I burned them in the barrel this morning. The smoke made my eyes smart for a whole hour." Curtain. Groaning, Mitka collapsed on the bed.

He was convinced it was every bit of it true. He saw the crazy dame dumping the manuscript into the barrel and stirring it until every blessed page was aflame. He groaned at the burning—years of precious work. The tale haunted him. He wanted to escape it—leave the room and abandon the dismal memory of misery, but where would he go and what do without a penny in his pocket? So he lay on the bed and whether awake or asleep dreamed the recurrent dream of the burning barrel (in it their books commingled), suffering her agony as well as his own. The barrel, a symbol he had not conceived before, belched flame, shot word-sparks, poured smoke as thick as oil. It turned red hot, a sickly yellow, black—loaded high with the ashes of human bones—guess whose. When his imagination calmed, a sorrow for her afflicted him. The last chapter—irony of it. He yearned all day to assuage her grief, express sympathy in some loving word or gesture, assure her she would write it again, only better. Around midnight he could bear his thoughts no longer. He thrust a sheet of paper into the portable, twirled the roller and in the strange stillness of the house clacked out to her a note c/o *Globe*, expressing his sorrow—a writer himself—but don't give up, write it again. Sincerely, Mitka. He found an envelope and sticky stamp in his desk drawer. Against his better judgment he sneaked out and mailed it.

Immediately he regretted it. Was he in his right mind? *All right*, so he had written to her, but what if she wrote back? Who wanted, who needed a correspondence? He simply hadn't the strength for it. Therefore he was glad there continued to be no mail—not since he had burned his book in November, and this was February. Yet on the way out to forage some food for himself when the house was sleeping, ridiculing himself, holding a lit match he peered into the mailbox. The next night he felt inside the slot with his fingers: empty, served him right. Silly business. He had all but forgotten her story; that is, thought of it less each day. Yet if the girl by some mischance should write, Mrs. Lutz usually opened the box and brought up whatever mail herself—any excuse to waste his time. The next morning he heard the courier carrying her bulk lightly up the stairs and knew the girl had answered. Steady, Mitka. Despite a warning to himself of the dream world he was in, his heart pounded as the old tease coyly knocked. He didn't answer. Gurgling, "For you, Mitka darling," she at last slipped it under the door—her favorite pastime. Waiting till she had moved on so as not to give her the satisfaction of hearing him go for it, he sprang off the bed and tore the envelope open. "Dear Mr. Mitka (a most feminine handwriting): Thank you for the expression of your kind sympathy, sincerely, M.T." That was all, no return address, no nothing. Giving himself a horse bray he dropped the business into the basket. He brayed louder the next day: there was another epistle, the story wasn't true—she had invented every word; but the truth was she was lonely and would he care to write again?

Nothing comes easy for Mitka but eventually he wrote to her. He had plenty of time and nothing else to do. He told himself he had answered her letter because she was lonely—all right, because they both were. Ultimately he admitted that he wrote because he couldn't do the other kind of writing, and this, though he was no escapist, solaced him a bit. Mitka sensed that although he had vowed never to go back to it, he hoped the correspondence would return him to his abandoned book. (Sterile writer seeking end of sterility through satisfying epistolary intercourse with lady writer.) Clearly then, he was trying with these letters to put an end to the hatred of self for not working, for having no ideas, for cutting himself off from them. Ah, Mitka. He sighed at this weakness, to depend on others. Yet though his letters were often harsh, provocative, even unkind, they drew from her warm responses, receptive, soft, willing; and so it was not long (who can resist it? he bitterly assailed himself) before he had brought up the subject of their meeting. He broached it first and she (with reluctance) gave in, for wasn't it better, she had asked, not to intrude the person?

The meeting was arranged for a Monday evening at the branch public library near where she worked—her bookish preference; himself, he would have chosen the freedom of a street corner. She would, she said, be wearing a sort of reddish babushka. Now Mitka found himself actively wondering what she looked like. Her letters showed her sensible, modest, honest but what of the human body? Though he liked his women, among other things, to be lookers, he guessed she wasn't. Partly from hints dropped by her, partly his intuition. He pictured her as comely yet hefty. But what of it as long as she was womanly, intelligent, brave? A man like him nowadays had need of something special.

The March evening was zippy outside but cupped in it the breath of spring. Mitka opened both windows and allowed the free air to blow on him. About to go—there came a quick knock on the door. "Telephone," a girl's voice sang out. Probably the advertising Beatrice. He waited till she was gone, then unlocked the door and stepped into the hall for his first phone call of the year. As he picked up the receiver a crack of light showed in the corner. He stared and the door shut tight. The landlady's fault, she built him up among the roomers as a sort of freak. "My writer upstairs."

"Mitka?" It was Madeleine.

"Speaking."

"Mitka, do you know why I'm calling?"

"How should I know?"

"I'm half drunk on wine."

"Save it till later."

"Because I am afraid."

"Afraid of what?"

"I do so love your letters and would hate to lose them. Do we have to meet?"

"Yes," he hissed.

"Suppose I am not what you expect?"

"Leave that to me."

She sighed. "All right then—"

"You'll be there?"

No sound from her.

"For God's sake, don't frustrate me now."

"Yes, Mitka." She hung up.

Sensitive kid. He plucked his very last buck out of the drawer and quickly left the room, to hurry to the library before she could change her mind and leave. But Mrs. Lutz, in flannel bathrobe, caught him at the bottom of the stairs. Her gray hair wild, her voice broken. "Mitka, why have you shunned me so long? I have waited months for a single word. How can you be so cruel?"

"Please." He shoved her aside and ran out of the house. Nutty dame. The balmy current in the air swept away the unpleasantness, carried a sob to his throat. He walked briskly, more alive than for many a season.

The library was an old stone structure. He searched in circulation amid rows of books on sagging floors but found only the yawning librarian. The children's room was dark. In reference, a lone middle-aged female sat at a long table, reading; on the table stood her bulky market bag. Mitka searched the room and was turning to look elsewhere when a monstrous insight tore at his scalp: *this was she.* He stared unbelievingly, his heart a dishrag. Rage possessed him. Hefty she was but yes, eyeglassed, and marvelously plain; Christ, didn't know color even—the babushka a sickly running orange. Ah, colossal trickery—was ever man so cruelly defrauded? His impulse was to escape into breathable air but she held him there by serenely reading the printed page—(sly one, she knew the tiger in the room). Had she for a split second gazed up with wavering lids he'd have bolted sure; instead she buttoned her eyes to the book and let him duck if he so willed. This infuriated him further. Who wanted charity from the old girl? Mitka strode (in misery) toward her table.

"Madeleine?" He mocked the name. (Writer maims bird in flight. Enough not enough.)

She looked up with a shy and stricken smile. "Mitka?"

"The same—" He cynically bowed.

"Madeleine is my daughter's name, which I borrowed for my story. Mine is Olga really."

A pox on her lies—yet he hopefully asked, "Did she send you?"

She smiled sadly. "No, I am the one. Sit, Mitka."

He sat sullenly, harboring murderous thoughts: to hack her to pieces and incinerate the remains in Mrs. Lutz's barrel.

"They'll be closing soon," she said. "Where shall we go?"

He was motionless, stunned.

"I know a beer place around the corner where we can refresh ourselves," Olga suggested.

She buttoned a drab coat over a gray sweater. At length he rose. She got up too and followed him, hauling her market bag down the stone steps.

In the street he took the bag—it felt full of rocks—and trailed her around the corner into the beer joint.

Along the wall opposite the beat-up bar ran a row of dark booths. Olga sought one in the rear.

"For peace and privacy."

He laid the bag on the table. "The place smells."

They sat facing each other. He grew increasingly depressed at the thought of spending the evening with her. The irony of it—immured for months in a rat hole, to come forth for this. He'd go back now and entomb himself forever.

She removed her coat. "You'd have liked me when I was young, Mitka. I had a sylphlike figure and glorious hair. I was much sought after by men. I was not what you would call sexy but they knew I had it."

Mitka looked away.

"I had verve and a quality of wholeness. I loved life. In many ways I was too rich for my husband. He couldn't understand my nature and this caused him to leave me—mind you, with two small children."

She saw he wasn't listening. Olga sighed and burst into tears.

The waiter came.

"One beer. Bring the lady whiskey."

She used two handkerchiefs, one to blow her nose in, the other to dry her eyes.

"You see, Mitka, I told you so."

Her humility touched him. "I see." Why hadn't he, fool, not listened?

She gazed at him with sadly smiling eyes. Without glasses she looked better.

"You're exactly the way I pictured you, except for your thinness which surprises me."

Olga reached into her market bag and brought out several packages. She unwrapped bread, sausage, herring, Italian cheese, soft salami, pickles and a large turkey drumstick.

"Sometimes I favor myself with these little treats. Eat, Mitka."

Another landlady. Set Mitka adrift and he enticed somebody's Mama. But he ate, grateful she had provided an occupation.

The waiter brought the drinks. "What's going on here, a picnic?"

"We're writers," Olga explained.

"The boss will be pleased."

"Never mind him, eat, Mitka."

He ate listlessly. A man had to live. Or did he? When had he felt this low? Probably never.

Olga sipped her whiskey. "Eat, it's self-expression."

He expressed himself by finishing off the salami, also half the loaf of bread, cheese, and herring. His appetite grew. Searching within the bag Olga brought out a package of sliced corned beef and a ripe pear. He made a sandwich of the meat. On top of that the cold beer was tasty.

"How is the writing going now, Mitka?"

He lowered the glass but changed his mind and gulped the rest.

"Don't speak of it."

"Be uphearted, not down. Work every day."

He gnawed the turkey drumstick.

"That's what I do. I've been writing for over twenty years and sometimes—for one reason or another—it gets so bad that I don't feel like going on. But what I do then is relax for a short while and then change to another story. After my juices are flowing again I go back to the other and usually that starts off once more. Or sometimes I discover that it isn't worth bothering over. After you've been writing so long as I you'll learn a system to keep yourself going. It depends on your view of life. If you're mature you'll find out how to work."

"My writing is a mess," he sighed, "a fog, a blot."

"You'll invent your way out," said Olga, "if you only keep trying."

They sat a while longer. Olga told him of her childhood and when she was a girl. She would have talked longer but Mitka was restless. He was wondering, what after this? Where would he drag that dead cat, his soul?

Olga put what was left of the food into the market bag.

In the street he asked where to.

"The bus I guess. I live on the other side of the river with my son, his vinegary wife and their little daughter."

He took her bag—a lightened load—and walked with it in one hand, a cigarette in the other, toward the bus terminal.

"I wish you'd known my daughter, Mitka."

"So why not?" he asked hopefully, surprised he hadn't brought up this before, because she was all the time in the back of his mind.

"She had flowing hair and a sweet hourglass figure. Her nature was beyond compare. You'd have loved her."

"What's the matter, is she married?"

"She died at twenty—at the fount of life. All my stories are actually about her. Someday I'll collect the best and see if I can get them published."

He all but crumpled, then walked unsteadily on. For Madeleine he had this night come out of his burrow, to hold her against his lonely heart, but she had burst into fragments, a meteor in reverse, scattered in the far-flung sky, as he stood below, a man mourning.

They came at last to the terminal and Mitka put Olga on the bus.

"Will we meet again, Mitka?"

"Better no," he said.

"Why not?"

"It makes me sad."

"Won't you write either? You'll never know what your letters meant to me. I was like a young girl waiting for the mailman."

"Who knows?" He got off the bus.

She called him to the window. "Don't worry about your

work, and get more fresh air. Build up your body. Good health
will help your writing."

His face showed nothing but he pitied her, her daughter,
the world. Who not?

"Character is what counts in the pinches, of course properly
mixed with talent. When you saw me in the library and stayed
I thought, there is a man of character."

"Good night," Mitka said.

"Good night, my dear. Write soon."

She sat back in her seat and the bus roared out of the depot.
As it turned the corner she waved from the window.

Mitka walked the other way. He was momentarily uneasy,
until he realized he felt no pangs of hunger. On what he had
eaten tonight he could live for a week. Mitka, the camel.

Spring. It gripped and held him. Though he fought the intimacy he was the night's prisoner as he moved toward Mrs.
Lutz's.

He thought of the old girl. He'd go home now and drape her
from head to foot in flowing white. They would jounce together
up the stairs, then (strictly a one-marriage man) he would swing
her across the threshold, holding her where the fat overflowed
her corset as they waltzed around his writing chamber.

1953

The Magic Barrel

NOT LONG ago there lived in uptown New York, in a small, almost meager room, though crowded with books, Leo Finkle, a rabbinical student at the Yeshiva University. Finkle, after six years of study, was to be ordained in June and had been advised by an acquaintance that he might find it easier to win himself a congregation if he were married. Since he had no present prospects of marriage, after two tormented days of turning it over in his mind, he called in Pinye Salzman, a marriage broker whose two-line advertisement he had read in the *Forward*.

The matchmaker appeared one night out of the dark fourth-floor hallway of the graystone rooming house where Finkle lived, grasping a black, strapped portfolio that had been worn thin with use. Salzman, who had been long in the business, was of slight but dignified build, wearing an old hat, and an overcoat too short and tight for him. He smelled frankly of fish, which he loved to eat, and although he was missing a few teeth, his presence was not displeasing, because of an amiable manner curiously contrasted with mournful eyes. His voice, his lips, his wisp of beard, his bony fingers were animated, but give him a moment of repose and his mild blue eyes revealed a depth of sadness, a characteristic that put Leo a little at ease although the situation, for him, was inherently tense.

He at once informed Salzman why he had asked him to come, explaining that but for his parents, who had married comparatively late in life, he was alone in the world. He had for six years devoted himself almost entirely to his studies, as a result of which, understandably, he had found himself without time for social life and the company of young women. Therefore he thought it the better part of trial and error—of embarrassing fumbling—to call in an experienced person to advise him on these matters. He remarked in passing that the function of the marriage broker was ancient and honorable, highly approved in the Jewish community, because it made practical the necessary without hindering joy. Moreover, his own parents had been brought together by a matchmaker. They had made, if not a financially profitable marriage—since neither had possessed any worldly goods to speak of—at least a suc-cessful one in the sense of their everlasting devotion to each other. Salzman listened in embarrassed surprise, sensing a sort of apology. Later, however, he experienced a glow of pride in his work, an emotion that had left him years ago, and he heart-ily approved of Finkle.

The two went to their business. Leo had led Salzman to the only clear place in the room, a table near a window that over-looked the lamp-lit city. He seated himself at the matchmaker's side but facing him, attempting by an act of will to suppress the unpleasant tickle in his throat. Salzman eagerly unstrapped his portfolio and removed a loose rubber band from a thin packet of much-handled cards. As he flipped through them, a gesture and sound that physically hurt Leo, the student pre-tended not to see and gazed steadfastly out the window. Al-though it was still February, winter was on its last legs, signs of which he had for the first time in years begun to notice. He now observed the round white moon, moving high in the sky through a cloud menagerie, and watched with half-open mouth as it penetrated a huge hen, and dropped out of her like an egg laying itself. Salzman, though pretending through eye-glasses he had just slipped on to be engaged in scanning the writing on the cards, stole occasional glances at the young man's distinguished face, noting with pleasure the long, severe scholar's nose, brown eyes heavy with learning, sensitive yet ascetic lips, and a certain almost hollow quality of the dark cheeks. He gazed around at shelves upon shelves of books and let out a soft, contented sigh.

When Leo's eyes fell upon the cards, he counted six spread out in Salzman's hand.

"So few?" he asked in disappointment.

"You wouldn't believe me how much cards I got in my of-fice," Salzman replied. "The drawers are already filled to the top, so I keep them now in a barrel, but is every girl good for a new rabbi?"

Leo blushed at this, regretting all he had revealed of himself in a curriculum vitae he had sent to Salzman. He had thought it best to acquaint him with his strict standards and specifica-tions, but in having done so, felt he had told the marriage broker more than was absolutely necessary.

He hesitantly inquired, "Do you keep photographs of your clients on file?"

"First comes family, amount of dowry, also what kind promises," Salzman replied, unbuttoning his tight coat and settling himself in the chair. "After comes pictures, rabbi."

"Call me Mr. Finkle. I'm not yet a rabbi."

Salzman said he would, but instead called him doctor, which he changed to rabbi when Leo was not listening too attentively.

Salzman adjusted his horn-rimmed spectacles, gently cleared his throat, and read in an eager voice the contents of the top card:

"Sophie P. Twenty-four years. Widow one year. No children. Educated high school and two years' college. Father promises eight thousand dollars. Has wonderful wholesale business. Also real estate. On the mother's side comes teachers, also one actor. Well known on Second Avenue."

Leo gazed up in surprise. "Did you say a widow?"

"A widow don't mean spoiled, rabbi. She lived with her husband maybe four months. He was a sick boy she made a mistake to marry him."

"Marrying a widow has never entered my mind."

"This is because you have no experience. A widow, especially if she is young and healthy like this girl, is a wonderful person to marry. She will be thankful to you the rest of her life. Believe me, if I was looking now for a bride, I would marry a widow."

Leo reflected, then shook his head.

Salzman hunched his shoulders in an almost imperceptible gesture of disappointment. He placed the card down on the wooden table and began to read another:

"Lily H. High school teacher. Regular. Not a substitute. Has savings and new Dodge car. Lived in Paris one year. Father is successful dentist thirty-five years. Interested in professional man. Well-Americanized family. Wonderful opportunity.

"I know her personally," said Salzman. "I wish you could see this girl. She is a doll. Also very intelligent. All day you could talk to her about books and theyater and what not. She also knows current events."

"I don't believe you mentioned her age?"

"Her age?" Salzman said, raising his brows. "Her age is thirty-two years."

Leo said after a while, "I'm afraid that seems a little too old."

Salzman let out a laugh. "So how old are you, rabbi?"

"Twenty-seven."

"So what is the difference, tell me, between twenty-seven and thirty-two? My own wife is seven years older than me. So what did I suffer?— Nothing. If Rothschild's daughter wants to marry you, would you say on account her age, no?"

"Yes," Leo said dryly.

Salzman shook off the no in the yes. "Five years don't mean a thing. I give you my word that when you will live with her for one week you will forget her age. What does it mean five years—that she lived more and knows more than somebody who is younger? On this girl, God bless her, years are not wasted. Each one that it comes makes better the bargain."

"What subject does she teach in high school?"

"Languages. If you heard the way she speaks French, you will think it is music. I am in the business twenty-five years, and I recommend her with my whole heart. Believe me, I know what I'm talking, rabbi."

"What's on the next card?" Leo said abruptly.

Salzman reluctantly turned up the third card:

"Ruth K. Nineteen years. Honor student. Father offers thirteen thousand cash to the right bridegroom. He is a medical doctor. Stomach specialist with marvelous practice. Brother-in-law owns own garment business. Particular people."

Salzman looked as if he had read his trump card.

"Did you say nineteen?" Leo asked with interest.

"On the dot."

"Is she attractive?" He blushed. "Pretty?"

Salzman kissed his fingertips. "A little doll. On this I give you my word. Let me call the father tonight and you will see what means pretty."

But Leo was troubled. "You're sure she's that young?"

"This I am positive. The father will show you the birth certificate."

"Are you positive there isn't something wrong with her?" Leo insisted.

"Who says there is wrong?"

"I don't understand why an American girl her age should go to a marriage broker."

A smile spread over Salzman's face.

"So for the same reason you went, she comes."

Leo flushed. "I am pressed for time."

Salzman, realizing he had been tactless, quickly explained. "The father came, not her. He wants she should have the best, so he looks around himself. When we will locate the right boy he will introduce him and encourage. This makes a better marriage than if a young girl without experience takes for herself. I don't have to tell you this."

"But don't you think this young girl believes in love?" Leo spoke uneasily.

Salzman was about to guffaw but caught himself and said soberly, "Love comes with the right person, not before."

Leo parted dry lips but did not speak. Noticing that Salzman had snatched a glance at the next card, he cleverly asked, "How is her health?"

"Perfect," Salzman said, breathing with difficulty. "Of course, she is a little lame on her right foot from an auto accident that it happened to her when she was twelve years, but nobody notices on account she is so brilliant and also beautiful."

Leo got up heavily and went to the window. He felt curiously bitter and upbraided himself for having called in the marriage broker. Finally, he shook his head.

"Why not?" Salzman persisted, the pitch of his voice rising.

"Because I detest stomach specialists."

"So what do you care what is his business? After you marry her do you need him? Who says he must come every Friday night in your house?"

Ashamed of the way the talk was going, Leo dismissed Salzman, who went home with heavy, melancholy eyes.

Though he had felt only relief at the marriage broker's departure, Leo was in low spirits the next day. He explained it as arising from Salzman's failure to produce a suitable bride for him. He did not care for his type of clientele. But when Leo found himself hesitating whether to seek out another matchmaker, one more polished than Pinye, he wondered if it could be—his protestations to the contrary, and although he honored his father and mother—that he did not, in essence, care for the matchmaking institution? This thought he quickly put out of mind yet found himself still upset. All day he ran around in the woods—missed an important appointment, forgot to give out his laundry, walked out of a Broadway cafeteria without paying and had to run back with the ticket in his hand; had even not recognized his landlady in the street when she passed with a friend and courteously called out, "A good evening to you, Doctor Finkle." By nightfall, however, he had regained sufficient calm to sink his nose into a book and there found peace from his thoughts.

Almost at once there came a knock on the door. Before Leo could say enter, Salzman, commercial cupid, was standing in the room. His face was gray and meager, his expression hungry, and he looked as if he would expire on his feet. Yet the marriage broker managed, by some trick of the muscles, to display a broad smile.

"So good evening. I am invited?"

Leo nodded, disturbed to see him again, yet unwilling to ask the man to leave.

Beaming still, Salzman laid his portfolio on the table. "Rabbi, I got for you tonight good news."

"I've asked you not to call me rabbi. I'm still a student."

"Your worries are finished. I have for you a first-class bride."

"Leave me in peace concerning this subject." Leo pretended lack of interest.

"The world will dance at your wedding."

"Please, Mr. Salzman, no more."

"But first must come back my strength," Salzman said weakly. He fumbled with the portfolio straps and took out of the leather case an oily paper bag, from which he extracted a hard, seeded roll and a small smoked whitefish. With a quick motion of his hand he stripped the fish out of its skin and began ravenously to chew. "All day in a rush," he muttered.

Leo watched him eat.

"A sliced tomato you have maybe?" Salzman hesitantly inquired.

"No."

The marriage broker shut his eyes and ate. When he had finished he carefully cleaned up the crumbs and rolled up the remains of the fish, in the paper bag. His spectacled eyes roamed the room until he discovered, amid some piles of books, a one-burner gas stove. Lifting his hat he humbly asked, "A glass tea you got, rabbi?"

Conscience-stricken, Leo rose and brewed the tea. He served it with a chunk of lemon and two cubes of lump sugar, delighting Salzman.

After he had drunk his tea, Salzman's strength and good spirits were restored.

"So tell me, rabbi," he said amiably, "you considered some more the three clients I mentioned yesterday?"

"There was no need to consider."

"Why not?"

"None of them suits me."

"What then suits you?"

Leo let it pass because he could give only a confused answer.

Without waiting for a reply, Salzman asked, "You remember this girl I talked to you—the high school teacher?"

"Age thirty-two?"

But, surprisingly, Salzman's face lit in a smile. "Age twenty-nine."

Leo shot him a look. "Reduced from thirty-two?"

"A mistake," Salzman avowed. "I talked today with the dentist. He took me to his safety deposit box and showed me the birth certificate. She was twenty-nine years last August. They made her a party in the mountains where she went for her vacation. When her father spoke to me the first time I forgot to write the age and I told you thirty-two, but now I remember this was a different client, a widow."

"The same one you told me about, I thought she was twenty-four?"

"A different. Am I responsible that the world is filled with widows?"

"No, but I'm not interested in them, nor, for that matter, in schoolteachers."

Salzman pulled his clasped hands to his breast. Looking at the ceiling he devoutly exclaimed, "Yiddishe kinder, what can I say to somebody that he is not interested in high school teachers? So what then you are interested?"

Leo flushed but controlled himself.

"In what else will you be interested," Salzman went on, "if you not interested in this fine girl that she speaks four languages and has personally in the bank ten thousand dollars? Also her father guarantees further twelve thousand. Also she has a new car, wonderful clothes, talks on all subjects, and she will give you a first-class home and children. How near do we come in our life to paradise?"

"If she's so wonderful, why wasn't she married ten years ago?"

"Why?" said Salzman with a heavy laugh. "—Why? Because she is *partikiler*. This is why. She wants the *best*."

Leo was silent, amused at how he had entangled himself. But Salzman had aroused his interest in Lily H., and he began seriously to consider calling on her. When the marriage broker observed how intently Leo's mind was at work on the facts he had supplied, he felt certain they would soon come to an agreement.

Late Saturday afternoon, conscious of Salzman, Leo Finkle walked with Lily Hirschorn along Riverside Drive. He walked briskly and erectly, wearing with distinction the black fedora he had that morning taken with trepidation out of the dusty hat box on his closet shelf, and the heavy black Saturday coat he had thoroughly whisked clean. Leo also owned a walking stick, a present from a distant relative, but quickly put temptation aside and did not use it. Lily, petite and not unpretty, had on something signifying the approach of spring. She was au courant, animatedly, with all sorts of subjects, and he weighed her words and found her surprisingly sound—score another for Salzman, whom he uneasily sensed to be somewhere around, hiding perhaps high in a tree along the street, flashing the lady signals with a pocket mirror; or perhaps a cloven-hoofed Pan, piping nuptial ditties as he danced his invisible way before them, strewing wild buds on the walk and purple grapes in their path, symbolizing fruit of a union, though there was of course still none.

Lily startled Leo by remarking, "I was thinking of Mr. Salzman, a curious figure, wouldn't you say?"

Not certain what to answer, he nodded.

She bravely went on, blushing, "I for one am grateful for his introducing us. Aren't you?"

He courteously replied, "I am."

"I mean," she said with a little laugh—and it was all in good taste, or at least gave the effect of being not in bad—"do you mind that we came together so?"

He was not displeased with her honesty, recognizing that she meant to set the relationship aright, and understanding that it took a certain amount of experience in life, and courage, to want to do it quite that way. One had to have some sort of past to make that kind of beginning.

He said that he did not mind. Salzman's function was traditional and honorable—valuable for what it might achieve, which, he pointed out, was frequently nothing.

Lily agreed with a sigh. They walked on for a while and she said after a long silence, again with a nervous laugh, "Would you mind if I asked you something a little bit personal? Frankly, I find the subject fascinating." Although Leo shrugged, she went on half embarrassedly, "How was it that you came to your calling? I mean, was it a sudden passionate inspiration?"

Leo, after a time, slowly replied, "I was always interested in the Law."

"You saw revealed in it the presence of the Highest?"

He nodded and changed the subject. "I understand that you spent a little time in Paris, Miss Hirschorn?"

"Oh, did Mr. Salzman tell you, Rabbi Finkle?" Leo winced but she went on, "It was ages ago and almost forgotten. I remember I had to return for my sister's wedding."

And Lily would not be put off. "When," she asked in a slightly trembly voice, "did you become enamored of God?"

He stared at her. Then it came to him that she was talking not about Leo Finkle but a total stranger, some mystical figure, perhaps even passionate prophet that Salzman had dreamed up for her—no relation to the living or dead. Leo trembled with rage and weakness. The trickster had obviously sold her a bill of goods, just as he had him, who'd expected to become acquainted with a young lady of twenty-nine, only to behold, the moment he had laid eyes upon her strained and anxious face, a woman past thirty-five and aging rapidly. Only his self-control had kept him this long in her presence.

"I am not," he said gravely, "a talented religious person," and in seeking words to go on, found himself possessed by shame and fear. "I think," he said in a strained manner, "that I came to God not because I loved Him but because I did not."

This confession he spoke harshly because its unexpectedness shook him.

Lily wilted. Leo saw a profusion of loaves of bread go flying like ducks high over his head, not unlike the winged loaves by which he had counted himself to sleep last night. Mercifully, then, it snowed, which he would not put past Salzman's machinations.

He was infuriated with the marriage broker and swore he would throw him out of the room the moment he reappeared. But Salzman did not come that night, and when Leo's anger had subsided, an unaccountable despair grew in its place. At first he thought this was caused by his disappointment in Lily, but before long it became evident that he had involved himself with Salzman without a true knowledge of his own intent. He gradually realized—with an emptiness that seized him with six hands—that he had called in the broker to find him a bride because he was incapable of doing it himself. This terrifying insight he had derived as a result of his meeting and conversation with Lily Hirschorn. Her probing questions had somehow irritated him into revealing—to himself more than her—the true nature of his relationship to God, and from that it had come upon him, with shocking force, that apart from his parents, he had never loved anyone. Or perhaps it went the other way, that he did not love God so well as he might, because he had not loved man. It seemed to Leo that his whole life stood starkly revealed and he saw himself for the first time as he truly was—unloved and loveless. This bitter but somehow not fully unexpected revelation brought him to a point of panic, controlled only by extraordinary effort. He covered his face with his hands and cried.

The week that followed was the worst of his life. He did not eat and lost weight. His beard darkened and grew ragged. He stopped attending seminars and almost never opened a book. He seriously considered leaving the Yeshiva, although he was deeply troubled at the thought of the loss of all his years of study—saw them like pages torn from a book, strewn over the city—and at the devastating effect of this decision upon his parents. But he had lived without knowledge of himself, and never in the Five Books and all the Commentaries—mea culpa—had the truth been revealed to him. He did not know where to turn, and in all this desolating loneliness there was no *to whom*, although he often thought of Lily but not once could bring himself to go downstairs and make the call. He became touchy and irritable, especially with his landlady, who asked him all manner of personal questions; on the other hand, sensing his own disagreeableness, he waylaid her on the stairs and apologized abjectly, until, mortified, she ran from him. Out of this, however, he drew the consolation that he was a Jew and that a Jew suffered. But gradually, as the long and terrible week drew to a close, he regained his composure and some idea of purpose in life: to go on as planned. Although he was imperfect, the ideal was not. As for his quest of a bride, the thought of continuing afflicted him with anxiety and heartburn, yet perhaps with this new knowledge of himself he would be more successful than in the past. Perhaps love would now come to him and a bride to that love. And for this sanctified seeking who needed a Salzman?

The marriage broker, a skeleton with haunted eyes, returned that very night. He looked, withal, the picture of frustrated expectancy—as if he had steadfastly waited the week at Miss Lily Hirschorn's side for a telephone call that never came.

Casually coughing, Salzman came immediately to the point: "So how did you like her?"

Leo's anger rose and he could not refrain from chiding the matchmaker: "Why did you lie to me, Salzman?"

Salzman's pale face went dead white, the world had snowed on him.

"Did you not state that she was twenty-nine?" Leo insisted.

"I give you my word—"

"She was thirty-five, if a day. *At least* thirty-five."

"Of this don't be too sure. Her father told me—"

"Never mind. The worst of it is that you lied to her."

"How did I lie to her, tell me?"

"You told her things about me that weren't true. You made me out to be more, consequently less than I am. She had in mind a totally different person, a sort of semi-mystical Wonder Rabbi."

"All I said, you was a religious man."

"I can imagine."

Salzman sighed. "This is my weakness that I have," he confessed. "My wife says to me I shouldn't be a salesman, but when I have two fine people that they would be wonderful to be married, I am so happy that I talk too much." He smiled wanly. "This is why Salzman is a poor man."

Leo's anger left him. "Well, Salzman, I'm afraid that's all."

The marriage broker fastened hungry eyes on him.

"You don't want any more a bride?"

"I do," said Leo, "but I have decided to seek her in another way. I am no longer interested in an arranged marriage. To be frank, I now admit the necessity of premarital love. That is, I want to be in love with the one I marry."

"Love?" said Salzman, astounded. After a moment he remarked, "For us, our love is our life, not for the ladies. In the ghetto they—"

"I know, I know," said Leo. "I've thought of it often. Love, I have said to myself, should be a product of living and worship rather than its own end. Yet for myself I find it necessary to establish the level of my need and fulfill it."

Salzman shrugged but answered, "Listen, rabbi, if you want love, this I can find for you also. I have such beautiful clients that you will love them the minute your eyes will see them."

Leo smiled unhappily. "I'm afraid you don't understand."

But Salzman hastily unstrapped his portfolio and withdrew a manila packet from it.

"Pictures," he said, quickly laying the envelope on the table.

Leo called after him to take the pictures away, but as if on the wings of the wind, Salzman had disappeared.

March came. Leo had returned to his regular routine. Although he felt not quite himself yet—lacked energy—he was making plans for a more active social life. Of course it would cost something, but he was an expert in cutting corners; and when there were no corners left he would make circles rounder. All the while Salzman's pictures had lain on the table, gathering dust. Occasionally as Leo sat studying, or enjoying a cup of tea, his eyes fell on the manila envelope, but he never opened it.

The days went by and no social life to speak of developed with a member of the opposite sex—it was difficult, given the circumstances of his situation. One morning Leo toiled up the stairs to his room and stared out the window at the city. Although the day was bright his view of it was dark. For some time he watched the people in the street below hurrying along and then turned with a heavy heart to his little room. On the table was the packet. With a sudden relentless gesture he tore it open. For a half hour he stood by the table in a state of excitement, examining the photographs of the ladies Salzman had included. Finally, with a deep sigh he put them down. There were six, of varying degrees of attractiveness, but look at them long enough and they all became Lily Hirschorn: all past their prime, all starved behind bright smiles, not a true personality in the lot. Life, despite their frantic yoohooings, had passed them by; they were pictures in a briefcase that stank of fish. After a while, however, as Leo attempted to return the photographs into the envelope, he found in it another, a snapshot of the type taken by a machine for a quarter. He gazed at it a moment and let out a low cry.

Her face deeply moved him. Why, he could at first not say. It gave him the impression of youth—spring flowers, yet age— a sense of having been used to the bone, wasted; this came from the eyes, which were hauntingly familiar, yet absolutely strange. He had a vivid impression that he had met her before, but try as he might he could not place her although he could almost recall her name, as if he had read it in her own handwriting. No, this couldn't be; he would have remembered her. It was not, he affirmed, that she had an extraordinary beauty—no, though her face was attractive enough; it was that *something* about her moved him. Feature for feature, even some of the ladies of the photographs could do better; but she leaped forth to his heart—had *lived*, or wanted to—more than just wanted, perhaps regretted how she had lived—had somehow deeply suffered: it could be seen in the depths of those reluctant eyes, and from the way the light enclosed and shone from her, and within her, opening realms of possibility: this was her own. Her he desired. His head ached and eyes narrowed with the intensity of his gazing, then as if an obscure fog had blown up in the mind, he experienced fear of her and was aware that he had received an impression, somehow, of evil. He shuddered, saying softly, it is thus with us all. Leo brewed some tea in a

small pot and sat sipping it without sugar, to calm himself. But
before he had finished drinking, again with excitement he examined the face and found it good: good for Leo Finkle. Only
such a one could understand him and help him seek whatever
he was seeking. She might, perhaps, love him. How she had
happened to be among the discards in Salzman's barrel he
could never guess, but he knew he must urgently go find her.

Leo rushed downstairs, grabbed up the Bronx telephone
book, and searched for Salzman's home address. He was not
listed, nor was his office. Neither was he in the Manhattan
book. But Leo remembered having written down the address
on a slip of paper after he had read Salzman's advertisement in
the "personals" column of the *Forward*. He ran up to his room
and tore through his papers, without luck. It was exasperating.
Just when he needed the matchmaker he was nowhere to be
found. Fortunately Leo remembered to look in his wallet.
There on a card he found his name written and a Bronx address. No phone number was listed, the reason—Leo now
recalled—he had originally communicated with Salzman by
letter. He got on his coat, put a hat on over his skullcap and
hurried to the subway station. All the way to the far end of the
Bronx he sat on the edge of his seat. He was more than once
tempted to take out the picture and see if the girl's face was as
he remembered, but he refrained, allowing the snapshot to
remain in his inside coat pocket, content to have her so close.
When the train pulled into the station he was waiting at the
door and bolted out. He quickly located the street Salzman
had advertised.

The building he sought was less than a block from the subway, but it was not an office building, nor even a loft, nor a
store in which one could rent office space. It was a very old
tenement house. Leo found Salzman's name in pencil on a
soiled tag under the bell and climbed three dark flights to his
apartment. When he knocked, the door was opened by a thin,
asthmatic, gray-haired woman, in felt slippers.

"Yes?" she said, expecting nothing. She listened without listening. He could have sworn he had seen her, too, before but
knew it was an illusion.

"Salzman—does he live here? Pinye Salzman," he said, "the
matchmaker?"

She stared at him a long minute. "Of course."

He felt embarrassed. "Is he in?"

"No." Her mouth, though left open, offered nothing more.

"The matter is urgent. Can you tell me where his office is?"

"In the air." She pointed upward.

"You mean he has no office?" Leo asked.

"In his socks."

He peered into the apartment. It was sunless and dingy, one large room divided by a half-open curtain, beyond which he could see a sagging metal bed. The near side of the room was crowded with rickety chairs, old bureaus, a three-legged table, racks of cooking utensils, and all the apparatus of a kitchen. But there was no sign of Salzman or his magic barrel, probably also a figment of the imagination. An odor of frying fish made Leo weak to the knees.

"Where is he?" he insisted. "I've got to see your husband."

At length she answered, "So who knows where he is? Every time he thinks a new thought he runs to a different place. Go home, he will find you."

"Tell him Leo Finkle."

She gave no sign she had heard.

He walked downstairs, depressed.

But Salzman, breathless, stood waiting at his door.

Leo was astounded and overjoyed. "How did you get here before me?"

"I rushed."

"Come inside."

They entered. Leo fixed tea, and a sardine sandwich for Salzman. As they were drinking he reached behind him for the packet of pictures and handed them to the marriage broker.

Salzman put down his glass and said expectantly, "You found somebody you like?"

"Not among these."

The marriage broker turned away.

"Here is the one I want." Leo held forth the snapshot.

Salzman slipped on his glasses and took the picture into his trembling hand. He turned ghastly and let out a groan.

"What's the matter?" cried Leo.

"Excuse me. Was an accident this picture. She isn't for you." Salzman frantically shoved the manila packet into his portfolio. He thrust the snapshot into his pocket and fled down the stairs.

Leo, after momentary paralysis, gave chase and cornered the marriage broker in the vestibule. The landlady made hysterical outcries but neither of them listened.

"Give me back the picture, Salzman."

"No." The pain in his eyes was terrible.

"Tell me who she is then."

"This I can't tell you. Excuse me."

He made to depart, but Leo, forgetting himself, seized the matchmaker by his tight coat and shook him frenziedly.

"Please," sighed Salzman. "*Please*."

Leo ashamedly let him go. "Tell me who she is," he begged. "It's very important for me to know."

"She is not for you. She is a wild one—wild, without shame. This is not a bride for a rabbi."

"What do you mean wild?"

"Like an animal. Like a dog. For her to be poor was a sin. This is why to me she is dead now."

"In God's name, what do you mean?"

"Her I can't introduce to you," Salzman cried.

"Why are you so excited?"

"Why, he asks," Salzman said, bursting into tears. "This is my baby, my Stella, she should burn in hell."

Leo hurried up to bed and hid under the covers. Under the covers he thought his life through. Although he soon fell asleep he could not sleep her out of his mind. He woke, beating his breast. Though he prayed to be rid of her, his prayers went unanswered. Through days of torment he endlessly struggled not to love her; fearing success, he escaped it. He then concluded to convert her to goodness, himself to God. The idea alternately nauseated and exalted him.

He perhaps did not know that he had come to a final decision until he encountered Salzman in a Broadway cafeteria. He was sitting alone at a rear table, sucking the bony remains of a fish. The marriage broker appeared haggard, and transparent to the point of vanishing.

Salzman looked up at first without recognizing him. Leo

had grown a pointed beard and his eyes were weighted with wisdom.

"Salzman," he said, "love has at last come to my heart."

"Who can love from a picture?" mocked the marriage broker.

"It is not impossible."

"If you can love her, then you can love anybody. Let me show you some new clients that they just sent me their photographs. One is a little doll."

"Just her I want," Leo murmured.

"Don't be a fool, doctor. Don't bother with her."

"Put me in touch with her, Salzman," Leo said humbly. "Perhaps I can be of service."

Salzman had stopped eating and Leo understood with emotion that it was now arranged.

Leaving the cafeteria, he was, however, afflicted by a tormenting suspicion that Salzman had planned it all to happen this way.

Leo was informed by letter that she would meet him on a certain corner, and she was there one spring night, waiting under a street lamp. He appeared, carrying a small bouquet of violets and rosebuds. Stella stood by the lamppost, smoking. She wore white with red shoes, which fitted his expectations, although in a troubled moment he had imagined the dress red, and only the shoes white. She waited uneasily and shyly. From afar he saw that her eyes—clearly her father's—were filled with desperate innocence. He pictured, in her, his own redemption. Violins and lit candles revolved in the sky. Leo ran forward with flowers outthrust.

Around the corner, Salzman, leaning against a wall, chanted prayers for the dead.

1954

The Mourners

KESSLER, FORMERLY an egg candler, lived alone on social security. Though past sixty-five, he might have found well-paying work with more than one butter and egg wholesaler, for he sorted and graded with speed and accuracy, but he was a quarrelsome type and considered a troublemaker, so the wholesalers did without him. Therefore, after a time he retired, living with few wants on his old-age pension. Kessler inhabited a small cheap flat on the top floor of a decrepit tenement on the East Side. Perhaps because he lived above so many stairs, no one bothered to visit him. He was much alone, as he had been most of his life. At one time he'd had a family, but unable to stand his wife or children, always in his way, he had after some years walked out on them. He never saw them thereafter because he never sought them, and they did not seek him. Thirty years had passed. He had no idea where they were, nor did he think much about it.

In the tenement, although he had lived there ten years, he was more or less unknown. The tenants on both sides of his flat on the fifth floor, an Italian family of three middle-aged sons and their wizened mother, and a sullen, childless German couple named Hoffman, never said hello to him, nor did he greet any of them on the way up or down the narrow wooden stairs. Others of the house recognized Kessler when they passed him in the street, but they thought he lived elsewhere on the block. Ignace, the small, bent-back janitor, knew him best, for they had several times played two-handed pinochle; but Ignace, usually the loser because he lacked skill at cards, had stopped going up after a time. He complained to his wife that he couldn't stand the stink there, that the filthy flat with its junky furniture made him sick. The janitor had spread the word about Kessler to the others on the floor, and they shunned him as a dirty old man. Kessler understood this but had contempt for them all.

One day Ignace and Kessler began a quarrel over the way the egg candler piled oily bags overflowing with garbage into the dumbwaiter, instead of using a pail. One word shot off another, and they were soon calling each other savage names, when Kessler slammed the door in the janitor's face. Ignace ran down five flights of stairs and loudly cursed out the old man to his impassive wife. It happened that Gruber, the land-lord, a fat man with a consistently worried face, who wore yards of baggy clothes, was in the building, making a check of plumbing repairs, and to him the enraged Ignace related the trouble he was having with Kessler. He described, holding his nose, the smell in Kessler's flat, and called him the dirtiest person he ever saw. Gruber knew his janitor was exaggerating, but he felt burdened by financial worries which shot his blood pressure up to astonishing heights, so he settled it quickly by saying, "Give him notice." None of the tenants in the house had held a written lease since the war, and Gruber felt confi-dent, in case somebody asked questions, that he could easily justify his dismissal of Kessler as an undesirable tenant. It had occurred to him that Ignace could then slap a cheap coat of paint on the walls, and the flat would be let to someone for five dollars more than the old man was paying.

That night after supper, Ignace victoriously ascended the stairs and knocked on Kessler's door. The egg candler opened it, and seeing who stood there, immediately slammed it shut. Ignace shouted through the door, "Mr. Gruber says to give notice. We don't want you around here. Your dirt stinks the whole house." There was silence, but Ignace waited, relishing what he had said. Although after five minutes he still heard no sound, the janitor stayed there, picturing the old Jew trem-bling behind the locked door. He spoke again, "You got two weeks' notice till the first, then you better move out or Mr. Gruber and myself will throw you out." Ignace watched as the door slowly opened. To his surprise he found himself fright-ened at the old man's appearance. He looked, in the act of opening the door, like a corpse adjusting his coffin lid. But if he appeared dead, his voice was alive. It rose terrifyingly harsh from his throat, and he sprayed curses over all the years of Ig-nace's life. His eyes were reddened, his cheeks sunken, and his wisp of beard moved agitatedly. He seemed to be losing weight as he shouted. The janitor no longer had any heart for the matter, but he could not bear so many insults all at once, so he cried out, "You dirty old bum, you better get out and don't make so much trouble." To this the enraged Kessler swore they would first have to kill him and drag him out dead.

On the morning of the first of December, Ignace found in his letter box a soiled folded paper containing Kessler's twenty-five dollars. He showed it to Gruber that evening when the landlord came to collect the rent money. Gruber, after a minute of absently contemplating the money, frowned disgustedly.

"I thought I told you to give notice."

"Yes, Mr. Gruber," Ignace agreed. "I gave him."

"That's a helluva chutzpah," said Gruber. "Gimme the keys."

Ignace brought the ring of passkeys, and Gruber, breathing heavily, began the lumbering climb up the long avenue of stairs. Although he rested on each landing, the fatigue of climbing, and his profuse flowing perspiration, heightened his irritation.

Arriving at the top floor he banged his fist on Kessler's door. "Gruber, the landlord. Open up here."

There was no answer, no movement within, so Gruber inserted his key into the lock and twisted. Kessler had barricaded the door with a chest and some chairs. Gruber had to put his shoulder to the door and shove before he could step into the hallway of the badly lit two-and-a-half-room flat. The old man, his face drained of blood, was standing in the kitchen doorway.

"I warned you to scram outa here," Gruber said loudly. "Move out or I'll telephone the city marshal."

"Mr. Gruber—" began Kessler.

"Don't bother me with your lousy excuses, just beat it." He gazed around. "It looks like a junk shop and it smells like a toilet. It'll take me a month to clean up here."

"This smell is only cabbage that I am cooking for my supper. Wait, I'll open a window and it will go away."

"When you go away, it'll go away." Gruber took out his bulky wallet, counted out twelve dollars, added fifty cents, and plunked the money on top of the chest. "You got two more weeks till the fifteenth, then you gotta be out or I will get a dispossess. Don't talk back talk. Get outa here and go somewhere that they don't know you and maybe you'll get a place."

"No, Mr. Gruber," Kessler cried passionately. "I didn't do nothing, and I will stay here."

"Don't monkey with my blood pressure," said Gruber. "If you're not out by the fifteenth, I will personally throw you on your bony ass."

Then he left and walked heavily down the stairs.

The fifteenth came and Ignace found the twelve-fifty in his letter box. He telephoned Gruber and told him.

"I'll get a dispossess," Gruber shouted. He instructed the janitor to write out a note saying to Kessler that his money was refused, and to stick it under his door. This Ignace did. Kessler returned the money to the letter box, but again Ignace wrote a note and slipped it, with the money, under the old man's door.

After another day Kessler received a copy of his eviction notice. It said to appear in court on Friday at 10 a.m. to show cause why he should not be evicted for continued neglect and destruction of rental property. The official notice filled Kessler with great fright because he had never in his life been to court. He did not appear on the day he had been ordered to.

That same afternoon the marshal came with two brawny assistants. Ignace opened Kessler's lock for them and as they pushed their way into the flat, the janitor hastily ran down the stairs to hide in the cellar. Despite Kessler's wailing and carrying on, the two assistants methodically removed his meager furniture and set it out on the sidewalk. After that they got Kessler out, though they had to break open the bathroom door because the old man had locked himself in there. He shouted, struggled, pleaded with his neighbors to help him, but they looked on in a silent group outside the door. The two assistants, holding the old man tightly by the arms and skinny legs, carried him, kicking and moaning, down the stairs. They sat him in the street on a chair amid his junk. Upstairs, the marshal bolted the door with a lock Ignace had supplied, signed a paper which he handed to the janitor's wife, and then drove off in an automobile with his assistants.

Kessler sat on a split chair on the sidewalk. It was raining and the rain soon turned to sleet, but he still sat there. People passing by skirted the pile of his belongings. They stared at Kessler and he stared at nothing. He wore no hat or coat, and the snow fell on him, making him look like a piece of his dispossessed goods. Soon the wizened Italian woman from the top floor returned to the house with two of her sons, each carrying a loaded shopping bag. When she recognized Kessler sitting amid his furniture, she began to shriek. She shrieked in Italian at Kessler although he paid no attention to her. She stood on the stoop, shrunken, gesticulating with thin arms, her loose mouth working angrily. Her sons tried to calm her, but still she shrieked. Several of the neighbors came down to see who was making the racket. Finally, the two sons, unable to think what else to do, set down their shopping bags, lifted Kessler out of the chair, and carried him up the stairs. Hoffman, Kessler's other neighbor, working with a small triangular file, cut open the padlock, and Kessler was carried into the flat from which he had been evicted. Ignace screeched at everybody, calling them filthy names, but the three men went downstairs and hauled up Kessler's chairs, his broken table, chest, and ancient metal bed. They piled all the furniture into the bedroom. Kessler sat on the edge of the bed and wept. After a while, after the old Italian woman had sent in a soup plate full of hot macaroni seasoned with tomato sauce and grated cheese, they left.

Ignace phoned Gruber. The landlord was eating and the food turned to lumps in his throat. "I'll throw them all out, the bastards," he yelled. He put on his hat, got into his car, and drove through the slush to the tenement. All the time he was thinking of his worries: high repair costs; it was hard to keep the place together; maybe the building would someday collapse. He had read of such things. All of a sudden the front of the building parted from the rest and fell like a breaking wave into the street. Gruber cursed the old man for taking him from his supper. When he got to the house, he snatched Ignace's keys and ascended the sagging stairs. Ignace tried to follow, but Gruber told him to stay the hell in his hole. When the landlord was not looking, Ignace crept up after him.

Gruber turned the key and let himself into Kessler's dark flat. He pulled the light chain and found the old man sitting limply on the side of the bed. On the floor at his feet lay a plate of stiffened macaroni.

"What do you think you're doing here?" Gruber thundered.

The old man sat motionless.

"Don't you know it's against the law? This is trespassing and you're breaking the law. Answer me."

Kessler remained mute.

Gruber mopped his brow with a large yellowed handkerchief.

"Listen, my friend, you're gonna make lots of trouble for yourself. If they catch you in here you might go to the workhouse. I'm only trying to advise you."

To his surprise Kessler looked at him with wet, brimming eyes.

"What did I did to you?" he bitterly wept. "Who throws out of his house a man that he lived there ten years and pays every month on time his rent? What did I do, tell me? Who hurts a man without a reason? Are you Hitler or a Jew?" He was hitting his chest with his fist.

Gruber removed his hat. He listened carefully, at first at a loss what to say, but then answered: "Listen, Kessler, it's not personal. I own this house and it's falling apart. My bills are sky high. If the tenants don't take care they have to go. You don't take care and you fight with my janitor, so you have to go. Leave in the morning, and I won't say another word. But if you don't leave the flat, you'll get the heave-ho again. I'll call the marshal."

"Mr. Gruber," said Kessler, "I won't go. Kill me if you want it, but I won't go."

Ignace hurried away from the door as Gruber left in anger. The next morning, after a restless night of worries, the landlord set out to drive to the city marshal's office. On the way he stopped at a candy store for a pack of cigarettes and there decided once more to speak to Kessler. A thought had occurred to him: he would offer to get the old man into a public home.

He drove to the tenement and knocked on Ignace's door.

"Is the old gink still up there?"

"I don't know if so, Mr. Gruber." The janitor was ill at ease.

"What do you mean you don't know?"

"I didn't see him go out. Before, I looked in his keyhole but nothing moves."

"So why didn't you open the door with your key?"

"I was afraid," Ignace answered nervously.

"What are you afraid?"

Ignace wouldn't say.

A fright went through Gruber but he didn't show it. He grabbed the keys and walked ponderously up the stairs, hurrying every so often.

No one answered his knock. As he unlocked the door he broke into heavy sweat.

But the old man was there, alive, sitting without shoes on the bedroom floor.

"Listen, Kessler," said the landlord, relieved although his head pounded. "I got an idea that, if you do it the way I say, your troubles are over."

He explained his proposal to Kessler, but the egg candler was not listening. His eyes were downcast, and his body swayed slowly sideways. As the landlord talked on, the old man was thinking of what had whirled through his mind as he had sat out on the sidewalk in the falling snow. He had thought through his miserable life, remembering how, as a young man, he had abandoned his family, walking out on his wife and three innocent children, without even in some way attempting to provide for them; without, in all the intervening years—so God help him—once trying to discover if they were alive or dead. How, in so short a life, could a man do so much wrong? This thought smote him to the heart and he recalled the past without end and moaned and tore at his flesh with his nails.

Gruber was frightened at the extent of Kessler's suffering. Maybe I should let him stay, he thought. Then as he watched the old man, he realized he was bunched up there on the floor engaged in an act of mourning. There he sat, white from fasting, rocking back and forth, his beard dwindled to a shade of itself.

Something's wrong here—Gruber tried to imagine what and found it all oppressive. He felt he ought to run out, get away, but then saw himself fall and go tumbling down the five flights of stairs; he groaned at the broken picture of himself lying at the bottom. Only he was still there in Kessler's bedroom, listening to the old man praying. Somebody's dead, Gruber muttered. He figured Kessler had got bad news, yet instinctively he knew he hadn't. Then it struck him with a terrible force that the mourner was mourning him: it was *he* who was dead.

The landlord was agonized. Sweating brutally, he felt an enormous constricted weight in him that forced itself up until his head was at the point of bursting. For a full minute he awaited a stroke; but the feeling painfully passed, leaving him miserable.

When after a while, he gazed around the room, it was clean, drenched in daylight, and fragrant. Gruber then suffered unbearable remorse for the way he had treated the old man. With a cry of shame he pulled the sheet off Kessler's bed, and wrapping it around himself, sank to the floor and became a mourner.

1955

Angel Levine

MANISCHEVITZ, A tailor, in his fifty-first year suffered many reverses and indignities. Previously a man of comfortable means, he overnight lost all he had, when his establishment caught fire, after a metal container of cleaning fluid exploded, and burned to the ground. Although Manischevitz was insured against fire, damage suits by two customers who had been hurt in the flames deprived him of every penny he had saved. At almost the same time, his son, of much promise, was killed in the war, and his daughter, without so much as a word of warning, married a lout and disappeared with him as off the face of the earth. Thereafter Manischevitz was victimized by excruciating backaches and found himself unable to work even as a presser—the only kind of work available to him—for more than an hour or two daily, because beyond that the pain from standing was maddening. His Fanny, a good wife and mother, who had taken in washing and sewing, began before his eyes to waste away. Suffering shortness of breath, she at last became seriously ill and took to her bed. The doctor, a former customer of Manischevitz, who out of pity treated them, at first had difficulty diagnosing her ailment, but later put it down as hardening of the arteries at an advanced stage. He took Manischevitz aside, prescribed complete rest for her, and in whispers gave him to know there was little hope.

Throughout his trials Manischevitz had remained somewhat stoic, almost unbelieving that all this had descended on his head, as if it were happening, let us say, to an acquaintance or some distant relative; it was, in sheer quantity of woe, incomprehensible. It was also ridiculous, unjust, and because he had always been a religious man, an affront to God. Manischevitz believed this in all his suffering. When his burden had grown too crushingly heavy to be borne he prayed in his chair with shut hollow eyes: "My dear God, sweetheart, did I deserve that this should happen to me?" Then recognizing the worthlessness of it, he set aside the complaint and prayed humbly for assistance: "Give Fanny back her health, and to me for myself that I shouldn't feel pain in every step. Help now or tomorrow is too late." And Manischevitz wept.

Manischevitz's flat, which he had moved into after the disastrous fire, was a meager one, furnished with a few sticks of chairs, a table, and bed, in one of the poorer sections of the city. There were three rooms: a small, poorly papered living room; an apology for a kitchen with a wooden icebox; and the comparatively large bedroom where Fanny lay in a sagging secondhand bed, gasping for breath. The bedroom was the warmest room in the house and it was here, after his outburst to God, that Manischevitz, by the light of two small bulbs overhead, sat reading his Jewish newspaper. He was not truly reading because his thoughts were everywhere; however the print offered a convenient resting place for his eyes, and a word or two, when he permitted himself to comprehend them, had the momentary effect of helping him forget his troubles. After a short while he discovered, to his surprise, that he was actively scanning the news, searching for an item of great interest to him. Exactly what he thought he would read he couldn't say—until he realized, with some astonishment, that he was expecting to discover something about himself. Manischevitz put his paper down and looked up with the distinct impression that someone had come into the apartment, though he could not remember having heard the sound of the door opening. He looked around: the room was very still, Fanny sleeping, for once, quietly. Half frightened, he watched her until he was satisfied she wasn't dead; then, still disturbed by the thought of an unannounced visitor, he stumbled into the living room and there had the shock of his life, for at the table sat a black man reading a newspaper he had folded up to fit into one hand.

"What do you want here?" Manischevitz asked in fright.

The Negro put down the paper and glanced up with a gentle expression. "Good evening." He seemed not to be sure of himself, as if he had got into the wrong house. He was a large man, bonily built, with a heavy head covered by a hard derby, which he made no attempt to remove. His eyes seemed sad, but his lips, above which he wore a slight mustache, sought to smile; he was not otherwise prepossessing. The cuffs of his sleeves, Manischevitz noted, were frayed to the lining, and the dark suit was badly fitted. He had very large feet. Recovering from his fright, Manischevitz guessed he had left the door open and was being visited by a case worker from the Welfare Department—some came at night—for he had recently applied for welfare. Therefore he lowered himself into a chair opposite the Negro, trying, before the man's uncertain smile, to feel comfortable. The former tailor sat stiffly but patiently at the table, waiting for the investigator to take out his pad and pencil and begin asking questions; but before long he became convinced the man intended to do nothing of the sort.

"Who are you?" Manischevitz at last asked uneasily.

"If I may, insofar as one is able to, identify myself, I bear the name of Alexander Levine."

In spite of his troubles Manischevitz felt a smile growing on his lips. "You said Levine?" he politely inquired.

The Negro nodded. "That is exactly right."

Carrying the jest further, Manischevitz asked, "You are maybe Jewish?"

"All my life I was, willingly."

The tailor hesitated. He had heard of black Jews but had never met one. It gave an unusual sensation.

Recognizing in afterthought something odd about the tense of Levine's remark, he said doubtfully, "You ain't Jewish any more?"

Levine at this point removed his hat, revealing a very white part in his black hair, but quickly replaced it. He replied, "I have recently been disincarnated into an angel. As such, I offer you my humble assistance, if to offer is within my province and power—in the best sense." He lowered his eyes in apology. "Which calls for added explanation: I am what I am granted to be, and at present the completion is in the future."

"What kind of angel is this?" Manischevitz gravely asked.

"A bona fide angel of God, within prescribed limitations," answered Levine, "not to be confused with the members of any particular sect, order, or organization here on earth operating under a similar name."

Manischevitz was thoroughly disturbed. He had been expecting something, but not this. What sort of mockery was it—provided that Levine was an angel—of a faithful servant who had from childhood lived in the synagogues, concerned with the word of God?

To test Levine he asked, "Then where are your wings?"

The Negro blushed as well as he could. Manischevitz understood this from his altered expression. "Under certain circumstances we lose privileges and prerogatives upon returning to earth, no matter for what purpose or endeavoring to assist whomsoever."

"So tell me," Manischevitz said triumphantly, "how did you get here?"

"I was translated."

Still troubled, the tailor said, "If you are a Jew, say the blessing for bread."

Levine recited it in sonorous Hebrew.

Although moved by the familiar words Manischevitz still felt doubt he was dealing with an angel.

"If you are an angel," he demanded somewhat angrily, "give me the proof."

Levine wet his lips. "Frankly, I cannot perform either miracles or near-miracles, due to the fact that I am in a condition of probation. How long that will persist or even consist depends on the outcome."

Manischevitz racked his brains for some means of causing Levine positively to reveal his true identity, when the Negro spoke again:

"It was given me to understand that both your wife and you require assistance of a salubrious nature?"

The tailor could not rid himself of the feeling that he was the butt of a jokester. Is this what a Jewish angel looks like? he asked himself. This I am not convinced.

He asked a last question. "So if God sends to me an angel, why a black? Why not a white that there are so many of them?"

"It was my turn to go next," Levine explained.

Manischevitz could not be persuaded. "I think you are a faker."

Levine slowly rose. His eyes indicated disappointment and worry. "Mr. Manischevitz," he said tonelessly, "if you should desire me to be of assistance to you any time in the near future, or possibly before, I can be found"—he glanced at his fingernails—"in Harlem."

He was by then gone.

The next day Manischevitz felt some relief from his backache and was able to work four hours at pressing. The day after, he put in six hours; and the third day four again. Fanny sat up a little and asked for some halvah to suck. But after the fourth day the stabbing, breaking ache afflicted his back, and Fanny again lay supine, breathing with blue-lipped difficulty.

Manischevitz was profoundly disappointed at the return of his active pain and suffering. He had hoped for a longer interval of easement, long enough to have a thought other than of himself and his troubles. Day by day, minute after minute, he lived in pain, pain his only memory, questioning the necessity of it, inveighing, though with affection, against God. Why *so much*, Gottenyu? If He wanted to teach His servant a lesson for some reason, some cause—the nature of His nature—to teach him, say, for reasons of his weakness, his pride, perhaps, during his years of prosperity, his frequent neglect of God—to give him a little lesson, why then any of the tragedies that had happened to him, any *one* would have sufficed to chasten him. But *all together*—the loss of both his children, his means of livelihood, Fanny's health and his—that was too much to ask one frail-boned man to endure. Who, after all, was Manischevitz that he had been given so much to suffer? A tailor. Certainly not a man of talent. Upon him suffering was largely wasted. It went nowhere, into nothing: into more suffering. His pain did not earn him bread, nor fill the cracks in the wall, nor lift, in the middle of the night, the kitchen table; only lay upon him, sleepless, so sharply oppressive that he could many times have cried out yet not heard himself this misery.

In this mood he gave no thought to Mr. Alexander Levine, but at moments when the pain wavered, slightly diminishing, he sometimes wondered if he had been mistaken to dismiss him. A black Jew and angel to boot—very hard to believe, but suppose he *had* been sent to succor him, and he, Manischevitz, was in his blindness too blind to understand? It was this thought that put him on the knife-point of agony.

Therefore the tailor, after much self-questioning and continuing doubt, decided he would seek the self-styled angel in
Harlem. Of course he had great difficulty because he had not
asked for specific directions, and movement was tedious to
him. The subway took him to 116th Street, and from there he
wandered in the open dark world. It was vast and its lights lit
nothing. Everywhere were shadows, often moving. Manischevitz hobbled along with the aid of a cane, and not knowing where to seek in the blackened tenement buildings, would
look fruitlessly through store windows. In the stores he saw
people and everybody was black. It was an amazing thing to
observe. When he was too tired, too unhappy to go farther,
Manischevitz stopped in front of a tailor's shop. Out of familiar-
ity with the appearance of it, with some sadness he entered. The
tailor, an old skinny man with a mop of woolly gray hair, was
sitting cross-legged on his workbench, sewing a pair of tuxedo
pants that had a razor slit all the way down the seat.

"You'll excuse me, please, gentleman," said Manischevitz,
admiring the tailor's deft thimbled fingerwork, "but you know
maybe somebody by the name Alexander Levine?"

The tailor, who, Manischevitz thought, seemed a little an-
tagonistic to him, scratched his scalp.

"Cain't say I ever heared dat name."

"Alex-ander Lev-ine," Manischevitz repeated it.

The man shook his head. "Cain't say I heared."

Manischevitz remembered to say: "He is an angel, maybe."

"Oh *him*," said the tailor, clucking. "He hang out in dat
honky-tonk down here a ways." He pointed with his skinny
finger and returned to sewing the pants.

Manischevitz crossed the street against a red light and was
almost run down by a taxi. On the block after the next, the
sixth store from the corner was a cabaret, and the name in
sparkling lights was Bella's. Ashamed to go in, Manischevitz
gazed through the neon-lit window, and when the dancing
couples had parted and drifted away, he discovered at a table
on the side, toward the rear, Alexander Levine.

He was sitting alone, a cigarette butt hanging from the
corner of his mouth, playing solitaire with a dirty pack of
cards, and Manischevitz felt a touch of pity for him, because
Levine had deteriorated in appearance. His derby hat was

dented and had a gray smudge. His ill-fitting suit was shabbier, as if he had been sleeping in it. His shoes and trouser cuffs were muddy, and his face covered with an impenetrable stubble the color of licorice. Manischevitz, though deeply disappointed, was about to enter, when a big-breasted Negress in a purple evening gown appeared before Levine's table, and with much laughter through many white teeth, broke into a vigorous shimmy. Levine looked at Manischevitz with a haunted expression, but the tailor was too paralyzed to move or acknowledge it. As Bella's gyrations continued Levine rose, his eyes lit in excitement. She embraced him with vigor, both his hands clasped around her restless buttocks, and they tangoed together across the floor, loudly applauded by the customers. She seemed to have lifted Levine off his feet and his large shoes hung limp as they danced. They slid past the windows where Manischevitz, white-faced, stood staring in. Levine winked slyly and the tailor left for home.

Fanny lay at death's door. Through shrunken lips she muttered concerning her childhood, the sorrows of the marriage bed, the loss of her children; yet wept to live. Manischevitz tried not to listen, but even without ears he would have heard. It was not a gift. The doctor panted up the stairs, a broad but bland, unshaven man (it was Sunday), and soon shook his head. A day at most, or two. He left at once to spare himself Manischevitz's multiplied sorrow; the man who never stopped hurting. He would someday get him into a public home.

Manischevitz visited a synagogue and there spoke to God, but God had absented himself. The tailor searched his heart and found no hope. When she died, he would live dead. He considered taking his life although he knew he wouldn't. Yet it was something to consider. Considering, you existed. He railed against God— Can you love a rock, a broom, an emptiness? Baring his chest, he smote the naked bones, cursing himself for having, beyond belief, believed.

Asleep in a chair that afternoon, he dreamed of Levine. He was standing before a faded mirror, preening small decaying opalescent wings. "This means," mumbled Manischevitz, as he broke out of sleep, "that it is possible he could be an angel." Begging a neighbor lady to look in on Fanny and occasionally wet her lips with water, he drew on his thin coat, gripped his walking stick, exchanged some pennies for a subway token, and rode to Harlem. He knew this act was the last desperate one of his woe: to go seeking a black magician to restore his wife to invalidism. Yet if there was no choice, he did at least what was chosen.

He hobbled to Bella's, but the place seemed to have changed hands. It was now, as he breathed, a synagogue in a store. In the front, toward him, were several rows of empty wooden benches. In the rear stood the Ark, its portals of rough wood covered with rainbows of sequins; under it a long table on which lay the sacred scroll unrolled, illuminated by the dim light from a bulb on a chain overhead. Around the table, as if frozen to it and the scroll, which they all touched with their fingers, sat four Negroes wearing skullcaps. Now as they read the Holy Word, Manischevitz could, through the plate-glass window, hear the singsong chant of their voices. One of them was old, with a gray beard. One was bubble-eyed. One was humpbacked. The fourth was a boy, no older than thirteen. Their heads moved in rhythmic swaying. Touched by this sight from his childhood and youth, Manischevitz entered and stood silent in the rear.

"Neshoma," said bubble eyes, pointing to the word with a stubby finger. "Now what dat mean?"

"That's the word that means soul," said the boy. He wore eyeglasses.

"Let's git on wid de commentary," said the old man.

"Ain't necessary," said the humpback. "Souls is immaterial substance. That's all. The soul is derived in that manner. The immateriality is derived from the substance, and they both, causally an' otherwise, derived from the soul. There can be no higher."

"That's the highest."

"Over de top."

"Wait a minute," said bubble eyes. "I don't see what is dat immaterial substance. How come de one gits hitched up to de odder?" He addressed the humpback.

"Ask me somethin' hard. Because it is substanceless immateriality. It couldn't be closer together, like all the parts of the body under one skin—closer."

"Hear now," said the old man.

"All you done is switched de words."

"It's the primum mobile, the substanceless substance from which comes all things that were incepted in the idea—you, me, and everything and -body else."

"Now how did all dat happen? Make it sound simple."

"It de speerit," said the old man. "On de face of de water moved de speerit. An' dat was good. It say so in de Book. From de speerit ariz de man."

"But now listen here. How come it become substance if it all de time a spirit?"

"God alone done dat."

"Holy! Holy! Praise His Name."

"But has dis spirit got some kind of a shade or color?" asked bubble eyes, deadpan.

"Man, of course not. A spirit is a spirit."

"Then how come we is colored?" he said with a triumphant glare.

"Ain't got nothing to do wid dat."

"I still like to know."

"God put the spirit in all things," answered the boy. "He put it in the green leaves and the yellow flowers. He put it with the gold in the fishes and the blue in the sky. That's how come it came to us."

"Amen."

"Praise Lawd and utter loud His speechless Name."

"Blow de bugle till it bust the sky."

They fell silent, intent upon the next word. Manischevitz, with doubt, approached them.

"You'll excuse me," he said. "I am looking for Alexander Levine. You know him maybe?"

"That's the angel," said the boy.

"Oh *him*," snuffed bubble eyes.

"You'll find him at Bella's. It's the establishment right down the street," the humpback said.

Manischevitz said he was sorry that he could not stay, thanked them, and limped across the street. It was already night. The city was dark and he could barely find his way.

But Bella's was bursting with jazz and the blues. Through the window Manischevitz recognized the dancing crowd and among them sought Levine. He was sitting loose-lipped at Bella's side table. They were tippling from an almost empty whiskey fifth. Levine had shed his old clothes, wore a shiny new checkered suit, pearl-gray derby hat, cigar, and big, two-tone, button shoes. To the tailor's dismay, a drunken look had settled upon his formerly dignified face. He leaned toward Bella, tickled her earlobe with his pinky while whispering words that sent her into gales of raucous laughter. She fondled his knee.

Manischevitz, girding himself, pushed open the door and was not welcomed.

"This place reserved."

"Beat it, pale puss."

"Exit, Yankel, semitic trash."

But he moved toward the table where Levine sat, the crowd breaking before him as he hobbled forward.

"Mr. Levine," he spoke in a trembly voice. "Is here Manischevitz."

Levine glared blearily. "Speak yo' piece, son."

Manischevitz shivered. His back plagued him. Tremors tormented his legs. He looked around, everybody was all ears.

"You'll excuse me. I would like to talk to you in a private place."

"Speak, Ah is a private pusson."

Bella laughed piercingly. "Stop it, boy, you killin' me."

Manischevitz, no end disturbed, considered fleeing but Levine addressed him:

"Kindly state the pu'pose of yo' communication with yo's truly."

The tailor wet cracked lips. "You are Jewish. This I am sure."

Levine rose, nostrils flaring. "Anythin' else yo' got to say?"

Manischevitz's tongue lay like a slab of stone.

"Speak now or fo'ever hold off."

Tears blinded the tailor's eyes. Was ever man so tried? Should he say he believed a half-drunk Negro was an angel?

The silence slowly petrified.

Manischevitz was recalling scenes of his youth as a wheel in his mind whirred: believe, do not, yes, no, yes, no. The pointer pointed to yes, to between yes and no, to no, no it was yes. He sighed. It moved but one still had to make a choice.

"I think you are an angel from God." He said it in a broken voice, thinking, If you said it it was said. If you believed it you must say it. If you believed, you believed.

The hush broke. Everybody talked but the music began and they went on dancing. Bella, grown bored, picked up the cards and dealt herself a hand.

Levine burst into tears. "How you have humiliated me."

Manischevitz apologized.

"Wait'll I freshen up." Levine went to the men's room and returned in his old suit.

No one said goodbye as they left.

They rode to the flat via subway. As they walked up the stairs Manischevitz pointed with his cane at his door.

"That's all been taken care of," Levine said. "You go in while I take off."

Disappointed that it was so soon over, but torn by curiosity, Manischevitz followed the angel up three flights to the roof. When he got there the door was already padlocked.

Luckily he could see through a small broken window. He heard an odd noise, as though of a whirring of wings, and when he strained for a wider view, could have sworn he saw a dark figure borne aloft on a pair of strong black wings.

A feather drifted down. Manischevitz gasped as it turned white, but it was only snowing.

He rushed downstairs. In the flat Fanny wielded a dust mop under the bed, and then upon the cobwebs on the wall.

"A wonderful thing, Fanny," Manischevitz said. "Believe me, there are Jews everywhere."

1955

A Summer's Reading

GEORGE STOYONOVICH was a neighborhood boy who had quit high school on an impulse when he was sixteen, run out of patience, and though he was ashamed every time he went looking for a job, when people asked him if he had finished and he had to say no, he never went back to school. This summer was a hard time for jobs and he had none. Having so much time on his hands, George thought of going to summer school, but the kids in his classes would be too young. He also considered registering in a night high school, only he didn't like the idea of the teachers always telling him what to do. He felt they had not respected him. The result was he stayed off the streets and in his room most of the day. He was close to twenty and had needs with the neighborhood girls, but no money to spend, and he couldn't get more than an occasional few cents because his father was poor, and his sister Sophie, who resembled George, a tall bony girl of twenty-three, earned very little and what she had she kept for herself. Their mother was dead, and Sophie had to take care of the house.

Very early in the morning George's father got up to go to work in a fish market. Sophie left at about eight for her long ride in the subway to a cafeteria in the Bronx. George had his coffee by himself, then hung around in the house. When the house, a five-room railroad flat above a butcher store, got on his nerves he cleaned it up—mopped the floors with a wet mop and put things away. But most of the time he sat in his room. In the afternoons he listened to the ball game. Otherwise he had a couple of old copies of the *World Almanac* he had bought long ago, and he liked to read in them and also the magazines and newspapers that Sophie brought home, that had been left on the tables in the cafeteria. They were mostly picture magazines about movie stars and sports figures, also usually the *News* and *Mirror*. Sophie herself read whatever fell into her hands, although she sometimes read good books.

She once asked George what he did in his room all day and he said he read a lot too.

"Of what besides what I bring home? Do you ever read any worthwhile books?"

"Some," George answered, although he really didn't. He had tried to read a book or two that Sophie had in the house but found he was in no mood for them. Lately he couldn't stand made-up stories, they got on his nerves. He wished he had some hobby to work at—as a kid he was good in carpentry, but where could he work at it? Sometimes during the day he went for walks, but mostly he did his walking after the hot sun had gone down and it was cooler in the streets.

In the evening after supper George left the house and wandered in the neighborhood. During the sultry days some of the storekeepers and their wives sat in chairs on the thick, broken sidewalks in front of their shops, fanning themselves, and George walked past them and the guys hanging out on the candy store corner. A couple of them he had known his whole life, but nobody recognized each other. He had no place special to go, but generally, saving it till the last, he left the neighborhood and walked for blocks till he came to a darkly lit little park with benches and trees and an iron railing, giving it a feeling of privacy. He sat on a bench here, watching the leafy trees and the flowers blooming on the inside of the railing, thinking of a better life for himself. He thought of the jobs he had had since he had quit school—delivery boy, stock clerk, runner, lately working in a factory—and he was dissatisfied with all of them. He felt he would someday like to have a good job and live in a private house with a porch, on a street with trees. He wanted to have some dough in his pocket to buy things with, and a girl to go with, so as not to be so lonely, especially on Saturday nights. He wanted people to like and respect him. He thought about these things often but mostly when he was alone at night. Around midnight he got up and drifted back to his hot and stony neighborhood.

One time while on his walk George met Mr. Cattanzara coming home very late from work. He wondered if he was drunk but then could tell he wasn't. Mr. Cattanzara, a stocky, bald-headed man who worked in a change booth on an IRT station, lived on the next block after George's, above a shoe repair store. Nights, during the hot weather, he sat on his stoop in an undershirt, reading the *New York Times* in the light of the shoemaker's window. He read it from the first page to the last, then went up to sleep. And all the time he was reading the paper, his wife, a fat woman with a white face, leaned out of the window, gazing into the street, her thick white arms folded under her loose breasts, on the window ledge.

Once in a while Mr. Cattanzara came home drunk, but it was a quiet drunk. He never made any trouble, only walked stiffly up the street and slowly climbed the stairs into the hall. Though drunk, he looked the same as always, except for his tight walk, the quietness, and that his eyes were wet. George liked Mr. Cattanzara because he remembered him giving him nickels to buy lemon ice with when he was a squirt. Mr. Cattanzara was a different type than those in the neighborhood. He asked different questions than the others when he met you, and he seemed to know what went on in all the newspapers. He read them, as his fat sick wife watched from the window.

"What are you doing with yourself this summer, George?" Mr. Cattanzara asked. "I see you walkin' around at nights."

George felt embarrassed. "I like to walk."

"What are you doin' in the day now?"

"Nothing much just right now. I'm waiting for a job." Since it shamed him to admit he wasn't working, George said, "I'm staying home—but I'm reading a lot to pick up my education."

Mr. Cattanzara looked interested. He mopped his hot face with a red handkerchief.

"What are you readin'?"

George hesitated, then said, "I got a list of books in the library once, and now I'm gonna read them this summer." He felt strange and a little unhappy saying this, but he wanted Mr. Cattanzara to respect him.

"How many books are there on it?"

"I never counted them. Maybe around a hundred."

Mr. Cattanzara whistled through his teeth.

"I figure if I did that," George went on earnestly, "it would help me in my education. I don't mean the kind they give you in high school. I want to know different things than they learn there, if you know what I mean."

The change maker nodded. "Still and all, one hundred books is a pretty big load for one summer."

"It might take longer."

"After you're finished with some, maybe you and I can shoot the breeze about them?" said Mr. Cattanzara.

"When I'm finished," George answered.

Mr. Cattanzara went home and George continued on his walk. After that, though he had the urge to, George did nothing different from usual. He still took his walks at night, ending up in the little park. But one evening the shoemaker on the next block stopped George to say he was a good boy, and George figured that Mr. Cattanzara had told him all about the books he was reading. From the shoemaker it must have gone down the street, because George saw a couple of people smiling kindly at him, though nobody spoke to him personally. He felt a little better around the neighborhood and liked it more, though not so much he would want to live in it forever. He had never exactly disliked the people in it, yet he had never liked them very much either. It was the fault of the neighborhood. To his surprise, George found out that his father and Sophie knew about his reading too. His father was too shy to say anything about it—he was never much of a talker in his whole life—but Sophie was softer to George, and she showed him in other ways she was proud of him.

As the summer went on George felt in a good mood about things. He cleaned the house every day, as a favor to Sophie, and he enjoyed the ball games more. Sophie gave him a buck a week allowance, and though it still wasn't enough and he had to use it carefully, it was a helluva lot better than just having two bits now and then. What he bought with the money— cigarettes mostly, an occasional beer or movie ticket—he got a big kick out of. Life wasn't so bad if you knew how to appreciate it. Occasionally he bought a paperback book from the newsstand, but he never got around to reading it, though he was glad to have a couple of books in his room. But he read thoroughly Sophie's magazines and newspapers. And at night was the most enjoyable time, because when he passed the storekeepers sitting outside their stores, he could tell they regarded him highly. He walked erect, and though he did not say much to them, or they to him, he could feel approval on all sides. A couple of nights he felt so good that he skipped the park at the end of the evening. He just wandered in the neighborhood, where people had known him from the time he was a kid playing punchball whenever there was a game of it going; he wandered there, then came home and got undressed for bed, feeling fine.

For a few weeks he had talked only once with Mr. Cattanzara, and though the change maker had said nothing more about the books, asked no questions, his silence made George a little uneasy. For a while George didn't pass in front of Mr. Cattanzara's house anymore, until one night, forgetting himself, he approached it from a different direction than he usually did when he did. It was already past midnight. The street, except for one or two people, was deserted, and George was surprised when he saw Mr. Cattanzara still reading his newspaper by the light of the street lamp overhead. His impulse was to stop at the stoop and talk to him. He wasn't sure what he wanted to say, though he felt the words would come when he began to talk; but the more he thought about it, the more the idea scared him, and he decided he'd better not. He even considered beating it home by another street, but he was too near Mr. Cattanzara, and the change maker might see him as he ran, and get annoyed. So George unobtrusively crossed the street, trying to make it seem as if he had to look in a store window on the other side, which he did, and then went on, uncomfortable at what he was doing. He feared Mr. Cattanzara would glance up from his paper and call him a dirty rat for walking on the other side of the street, but all he did was sit there, sweating through his undershirt, his bald head shining in the dim light as he read his *Times*, and upstairs his fat wife leaned out of the window, seeming to read the paper along with him. George thought she would spy him and yell out to Mr. Cattanzara, but she never moved her eyes off her husband.

George made up his mind to stay away from the change maker until he had got some of his softback books read, but when he started them and saw they were mostly story books, he lost his interest and didn't bother to finish them. He lost his interest in reading other things too. Sophie's magazines and newspapers went unread. She saw them piling up on a chair in his room and asked why he was no longer looking at them, and George told her it was because of all the other reading he had to do. Sophie said she had guessed that was it. So for most of the day, George had the radio on, turning to music when he was sick of the human voice. He kept the house fairly neat, and Sophie said nothing on the days when he neglected it. She was still kind and gave him his extra buck, though things weren't so good for him as they had been before.

But they were good enough, considering. Also his night walks invariably picked him up, no matter how bad the day was. Then one night George saw Mr. Cattanzara coming down the street toward him. George was about to turn and run but he recognized from Mr. Cattanzara's walk that he was drunk, and if so, probably he would not even bother to notice him. So George kept on walking straight ahead until he came abreast of Mr. Cattanzara and though he felt wound up enough to pop into the sky, he was not surprised when Mr. Cattanzara passed him without a word, walking slowly, his face and body stiff. George drew a breath in relief at his narrow escape, when he heard his name called, and there stood Mr. Cattanzara at his elbow, smelling like the inside of a beer barrel. His eyes were sad as he gazed at George, and George felt so intensely uncomfortable he was tempted to shove the drunk aside and continue on his walk.

But he couldn't act that way to him, and, besides, Mr. Cattanzara took a nickel out of his pants pocket and handed it to him.

"Go buy yourself a lemon ice, Georgie."

"It's not that time anymore, Mr. Cattanzara," George said, "I am a big guy now."

"No, you ain't," said Mr. Cattanzara, to which George made no reply he could think of.

"How are all your books comin' along now?" Mr. Cattanzara asked. Though he tried to stand steady, he swayed a little.

"Fine, I guess," said George, feeling the red crawling up his face.

"You ain't sure?" The change maker smiled slyly, a way George had never seen him smile.

"Sure I'm sure. They're fine."

Though his head swayed in little arcs, Mr. Cattanzara's eyes were steady. He had small blue eyes which could hurt if you looked at them too long.

"George," he said, "name me one book on that list that you read this summer, and I will drink to your health."

"I don't want anybody drinking to me."

"Name me one so I can ask you a question on it. Who can tell, if it's a good book maybe I might wanna read it myself."

George knew he looked passable on the outside, but inside he was crumbling apart.

Unable to reply, he shut his eyes, but when—years later—he opened them, he saw that Mr. Cattanzara had, out of pity, gone away, but in his ears he still heard the words he had said when he left: "George, don't do what I did."

The next night he was afraid to leave his room, and though Sophie argued with him he wouldn't open the door.

"What are you doing in there?" she asked.

"Nothing."

"Aren't you reading?"

"No."

She was silent a minute, then asked, "Where do you keep the books you read? I never see any in your room outside of a few cheap trashy ones."

He wouldn't tell her.

"In that case you're not worth a buck of my hard-earned money. Why should I break my back for you? Go on out, you bum, and get a job."

He stayed in his room for almost a week, except to sneak into the kitchen when nobody was home. Sophie railed at him, then begged him to come out, and his old father wept, but George wouldn't budge, though the weather was terrible and his small room stifling. He found it very hard to breathe, each breath was like drawing a flame into his lungs.

One night, unable to stand the heat anymore, he burst into the street at one A.M., a shadow of himself. He hoped to sneak to the park without being seen, but there were people all over the block, wilted and listless, waiting for a breeze. George lowered his eyes and walked, in disgrace, away from them, but before long he discovered they were still friendly to him. He figured Mr. Cattanzara hadn't told on him. Maybe when he woke up out of his drunk the next morning, he had forgotten all about meeting George. George felt his confidence slowly come back to him.

That same night a man on a street corner asked him if it was true that he had finished reading so many books, and George admitted he had. The man said it was a wonderful thing for a boy his age to read so much.

"Yeah," George said, but he felt relieved. He hoped nobody would mention the books anymore, and when, after a couple of days, he accidentally met Mr. Cattanzara again, *he* didn't, though George had the idea he was the one who had started the rumor that he had finished all the books.

One evening in the fall, George ran out of his house to the library, where he hadn't been in years. There were books all over the place, wherever he looked, and though he was struggling to control an inward trembling, he easily counted off a hundred, then sat down at a table to read.

1956

Take Pity

D AVIDOV, THE census-taker, opened the door without knocking, limped into the room, and sat wearily down. Out came his notebook and he was on the job. Rosen, the ex-coffee salesman, wasted, eyes despairing, sat motionless, cross-legged, on his cot. The square, clean but cold room, lit by a dim globe, was sparsely furnished: the cot, a folding chair, small table, old unpainted chests—no closets but who needed them?—and a small sink with a rough piece of green, institutional soap on its holder—you could smell it across the room. The worn black shade over the single narrow window was drawn to the ledge, surprising Davidov.

"What's the matter you don't pull the shade up?" he remarked.

Rosen ultimately sighed. "Let it stay."

"Why? Outside is light."

"Who needs light?"

"What then you need?"

"Light I don't need," replied Rosen.

Davidov, sour-faced, flipped through the closely scrawled pages of his notebook until he found a clean one. He attempted to scratch in a word with his fountain pen but it had run dry, so he fished a pencil stub out of his vest pocket and sharpened it with a cracked razor blade. Rosen paid no attention to the feathery shavings falling to the floor. He looked restless, seemed to be listening to or for something, although Davidov was convinced there was absolutely nothing to listen to. It was only when the census-taker somewhat irritably and with increasing loudness repeated a question that Rosen stirred and identified himself. He was about to furnish an address but caught himself and shrugged.

Davidov did not comment on the salesman's gesture. "So begin," he nodded.

"Who knows where to begin?" Rosen stared at the drawn shade. "Do they know here where to begin?"

"Philosophy we are not interested," said Davidov. "Start in how you met her."

"Who?" pretended Rosen.

"Her," he snapped.

"So if I got to begin, how you know about her already?" Rosen asked triumphantly.

Davidov spoke wearily, "You mentioned before."

Rosen remembered. They had questioned him upon his arrival and he now recalled blurting out her name. It was perhaps something in the air. It did not permit you to retain what you remembered. That was part of the cure, if you wanted a cure.

"Where I met her—?" Rosen murmured. "I met her where she always was—in the back room there in that hole in the wall that it was a waste of time for me I went there. Maybe I sold them a half a bag of coffee a month. This is not business."

"In business we are not interested."

"What then you are interested?" Rosen mimicked Davidov's tone.

Davidov clammed up coldly.

Rosen knew they had him where it hurt, so he went on: "The husband was maybe forty, Axel Kalish, a Polish refugee. He worked like a blind horse when he got to America, and saved maybe two, three thousand dollars that he bought with the money this pisher grocery in a dead neighborhood where he didn't have a chance. He called my company up for credit and they sent me I should see. I recommended okay because I felt sorry. He had a wife, Eva, you know already about her, and two darling girls, one five and one three, little dolls, Fega and Surale, that I didn't want them to suffer. So right away I told him, without tricks, 'Kiddo, this is a mistake. This place is a grave. Here they will bury you if you don't get out quick!'"

Rosen sighed deeply.

"So?" Davidov had thus far written nothing, irking the ex-salesman.

"So?— Nothing. He didn't get out. After a couple months he tried to sell but nobody bought, so he stayed and starved. They never made expenses. Every day they got poorer you couldn't look in their faces. 'Don't be a damn fool,' I told him, 'go in bankruptcy.' But he couldn't stand to lose all his capital, and he was also afraid it would be hard to find a job. 'My God,' I said, 'do anything. Be a painter, a janitor, a junk man, but get out of here before everybody is a skeleton.'

"This he finally agreed with me, but before he could go in auction he dropped dead."

Davidov made a note. "How did he die?"

"On this I am not an expert," Rosen replied. "You know better than me."

"How did he die?" Davidov spoke impatiently. "Say in one word."

"From what he died?—he died, that's all."

"Answer, please, this question."

"Broke in him something. That's how."

"Broke what?"

"Broke what breaks. He was talking to me how bitter was his life, and he touched me on my sleeve to say something else, but the next minute his face got small and he fell down dead, the wife screaming, the little girls crying that it made in my heart pain. I am myself a sick man and when I saw him laying on the floor, I said to myself, 'Rosen, say goodbye, this guy is finished.' So I said it."

Rosen got up from the cot and strayed despondently around the room, avoiding the window. Davidov was occupying the only chair, so the ex-salesman was finally forced to sit on the edge of the bed again. This irritated him. He badly wanted a cigarette but disliked asking for one.

Davidov permitted him a short interval of silence, then leafed impatiently through his notebook. Rosen, to needle the census-taker, said nothing.

"So what happened?" Davidov finally demanded.

Rosen spoke with ashes in his mouth. "After the funeral—" He paused, tried to wet his lips, then went on, "He belonged to a society that they buried him, and he also left a thousand dollars' insurance, but after the funeral I said to her, 'Eva, listen to me. Take the money and your children and run away from here. Let the creditors take the store. What will they get?— Nothing.'

"But she answered me, 'Where will I go, where, with my two orphans that their father left them to starve?'

"'Go anywhere,' I said. 'Go to your relatives.'

"She laughed like laughs somebody who hasn't got no joy. 'My relatives Hitler took away from me.'

"'What about Axel—surely an uncle somewheres?'

"'Nobody,' she said. 'I will stay here like my Axel wanted. With the insurance I will buy new stock and fix up the store. Every week I will decorate the window, and in this way gradually will come in new customers—'

"'Eva, my darling girl—'

"'A millionaire I don't expect to be. All I want is I should make a little living and take care of my girls. We will live in the back here like before, and in this way I can work and watch them, too.'

"'Eva,' I said, 'you are a nice-looking young woman, only thirty-eight years. Don't throw away your life here. Don't flush in the toilet—you should excuse me—the thousand poor dollars from your dead husband. Believe me, I know from such stores. After thirty-five years' experience I know a graveyard when I smell it. Go better someplace and find a job. You're young yet. Sometime you will meet somebody and get married.'

"'No, Rosen, not me,' she said. 'With marriage I am finished. Nobody wants a poor widow with two children.'

"'This I don't believe it.'

"'I know,' she said.

"Never in my life I saw so bitter a woman's face.

"'No,' I said. 'No.'

"'Yes, Rosen, yes. In my whole life I never had anything. In my whole life I always suffered. I don't expect better. This is my life.'

"I said no and she said yes. What could I do? I am a man with only one kidney, and worse than that, that I won't mention it. When I talked she didn't listen, so I stopped to talk. Who can argue with a widow?"

The ex-salesman glanced up at Davidov but the census-taker did not reply. "What happened then?" he asked.

"What happened?" mocked Rosen. "Happened what happens."

Davidov's face grew red.

"What happened, happened," Rosen said hastily. "She ordered from the wholesalers all kinds goods that she paid for them cash. All week she opened boxes and packed on the shelves cans, jars, packages. Also she cleaned, and she washed, and she mopped with oil the floor. With tissue paper she made

new decorations in the window, everything should look nice—
but who came in? Nobody except a few poor customers from
the tenement around the corner. And when they came? When
was closed the supermarkets and they needed some little item
that they forgot to buy, like a quart milk, fifteen cents' cheese,
a small can sardines for lunch. In a few months was again dusty
the cans on the shelves, and her money was gone. Credit she
couldn't get except from me, and from me she got because I
paid out of my pocket the company. This she didn't know. She
worked, she dressed clean, she waited that the store should get
better. Little by little the shelves got empty, but where was the
profit? They ate it up. When I looked on the little girls I knew
what she didn't tell me. Their faces were white, they were thin,
they were hungry. She kept the little food that was left, on the
shelves. One night I brought in a nice piece of sirloin, but I
could see from her eyes that she didn't like that I did it. So
what else could I do? I have a heart and I am human."

Here the ex-salesman wept.

Davidov pretended not to see though once he peeked.

Rosen blew his nose, then went on more calmly, "When the
children were sleeping we sat in the dark there, in the back,
and not once in four hours opened the door should come in a
customer. 'Eva, for Godsakes, *run away*,' I said.

"'I have no place to go,' she said.

"'I will give you where you can go, and please don't say to
me no. I am a bachelor, this you know. I got whatever I need
and more besides. Let me help you and the children. Money
don't interest me. Interests me good health, but I can't buy it.
I'll tell you what I will do. Let this place go to the creditors
and move into a two-family house that I own, which the top
floor is now empty. Rent will cost you nothing. In the meantime you can go and find a job. I will also pay the downstairs
lady to take care of the girls—God bless them—until you will
come home. With your wages you will buy the food, if you
need clothes, and also save a little. This you can use when you
get married someday. What do you say?'

"She didn't answer me. She only looked on me in such a
way, with such burning eyes, like I was small and ugly. For the
first time I thought to myself, 'Rosen, this woman don't like
you.'

"'Thank you very kindly, my friend Mr. Rosen,' she answered me, 'but charity we are not needing. I got yet a paying business, and it will get better when times are better. Now is bad times. When comes again good times will get better the business.'

"'Who charity?' I cried to her. 'What charity? Speaks to you your husband's a friend.'

"'Mr. Rosen, my husband didn't have no friends.'

"'Can't you see that I want to help the children?'

"'The children have their mother.'

"'Eva, what's the matter with you?' I said. 'Why do you make sound bad something that I mean it should be good?'

"This she didn't answer. I felt sick in my stomach, and was coming also a headache so I left.

"All night I didn't sleep, and then all of a sudden I figured out a reason why she was worried. She was worried I would ask for some kind of payment except cash. She got the wrong man. Anyway, this made me think of something that I didn't think about before. I thought now to ask her to marry me. What did she have to lose? I could take care of myself without any trouble to them. Fega and Surale would have a father he could give them for the movies, or sometime to buy a little doll to play with, and when I died, would go to them my investments and insurance policies.

"The next day I spoke to her.

"'For myself, Eva, I don't want a thing. Absolutely not a thing. For you and your girls—everything. I am not a strong man, Eva. In fact, I am sick. I tell you this you should understand I don't expect to live long. But even for a few years would be nice to have a little family.'

"She was with her back to me and didn't speak.

"When she turned around again her face was white but the mouth was like iron.

"'No, Mr. Rosen.'

"'Why not, tell me?'

"'I had enough with sick men.' She began to cry. 'Please, Mr. Rosen. Go home.'

"I didn't have strength I should argue with her, so I went home. I went home but hurt me in my mind. All day long and all night I felt bad. My back pained me where was missing my kidney. Also too much smoking. I tried to understand this woman but I couldn't. Why should somebody that her two children were starving always say no to a man that he wanted to help her? What did I do to her bad? Am I maybe a murderer she should hate me so much? All that I felt in my heart was pity for her and the children, but I couldn't convince her. Then I went back and begged her she should let me help them, and once more she told me no.

"'Eva,' I said, 'I don't blame you that you don't want a sick man. So come with me to a marriage broker and we will find you a strong, healthy husband that he will support you and your girls. I will give the dowry.'

"She screamed, 'On this I don't need your help, Rosen!'

"I didn't say no more. What more could I say? All day long, from early in the morning till late in the night she worked like an animal. All day she mopped, she washed with soap and a brush the shelves, the few cans she polished, but the store was still rotten. The little girls I was afraid to look at. I could see in their faces their bones. They were tired, they were weak. Little Surale held with her hand all the time the dress of Fega. Once when I saw them in the street I gave them some cakes, but when I tried the next day to give them something else, the mother shouldn't know, Fega answered me, 'We can't take, Momma says today is a fast day.'

"I went inside. I made my voice soft. 'Eva, on my bended knees, I am a man with nothing in this world. Allow me that I should have a little pleasure before I die. Allow me that I should help you to stock up once more the store.'

"So what did she do? She cried, it was terrible to see. And after she cried, what did she say? She told me to go away and I shouldn't come back. I felt like to pick up a chair and break her head.

"In my house I was too weak to eat. For two days I took in my mouth nothing except maybe a spoon of chicken noodle soup, or maybe a glass tea without sugar. This wasn't good for me. My health felt bad.

"Then I made up a scheme that I was a friend of Axel's who lived in Jersey. I said I owed Axel seven hundred dollars that he lent me this money fifteen years ago, before he got married. I said I did not have the whole money now, but I would send her every week twenty dollars till it was paid up the debt. I put inside the letter two tens and gave it to a friend of mine, also a salesman, he should mail it in Newark so she wouldn't be suspicious who wrote the letters."

To Rosen's surprise Davidov had stopped writing. The book was full, so he tossed it onto the table, yawned, yet listened amiably. His curiosity had died.

Rosen got up and fingered the notebook. He tried to read the small distorted handwriting but could not make out a single word.

"It's not English and it's not Yiddish," he said. "Could it be in Hebrew?"

"No," answered Davidov. "It's an old-fashioned language they don't use it nowadays."

"Oh?" Rosen returned to the cot. He saw no purpose in going on now that it was not required, but he felt he had to.

"Came back all the letters," he said dully. "The first she opened it, then pasted back again the envelope, but the rest she didn't even open."

"'Here,' I said to myself, 'is a very strange thing—a person that you can never give her anything. —*But I will give.*'

"I went then to my lawyer and we made out a will that everything I had—all my investments, my two houses that I owned, also furniture, my car, the checking account—every cent would go to her, and when she died, the rest would be left for the two girls. The same with my insurance. They would be my beneficiaries. Then I signed and went home. In the kitchen I turned on the gas and put my head in the stove.

"Let her say now no."

Davidov, scratching his stubbled cheek, nodded. This was the part he already knew. He got up and, before Rosen could cry no, idly raised the window shade.

It was twilight in space but a woman stood before the window.

Rosen with a bound was off his cot to see.

It was Eva, staring at him with haunted, beseeching eyes. She raised her arms to him.

Infuriated, the ex-salesman shook his fist.

"Whore, bastard, bitch," he shouted at her. "Go 'way from here. Go home to your children."

Davidov made no move to hinder him as Rosen rammed down the window shade.

1956

The Lady of the Lake

Henry Levin, an ambitious, handsome thirty, who walked the floors in Macy's book department wearing a white flower in his lapel, having recently come into a small inheritance, quit, and went abroad seeking romance. In Paris, for no reason he was sure of, except that he was tired of the past—tired of the limitations it had imposed upon him; although he had signed the hotel register with his right name, Levin took to calling himself Henry R. Freeman. Freeman lived for a short while in a little hotel on a narrow gas lamp-lit street near the Luxembourg Gardens. In the beginning he liked the sense of foreignness of the city—of things different, anything likely to happen. He liked, he said to himself, the possible combinations. But not much did happen; he met no one he particularly cared for (he had sometimes in the past deceived himself about women, they had come to less than he had expected); and since the heat was hot and tourists underfoot, he felt he must flee. He boarded the Milan express, and after Dijon, developed a painful, palpitating anxiety. This grew so troublesome that he had serious visions of leaping off the train, but reason prevailed and he rode on. However, he did not get to Milan. Nearing Stresa, after a quick, astonished look at Lake Maggiore, Freeman, a nature lover from early childhood, pulled his suitcase off the rack and hurriedly left the train. He at once felt better.

An hour later he was established in a pensione in a villa not far from the line of assorted hotels fronting the Stresa shore. The padrona, a talkative woman, much interested in her guests, complained that June and July had been lost in unseasonable cold and wet. Many had cancelled; there were few Americans around. This didn't exactly disturb Freeman, who had had his full share of Coney Island. He lived in an airy, French-windowed room, including soft bed and spacious bath, and though personally the shower type, was glad of the change. He was very fond of the balcony at his window, where he loved to read, or study Italian, glancing up often to gaze at the water. The long blue lake, sometimes green, sometimes gold, went out of sight among distant mountains. He liked the red-roofed

574

town of Pallanza on the opposite shore, and especially the four beautiful islands in the water, tiny but teeming with palazzi, tall trees, gardens, visible statuary. The sight of these islands aroused in Freeman a deep emotion; each a universe—how often do we come across one in a lifetime?—filled him with expectancy. Of what, he wasn't sure. Freeman still hoped for what he hadn't, what few got in the world and many dared not think of; to wit, love, adventure, freedom. Alas, the words by now sounded slightly comical. Yet there were times, when he was staring at the islands, if you pushed him a little he could almost cry. Ah, what names of beauty: Isola Bella, dei Pescatori, Madre, and del Dongo. Travel is truly broadening, he thought; who ever got emotional over Welfare Island?

But the islands, the two he visited, let him down. Freeman walked off the vaporetto at Isola Bella amid a crowd of late-season tourists in all languages, especially German, who were at once beset by many vendors of cheap trinkets. And he discovered there were guided tours only—strictly no unsupervised wandering—the pink palazzo full of old junk, surrounded by artificial formal gardens, including grottoes made of seashells, the stone statuary a tasteless laugh. And although Isola dei Pescatori had some honest atmosphere, old houses hugging crooked streets, thick nets drying in piles near fishermen's dories drawn up among trees; again there were tourists snapping all in pictures, and the whole town catering to them. Everybody had something to sell you could buy better in Macy's basement. Freeman returned to his pensione, disappointed. The islands, beautiful from afar, up close were so much stage scenery. He complained thus to the padrona and she urged him to visit Isola del Dongo. "More natural," she persuaded him. "You never saw such unusual gardens. And the palazzo is historical, full of the tombs of famous men of the region, including a cardinal who became a saint. Napoleon, the emperor, slept there. The French have always loved this island. Their writers have wept at its beauty."

However, Freeman showed little interest. "Gardens I've seen in my time." So, when restive, he wandered in the back streets of Stresa, watching the men playing at boccia, avoiding the laden store windows. Drifting by devious routes back to the lake, he sat at a bench in the small park, watching the

lingering sunset over the dark mountains and thinking of a life
of adventure. He watched alone, talked now and then to stray
Italians—almost everybody spoke a good broken English—
and lived too much on himself. On weekends, there was,
however, a buzz of merriment in the streets. Excursionists
from around Milan arrived in busloads. All day they hurried to
their picnics; at night one of them pulled an accordion out of
the bus and played sad Venetian or happy Neapolitan songs.
Then the young Italians and their girls got up and danced in
tight embrace in the public square; but not Freeman.

One evening at sunset, the calm waters so marvelously
painted they drew him from inactivity, he hired a rowboat, and
for want of anyplace more exciting to go, rowed toward the
Isola del Dongo. He had no intention other than reaching it,
then turning back, a round trip completed. Two-thirds of the
way there, he began to row with growing uneasiness which
soon became dread, because a stiff breeze had risen, driving
the sucking waves against the side of the boat. It was a warm
wind, but a wind was a wind and the water was wet. Freeman
didn't row well—had learned late in his twenties, despite the
nearness of Central Park—and he swam poorly, always swallowing water, never enough breath to get anywhere; clearly a
landlubber from the word go. He strongly considered returning to Stresa—it was at least a half mile to the island, then a
mile and a half in return—but chided himself for his timidity.
He had, after all, hired the boat for an hour; so he kept rowing
though he feared the risk. However, the waves were not too
bad and he had discovered the trick of letting them hit the
prow head-on. Although he handled his oars awkwardly, Freeman, to his surprise, made good time. The wind now helped
rather than hindered; and daylight—reassuring—still lingered
in the sky among streaks of red.

At last Freeman neared the island. Like Isola Bella, it rose in
terraces through hedged gardens crowded with statuary, to a
palazzo on top. But the padrona had told the truth—this island looked more interesting than the others, the vegetation
lush, wilder, exotic birds flying around. By now the place was
bathed in mist, and despite the thickening dark, Freeman re-
captured the sense of awe and beauty he had felt upon first
beholding the islands. At the same time he recalled a sad

memory of unlived life, his own, of all that had slipped through his fingers. Amidst these thoughts he was startled by a movement in the garden by the water's edge. It had momentarily seemed as though a statue had come to life, but Freeman quickly realized a woman was standing this side of a low marble wall, watching the water. He could not, of course, make out her face, though he sensed she was young; only the skirt of her white dress moved in the breeze. He imagined someone waiting for her lover, and was tempted to speak to her, but then the wind blew up strongly and the waves rocked his rowboat. Freeman hastily turned the boat with one oar, and pulling hard, took off. The wind drenched him with spray, the rowboat bobbed among nasty waves, the going grew frighteningly rough. He had visions of drowning, the rowboat swamped, poor Freeman slowly sinking to the bottom, striving fruitlessly to reach the top. But as he rowed, his heart like a metal disk in his mouth, and still rowed on, gradually he overcame his fears; also the waves and wind. Although the lake was by now black, though the sky still dimly reflected white, turning from time to time to peer ahead, he guided himself by the flickering lights of the Stresa shore. It rained hard as he landed, but Freeman, as he beached the boat, considered his adventure an accomplishment and ate a hearty supper at an expensive restaurant.

The curtains billowing in his sunny room the next morning, awoke him. Freeman rose, shaved, bathed, and after breakfast got a haircut. Wearing his bathing trunks under slacks, he sneaked onto the Hotel Excelsior beach for a dip, short but refreshing. In the early afternoon he read his Italian lesson on the balcony, then snatched a snooze. At four-thirty—he felt he really hadn't made up his mind until then—Freeman boarded the vaporetto making its hourly tour of the islands. After touching at Isola Madre, the boat headed for the Isola del Dongo. As they were approaching the island, coming from the direction opposite that which Freeman had taken last night, he observed a lanky boy in bathing trunks sunning himself on a raft in the lake—nobody he recognized. When the vaporetto landed at the dock on the southern side of the island, to Freeman's surprise and deep regret, the area was crowded with the usual stalls piled high with tourist gewgaws. And though he had hoped otherwise, inspection of the island was strictly in the guide's footsteps, and *vietato* trying to go anywhere alone. You paid a hundred lire for a ticket, then trailed behind this unshaven, sad-looking clown, who stabbed a jaunty cane at the sky as he announced in three languages to the tourists who followed him: "Please not stray nor wander. The family del Dongo, one of the most illustrious of Italy, so requests. Only thus ees eet able to remain open thees magnificent 'eestorical palatz and supreme jardens for the inspection by the members of all nations."

They tailed the guide at a fast clip through the palace, through long halls hung with tapestries and elaborate mirrors, enormous rooms filled with antique furniture, old books, paintings, statuary—a lot of it in better taste than the stuff he had seen on the other island; and he visited where Napoleon had slept—a bed. Yet Freeman secretly touched the counterpane, though not quickly enough to escape the all-seeing eye of the Italian guide, who wrathfully raised his cane to the level of Freeman's heart and explosively shouted, "Basta!" This embarrassed Freeman and two British ladies carrying parasols. He felt bad until the group—about twenty—were led into the garden. Gazing from here, the highest point of the island, at the panorama of the golden-blue lake, Freeman gasped. And the luxuriant vegetation of the island was daring, voluptuous. They went among orange and lemon trees (he had never known that lemon was a perfume), magnolia, oleander—the guide called out the names. Everywhere were flowers in great profusion, huge camellias, rhododendron, jasmine, roses in innumerable colors and varieties, all bathed in intoxicating floral fragrance. Freeman's head swam; he felt dizzy, slightly off his rocker at this extraordinary assailment of his senses. At the same time, though it was an "underground" reaction, he experienced a painful, contracting remembrance—more like a warning—of personal poverty. This he had difficulty accounting for, because he usually held a decent opinion of himself. When the comical guide bounced forward, with his cane indicating cedar, eucalyptus, camphor and pepper trees, the former floorwalker, overcome by all he was for the first time seeing, at the same moment choked by almost breathless excitement, fell behind the group of tourists, and pretended to inspect the berries of a pepper tree. As the guide hurried forward, Free-

man, although not positive he had planned it so, ducked behind the pepper tree, ran along a path beside a tall laurel shrub
and down two flights of stairs; he hopped over a marble wall
and went hastily through a small wood, expectant, seeking, he
thought only God knew what.

He figured he was headed in the direction of the garden by
the water where he had seen the girl in the white dress last
night, but after several minutes of involved wandering, Freeman came upon a little beach, a pebbly strand, leading down
stone steps into the lake. About a hundred feet away a raft was
anchored, nobody on it. Exhausted by the excitement, a little
moody, Freeman sat down under a tree, to rest. When he
glanced up, a girl in a white bathing suit was coming up the steps
out of the water. Freeman stared as she sloshed up the shore,
her wet skin glistening in bright sunlight. She had seen him
and quickly bent for a towel she had left on a blanket, draped
it over her shoulders and modestly held the ends together over
her high-arched breast. Her wet black hair fell upon her shoulders. She stared at Freeman. He rose, forming words of apology
in his mind. A haze that had been before his eyes, evaporated.
Freeman grew pale and the girl blushed.

Freeman was, of course, a New York City boy from away
back. As the girl stood there unselfconsciously regarding him—
it could not have been longer than thirty seconds—he was
aware of his background and certain other disadvantages; but
he also knew he wasn't a bad-looking guy, even, it could be
said, quite on the handsome side. Though a pinprick bald at
the back of his noggin—not more than a dime could adequately
cover—his head of hair was alive, expressive; Freeman's gray
eyes were clear, unenvious, nose well-molded, the mouth
generous. He had well-proportioned arms and legs and his
stomach lay respectfully flat. He was a bit short, but on him,
he knew, it barely showed. One of his former girl friends had
told him she sometimes thought of him as tall. This counter-
balanced the occasions when he had thought of himself as
short. Yet though he knew he made a good appearance, Freeman feared this moment, partly because of all he hungered for
from life, and partly because of the uncountable obstacles ex-
isting between strangers, may the word forever perish.

She, apparently, had no fear of their meeting; as a matter of

surprising fact, seemed to welcome it, immediately curious
about him. She had, of course, the advantage of position—
which included receiving, so to speak, the guest-intruder. And
she had grace to lean on; herself also favored physically—
mama, what a queenly high-assed form—itself the cause of
grace. Her dark, sharp Italian face had that quality of beauty
which holds the mark of history, the beauty of a people and
civilization. The large brown eyes, under straight slender
brows, were filled with sweet light; her lips were purely cut as
if from red flowers; her nose was perhaps the one touch of
imperfection that perfected the rest—a trifle long and thin.
Despite the effect, a little of sculpture, her ovoid face, tapering
to a small chin, was soft, suffused with the loveliness of youth.
She was about twenty-three or -four. And when Freeman had,
to a small degree, calmed down, he discovered in her eyes a
hidden hunger, or memory thereof; perhaps it was sadness;
and he felt he was, for this reason, if not unknown others, sincerely welcomed. Had he, Oh God, at last met his fate?

"Si è perduto?" the girl asked, smiling, still tightly holding
her white towel. Freeman understood and answered in English. "No, I came on my own. On purpose you might say."
He had in mind to ask her if she remembered having seen him
before, namely in last night's rowboat, but didn't.

"Are you an American?" she inquired, her Italian accent
pleasantly touched with an English one.

"That's right."

The girl studied him for a full minute, and then hesitantly
asked, "Are you, perhaps, Jewish?"

Freeman suppressed a groan. Though secretly shocked by
the question, it was not, in a way, unexpected. Yet he did not
look Jewish, could pass as not—had. So without batting an
eyelash, he said, no, he wasn't. And a moment later added,
though he personally had nothing against them.

"It was just a thought. You Americans are so varied," she
explained vaguely.

"I understand," he said, "but have no worry." Lifting his
hat, he introduced himself: "Henry R. Freeman, traveling
abroad."

"My name," she said, after an absent-minded pause, "is Isabella del Dongo."

Safe on first, thought Freeman. "I'm proud to know you."
He bowed. She gave him her hand with a gentle smile. He was
about to surprise it with a kiss when the comical guide appeared at a wall a few terraces above. He gazed at them in astonishment, then let out a yell and ran down the stairs, waving
his cane like a rapier.

"Transgressor," he shouted at Freeman.

The girl said something to calm him, but the guide was too
furious to listen. He grabbed Freeman's arm, yanking him toward the stairs. And though Freeman, in the interest of good
manners, barely resisted, the guide whacked him across the
seat of the pants; but the ex-floorwalker did not complain.

Though his departure from the island had been, to put it
mildly, an embarrassment (the girl had vanished after her unsuccessful momentary intercession), Freeman dreamed of a
triumphant return. The big thing so far was that she, a knock-
out, had taken to him; he had been favored by her. Just why,
he couldn't exactly tell, but he could tell yes, had seen in her
eyes. Yet wondering if yes why yes—an old habit—Freeman,
among other reasons he had already thought of, namely the
thus and therefore of man-woman attraction—laid it to the
fact that he was different, had dared. He had, specifically, dared
to duck the guide and be waiting for her at the edge of the lake
when she came out of it. And she was different too (which of
course quickened her response to him). Not only in her looks
and background, but of course different as regards past. (He
had been reading with fascination about the del Dongos in all
the local guide books.) Her past he could see boiling in her all
the way back to the knights of old, and then some; his own
history was something else again, but men were malleable, and
he wasn't afraid of attempting to create certain daring combinations: Isabella and Henry Freeman. Hoping to meet someone like her was his main reason for having come abroad. And
he had also felt he would be appreciated more by a European
woman; his personality, that is. Yet, since their lives were *so*
different, Freeman had moments of grave doubt, wondered
what trials he was in for if he went after her, as he had every
intention of doing: with her unknown family—other things of
that sort. And he was in afterthought worried because she had
asked him if he was Jewish. Why had the question popped out

of her pretty mouth before they had even met? He had never before been asked anything like this by a girl, under let's call it similar circumstances. Just when they were looking each other over. He was puzzled because he absolutely did not look Jewish. But then he figured her question might have been a "test" of some kind, she making it a point, when a man attracted her, quickly to determine his "eligibility." Maybe she had once had some sort of unhappy experience with a Jew? Unlikely, but possible, they were now everywhere. Freeman finally explained it to himself as "one of those things," perhaps a queer thought that had for no good reason impulsively entered her mind. And because it was queer, his answer, without elaboration, was sufficient. With ancient history why bother? All these things— the odds against him, whetted his adventurous appetite.

He was in the grip of an almost unbearable excitement and must see her again soon, often, become her friend—not more than a beginning but where begin? He considered calling her on the telephone, if there was one in a palazzo where Napoleon had slept. But if the maid or somebody answered the phone first, he would have a ridiculous time identifying himself; so he settled for sending her a note. Freeman wrote a few lines on good stationery he had bought for the purpose, asking if he might have the pleasure of seeing her again under circumstances favorable to leisurely conversation. He suggested a carriage ride to one of the other lakes in the neighborhood, and signed his name not Levin, of course, but Freeman. Later he told the padrona that anything addressed to that name was meant for him. She was always to refer to him as Mr. Freeman. He gave no explanation, although the padrona raised interested brows; but after he had slipped her—for reasons of friendship—a thousand lire, her expression became serene. Having mailed the letter, he felt time descend on him like an intricate trap. How would he ever endure until she answered? That evening he impatiently hired a rowboat and headed for Isola del Dongo. The water was glassy smooth but when he arrived, the palazzo was dark, almost gloomy, not a single window lit; the whole island looked dead. He saw no one, though he imagined her presence. Freeman thought of tying up at a dock and searching around a bit, but it seemed like folly. Rowing back to Stresa, he was stopped by the lake patrol and compelled to show his passport. An officer advised him not to row on the lake after dark; he might have an accident. The next morning, wearing sunglasses, a light straw, recently purchased, and a seersucker suit, he boarded the vaporetto and soon landed on the island of his dreams, together with the usual group of tourists. But the fanatic guide at once spied Freeman, and waving his cane like a schoolmaster's rod, called on him to depart peacefully. Fearing a scene that the girl would surely hear of, Freeman left at once, greatly annoyed. The padrona, that night, in a confidential mood, warned him not to have anything to do with anybody on the Isola del Dongo. The family had a perfidious history and was known for its deceit and trickery.

On Sunday, at the low point of a depression after an afternoon nap, Freeman heard a knock on his door. A long-legged boy in short pants and a torn shirt handed him an envelope, the corner embossed with somebody's coat of arms. Breathlessly, Freeman tore it open and extracted a sheet of thin bluish paper with a few lines of spidery writing on it: "You may come this afternoon at six. Ernesto will accompany you. I. del D." It was already after five. Freeman was overwhelmed, giddy with pleasure.

"Tu sei Ernesto?" he asked the boy.

The boy, perhaps eleven or twelve, who had been watching Freeman with large curious eyes, shook his head. "No, Signore. Sono Giacobbe."

"Dov'è Ernesto?"

The boy pointed vaguely at the window, which Freeman took to mean that whoever he was was waiting at the lake front.

Freeman changed in the bathroom, emerging in a jiffy with his new straw hat on and the seersucker suit. "Let's go." He ran down the stairs, the boy running after him.

At the dock, to Freeman's startled surprise, "Ernesto" turned out to be the temperamental guide with the pestiferous cane, probably a majordomo in the palazzo, long with the family. Now a guide in another context, he was obviously an unwilling one, to judge from his expression. Perhaps a few wise words had subdued him and though haughty still, he settled for a show of politeness. Freeman greeted him courteously.

The guide sat not in the ritzy launch Freeman had expected to see, but at the stern of an oversize, weatherbeaten rowboat, a cross between a fishing dory and small lifeboat. Preceded by the boy, Freeman climbed in over the unoccupied part of the rear seat, then, as Giacobbe took his place at the oars, hesitantly sat down next to Ernesto. One of the boatmen on the shore gave them a shove off and the boy began to row. The big boat seemed hard to maneuver, but Giacobbe, working deftly with a pair of long, heavy oars, managed with ease. He rowed quickly from the shore and toward the island where Isabella was waiting.

Freeman, though heartened to be off, contented, loving the wide airy world, wasn't comfortable sitting so snug with Ernesto, who smelled freshly of garlic. The talkative guide was a silent traveler. A dead cheroot hung from the corner of his mouth, and from time to time he absently poked his cane in the slats at the bottom of the boat; if there was no leak, Freeman thought, he would create one. He seemed tired, as if he had been carousing all night and had found no time to rest. Once he removed his black felt hat to mop his head with a handkerchief, and Freeman realized he was bald and looked surprisingly old.

Though tempted to say something pleasant to the old man—no hard feelings on this marvelous journey—Freeman had no idea where to begin. What would he reply to a grunt? After a time of prolonged silence, now a bit on edge, Freeman remarked, "Maybe I'd better row and give the boy a rest?"

"As you weesh." Ernesto shrugged.

Freeman traded places with the boy, then wished he hadn't. The oars were impossibly heavy; he rowed badly, allowing the left oar to sink deeper into the water than the right, thus twisting the boat off course. It was like pulling a hearse, and as he awkwardly splashed the oars around, he was embarrassedly aware of the boy and Ernesto, alike in their dark eyes and greedy beaks, a pair of odd birds, openly staring at him. He wished them far far away from the beautiful island and in exasperation pulled harder. By dint of determined effort, though his palms were painfully blistered, he began to row rhythmically, and the boat went along more smoothly. Freeman gazed up in triumph but they were no longer watching him, the boy trailing a straw in the water, the guide staring dreamily into the distance.

After a while, as if having studied Freeman and decided, when all was said and done, that he wasn't exactly a villain, Ernesto spoke in a not unfriendly tone.

"Everybody says how reech ees America?" he remarked.

"Rich enough," Freeman grunted.

"Also thees ees the same with you?" The guide spoke with a half-embarrassed smile around his drooping cheroot butt.

"I'm comfortable," Freeman replied, and in honesty added, "but I have to work for a living."

"For the young people ees a nice life, no? I mean there ees always what to eat, and for the woman een the house many remarkable machines?"

"Many," Freeman said. Nothing comes from nothing, he thought. He's been asked to ask questions. Freeman then gave the guide an earful on the American standard of living, and he meant living. This for whatever it was worth to such as the Italian aristocracy. He hoped for the best. You could never tell the needs and desires of others.

Ernesto, as if memorizing what he had just heard, watched Freeman row for a while.

"Are you in biziness?" he ultimately asked.

Freeman searched around and came up with, "Sort of in public relations."

Ernesto now threw away his butt. "Excuse me that I ask. How much does one earn in thees biziness in America?"

Calculating quickly, Freeman replied, "I personally average about a hundred dollars a week. That comes to about a quarter million lire every month."

Ernesto repeated the sum, holding onto his hat in the breeze. The boy's eyes had widened. Freeman hid a satisfied smile.

"And your father?" Here the guide paused, searching Freeman's face.

"What about him?" asked Freeman, tensing.

"What ees hees trade?"

"Was. He's dead—insurance."

Ernesto removed his respectful hat, letting the sunlight bathe his bald head. They said nothing more until they had reached the island, then Freeman, consolidating possible gain, asked him in a complimentary tone where he had learned his English.

"Everywhere," Ernesto replied, with a weary smile, and, Freeman, alert for each shift in prevailing wind, felt that if he hadn't made a bosom friend, he had at least softened an enemy; and that, on home grounds, was going good.

They landed and watched the boy tie up the boat; Freeman asked Ernesto where the signorina was. The guide, now looking bored by it all, pointed his cane at the top terraces, a sweeping gesture that seemed to take in the whole upper half of the luscious island. Freeman hoped the man would not insist on accompanying him and interfering with his meeting with the girl; but when he looked down from looking up without sighting Isabella, both Ernesto and Giacobbe had made themselves scarce. Leave it to the Italians at this sort of thing, Freeman thought.

Warning himself to be careful, tactful, he went quickly up the stairs. At each terrace he glanced around, then ran up to the next, his hat already in his hand. He found her, after wandering through profusions of flowers, where he had guessed she would be, alone in the garden behind the palazzo. She was sitting on an old stone bench near a little marble fountain, whose jets from the mouths of mocking elves sparkled in mellow sunlight.

Beholding her, the lovely face, sharply incised, yet soft in its femininity, the dark eyes pensive, her hair loosely knotted at the nape of her graceful neck, Freeman ached to his oar-blistered fingers. She was wearing a linen blouse of some soft shade of red that fell gently upon her breasts, and a long, slender black skirt; her tanned legs were without stockings; and on her narrow feet she wore sandals. As Freeman approached her, walking slowly to keep from loping, she brushed back a strand of hair, a gesture so beautiful it saddened him, because it was gone in the doing; and though Freeman, on this miraculous Sunday evening, was aware of his indefatigable reality, he could not help thinking as he dwelt upon her lost gesture, that she might be as elusive as it, as evanescent; and so might this island be, and so, despite all the days he had lived through, good, bad and boring, that too often sneaked into his thoughts—so, indeed, might he today, tomorrow. He went toward her with a deep sense of the transitoriness of things, but this feeling was overwhelmed by one of pure joy when she rose to give him her hand.

"Welcome," Isabella said, blushing; she seemed happy, yet, in her manner, a little agitated to see him—perhaps one and the same thing—and he wanted then and there to embrace her but could not work up the nerve. Although he felt in her presence a fulfillment, as if they had already confessed love for one another, at the same time Freeman sensed an uneasiness in her which made him think, though he fought the idea, that they were far away from love; or at least were approaching it through opaque mystery. But that's what happened, Freeman, who had often been in love, told himself. Until you were lovers you were strangers.

In conversation he was at first formal. "I thank you for your kind note. I have been looking forward to seeing you."

She turned toward the palazzo. "My people are out. They have gone to a wedding on another island. May I show you something of the palace?"

He was at this news both pleased and disappointed. He did not at the moment feel like meeting her family. Yet if she had presented him, it would have been a good sign.

They walked for a while in the garden, then Isabella took Freeman's hand and led him through a heavy door into the large rococo palazzo.

"What would you care to see?"

Though he had superficially been through two floors of the building, wanting to be led by her, this close to him, Freeman replied, "Whatever you want me to."

She took him first to the chamber where Napoleon had slept. "It wasn't Napoleon himself, who slept here," Isabella explained. "He slept on Isola Bella. His brother Joseph may have been here, or perhaps Pauline, with one of her lovers. No one is sure."

"Oh ho, a trick," said Freeman.

"We often pretend," she remarked. "This is a poor country."

They entered the main picture gallery. Isabella pointed out the Titians, Tintorettos, Bellinis, making Freeman breathless; then at the door of the room she turned with an embarrassed

smile and said that most of the paintings in the gallery were
copies.

"Copies?" Freeman was shocked.

"Yes, although there are some fair originals from the Lom-
bard school."

"All the Titians are copies?"

"All."

This slightly depressed him. "What about the statuary—also
copies?"

"For the most part."

His face fell.

"Is something the matter?"

"Only that I couldn't tell the fake from the real."

"Oh, but many of the copies are exceedingly beautiful,"
Isabella said. "It would take an expert to tell they weren't
originals."

"I guess I've got a lot to learn," Freeman said.

At this she squeezed his hand and he felt better.

But the tapestries, she remarked as they traversed the long
hall hung with them, which darkened as the sun set, were
genuine and valuable. They meant little to Freeman: long
floor-to-ceiling, bluish-green fabrics of woodland scenes: stags,
unicorns and tigers disporting themselves, though in one picture, the tiger killed the unicorn. Isabella hurried past this and
led Freeman into a room he had not been in before, hung with
tapestries of somber scenes from the *Inferno*. One before
which they stopped, was of a writhing leper, spotted from head
to foot with pustulating sores which he tore at with his nails
but the itch went on forever.

"What did he do to deserve his fate?" Freeman inquired.

"He falsely said he could fly."

"For that you go to hell?"

She did not reply. The hall had become gloomily dark, so
they left.

From the garden close by the beach where the raft was
anchored, they watched the water turn all colors. Isabella had
little to say about herself—she seemed to be quite often
pensive—and Freeman, concerned with the complexities of
the future, though his heart contained multitudes, found himself comparatively silent. When the night was complete, as the

moon was rising, Isabella said she would be gone for a moment, and stepped behind a shrub. When she came forth, Freeman had this utterly amazing vision of her, naked, but before he could even focus his eyes on her flowerlike behind, she was already in the water, swimming for the raft. After an anguished consideration of could he swim that far or would he drown, Freeman, eager to see her from up close (she was sitting on the raft, showing her breasts to the moon) shed his clothes behind the shrub where her delicate things lay, and walked down the stone steps into the warm water. He swam awkwardly, hating the picture he must make in her eyes, Apollo Belvedere slightly maimed; and still suffered visions of drowning in twelve feet of water. Or suppose she had to jump in to rescue him? However, nothing risked, nothing gained, so he splashed on and made the raft with breath to spare, his worries always greater than their cause.

But when he had pulled himself up on the raft, to his dismay, Isabella was no longer there. He caught a glimpse of her on the shore, darting behind the shrub. Nursing gloomy thoughts, Freeman rested a while, then, when he had sneezed twice and presupposed a nasty cold, jumped into the water and splashed his way back to the island. Isabella, already clothed, was waiting with a towel. She threw it to Freeman as he came up the steps, and withdrew while he dried himself and dressed. When he came forth in his seersucker, she offered salami, prosciutto, cheese, bread, and red wine, from a large platter delivered from the kitchen. Freeman, for a while angered at the runaround on the raft, relaxed with the wine and feeling of freshness after a bath. The mosquitoes behaved long enough for him to say he loved her. Isabella kissed him tenderly, then Ernesto and Giacobbe appeared and rowed him back to Stresa.

Monday morning Freeman didn't know what to do with himself. He awoke with restless memories, enormously potent, many satisfying, some burdensome; they ate him, he ate them. He felt he should somehow have made every minute with her better, hadn't begun to say half of what he had wanted—the kind of man he was, what they could get out of life together. And he regretted that he hadn't gotten quickly to the raft, still excited by what might have happened if he had reached it before she had left. But a memory was only a memory—you could forget, not change it. On the other hand, he was pleased, surprised by what he had accomplished: the evening alone with her, the trusting, intimate sight of her beautiful body, her kiss, the unspoken promise of love. His desire for her was so splendid it hurt. He wandered through the afternoon, dreaming of her, staring often at the glittering islands in the opaque lake. By nightfall he was exhausted and went to sleep oppressed by all he had lived through.

It was strange, he thought, as he lay in bed waiting to sleep, that of all his buzzing worries he was worried most about one. If Isabella loved him, as he now felt she did or would before very long, with the strength of this love they could conquer their problems as they arose. He anticipated a good handful, stirred up, in all probability, by her family; but life in the U.S.A. was considered by many Italians, including aristocrats (else why had Ernesto been sent to sniff out conditions there?) a fine thing for their marriageable daughters. Given this additional advantage, things would somehow get worked out, especially if Isabella, an independent girl, gazed a little eagerly at the star-spangled shore. Her family would give before flight in her eyes. No, the worry that troubled him most was the lie he had told her, that he wasn't a Jew. He could, of course, confess, say she knew Levin, not Freeman, man of adventure, but that might ruin all, since it was quite clear she wanted nothing to do with a Jew, or why, at first sight, had she asked so searching a question? Or he might admit nothing and let her, more or less, find out after she had lived a while in the States and seen it was no crime to be Jewish; that a man's past was, it could safely be said, expendable. Yet this treatment, if the surprise was upsetting, might cause recriminations later on. Another solution might be one he had thought of often: to change his name (he had considered Le Vin but preferred Freeman) and forget he had ever been born Jewish. There was no question of hurting family, or being embarrassed by them, he the only son of both parents dead. Cousins lived in Toledo, Ohio, where they would always live and never bother. And when he brought Isabella to America they could skip N.Y.C. and go to live in a place like San Francisco, where nobody knew him and nobody "would know." To arrange such details and prepare other

minor changes was why he figured on a trip or two home before they were married; he was prepared for that. As for the
wedding itself, since he would have to marry her here to get
her out of Italy, it would probably have to be in a church, but
he would go along with that to hasten things. It was done
every day. Thus he decided, although it did not entirely satisfy
him; not so much the denial of being Jewish—what had it
brought him but headaches, inferiorities, unhappy memories?—
as the lie to the beloved. At first sight love and a lie; it lay on
his heart like a sore. Yet, if that was the way it had to be, it was
the way.

He awoke the next morning, beset by a swarm of doubts
concerning his plans and possibilities. When would he see Isabella again, let alone marry her? ("When?" he had whispered
before getting into the boat, and she had vaguely promised,
"Soon.") Soon was brutally endless. The mail brought nothing
and Freeman grew dismayed. Had he, he asked himself, been
constructing a hopeless fantasy, wish seducing probability?
Was he inventing a situation that didn't exist, namely, her feeling for him, the possibility of a future with her? He was desperately casting about for something to keep his mood from
turning dark blue, when a knock sounded on his door. The
padrona, he thought, because she often came up for one unimportant thing or another, but to his unspeakable joy it was
Cupid in short pants—Giacobbe holding forth the familiar
envelope. She would meet him, Isabella wrote, at two o'clock
in the piazza where the electric tram took off for Mt. Mot-
tarone, from whose summit one saw the beautiful panorama of
lakes and mountains in the region. Would he share this with
her?

Although he had quashed the morning's anxiety, Freeman
was there at one P.M., smoking impatiently. His sun rose as
she appeared, but as she came towards him he noticed she was
not quite looking at him (in the distance he could see Giacobbe rowing away), her face neutral, inexpressive. He was at
first concerned, but she had, after all, written the letter to him,
so he wondered what hot nails she had had to walk on to get
off the island. He must sometime during the day drop the
word "elope" to see if she savored it. But whatever was bothering her, Isabella immediately shook off. She smiled as she

greeted him; he hoped for her lips but got instead her polite fingers. These he kissed in broad daylight (let the spies tell papa) and she shyly withdrew her hand. She was wearing—it surprised him, though he gave her credit for resisting foolish pressures—exactly the same blouse and skirt she had worn on Sunday. They boarded the tram with a dozen tourists and sat alone on the open seat in front; as a reward for managing this she permitted Freeman to hold her hand. He sighed. The tram, drawn by an old electric locomotive, moved slowly through the town and more slowly up the slope of the mountain. They rode for close to two hours, watching the lake fall as the mountains rose. Isabella, apart from pointing to something now and then, was again silent, withdrawn, but Freeman, allowing her her own rate at flowering, for the moment without plans, was practically contented. A long vote for an endless journey; but the tram at last came to a stop and they walked through a field thick with wildflowers, up the slope to the summit of the mountain. Though the tourists followed in a crowd, the mountain top was broad and they stood near its edge, to all intents and purposes alone. Below them, on the green undulating plains of Piedmont and Lombardy, seven lakes were scattered, each a mirror reflecting whose fate? And high in the distance rose a ring of astonishing snow-clad Alps. Ah, he murmured, and fell silent.

"We say here," Isabella said, "'un pezzo di paradiso caduto dal cielo.'"

"You can say it again." Freeman was deeply moved by the sublimity of the distant Alps. She named the white peaks from Mt. Rosa to the Jungfrau. Gazing at them, he felt he had grown a head taller and was inspired to accomplish a feat men would wonder at.

"Isabella—" Freeman turned to ask her to marry him; but she was standing apart from him, her face pale.

Pointing to the snowy mountains, her hand moving in a gentle arc, she asked, "Don't those peaks—those seven—look like a Menorah?"

"Like a what?" Freeman politely inquired. He had a sudden frightening remembrance of her seeing him naked as he came out of the lake and felt constrained to tell her that circumcision was de rigueur in stateside hospitals; but he didn't dare. She may not have noticed.

"Like a seven-branched candelabrum holding white candles in the sky?" Isabella asked.

"Something like that."

"Or do you see the Virgin's crown adorned with jewels?"

"Maybe the crown," he faltered. "It all depends how you look at it."

They left the mountain and went down to the water. The tram ride was faster going down. At the lake front, as they were waiting for Giacobbe to come with the rowboat, Isabella, her eyes troubled, told Freeman she had a confession to make. He, still eager to propose, hoped she would finally say she loved him. Instead, she said, "My name is not del Dongo. It is Isabella della Seta. The del Dongos have not been on the island in years. We are the caretakers of the palace, my father, brother and I. We are poor people."

"Caretakers?" Freeman was astonished.

"Yes."

"Ernesto is your father?" His voice rose.

She nodded.

"Was it his idea for you to say you were somebody else?"

"No, mine. He did what I asked him to. He has wanted me to go to America, but under the right circumstances."

"So you had to pretend," he said bitterly. He was more greatly disturbed than he could account for, as if he had been expecting just this to happen.

She blushed and turned away. "I was not sure of the circumstances. I wanted you to stay until I knew you better."

"Why didn't you say so?"

"Perhaps I wasn't serious in the beginning. I said what I thought you wanted to hear. At the same time I wished you to stay. I thought you would be clearer to me after a while."

"Clearer how?"

"I don't really know." Her eyes searched his, then she dropped her glance.

"I'm not hiding anything," he said. He wanted to say more but warned himself not to.

"That's what I was afraid of."

Giacobbe had come with the boat and steadied it for his sister. They were alike as the proverbial peas—two dark Italian faces, the Middle Ages looking out of their eyes. Isabella got into the boat and Giacobbe pushed off with one oar. She waved from afar.

Freeman went back to his pensione in a turmoil, hurt where it hurts—in his dreams, thinking he should have noticed before how worn her blouse and skirt were, should have seen more than he had. It was this that irked. He called himself a damn fool for making up fairy tales—Freeman in love with the Italian aristocracy. He thought of taking off for Venice or Florence, but his heart ached for love of her, and he could not forget that he had originally come in the simple hope of finding a girl worth marrying. If the desire had developed complications, the fault was mostly his own. After an hour in his room, burdened by an overpowering loneliness, Freeman felt he must have her. She mustn't get away from him. So what if the countess had become a caretaker? She was a natural-born queen, whether by del Dongo or any other name. So she had lied to him, but so had he to her; they were quits on that score and his conscience was calm. He felt things would be easier all around now that the air had been cleared.

Freeman ran down to the dock; the sun had set and the boatmen were home, swallowing spaghetti. He was considering untying one of the rowboats and paying tomorrow, when he caught sight of someone sitting on a bench—Ernesto, in his hot winter hat, smoking a cheroot. He was resting his wrists on the handle of his cane, his chin on them.

"You weesh a boat?" the guide asked in a not unkindly tone.

"With all my heart. Did Isabella send you?"

"No."

He came because she was unhappy, Freeman guessed—maybe crying. There's a father for you, a real magician despite his appearance. He waves his stick and up pops Freeman for his little girl.

"Get een," said Ernesto.

"I'll row," said Freeman. He had almost added "father," but had caught himself. As if guessing the jest, Ernesto smiled, a little sadly. But he sat at the stern of the boat, enjoying the ride.

In the middle of the lake, seeing the mountains surrounding it lit in the last glow of daylight, Freeman thought of the "Menorah" in the Alps. Where had she got the word, he wondered, and decided anywhere, a book or picture. But wherever she had, he must settle this subject once and for all tonight.

When the boat touched the dock, the pale moon rose. Ernesto tied up, and handed Freeman a flashlight.

"Een the jarden," he said tiredly, pointing with his cane.

"Don't wait up." Freeman hastened to the garden at the lake's edge, where the roots of trees hung like hoary beards above the water; the flashlight didn't work, but the moon and his memory were enough. Isabella, God bless her, was standing at the low wall among the moonlit statuary: stags, tigers and unicorns, poets and painters, shepherds with pipes, and playful shepherdesses, gazing at the light shimmering on the water.

She was wearing white, the figure of a future bride; perhaps it was an altered wedding dress—he would not be surprised if a hand-me-down, the way they saved clothes in this poor country. He had pleasant thoughts of buying her some nifty outfits.

She was motionless, her back toward him—though he could picture her bosom breathing. When he said good evening, lifting his light straw, she turned to him with a sweet smile. He tenderly kissed her lips; this she let him do, softly returning the same.

"Goodbye," Isabella whispered.

"To whom goodbye?" Freeman affectionately mocked. "I have come to marry you."

She gazed at him with eyes moistly bright, then came the soft, inevitable thunder: "Are you a Jew?"

"Why should I lie?" he thought; she's mine for the asking. But then he trembled with the fear of at the last moment losing her, so Freeman answered, though his scalp prickled, "How many no's make never? Why do you persist with such foolish questions?"

"Because I hoped you were." Slowly she unbuttoned her bodice, arousing Freeman, though he was thoroughly confused as to her intent. When she revealed her breasts—he could have wept at their beauty (now recalling a former invitation to gaze at them, but he had arrived too late on the raft)—to his horror he discerned tattooed on the soft and tender flesh a bluish line of distorted numbers.

"Buchenwald," Isabella said, "when I was a little girl. The Fascists sent us there. The Nazis did it."

Freeman groaned, incensed at the cruelty, stunned by the desecration.

"I can't marry you. We are Jews. My past is meaningful to me. I treasure what I suffered for."

"Jews," he muttered, "—you? Oh, God, why did you keep this from me, too?"

"I did not wish to tell you something you would not welcome. I thought at one time it was possible you were—I hoped but was wrong."

"Isabella—" he cried brokenly. "Listen, I—I am—"

He groped for her breasts, to clutch, kiss or suckle them; but she had stepped among the statues, and when he vainly sought her in the veiled mist that had risen from the lake, still calling her name, Freeman embraced only moonlit stone.

1958

Behold the Key

ONE BEAUTIFUL late-autumn day in Rome, Carl Schneider, a graduate student in Italian studies at Columbia University, left a real estate agent's office after a depressing morning of apartment hunting and walked up Via Veneto, disappointed in finding himself so dissatisfied in this city of his dreams. Rome, a city of perpetual surprise, had surprised unhappily. He felt unpleasantly lonely for the first time since he had been married, and found himself desiring the lovely Italian women he passed in the street, especially the few who looked as if they had money. He had been a damn fool, he thought, to come here with so little of it in his pocket.

He had, last spring, been turned down for a Fulbright fellowship and had had no peace with himself until he decided to go to Rome anyway to do his Ph.D. on the Risorgimento from first-hand sources, at the same time enjoying Italy. This plan had for years aroused his happiest expectations. Norma thought he was crazy to want to take off with two kids under six and all their savings—$3,600, most of it earned by her, but Carl argued that people had to do something different with their lives occasionally or they went to pot. He was twenty-eight—his years weighed on him—and she was thirty, and when else could they go if not now? He was confident, since he knew the language, that they could get settled satisfactorily in a short time. Norma had her doubts. It all came to nothing until her mother, a widow, offered to pay their passage across; then Norma said yes, though still with misgiving.

"We've read prices are terrible in Rome. How do we know we'll get along on what we have?"

"You got to take a chance once in a while," Carl said.

"Up to a point, with two kids," Norma replied; but she took the chance and they sailed out of season—the sixteenth of October, arriving in Naples on the twenty-sixth and going on at once to Rome, in the hope they would save money if they found an apartment quickly, though Norma wanted to see Capri and Carl would have liked to spend a little time in Pompeii.

In Rome, though Carl had no trouble getting around or making himself understood, they had immediate rough going trying to locate an inexpensive furnished flat. They had figured on a two-bedroom apartment, Carl to work in theirs; or one bedroom and a large maid's room where the kids would sleep. Although they searched across the city they could locate nothing decent within their means, fifty to fifty-five thousand lire a month, a top of about ninety dollars. Carl turned up some inexpensive places but in hopeless Trastevere sections; elsewhere there was always some other fatal flaw: no heat, missing furniture, sometimes no running water or sanitation.

To make bad worse, during their second week at the dark little pensione where they were staying, the children developed nasty intestinal disorders, little Mike having to be carried to the bathroom ten times one memorable night, and Christine running a temperature of 105; so Norma, who didn't trust the milk or cleanliness of the pensione, suggested they would be better off in a hotel. When Christine's fever abated they moved into the Sora Cecilia, a second-class albergo recommended by a Fulbright fellow they had met. It was a four-story building full of high-ceilinged, boxlike rooms. The toilets were in the hall, but the rent was comparatively low. About the only other virtue of the place was that it was near the Piazza Navona, a lovely 17th-century square, walled by many magnificently picturesque, wine-colored houses. Within the piazza three fountains played, whose water and sculpture Carl and Norma enjoyed, but which they soon became insensible to during their sad little walks with the kids, as the days passed and they still found themselves homeless.

Carl had in the beginning avoided the real estate agents to save the commission—5 per cent of the full year's rent; but when he gave in and visited their offices they said it was too late to get anything at the price he wanted to pay.

"You should have come in July," one agent said.

"I'm here now."

He threw up his hands. "I believe in miracles but who can make them?" Better to pay seventy-five thousand and so live comfortable like other Americans.

"I can't afford it, not with heat extra."

"Then you will sit out the winter in the hotel."

"I appreciate your concern." Carl left, embittered.

However, they sometimes called him to witness an occasional "miracle." One man showed him a pleasant apartment overlooking some prince or other's formal garden. The rent was sixty thousand, and Carl would have taken it had he not later learned from the tenant next door—he had returned because he distrusted the agent—that the flat was heated electrically, which would cost twenty thousand a month over the sixty thousand rent. Another "miracle" was the offer by this agent's cousin of a single studio room on the Via Margutta, for forty thousand. And from time to time a lady agent called Norma to tell her about this miraculous place in the Parioli: eight stunning rooms, three bedrooms, double service, American-style kitchen with refrigerator, garage—marvelous for an American family: price, two hundred thousand.

"Please, no more," Norma said.

"I'll go mad," said Carl. He was nervous over the way time was flying, almost a month gone, he having given none of it to his work. And Norma, washing the kids' things in the hotel sink, in an unheated, cluttered room, was obviously unhappy. Furthermore, the hotel bill last week had come to twenty thousand lire, and it was costing them two thousand more a day to eat badly, even though Norma was cooking the children's food in their room on a hotplate they had bought.

"Carl, maybe I'd better go to work?"

"I'm tired of your working," he answered. "You'll have no fun."

"What fun am I having? All I've seen is the Colosseum." She then suggested they could rent an unfurnished flat and build their own furniture.

"Where would I get the tools?" he said. "And what about the cost of wood in a country where it's cheaper to lay down marble floors? And who'll do my reading for me while I'm building and finishing the stuff?"

"All right," Norma said. "Forget I said anything."

"What about taking a seventy-five thousand place but staying only for five or six months?" Carl said.

"Can you get your research done in five or six months?"

"No."

"I thought your research was the main reason we came here." Norma then wished she had never heard of Italy.

"That's enough of that," said Carl.

He felt helpless, blamed himself for coming—bringing all this on Norma and the kids. He could not understand why things were going so badly. When he was not blaming himself he was blaming the Italians. They were aloof, evasive, indifferent to his plight. He couldn't communicate with them in their own language, whatever it was. He couldn't get them to say what was what, to awaken their hearts to his needs. He felt his plans, his hopes caving in, and feared disenchantment with Italy unless they soon found an apartment.

At the Porta Pinciana, near the tram, Carl felt himself tapped on the shoulder. A bushy-haired Italian, clutching a worn briefcase, was standing in the sun on the sidewalk. His hair rose in all directions. His eyes were gentle; not sad, but they had been. He wore a clean white shirt, rag of a tie, and a black jacket that had crawled a little up his back. His trousers were of denim, and his porous, sharp-pointed shoes, neatly shined, were summer shoes.

"Excuse me," he said with an uneasy smile. "I am Vasco Bevilacqua. Weesh you an apotament?"

"How did you guess?" Carl said.

"I follow you," the Italian answered, making a gesture in the air, "when you leave the agencia. I am myself agencia. I like to help Americans. They are wonderful people."

"You're a real estate agent?"

"Eet is just."

"Parliamo italiano?"

"You spik?" He seemed disappointed. "Ma non è italiano?"

Carl told him he was an American student of Italian history and culture, had studied the language for years.

Bevilacqua then explained that, although he had no regular office, nor, for that matter, a car, he had managed to collect several exclusive listings. He had got these, he said, from friends who knew he was starting a business, and they made it a habit to inform him of apartments recently vacated in their buildings or those of friends, for which service, he of course tipped them out of his commissions. The regular agents, he went on, demanded a heartless five per cent. He requested only three. He charged less because his expenses, frankly, were low, and also because of his great affection for Americans. He asked Carl how many rooms he was looking for and what he was willing to pay.

Carl hesitated. The man, though pleasant, was no bona fide agent, probably had no license. He had heard about these two-bit operators and was about to say he wasn't interested but Bevilacqua's eyes pleaded with him not to say it.

Carl figured he had nothing to lose. Maybe he does have a place I might be interested in. He told the Italian what he was looking for and how much he expected to pay.

Bevilacqua's face lit up. "In weech zone do you seek?" he asked with emotion.

"Any place fairly decent," Carl said in Italian. "It doesn't have to be perfect."

"Not the Parioli?"

"Not the Parioli only. It would depend on the rent."

Bevilacqua held his briefcase between his knees and fished in his shirt pocket. He drew out a sheet of very thin paper, unfolded it, and read the penciled writing, with wrinkled brows. After a while he thrust the paper back into his pocket and retrieved his briefcase.

"Let me have your telephone number," he said in Italian. "I will examine my other listings and give you a ring."

"Listen," Carl said, "if you've got a good place to show me, all right. If not, please don't waste my time."

Bevilacqua looked hurt. "I give you my word," he said, placing his big hand on his chest, "tomorrow you will have your apartment. May my mother give birth to a goat if I fail you."

He put down in a little book where Carl was staying. "I'll be over at thirteen sharp to show you some miraculous places," he said.

"Can't you make it in the morning?"

Bevilacqua was apologetic. "My hours are now from thirteen to sixteen." He said he hoped to expand his time later, and Carl guessed he was working his real estate venture during his lunch and siesta time, probably from some underpaid clerk's job.

He said he would expect him at thirteen sharp.

Bevilacqua, his expression now so serious he seemed to be listening to it, bowed, and walked away in his funny shoes.

He showed up at the hotel at ten to two, wearing a small black fedora, his hair beaten down with pomade whose odor sprang into the lobby. Carl was waiting restlessly near the desk, doubting he would show up, when Bevilacqua came running through the door, clutching his briefcase.

"Ready?" he said breathlessly.

"Since one o'clock," Carl answered.

"Ah, that's what comes of not owning your own car," Bevilacqua explained. "My bus had a flat tire."

Carl looked at him but his face was deadpan. "Well, let's get on," the student said.

"I have three places to show you." Bevilacqua told him the first address, a two-bedroom apartment at just fifty thousand.

On the bus they clung to straps in a tight crowd, the Italian raising himself on his toes and looking around at every stop to see where they were. Twice he asked Carl the time, and when Carl told him, his lips moved soundlessly. After a time Bevilacqua roused himself, smiled, and remarked, "What do you think of Marilyn Monroe?"

"I haven't much thought of her," Carl said.

Bevilacqua looked puzzled. "Don't you go to the movies?"

"Once in a while."

The Italian made a short speech on the wonder of American films. "In Italy they always make us look at what we have just lived through." He fell into silence again. Carl noticed that he was holding in his hand a wooden figurine of a hunchback with a high hat, whose poor gobbo he was rubbing with his thumb, for luck.

"For us both," Carl hoped. He was still restless, still worried.

But their luck was nil at the first place, an ochre-colored house behind an iron gate.

"Third floor?" Carl asked, after the unhappy realization that he had been here before.

"Exactly. How did you guess?"

"I've seen the apartment," he answered gloomily. He remembered having seen an ad. If that was how Bevilacqua got his listings, they might as well quit now.

"But what's wrong with it?" the Italian asked, visibly disappointed.

"Bad heating."

"How is that possible?"

"They have a single gas heater in the living room but nothing in the bedrooms. They were supposed to have steam heat installed in the building in September, but the contract fell through when the price of steam pipe went up. With two kids, I wouldn't want to spend the winter in a cold flat."

"Cretins," muttered Bevilacqua. "The portiere said the heat was perfect."

He consulted his paper. "I have a place in the Prati district, two fine bedrooms and combined living and dining room. Also an American-type refrigerator in the kitchen."

"Has the apartment been advertised in the papers?"

"Absolutely no. My cousin called me about this one last night—but the rent is fifty-five thousand."

"Let's see it anyway," Carl said.

It was an old house, formerly a villa, which had been cut up into apartments. Across the street stood a little park with tall, tufted pine trees, just the thing for the kids. Bevilacqua located the portiere, who led them up the stairs, all the while saying how good the flat was. Although Carl discovered at once that there was no hot water in the kitchen sink and it would have to be carried in from the bathroom, the flat made a good impression on him. But then in the master bedroom he noticed that one wall was wet and there was a disagreeable odor in the room.

The portiere quickly explained that a water pipe had burst in the wall, but they would have it fixed in a week.

"It smells like a sewer pipe," said Carl.

"But they will have it fixed this week," Bevilacqua said.

"I couldn't live a week with that smell in the room."

"You mean you are not interested in the apartment?" the Italian said fretfully.

Carl nodded. Bevilacqua's face fell. He blew his nose and they left the house. Outside he regained his calm. "You can't trust your own mother nowadays. I called the portiere this morning and he guaranteed me the house was without a fault."

"He must have been kidding you."

"It makes no difference. I have an exceptional place in mind for you now, but we've got to hurry."

Carl half-heartedly asked where it was.

The Italian looked embarrassed. "In the Parioli, a wonderful section, as you know. Your wife won't have to look far for friends—there are Americans all over. Also Japanese and Indians, if you have international tastes."

"The Parioli," Carl muttered. "How much?"

"Only sixty-five thousand," Bevilacqua said, staring at the ground.

"Only? Still, it must be a dump at that price."

"It's really very nice—new, and with a good-size nuptial bedroom and one small, besides the usual things, including a fine kitchen. You will personally love the magnificent terrace."

"Have you seen the place?"

"I spoke to the maid and she says the owner is very anxious to rent. They are moving, for business reasons, to Turin next week. The maid is an old friend of mine. She swears the place is perfect."

Carl considered it. Sixty-five thousand meant close to a hundred and five dollars. "Well," he said after a while, "let's have a look at it."

They caught a tram and found seats together, Bevilacqua impatiently glancing out of the window whenever they stopped. On the way he told Carl about his hard life. He was the eighth of twelve children, only five now alive. Nobody was really ever not hungry, though they ate spaghetti by the bucketful. He had to leave school at ten and go to work. In the war he was wounded twice, once by the Americans advancing, and once by the Germans retreating. His father was killed in an Allied bombardment of Rome, the same that had cracked open his mother's grave in the Cimitero Verano.

"The British pinpointed their targets," he said, "but the Americans dropped bombs everywhere. This was the advantage of your great wealth."

Carl said he was sorry about the bombardments.

"Nevertheless, I like the Americans better," Bevilacqua went on. "They are more like Italians—open. That's why I like to help them when they come here. The British are more closed. They talk with tight lips." He made sounds with tight lips.

As they were walking towards Piazza Euclide, he asked Carl if he had an American cigarette on him.

"I don't smoke," Carl said apologetically.

Bevilacqua shrugged and walked faster.

The house he took Carl to was a new one on Via Archimede, an attractive street that wound up and around a hill. It was crowded with long-balconied apartment buildings in bright colors. Carl thought he would be happy to live in one of them. It was a short thought, he wouldn't let it get too long.

They rode up to the fifth floor, and the maid, a dark girl with fuzzy cheeks, showed them through the neat apartment.

"Is sixty-five thousand correct?" Carl asked her.

She said yes.

The flat was so good that Carl, moved by elation and fear, began to pray.

"I told you you'd like it," Bevilacqua said, rubbing his palms. "I'll draw up the contract tonight."

"Let's see the bedroom now," Carl said.

But first the maid led them onto a broad terrace to show them the view of the city. The sight excited Carl—the variety of architecture from ancient to modern times, where history had been and still, in its own aftermath, sensuously flowed, a sea of roofs, towers, domes; and in the background, golden-domed St. Peter's. This marvelous city, Carl thought.

"Now the bedroom," he said.

"Yes, the bedroom." The maid led them through double doors into the "camera matrimoniale," spacious, and tastefully furnished, containing handsome mahogany twin beds.

"They'll do," Carl said, to hide his joy, "though I personally prefer a double bed."

"I also," said the maid, "but you can move one in."

"These will do."

"But they won't be here," she said.

"What do you mean they won't be here?" Bevilacqua demanded.

"Nothing will be left. Everything goes to Turin."

Carl's beautiful hopes took another long dive into a dirty cellar.

Bevilacqua flung his hat on the floor, landed on it with both feet and punched himself on the head with his fists.

The maid swore she had told him on the phone that the apartment was for rent unfurnished.

He began to yell at her and she shouted at him. Carl left, broken-backed. Bevilacqua caught up with him in the street. It was a quarter to four and he had to rush off to work. He held his hat and ran down the hill.

"I weel show you a terreefic place tomorrow," he called over his shoulder.

"Over my dead body," said Carl.

On the way to the hotel he was drenched in a heavy rainfall, the first of many in the late autumn.

The next morning the hotel phone rang at seven-thirty. The children awoke, Mike crying. Carl, dreading the day, groped for the ringing phone. Outside it was still raining.

"Pronto."

It was a cheery Bevilacqua. "I call you from my job. I 'ave found for you an apotament een weech you can move tomorrow if you like."

"Go to hell."

"Cosa?"

"Why do you call so early? You woke the children."

"Excuse me," Bevilacqua said in Italian. "I wanted to give you the good news."

"What goddamn good news?"

"I have found a first-class apartment for you near the Monte Sacro. It has only one bedroom but also a combined living and dining room with a double day bed, and a glass-enclosed terrace studio for your studies, and a small maid's room. There is no garage but you have no car. Price forty-five thousand—less than you expected. The apartment is on the ground floor and there is also a garden for your children to play in. Your wife will go crazy when she sees it."

"So will I," Carl said. "Is it furnished?"

Bevilacqua coughed. "Of course."

"Of course. Have you been there?"

He cleared his throat. "Not yet. I just discovered it this minute. The secretary of my office, Mrs. Gaspari, told me about it. The apartment is directly under hers. She will make a wonderful neighbor for you. I will come to your hotel precisely at thirteen and a quarter."

"Give yourself time. Make it fourteen."

"You will be ready?"

"Yes."

But when he had hung up, his feeling of dread had grown. He felt afraid to leave the hotel and confessed this to Norma.

"Would you like me to go this time?" she asked.

He considered it but said no.

"Poor Carl."

"'The great adventure.'"

"Don't be bitter. It makes me miserable."

They had breakfast in the room—tea, bread and jam, fruit. They were cold, but there was to be no heat, it said on a card tacked on the door, until December. Norma put sweaters on the kids. Both had colds. Carl opened a book but could not concentrate and settled for *Il Messaggero*. Norma telephoned the lady agent; she said she would ring back when there was something new to show.

Bevilacqua called up from the lobby at one-forty.

"Coming," Carl said, his heart heavy.

The Italian was standing in wet shoes near the door. He held his briefcase and a dripping large umbrella but had left his hat home. Even in the damp his bushy hair stood upright. He looked slightly miserable.

They left the hotel. Bevilacqua walking quickly by Carl's side, maneuvering to keep the umbrella over both of them. On the Piazza Navona a woman was feeding a dozen stray cats in the rain. She had spread a newspaper on the ground and the cats were grabbing hard strings of last night's macaroni. Carl felt the recurrence of his loneliness.

A packet of garbage thrown out of a window hit their umbrella and bounced off. The garbage spilled on the ground. A white-faced man, staring out of a third-floor window, pointed to the cats. Carl shook his fist at him.

Bevilacqua was moodily talking about himself. "In eight years of hard work I advanced myself only from thirty thousand lire to fifty-five thousand a month. The cretin who sits on my left in the office has his desk at the door and makes forty thousand extra in tips just to give callers an appointment with the big boss. If I had that desk I would double what he takes in."

"Have you thought of changing jobs?"

"Certainly, but I could never start at the salary I am now earning. And there are twenty people who will jump into my job at half the pay."

"Tough," Carl said.

"For every piece of bread, we have twenty open mouths. You Americans are the lucky ones."

"Yes, in that way."

"In what way no?"

"We have no piazzas."

Bevilacqua shrugged one shoulder. "Can you blame me for wanting to advance myself?"

"Of course not. I wish you the best."

"I wish the best to all Americans," Bevilacqua declared. "I like to help them."

"And I to all Italians and pray them to let me live among them for a while."

"Today it will be arranged. Tomorrow you will move in. I feel luck in my bones. My wife kissed St. Peter's toe yesterday."

Traffic was heavy, a stream of gnats—Vespas, Fiats, Renaults—roared at them from both directions, nobody slowing down to let them pass. They plowed across dangerously. At the bus stop the crowd rushed for the doors when the bus swerved to the curb. It moved away with its rear door open, four people hanging on the step.

I can do as well in Times Square, Carl thought.

In a half hour, after a short walk from the bus stop, they arrived at a broad, tree-lined street. Bevilacqua pointed to a yellow apartment house on the corner they were approaching. All over it were terraces, the ledges loaded with flower pots and stone boxes dropping ivy over the walls. Carl would not allow himself to think the place had impressed him.

Bevilacqua nervously rang the portiere's bell. He was again rubbing the hunchback's gobbo. A thick-set man in a blue smock came up from the basement. His face was heavy and he wore a full black mustache. Bevilacqua gave him the number of the apartment they wanted to see.

"Ah, there I can't help you," said the portiere. "I haven't got the key."

"Here we go again," Carl muttered.

"Patience," Bevilacqua counseled. He spoke to the portiere in a dialect Carl couldn't follow. The portiere made a long speech in the same dialect.

"Come upstairs," said Bevilacqua.

"Upstairs where?"

"To the lady I told you about, the secretary of my office. She lives on the first floor. We will wait there comfortably until we can get the key to the apartment."

"Where is it?"

"The portiere isn't sure. He says a certain Contessa owns the apartment but she let her lover live in it. Now the Contessa decided to get married so she asked the lover to move, but he took the key with him."

"It's that simple," said Carl.

"The portiere will telephone the Contessa's lawyer who takes care of her affairs. He must have another key. While he makes the call we will wait in Mrs. Gaspari's apartment. She will make you an American coffee. You'll like her husband too, he works for an American company."

"Never mind the coffee," Carl said. "Isn't there some way we can get a look into the flat? For all I know it may not be worth waiting for. Since it's on the ground floor maybe we can have a look through the windows?"

"The windows are covered by shutters which can be raised from the inside only."

They walked up to the secretary's apartment. She was a dark woman of thirty, with extraordinary legs, and bad teeth when she smiled.

"Is the apartment worth seeing?" Carl asked her.

"It's just like mine, with the exception of having a garden. Would you care to see mine?"

"If I may."

"Please."

She led him through her rooms. Bevilacqua remained on the sofa in the living room, his damp briefcase on his knees.

He opened the straps, took out a chunk of bread, and chewed thoughtfully.

Carl admitted to himself that he liked the flat. The building was comparatively new, had gone up after the war. The one bedroom was a disadvantage, but the kids could have it and he and Norma would sleep on the day bed in the living room. The terrace studio was perfect for a workroom. He had looked out of the bedroom window and seen the garden, a wonderful place for children to play.

"Is the rent really forty-five thousand?" he asked.

"Exactly."

"And it is furnished?"

"In quite good taste."

"Why doesn't the Contessa ask more for it?"

"She has other things on her mind," Mrs. Gaspari laughed. "Oh, see," she said, "the rain has stopped and the sun is coming out. It is a good sign." She was standing close to him.

"What's in it for her?" Carl thought and then remembered she would share Bevilacqua's poor three per cent.

He felt his lips moving. He tried to stop the prayer but it went on. When he had finished, it began again. The apartment was fine, the garden just the thing for the kids. The price was better than he had hoped.

In the living room Bevilacqua was talking to the portiere. "He couldn't reach the lawyer," he said glumly.

"Let me try," Mrs. Gaspari said. The portiere gave her the number and left. She dialed the lawyer but found he had gone for the day. She got his house number and telephoned there. The busy signal came. She waited a minute, then dialed again.

Bevilacqua took two small hard apples from his briefcase and offered one to Carl. Carl shook his head. The Italian peeled the apples with his penknife and ate both. He dropped the skins and cores into his briefcase, then locked the straps.

"Maybe we could take the door down," Carl suggested. "It shouldn't be hard to pull the hinges."

"The hinges are on the inside," Bevilacqua said.

"I doubt if the Contessa would rent to you," said Mrs. Gaspari from the telephone, "if you got in by force."

"If I had the lover here," Bevilacqua said, "I would break his neck for stealing the key."

"Still busy," said Mrs. Gaspari.

"Where does the Contessa live?" Carl asked. "Maybe I could take a taxi over."

"I believe she moved recently," Mrs. Gaspari said. "I once had her address but I have no longer."

"Would the portiere know it?"

"Possibly." She called the portiere on the house phone but all he would give her was the Contessa's telephone number. The Contessa wasn't home, her maid said, so they telephoned the lawyer and again got a busy signal. Carl was by now irritated.

Mrs. Gaspari called the telephone operator, giving the Contessa's number and requesting her home address. The telephone operator found the old one but could not locate the new.

"Stupid," said Mrs. Gaspari. Once more she dialed the lawyer.

"I have him," she announced over the mouthpiece. "Buon giorno, Avvocato." Her voice was candy.

Carl heard her ask the lawyer if he had a duplicate key and the lawyer replied for three minutes.

She banged down the phone. "He has no key. Apparently there is only one."

"To hell with all this." Carl got up. "I'm going back to the United States."

It was raining again. A sharp crack of thunder split the sky, and Bevilacqua, abandoning his briefcase, rose in fright.

"I'm licked," Carl said to Norma, the next morning. "Call the agents and tell them we're ready to pay seventy-five. We've got to get out of this joint."

"Not before we speak to the Contessa. I'll tell her my troubles and break her heart."

"You'll get involved and you'll get nowhere," Carl warned her.

"Please call her anyway."

"I haven't got her number. I didn't think of asking for it."

"Find it. You're good at research."

He considered phoning Mrs. Gaspari for the number but remembered she was at work, and he didn't have that number.

Recalling the address of the apartment house, he looked it up in the phone book. Then he telephoned the portiere and asked for the Contessa's address and her phone number.

"I'll call you back," said the portiere, eating as he spoke. "Give me your telephone."

"Why bother? Give me her number and save yourself the trouble."

"I have strict orders from the Contessa never to give her number to strangers. They call up on the phone and annoy her."

"I'm not a stranger. I want to rent her flat."

The portiere cleared his throat. "Where are you staying?"

"Albergo Sora Cecilia."

"I'll call you back in a quarter of an hour."

"Have it your way." He gave the portiere his name.

In forty minutes the phone rang and Carl reached for it. "Pronto."

"Signore Schneider?" It was a man's voice—a trifle high.

"Speaking."

"Permit me," the man said, in fluent though accented English. "I am Aldo De Vecchis. It would please me to speak to you in person."

"Are you a real estate agent?"

"Not precisely, but it refers to the apartment of the Contessa. I am the former occupant."

"The man with the key?" Carl asked quickly.

"It is I."

"Where are you now?"

"In the foyer downstairs."

"Come up, please."

"Excuse me, but if you will permit, I would prefer to speak to you here."

"I'll be right down."

"The lover," he said to Norma.

"Oh, God."

He rushed down in the elevator. A thin man in a green suit with cuffless trousers was waiting in the lobby. He was about forty, his face small, his hair wet black, and he wore at a tilt the brownest hat Carl had ever seen. Though his shirt collar was frayed, he looked impeccable. Into the air around him leaked the odor of cologne.

"De Vecchis," he bowed. His eyes, in a slightly pockmarked face, were restless.

"I'm Carl Schneider. How'd you get my number?"

De Vecchis seemed not to have heard. "I hope you are enjoying your visit here."

"I'd enjoy it more if I had a house to live in."

"Precisely. But what is your impression of Italy?"

"I like the people."

"There are too many of them." De Vecchis looked restlessly around. "Where may we speak? My time is short."

"Ah," said Carl. He pointed to a little room where people wrote letters. "In there."

They entered and sat at a table, alone in the room.

De Vecchis felt in his pocket for something, perhaps a cigarette, but came up with nothing. "I won't waste your time," he said. "You wish the apartment you saw yesterday? I wish you to have it, it is most desirable. There is also with it a garden of roses. You will love it on a summer night when Rome is hot. However, the practical matter is this. Are you willing to invest a few lire to obtain the privilege of entry?"

"The key?" Carl knew but asked.

"Precisely. To be frank I am not in good straits. To that is added the psychological disadvantage of the aftermath of a love affair with a most difficult woman. I leave you to imagine my present condition. Notwithstanding, the apartment I offer is attractive and the rent, as I understand, is for Americans not too high. Surely this has its value for you?" He attempted a smile but it died in birth.

"I am a graduate student of Italian studies," Carl said, giving him the facts. "I've invested all of my savings in this trip abroad to get my Ph.D. dissertation done. I have a wife to support and two children."

"I hear that your government is most generous to the Fulbright Fellows?"

"You don't understand. I am not a Fulbright Fellow."

"Whatever it is," De Vecchis said, drumming his fingertips on the table, "the price of the key is eighty thousand lire."

Carl laughed mirthlessly.

"I beg your pardon?"

Carl rose.

"Is the price too high?"

"It's impossible."

De Vecchis rubbed his brow nervously. "Very well, since not all Americans are rich Americans—you see, I am objective—I will reduce the sum by one half. For less than a month's rent the key is yours."

"Thanks. No dice."

"Please? I don't understand your expression."

"I can't afford it. I'd still have a commission to pay the agent."

"Oh? Then why don't you forget him? I will issue orders to the portiere to allow you to move in immediately. This evening, if you prefer. The Contessa's lawyer will draw up the lease free of charge. And although she is difficult to her lovers, she is an angel to her tenants."

"I'd like to forget the agent," Carl said, "but I can't."

De Vecchis gnawed his lip. "I will make it twenty-five thousand," he said, "but this is my last and absolute word."

"No, thanks. I won't be a party to a bribe."

De Vecchis rose, his small face tight, pale. "It is people like you who drive us to the hands of the Communists. You try to buy us—our votes, our culture, and then you dare speak of bribes."

He strode out of the room and through the lobby.

Five minutes later the phone rang. "Fifteen thousand is my final offer." His voice was thick.

"Not a cent," said Carl.

Norma stared at him.

De Vecchis slammed the phone.

The portiere telephoned. He had looked everywhere, he said, but had lost the Contessa's address.

"What about her phone number?" Carl asked.

"It was changed when she moved. The numbers are confused in my mind, the old with the new."

"Look here," Carl said, "I'll tell the Contessa you sent De Vecchis to see me about her apartment."

"How can you tell her if you don't know her number?" the portiere asked with curiosity. "It isn't listed in the book."

"I'll ask Mrs. Gaspari for it when she gets home from work, then I'll call the Contessa and tell her what you did."

"What did I do? Tell me exactly."

"You sent her former lover, a man she wants to get rid of, to try to squeeze money out of me for something that is none of his business—namely her apartment."

"Is there no other way than this?" asked the portiere.

"If you tell me her address I will give you one thousand lire." Carl felt his tongue thicken.

"How shameful," Norma said from the sink, where she was washing clothes.

"Not more than one thousand?" asked the portiere.

"Not till I move in."

The portiere then told him the Contessa's last name and her new address. "Don't repeat where you got it."

Carl swore he wouldn't.

He left the hotel on the run, got into a cab, and drove across the Tiber to the Via Cassia, in the country.

The Contessa's maid admitted him into a fabulous place with mosaic floors, gilded furniture, and a marble bust of the Contessa's great-grandfather in the foyer where Carl waited. In twenty minutes the Contessa appeared, a plain-looking woman, past fifty, with dyed blonde hair, black eyebrows, and a short, tight dress. The skin on her arms was wrinkled, but her bosom was enormous and she smelled like a rose garden.

"Please, you must be quick," she said impatiently. "There is so much to do. I am preparing for my wedding."

"Contessa," said Carl, "excuse me for rushing in like this, but my wife and I have a desperate need for an apartment and we know that yours on the Via Tirreno is vacant. I'm an American student of Italian life and manners. We've been in Italy almost a month and are still living in a third-rate hotel. My wife is unhappy. The children have miserable colds. I'll be glad to pay you fifty thousand lire, instead of the forty-five you ask, if you will kindly let us move in today."

"Listen," said the Contessa, "I come from an honorable family. Don't try to bribe me."

Carl blushed. "I mean nothing more than to give you proof of my good will."

"In any case, my lawyer attends to my real estate matters."

"He hasn't the key."

"Why hasn't he?"

"The former occupant took it with him."

"The fool," she said.

"Do you happen to have a duplicate?"

"I never keep duplicate keys. They all get mixed up and I never know which is which."

"Could we have one made?"

"Ask my lawyer."

"I called this morning but he's out of town. May I make a suggestion, Contessa? Could we have a window or a door forced? I will pay the cost of repair."

The Contessa's eyes glinted. "Of course not," she said huffily. "I will have no destruction of my property. We've had enough of that sort of thing here. You Americans have no idea what we've lived through."

"But doesn't it mean something to you to have a reliable tenant in your apartment? What good is it standing empty? Say the word and I'll bring you the rent in an hour."

"Come back in two weeks, young man, after I finish my honeymoon."

"In two weeks I may be dead," Carl said.

The Contessa laughed.

Outside, he met Bevilacqua. He had a black eye and a stricken expression.

"So you've betrayed me?" the Italian said hoarsely.

"What do you mean 'betrayed'? Who are you, Jesus Christ?"

"I hear you went to De Vecchis and begged for the key, with plans to move in without telling me."

"How could I keep that a secret with your pal Mrs. Gaspari living right over my head? The minute I moved in she'd tell you, then you'd be over on horseback to collect."

"That's right," said Bevilacqua. "I didn't think of it."

"Who gave you the black eye?" Carl asked.

"De Vecchis. He's as strong as a wild pig. I met him at the apartment and asked for the key. He called me dirty names. We had a fight and he hit me in the eye with his elbow. How did you make out with the Contessa?"

"Not well. Did you come to see her?"

"Vaguely."

"Go in and beg her to let me move in, for God's sake. Maybe she'll listen to a countryman."

"Don't ask me to eat a horse," said Bevilacqua.

That night Carl dreamed they had moved out of the hotel into the Contessa's apartment. The children were in the garden, playing among the roses. In the morning he decided to go to the portiere and offer him ten thousand lire if he would have a new key made, however they did it—door up or door down.

When he arrived at the apartment house the portiere and Bevilacqua were there with a toothless man, on his knees, poking a hooked wire into the door lock. In two minutes it clicked open.

With a gasp they all entered. From room to room they wandered like dead men. The place was a ruin. The furniture had been smashed with a dull axe. The slashed sofa revealed its inner springs. Rugs were cut up, crockery broken, books wildly torn and scattered. The white walls had been splashed with red wine, except one in the living room which was decorated with dirty words in six languages, printed in orange lipstick.

"Mamma mia," muttered the toothless locksmith, crossing himself. The portiere slowly turned yellow. Bevilacqua wept.

De Vecchis, in his pea green suit, appeared in the doorway. "Ecco la chiave!" He held it triumphantly aloft.

"Assassin!" shouted Bevilacqua. "Turd! May your bones grow hair and rot."

"He lives for my death," he cried to Carl, "I for his. This is our condition."

"You lie," said Carl. "I love this country."

De Vecchis flung the key at them and ran. Bevilacqua, the light of hatred in his eyes, ducked, and the key hit Carl on the forehead, leaving a mark he could not rub out.

1958

The Maid's Shoes

THE MAID had left her name with the porter's wife. She said she was looking for steady work and would take anything but preferred not to work for an old woman. Still, if she had to she would. She was forty-five and looked older. Her face was worn but her hair was black, and her eyes and lips were pretty. She had few good teeth. When she laughed she was embarrassed around the mouth. Although it was cold in early October, that year in Rome, and the chestnut vendors were already bent over their pans of glowing charcoals, the maid wore only a threadbare black cotton dress which had a split down the left side, where about two inches of seam had opened on the hip, exposing her underwear. She had sewn the seam several times but this was one of the times it was open again. Her heavy but well-formed legs were bare and she wore house slippers as she talked to the portinaia; she had done a single day's washing for a signora down the street and carried her shoes in a paper bag. There were three comparatively new apartment houses on the hilly street and she left her name in each.

The portinaia, a dumpy woman wearing a brown tweed skirt she had got from an English family that had once lived in the building, said she would remember the maid but then she forgot; she forgot until an American professor moved into a furnished apartment on the fifth floor and asked her to help him find a maid. The portinaia brought him a girl from the neighborhood, a girl of sixteen, recently from Umbria, who came with her aunt. But the professor, Orlando Krantz, did not like the way the aunt played up certain qualities of the girl, so he sent her away. He told the portinaia he was looking for an older woman, someone he wouldn't have to worry about. Then the portinaia thought of the maid who had left her name and address, and she went to her house on the Via Appia Antica near the catacombs and told her an American was looking for a maid, mezzo servizio; she would give him her name if the maid agreed to make it worth her while. The maid, whose name was Rosa, shrugged her shoulders and looked stiffly down the street. She said she had nothing to offer the portinaia.

"Look at what I'm wearing," she said. "Look at this junk pile, can you call it a house? I live here with my son and his bitch of a wife who counts every spoonful of soup in my mouth. They treat me like dirt and dirt is all I have to my name."

"In that case I can do nothing for you," the portinaia said. "I have myself and my husband to think of." But she returned from the bus stop and said she would recommend the maid to the American professor if she gave her five thousand lire the first time she was paid.

"How much will he pay?" the maid asked the portinaia.

"I would ask for eighteen thousand a month. Tell him you have to spend two hundred lire a day for carfare."

"That's almost right," Rosa said. "It will cost me forty one way and forty back. But if he pays me eighteen thousand I'll give you five if you sign that's all I owe you."

"I will sign," said the portinaia, and she recommended the maid to the American professor.

Orlando Krantz was a nervous man of sixty. He had mild gray eyes, a broad mouth, and a pointed clefted chin. His round head was bald and he had a bit of a belly, although the rest of him was quite thin. He was a somewhat odd-looking man but an authority in law, the portinaia told Rosa. The professor sat at a table in his study, writing all day, yet was up every half hour on some pretext or other to look nervously around. He worried how things were going and often came out of his study to see. He would watch Rosa working, then went in and wrote. In a half hour he would come out, ostensibly to wash his hands in the bathroom or drink a glass of cold water, but he was really passing by to see what she was doing. She was doing what she had to. Rosa worked quickly, especially when he was watching. She seemed, he thought, to be unhappy, but that was none of his business. Their lives, he knew, were full of troubles, often sordid; it was best to be detached.

This was the professor's second year in Italy; he had spent the first in Milan, and the second was in Rome. He had rented a large three-bedroom apartment, one of which he used as a study. His wife and daughter, who had returned for a visit to the States in August, would have the other bedrooms; they were due back before not too long. When the ladies returned, he had told Rosa, he would put her on full time. There was a maid's room where she could sleep; indeed, which she already used as her own though she was in the apartment only from nine till four. Rosa agreed to a full-time arrangement because it would mean all her meals in and no rent to pay her son and his dog-faced wife.

While they were waiting for Mrs. Krantz and the daughter to arrive, Rosa did the marketing and cooking. She made the professor's breakfast when she came in, and his lunch at one. She offered to stay later than four, to prepare his supper, which he ate at six, but he preferred to take that meal out. After shopping she cleaned the house, thoroughly mopping the marble floors with a wet rag she pushed around with a stick, though the floors did not look particularly dusty to him. She also washed and ironed his laundry. She was a good worker, her slippers clip-clopping as she hurried from one room to the next, and she frequently finished up about an hour or so before she was due to go home; so she retired to the maid's room and there read *Tempo* or *Epoca*, or sometimes a love story in photographs, with the words printed in italics under each picture. Often she pulled her bed down and lay in it under blankets, to keep warm. The weather had turned rainy, and now the apartment was uncomfortably cold. The custom of the condominium in this apartment house was not to heat until the fifteenth of November, and if it was cold before then, as it was now, the people of the house had to do the best they could. The cold disturbed the professor, who wrote with his gloves and hat on, and increased his nervousness so that he was out to look at her more often. He wore a heavy blue bathrobe over his clothes; sometimes the bathrobe belt was wrapped around a hot-water bottle he had placed against the lower part of his back, under the suit coat. Sometimes he sat on the hot-water bag as he wrote, a sight that caused Rosa, when she once saw this, to smile behind her hand. If he left the hot-water bag in the dining room after lunch, Rosa asked if she might use it. As a rule he allowed her to, and then she did her work with the rubber bag pressed against her stomach with her elbow. She said she had trouble with her liver. That was why the professor did not mind her going to the maid's room to lie down before leaving, after she had finished her work.

Once after Rosa had gone home, smelling tobacco smoke in the corridor near her room, the professor entered it to investigate. The room was not more than an elongated cubicle with a narrow bed that lifted sideways against the wall; there was also a small green cabinet, and an adjoining tiny bathroom containing a toilet and a sitz bath fed by a cold-water tap. She often did the laundry on a washboard in the sitz bath, but never, so far as he knew, had bathed in it. The day before her daughter-in-law's name day she had asked permission to take a hot bath in his tub in the big bathroom, and though he had hesitated a moment, the professor finally said yes. In her room, he opened a drawer at the bottom of the cabinet and found a hoard of cigarette butts in it, the butts he had left in ashtrays. He noticed, too, that she had collected his old newspapers and magazines from the wastebaskets. She also saved cord, paper bags, and rubber bands; also pencil stubs he had thrown away. After he found that out, he occasionally gave her some meat left over from lunch, and cheese that had gone dry, to take with her. For this she brought him flowers. She also brought a dirty egg or two her daughter-in-law's hen had laid, but he thanked her and said the yolks were too strong for his taste. He noticed that she needed a pair of shoes, for those she put on to go home in were split in two places, and she wore the same black dress with the tear in it every day, which embarrassed him when he had to speak to her; however, he thought he would refer these matters to his wife when she arrived.

As jobs went, Rosa knew she had a good one. The professor paid well and promptly, and he never ordered her around in the haughty manner of some of her Italian employers. This one was nervous and fussy but not a bad sort. His main fault was his silence. Though he could speak a better than passable Italian, he preferred, when not at work, to sit in an armchair in the living room, reading. Only two souls in the whole apartment, you would think they would want to say something to each other once in a while. Sometimes when she served him a cup of coffee as he read, she tried to get in a word about her troubles. She wanted to tell him about her long, impoverished widowhood, how badly her son had turned out, and what her miserable daughter-in-law was like to live with. But though he listened courteously, although they shared the same roof, and even the same hot-water bottle and bathtub, they almost never shared speech. He said no more to her than a crow would, and clearly showed he preferred to be left alone. So she left him alone and was lonely in the apartment. Working for foreigners had its advantages, she thought, but it also had disadvantages.

After a while the professor noticed that the telephone was ringing regularly for Rosa each afternoon during the time she usually was resting in her room. In the following week, instead of staying in the house until four, after her telephone call she asked permission to leave. At first she said her liver was bothering her, but later she stopped giving excuses. Although he did not much approve of this sort of thing, suspecting she would take advantage of him if he was too liberal in granting favors, he informed her that, until his wife arrived, she might leave at three on two afternoons of the week, provided that all her duties were fully discharged. He knew that everything was done before she left but thought he ought to say it. She listened meekly—her eyes aglow, lips twitching—and meekly agreed. He presumed, when he happened to think about it afterwards, that Rosa had a good spot here, by any standard, and she ought soon to show it in her face, change her unhappy expression for one less so. However, this did not happen, for when he chanced to observe her, even on days when she was leaving early, she seemed sadly preoccupied, sighed much, as if something on her heart was weighing her down.

He never asked what, preferring not to become involved in whatever it was. These people had endless troubles, and if you let yourself get involved in them you got endlessly involved. He knew of one woman, the wife of a colleague, who had said to her maid: "Lucrezia, I am sympathetic to your condition but I don't want to hear about it." This, the professor reflected, was basically good policy. It kept employer-employee relationships where they belonged—on an objective level. He was, after all, leaving Italy in April and would never in his life see Rosa again. It would do her a lot more good if, say, he sent her a small check at Christmas, than if he needlessly immersed himself in her miseries now. The professor knew he was nervous and often impatient, and he was sometimes sorry for his nature; but he was what he was and preferred to stay aloof from what did not closely and personally concern him.

But Rosa would not have it so. One morning she knocked on his study door, and when he said avanti, she went in embarrassedly, so that even before she began to speak he was himself embarrassed.

"Professore," Rosa said, unhappily, "please excuse me for bothering your work, but I have to talk to somebody."

"I happen to be very busy," he said, growing a little angry. "Can it wait a while?"

"It'll take only a minute. Your troubles hang on all your life but it doesn't take long to tell them."

"Is it your liver complaint?" he asked.

"No. I need your advice. You're an educated man and I'm no more than an ignorant peasant."

"What kind of advice?" he asked impatiently.

"Call it anything you like. The fact is I have to speak to somebody. I can't talk to my son, even if it were possible in this case. When I open my mouth he roars like a bull. And my daughter-in-law isn't worth wasting my breath on. Sometimes, on the roof, when we're hanging the wash, I say a few words to the portinaia, but she isn't a sympathetic person so I have to come to you, I'll tell you why."

Before he could say how he felt about hearing her confidences, Rosa had launched into a story about this middle-aged government worker in the tax bureau, whom she had happened to meet in the neighborhood. He was married, had four children, and sometimes worked as a carpenter after leaving his office at two o'clock each day. His name was Armando; it was he who telephoned her every afternoon. They had met recently on a bus, and he had, after two or three meetings, seeing that her shoes weren't fit to wear, urged her to let him buy her a new pair. She had told him not to be foolish. One could see he had very little, and it was enough that he took her to the movies twice a week. She had said that, yet every time they met he talked about the shoes he wanted to buy her.

"I'm only human," Rosa frankly told the professor, "and I need the shoes badly, but you know how these things go. *If* I put on his shoes they may carry me to his bed. That's why I thought I would ask you if I ought to take them."

The professor's face and bald head were flushed. "I don't see how I can possibly advise you—"

"You're the educated one," she said.

"However," he went on, "since the situation is still essentially hypothetical, I will go so far as to say you ought to tell this generous gentleman that his responsibilities should be to his family. He would do well not to offer you gifts, as you will do, not to accept them. If you don't, he can't possibly make any claims upon you or your person. This is all I care to say. Since you have requested advice, I've given it, but I won't say any more."

Rosa sighed. "The truth of it is I could use a pair of shoes. Mine look as though they've been chewed by goats. I haven't had a new pair in six years."

But the professor had nothing more to add.

After Rosa had gone for the day, in thinking about her problem, he decided to buy her a pair of shoes. He was concerned that she might be expecting something of the sort, had planned, so to speak, to have it work out this way. But since this was conjecture only, evidence entirely lacking, he would assume, until proof to the contrary became available, that she had no ulterior motive in asking his advice. He considered giving her five thousand lire to make the purchase of the shoes herself and relieve him of the trouble, but he was doubtful, for there was no guarantee she would use the money for the agreed purpose. Suppose she came in the next day, saying she had had a liver attack that had necessitated calling the doctor, who had charged three thousand lire for his visit; therefore would the professor, in view of these unhappy circumstances, supply an additional three thousand for the shoes? That would never do, so the next morning, when the maid was at the grocer's, the professor slipped into her room and quickly traced on paper the outline of her miserable shoe—a task but he accomplished it quickly. That evening, in a store on the same piazza as the restaurant where he liked to eat, he bought Rosa a pair of brown shoes for fifty-five hundred lire, slightly more than he had planned to spend; but they were a solid pair of ties, walking shoes with a medium heel, a practical gift.

He gave them to Rosa the next day, a Wednesday. He felt embarrassed to be doing that, because he realized that despite his warnings to her, he had permitted himself to meddle in her affairs; but he considered giving her the shoes a psychologically proper move in more ways than one. In presenting her with them he said, "Rosa, I have perhaps a solution to suggest in the matter you discussed with me. Here are a pair of new shoes for you. Tell your friend you must refuse his. And when you do, perhaps it would be advisable also to inform him that you intend to see him a little less frequently from now on."

Rosa was overjoyed at the professor's kindness. She attempted to kiss his hand but he thrust it behind him and retired to his study. On Thursday, when he opened the apartment door to her ring, she was wearing his shoes. She carried a large paper bag from which she offered the professor three small oranges still on a branch with green leaves. He said she needn't have brought them, but Rosa, smiling half hiddenly in order not to show her teeth, said that she wanted him to see how grateful she was. Later she requested permission to leave at three so she could show Armando her new shoes.

He said dryly, "You may go at that hour if your work is done."

She thanked him profusely. Hastening through her tasks, she left shortly after three, but not before the professor, in his hat, gloves, and bathrobe, standing at his open study door as he was inspecting the corridor floor she had just mopped, saw her hurrying out of the apartment, wearing a pair of dressy black needle-point pumps. This angered him; and when Rosa appeared the next morning, though she begged him not to when he said she had made a fool of him and he was firing her to teach her a lesson, the professor did. She wept, pleading for another chance, but he would not change his mind. So she desolately wrapped up the odds and ends in her room in a newspaper and left, still crying. Afterwards he was upset and very nervous. He could not stand the cold that day and he could not work.

A week later, the morning the heat was turned on, Rosa appeared at the apartment door, and begged to have her job back. She was distraught, said her son had hit her, and gently touched her puffed black-and-blue lip. With tears in her eyes, although she didn't cry, Rosa explained it was no fault of hers that she had accepted both pairs of shoes. Armando had given her his pair first; had, out of jealousy of a possible rival, forced her to take them. Then when the professor had kindly offered his pair of shoes, she had wanted to refuse them but was afraid of angering him and losing her job. This was God's truth, so help her St. Peter. She would, she promised, find Armando, whom she had not seen in a week, and return his shoes if the professor would take her back. If he didn't, she would throw herself into the Tiber. He, though he didn't care for talk of this kind, felt a certain sympathy for her. He was disappointed in himself at the way he had handled her. It would have been better to have said a few appropriate words on the subject of honesty and then philosophically dropped the matter. In firing her he had only made things difficult for them both, because, in the meantime, he had tried two other maids and found them unsuitable. One stole, the other was lazy. As a result the house was a mess, impossible for him to work in, although the portinaia came up for an hour each morning to clean. It was his good fortune that Rosa had appeared at the door just then. When she removed her coat, he noticed with satisfaction that the tear in her dress had finally been mended.

She went grimly to work, dusting, polishing, cleaning everything in sight. She unmade beds, then made them, swept under them, mopped, polished head- and footboards, adorned the beds with newly pressed spreads. Though she had just got her job back and worked with her usual efficiency, she worked, he observed, in sadness, frequently sighing, attempting a smile only when his eye was on her. This is their nature, he thought; they have hard lives. To spare her further blows by her son he gave her permission to live in. He offered extra money to buy meat for her supper but she refused it, saying pasta would do. Pasta and green salad was all she ate at night. Occasionally she boiled an artichoke left over from lunch and ate it with oil and vinegar. He invited her to drink the white wine in the cupboard and take fruit. Once in a while she did, always telling what and how much, though he repeatedly asked her not to. The apartment was nicely in order. Though the phone rang, as usual, daily at three, only seldom did she leave the house after she had talked to Armando.

Then one dismal morning Rosa came to the professor and in her distraught way confessed she was pregnant. Her face was lit in despair; her white underwear shone through her black dress.

He felt annoyance, disgust, blaming himself for having re-employed her.

"You must leave at once," he said, trying to keep his voice from trembling.

"I can't," she said. "My son will kill me. In God's name, help me, professore."

He was infuriated by her stupidity. "Your sexual adventures are none of my responsibility.

"Was it this Armando?" he asked almost savagely.

She nodded.

"Have you informed him?"

"He says he can't believe it." She tried to smile but couldn't.

"I'll convince him," he said. "Do you have his telephone number?"

She told it to him. He called Armando at his office, identi-fied himself, and asked the government clerk to come at once to the apartment. "You have a grave responsibility to Rosa."

"I have a grave responsibility to my family," Armando answered.

"You might have considered them before this."

"All right, I'll come over tomorrow after work. It's impossi-ble today. I have a carpentering contract to finish up."

"She'll expect you," the professor said.

When he hung up he felt less angry, although still more emotional than he cared to feel. "Are you quite sure of your condition?" he asked her, "that you are pregnant?"

"Yes." She was crying now. "Tomorrow is my son's birthday. What a beautiful present it will be for him to find out his mother's a whore. He'll break my bones, if not with his hands, then with his teeth."

"It hardly seems likely you can conceive, considering your age."

"My mother gave birth at fifty."

"Isn't there a possibility you are mistaken?"

"I don't know. It's never been this way before. After all, I've been a widow—"

"Well, you'd better find out."

"Yes, I want to," Rosa said. "I want to see the midwife in my neighborhood but I haven't got a single lira. I spent all I had left when I wasn't working, and I had to borrow carfare to get here. Armando can't help me just now. He has to pay for his wife's teeth this week. She has very bad teeth, poor thing. That's why I came to you. Could you advance me two thousand of my pay so I can be examined by the midwife?"

After a minute he counted two one-thousand-lire notes out of his wallet. "Go to her now," he said. He was about to add that if she was pregnant, not to come back, but he was afraid she might do something desperate, or lie to him so she could go on working. He didn't want her around any more. When he thought of his wife and daughter arriving amid this mess, he felt sick with nervousness. He wanted to get rid of the maid as soon as possible.

The next day Rosa came in at twelve instead of nine. Her dark face was pale. "Excuse me for being late," she murmured. "I was praying at my husband's grave."

"That's all right," the professor said. "But did you go to the midwife?"

"Not yet."

"Why not?" Though angry he spoke calmly.

She stared at the floor.

"Please answer my question."

"I was going to say I lost the two thousand lire on the bus, but after being at my husband's grave I'll tell you the truth. After all, it's bound to come out."

This is terrible, he thought, it's unending. "What did you do with the money?"

"That's what I mean," Rosa sighed. "I bought my son a present. Not that he deserves it, but it was his birthday." She burst into tears.

He stared at her a minute, then said, "Please come with me."

The professor left the apartment in his bathrobe, and Rosa followed. Opening the elevator door he stepped inside, holding the door for her. She entered the elevator.

They stopped two floors below. He got out and nearsightedly scanned the names on the brass plates above the bells. Finding the one he wanted, he pressed the button. A maid opened the door and let them in. She seemed frightened by Rosa's expression.

"Is the doctor in?" the professor asked the doctor's maid.

"I will see."

"Please ask him if he'll see me for a minute. I live in the building, two flights up."

"Sì, signore." She glanced again at Rosa, then went inside.

The Italian doctor came out, a short middle-aged man with a beard. The professor had once or twice passed him in the cortile of the apartment house. The doctor was buttoning his shirt cuff.

"I am sorry to trouble you, sir," said the professor. "This is my maid, who has been having some difficulty. She would like to determine whether she is pregnant. Can you assist her?"

The doctor looked at him, then at the maid, who had a handkerchief to her eyes.

"Let her come into my office."

"Thank you," said the professor. The doctor nodded.

The professor went up to his apartment. In a half hour the phone rang.

"Pronto."

It was the doctor. "She is not pregnant," he said. "She is frightened. She also has trouble with her liver."

"Can you be certain, doctor?"

"Yes."

"Thank you," said the professor. "If you write her a prescription, please have it charged to me, and also send me your bill."

"I will," said the doctor and hung up.

Rosa came into the apartment. "The doctor told you?" the professor said. "You aren't pregnant."

"It's the Virgin's blessing," said Rosa.

Speaking quietly, he then told her she would have to go. "I'm sorry, Rosa, but I simply cannot be constantly caught up in this sort of thing. It upsets me and I can't work."

She turned her head away.

The doorbell rang. It was Armando, a small thin man in a long gray overcoat. He was wearing a rakish black Borsalino and a slight mustache. He had dark, worried eyes. He tipped his hat to them.

Rosa told him she was leaving the apartment.

"Then let me help you get your things," Armando said. He followed her to the maid's room and they wrapped Rosa's things in newspaper.

When they came out of the room, Armando carrying a shopping bag, Rosa holding a shoe box wrapped in a newspaper, the professor handed Rosa the remainder of her month's wages.

"I'm sorry," he said, "but I have my wife and daughter to think of. They'll be here in a few days."

She answered nothing. Armando, smoking a cigarette butt, gently opened the door for her and they left together.

Later the professor inspected the maid's room and saw that Rosa had taken all her belongings but the shoes he had given her. When his wife arrived in the apartment, shortly before Thanksgiving, she gave the shoes to the portinaia, who wore them a week, then gave them to her daughter-in-law.

1959

POSTHUMOUSLY PUBLISHED
STORIES

Armistice

WHEN HE was a boy, Morris Lieberman saw a burly Russian peasant seize a wagon wheel that was lying against the side of a blacksmith's shop, swing it around, and hurl it at a fleeing Jewish sexton. The wheel caught the Jew in the back, crushing his spine. In speechless terror, he lay on the ground before his burning house, waiting to die.

Thirty years later Morris, a widower who owned a small grocery and delicatessen store in a Scandinavian neighborhood in Brooklyn, could recall the scene of the pogrom with the twisting fright that he had felt at fifteen. He often experienced the same fear since the Nazis had come to power.

The reports of their persecution of the Jews that he heard over the radio filled him with dread, but he never stopped listening to them. His fourteen-year-old son, Leonard, a thin, studious boy, saw how overwrought his father became and tried to shut off the radio, but the grocer would not allow him to. He listened, and at night did not sleep, because in listening he shared the woes inflicted upon his race.

When the war began, Morris placed his hope for the salvation of the Jews in his trust of the French army. He lived close to his radio, listening to the bulletins and praying for a French victory in the conflict which he called "this righteous war."

On the May day in 1940 when the Germans ripped open the French lines at Sedan, his long-growing anxiety became intolerable. Between waiting on customers, or when he was preparing salads in the kitchen at the rear of the store, he switched on the radio and heard, with increasing dismay, the flood of reports which never seemed to contain any good news. The Belgians surrendered. The British retreated at Dunkerque, and in mid-June, the Nazis, speeding toward Paris in their lorries, were passing large herds of conquered Frenchmen resting in the fields.

Day after day, as the battle progressed, Morris sat on the edge of the cot in the kitchen listening to the additions to his sorrow, nodding his head the way the Jews do in mourning, then rousing himself to hope for the miracle that would save the French as it had saved the Jews in the wilderness. At three o'clock, he shut off the radio, because Leonard came home from school about then. The boy, seeing the harmful effect of the war on his father's health, had begun to plead with him not to listen to so many news broadcasts, and Morris pacified him by pretending that he no longer thought of the war. Each afternoon Leonard remained behind the counter while his father slept on the cot. From the dream-filled, raw sleep of these afternoons, the grocer managed to derive enough strength to endure the long day and his own bitter thoughts.

The salesmen from the wholesale grocery houses and the drivers who served Morris were amazed at the way he suffered. They told him that the war had nothing to do with America and that he was taking it too seriously. Some of the others made him the object of their ridicule outside the store. One of them, Gus Wagner, who delivered the delicatessen meats and provisions, was not afraid to laugh at Morris to his face.

Gus was a heavy man, with a strong, full head and a fleshy face. Although born in America, and a member of the AEF in 1918, his imagination was fired by the Nazi conquests and he believed that they had the strength and power to conquer the world. He kept a scrapbook filled with clippings and pictures of the German army. He was deeply impressed by the Panzer divisions, and when he read accounts of battles in which they tore through the enemy's lines, his mind glowed with excitement. He did not reveal his feelings directly because he considered his business first. As it was, he poked fun at the grocer for wanting the French to win.

Each afternoon, with his basket of liverwursts and bolognas on his arm, Gus strode into the store and swung the basket onto the table in the kitchen. The grocer as usual was sitting on the cot, listening to the radio.

"Hello Morris," Gus said, pretending surprise. "What does it say on the radio?" He sat down heavily and laughed.

When things were going especially well for the Germans, Gus dropped his attitude of pretense and said openly, "You better get used to it, Morris. The Germans will wipe out the Frenchmen."

Morris disliked these remarks, but he said nothing. He allowed Gus to talk as he did because he had known the meat man for nine years. Once they had nearly been friends. After the death of Morris's wife four years ago, Gus stayed longer than usual and joined Morris in a cup of coffee. Occasionally he repaired a hole in the screen door or fixed the plug for the electric slicing machine.

Leonard had driven them apart. The boy disliked the meat man and always tried to avoid him. He was nauseated by Gus's laughter, which he called a cackle, and he would not allow his father to do business with Gus in the kitchen when he was having his milk and crackers after school.

Gus knew how the boy felt about him and he was deeply annoyed. He was angered too when the boy added up the figures on the meat bills and found errors. Gus was careless in arithmetic, which often caused trouble. Once Morris mentioned a five-dollar prize that Leonard had won in mathematics and Gus said, "You better watch out, Morris. He's a skinny kid. If he studies too much, he'll get consumption."

Morris was frightened. He felt that Gus was wishing harm upon Leonard. Their relations became cooler, and after that Gus spoke more freely about politics and the war, often expressing his contempt for the French.

The Germans took Paris and pushed on toward the west and south. Morris, drained of his energy, prayed that the ordeal would soon be over. Then the Reynaud cabinet fell. Marshal Pétain addressed a request to the Germans for "peace with honor." In the dark Compiègne forest, Hitler sat in Marshal Foch's railroad car, listening to his terms being read to the French delegation.

That night, after closing his store, Morris disconnected the radio and carried it upstairs. In his bedroom, the door shut tightly so Leonard would not be awakened, he tuned in softly to the midnight broadcast and learned that the French had accepted Hitler's terms and would sign the armistice tomorrow. Morris shut off the radio. An age-old weariness filled him. He wanted to sleep but he knew that he could not.

Morris turned out the lights, removed his shirt and shoes in the dark, and sat smoking in the large bedroom that had once belonged to him and his wife.

The door opened softly, and Leonard looked into the room. By the light of the street lamp which shone through the window, the boy could see his father in the chair. It made him think of the time when his mother was in the hospital and his father sat in the chair all night.

Leonard entered the bedroom in his bare feet. "Pa," he said, putting his arm around his father's shoulders, "go to sleep."

"I can't sleep, Leonard."

"Pa, you got to. You work sixteen hours."

"Oh, my son," cried Morris, with sudden emotion, putting his arms around Leonard, "what will become of us?"

The boy became afraid.

"Pa," he said, "go to sleep. Please, you got to."

"All right, I'll go," said Morris. He crushed his cigarette in the ashtray and got into bed. The boy watched him until he turned over on his right side, which was the side he slept on; then he returned to his room.

Later Morris rose and sat by the window, looking into the street. The night was cool. The breeze swayed the street lamp, which creaked and moved the circle of light that fell upon the street.

"What will become of us?" he muttered to himself. His mind went back to the days when he was a boy studying Jewish history. The Jews lived in an interminable exodus. Long lines trudged forever with their bundles on their shoulders.

He dozed and dreamed that he had fled from Germany into France. The Nazis had found out where he lived in Paris. He sat in a chair in a dark room waiting for them to come. His hair had grown grayer. The moonlight fell on his sloping shoulders, then moved into the darkness. He rose and climbed out onto a ledge overlooking the lighted city of Paris. He fell. Something clumped to the sidewalk. Morris groaned and awoke. He heard the purring of a truck's motor and he knew that the driver was dropping the bundles of morning newspapers in front of the stationery store on the corner.

The dark was soft with gray. Morris crawled into bed and began to dream again. It was Sunday at suppertime. The store was crowded with customers. Suddenly Gus was there. He waved a copy of *Social Justice* and cried out, "The Protocols of Zion! The Protocols of Zion!" The customers began to leave. "Gus," Morris pleaded, "the customers, the customers—"

He awoke shivering and lay awake until the alarm rang.

After he had dragged in the bread and milk boxes and had waited on the deaf man who always came early, Morris went to the corner for a paper. The armistice was signed. Morris looked around to see if the street had changed, but everything was the same, though he could hardly understand why. Leonard came down for his coffee and roll. He took fifty cents from the till and left for school.

The day was warm and Morris was tired. He grew uneasy when he thought of Gus. He knew that today he would have difficulty controlling himself if Gus made some of his remarks.

At three o'clock, when Morris was slicing small potatoes for potato salad, Gus strode into the store and swung his basket onto the table.

"Well, Morris"—he laughed—"why don't you turn the radio on? Let's hear the news."

Morris tried to control himself, but his bitterness overcame him. "I see you're happy today, Gus. What great cause has died?"

The meat man laughed, but he did not like that remark.

"Come on, Morris," he said, "let's do business before your skinny kid comes home and wants the bill signed by a certified public accountant."

"He looks out for my interests," answered Morris. "He's a good mathematics student," he added.

"That's the sixth time I heard that," said Gus.

"You'll never hear it about your children."

Gus lost his temper. "What the hell's the matter with you Jews?" he asked. "Do you think you own all the brains in the world?"

"Gus," Morris cried, "you talk like a Nazi."

"I'm a hundred percent American. I fought in the war," answered Gus.

Leonard came into the store and heard the loud voices. He ran into the kitchen and saw the two men arguing. A feeling of shame and nausea overcame him.

"Pa," he begged, "don't fight."

Morris was still angry. "If you're not a Nazi," he said to Gus, "why are you so glad the French lost?"

"Who's glad?" asked Gus. Suddenly he felt proud and he said, "They deserved to lose, the way they starved the German people. Why the hell do you want them to win?"

"Pa," said Leonard again.

"I want them to win because they are fighting for democracy."

"Like hell," said Gus. "You want them to win because they're protecting the Jews—like that lousy Léon Blum."

"You Nazi, you," Morris shouted angrily, coming from behind the table. "You Nazi. You don't deserve to live in America!"

"Papa," cried Leonard, holding him, "don't fight, please, please."

"Mind your own business, you little bastard," said Gus, pushing Leonard away.

A sob broke from Leonard's throat. He began to cry.

Gus paused, seeing that he had gone too far.

Morris Lieberman's face was white. He put his arm around the boy and kissed him again and again.

"No, no. No more, Leonard. Don't cry. I'm sorry. I give you my word. No more."

Gus looked on without speaking. His face was still red with anger, but he was afraid that he would lose Morris's business. He pulled two liverwursts and a bologna from his basket.

"The meat's on the table," he said. "Pay me tomorrow."

Gus glanced contemptuously at the grocer comforting his son, who was quiet now, and he walked out of the store. He threw the basket into his truck, got in, and drove off.

As he rode amid the cars on the avenue, he thought of the boy crying and his father holding him. It was always like that with the Jews. Tears and people holding each other. Why feel sorry for them?

Gus sat up straight at the wheel, his face grim. He thought of the armistice and imagined that he was in Paris. His truck was a massive tank rumbling with the others through the wide boulevards. The French, on the sidewalks, were overpowered with fear.

He drove tensely, his eyes unsmiling. He knew that if he relaxed the picture would fade.

1940

Spring Rain

GEORGE FISHER was still lying awake, thinking of the accident which he had seen on 121st Street. A young man had been struck by an automobile, and they had carried him to the drugstore on Broadway. The druggist couldn't do anything for him, so they waited for an ambulance. The man lay on the druggist's table in the back of the store looking at the ceiling. He knew he was going to die.

George felt deeply sorry for the man, who seemed to be in his late twenties. The stoical way in which he took the accident convinced George that he was a person of fine character. He knew that the man was not afraid of death, and he wanted to speak to him and tell him that he too was not afraid to die; but the words never formed themselves on his thin lips. George went home, choked with unspoken words.

Lying in bed in his dark room, George heard his daughter, Florence, put the key in the lock. He heard her whisper to Paul, "Do you want to come in for a minute?"

"No," said Paul after a while, "I've got a nine o'clock class tomorrow."

"Then good night," said Florence and she closed the door hard.

George thought, This is the first decent boy Florence has gone out with, and she can't get anywhere with him. She's like her mother. She doesn't know how to handle decent people. He raised his head and looked at Beatie, half expecting her to wake up because his thoughts sounded so loud to him, but she didn't move.

This was one of George's sleepless nights. They came just after he had finished reading an interesting novel, and he lay awake imagining that all those things were happening to him. In his sleepless nights George thought of the things that had happened to him during the day, and he said those words that people saw on his lips, but which they never heard him speak. He said to the dying young man, "I'm not afraid to die either." He said to the heroine in the novel, "You understand my loneliness. I can tell you these things." He told his wife and daughter what he thought of them.

"Beatie," he said, "you made me talk once, but it wasn't you. It was the sea and the darkness and the sound of the water sucking the beams of the pier. Those poetical things I said about how lonely men are—I said them because you were pretty, with dark red hair, and I was afraid because I was a small man with thin lips, and I was afraid that I could not have you. You didn't love me, but you said yes for Riverside Drive and your apartment and your two fur coats and the people who come here to play bridge and mah-jongg."

He said to Florence, "What a disappointment you are. I loved you when you were a child, but now you're selfish and small. I lost my last bit of feeling for you when you didn't want to go to college. The best thing you ever did was to bring an educated boy like Paul into the house, but you'll never keep him."

George spoke these thoughts to himself until the first gray of the April dawn drifted into the bedroom and made the silhouette of Beatie in the other bed clearer. Then George turned over and slept for a while.

In the morning, at breakfast, George said to Florence, "Did you have a good time?"

"Oh, leave me alone," answered Florence.

"Leave her alone," said Beatie. "You know she's cranky in the morning."

"I'm not cranky," said Florence, almost crying. "It's Paul. He never takes me anyplace."

"What did you do last night?" asked Beatie.

"What we always do," answered Florence. "We went for a walk. I can't even get him into a movie."

"Does he have money?" asked Beatie. "Maybe he's working his way through college."

"No," said Florence, "he's got money. His father is a big buyer. Oh, what's the use? I'll never get him to take me out."

"Be patient," Beatie told her. "Next time, either I or your father will suggest it to him."

"I won't," said George.

"No, you won't," answered Beatie, "but I will."

George drank his coffee and left.

When he came home for dinner, there was a note for George saying that Beatie and Florence had eaten early because Beatie was going to Forest Hills to play bridge and Florence had a date to go to the movies with her girl friend. The maid served George, and later he went into the living room to read the papers and listen to the war news.

The bell rang. George rose, calling out to the maid, who was coming from her room, that he would answer the bell. It was Paul, wearing an old hat and a raincoat, wet on the shoulders.

George was glad that Florence and Beatie were not there.

"Come in, Paul. Is it raining?"

"It's drizzling."

Paul entered without taking off his raincoat. "Where's Florence?" he asked.

"She went to the pictures with a friend of hers. Her mother is playing bridge or mah-jongg somewhere. Did Florence know you were coming?"

"No, she didn't know."

Paul looked disappointed. He walked to the door.

"Well, I'm sorry," said George, hoping that the boy would stay.

Paul turned at the door. "Mr. Fisher."

"Yes?" said George.

"Are you busy now?"

"No, I'm not."

"How about going for a walk with me?"

"Didn't you say it was raining?"

"It's only spring rain," said Paul. "Put on your raincoat and an old hat."

"Yes," said George, "a walk will do me good." He went into his room for a pair of rubbers. As he was putting them on, he could feel a sensation of excitement, but he didn't think of it. He put on his black raincoat and last year's hat.

As soon as they came into the street and the cold mist fell on his face, George could feel the excitement flow through his body. They crossed the street, passed Grant's Tomb, and walked toward the George Washington Bridge.

The sky was filled with a floating white mist which clung to the street lamps. A wet wind blew across the dark Hudson from New Jersey and carried within it the smell of spring.

Sometimes the wind blew the cold mist into George's eyes, and it shocked him as if it were electricity. He took long steps to keep up with Paul, and he secretly rejoiced in what they were doing. He felt a little like crying, but he did not let Paul guess.

Paul was talking. He told stories about his professors in Columbia at which George laughed. Then Paul surprised George by telling him that he was studying architecture. He pointed out the various details of the houses they were passing and told him what they were derived from. George was very much interested. He always liked to know where things came from.

They slowed down, waited for traffic to stop, crossed Riverside Drive again, and walked over to Broadway to a tavern. Paul ordered a sandwich and a bottle of beer, and George did the same. They talked about the war; then George ordered two more bottles of beer for Paul and him, and they began to talk about people. George told the boy the story of the young man who had died in the drugstore. He felt a strange happiness to see how the story affected Paul.

Somebody put a nickel into the electric phonograph, and it played a tango. The tango added to George's pleasure, and he sat there thinking how fluently he had talked.

Paul had grown quiet. He drank some beer, then he began to speak about Florence. George was uneasy and a little bit frightened. He was afraid that the boy was going to tell him something that he did not want to know and that his good time would be over.

"Florence is beautiful with that red hair," said Paul, as if he were talking to himself.

George said nothing.

"Mr. Fisher," said Paul, lowering his glass and looking up, "there's something I want you to know."

"Me?"

"Mr. Fisher," Paul told him earnestly, "Florence is in love with me. She told me that. I want to love her because I'm lonely, but I don't know—I can't love her. I can't reach her. She's not like you. We go for a walk along the Drive, and I can't reach her. Then she says I'm moody, and she wants to go to the movies."

George could feel his heart beating strongly. He felt that he was listening to secrets, yet they were not secrets because he had known them all his life. He wanted to talk—to tell Paul that he was like him. He wanted to tell him how lonely he had been all his life and how he lay awake at night, dreaming and thinking until the gray morning drifted into the room. But he didn't.

"I know what you mean, Paul," he said.

They walked home in the rain, which was coming down hard now.

When he got in, George saw that both Beatie and Florence had gone to bed. He removed his rubbers and hung his wet hat and raincoat in the bathroom. He stepped into his slippers, but he decided not to undress because he did not feel like sleeping. He was aware of a fullness of emotion within him.

George went over to the radio and turned on some jazz softly. He lit a cigar and put out the lamps. For a while he stood in the dark, listening to the soft music. Then he went to the window and drew aside the curtain.

The spring rain was falling everywhere. On the dark mass of the Jersey shore. On the flowing river. Across the street the rain was droning on the leaves of the tall maples, wet in the lamplight, and swaying in the wind. The wind blew the rain hard and sharp across the window, and George felt tears on his cheeks.

A great hunger for words rose in him. He wanted to talk. He wanted to say things that he had never said before. He wanted to tell them that he had discovered himself and that never again would he be lost and silent. Once more he possessed the world and loved it. He loved Paul, and he loved Florence, and he loved the young man who had died.

I must tell her, he thought. He opened the door of Florence's room. She was sleeping. He could hear her quiet breathing.

"Florence," he called softly, "Florence."

She was instantly awake. "What's the matter?" she whispered.

The words rushed to his lips. "Paul, Paul was here."

She rose on her elbow, her long hair falling over her shoulder. "Paul? What did he say?"

George tried to speak, but the words were suddenly immovable. He could never tell her what Paul had said. A feeling of sorrow for Florence stabbed him.

"He didn't say anything," he stammered. "We walked—went for a walk."

Florence sighed and lay down again. The wind blew the spring rain against the windows and they listened to the sound it made falling in the street.

1942

The Grocery Store

THEY SAT in the kitchen in the rear of the grocery store, and Rosen, the salesman from G. and S., chewing a cigar stump in the corner of his mouth, quickly and monotonously read off the items from a mimeographed list that was clipped to the inside cover of his large pink-sheeted order book. Ida Kaplan, her small, fleshy chin raised, was listening attentively as Rosen read this week's specials and their prices. She looked up, annoyed at her husband, whose eyes showed that he wasn't listening.

"Sam," she called sharply, "listen please to Rosen."

"I'm listening," said Sam absently. He was a heavy man with thick, sloping shoulders and graying hair which looked grayer still in the glare of the large, unshaded electric bulb. The sharp light bothered his eyes, and water constantly trickled over his reddened eyelids. He was tired and he yawned ceaselessly.

Rosen stopped for a minute and smiled cynically at the grocer. The salesman shifted his large body into a more comfortable position on the backless chair and automatically continued to drone forth the list of grocery items: "G. and S. grape jam, $1.80 a dozen; G. and S. grape jelly, $1.60 a dozen; Gulden's mustard, $2.76 a carton; G. and S. canned grapefruit juice Number 2, $1.00 a dozen; Heckers flour, 3½ lbs., $2.52 a half barrel—"

Rosen stopped abruptly, removed his cigar, and said, "Well, whaddayasay, Sam, you gonna order one item at least?"

"Read," said Sam, stirring a bit, "I'm listening."

"You listening, yes," said Ida, "but you not thinking."

Rosen gripped the wet cigar butt between his teeth and went on reading: "Kippered herrings, $2.40 a dozen; Jell-O, 65¢ a dozen; junket, $1.00 a dozen."

Sam forced himself to listen for a moment, then his mind wandered. What was the use? True, the shelves were threadbare and the store needed goods, but how could he afford to place an order? Ever since the A&P supermarket had moved into the neighborhood, he had done less than half his original business. The store was down to $160 a week, just barely enough to pay for rent, gas, electricity, and a few other expenses. A dull feeling of misery gnawed at his heart. Eighteen hours a day, from 6:00 A.M. to midnight, sitting in the back of a grocery store waiting for a customer to come in for a bottle of milk and a loaf of bread and maybe—*maybe* a can of sardines. Nineteen impoverished years in the grocery business to this end. Nineteen years of standing on his feet for endless hours until the blue veins bulged out of his legs and grew hard and stiff so that every step he took was a step of pain. For what? For what, dear God? The feeling of misery crept to his stomach. Sam shivered. He felt sick.

"Sam," cried Ida, "listen, for godsake."

"I'm listening," Sam said, in a loud, annoyed tone.

Rosen looked up in surprise. "I read the whole list," he declared.

"I heard," Sam said.

"So what did you decide to order?" asked Ida.

"Nothing."

"Nothing!" she cried shrilly.

In disgust, Rosen snapped his order book shut. He put on his woolen muffler and began to button his overcoat.

"Jack Rosen takes the trouble to come out on a windy, snowy February night and he don't even get an order for a lousy box of matches. That's a nice how-d'ye-do," he said sarcastically.

"Sam, we need goods," said Ida.

"So how'll we pay for the goods—with toothpicks?"

Ida grew angry. "Please," she said haughtily, "please, to me you will speak with respect. I wasn't brought up in my father's house a grocer should—you'll excuse me—a grocer should spit on me every time he talks."

"She's right," said Rosen.

"Who asked you?" Sam said, looking up at the salesman.

"I'm talking for your own good," said Rosen.

"Please," said Sam, "you'll be quiet. You are a salesman of groceries, not a counselor of human relations."

"It happens that I am also a human being."

"This is not the point," Sam declared. "I'm doing business with Rosen, the salesman, not the human being, if any."

Rosen quickly snatched his hat off the table. "What

business?" he cried. "Who's doing business? On a freezing February night in winter I leave my wife and child and my warm house and drive twelve miles through the snow and the ice to give you a chance to fill up your fly-specked shelves with some goods, and you act like you're doing me a favor to say no. To hell with such business. It's not for Jack Rosen."

"Rosen," said Sam, looking at him calmly, "in my eyes you are common."

"Common?" spluttered the salesman. "I'm common?" he asked in astonishment. His manner changed. He slipped his book into the briefcase, snapped it shut, and gripped the handle with his gloved hand. "What's the use," he said philosophically. "Why should Jack Rosen waste his time talking to a two-bit grocer who don't think enough of his place of business to wash the windows or to sweep the snow off the sidewalk so that a customer can come in? Such a person is a peasant in his heart. He belongs in czarist Russia. The advantages of the new world he don't understand or appreciate."

"A philosopher," sneered Sam, "a G. and S. wholesale groceries' philosopher."

The salesman snatched up his bag and strode out of the store. He slammed the front door hard. Several cans in the window toppled and fell.

Ida looked at her husband with loathing. Her small, stout body trembled with indignation.

"His every word was like it come from God," she said vehemently. "Who ever saw a man should sit in the back of the store all day long and never go inside, maybe to wipe off the shelves or clean out under the counter the boxes, or to think how to improve his store a customer should come in?"

Sam said nothing.

"Who ever heard there should be a grocer," continued Ida, shaking her head scornfully, "who don't think enough about his place of business and his wife, he should go outside and sweep off the snow from the sidewalk a customer should be able to come to the door. It's a shame and a disgrace that a man with a place of business is so lazy he won't get up from a chair. A shame and a disgrace."

"Enough," said Sam quietly.

"I deserve better," she said, raising her voice.

"Enough," he said again.

"Get up," she cried. "Get up and clean the sidewalk."

He turned to her angrily. "Please," he cried, "don't give me orders."

Ida rose and stood near his chair. "Sam, clean off the sidewalk," she shouted in her shrill voice.

"Shut up!" he shouted.

"Clean off the sidewalk!" Her voice was thick with rage.

"Shut up," he roared, rising angrily. "Shut up, you bastard, you."

Ida looked at him uncomprehendingly; then her lips twisted grotesquely, her cheeks bunched up like a gargoyle's, and her body shook with sobs as the hot tears flowed. She sank down into her chair, lowered her head on her arms, and cried with a bitter squealing sound.

Sam groaned inwardly. The words had leaped from his tongue, and now she was crying again. The miserable feeling ground itself into his bones. He cursed the store and his profitless life.

"Where's the shovel?" he asked, defeated.

She did not look up.

He searched for it in the store and found it in the hallway near the cellar door. Sam bounced the shovel against the floor to shake off the cobwebs and then went outside.

The icy February wind wrapped him in a tight, cold jacket, and the frozen snow on the ground gripped his feet like a steel vise. His apron flapped, and the wind blew his thin hair into his eyes. A wave of desperation rolled over him, but he fought against it. Sam bent over, scooped up a pile of snow, and heaved it into the gutter, where it fell and broke. His face was whipped into an icy ruddiness, and cold water ran from his eyes.

Mr. Fine, a retired policeman, one of Sam's customers, trudged by, heavily bundled up.

"For godsake, Sam," he boomed in his loud voice, "put on something warm."

The tenants on the top floor, a young Italian couple, came out of the house on their way to the movies. "You'll catch pneumonia, Mr. Kaplan," said Mrs. Costa.

"That's what I told him," Mr. Fine called back.

"At least put a coat on, Sam," advised Patsy Costa.

"I'm almost through," Sam grunted.

"It's your health," said Patsy. He and his wife pushed their way through the wind and the snow, going to the movies. Sam continued to shovel up the snow and heave it into the gutter.

When he finished cleaning the sidewalk, Sam was half frozen. His nose was running and his eyes were bleary. He went inside quickly. The warmth of the store struck him so hard that the back of his head began to ache, and he knew at once that he had made a mistake in not putting on an overcoat and gloves. He reeled and suddenly felt weak, as if his bones had dissolved and were no longer holding up his body. Sam leaned against the counter to keep himself from falling. When the dizziness went away, he dragged the wet shovel across the floor and put it back in the hall.

Ida was no longer crying. Her eyes were red and she looked away from him as he came into the kitchen. Sam still felt cold. He moved his chair close to the stove and picked up the Jewish paper, but his eyes were so tired that he could not make out the words. He closed them and let the paper slip to the floor. The overpowering warmth of the stove thawed out his chilled body, and he grew sleepy. As he was dozing off, he heard the front door open. With a start, Sam opened his eyes to see if Ida had gone inside. No, she sat at the table in frigid silence. His eyelids shut and opened again. Sam rose with an effort and shuffled into the store. The customer wanted a loaf of bread and ten cents' worth of store cheese. Sam waited on her and returned to his place by the stove. He closed his eyes again and sneezed violently. His nose was running. As he was searching for his handkerchief, the store door opened again.

"Go inside," he said to Ida, "I must take a aspirin."

She did not move.

"I have a cold," he said.

She gave no sign that she had heard.

With a look of disgust, he walked into the store and waited on the customer. In the kitchen, he began to sneeze again. Sam shook two aspirins out of the bottle and lifted them to his mouth with his palm, then he drank some water. As he sat down by the stove, he felt the cold grip him inside and he shivered.

"I'm sick," he said to his wife, but Ida paid no attention to him.

"I'm sick," he repeated miserably. "I'm going upstairs to sleep. Maybe tomorrow I'll feel a little better."

"If you go upstairs now," Ida said, with her back turned toward him, "I will not go in the store."

"So don't go," he said angrily.

"I will not come downstairs tomorrow," she threatened coldly.

"So don't come down," he said brokenly. "The way I feel, I hope the store drops dead. Nineteen years is enough. I can't stand any more. My heart feels dried up. I suffered too much in my life."

He went into the hall. She could hear his slow, heavy footsteps on the stairs and the door closing upstairs.

Ida looked at the clock. It was ten-thirty. For a moment she was tempted to close the store, but she decided not to. The A&P was closed. It was the only time they could hope to make a few cents. She thought about her life and grew despondent. After twenty-two years of married life, a cold flat and an impoverished grocery store. She looked out at the store, hating every inch of it, the dirty window, the empty shelves, showing old brown wallpaper where there were no cans, the old-fashioned wooden icebox, the soiled marble counters, the hard floor, the meagerness, the poverty, and the hard years of toil—for what?—to be insulted by a man without understanding or appreciation of her sacrifices, and to be left alone while he went upstairs to sleep. She could hear the wind blowing outside and she felt cold. The stove needed to be shaken and filled with coal, but she was too tired. Ida decided to close the store. It wasn't worth keeping open. Better for her to go to sleep and come down as late as she chose tomorrow. Let him have to prepare his own breakfast and dinner. Let him wash the kitchen floor and scrub out the icebox. Let him do all the things she did, then he would learn how to speak to her. She locked the front door, put out the window lights, and pulled the cord of each ceiling lamp, extinguishing the light, as she made her way toward the hall door.

Suddenly she heard a sharp tapping against the store window. Ida looked out and saw the dark form of a man who was rapping a coin against the glass.

A bottle of milk, thought Ida.

"Tomorrow," she called out. "The store is now closed."

The man stopped for a second, and she thought with relief that he was going away, but once again he began to rap the coin sharply and insistently. He waved his hands and shouted at her. A woman joined him.

"Mrs. Kaplan!" she called, "Mrs. Kaplan!"

Ida recognized Mrs. Costa. A great fright tore at her heart, and she rushed over to the door.

"What's the matter?" she cried when she opened it.

"Gas," said Patsy. "Gas in the hall. Where's Sam?"

"Oh, my God," cried Ida, pressing her hands against her bosom. "Oh, my God," she cried, "Sam is upstairs."

"Gimme the key, quick," said Patsy.

"Give him the key, Mrs. Kaplan," said Mrs. Costa excitedly.

Ida grew faint. "Oh, my God," she cried.

"Gimme the key," Patsy repeated urgently.

Ida found it in the pocket of her sweater and handed it to Patsy. He ran upstairs, two steps at a time, his wife running after him. Ida closed the store and followed them upstairs. The odor of gas was heavy.

"Oh, my God," she cried over and over again.

Patsy was opening all the windows, and his wife was shaking Sam in his bed. The sharp heavy stink of the gas tore at Ida's nostrils as she came into the room.

"Sam!" she shrieked, "Sam!"

He woke from his sleep with a shock. "What's the matter?" he cried, his voice filled with fear.

"Oh, why did you do it?" cried Mrs. Costa in the dark. "Why did you do it?"

"I thank God he's alive," said Patsy.

Ida moaned and squeezed her hands against her bosom.

"What's the matter?" cried Sam. Then he smelled the gas, and for a moment he was paralyzed with fright.

Patsy put on the light. Sam's face was a dark red. He was perspiring from every pore. He pulled up the quilt to cover his shoulders.

"Why did you do it for, Sam?" asked Patsy.

"What? What?" Sam said excitedly, "what did I do?"

"The gas. You turned on the gas radiator without making the light."

"It wasn't lit?" cried Sam in astonishment.

"No," said Mrs. Costa.

Sam grew quieter. He lay back. "I made a mistake," he said. "This is the first time I made such a mistake."

"Didn't you do it on purpose?" asked Mrs. Costa.

"What on purpose? Why on purpose?" Sam asked.

"We thought—"

"No," said Sam, "no, I made a mistake. Maybe the match was no good."

"Then you shoulda smelled the gas," said Patsy.

"No, I got a cold."

"The only thing that saved you was you got a lot of air. You're lucky this flat ain't windproof."

"Yes, I'm lucky," Sam agreed.

"I told you to put on a coat," said Mrs. Costa. "He was standing out in the snow without a coat," she said to Ida.

Ida was pale and silent.

"Well, come on," said Patsy, taking his wife by the arm, "everybody wants to go to sleep."

"Good night," said Mrs. Costa.

"Leave the windows open for a coupla minutes more, and don't light no matches," advised Patsy.

"I'm much obliged to you for your trouble you took," said Sam.

"Don't mention it at all," said Patsy, "but next time take more care."

"It was a mistake," said Sam. "Nothing more, I assure you."

The Costas left. Ida saw them to the door and turned the lock. Sam covered himself more securely with the quilt. The house was freezing with the windows open. He was afraid he would begin to sneeze again. Ida said nothing. Sam fell asleep very soon.

Ida waited until the house was free of the smell of gas. Then she closed the windows. Before undressing, she looked at the radiator and saw that the stopcock was closed. She got into bed, utterly fatigued, and fell asleep immediately.

It seemed to Ida that she had slept only a short time when she awoke suddenly. Frightened, she looked at Sam, but he was bulked up beside her with the covers over his head. She listened to his deep, heavy breathing, and the momentary fear left her. Ida was fully awake now, and the events of the day tumbled quickly through her brain. She thought of the episode of the gas, and a sharp streak of pain ripped through every nerve in her body. Had Sam really tried to take his life? Had he? She wanted to wake him and ask him, but she was afraid. She turned over and tried to sleep again, but she couldn't.

Ida reached over to the night table and looked at the luminous face of the clock. It was four-twenty-five. The alarm would ring at six. Sam would get up and she would ask him, then maybe she could sleep. She closed her eyes, but still no sleep came. She opened them and kept them open.

A faint tinkling on the window caused her to look out. By the light of the street lamp she could see that it was snowing again. The flakes drifted down slowly and silently. They seemed to hang in the air, then the wind rose and blew them against the windows. The windows rattled softly; then everything became quiet again, except for the ticking of the clock.

Ida reached over for the clock and shut off the alarm. It was nearly five. At six o'clock she would get up, dress, and go downstairs. She would pull in the milk box and the bread. Then she would sweep the store, and then the snow from the sidewalk. Let Sam sleep. Later, if he felt better, he could come downstairs. Ida looked at the clock again. Five past five. The sleep would do him good.

1943

A Confession of Murder

WITH THE doing of the deed embedded in his mind like a child's grave in the earth, Farr shut the door and walked heavy-hearted down the stairs. At the third-floor landing he stopped to look out the small dirty window, across the harbor. The late-winter day was sullen, but Farr could see the ocean in the distance. Although he was carrying the weapon, a stone sash weight in a brown paper bag, heedless of the danger he set it down on the window ledge and stared at the water. It seemed to Farr that he had never loved the sea as he did now. Although he had not crossed it—he thought he would during the war but didn't—and had never gone any of the different ways it led, he felt he someday ought to. As he gazed, the water seemed to come alive in sunlight, flowing with slanted white sails. Moved to grief at the lovely sight he remained at the window with unseeing eyes until he remembered to go.

He went down the creaking stairs to the black, airless cellar. Farr pulled the rasping chain above the electric bulb and, when the dim light fell on him, searched around for a hiding place. As his hand uncoiled he realized with horror that he had forgotten the sash weight. He bounded up three flights of stairs, coming to a halt as he saw through the banister that an old woman was standing at the window, resting her bundle on the ledge—on the sash weight itself! Agitated, Farr watched to see whether she would discover the bloody thing, but she too was looking at the water and made no move to go. When she finally left, Farr, who had been lurking on the landing below, ran up, seized the package, and fled down to the cellar.

There he was tempted to draw the weapon out of the paper to inspect it but did not dare. He hunted for a place to bury it but felt secure nowhere. At last he tore open the asbestos covering of an insulated water pipe overhead and shoved the sash weight into the wool. As he was smoothing the asbestos he heard footsteps above and broke into a chilling sweat at the fear he was being followed. Stealthily he put out the light, sneaked close to the wall, and crouched in the pitch dark behind a dusty dresser abandoned there. He waited with indrawn breath for whoever he was to come limping down. Farr planned to yell into his face, escape up the stairs.

No one came down. Farr was afraid to abandon the hiding place, stricken at the thought that it was not a stranger but his father, miraculously recovered from his wound, who sought him there, as he had in the past, shouting in drunken rage against his son, stalking him in the dark, threatening to beat his head off with his belt buckle if he did not reveal himself. The memory of this so deeply affected Farr that he groaned aloud. It did not console him that his father had at last paid a terrible price for all the misery he had inflicted on him.

Farr trudged up the steps out of the cellar. In the street he felt unspeakable relief to be out of the grimy tenement house. He brushed the cobwebs off his brown hat and spanked a whitewash smear off the back of his long overcoat. Then he went down the block to where the houses ended and stood at the water's edge. The wind, whipping whitecaps along the surface of the harbor water, struck him with force. He held tightly to his hat. A flight of sparrows sprang across the sky, flying over the ships at anchor and disappearing in the distance. The aroma of roasting coffee filled Farr's hungry nostrils, but just then he saw some eggshells bobbing in the water and a dead rat floating. Surfeited, he turned away.

A skinny man in a green suit was standing at his elbow. "Sure looks like snow." The man wore no overcoat and his soiled shirt was open at the collar. His face and hands were tinged blue. Farr cupped a match to his cigarette, puffing quickly. He would have walked away but was afraid of being followed, so he stayed.

"Just a whiff of a butt makes me hungry to the bottom of my belly," said the man.

Farr listened, looking away.

After a minute the man, staring absently at the water, said, "The chill bites deep when there's no food between it and the marrow."

Suspecting him of planning to trick him, Farr warned himself to confess nothing. They'd have to ram a crowbar through his teeth to pry his jaws open.

"You wouldn't know it from the look of me," said the man, "but I'm a gentleman at heart." He wore a strained smile and held forth a trembling hand. Farr reached into his pants pocket, where he had five crumpled dollars plus a large assortment of coins. He pulled out a fistful of change, selected a nickel and five pennies, and dropped them into the man's outstretched hand.

Without thanking Farr, he drew back his arm and pitched the money into the water. Farr's suspicions awoke. He hurried up the block, glancing back from time to time to see if he was being followed, but the man had dropped out of sight.

He turned on the half run up the treeless avenue, angered with the bum for spoiling his view of the harbor. Yet though Farr was now passing the pawnshops, which reminded him of things he did not like to remember, his spirits rose. He accounted for this strange and unexpected change in him by his having done the deed. For an age he had been tormented by the desire to do it, had grown silent, lonely, sullen, until the decision came that the doing was the only way out. Much too long the plan had festered in his mind, waiting for an action, but now that it was done he at last felt free of the rank desire, the suppressed rage and fear that had embittered and thwarted his existence. It was done; he was content. As he walked, the vista of the narrow avenue, a street he had lived his life along, broadened, and he could see miles ahead, down to the suspension bridge in the distance, and was aware of people walking along as separate beings, not part of the mass he remembered avoiding so often as he'd trudged along here at various times of day and night.

One of the pawnshop windows caught his eye. Farr reluctantly stopped, yet he scanned it eagerly. There among the wedding bands, watches, knives, crucifixes, and the rest, among the stringed musical instruments and brasses hanging on pegs on the wall, he found what his eye sought—his mandolin—and felt a throb of pity for it. But Farr had not been working for more than a year—had left the place one rainy day in the fall—and the only way, thereafter, that he could keep himself in cigarette, newspaper, and movie money was to part, one by one, with the things he had bought for himself in a better time: a portable typewriter, used perhaps now and then to peck out a letter ordering a magazine; a pair of ice skates worn twice; a fine wristwatch he had bought on his birthday; and lately, with everything else gone, he had sold this little mandolin he'd liked so well, which he had taught himself to strum as he sang, and it was this bit of self-made music that he missed most. He considered redeeming it with the same five one-dollar bills he had got for it a month ago, but didn't relish the thought of strumming alone in his room; so sighing, Farr tore himself away from the window.

At the next corner stood Gus's Tavern. Farr, who had not gone in in an age, after a struggle entered, gazing around as if in a cathedral. Gus, older, with a folded apron around his paunch and an open vest over his white shirt, was standing behind the bar polishing beer glasses. When he saw Farr he put down the glass he was shining and observed him in astonishment.

"Well, throw me for a jackass if 'tisn't the old Punch-Ball King of South Second!"

Farr grunted awkwardly at the old appellation. "Surprised, Gus?"

"That's the least of it. Where in the name of mud have you been these many months—or is it years?"

"In the house mostly," Farr answered huskily.

Gus continued to regard him closely, to Farr's discomfort. "You've changed a lot, Eddie, haven't you now? I ask everybody whatever has become of the old Punch-Ball King and nobody says they ever see you. You used to haunt the streets when you were a kid."

Farr blinked but didn't reply.

"Married?" Gus winked.

"No," Farr said, embarrassed. He stole a glance at the door. It was still there.

Gus clucked. "How well I remember standing on the curbstone watching you play. *Flippo* with his left hand and the ball spins up. *Biffo* with his right, a tremendous sock lifting it far over the heads of all the fielders. How old were you then, Eddie?"

Farr made no attempt to think. "Fifteen, I guess."

An expression of sorrow lit Gus's eyes. "It comes back to me now. You were the same age as my Marty."

Farr's tongue tightened. It was beyond him to speak of the dead.

Himself again after a while, Gus sighed, "Ah yes, Eddie, you missed your true calling."

"One beer," Farr said, digging into his pocket for the change.

Gus drew a beer, shaved it, and set it before him.

"Put your pennies away. Any old friend of my Marty's needn't be thirsty here."

Farr gulped through the froth. A cold beer went with how good he now felt. He thought he might even break into a jig step or two.

Gus was still watching him. Farr, finding he couldn't drink, set the glass down.

After a pause Gus asked, "Do you still ever sing, Eddie?"

"Not so much anymore."

"Do me a favor and sing some old-time tune."

Farr looked around, but they were alone. Pretending to be strumming his mandolin, he sang, "In the good old summertime, in the good old summertime."

"Your voice has changed, Eddie," said Gus, "but it's still pleasing to the ear."

Farr then sang, "Ah, sweet mystery of life, at last I've found you."

Gus's eyes went wet and he blew his nose. "A fine little singer was lost to the world somewhere along the line."

Farr hung his head.

"What are your plans now, Eddie?"

The question scared him. Luckily, two customers came in and stood at the bar. Gus went to them, and Farr did not have to answer.

He picked up the beer and pointed with one finger to a booth in the rear.

Gus nodded. "Only don't leave without saying goodbye."

Farr promised.

He sat in the booth, thinking of Marty. Farr often thought and dreamed about him, but though he knew him best as a boy he dreamed of him as a man, mostly as he was during the days and nights they stood on street corners, waiting to be called into the army. There didn't seem anything to do then but wait till they were called in, so they spent most of their time smoking, throwing the bull, and making wisecracks at the girls who passed by. Marty, strangely inactive for the wild kid he had been—never knowing what wild thing to do next—was a blond fellow whose good looks the girls liked, but he never stopped wisecracking at them, whether he knew them or not. One day he said something dirty to this Jewish girl who passed by and she burst into tears. Gus, who had happened to be watching out of the upstairs window, heard what Marty said, ran down in his slippers, and smacked him hard across the teeth. Marty spat blood. Farr went sick to the pit of his stomach at the sound of the sock. He later threw up. And that was the last any of them had ever seen of Marty, because he enlisted in the army and never came out again. Gus got a telegram one day saying that he was killed in action, and he never really got over it.

Farr was whispering to himself about Marty when he gazed up and saw this dark-haired woman standing by his table, looking as if she had slyly watched his startled eyes find her. Half rising, he remembered to remove his hat.

"Remember me, Ed? Helen Melisatos—Gus told me to say hello."

He knew she was this Greek girl—only she'd been very pretty then—who had once lived in the same tenement house with him. One summer night they had gone together up to the roof.

"Sure," said Farr. "Sure I remember you."

Her body had broadened but her face and hair were not bad, and her dark brown eyes seemed still to be expecting something that she would never get.

She sat down, telling him to sit.

He did, placing his hat next to him on the seat.

She lit a cigarette and smoked for a long time. A man called her from the bar but she shook her head. He left without her.

Her lips moved hungrily. Although he could at first hear no voice, she seemed, against his will, to be telling him a story he didn't want to hear. It was about this boy and a girl, a slim dark girl with soft eyes, seventeen then, wearing this nice white dress on a hot summer night. They'd been kissing. Then she had slipped off her undergarment and lain back, uncovered, on the tar-papered roof. With heart thudding he watched her, and when she said to kneel he kneeled, and then she said it was hot and why didn't he take off his pants. He wanted to love her with their clothes on. When he got his pants off he stopped and couldn't go on. What do you think of a guy who would do a thing like that to a girl? He wasn't much of a lover, was he? She was smiling broadly now, and she spoke in an older, disillusioned voice, "You're different, Ed." And she said, "You used to talk a lot."

He listened intently but said nothing.

"But you still ain't a bad-looking guy. How old are you, anyway?"

"Twenty-eight, going on twenty-nine."

"Married?"

"Not yet," he said quickly. "How about you?"

"I had enough," Helen said.

He cagily asked her another question to keep her talking about herself. "How's your brother George?"

"He lives in Athens now. He went back with my mother after the war. My father died here."

Farr put on his hat.

"Going someplace, Ed?"

"No." He whispered to himself that he must say nothing about his own father.

She shrugged.

"Drink?" he asked.

She lifted her half-full whiskey glass. "Order yourself."

"I got my beer." But when he took up the glass it was empty.

"Still absentminded?" She smiled.

"My mind's okay," Farr said.

"I bet you're still a virgin?"

"I bet you're not." Farr grinned and drained a drop from the glass.

"Remember that night on the roof?"

He harshly said he didn't want to hear about it.

"I couldn't believe in myself for a long time after that," Helen said.

"I don't want to hear about it."

She sat silent, not looking at him. She sat silent so long his confidence finally ebbed back.

"Remember," he said, "when you had that sweet-sixteen party in your house, your mother gave us that Greek coffee that had jelly in the bottom of the little cup?"

She said she remembered.

"Let me buy you a drink." Farr reached into his pocket. He was smoking and squinted as he counted the coins.

He caught Gus's eye and ordered whiskey for her, but Gus wouldn't take anything for it. Farr then slid a coin into the jukebox.

"Dance?" he said, fighting a panicky feeling.

"No."

Vastly relieved, he went to the bar and ordered another beer. This time Gus let him pay. Farr cashed one of his dollar bills.

"Nothing like old friends, eh, Eddie?"

"Yeah," said Farr happily. He lit a cigarette and steered the beer over to the table. Helen had another whiskey and Farr another beer. He got used to the way her eyes looked at him over her glass.

After a time Helen asked him if he had had supper.

A violent hunger seized him as he remembered his last meal had been breakfast.

He said no.

"Come on up to my place. I'll fix you something good."

Farr whispered to himself that he ought to go. He ought to, and later talk her into going up to the roof with him. If he did it to her now, maybe he would feel better and then things that had gone wrong would go right. You could never tell.

Her face was flushed, and all the time she was grinning at him in a dirty way.

Farr whispered something and she strained to catch it but couldn't. "What the hell are you saying?"

"Nothing."

"Come on up with me, kid," she urged. "After, I'll show you how to make a man out of yourself."

His head fell with a bang against the tabletop. His eyes were shut, and he wouldn't move.

"Imagine a guy your age who never made love," Helen taunted.

He answered nothing and she began cursing him, her face lit in livid anger. Finally she got up, a little unsteady on her feet. "Why don't you go and drop dead?"

He said he would.

Farr walked again in the darkened streets. He stopped at the heavy wooden doors of the Catholic church. Pulling one open, he glanced hastily inside and saw the holy-water basin. He wondered what would happen if he went in and gargled a mouthful. A girl in a brown coat and purple bandanna came out of the church and Farr asked her when was confession.

She looked up at him in fright and quickly said, "Saturday."

He thanked her and walked away. It was Monday.

She ran after him and said she could arrange for him to see the priest if he wanted to.

He said no, that he was not a Catholic.

Though his coat reached to his ankles, his legs were cold. So were the soles of his feet. He walked as if he were dragging a burden. The burden was the way he felt. The good feeling had gone and this old one was heavier now than anything he remembered. He would not mind the cold so much if he could only get rid of this dismal heaviness. His brain felt like a rock. Still it grew heavier. That was the unaccountable thing. He wondered how heavy it could get. If it got any heavier, he would keel over in the street and nobody'd be able to lift him. They would all give up and leave him lying with his head sunk in asphalt.

On the next street shone two green lamps on both sides of some stone steps leading into a dark and dirty building. It was a police station. Farr stood across the street from it, but nobody went in or came out. Finally it grew freezing cold. He blew into his fists, looked around to see if he was being followed, and then went in.

He was grateful for the warmth. The sergeant sat at the desk writing. He was a bald-headed man with a bulbous nose, which he frequently scratched with his little finger. His second and third fingers had ink stains on them from a leaky fountain pen. The sergeant glanced up in surprise, and Farr did not care for his face.

"What's yours?" he said.

Farr's tongue was like a sash weight. Unable to speak, he hung his head.

"Remove your hat."

Farr took it off.

"Come to the point," said the sergeant, scratching his nose.

Farr at last confessed to a crime.

"Such as what?" said the sergeant.

Farr's lips twitched and assumed odd shapes. "I killed somebody."

"Who, for instance?"

"My father."

The sergeant's incredulous look vanished. "Ah, that's too bad."

He wrote Farr's name down in a large ledger, blotted it, and told him to wait on a bench by the wall.

"I got to locate a detective to talk to you, but as it happens nobody's around just now. You picked suppertime to come in."

Farr sat on the bench with his hat on. After a while a heavy-set man came through the door, carrying a paper bag and a pint container of coffee.

"Say, Wolff," called the sergeant.

Wolff slowly turned around. He had broad, bent shoulders and a thick mustache. His large black hat was broad-brimmed.

The sergeant pointed his pen at Farr. "A confession of murder."

Wolff's eyebrows went up slightly. "Where's Burns or Newman?"

"Supper. You're the only one that's around right now."

The detective glanced uneasily at Farr. "Come on," he said.

Farr got up and followed him. The detective walked heavily up the wooden stairs. Halfway up he stopped, sighed inaudibly, and went up more slowly.

"Hold this," he said at the top of the stairs.

Farr held the bag of food and the coffee. The hot container warmed his cold hand. Wolff unlocked a door with a key, then took his supper from Farr, and they went inside. The church bell in the neighborhood bonged seven times.

Wolff routinely frisked Farr. He sat down heavily at his desk, tore open the paper bag, and unwrapped his food. He had three meat-and-cheese sandwiches and a paper dish of cabbage salad which he ate with a small plastic fork that annoyed him. As he was eating he remembered the coffee and twisted the top off the container. His hand shook a little as he poured the steaming coffee into a white cup without a handle.

He ate with his hat on. Farr held his in his lap. He enjoyed the warmth of the room and the peaceful sight of someone eating.

"My first square today," said Wolff. "Busy from morning."

Farr nodded.

"One thing after another."

"I know."

Wolff, as he ate, kept his eyes fastened on Farr. "Take your coat off. It's hot here."

"No, thanks." He was now sorry he had come.

The detective finished up quickly. He rolled the papers on his desk and what remained of the food into a ball and dumped it into the wastebasket. Then he got up and washed his hands in a closet sink. At his desk he lit a cigar, puffed with pleasure two or three times, put it to the side in an ashtray, and said, "What's this confession?"

Although Farr struggled with himself to speak, he couldn't.

Wolff grew restless. "Murder, did somebody say?"

Farr sighed deeply.

"Your mother?" Wolff asked sympathetically.

"No, my father."

"Oh ho," said Wolff.

Farr gazed at the floor.

The detective opened a black pocket notebook and found a pencil stub.

"Name?" he said.

"You mean mine?" asked Farr.

"Yours—who else?"

"My father's."

"First yours."

"Farr, Edward."

"His?"

"Herman J. Farr."

"Age of victim?"

Farr tried to think. "I don't know."

"You don't know your own father's age?"

"No."

"How old are you?"

"Twenty-nine, going on thirty."

"That you know?"

Farr didn't answer.

Wolff wrote down something in the book.

"What was his occupation?"

"Upholsterer."

"And yours?"

"None," Farr said, in embarrassment.

"Unemployed?"

"Yes."

"What's your regular work?"

"I have none in particular."

"A jack of all trades." Wolff broke the ash off in the tray and took another puff of the cigar. "Address?"

"80 South Second."

"Your father too?"

"Yes."

"That where the body is?"

Farr nodded absently.

The detective then slipped the notebook into his pocket.

"What did you use to kill him with?"

Farr paused, wet his dry lips, and said, "A blunt instrument."

"You don't say? What kind of a blunt instrument?"

"A window sash weight."

"What'd you do with it?"

"I hid it."

"Whereabouts?"

"In the cellar where we live."

Wolff carefully tapped his cigar out in the ashtray and leaned forward. "So tell me," he said, "why does a man kill his father?"

Alarmed, Farr half rose from his chair.

"Sit down," said the detective.

Farr sat down.

"I asked you why did you kill him?"

Farr gnawed on his lip till it bled.

"Come on, come on," said Wolff, "we have to have the motive."

"I don't know."

"Who then should know—I?"

Farr tried frantically to think why. Because he had had nothing in his life and what he had done was a way of having something?

"What did you do it for, I said," Wolff asked sternly.

"I had to—" Farr had risen.

"What do you mean 'had to'?"

"I had no love for him. He ruined my life."

"Is that a reason to kill your father?"

"Yes," Farr shouted. "For that and everything else."

"What else?"

"Leave me alone. Can't you see I'm an unhappy man?"

Wolff sat back in his chair. "You don't say?"

"Sarcasm won't get you anyplace," Farr cried angrily. "Be humble with suffering people."

"I don't need any advice on how to run my profession."

"Try to remember a man is not a beast." Trembling, Farr resumed his seat.

"Are you a man?" Wolff asked slyly.

"No, I have failed."

"Then you are a beast?"

"Insofar as I am not a man."

They stared at each other. Wolff flattened his mustache with his fingertips. Suddenly he opened his drawer and took out a picture.

"Do you recognize this woman?"

Farr stared at the wrinkled face of an old crone. "No."

"She was raped and murdered on the top floor of an apartment house in your neighborhood."

Farr covered his ears with his hands.

The detective laid the picture back in the drawer. He fished out another.

"Here's a boy aged about six or seven. He was brutally stabbed to death in an empty lot on South Eighth. Did you ever see him before?"

He thrust the picture close to Farr's face.

When Farr looked into the boy's innocent eyes he burst into tears.

Wolff put the picture away. He pulled on the dead cigar, then examined it and threw it away.

"Come on," he said, tiredly rising.

The cellar was full of violent presences. Farr went fearfully down the steps.

Wolff flashed his light on the crisscrossed pipes overhead. "Which one?"

Farr pointed.

The detective brushed aside some cobwebs and felt along the pipe with his fingers. He found the loose asbestos and from the wool inside plucked forth the sash weight.

Farr audibly sucked in his breath.

In the yellow glow of the hall lamp upstairs the detective took the sash weight out of the bag and examined it. Farr shut his eyes.

"What floor do you live on?"

"Fourth."

Wolff looked up uneasily. They trudged up the stairs, Farr leading.

"Not so fast," said Wolff.

Farr slowed down. As they passed the third-floor window he looked out to sea, but all was dark. On the next floor he stopped before a warped door with a top panel of frosted glass.

"In here," Farr said at last.

"Have you got the key?"

Farr turned the knob and the door fell open, bumping loudly against the wall. The corridor to the kitchen was black. The detective's light pierced it, lighting up a wooden table and two wooden chairs.

"Go on in."

"I'm afraid," whispered Farr.

"Go on, I said."

He stepped reluctantly forward.

"Where is he?" said the detective.

"In the bedroom." He spoke hoarsely.

"Show me."

Farr led him through a small windowless room containing a

cot and some books and magazines on the floor. Wolff's light shone on him.

"In there." Farr pointed to the door.

"Open it."

"No."

"Open, I said."

"For godsake, don't make me."

"Open."

Farr thought quickly: in the dark there he would upset the detective and make a hasty escape into the street.

"For the last time I said open."

Farr pushed the door and it squeaked open on its hinges. The long narrow bedroom was heavy with darkness. Wolff's light hit the metal headboard of an old double bed, sunken in the middle.

A groan rose from the bed. Farr groaned too, his hair on end.

"Murder," said the groan, "terrible, terrible."

A white bloodless face rose into the light, old and staring.

"Who's there?" cried Wolff.

"Oh, my dreams, my dreams," wept the old man, "I dreamed I was bein murdered."

Flinging aside the worn quilt, he slid out of bed and hopped in bare feet on the cold floor, skinny in his long underwear. He groped toward them.

Farr whispered wild things to himself.

The detective found the light chain and pulled it.

The old man saw the stranger in the room. "And who are you, might I ask?"

"Theodore Wolff, detective from the Sixty-second Precinct." He flashed his shield.

Herman Farr blinked in surprise and shame. He hastily got into the pants that had been draped across a chair and, stepping into misshapen slippers, raised suspenders over his shoulders.

"I must've overslept my nap. I usually have supper cookin at six and we eat half past six, him and I." He suddenly asked, "What are you doin here if you're a detective?"

"I came here with your son."

"He didn't do anything wrong?" asked the old man, frightened.

"I don't know. That's what I came to find out."

"Come into the kitchen," said Herman Farr. "The light's better."

They went into the kitchen. Herman Farr got a third chair from the bedroom and they sat around the wooden table, Farr waxen and fatigued, his father gaunt and bony-faced, with loose skin sprouting gray stubble, and on the long side of the table, the heavyset Wolff, wearing his black hat.

"Where are my glasses?" complained Herman Farr. He got up and found them on a shelf above the gas stove. The lenses were thick and magnified his watery eyes.

"Until now I couldn't tell the nature of your face," he said to the detective.

Wolff grunted.

"Now what's the trouble here?" said Herman Farr, staring at his son.

Farr sneered at him.

The detective removed the sash weight from the paper bag and laid it on the table. Farr gazed at it as if it were a snake uncoiling.

"Ever see this before?"

Herman Farr stared stupidly at the sash weight, one hand clawing the back of the other.

"Where'd you get it?" he cried in a quavering voice.

"Answer my question first."

"Yes. It belongs to me, though I wish to Christ I had never seen it."

"It's yours?" said Wolff.

"That's right. I had it hid in my trunk."

"What's this stain on it here?"

Farr gazed in fascination where the detective pointed.

Herman Farr said he didn't know.

"It's a bloodstain," Wolff said.

"Ah, so it is," sighed Herman Farr, his mouth trembling. "I'll tell you the truth. My wife—may God rest her soul—once tried to hit me with it."

Farr laughed out loud.

"Is this your blood?" asked Wolff.

"No, by the livin mercy. It's hers."

They were all astonished.

"Are you telling the truth?" said Wolff sternly.

"I'd give my soul if I only wasn't."

"Did you hit her with it?"

Herman Farr lifted his glasses and with a clotted yellow handkerchief wiped the tears from his flowing eyes.

"A sin is never lost. Once in a drunken fit, enraged as I was by my long-lastin poverty, I swung it at her and opened a wound on her head. The blood is hers. I could never blame her for wantin to kill me with it. She tried it one night when I was at my supper, but the thing fell out of her hand and smashed the plate. I nearly jumped out of my shoes. Seein it fall I realized the extent of my wickedness and kept the sash weight hid away at the bottom of my trunk as a memory of my sins."

Wolff scratched a match under the table, paused, and shook it out. Farr smoked the last cigarette in his crushed pack. The old man wept into his dirty handkerchief.

"I have deserved a violent endin of my life if anybody ever did. In my younger days I was a beast—cruel, and a weaklin. I treated them both very badly." He nodded to Farr. "As he more than once said it, I killed her a little every day. Many times—may the livin God keep torturin me for it—I beat her black and blue, once bloodyin her nose on a frosty morning when she complained of the cold, and another time pushin her down a flight of stairs. As for him, I more than once skinned his back with my belt buckle."

Farr crushed his cigarette and snapped it into the sink.

Wolff then lit a cigar and puffed slowly.

The old man wept openly. "This young man is the livin witness of my terrible deeds, but he don't know half the depths of my sufferin since that poor soul left this world, or the terrible nature of my nightly dreams."

"When did she die?" the detective asked.

"Sixteen years ago, and he has never forgiven me, carryin his hatred like a fire in his heart, although she, good soul, forgave me in his presence at the time of her last illness. 'Herman,' she said, 'I'm goin to a place where I would be ill at ease if I didn't forgive you,' and with that she went to her peace. But my son has hated me throughout the years, and I can't look at him without seein it in his eyes. 'Tis true, he has sometimes been kind to a helpless old man, and when my arthritis was so bad that I couldn't move, he more than once brought a plate of soup to my bed and fed me with a spoon, but in the depths of his soul my change has made no difference to him and he hates me now as he did then, though I've repented on sore knees a thousand times. I have often said to him, 'What's done is done, and judge me for what I have since become'—for he is an intelligent man and reads books you and I never heard of—but on this thing he won't yield or be reasoned with."

"Did he ever try to hurt you?"

"No more than to nag or snarl at me. No, for all he does nowadays is to sit alone in his room and read and reflect, although his learnin doesn't in the least unbend his mind to me. Of course I don't approve him givin up his job, because with these puffed and crippled hands I am lucky when I can work half time, but there are all sorts in the world and some have greater need for reflection than others. He has been inclined in that direction since he was a lad, although I did not notice his quiet and solitary ways until after he had returned from the army."

"What did he do then?" said Wolff.

"He worked for a year at his old job, then gave it up and became a hospital orderly. But he couldn't stand it long and he quit and stayed home."

Farr looked out the dark fire-escape window and saw himself walking along the dreary edge of a desolate beach, the wind wailing at his feet, driftwood taking on frightening shapes, and his footsteps fading behind, to appear on the ground before him as he walked along the vast, silent shore . . .

Wolff rubbed the cigar out against the sole of his shoe. "You want to know why I'm here?" he said to Herman Farr.

"Yes."

"He came to the station house around suppertime and made a statement that he had murdered you with this sash weight."

The old man groaned. "Not that I don't deserve the fate."

"He thought he actually did it," Wolff said.

"It's his overactive imagination on account of not gettin any exercise to speak of. I've told him that many times but he don't listen to what I say. I can't describe to you the things he talks about in his sleep. Many a night they keep me awake."

"Do you see this sash weight?" Wolff asked Farr.

"I do," he said, with eyes shut.

"Do you still maintain that you hit or attempted to hit your father with it?"

Farr stared rigidly at the wall. He thought, If I answer I'll go crazy. *I mustn't. I mustn't.*

"He thinks he did," Wolff said. "You can see he's insane."

Herman Farr cried out as though he had been stabbed in the throat.

Farr shouted, "What about that boy I killed? You showed me his picture."

"That boy was my son," Wolff said. "He died ten years ago of terrible sickness."

Farr rose and thrust forth his wrists.

The detective shook his head. "No cuffs. We'll just call the ambulance."

Farr wildly swung his fist, catching the detective on the jaw. Wolff's chair toppled and he fell heavily to the floor. Amid the confusion and shouting by Herman Farr that he was the one who deserved hanging, Farr fled down the ill-lighted stairs with murder in his heart. In the street he flung his coins into the sky.

1953

Riding Pants

AFTER A supper of fried kidneys and brains—he was thoroughly sick of every kind of meat—Herm quickly cleared the table and piled the dirty dishes in with the oily pans in the metal sink. He planned to leave like the wind, but in the thinking of it hesitated just long enough for his father to get his tongue free.

"Herm," said the butcher in a tired but angry voice as he stroked the fat-to-bursting beef-livered cat that looked like him, "you better think of getting them fancy pants off and giving me a hand. I never heard of a boy of sixteen years wearing riding pants for all day when he should be thinking to start some steady work."

He was sitting, with the cat on his knees, in a rocker in the harshly lit kitchen behind the butcher shop where they always ate since the death of the butcher's wife. He had on—it never seemed otherwise—his white store jacket with the bloody sleeves, an apron, also blood-smeared and tight around his bulging belly, and the stupid yellow pancake of a straw hat that he wore in storm, sleet, or dead of winter. His mustache was gray, his lips thin, and his eyes, once blue as ice, were dark with fatigue.

"Not in a butcher store, Pa," Herm answered.

"What's the matter with one?" said the butcher, sitting up and looking around with exaggerated movements of the head.

Herm turned away. "Blood," he said sideways, "and chicken feathers."

The butcher slumped back in the chair.

"The Lord made certain creatures designed for man to satisfy his craving for food. Meat and fowl are full of proteins and vitamins. Somebody has to carve the animal and trim the meat clear of bone and gristle. There's no shame attached to such work. I did it my whole life long and never stole a cent from no one."

Herm considered whether there was a concealed stab in his words but he could find none. He had not stolen anything since he was thirteen and the butcher was never one to carry a long grudge.

"Meat might be good, but I don't have to like it."

"What *do* you like, Herm?"

Herm thought of his riding pants and the leather boots he was saving for. He knew, though, what his father meant—that he never stuck to a job. After he quit school he had a paper route, but the pay was chicken feed, so he left that and did lawn-mowing and cellar-cleaning, but that was not steady enough, so he quit that too, but not before he had enough to buy a pair of riding pants.

Since he could think of nothing to say, he tried to walk out, but his father called him back.

"Herm, I'm a mighty tired man since your momma died. I don't get near enough rest and I need it. I can't afford to pay a butcher's clerk because my take is not good. As a matter of fact it's bad. I'm every day losing customers for the reason that I can't give them the service they're entitled to. I know you're favorable to delivering orders but I need more of your help. You didn't like high school and asked me to sign you out. I did that, but you haven't been doing anything worthwhile for the past two months, so I decided I could use you in here. What do you say?"

"What am I supposed to say?"

"Yes or no, damn it."

"Then no, damn it," Herm said, his face flaring. "I hate butcher stores. I hate guts and chicken feathers, and I want to live my own kind of life and not yours."

And though the butcher called and called, he ran out of the store.

That night, while Herm was asleep, the butcher took his riding pants and locked them in the closet of his bedroom, but Herm guessed where they were and the next day went to the hardware store down the block, bought a skeleton key for a dime, and sneaked his riding pants out of his father's closet.

When Herm had just learned to ride he liked to go often, though he didn't always enjoy it. In the beginning he was too conscious of the horse's body, the massive frame he had to straddle, each independent rippling muscle, and the danger that he might have his head kicked in if he fell under the thundering hooves. And the worst of it was that sometimes while riding he was conscious of the interior layout of the horse, where the different cuts of round, rump, and flank were, as if the horse were stripped and labeled on a chart, posted, as a steer was, on the wall in the back of the store. He kept thinking of this the night he was out on Girlie, the roan they told him he wasn't ready for, and she had got the reins from him and turned and ran the way she wanted, shaking him away when he tried to hold her back, till she came to the stable with him on her like a sack of beans and everybody laughing. After that he had made up his mind to quit horses, and did, but one spring night he went back and took out Girlie, who, though lively, was docile to his touch and went with him everywhere and did everything he wanted; and the next morning he took his last twenty-five dollars out of the savings account and bought the riding pants, and that same night dreamed he was on a horse that dissolved under him as he rode but there he was with his riding pants on galloping away on thin air.

Herm woke to hear the sound of a cleaver on the wooden block down in the store. As it was still night he jumped out of bed frightened and searched for his riding pants. They were not in the bottom drawer where he had hidden them under a pile of his mother's clothes, so he ran to his father's closet and saw it was open and the butcher not in bed. In his pajamas Herm raced downstairs and tried to get into the butcher shop, but he was locked out and stood by the door crying as his father chopped the tightly rolled pants as if they were a bologna, with the slices falling off at each sock of the cleaver onto the floor, where the cat sniffed the uncurled remains.

He woke with the moon on his bed, rose and went on bare toes into his father's room, which looked so different now that it was no longer his mother's, and tried to find the butcher's trousers. They were hanging on a chair but without the store keys in the pockets, or the billfold, he realized blushing. Some loose change clinked and the butcher stirred in the creaking bed. Herm stood desperately still but, when his father had quieted, hung the pants and tiptoed back to his room. He pushed up the window softly, deciding he would slide down the telephone wires to the back yard and get in that way. Once within the store he would find a knife, catch the cat, and dismember it, leaving the pieces for his father to find in the morning; but not his son.

Testing the waterspout, he found it too shaky, but the wires held his weight, so he slid slowly down to the ground. Then he climbed up the sill and tried to push on the window. The butcher had latched it, not knowing Herm had loosened the screws of the latch; it gave and he was able to climb in. As his foot touched the floor, he thought he heard something scamper away but wasn't sure. Afraid to pull the light on because the Holmes police usually passed along the block this time of night, he said softly in the dark, "Here, kitty, here, kitty kitty," and felt around on the pile of burlap bags, but the cat was not where she usually slept.

He felt his way into the store and looked in the windows and they too were empty except for the pulpy blood droppings from the chickens that had hung on the hooks. He tried the paper-bag slots behind the counter and the cat was not there either, so he called again, "Here, kitty kitty kitty," but could not find it. Then he noticed the icebox door had been left ajar, which surprised him, because the butcher always yelled whenever anyone kept it open too long. He went in thinking of course the damn cat was there, poking its greedy head into the bowl of slightly sour chicken livers the butcher conveniently kept on the bottom shelf.

"Here, kitty," he whispered as he stepped into the box, and was completely unprepared when the door slammed shut behind him. He thought at first, so what, it could be opened from the inside, but then it flashed on him that the butcher had vaguely mentioned he was having trouble with the door handle and the locksmith was taking it away till tomorrow. He thought then, Oh, my God, I'm trapped here and will freeze to death, and his skull all but cracked with terror. Fumbling his way to the door, he worked frantically on the lock with his numbed fingers, wishing he had at least switched on the light from outside where the switch was, and he could feel the hole where the handle had been but was unable to get his comb or house key in to turn it. He thought if he had a screwdriver that might do it, or he could unscrew the metal plate and pick the lock apart, and for a second his heart leaped in expectation that he had taken a knife with him, but he hadn't.

Holding his head back to escape the impaling hooks, he reached his hand along the shelves on the side of the icebox and then the top shelf, cautiously feeling if the butcher had maybe left some tool around. His hand moved forward and stopped; it took him a minute to comprehend it was not going farther, because his fingers had entered a moist bony cavern; he felt suddenly shocked, as if he were touching the inside of an electric socket, but the hole was in a pig's head where an eye had been. Stepping back, he tripped over something he thought was the cat, but when he touched it, it was a bag of damp squirmy guts. As he flung it away he lost his balance and his face brushed against the clammy open side of a bleeding lamb. He sat down in the sawdust on the floor and bit his knuckles.

After a time, his fright prevented any further disgust. He tried to reason out what to do, but there was nothing he could think of, so he tried to think what time it was and could he live till his father came down to open the store. He had heard of people staying alive by beating their arms together and walking back and forth till help came, but when he tried that it tired him more, so that he began to feel very sleepy, and though he knew he oughtn't, he sat down again. He might have cried, but the tears were frozen in, and he began to wonder from afar if there was some quicker way to die. By now the icebox had filled with white mist, and from the distance, through the haze, a winged black horse moved toward him. This is it, he thought, and got up to mount it, but his foot slipped from the stirrup and he fell forward, his head bonging against the door, which opened, and he fell out on the floor.

He woke in the morning with a cutting headache and would have stayed in bed but was too hungry, so he dressed and went downstairs. He had six dollars in his pocket, all he owned in the world; he intended to have breakfast and after that pretend to go for a newspaper and never come back again.

The butcher was sitting in the rocker, sleepily stroking the cat. Neither he nor Herm spoke. There were some slices of uncooked bacon on a plate on the table and two eggs in a cardboard carton, but he could not look at them. He poured himself a cup of black coffee and drank it with an unbuttered roll.

A customer came into the store and the butcher rose with a sigh to serve her. The cat jumped off his lap and followed him. They looked like brothers. Herm turned away. This was the last he would see of either of them.

He heard a woman's resounding voice ordering some porterhouse steak and a chunk of calf's liver, nice and juicy for the dogs, and recognized her as Mrs. Gibbs, the doctor's wife, whom all the storekeepers treated like the Empress of Japan, all but kissing her rear end, especially his father, and this was what he wanted his own son to do. Then he heard the butcher go into the icebox and he shivered. The butcher came out and hacked at something with the cleaver and Herm shivered again. Finally the lady, who had talked loud and steadily, the butcher always assenting, was served. The door closed behind her corpulent bulk and the store was quiet. The butcher returned and sat in his chair, fanning his red face with his straw hat, his bald head glistening with sweat. It took him a half hour to recover every time he waited on her.

When the door opened again a few minutes later, it almost seemed as if he would not be able to get up, but Mrs. Gibbs's bellow brought him immediately to his feet. "Coming," he called with a sudden frog in his throat and hurried inside. Then Herm heard her yelling about something, but her voice was so powerful the sound blurred. He got up and stood at the door.

It was her, all right, a tub of a woman with a large hat, a meaty face, and a thick rump covered in mink.

"You stupid dope," she shouted at the butcher, "you don't even know how to wrap a package. You let the liver blood run all over my fur. My coat is ruined."

The anguished butcher attempted to apologize, but her voice beat him down. He tried to apologize with his hands and his rolling eyes and with his yellow straw hat, but she would have none of it. When he went forth with a clean rag and tried to wipe the mink, she drove him back with an angry yelp. The door shut with a bang. On the counter stood her dripping bag. Herm could see his father had tried to save paper.

He went back to the table. About a half hour later the butcher came in. His face was deathly white and he looked like a white scarecrow with a yellow straw hat. He sat in the rocker without rocking. The cat tried to jump into his lap but he wouldn't let it and sat there looking into the back yard and far away.

Herm too was looking into the back yard. He was thinking of all the places he could go where there were horses. He wanted to be where there were many and he could ride them all.

But then he got up and reached for the blood-smeared apron hanging on a hook. He looped the loop over his head and tied the strings around him. They covered where the riding pants had been, but he felt as though he still had them on.

1953

The Elevator

ELEONORA WAS an Umbrian girl whom the portiere's wife had brought up to the Agostinis' first-floor apartment after their two unhappy experiences with Italian maids, not long after they had arrived in Rome from Chicago. She was about twenty-three, thin, and with bent bony shoulders which she embarrassedly characterized as gobbo—hunchbacked. But she was not unattractive and had an interesting profile, George Agostini thought. Her full face was not so interesting; like the portinaia's, also an Umbrian, it was too broad and round, and her left brown eye was slightly wider than her right. It also looked sadder than her right eye.

She was an active girl, always moving in her noisy slippers at a half trot across the marble floors of the furnished two-bedroom apartment, getting things done without having to be told, and handling the two children very well. After the second girl was let go, George had wished they didn't have to be bothered with a full-time live-in maid. He had suggested that maybe Grace ought to go back to sharing the signora's maid—their landlady across the hall—for three hours a day, paying her on an hourly basis, as they had when they first moved in after a rough month of apartment hunting. But when George mentioned this, Grace made a gesture of tearing her red hair, so he said nothing more. It wasn't that he didn't want her to have the girl—she certainly needed one with all the time it took to shop in six or seven stores instead of one supermarket, and she was even without a washing machine, with all the kids' things to do; but George felt he wasn't comfortable with a maid always around. He didn't like people waiting on him, or watching him eat. George was heavy, and sensitive about it. He also didn't like her standing back to let him enter a room first. He didn't want her saying "Comanda" the minute he spoke her name. Furthermore he wasn't happy about the tiny maid's room the girl lived in, or her sinkless bathroom, with its cramped sitzbath and no water heater. Grace, whose people had always been much better off than his, said everybody in Italy had maids and he would get used to it. George hadn't got used to the first two girls, but he did find that Eleonora bothered him less. He liked her more as a person and felt sorry for her. She looked as though she had more on her back than her bent shoulders.

One afternoon about a week and a half after Eleonora had come to them, when George arrived home from the FAO office where he worked, during the long lunch break, Grace said the maid was in her room crying.

"What for?" George said, worried.

"I don't know."

"Didn't you ask her?"

"Sure I did, but all I could gather was that she's had a sad life. You're the linguist around here, why don't you ask her?"

"What are you so annoyed about?"

"Because I feel like a fool, frankly, not knowing what it's all about."

"Tell me what happened."

"She came out of the hall crying, about an hour ago," Grace said. "I had sent her up to the roof with a bundle of wash to do in one of the tubs up there instead of our bathtub, so she doesn't have to lug the heavy wet stuff up to the lines on the roof but can hang it out right away. Anyway, she wasn't gone five minutes before she was back crying, and that was when she answered me about her sad life. I wanted to tell her I have a sad life too. We've been in Rome close to two months and I haven't even been able to see St. Peter's. When will I ever see anything?"

"Let's talk about her," George said. "Do you know what happened in the hall?"

"I told you I didn't. After she came back, I went down to the ground floor to talk to the portinaia—she has some smattering of English—and she told me that Eleonora had been married but had lost her husband. He died or something when she was eighteen. Then she had a baby by another guy who didn't stay around long enough to see if he recognized it, and that, I suppose, is why she finds life so sad."

"Did the portinaia say whether the kid is still alive?" George asked.

"Yes. She keeps it in a convent school."

"Maybe that's what got her down," he suggested. "She thinks of her kid being away from her and then feels bad."

"So she starts to cry in the hall?"

"Why not in the hall? Why not anywhere so long as you feel like crying? Maybe I ought to talk to her."

Grace nodded. Her face was flushed, and George knew she was troubled.

He went into the corridor and knocked on the door of the maid's room. "Permesso," George said.

"Prego." Eleonora had been lying on the bed but was respectfully on her feet when George entered. He could see she had been crying. Her eyes were red and her face pale. She looked scared, and George's throat went dry.

"Eleonora, I am sorry to see you like this," he said in Italian. "Is there something either my wife or I can do to help you?"

"No, Signore," she said quietly.

"What happened to you out in the hall?"

Her eyes glistened but she held back the tears. "Nothing. One feels like crying, so she cries. Do these things have a reason?"

"Are you satisfied with conditions here?" George asked her. "Yes."

"If there is something we can do for you, I want you to tell us."

"Please don't trouble yourself about me." She lifted the bottom of her skirt, at the same time bending her head to dry her eyes on it. Her bare legs were hairy but shapely.

"No trouble at all," George said. He closed the door softly.

"Let her rest," he said to Grace.

"Damn! Just when I have to go out."

But in a few minutes Eleonora came out and went on with her work in the kitchen. They said nothing more and neither did she. Then at three George left for the office, and Grace put on her hat and went off to her Italian class and then to St. Peter's.

That night when George got home from work, Grace called him into their bedroom and said she now knew what had created all the commotion that afternoon. First the signora, after returning from an appointment with her doctor, had bounded in from across the hall, and Grace had gathered from the hot stew the old woman was in that she was complaining about their maid. The portinaia then happened to come up with the six o'clock mail, and the signora laced into her for bringing an inferior type of maid into the house. Finally, when the signora had left, the portinaia told Grace that the old lady had been the one who had made Eleonora cry. She had apparently forbidden the girl to use the elevator. She would listen behind the door, and as soon as she heard someone putting the key into the elevator lock, she would fling open her door, and if it was Eleonora, as she had suspected, she would cry out, "The key is not for you. The key is not for you." She would stand in front of the elevator, waving her arms to prevent her from entering. "Use the stairs," she cried, "the stairs are for walking. There is no need to fly, or God would have given you wings."

"Anyway," Grace went on, "Eleonora must have been outwitting her or something, because what she would do, according to the portinaia, was go upstairs to the next floor and call the elevator from there. But today the signora got suspicious and followed Eleonora up the stairs. She gave her a bad time up there. When she blew in here before, Eleonora got so scared that she ran to her room and locked the door. The signora said she would have to ask us not to give our girl the key anymore. She shook her keys at me."

"What did you say after that?" George asked.

"Nothing. I wasn't going to pick a fight with her even if I could speak the language. A month of hunting apartments was enough for me."

"We have a lease," said George.

"Leases have been broken."

"She wouldn't do it—she needs the money."

"I wouldn't bet on it," said Grace.

"It burns me up," George said. "Why shouldn't the girl use the elevator to lug the clothes up to the roof? Five floors is a long haul."

"Apparently none of the other girls does," Grace said. "I saw one of them carrying a basket of wash up the stairs on her head."

"They ought to join the acrobats' union."

"We have to stick to their customs."

"I'd still like to tell the old dame off."

"This is Rome, George, not Chicago. You came here of your own free will."

"Where's Eleonora?" George asked.

"In the kitchen."

George went into the kitchen. Eleonora was washing the children's supper dishes in a pan of hot water. When George came in she looked up with fear, the fear in her left eye shining more brightly than in her right.

"I'm sorry about the business in the hall," George said with sympathy, "but why didn't you tell me about it this afternoon?"

"I don't want to make trouble."

"Would you like me to talk to the signora?"

"No, no."

"I want you to ride in the elevator if you want to."

"Thank you, but it doesn't matter."

"Then why are you crying?"

"I'm always crying, Signore. Don't bother to notice it."

"Have it your own way," George said.

He thought that ended it, but a week later as he came into the building at lunchtime he saw Eleonora getting into the elevator with a laundry bundle. The portinaia had just opened the door for her with her key, but when she saw George she quickly ducked down the stairs to the basement. George got on the elevator with Eleonora. Her face was crimson.

"I see you don't mind using the elevator," he said.

"Ah, Signore"—she shrugged—"we must all try to improve ourselves."

"Are you no longer afraid of the signora?"

"Her girl told me the signora is sick," Eleonora said happily.

Eleonora's luck held, George learned, because the signora stayed too sick to be watching the elevator, and one day after the maid rode up in it to the roof, she met a plumber's helper working on the washtubs, Fabrizio Occhiogrosso, who asked her to go out with him on her next afternoon off. Eleonora, who had been doing little on her Thursday and Sunday afternoons off, mostly spending her time with the portinaia, readily accepted. Fabrizio, a short man with pointed shoes, a thick trunk, hairy arms, and the swarthy face of a Spaniard, came for her on his motorbike and away they would go together, she sitting on the seat behind him, holding both arms around his belly. She sat astride the seat, and when Fabrizio, after impatiently revving the Vespa, roared up the narrow street, the wind fluttered her skirt and her bare legs were exposed above the knees.

"Where do they go?" George once asked Grace.

"She says he has a room on the Via della Purificazióne."

"Do they always go to his room?"

"She says they sometimes ride to the Borghese Gardens or go to the movies."

One night in early December, after the maid had mentioned that Fabrizio was her fiancé now, George and Grace stood at their living-room window looking down into the street as Eleonora got on the motorbike and it raced off out of sight.

"I hope she knows what she's doing," he muttered in a worried tone. "I don't much take to Fabrizio."

"So long as she doesn't get pregnant too soon. I'd hate to lose her."

George was silent for a time, then remarked, "How responsible do you suppose we are for her morals?"

"Her morals?" laughed Grace. "Are you batty?"

"I never had a maid before," George said.

"This is our third."

"I mean in principle."

"Stop mothering the world," said Grace.

Then one Sunday after midnight Eleonora came home on the verge of fainting. What George had thought might happen had. Fabrizio had taken off into the night on his motorbike. When they had arrived at his room early that evening, a girl from Perugia was sitting on his bed. The portiere had let her in after she had showed him an engagement ring and a snapshot of her and Fabrizio in a rowboat. When Eleonora demanded to know who this one was, the plumber's helper did not bother to explain but ran down the stairs, mounted his Vespa, and drove away. The girl disappeared. Eleonora wandered the streets for hours, then returned to Fabrizio's room. The portiere told her that he had been back, packed his valise, and left for Perugia, the young lady riding on the back seat.

Eleonora dragged herself home. When she got up the next morning to make breakfast she was a skeleton of herself and the gobbo looked like a hill. She said nothing and they asked nothing. What Grace wanted to know she later got from the portinaia. Eleonora no longer ran through her chores but did everything wearily, each movement like flowing stone. Afraid she would collapse, George advised her to take a week off and go home. He would pay her salary and give her something extra for the bus.

"No, Signore," she said dully, "it is better for me to work." She said, "I have been through so much, more is not noticeable."

But then she had to notice it. One afternoon she absent-mindedly picked up Grace's keys and got on the elevator with a bag of clothes to be washed. The signora, having recovered her health, was waiting for her. She flung open the door, grabbed Eleonora by the arm as she was about to close the elevator door, and dragged her out.

"Whore," she cried, "don't steal the privileges of your betters. Use the stairs."

Grace opened the apartment door to see what the shouting was about, and Eleonora, with a yowl, rushed past her. She locked herself in her room and sat there all afternoon without moving. She wept copiously. Grace, on the verge of exhaustion, could do nothing with her. When George came home from work that evening he tried to coax her out, but she shouted at him to leave her alone.

George was thoroughly fed up. "I've had enough," he said. He thought out how he would handle the signora, then told Grace he was going across the hall.

"Don't do it," she shouted, but he was already on his way.

George knocked on the signora's door. She was a woman of past sixty-five, a widow, always dressed in black. Her face was long and gray, but her eyes were bright black. Her husband had left her these two apartments across the hall from each other that he had owned outright. She lived in the smaller and rented the other, furnished, at a good rent. George knew that this was her only source of income. She had once been a schoolteacher.

"Scusi, Signora," said George, "I have come with a request."

"Prego." She asked him to sit.

George took a chair near the terrace window. "I would really appreciate it, Signora, if you will let our girl go into the elevator with the laundry when my wife sends her up to the tubs. She is not a fortunate person and we would like to make her life a little easier for her."

"I am sorry," answered the signora with dignity, "but I can't permit her to enter the elevator."

"She's a good girl and you have upset her very much."

"Good," said the signora, "I am glad. She must remember her place, even if you don't. This is Italy, not America. You must understand that we have to live with these people long after you, who come to stay for a year or two, return to your own country."

"Signora, she does no harm in the elevator. We are not asking you to ride with her. After all, the elevators are a convenience for all who live in this house and therefore ought to be open for those who work for us here."

"No," said the signora.

"Why not think it over and let me know your answer tomorrow? I assure you I wouldn't ask this if I didn't think it was important."

"I have thought it over," she said stiffly, "and I have given you the same answer I will give tomorrow."

George got up. "In that case," he said, "if you won't listen to reason, I consider my lease with you ended. You have had your last month's rent. We will move on the first of February."

The signora looked as if she had just swallowed a fork.

"The lease is a sacred contract," she said, trembling. "It is against the law to break it."

"I consider that you have already broken it," George said quietly, "by creating conditions that make it very hard for my family to function in this apartment. I am simply acknowledging a situation that already exists."

"If you move out, I will take a lawyer and make you pay for the whole year."

"A lawyer will cost you half the rent he might collect," George answered. "And if my lawyer is better than yours, you will get nothing and owe your lawyer besides."

"Oh, you Americans," said the signora bitterly. "How well I understand you. Your money is your dirty foot with which you kick the world. Who wants you here," she cried, "with your soaps and toothpastes and your dirty gangster movies!"

"I would like to remind you that my origin is Italian," George said.

"You have long ago forgotten your origin," she shouted.

George left the apartment and went back to his own.

"I'll bet you did it," Grace greeted him. Her face was ashen.

"I did," said George.

"I'll bet you fixed us good. Oh, you ought to be proud. How will we ever find another apartment in the dead of winter with two kids?"

She left George and locked herself in the children's bedroom. They were both awake and got out of bed to be with her.

George sat in the living room in the dark. I did it, he was thinking.

After a while the doorbell rang. He got up and put on the light. It was the signora and she looked unwell. She entered the living room at George's invitation and sat there with great dignity.

"I am sorry I raised my voice to a guest in my house," she said. Her mouth was loose and her eyes glistened.

"I am sorry I offended you," George said.

She did not speak for a while, then said, "Let the girl use the elevator." The signora broke into tears.

When she had dried her eyes, she said, "You have no idea how bad things have become since the war. The girls are disrespectful. Their demands are endless, it is impossible to keep up with them. They talk back, they take every advantage. They crown themselves with privileges. It is a struggle to keep them in their place. After all, what have we left when we lose our self-respect?" The signora wept heartbrokenly.

After she had gone, George stood at the window. Across the street a beggar played a flute.

I didn't do it well, George thought. He felt depressed.

On her afternoon off Eleonora rode up and down on the elevator.

1957

CHRONOLOGY

NOTE ON THE TEXTS

NOTES

Chronology

1914   Bernard Malamud born April 26 in Brooklyn, New York, the first child of Max (Mendel) Malamud and Bertha (Brucha) Fidelman. (Max, born 1885, a poor, uneducated grocer, had come to America in 1905 from a Jewish shtetl near Kamianets-Podilsky in Ukraine, then part of the Russian Empire, fleeing from pogroms and the threat of conscription to join two of his brothers who had established themselves in Brooklyn. Born to a somewhat better-off family, the daughter of a *shochet* [a ritual slaughterer of meat], Bertha, born 1888, left Kamianets-Podilskyi in 1909 to join her brother in America, and married Max the following year. They lived first on Flushing Avenue, then above and behind a series of unsuccessful grocery stores in the Brooklyn neighborhoods of Williamsburg and Flatbush. A son had been delivered stillborn in 1912.)

1917   Brother Eugene born in May. Family believes that damage to mother's left leg was due to the birth of one of her sons; during his boyhood Malamud would feel guilty about causing the injury. Mother is increasingly depressed, reclusive, and overweight, and probably suffers from schizophrenia. Yiddish is the primary language spoken at home, with occasional Russian.

1919   With a partner, father buys grocery on 15th Avenue in the Borough Park section of Brooklyn, the largest and fanciest of his stores, but is forced to sell within a year after partner takes off with the money that had been invested. Malamud enters kindergarten and his English rapidly improves.

1920–23   Attends elementary school on Cortelyou Road in Brooklyn where he first finds access to books; reads *Robinson Crusoe, A Tale of Two Cities,* and *Treasure Island,* as well as dime novels and Horatio Alger's boys' adventure books. At home, would listen through living room window to piano-playing across the street: "I was moved by the music being played by someone in one of the houses nearby, perhaps a girl my age, and was hungry to hear more of it." Enrolls in the third grade at P.S. 181, an outstanding new school with a middle-class and largely Jewish student body, to which Malamud traveled via trolley five miles every day on his own. Thrives and is challenged at the school, which he will recall as being "the most important school in my life," and displays a talent for telling and writing stories. Avidly goes to the movies and is enchanted by silent films. Catches pneumonia at age nine and is close to being pronounced dead when an injection of digitalis restores his heartbeat; in celebration of his recovery, father buys him *The Book of Knowledge*, a twenty-volume children's encyclopedia.

1924–26   After several of his grocery ventures have failed, father settles in to operating a German-style delicatessen at 1111 Gravesend Avenue (now McDonald Avenue), so called for its proximity to Washington Cemetery. Brother Eugene shows early signs of lifelong mental illness, and Malamud, sometimes reluctantly, takes a parental role toward him, especially during Eugene's unhappy experience at school, where he is mocked and bullied.

1927   Turns thirteen but is not given a bar mitzvah ceremony. Returns from school one afternoon to find his mother on the kitchen floor after she had swallowed a can of disinfectant in a suicide attempt. She is committed to Kings County Hospital; father manages to pay for her to be sent to a private mental hospital in Queens. Malamud works part-time in father's store.

1928   Enters Erasmus Hall High School in Flatbush, where he will edit the school magazine and act in the school's theater group.

1929   Mother dies in May in mental hospital; Malamud is not told the cause of death but in later years he will suspect suicide. His last view of mother was her waving through the window of the institution.

1931   Father marries Liza (Elizabeth) Merov. "Neither of the boys had any affection for their step-mother," Malamud would recall in 1951. The grocery store remains barely profitable: "It was not very good anywhere until the Depression, then it was bad."

1932–35   Wins Richard Young prize in 1932 for autobiographical essay "Life—From Behind a Counter," finishing second in the national Scholastic Awards. After graduating from Erasmus Hall, enters City College in Manhattan. Is praised by his professor Theodore Goodman for his stories, including an early version of "The Bill," which is later included in *The Magic Barrel*. Works part-time, including summers, at hotels in the Catskills.

1936–37 Graduates from City College with a B.A. in 1936. Works for $4.50 a day as teacher-in-training in New York public schools, but over the next two years twice fails teaching exams to become a permanent substitute teacher, first because of oversimplifying his writing style, then apparently because of his slight lisp. Takes out government loan to pay for graduate study in English at Columbia University.

1938–39 Works sporadically, taking odd jobs in factories and department stores and tutoring German-Jewish refugees in English (which will provide subject matter for story "The German Refugee," first published in 1963). Passes civil service examinations that lead to work as postal clerk and letter carrier. Receives first temporary teaching position as a substitute at Lafayette High School in Brooklyn in 1939.

1940 Accepts job as a clerk for U.S. Census Bureau in Washington, D.C., and is soon promoted; writes at his office in afternoons after his work is finished. Begins to submit short sketches of real life to the *Washington Post*, and for the first time is paid for his writing when several are published in column "The Post Impressionist" (including "The Refugee," "Sunday in the Park," "The People's Gallery," "Vacancy"). Writes story "Armistice." Returns to Brooklyn to teach at his former school, Erasmus Hall High, at evening classes there and at other New York City schools, while writing short stories during the day.

1942 Works on long autobiographical novel, "The Light Sleeper," about a young man's loneliness and despair. At a party in February, meets Ann deChiara (b. 1917), from New Rochelle, New York, of Italian immigrant parentage, who had graduated from Cornell University three years earlier with a degree in French; they soon become romantically involved, though during their long courtship Malamud worries about how he can combine marriage with a writer's life. Is exempted from military service as a result of stomach condition and teaching profession, though Eugene was called up for active service over four years, mainly in the Pacific, until discharged as a result of battle fatigue. Malamud moves out of family home to lodgings in

Flatbush. Receives M.A. from Columbia after submitting thesis, "Thomas Hardy's Reputation as Poet in American Periodicals." Writes story "Spring Rain." Continues teaching in the evening, though he also works for a short time in a war materials factory. Briefly consults a psychiatrist.

1943–44   Writes posthumously published story "The Grocery Store" in 1943, the year his short stories are first published: "Benefit Performance" in *Threshold* (February); "The Place is Different Now," a forerunner of *The Assistant*, in *American Prefaces* (Spring); "Steady Customer" in *New Threshold* (August); and "The Literary Life of Laban Goldman" in *Assembly* (November).

1945   Marries Ann on November 6 in a civil ceremony at the New York Society for Ethical Culture. Is estranged from father because he has married a Gentile woman; Ann's father also refuses to receive them in his house for more than two years. Moves from Brooklyn to 1 King Street in Greenwich Village.

1947   On the basis of his published work, receives invitation to spend summer working on his novel at Yaddo artists' colony at Saratoga Springs, New York, but is unable to accept for family and economic reasons; Ann, who had worked for the advertising agency Young & Rubicam, is now pregnant with their first child, and will no longer be contributing to the family finances. Birth of son, Paul Francis, in October, which brings about reconciliation with father.

1948   At Malamud's urging, Eugene undergoes psychoanalytic treatment for anxiety, depression, and paranoia and visits the Malamuds weekly, struggling with employment while still living with father and stepmother. Malamud completes "The Light Sleeper" and his agent, Diarmuid Russell of Russell & Volkening, begins sending it to prospective publishers. Teaches evening classes at Harlem Evening High School, but to support his family must now also teach during the day at Chelsea Vocational High School.

1949   In response to the opportunities offered by the G.I. Bill, Ann types more than two hundred standard letters for Malamud in application for posts in the teaching of literature. One of the few replies is from Oregon State College in Corvallis, Oregon, a state-endowed institution of six thousand students providing practical education in agriculture in particular, with the liberal arts constituting merely "the Lower Division." Appointed in July, he is allowed to teach freshman composition but not literature because he lacks a Ph.D. Moves family to Oregon, where the landscape is a revelation to him. Teaches three days a week for an initial annual salary of $3,600; spends the other four days writing.

1950　Works on a novel combining baseball and myth that would become *The Natural.* Publishes "The Cost of Living," story about a struggling grocery store in Brooklyn, in *Harper's Bazaar* in March and sends copy to his father. Publishes "The Prison" in *Commentary* (September) and "The First Seven Years" in *Partisan Review* (September–October); these stories are admired by Harcourt, Brace and Company editor Robert Giroux, who writes Malamud to show interest in publishing a novel and a collection of short stories.

1951　Publishes "The Death of Me" in *World Review* (April), and "The Bill" and "An Apology" in *Commentary* (April and November). Burns manuscript of "A Light Sleeper" after it has been rejected by numerous publishers: "My only triumph was in completing it after so many years of toil." Completes *The Natural* in October, having worked through only two main drafts, fewer than those of his later, more continuously laborious process of revision. Writes on October 15 to brother Eugene, who is increasingly delusional, paranoid, and suicidal, that he felt he had to leave New York "to be an effective man, to provide for my family and do my work—the writing I had to do. . . . That this should hurt you was, as you describe it, a bad break." Eugene is committed in early November to Kings County Hospital, the facility where their mother had been taken after her suicide attempt in 1927; he is transferred to Kings Park State Hospital and then to Kings Park Veterans' Memorial Hospital on Long Island, where he is diagnosed as schizophrenic.

1952　Malamud receives telegram from Giroux on January 7 that *The Natural* has been accepted by Harcourt, Brace and Company. Daughter Janna Ellen born January 19. To congratulate the family father sends $350 toward the purchase of a washing machine; not long afterward, in March, he suffers a heart attack, though at first he tells

Malamud that he is taking bed rest merely because of a cold. Eugene is declared an incompetent person by order of the New York Supreme Court in May. Malamud takes train cross-country to see his father and visit Eugene in hospital in June. Publishes "The Loan" in July in *Commentary*. Eugene is allowed home in July; hereafter he writes to his brother weekly or fortnightly for twenty years and just as regularly Malamud replies. Under the editorship of Giroux, *The Natural*, dedicated to Malamud's father, is published in July to mixed reviews. In the summer, Malamud begins novel "The Broken Snow," later "The Man Nobody Could Lift," about a schizophrenic. Earns $1,225 in income from royalties, rising to $2,700 the following year.

1953   Publishes "The Girl of My Dreams" in *American Mercury* in January. Submits draft of "The Man Nobody Could Lift" to Giroux, who in November advises against publication on grounds of overall quality (the first chapter will be published posthumously in 1997 as "A Confession of Murder" in *The Complete Stories of Bernard Malamud*, edited by Giroux).

1954   Father dies of a heart attack in March. In April, Malamud begins a novel about a Brooklyn grocery store, with working title "The Apprentice," that will become *The Assistant*. Receives promotion to assistant professor at Oregon State and is allowed to teach literature. Publishes "The Magic Barrel" in *Partisan Review* in November.

1955   Continues working steadily on *The Assistant*; as with all of his subsequent novels, the manuscript goes through multiple drafts and repetitions since revision was for Malamud the essential life of a writer: "I have succeeded in afterthought. I connect revisions with reformation." Thinks of himself as one of what William James called "twice-born souls" who struggle to establish themselves from a poor start through second chances: "Some are born whole; others must seek this blessed state in a struggle to achieve order. That is no loss to speak of; ultimately such seeking becomes the subject matter of fiction." Publishes under pen name Peter Lumm a children's novel, *Kim of Korea*, coauthored with Faith Norris, a colleague at Oregon State who wrote the first, main version that was then revised by Malamud. Publishes "The Mourners" in *Discovery*

(January) and "The Angel Levine" in *Commentary* (December). Having lived in rented houses since arriving in Oregon, buys house at 445 North 31st Street in Corvallis. Critic Leslie Fiedler publishes a brief appreciative essay on *The Natural* in *Folio*, which he sends to Malamud: "I shan't forget," Malamud would later write, "that he appreciated the quality of my imaginative writing before anyone else wrote about it."

1956 Under contract to Harcourt, Brace, submits *The Assistant* in spring but it is rejected, as it would be by Viking. Sends manuscript to Robert Giroux (now at Farrar, Straus & Cudahy), who is shocked by Harcourt's rejection. Receives $4,000 *Partisan Review*–Rockefeller Foundation fellowship in fiction and obtains sabbatical from Oregon State; takes family to live and write in Rome from autumn until the following summer. Departs by ship from New York in late August, and receives word on transatlantic crossing from Giroux that Farrar, Straus & Cudahy will publish *The Assistant*. Arrives in Rome, and the family settles into a two-bedroom apartment near Piazza Bologna: "Italy unrolled like a foreign film; what was going on before my eyes seemed close to unreality." Publishes "A Summer's Reading" in *The New Yorker* (September 22) and "Take Pity" in *America* (September 25).

1957 Travels throughout Italy and visits Austria and France. Makes final revisions to page proofs of *The Assistant*, which is published in April by Farrar, Straus & Cudahy to favorable reviews. Writes posthumously published story "The Elevator." Returns with family to the United States in the summer. In December, begins writing *A New Life*, novel loosely based on his experience at Oregon State. Earns $6,500 this year, including $2,800 in royalties.

1958 Publishes "The Last Mohican" in *Partisan Review* (Spring) and "Behold the Key" in *Commentary* (May), both included in *The Magic Barrel*, collection of thirteen short stories dedicated to Eugene and published by Farrar, Straus & Cudahy in May. Receives Rosenthal Foundation Award from the National Institute of Arts and Letters and the Daroff Memorial Fiction Award of the Jewish Book Council of America for *The Assistant*. Spends two months at Yaddo on a summer fellowship, working on *A New Life*. Promoted to associate professor at Oregon State "through his distinction as a writer," he no longer has to teach freshman composition and can focus his teaching on literature and creative writing instead.

1959   Publishes "The Maid's Shoes" in *Partisan Review* (Winter). Wins National Book Award for *The Magic Barrel*. Receives Ford Foundation grant of $15,000 providing two years' time to devote himself to his writing; refuses invitation to teach at Harvard because it would violate the terms of the award.

1960–61 Works steadily on *A New Life* throughout 1960 and completes the novel early the following year. Eugene is again hospitalized, as suicidal, in Brooklyn State Hospital, from early 1961 to August. Malamud teaches creative writing in summer school at Harvard. Largely through the initiative of the poet Howard Nemerov, obtains teaching post in Division of Language and Literature at Bennington College in Bennington, Vermont, a progressive liberal arts college for women (until 1969, when it becomes coeducational), at a salary of around $8,000. Arrives with family in Bennington in September. Publishes *A New Life* with Farrar, Straus & Cudahy in October. Publishes "Idiots First" in *Commentary* in December.

1962   Publishes "Still Life" in *Partisan Review* (Winter). Searching for the subject of his next novel, spends several months reading about social injustice in the United States.

1963   Publishes "Suppose a Wedding" in *New Statesman* (February 8), "The Jewbird" and "Black Is My Favorite Color" in *Reporter* (April 11 and July 18), "Life Is Better than Death" in *Esquire* (May), "Naked Nude" in *Playboy* (August), "The German Refugee" in *The Saturday Evening Post* (September 14), and "A Choice of Profession" in *Commentary* (September); these are among the twelve stories he collects in *Idiots First*, published by Farrar, Straus & Company in the fall. Travels to England and Italy. In the fall, begins *The Fixer*, novel about anti-Semitism drawing on the Dreyfus affair and the case of Mendel Beilis, a Jew arrested in Kiev in 1911 on false charges of having committed a ritual murder of a Christian boy.

1964   Is elected in February as a member of the National Institute of Arts and Letters.

1965   Completes first draft of *The Fixer*. In summer, travels in Spain, France, and, to research *The Fixer*, the Soviet Union.

1966   Completes *The Fixer* in early spring after more laborious revising than ever before: "The book nearly killed me." Moves to Cambridge, Massachusetts, for two years after being named visiting lecturer in the English Department at Harvard.

1967   Wins both National Book Award and Pulitzer Prize for *The Fixer*. Is elected member of American Academy of Arts and Sciences. *A Malamud Reader*, anthology with an introduction by Philip Rahv, is published by Farrar, Straus & Giroux. Malamud makes $230,000 in gross income, compared to $20,000 per year in the early 1960s.

1968   Visits Israel in March. Returns to Bennington after Harvard position ends. Buys 1930s colonial-style house on two-and-a-half acres at 11 Catamount Lane, Old Bennington, at cost of $35,000. Publishes "A Pimp's Revenge" in *Playboy* (September), "My Son the Murderer" in *Esquire* (November), "An Exorcism" in *Harper's* (December), and both "Man in the Drawer" and "Pictures of the Artist" (later "Pictures of Fidelman") in *The Atlantic* (April and December). Refuses offer to travel to the set of the film adaptation of *The Fixer* in Hungary, partly because the filmmakers tell him they do not wish to make the movie too Jewish; released in December, the film (directed by John Frankenheimer and starring Alan Bates) makes him more financially secure, earning him around $200,000.

1969   Begins novel *The Tenants*, set against the background of race relations in the 1960s. Publishes with Farrar, Straus & Giroux *Pictures of Fidelman: An Exhibition*: inspired by his stay in Italy, it is a picaresque novel in six linked stories, including one previously published in *The Magic Barrel* and two in *Idiots First*. Receives O. Henry Prize for "Man in the Drawer," story inspired by his trip to the Soviet Union. Writes screenplay for *The Assistant* but option not taken up. Rents apartment in Manhattan; the Malamuds will increasingly spend the fall and winter in New York City. Begins giving his papers to the Library of Congress.

1970   Begins writing in notebooks labeled "The Juggler," working title for the novel that will become *Dubin's Lives*. Film adaptation *The Angel Levine*, directed by Ján Kadár and starring Zero Mostel and Harry Belafonte, is released in July.

1971   *The Tenants* is published in the fall by Farrar, Straus &

Giroux. Malamud travels with Ann in the fall to London, where they live for five months.

1972   Purchases two-bedroom apartment in Lincoln Towers complex on Manhattan's Upper West Side. Publishes "God's Wrath" and "Talking Horse" in *The Atlantic* (February and April), "The Letter" in *Esquire* (August), and "The Silver Crown" in *Playboy* (December).

1973   Begins writing "The Juggler" in February: the first draft, instead of taking the usual one year, takes three. Settles for $39,000 in reluctant lawsuit with Elliott Gould and associates over bankruptcy in relation to proposed filming of *A New Life*. Publishes "Notes from a Lady at a Dinner Party" in *Harper's* (February), "In Retirement" in *The Atlantic* (March), and "Rembrandt's Hat" in *The New Yorker* (March), all of which are collected in a volume of eight short stories, *Rembrandt's Hat*, published by Farrar, Straus & Giroux in March. Eugene Malamud dies of heart attack, October 30, aged 55: he had carried on living above his father's old store, with stepmother Liza until her death in 1967 and thereafter alone. Malamud wrote the funeral eulogy ("He was a wounded man trying to keep going") but did not deliver it in person because he is admitted to hospital on October 31, with suspected heart problems of his own.

1974   Is interviewed by his friend Daniel Stern for *The Paris Review*'s "Writers at Work" series.

1976   Marriage of daughter Janna to David Smith. Writes in notebook on 21 October "[Saul] Bellow gets Nobel Prize, I win $24.25 in poker."

1977   In February, receives annual B'nai B'rith Jewish Heritage Award. Publishes excerpts from forthcoming *Dubin's Lives* in *The New Yorker* (April 18 and 25) and *Playboy* (December).

1978   Publishes excerpt from *Dubin's Lives* in *The Atlantic* (January). Completes *Dubin's Lives* in August. Makes visit with Ann to Hungary, arranged by translator and scholar Tamas Ungvari. Signs five hundred copies of *The Fixer* for Hungarian admirers; the Hungarian reception of the novel now gives him back his belief in that book.

1979   Publishes *Dubin's Lives* with a first printing of fifty thousand copies from Farrar, Straus & Giroux, his largest ever, and an advance of $150,000. Begins two-year term as president of PEN American Center, concerning himself in particular with writers' freedom throughout the world, the state of the publishing industry, and the provision of books within prisons in the United States.

1980   Publishes "A Wig" in *The Atlantic* (January). Begins novel *God's Grace*. Receives the Governor's Award for Excellence in the Arts from the Vermont Council on the Arts.

1981   Receives Brandeis Creative Arts Award. Awarded one-year fellowship of the Center for Advanced Study in the Behavioral Sciences at Stanford University; arrives with Ann in California in September. Increasingly concerned about his history of angina, decides on three-vessel coronary bypass operation at Stanford, requiring two weeks' hospitalization and two months' convalescence, to be delayed until following year so he can finish *God's Grace*.

1982   Completes *God's Grace*, published in the summer by Farrar, Straus & Giroux. Undergoes bypass surgery on March 10 and suffers a stroke on the operating table. When coming round, he is asked his name and age, and replies "William Dubin, 57." He is 68 and the name he gives is that of the biographer protagonist of *Dubin's Lives*. By December, though he has recovered many of his functions, including use of his right arm, he experiences difficulty in reading, handwriting, memory, and spatial awareness. He has to relearn much vocabulary and reports feeling "diminished," registering an increased inability in social life to get people involved with him. His ability to write creatively is thereafter impaired.

1983   In May, receives Gold Medal for Fiction from American Academy and Institute of Arts and Letters. Publishes "The Model" in *The Atlantic* (August), the only new story to be included in *The Stories of Bernard Malamud*, his selection of his shorter fiction, which is brought out by Farrar, Straus & Giroux in the fall.

1984   Publishes brief stories "Alma Redeemed" in *Commentary* (July), and "In Kew Gardens" in *Partisan Review* (Fall–Winter), on Alma Mahler and Virginia Woolf, respectively, written as if through the interests of Dubin, his fictional biographer. Film of *The Natural*, starring Robert Redford, earns him $125,000, but he does not admire the adaptation, particularly the changed, more optimistic ending.

Determined to write a new novel, he struggles to begin draft of *The People*, about a Jewish peddler who becomes chief of an American Indian tribe in the Pacific Northwest. Concerned about future, has worth of his total estate estimated at about $1,200,000. Prepares memoir "Long Work, Short Life," delivered at Bennington College in the Ben Belitt memorial lectureship series, October 13.

1985   Publishes "Zora's Noise" in *GQ* (January) and "A Lost Grave" in *Esquire* (May). Wins Premio Mondello, Italian literary prize. Struggling still to write *The People* (which was posthumously published in draft state by the estate with most of his uncollected stories in 1989), he reads opening chapters in July to Philip Roth, who later wrote: "He wanted to be told that what he had painfully composed while enduring all his burdens was something more than he himself must have known it to be in his heart."

1986   Dies of heart attack, March 18, in apartment in Lincoln Towers. Last note to self, found by his son Paul on writing desk, repeats four times "Don't be fragile." Is cremated; ashes buried in Mount Auburn Cemetery, Cambridge, Massachusetts.

Note on the Texts

This volume contains Bernard Malamud's novels *The Natural* (1952) and *The Assistant* (1957), twenty stories published from 1943 to 1959, and six works of short fiction (five stories and the first chapter of an abandoned novel) first published after Malamud's death in 1986.

Malamud began planning the novel that would become *The Natural* in the late 1940s, when he was living in New York City, and started writing the first of the novel's two primary drafts early in 1950, not long after he moved to Corvallis, Oregon, to teach at Oregon State University. Later that year, in November, he was contacted by Robert Giroux, then an editor at Harcourt, Brace and Company, who had read Malamud's stories in periodicals and had learned from the critic Alfred Kazin that Malamud was working on a novel about baseball. Writing that "we prefer to publish a writer, rather than a book," Giroux expressed interest in acquiring the novel and a collection of stories. Malamud completed *The Natural* in October 1951 and submitted it to Harcourt, Brace, which accepted it for publication on January 7, 1952, and offered suggestions for revisions, only some of which Malamud agreed to. *The Natural* was published in July 1952. It was later included in the 1964 Modern Library edition *Two Novels: The Natural and The Assistant*; the text differs slightly from that of the Harcourt, Brace edition because of a few corrections, though errors were also introduced, such as the omission of two unambiguous section breaks. The novel was later published in England by Eyre and Spottiswoode in 1963. The text printed here is taken from the 1952 Harcourt, Brace and Company edition of *The Natural*.

The Assistant has its origins in "The Cost of Living," a short story first published in 1950, which is set in a Brooklyn grocery store modeled on the shop run by Malamud's father. In 1954, not long after his father's death, Malamud started to write "The Apprentice," the working title of the novel that would become *The Assistant*, and over the next two years he wrote and revised several drafts. After he finished the novel he submitted it in the spring of 1956 to Harcourt, Brace, where he was still under contract, though Giroux had left the firm and was now an editor at Farrar, Straus & Cudahy. Harcourt rejected it—"on the whole," wrote vice-president John H. McCallum to Malamud's agent, Diarmuid Russell, "we find it more unsatisfying than satisfying; we believe it would not be a step upward from THE NATURAL"—as did Viking Press. Giroux, quite surprised at Harcourt's rejection, was sent the manuscript, which was accepted for publication by Farrar, Straus & Cudahy in the fall of 1956. It was published in April of the following year. Malamud did not subsequently revise *The Assistant*, though it was included in the 1964 Modern Library edition *Two Novels* and the omnibus volume *A Malamud Reader* (New York: Farrar, Straus & Giroux, 1967). It was published in England by Eyre and Spottiswoode in 1959. The 1957 Farrar, Straus & Cudahy edition contains the text printed here. The text of "A Note to My Norwegian Readers on *The Assistant*," written for the novel's 1963 translation into Norwegian, is taken from *Talking Horse: Bernard Malamud on Life and Work*, eds. Alan Cheuse and Nicholas Delbanco (New York: Columbia University Press, 1996).

Most of Malamud's short stories written in the 1940s and 1950s were first published in periodicals, then collected in the volumes *The Magic Barrel* (1958) and *Idiots First* (1963). The texts of the stories later included in *The Stories of Bernard Malamud* (1983), a collection spanning his entire career, contain light revisions by Malamud. These changes are sentence-level revisions that correct errors, improve occasionally awkward phrasing, add a clarifying detail, or eliminate verbal redundancy. In the few instances where he cuts more than a single word, Malamud deletes only a short sentence.

In the section "Twenty Stories," the texts are taken from the final version of a story or, for the five uncollected stories included in this section, the posthumous editions *The People, and Uncollected Stories* (1989), edited by Malamud's longtime editor, Robert Giroux, or *The Complete Stories of Bernard Malamud* (1997). Listed below are the sources and other information about the publication history of the stories, keyed to the following abbreviations:

MB   *The Magic Barrel.* New York: Farrar, Straus & Cudahy, 1958.
IF   *Idiots First.* New York: Farrar, Straus & Company, 1963.
SBM   *The Stories of Bernard Malamud.* New York: Farrar, Straus & Giroux, 1983.
TP   *The People and Uncollected Stories*, ed. Robert Giroux. New York: Farrar, Straus & Giroux, 1989.

Benefit Performance. *TP.* First published in *Threshold*, February 1943.
The Place Is Different Now. *TP.* First published in *American Prefaces*, Spring 1943.
Steady Customer. *The Complete Stories of Bernard Malamud* (New York: Farrar, Straus & Giroux, 1997). First published in *New Threshold*, August 1943.
The Literary Life of Laban Goldman. *TP.* First published in *Assembly*, November 1943.

The Cost of Living. *SBM*. First published in *Harper's Bazaar*, March 1950. Included in *IF*.

The Prison. *MB*. First published in *Commentary*, September 1950.

The First Seven Years. *SBM*. First published in *Partisan Review*, September–October 1950. Included in *MB*.

The Death of Me. *SBM*. First published in *World Review*, April 1951. Included in *IF*.

The Bill. *SBM*. First published in *Commentary*, April 1951. Included in *MB*.

An Apology. *TP* (incorrectly dated 1957). First published in *Commentary*, November 1951.

The Loan. *SBM*. First published in *Commentary*, July 1952. Included in *MB*.

The Girl of My Dreams. *MB*. First published in *The American Mercury*, January 1953.

The Magic Barrel. *SBM*. First published in *Partisan Review*, November 1954. Included in *MB*.

The Mourners. *SBM*. First published in *Discovery*, January 1955. Included in MB.

Angel Levine. *SBM*. First published (as "The Angel Levine") in *Commentary*, December 1955. MB.

A Summer's Reading. *MB*. First published in *The New Yorker*, September 22, 1956.

Take Pity. *SBM*. First published in *America*, September 26, 1956. Included in *MB*.

The Lady of the Lake. *MB*.

Behold the Key. *MB*. Published in *Commentary*, May 1958.

The Maid's Shoes. *SBM*. First published in *Partisan Review*, Winter 1959. Included in *IF*.

In 1989, six previously unpublished works of fiction written by Malamud in the 1940s and 1950s were gathered in *The People and Uncollected Stories*. Five of these—"Armistice" (1940), "Spring Rain" (1942), "The Grocery Store" (1943), "Riding Pants" (1953), and "The Elevator" (1957)—are short stories. "A Confession of Murder" was not conceived by Malamud as a story but was the first chapter of an abandoned novel, with working titles "The Broken Snow" and "The Man Nobody Could Lift," that Malamud drafted in 1952–53. The texts of these six works printed here are taken from the 1989 edition of *The People and Uncollected Stories*.

This volume presents the texts of the original printings chosen for inclusion here, but it does not attempt to reproduce nontextual features of their typographic design. The texts are presented without change, except for the correction of typographical errors. Spelling, punctuation, and capitalization are often expressive features and are not altered, even when inconsistent or irregular. The following is a list of typographical errors corrected, cited by page and line number: 18.18–19, and baby; 23.4, the worm's; 36.23, first place; 57.21, half-moon; 61.13, cross-eyed; 66.28, Flores' (and *passim*); 82.31, anymore; 112.6–7, which ever; 121.12, Cubs half; 128.15, Knights fan; 132.32–33, appeal that you; 153.31–32, orphan's home; 155.34, Iris' (and *passim*); 177.19, PA; 210.9, *Don Quixote*"?; 216.31, yet You; 217.19, half-past; 224.4, presence complained; 236.20–21, said, "That's; 238.12, happen.; 241.3, Papadopolous' door.; 250.38, brassières (and *passim*); 251.2, cents spending; 281.39, Helen said,; 282.34, *Napoleon*"?; 285.11, I like; 294.21, time?'; 306.6, Frank squirming; 306.21, startled,; 306.22, "But; 347.23, fright, "Did; 358.2, half hour; 358.13, cheese cake; 365.10, figure it out; 380.26, home papa?; 383.15, half hour; 384.18, Christ sake; 387.14–15, with with a; 413.4, who, as; 413.25, characters, who; 455.11, embarrassment, "What; 462.17–18, buy television; 514.14, years college; 515.8, Rothschild's a daughter; 537.31, was in; 548.4, everytime; 550.6, breast; 558.30–31, dollars insurance; 559.7, care on; 566.38, mir,"; 578.7, 'eestorical; 578.36, cedars; 581.24, too, (which; 583.36, major domo; 584.24, journey, Freedom; 586.36, evening was; 587.31, were Napoleon; 590.13, long; with; 591.35, away) her; 592.9, locomotive moved; 593.3, candalabrum; 598.23, Piazza Navone; 613.31, my Ph.D; 613.32, children.; 621.40, courteously;; 651.24, nostils; 678.10, calves' liver.

Notes

In the notes below, the reference numbers denote page and line of this volume (the line count includes chapter headings). Biblical quotations are keyed to the King James Version. Quotations from Shakespeare are keyed to *The Riverside Shakespeare*, ed. G. Blakemore Evans (Boston: Houghton Mifflin, 1974). For more biographical information than is contained in the Chronology, see *Talking Horse: Bernard Malamud on Life and Work*, eds. Alan Cheuse and Nicholas Delbanco (New York: Columbia University Press, 1996); Philip Davis, *Bernard Malamud: A Writer's Life* (Oxford: Oxford University Press, 2007); *Conversations with Bernard Malamud*, ed. Lawrence Lasher (Jackson: University Press of Mississippi, 1991); and Janna Malamud Smith, *My Father Is a Book: A Memoir of Bernard Malamud* (Boston: Houghton Mifflin, 2006).

THE NATURAL

24.25   Sir Percy] Percival, one of the Arthurian Knights of the Round Table, who embarked on a quest for the Holy Grail.

32.13   She pulled the trigger] The incident echoes the shooting of Philadelphia Phillies first baseman Eddie Waitkus (1919–1972) in a Chicago hotel room by Ruth Ann Steinhagen (1929–2012) on June 14, 1949.

43.18–19   hawkshaw] Slang for detective.

45.5   "Many brave hearts are asleep in the deep."] From popular seafaring song "Asleep in the Deep" (1897), words by English lyricist Arthur J. Lamb (1870–1928), music by American composer Henry W. Petrie (1857–1925).

68.40   bucket foots] Batters who use an unorthodox stance, stepping toward third base (if a right-handed batter) with the left foot when swinging. The batter was said to be "stepping into the bucket" because the water bucket for players used to be in the dugout on the third-base side.

78.25   *"Be it ever . . . home"*] From "Home, Sweet Home" (1823), song with words by American writer John Howard Payne (1791–1852), music by English composer Henry R. Bishop (1786–1855).

78.26   *"Nihil nisi bonum"*] From Latin adage "De mortuis nihil nisi bonum": "Speak nothing but good of the dead."

78.27   *"All is not gold that glitters"*] English proverb, cited in English literature as early as "The Canon's Yeoman's Tale" (c. 1387) in Chaucer's *The Canterbury Tales*.

78.28   "The dog is turned to his vomit again"] 2 Peter 2:22, referring to Proverbs 26:11: "As a dog returneth to his vomit, so a fool returneth to his folly."

81.25   'The love of money is the root of all evil,'] 1 Timothy 6:10.

82.34   'He that maketh haste to be rich shall not be innocent,'] Proverbs 28:20.

83.1–2   'Put a knife to thy throat if thou be a man given to appetite.'] Proverbs 23:2.

118.27   if you hit one it will save him] During Game 4 of the 1926 World Series, Babe Ruth (1895–1948) famously kept his promise to hit a home run on behalf of Johnny Sylvester (1915–1990), a seriously ill eleven-year-old boy. In newspaper accounts, and later in the movie *The Babe Ruth Story* (1948), Sylvester's recovery was attributed to Ruth's performance in the game, when he hit three home runs.

146.29   Rube Goldberg contraption] An elaborate invention designed to perform mundane tasks by outlandishly circuitous methods, as imagined by American cartoonist Rube Goldberg (1883–1970).

152.15   "Down by the Old Mill Stream."] Popular song (1910) by American songwriter Tell Taylor (1876–1937).

171.8–9   "Honi soit qui mal y pense."] "Shame to him who thinks evil," the motto of the British Order of the Garter.

175.4   "Woe unto him who calls evil good and good evil."] Cf. Isaiah 5:20: "Woe unto them that call evil good, and good evil."

198.36   "Say it ain't true, Roy,"] Cf. "Say it ain't so, Joe," words said to have been spoken by a young fan to Chicago White Sox outfielder "Shoeless Joe" Jackson (1889–1951) after he and seven other teammates were accused of throwing the 1919 World Series against the Cincinnati Reds. The eight players were acquitted in court but banned from playing in organized baseball for life.

THE ASSISTANT

201.6   Poilisheh] Polish person. As with much of the dialect in *The Assistant*, a German-Yiddish amalgam.

204.13   schmerz] Yiddish: pain, ache.

205.18   landsleit] Yiddish: people from the same shtetl or village, neighbors from the old country; also singular "landsman" (see 269.7).

205.18   parnusseh] Yiddish: way of making a living.

214.4   Der oilem iz a goilem] Yiddish: The people are fools.

214.4   *Forward*] Yiddish-language daily newspaper, first published in 1897.

218.22   gesheft] Yiddish: business establishment.

237.31   pisher] Yiddish: a small, negligible person or enterprise; literally, one who urinates.

239.35   goniff] Yiddish: thief.

270.24–25   Come . . . play] From "Come, Little Leaves," anonymous nineteenth-century poem found in primers for young children.

274.21–22   seven-year itch] Scabies.

282.34   *The Life of Napoleon*] Biography (1901) by English historian John Holland Rose (1855–1942).

283.6   *The Idiot*] Novel (1868–69) by Russian writer Fyodor Dostoevsky (1821–1881).

290.32–33   *Madame Bovary*, *Anna Karenina* and *Crime and Punishment*] Novels by French writer Gustave Flaubert (1821–1880), Russian writer Leo Tolstoy (1828–1910), and Fyodor Dostoevsky (1821–1881), published in 1857, 1877, and 1866, respectively.

326.19   shikse] Yiddish: non-Jewish woman, often used pejoratively, as with "goy" (326.10), meaning "gentile."

329.16   shlimozel] Yiddish: an unlucky person for whom nothing goes right.

345.22   uncircumcised dog!] See Shakespeare, *Othello* (1602–4), V.ii.352–56, Othello's last words before stabbing himself: ". . . in Aleppo once, / Where a malignant and a turban'd Turk / Beat a Venetian and traduc'd the state, / I took by th' throat the circumcised dog, / And smote him—thus."

347.40   Vey is mir] Yiddish: Woe is me.

374.18   gelt] Yiddish: money.

378.21   balabos] Yiddish: master of the house.

381.25   A gut shabos] Yiddish: "Good Sabbath," a greeting from sundown Friday to sundown Saturday.

382.7   macher] Yiddish: a doer, big shot, someone who makes things happen.

382.38   tsu] Yiddish: if (also to, whether).

398.10–11   Yaskadal v'yiskadash . . . B'olmo divro] Hebrew: the opening words of the Kaddish, or prayer for the dead: "Magnificent and sanctified be His great name in the world which He has created [according to His will]."

411.33   schwer] Yiddish: heavy, tough, painfully difficult.

TWENTY STORIES

420.1–2   greatest Jewish actors . . . Goldenburg] Stars of Yiddish theater in the United States: Jacob Adler (1853–1926), perhaps best known for his leading role in Jacob Gordin's *The Yiddish King Lear* (1892) and as Shylock in Yiddish version of *The Merchant of Venice*; Maurice Schwartz (1889–1960), actor and founder of the Yiddish Art Theatre in 1918; Jacob Ben-Ami (1890–1977), actor and founder of the Jewish Art Theater in 1919; Isidor Goldenburg (1870–?), Romanian-born actor who came to America in 1903 and spent about a decade of his career acting in Manhattan.

424.3   Welfare Island] Island in the East River of New York City, now known as Roosevelt Island.

437.37–38   *World-Telegram*] New York City daily newspaper, 1931–66.

442.7   *The Brooklyn Eagle*] Brooklyn daily newspaper, 1841–1955.

446.34   Passions spin the plot] In *Modern Love* (1862), st. 43, by English novelist and poet George Meredith (1828–1909).

447.28–29   *Quod Erat Demonstrandum*] Latin: that which was to be proved; phrase used at the end of a mathematical proof.

453.15–16   Kamenets-Podolski] City in western Ukraine, birthplace of Malamud's father.

478.7   two years more] So that Sobel will have worked seven years for Feld, corresponding to how long Jacob served Laban in the book of Genesis in order to marry his daughter Rachel. Laban then tricks Jacob into marrying Leah, his older daughter, but allows the marriage to Rachel in exchange for seven more years of labor. See Genesis 29:20–30.

480.40   his *Corriere*] *Corriere della Serra* ("Evening Courier"), Italian daily newspaper.

503.18   Haben, hatte, gehabt] From the conjugation of "to have" in German: have, had (past indicative), had (past participle).

503.23–24   Come, . . . Come over the meadow with me and play] See note 270.24–25.

521.4   the Yeshiva University] Private Jewish university in upper Manhattan, which includes the Rabbi Isaac Elchanan Theological Seminary.

524.8   Rothschild's] The Rothschilds, family of German Jews with family ties to other nations who have been prominent in investment banking and philanthropy in Europe since the late eighteenth century.

527.36   Yiddishe kinder] Yiddish: Jewish children.

550.17   Gottenyu] Yiddish: dear God.

557.28   *World Almanac*] *The World Almanac and Book of Facts*, reference annual first published in 1868.

578.18   Basta!] Italian: Enough!

580.19   Si è perduto?] Italian: Are you lost?

587.33–34   brother Joseph . . . Pauline] Joseph Bonaparte (1768–1844), older brother of Napoleon and king of Naples, 1806–8; Pauline Bonaparte (1780–1825), Napoleon's sister, who lived in Italy after her marriage to a Roman nobleman in 1803.

589.11–12   Apollo Belvedere] Classical marble statue of the Greek god.

592.25–26   un pezzo di paradiso caduto dal cielo.] Italian: a piece of paradise fallen from the sky.

597.15   Risorgimento] Literally "resurgence," the Italian unification movement, 1815–70.

599.13   Parioli] Elegant upper-class area in Rome. Other districts in the story include Trastevere on the west bank of the river Tiber, the wealthy Prati neighborhood, the areas around the hill Monte Sacro, and the ancient Roman road Via Cassia.

602.30   gobbo] Italian: hunchback.

607.18   *Il Messaggero*] Italian daily newspaper ("The Messenger").

605.26   St. Peter's] St. Peter's Basilica, the great Renaissance church in Vatican City.

617.23   Ecco la chiave!] Italian: Behold the key!

618.34   mezzo servizio] Italian: employed on a half-day basis.

620.19   *Tempo* or *Epoca*] Glossy popular postwar Italian magazines ("Time" and "Epoch") modeled on *Life* magazine.

POSTHUMOUSLY PUBLISHED STORIES

633.24–25   May day in 1940 . . . Sedan] Nazi Germany attacked France and the Low Countries on May 10, 1940. On May 13 a German armored corps, supported by the Luftwaffe, crossed the Meuse River and broke through the French defenses at Sedan. German armored forces then rapidly advanced across northeastern France and reached the English Channel near Abbeville on May 20, completing the encirclement of the British and French armies in Belgium.

633.29–30   The Belgians surrendered . . . Dunkerque] The Belgian army surrendered to the Germans on May 28, 1940. After the Allied retreat to the port of Dunkirk in northern France, approximately 225,000 British and 110,000 French soldiers were evacuated across the English Channel, May 27–June 4, 1940.

634.19   AEF] American Expeditionary Forces, which fought in World War I under the command of General of the Armies John J. Pershing (1860–1948).

634.23–24   Panzer divisions] Armored divisions in the German armed forces.

635.22–24   took Paris . . . Reynaud cabinet fell] After the fall of Paris on

June 14, 1940, the French prime minister Paul Reynaud (1878–1966) was ousted by those who favored surrender to the Germans and was succeeded by Henri-Philippe Pétain (1856–1951), who led a collaborationist government through 1944.

635.25–26 Pétain . . . "peace with honor."] In a radio broadcast to the nation on June 17, 1940, Pétain announced that he was seeking an armistice with Germany.

635.26–28 In the dark Compiègne . . . delegation] In the forest near Compiègne where, on November 11, 1918, the armistice ending World War I had been signed, Adolf Hitler presented his armistice terms to France on June 21, 1940. To make German revenge complete, the meeting of the German and French delegations took place in the private railroad car of Ferdinand Foch (1851–1929), supreme commander of the Allied Forces in 1918, with Hitler sitting where Foch had sat when he dictated the 1918 armistice.

636.37–38 *Social Justice* . . . Zion!] Magazine of demagogic American Catholic priest Charles Coughlin (1891–1971), which printed in installments the forgery known as "The Protocols of the Elders of Zion," claiming that it was evidence of a secret Jewish plan for world domination. Coughlin also broadcast radio sermons in the 1930s in support of Nazi Germany.

638.4 Jews—like that lousy Léon Blum] French Socialist leader Léon Blum (1872–1950), a Jew, was the premier of two Popular Front governments, June 1936–June 1937 and March–April 1938; he was imprisoned by the Vichy government in September 1940 and deported to Germany in 1943.

657.16 Punch-Ball] Street baseball, played with a rubber ball and the fist used in lieu of a bat.

658.19–20 In the good old summertime] From popular American song "In the Good Old Summertime" (1902), words by Ren Shields (1868–1913), music by George Evans (1879–1915).

658.23–24 "Ah, sweet mystery of life"] From "Ah! Sweet Mystery of Life," hit song from *Naughty Marietta* (1910), operetta by Irish-born American composer Victor Herbert (1859–1924), with words by American playwright and songwriter Rida Johnson Young (1875–1926).

680.2 Umbrian] From Umbria, region of central Italy.

681.6 FAO] Food and Agriculture Organization, an agency of the United Nations with headquarters in Rome.

681.30 portinaia] Italian: female concierge or caretaker.

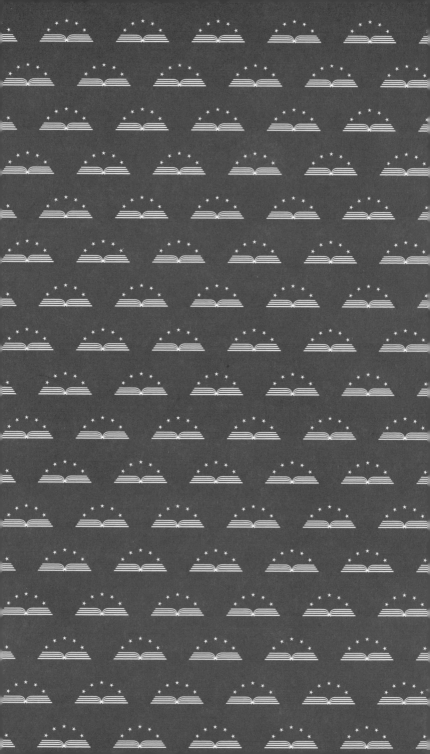